Somewhere Hidden
Between the Cracks

Somewhere Hidden Between the Cracks

✦

Part 1

Sandra Williams
cover by chicare j. brassell

iUniverse, Inc.

New York Lincoln Shanghai

Somewhere Hidden Between the Cracks
Part 1

iUniverse books may be ordered through booksellers or by contacting:

iUniverse
2021 Pine Lake Road, Suite 100
Lincoln, NE 68512
www.iuniverse.com
1-800-Authors (1-800-288-4677)

Because of the dynamic nature of the Internet, any Web addresses or links contained in this book may have changed since publication and may no longer be valid.

This is a work of fiction. All of the characters, names, incidents, organizations, and dialogue in this novel are either the products of the author's imagination or are used fictitiously.

Designer of Cover: Chicara J. Brassell
Design Implemented by: Sandra Williams
Editors: Moyna Uddin, Chicara J. Brassell, and Nadine Waller

ISBN: 978-0-595-46029-8 (pbk)
ISBN: 978-0-595-90330-6 (ebk)

Printed in the United States of America

INTRODUCTION

How far have we really come with discrimination since the 1950's? This book will take you on a journey through massive cover-ups and scandals by *the company* and *the union*. It emphasizes how discrimination is still prevalent among unions, private companies, and government entities. *Somewhere Hidden Between The Cracks* explains how companies and unions illegally intertwine to work together against employees in secrecy while breaking discrimination, labor, and/ or contract laws. This story is mainly about the experiences of Andrea Smith, Linda Jackson, Mazzie Cane, and me, Crista Carrie. However it also entails the extent other employees went through to achieve and maintain justice at the workplace. In this book I'll explain how the *union* failed the very same employees that it should have been protecting.

Through the years, the union decided to change sides. It's more profitable to work for the large companies instead of representing the union members who pay for their protection and services. The tables have turned and the union has totally started protecting the company. The benefits are greater for the elected union member who decides to accept pay-off's opposed to working for the union members. In my experiences I've found the benefits paid by the company, served as advertising to the elected union member. Therefore they'd decide to jump ship and support big business. The same tactics used by Local 783 against the company to protect us as union members, are the same tactics used to defeat the union member by not representing us through the grievance process. This is how the grievance process became so corrupt and the company began dishonoring the contract and/or labor laws. This leaves the union member with no resource to help themselves. All avenues are blocked which prevents the employee from filing lawsuits against the company in a court of law.

I recently ran into a problem while writing this book because the wrong version was printed instead of the current version. It was really embarrassing but I had to continue my efforts in telling my story. After having the proof edited twice by two separate people, I was confident the book was ready. When I received the proof (after having it edited twice and after reading the book three times myself), I assumed that the original version went to print, therefore having no need to read it again. My publisher never looked through the book. She just printed it. I assumed that she had read the manu-

script since she had it from February 2005 until May 2005. I take fault of my assumptions. If I read the proof when I received it, I would have known the unedited version was printed. I had started working on Part 2 in hopes that it would be on the market shortly after Part 1. I had many edits from Part 1 on my computer. Since it took up so much space on my computer I deleted all files pertaining to Part 1. I had no idea I'd saved the unedited version and deleted the original files. I had to almost start writing this book from the beginning using the unedited version as a guideline. This has been a very costly lesson that I will always remember.

I feel my story is enlightening especially regarding how Andrea and I were treated while employed at Woodrow Stamping Plant. Andrea was in the most extreme hostile working environment I'd ever seen in my life. The pilfering that no agency or organization cared to investigate caused the company and the union to continue doing such injustices to employees. This gave me that much more determination to print my story. We were told we had civil rights, but when they were violated nothing was ever done in our defense. We had no voice in anything that happened—not even through the grievance procedures. Local 783 never officially wrote a grievance. The outside government agencies never gave us an opportunity to tell our side of what transpired. Instead we were told if we didn't drop and/or withdraw our complaint against Woodrow Stamping Plant and/or Local 783, the government agencies would drop the complaints themselves. We weren't guilty of anything Woodrow Stamping Plant and Local 783 said we did. But simply by them saying so, we were guilty just the same. What they said and did was final. That's a horrific position to be in.

Famous Parts Company had their story and Local 783 had theirs. Andrea and I were never given the opportunity to tell *our* stories—even in a court of law. When a company makes their employees pay money back the employees never received, it's wrong. I feel the most important thing at this point, is to put my pride in my pocket and put my best efforts in finally publishing my side of the story. I wanted the world to know how Woodrow Stamping Plant and Local 783 have shafted me and others involved in this book. What was so horrific about my experiences was how Woodrow Stamping Plant had no conscience while pilfering money meant for me and other employees. It didn't matter the employees knew Woodrow Stamping Plant was pilfering their money because there was no one to stop them. No union, no court of law, no government agency, no local politician, no local news station, and no local newspaper. So why not continue pilfering from employees? Woodrow Stamping Plant and Local 783 had all their areas covered. Therefore they had no fear of ever being caught. They were bold and blatant. Woodrow Stamping Plant with the help of Local 783 took many dollars through retirement and Worker's Compensation benefits from those who had occupational injuries. These employees should have received compensation for their occupational injuries but didn't because the company pilfered their money. The most compelling story is how the company allowed employees suffering from occupational injuries to work without restrictions until their condition become so grave they were put on a 'no work available status'. Woodrow Stamping Plant pilfered Worker's Compensation benefits and retired these same employees without them having knowledge.

I have finally learned how the union became incorporated with the companies and the government agencies. The government agencies such as the National Labor Relations Board (NLRB), Department of Labor, and the Department of Civil Rights, worked in harmony with Woodrow Stamping Plant giving them what they needed—protection. The Department of Labor and the Department of Civil Rights were established to protect the working people against companies who violate labor and/or contract laws. The NLRB is supposed to protect the employee from unfair labor practices by the union. When a complaint was filed, an investigation should've been enacted against the union to see if Woodrow Stamping Plant and/or Local 783 were in violation of not representing their union member. The union was supposed to be my representation if the company violated contract and/or labor laws. Since I received none of the services from the union, I should have received all my money back. There were deals made with the National Labor Relations Board in an effort to get charges dropped against Local 783. The NLRB does everything they can to get charges dropped. When their decision is appealed, it is upheld in Washington D.C. I've even had one lawyer tell me I was being spiteful by not dropping the charges against Local 783. The National Labor Relations Board eventually dropped charges against Local 783 because I wouldn't.

It really didn't make much difference because the National Labor Relations Board never investigated complaints regarding Local 783. When complaints were filed, there were many employees forced to withdraw. What I mean by that is the Department of Civil Rights and the National Labor Relations Board basically gave employees the ultimatum of withdrawing their complaint or catching pure *Hell* at the workplace. This kind of action put the employee in a compromising position. When they'd go back to work, management would retaliate against them. I don't know of anyone who has successfully won an appeal requesting for Local 783 to be investigated. For various violations of federal, state, contract and/ or labor laws for discrimination, harassment, retaliation, and the pilfering of money through unfair labor practices. This allowed the company to continue pilfering money from employees without their knowledge.

Woodrow Stamping Plant and Local 783 kept at least two sets of records. Local 783 had records on the employees they were pilfering from. Those working on the cases at the government agencies took bribes and favors for their secrecy. Local 783 worked in unison with Woodrow Stamping Plant as they violated many labor and/or contract laws and civil rights laws as well. This conduct ranged from non-compliance of the National Labor Relations Board to other government agencies supposedly protecting the union member from contract violation. The Department of Labor is supposed to protect and oversee that large companies or small private businesses are not violating labor laws or using unfair labor practices.

My money was pilfered for three years at the same time the Department of Labor investigated my complaint. Woodrow Stamping Plant wasn't forced to repay the money. As my reader, do you think this qualifies as unfair labor practice? When a complaint with merit was filed, the organizations in this book had the opportunity to stop the harassment, discrimination, retaliation, and the pilfering the women in this book experienced. Has anyone noticed that the number of cases of discrimination have grown to an all time low with regards to complaints filed? The number has decreased in our state and federal court systems because the numbers of withdrawals are not counted. In my opinion, all withdrawals need to be investigated because of the way they're handled. If a person is going to take the initiative by filing a complaint against the company or the union for unfair labor practices, and then that employee suddenly withdraws from the investigation process, the complaints should yet be investigated.

When a person withdraws their complaint, that's when outside agencies should become concerned. They should investigate because of the pressure experienced by the complaining employee from the company. These employees are put in danger in some instances. For example with Andrea Smith when she was hit in the chest with a broom by a Caucasian co-worker, then hit by a hi-lo truck. All this occurred after she filed a complaint with these outside agencies. When it was all over, Andrea was terminated and Woodrow Stamping Plant had no record of these incidents ever occurring.

Complaints need to be investigated in order to make sure an employee isn't withdrawing their complaint under duress. Since so much fraud is involved regarding these government agencies, the real reason for a client to withdraw their complaint needs to be determined. There should be a written response from the agencies accepting the withdrawal and why they are accepting it. If complaints against the company continue to arise after a withdrawal has been granted by the same employee, common sense would tell anyone there was a problem with the company and the union which needed investigating. In our cases many complaints were filed. It doesn't take a rocket scientist to know the agencies are not doing their jobs by investigating the complaints filed. The laws in which the union and/or company violated when the client first filed the complaint should be quoted just to acknowledge a violation was made. There should also be a written response from the complainant detailing if they are withdrawing under duress or by choice. Safeguards need to be implemented for the complainant.

From my experiences when the Department of Civil Rights stated the claimant made a written request, they weren't telling the truth. I received a withdrawal form in the mail, but had never written a statement saying the reason I was withdrawing. Why were we forced to withdraw our complaint and did the Department of Civil Rights duplicate a written document to their superiors? If this is the case, there maybe needs to be a taped withdrawal statement from the client. This way it wouldn't come from the agent handling the claim for profit, which is what went on at the Michigan Branch of the Department of Civil Rights. Complaints filed in the courts are rarely heard of anymore, but discrimination is yet prevalent. It's almost as though discrimination doesn't exist any longer in the eyes of the court.

All those noted in this book have experienced discrimination in one form or another during employment at Woodrow Stamping Plant. In these cases, the union served as the overseer by making sure the grievance process didn't work for the employees. Discrimination isn't something of the past. It is alive, well, and growing stronger each day. Racism is growing in the state of Michigan at an alarming rate. Some may not think so because the tactics used in this day and age are much more subliminal. However they remain bold, blatant, and straightforward in letting one know who's superior. Andrea and I trusted the NLRB and they sided with the union by not investigating any complaints we filed. They didn't file charges against the union and the union didn't file charges against the company. The law is the law and the union and company was not following it. It's difficult for me to understand why it was so hard for Woodrow Stamping Plant and Local 783 to treat employees with a little dignity and respect. We all worked for Woodrow Stamping Plant for the same reason—to make a living and support our family and ourselves.

Pilfering money from employees is clearly an unfair labor practice that was condoned by government agencies. I complained for 14 years with no results. There was one particular grievance I filed in June 2000 against Woodrow Stamping Plant's Medical Department. The grievance was granted in my favor, but I still lost because the union lied and said settlement money wasn't discussed. The company also lied on Andrea stating she'd threatened the doctor and nurse in the Medical Department. Andrea was terminated and wasn't allowed to say anything in her own defense. The protocol used in a grievance procedure should have been used in accordance with the federal and state courts.

I must say Local 783 is a powerful organization of crime. They break laws, lie on people, and aren't held accountable for their actions. Local 783's elected union members are paid for their protection against complaints filed by the working people. Lawsuits are a thing of the past. Companies can do as they please when they have the union backing them. The reason you don't hear about stories such as mine or Andrea's is not because discrimination doesn't exist. It's because this information has to be carried to the public by someone. If local news stations or newspapers won't carry the information to the public, then the information remains censored. The media is afraid to report this controversial sort of news for fear of jeopardizing their jobs. Former News Anchor, Dan Rather, covered the evening news for years. I was truly saddened when his contract wasn't renewed because of a story he covered which cost him his job. If the news stations can't carry newsworthy information, they have to replace it with something other than what's happening in our federal and local governments. The news has become a bearer of bad news by covering murders, rapes, robberies, and private lives of the famous or other unworthy news stories. Routine propaganda surfaces across the airways telling us what they *think* we want to hear instead of the reality of a newsworthy story. Big business corruption is at an all time high and Woodrow Stamping Plant, Local 783, and these government agencies condone this corruption by censoring information that the public should be hearing. We are losing so many of our civil rights—especially our freedom of speech. That too, will soon become a thing of the past if something isn't done fast.

In this book, you'll see how *the company* outright pilfered money from characters Crista, Andrea, Linda, Mazzie, and others—without them being able to do anything about it. Is this what democracy is all about? When the hi-lo truck hit Andrea, the company literally hid the fact that it ever happened. Do you think we had due process of the law when we couldn't get a lawyer to represent our cases? It may not be important to others but it is important to those who are in need of help that's not democracy. Do you think we had civil rights when we couldn't even get a judge to appoint a lawyer regarding a case of a crime being committed by our employing company? We were limited to little or no assistance, in an effort for the company to continue pilfering from the employees. We no longer live in a democratic society if our rights are going to be stripped away.

Woodrow Stamping Plant was improperly labeling employees with 'occupational injuries' as "personal injuries". When the Medical Department became aware of an employee with an occupational injury, they changed the employee's diagnosis from occupational to personal. This is why Nurse Tootie was fired for embezzlement, falsifying medical records, and falsifying government documents. She was only doing her job from what I can see because she had a supervisor to answer to. She wasn't the only one involved at Woodrow Stamping Plant. Nurse Tootie was fired for doing her job very well. Famous Parts Company was aware of what she was doing in the Medical Department. It was done with Woodrow Stamping Plant's approval. At the point of my employment with Woodrow Stamping Plant, it didn't matter what you saw or heard there were those paid to say you didn't hear or see anything. Whatever documents in your possession to substantiate the truth were meaningless against Woodrow Stamping Plant. For government agencies and the courts would act as though you had no documents at all.

They are a powerful group of entities being able to make up lies and not allowing employees the opportunity to open their mouths. No one would listen anyway. Since many had to step down when Andrea's story broke, she was retaliated against by being stripped of all her financial security. After they did this, Andrea became a victim left on the streets with no means of support at all. This was a serious wrong committed against Andrea and Woodrow Stamping Plant and Local 783 knew just what they were doing. Woodrow Stamping Plant and Local 783 were the cause of her problems—not Andrea. She was only trying to find solutions, yet having to pay a high price to sustain and maintain the life she has left. What Woodrow Stamping Plant and Local 783 were doing was wrong and illegal. They were getting paid for disbursing injustices to others and they succeeded for many years.

I blame Metro Craft Insurance Company in part. They were aware they should not have been paying benefits to occupational injuries and that Worker's Compensation should have been liable. Metro Craft kept employees on long term medical leaves. This way Worker's Compensation would not have to pay the cost for the occupational injury of years. Being on medical leave or a 'no work available' status for 6-10 years should cause many red flags to the company—bottom line. If an employee is off work for this length of time, it's likely they will not be returning back to work. So why were they yet receiving payment from the company's insurance fund and not the retirement fund? If you have not returned

xii   Somewhere Hidden Between the Cracks

back to work, whether personal or occupational after 6-10 years, there is clearly something wrong with the situation. The employee is either employable or not. After eight years someone should have noticed these people should've been off company payrolls. They should have been declared disabled by the Social Security Administration standards. Many of them were, but were not receiving money from the Retirement Board for their occupational injury. Employees only need to be employed with the company for 4 years to retire with an occupational injury.

Woodrow Stamping Plant continued to drain money from the company's insurance fund. Woodrow Stamping Plant had employees on long-term benefits when *they* received their Social Security. Employees would have to pay the money back they received from Metro Craft Insurance Company. If the employee only received 'sick & accident' benefits from Metro Craft, Worker's Compensation has the responsibility to pay them back. It's not the employee's responsibility. Woodrow Stamping Plant had employees paying the money back which they pilfered from them and the employee was unaware the money had been pilfered until much later. Woodrow Stamping Plant continued to have employees on record as drawing Worker's Compensation. Woodrow Stamping Plant was keeping all monies having to do with Worker's Compensation. The company paid 100% of employee's salary when injured on the job. This is how Woodrow Stamping Plant was pilfering from the Worker's Compensation fund.

The employee was the one to pay the money back because Woodrow Stamping Plant stated they paid out weekly benefits. This made it look as though Woodrow Stamping Plant was paying employees at the same time as Metro Craft. Metro Craft Insurance Company would state the employee collected twice. (They call this *double dipping*.) If the employee was being paid Worker's Compensation Benefits, why would Metro Craft pay more benefits? In fact, how can you continue receiving 'sick & accident' insurance payments from Metro Craft Insurance Company while you're in the plant working at the same time? I complained about the ongoing fraud but again no one cared to investigate. My complaints went ignored. This was a joint venture between Woodrow Stamping Plant and Metro Craft Insurance Company.

The Medical Department was sending employees with occupational injuries to Metro Craft while the company put that same person on a 'no work available' status for a personal injury. The company would get their doctors to say the employee's medical problems were of a personal nature and to continue working the employee without restrictions. This ensured worsening of the employee's condition. Woodrow Stamping had employees receiving their retirement benefits while they were working at the same time under a different set of records. This, among many other extortions, served very profitable to Woodrow Stamping Plant. I blame the greedy lawyers or attorneys—whichever they want to be called. It would not have been possible to continue this kind of fraud without the help of others like them.

Lawyers allowed their doors to be shut in the faces of Mazzie Cane, Andrea Smith, myself, and others like us. They didn't lift a finger to help the employees who had been discriminated against, retaliated against, harassed, and pilfered from. In my opinion, all those who took part in the massive scheme should be punished. There was no justification for how they left others with no defense. I even have to blame the Social Security Administration for not reporting questionable events taking place. Suspicions should have been peaked when things didn't seem to be in line with normalcy. Nevertheless, these incidents ultimately went ignored.

I blame the Michigan Supreme Court for not hearing Andrea's court case when she herself, took her case first to the Worker's Compensation Appeal Board. Referee, Jackie Arnold, had already made a decision on Andrea's Worker's Compensation claim, but Andrea had no knowledge of this occurring. Andrea thought she was amending her prior claim to include the hi-lo incident at Woodrow Stamping Plant prior to her termination. She had no indication that the same referee she stood in front of, had already made a decision on the previous case that had been in the court since 1995.

Andrea didn't find out until after she'd made what she thought was an amendment to her claim, that a new claim was filed on her behalf. This new claim was filed as though there had been no prior claim. This is why Andrea appealed her Worker's Compensation claim and was denied. Andrea appealed her case to the Appellate Court the second time around then took it to the Michigan Supreme Court. Andrea was disappointed when she was told they weren't going to hear her argument. They wouldn't allow Andrea to say anything because she would put the pilfering scheme out in the open. Andrea had to be terminated because she had proof they filed her last Worker's Compensation claim as a new claim. This made Andrea a threat if she was allowed to officially speak on her behalf.

I blame the Worker's Compensation judges and referee for giving the company favorable judgment and giving the company the right to pilfer money. I blame the Michigan Supreme Court for not hearing Andrea's court case when she herself, took her case to the Appellate Court first. If I were a judge or referee, I would question a person who has such motivation to challenge a decision without an attorney. If I were a judge handling Andrea's Worker's Compensation case, there would be a few questions in need of answering with all honesty.

My first question: why was her case held up in Worker's Compensation court for many years? It doesn't take that long to determine if a person has a valid claim with documentation proving the injuries to be occupational. My second question: Why didn't Andrea have a lawyer representing her case being that she was *pro se*? *This is a person appearing in court that does not have a lawyer who represents oneself.* I would assume Andrea had no other choice than to represent herself. Third question: Why is it that no lawyer would take her case seeing that she was in court alone handling a case of that magnitude? Fourth: I would ask why is a person *pro se* taking their case to the highest court possible in Michigan? If a person went to this extent with relative facts supporting their claim and the court refused to hear their case, I would give them the benefit of doubt and at least hear their argument. Something just doesn't seem right when a person can't get their case heard in a court of law. I would assume this person wanting their case heard was unable to obtain counsel. Evidence proved Andrea had been hit by the hi-lo in the plant, where she worked and was treated at the local hospital. I would wonder why her case was in the Michigan Appellate Court before filed in the Supreme Court. Why wouldn't they hear her case? They had to review the case before denying they would hear her case. A person not obtaining representation for their case in a court of law would be crazy unless they're experienced in underlying situations.

Andrea Smith is a long way from being crazy. If I were a judge deciding an argument, I would gather the circumstances and consider first why a person was determined to have their voice heard—especially if they were determined enough to bring their claim in a court of law without an attorney. According to the law citizens have a right to have their cases heard in a court of law. If they can't afford an attorney, the judge is supposed to appoint counsel. In Andrea's case, I'd question why she was unable to obtain counsel. I would entertain the idea that she possibly had information to substantiate something someone didn't want to be known.

Everyone wants the best person representing them. Why would someone who knows nothing about the law choose to represent theirself? That doesn't make much sense. Not everyone can take a crash course in law and make it to the Michigan Supreme Court. This is exactly what Andrea did. She was desperate and had no other options. She completed her brief and followed the same court rules that all lawyers had to follow. For Andrea to get as far as she did, should have expressed to the court something was really out of order. But instead the justice system denied Andrea's appeal because of big business fraud. Famous Parts Company made sure Andrea Smith's case wasn't heard in any court she entered.

Andrea was silenced so Woodrow Stamping Plant and Local 783 could continue pilfering from her and other employees. There was a time Andrea should have won her case by default because Famous Parts Company's attorney was late filing their papers in the Appellate Court. Mind you, Andrea had to honor all the deadlines. Why didn't Famous Parts Company have to follow the same rules? I feel someone should have given Andrea's Worker's Compensation case the benefit of doubt and listened to what she had to say. I blame those who made sure this court or any other court didn't hear Andrea's case. If these judges or referees were paid, they should have stepped down from their judicial position. It's not as though Andrea didn't have proof she was hit by the hi-lo at work. No one cared to listen or take the initiative to read her paperwork. They could have even gone back to her old case filed with the court in 1995. This same case that was settled in July 2002 should have been reviewed to verify validity of the circumstances surrounding her medical condition already on record. But that didn't happen either.

Andrea's medical condition derived from the work she did in the plant going as far back as 1992. Why was there no record of the last decision on file to refer back to? This was the second claim filed even though it was filed as a new claim. What happened to Andrea's old claim dating injuries from 1995 until 2002? Andrea was employed at Woodrow Stamping Plant long before she was hit with the hi-lo in 2002, but all this seemed to have been forgotten. It was as though Andrea had no history. The referee/judge made a decision in July 2002. This was only a few weeks prior to the new claim being filed and denied. The referee made no reference to Andrea's prior settlement on the first claim.

Woodrow Stamping Plant denied Andrea was hit by a hi-lo in the plant. Woodrow Stamping Plant kept Andrea's Worker's Compensation money from her first settlement. They used their other set of records on Andrea in order for her to re-enter a new claim. There was no mention of any previous settlement regarding the Worker's Compensation settlement. Andrea was in front of the same judge and Woodrow Stamping Plant got away with pilfering from her first settlement.

All this was done because Woodrow Stamping Plant had retired Andrea many years prior. Someone had to take the rap. Of course no one knew what was going on at Woodrow Stamping Plant since they were handing out favors. In order for this kind of pilfering to take place, there had to be many involved. Clearly there were. This money-laundering scheme was so large that it took many to participate such as doctors, lawyers, insurance companies, government organizations, and union representatives. Woodrow Stamping Plant used much persuasion to the outside doctors of those suffering from occupational injuries. Woodrow Stamping Plant had much clout and they would simply sanction other doctors to make fraudulent diagnoses to the patients. The diagnoses were given only after tests and x-rays had been administered. Then Woodrow Stamping Plant would attempt to persuade the patients to quit their jobs.

I have been through a lot mentally and physically. Andrea has been through even more. Woodrow Stamping Plant and Local 783 should be accountable for their actions. There were contracts broken and labor laws violated, but we couldn't so much as get our cases heard in a court of law. We were angry because everything we said was true, but we had no one to stand up and say enough is enough. I had said for years that Woodrow Stamping and Local 783 were pilfering money from employees. Andrea Smith and I were discriminated against-not only by Woodrow Stamping Plant, but also by the federal courts that left us nowhere to seek solace. The tactics used were fierce. This was cruel and unusual punishment. I even won a grievance against the Medical Department for harassment in July 2002. This will be further discussed in *Part II*. Needless to say, I never received a dime of that money either.

This book was only written to expose the union and big businesses and the bigotry that existed in their money laundering schemes. This conduct was acknowledged throughout the Executive Branches of the Company and Union and the government entities, who failed to uphold the laws. The court system's failure to seek justice when a wrong had been committed left Andrea and me with no recourses when seeking help.

We couldn't and didn't have access to counsel because they either surrendered to the demands of big businesses, or it was simply a case no lawyer wanted to touch. This made it impossible to prevail in filing suit for accountability when various civil laws, labor laws, and contract laws were violated—unless we filed the case in court ourselves as we did. The judges made sure that the cases didn't make it in front of a jury. Judges for both Andrea and me took the initiative to give us a bench trial, when we both asked for a trial by jury. The Judge should have appointed us counsel upon our request and that was denied too. Our right as a citizen of the United States is to have representation in a court of law for our claim, but we were denied that too. Our court experiences will be explained in greater detail in *Part II* of this book.

We couldn't get any help when we contacted the elected officials in Michigan, when trying to obtain help for the money being pilfered from us. Instead, we were sent in a vicious circle that would always lead to nowhere. Especially, by our own democratic State Senator, Governor, and the Attorney General, who we contacted on many occasions for help. It's a sad position to be in when a wrong is committed against you and you're unable to protect yourself. We were unable to obtain help while helplessly watching our money being pilfered away, and our rights being disregarded as though we didn't count for anything. We were only doing our jobs.

There is some information in this book that is repeated for clarity only. When we were seeking help from the various government agencies, I needed to prove my claims were valid. These organizations included but were not limited to the Department of Labor, the National Labor Relations Board, the Equal Employment Opportunity Commission (EEOC), and the Department of Civil Rights. Our last resort was to contact the President of the United States. All those agencies, doors were slammed shut in the faces of Andrea and me. They sent us packing with no help to be found from anyone, which made all of our fighting for justice invalid. This allowed them to continued doing as they pleased to Andrea and me without any accountability.

I have never experienced so much discrimination, retaliation, pilfering, and other forms of big businesses corruption. They have the court system in the palm of their hands. The courts accommodate anything big businesses want. I never thought this kind of corruption could exist in the United States while living in a democratic society. Democracy is supposed to be freedom to the people over dictatorship. It's been proven that as minority women we can't get any justice. Big businesses have taken control of the world as we once knew it.

I can truly understand why big businesses are putting the lawyers out of business by limiting the amount one can sue for regarding punitive damages. There shouldn't be a cap on something these companies knowingly did to people like Andrea, others, and me. When big businesses knowingly commit fraud and crimes against humanity while violating laws, they should have to pay. What other way is there that big businesses can be taught a lesson for their accountability? Our own government is working with the big businesses to keep lawsuits at a minimum. By doing so, this sends a message that big businesses can break laws and have no accountability for their actions.

Our cases (Andrea and mine) were similar to that of the Whistle Blowers' cases, involving the Mayor of the City of Detroit. Two city police officers were unjustly discharged for investigating a party that occurred at the Mayor's Mansion. They were awarded millions. The jury found the city and the mayor of the city guilty of firing the two officers (under the Whistle Blower's Act) because of what they'd learned while investigating a party that got out of hand. The difference between us and them is those police officers were able to obtain attorneys, whereas we were not. We couldn't find any attorney to represent our interests or who was willing to challenge the Big Auto Giant and its union. One entity protected the other. Our cases are a perfect example of such.

1

CRISTA BECOMES PREPARED

I am the kind of young lady that loves to laugh and have fun. That's what life is all about. When the dual calamities of the universe collide, I try to find whatever I can to make me laugh in order to remove the stress dealt to me. When I have time in between dealing with circumstances, I have no idea from moment to moment what I'll have to encounter next. Laughter seems to work miracles for me. It allows me to take my mind off my problems for a moment. When I return to my stressful situation, I can see a clearer picture on how to handle things. It makes me wonder how strong I really have to be to survive. I try to stay focused in dealing with whatever circumstances are at hand and do whatever I can to make the best decisions. I suffer the feedback if I make the wrong decision. Laughter helps me readjust my frame of thinking and escape from the existing problems—kind of like a temporary vacation. When the madness subsides just for a few moments, soon there's another set of problems I have to face in my life. This occurs in everyone's life at one time or another. Laughter rejuvenates my sense of humor. I soon come into a better mood with an outburst of laughter. Things aren't so unbearable after that.

I am and have always been a strong-willed person who stands firmly in what I believe. If I feel I am right, then I will always debate the fact even at the cost of research. I will find facts supporting my argument and expressing those findings. In further chapters you will understand how I was plagued with multiple problems during my quest to maintain my job and my sanity. I experienced many problems with my employer, my union, and my health.

I am a fairly short young lady. My height is only 5 feet 1 inch and I weighed about 145 pounds at the time of being hired with Famous Parts Company. My skin color is of a medium dark brown—almost like a dark caramel. My hair is very fine and thin and was always hard to manage due to it being limp and life-

1

less. It was never able to hold a hairstyle very long. Many people ask me if I am foreigner because of my hair and the way I speak. I have always been teased and made fun of because of the way I talk—even as a child attending elementary on through high school.

I was a very active and well-known young lady during my school years. I attended Webster Elementary School in Detroit from Kindergarten through 8th grade. I was very good in every sport I tried out for. In my 5th or 6th grade year, I was the school's overall champion in the physical fitness programs, being the fastest runner. I won trophies and other awards eventually lost through years of moving. These awards were very important to me because they gave me a sense of accomplishment.

As a student at Earhart Junior High School, I did very little academically in my junior year. Earhart was a newly built school and when the school was completed, Webster's children moved grades 6 through 8 into Earhart. Webster became a K through 5 school. I completed the 11th grade at Western High School. I was very active in sports there too. I was on the cheerleading team. I played on the field hockey team and held the position as Guard on the girl's basketball team. I loved modern dance as well as other forms of art, but didn't take my grades too serious.

I started having problems at home when I was about 16 years old. I left my mother and father's home. Soon after that, my mother and father separated which eventually resulted in their divorce after 27 years of marriage. From that point my life became a total disaster. I desperately wanted to finish school. I resided with my sister Janet, On Detroit East Side, which wasn't a very pleasant experience for me. We lived on Watson Street. My sister Janet lived the fast life. It was adventurous but I didn't agree with the kind of lifestyle she lived. My life didn't go in the direction I felt it should've been going, but I did have plans to finish school. I eventually had to quit school due to lack of money for getting to & from school each day. I had a job working after school but it wasn't enough money to travel to & from school and purchase my personal needs and clothes. I weighed about 110 pounds at the time and wore a size 3. I could sew and I altered my sister's clothes to fit my small-framed body, but money was still an issue.

At that time I was dealing with many issues and was wondering how to handle my problems. That seemed to be very difficult due to my being underage. I had no one to truly confide in other than my older sister Janet. I later found that my sister, who I dearly trusted, had betrayed me. This was devastating and left me in a world of not knowing where to go for advice. I left my sister's home and went back to my father's house just before I was to be married. My mother and I weren't very close. I was always closer to my father. A few months after my mother left my father, my mother was nowhere to be found—nor did she want to be found.

I met Lee before I left my parent's home and we eventually married. He was more of a friend than a lover. I really didn't like him that way. Since I was a nice looking young lady, there were many young men calling for dates. Lee pursued me for a couple of years. He was always there to lean on trying to make sure he would be the winner over all my friends. As a result he was. He was there when I needed a friend showing genuine concern for my well-being.

Lee and I were married December 16, 1968 when he was 19 years old and I was 17. My father William signed for me to marry. Lee worked at Great Lakes Steel with his father. His father got him a job at the steel mill when he was only 17 years old. When applying for employment at that time, your word was taken at face value in terms of your name and social security number. In the 60's and 70's employers assumed the person seeking employment knew their name, address, age, and social security number. Therefore many employers didn't ask for actual proof of identification. Several labor employees at that time couldn't read or write. They were just hard working people. That's what employers were interested in when they were searching for workers.

I was staying with my father when Lee and I married. The day I married was the saddest day of my life because I knew I was marrying for all the wrong reasons. Lee loved me very much and I wanted my independence. The guilt I felt resulted from getting into something I really didn't know I could handle. Lee and I were married at the City County Building in Detroit, Michigan by a judge. The wedding was informal with 150 other people being married on that day at the same time. After leaving the City County Building, we walked through the crowd of people to our car in the parking lot across from the Greyhound Bus Station.

This day was the happiest day of Lee's life. He was elated. I looked at him with tears streaming down my face and tried not to show how I really felt. Lee was a very loving and respectful young man even though I felt this wasn't the man for me to be marrying. Lee looked at me and asked, "Are you crying because you're sorry you married me?" I lied because I didn't want to spoil the happiest day of his life. "They're tears of joy", I explained. "I'm very happy to be your wife." I made a promise to myself that day, even if I didn't love Lee, I would learn to love him. I felt he didn't deserve any pain for marrying a woman he was sincerely in love with.

From the day we were married I had to take on the responsibility of being a housewife. After all women in my era were raised to be wives to their working husbands and have babies while staying at home to care for them. As my mother would always say, "Men are the sole breadwinners in the family". In the 50's and early 60's there were a few women in the workforce but their jobs paid very little in comparison to what men were earning.

Being married and a high school dropout, I later decided to be a stay-at-home mom and raise my children. That was the trend in the early 70's but it didn't last very long. Women's liberation was just getting off the ground. I decided I would go back to school and further my education. It seemed to be the best decision I could come up with at the time. I thought by completing a portion of my education and by attending high school and college on a part-time basis, it would put me that much closer to my goal of obtaining a degree. The children will have graduated from high school by the time I reached my goal. After having problems obtaining childcare for my children, I decided to put my education on hold until a later time. It wasn't an easy decision but I didn't have much of a choice.

Lee was a good provider although I didn't like the dominance I had to put up with to keep him happy and to keep our marriage in working order. I didn't like the fact he was the only working adult—the sole supporter of the family. Lee always had the last word of any conversation whether he was right or wrong. I felt I had little or no control of my life being totally dependent on my husband. When Lee and I would argue or disagree about something the first words out of his mouth was what he had done for me or was doing for me. It was as if I had not contributed anything to the marriage. Instantly I'd defend myself stating my duties as a wife.

"I get up each morning before you go to work and make breakfast. I make you lunch. Your dinner is always ready when you come home from work every day. I clean the house. I am your sex partner when there is a need ... What more do you want?"

After our children were born, I was a good mother to them. I attended their daily needs. All I did to keep my family together went unappreciated. This left me feeling useless and unimportant in my marriage. After we were married my husband and I moved out of my father's house. After being unappreciated after two years or so, I left my husband. I moved back to my father's house and decided to go back to school. My aunt Jimmy Lee moved into my father's house to help me with my children. I attended Trombly Adult Day School located on

Mack Avenue and East Grand Boulevard on Detroit's East Side. I hadn't learned to drive so I took a bus each day.

On May 31, of 1974 (the day after my youngest son's birthday), my husband became ill and died at Henry Ford Hospital due to spinal meningitis. After Lee's death, he left me tending to our two children Johnny and Dorthia. I had two other children, Cella and Kamicka, in my later years. I eventually adopted my niece Shantell, which totaled five children in all. I worked for a short while at a warehouse and decided it wasn't beneficial to work making a little over minimum wage. I was receiving Social Security benefits from my deceased husband and my children were receiving survivor's benefits. (One rule of fact was if you wanted to work while drawing Social Security benefits, you had to pay one dollar for every two dollars for the amount allotted to work.) I worked a few years and determined I was paying more money back than I was earning. When the warehouse moved to the suburbs, I moved along with the company for a short period of time. I decided after a few months I'd discontinue working and go back to school. I felt this would be more beneficial to my family and me in the future.

I went to Chadsey Adult Evening School to complete the remaining high school requirements and graduated with a high school diploma. It seemed to have taken forever. It seemed like I was trying to do everything at once-finding ways to accomplish my goals and get my Associate's Degree. I decided to leave Wayne County Community College after one year to attend business school. I thought if I went to an accredited business school, I'd be able to transfer my credits to another higher learning institution. After deciding not to return to Wayne County Community College, the following semester I attended Payne Pulliam School of Trade and Commerce for nine months and graduated with honors.

After graduating from Payne Pulliam, I signed up for the fall semester at Wayne County Community College. I figured I'd have my two-year degree in no time. After trying to acquire my transcript from Payne Pulliam to send to Wayne County Community College, I discovered Wayne County Community College didn't accept credits from Payne Pulliam. I was disappointed to say the least when I heard this news, but I couldn't just stop with one disappointment. I was on my way—or so I thought towards a degree I very much wanted.

There were other community colleges and business schools in the metro area that accepted credits from Payne Pulliam School of Trade and Commerce, but Wayne County Community did not. I didn't want to enroll at another school. Therefore I took the loss. I felt one day if I ever decided to change my major or change my curriculum altogether, I could always use my credits. Once I received the news that my attempt to a shortcutting degree failed, I had to start from where I left off. I decided to enroll back at Wayne County Community College and complete my degree in Computer and Data Processing.

Returning to the Computer and Data Processing program was disappointing. Many of the computer languages I was familiar with had changed and I needed the second portion of my computer language courses. Computer technology was changing at a faster pace than I was able to keep up with. Going to school on a part-time basis complicated things for me. That's when I decided to change my major from Computer and Data Processing to Criminal Justice. I thought 'law' was a curriculum that basically never changed—at least not at the same rate as technology.

This is how I found my way to where I am now. After graduating from business school, I became employed at Glenn Walsh and Associates. This was an architectural firm in Detroit which laid-out foundations for new buildings from blueprints. I worked there for a year as a secretary, but was laid off due to lack of work. I was still undecided regarding what to do with my life. I just knew I wanted to attend school.

There is a fourteen-year age difference between my two youngest children. Cella is the older of the last two children and Kamicka is the youngest of all my children. There were so many different issues arising out of my last two relationships. I was sure I never wanted to tie the knot again. I became unable to trust men because of the lies taking place during my last two long-term relationships.

Just the same, I was an unmarried single mother with four children and one adopted. I'd always wanted to be accepted for who I was as a person, not for what people wanted me to be molded as. This type of acceptance meant very much to me because I didn't want to be made into something I wasn't. I felt if I was not the type of woman a man was looking for, then that man should move on and try to find someone more suitable of his taste.

I wanted to stay away from male dominance, which had played a major role in my prior environment. Even now being a 'Baby Boomer', I find many males are dominant in their relationships because of the era in which I was raised. Many of my peers were teens when women's liberation was adopted for the working-women. At first men had a hard time accepting these changes. Many men (still living from my generation) 'til this day haven't successfully changed their male dominant mindsets. In the 70's the men were more acceptable than they were in the 60's. The male generation of today's world is more tolerable of women's liberation than they were in the past. Now our society has more women in the working field than ever before. This is because of the many single parent households.

In the spring of 1990, my niece Carla called me. She said Woodrow Stamping Plant was going to be hiring soon and wondered if I would be interested in putting my name on a list to be tested for employment. "Yes!" I replied. I gave her my name, social security number, and that was the end of the conversation. My brother-in-law Bob turned the names in to Woodrow Stamping Plant. I didn't think very much about the matter because I didn't think I would be called-even though I was in the market for a job. When I was first called, I had a fourteen-year-old daughter, a five-month-old little girl, and my eight-year-old adopted niece.

At the time I was hired at Woodrow Stamping Plant, there was a massive amount of people being hired. The anticipation was that in the next ten years the majority of the plant's employees would be eligible to retire. The late 80's and 90's were prosperous years for the factories. Woodrow Stamping Plant needed new employees to replenish the work force.

In June 1990, I received a call from Famous Parts Company—Woodrow Stamping Plant, asking if I'd be interested in being tested for employment qualification. The gentleman had a very warm and pleasant voice. I was excited to be called, and asked myself if I really was ready to work at Famous Parts Company. I knew I would be able to accomplish quite a few more things I wanted to do with a good paying job. This would start me on the road to recovery. I started many processes trying to bring my life into focus while being a self-supporting single mom. Cella would be graduating from high school in a few years or so. Dorthia, my oldest child had already graduated and left home and my oldest son was incarcerated at the time. I wanted to get my education—so I could be qualified to work in a field I so desired.

When I was hired at Famous Parts Company I was proud of the fact I worked for them. The mere fact of working for a company like Famous Parts Company was enough to make me proud. It represented hard work and dignity. I'd always heard how Famous Parts Company took pride in their jobs and put out the best product they could. My conception was that their union stood behind their members at all costs. I was dumbfounded when I found out that was a lie. I heard the union was strong and fair when a union member had been treated unjustly. The concept of being in the union was well worth the union dues we had to pay, or so I thought.

When I was hired at Famous Parts Company I went through two weeks of orientation. This consisted of a variety of information on the history of Famous Parts Company and Local 783. I had my hopes up and had a vision of people being treated fairly. I had no idea of how disappointed I would be when I found out this picture didn't exist. I guess I was experiencing the calm before the storm. I came to work with the company being realistic. I was indeed calm and ready to do whatever needed to be done. The storm came and things eventually got out of control.

I was making more money than I had ever made in my life. When I worked part-time two days a week, I earned twice as much money per hour than I'd ever made on any other job. I went from making $5.00 per hour to $14.00 per hour. I was elated—being able to provide for my family while working only one job. When asked where I worked, "Famous Parts Company" was my proud response. I'd hold my head up high and my small chest would stick out as far as it would go. To me, my job was prestigious. It was a once in a lifetime opportunity to get a job such as this. I never dreamed I would be working in a factory. I heard about the advantages of working with a union versus working without one. But in my experiences, I'd always been dealt a bad hand with regards to union representation at Woodrow Stamping and Local 783. As you will see, this was from the very beginning.

I would like to express to you the false expectation I had of what working for Famous Parts Company consisted of. No matter how many classes employees took on diversity paid for by the company, it was a waste of time and money. The company didn't practice what they preached. If Woodrow Stamping and Sarrow Stamping were so diverse, why didn't they have more diversity in upper management? Woodrow Stamping and Sarrow Stamping both at one point had an all—Caucasian management in the late 90's and early 2000's. How can you call yourself diverse when the entire top level of the company is Caucasian? To me this was the first sign of discrimination. If you look at all the skilled tradesmen from Woodrow Stamping and Sarrow Stamping Plant, you'd find the majority of them were Caucasian as well. This was during all the years I had worked for the company until 2004, although Famous Parts Company was sued for discrimination in the end. All employees who took the skilled trades test were compensated because of unfair hiring practices in the field of skilled trades. In 2002, a settlement was granted against Famous Parts Company for discrimination by the court. Famous Parts Company paid out compensation in 2005 and throughout 2006.

I would presume the Department of Civil Rights was involved in 'recruitment' when the company began asking, if there were any minority women interested in becoming skilled trade's people. This recruitment took place in April of 2002 at Woodrow Stamping Plant. At one point I remembered asking John Hail, Plant Chairman, "You mean to tell me the only people that can pass a skilled trades test are Caucasian?" Famous Parts Company hired such a large volume of employees. For some reason, at that point, they hired no more than 3% minorities. None were in upper management. Indeed they practiced discrimination rather than diversity. If they were more diverse, there would've been more minorities-and I don't mean just Blacks.

I have worked in two Famous Parts Company factories, Woodrow Stamping Plant and Sarrow Stamping Plant. I've seen enough discrimination within these two institutions to know discrimination was a factor. In my opinion, Woodrow Stamping Plant and Sarrow Stamping Plant only hired the majority of their own skin color because they wanted to keep minorities at a certain level. This allowed the Caucasians to stay in control. Management would always hire just enough minorities to be able to say they didn't discriminate. I heard rumors that Sarrow Stamping and Woodrow Stamping Plants were full of KKK members. Sarrow Stamping was a haven for KKK members. This is where they lived and worked. Some were adamant and open about how they felt about minorities. Others were not.

When I was first hired at Woodrow Stamping in 1990, I really couldn't understand how management was so disrespectful to the minority supervisors. I had never seen so many supervisors that were "sons of b*tches", "mother f*ckers", or whatever other vulgarities you've heard in your life. This definitely came out of the mouths of the company's management workforce. When I first started working, there were no women in supervision. There was plenty of disrespect to women by management's male employees. A lot of sexual harassment was taking place. A year after I started working, things began to get a little less stressful for the women.

I was prideful about the work I did. I think everyone started out doing the best job as possible when first hired. We were taught and rehearsed regarding putting out a 'good product'. But it seemed the more we tried to do the best job as possible, the less management cared about the product they were putting out. I learned while in orientation if you see bad parts or scrap going down the line, tell your supervisor. But in reality, employees were told to run the parts—knowing for a fact the parts were no good.

Once I got on the floor, I learned to adapt to the plant's way of thinking. It wasn't always about the quality of the product, but how many parts could be put out per hour. Having worked at Woodrow Stamping for years, I can't tell you how this place kept their doors open without ever making a profit. I am aware that for at least ten years Woodrow Stamping Plant had never been in 'the black' in terms of profit margin.

After a short time working in the plant, my expectations went from an all time high to an all time low. It seemed as though when I started working for the company I painted a beautiful picture of how the plant should work. They had rules that were supposed to be followed regarding 'safety' but they rarely followed safety procedures unless they were forced to. This was usually when someone had gotten seriously injured on the job or died in the plant.

I recall when I was a child and we had houseguests visiting, the house was to be cleaned from top to bottom. But when no one was coming to visit, we didn't keep our house as tidy. I learned that in Woodrow Stamping Plant and Sarrow Stamping Plant, things weren't always what they seemed. It was a facade. I can say that in the truest sense of the word.

2

REQUIREMENTS FOR HIRE

On September 20, 1990, I had no problem finding Woodrow Stamping Plant. I parked in the large parking lot. You could place another plant the size of Woodrow Stamping Plant in this parking lot. I then walked to the building where the security window was located. There was a section that had a glass partition with two gentlemen sitting behind the glass. When I walked in I said, "Good morning". The larger gentleman slid the small glass compartment open. "Can I help you?" he said. "I am here for a physical", I said to the security guard. He directed me across the street where the sign said Medical Department. He asked me to sign the visitor's log. I said "Thank you." I then told him to "Have a blessed day". When I made that statement he said, "Thank you". The large teddy-bear-looking gentleman had a smile on his face from ear to ear.

When I reached the Medical Department, I walked through the heavy glass doors. About ten people were lounging around waiting for their names to be called. As I was standing in the aisle I saw my nephew, Bud. He was also scheduled to take his physical on the same day as I. "Hello", I said while walking up to him. We began some small talk about how thrilled we were to have advanced to this point. It meant we had achieved all the necessary steps to be hired with Famous Parts Company. We spoke about how we didn't expect to be called. I said to Bud the timing couldn't have been better. Bud was staying with his grandmother on the city's East Side of town. Bud stated he was looking for a good paying job. He was trying to support his wife who had one child before they were married. This job would help him to better support his family without much struggle.

I had been in the process of looking for a job. My daughter Kameica was only 9 months old when I completed the hiring process. Bud and I talked about my brother (his father) who had died a year prior. He and Bud were very close before his mother moved to St. Louis. Bud returned to Detroit, Michigan when his father became ill. His father died the same year Bud graduated from high school. He decided to make Detroit his home, if he was able to find ample employment.

After we talked for a while, he was called for his medical examination. When the Medical Department was complete with Bud he was instructed to go to the Personnel Department. He walked from the Medical Department to the Personnel Office where the employment applications were to be completed. As Bud was leaving Personnel, I was just being called to see the doctor.

When I completed my medical examination and the rigorous process to be hired by Famous Parts Company, my nerves were completely shattered. I didn't know why. It wasn't as though I hadn't ever applied for a job before. Maybe it was the fact starting something new always made me feel a little uneasy. A drug test was given and the results were to be given at a later date due to the drug-testing lab being off plant grounds.

The company doctor felt I should be on restricted work due to my height. He issued me a signed document called, "Ability to Work Report". On this report I was assigned "B Status". This meant I was to be given lightweight work or work suitable for a small stature body. He informed me the restriction was given for my benefit. He stated he was giving me this restriction because he knew I'd be placed on many jobs that weren't structured for my height. I assumed the doctor knew what he was doing while giving me this restriction. Afterall, he *was* experienced in working in the plant. I felt confident the restriction served as my safety's assurance. He further informed me, "If you are placed on a job that isn't suitable for your height due to the non-consideration of supervision, have the supervisor look into the computer and the restrictions will appear". He then explained that the supervisor would have to place me on another job assignment more suitable for my body structure.

At the time, I didn't understand what the doctor was telling me since I had never worked in a plant before. I personally felt I could do any job set before me. I was also considered an excellent worker. This restriction was given and signed on September 20, 1990, which is the date I had my physical. In average cases this would be the actual day of hire, but on Woodrow Stamping Plant's records my seniority date was September 28, 1990. However, in 1993, someone who worked in the Medical Department terminated this restriction. I wondered the reasoning behind this. My height was something that wasn't ever going to change. The boxes checked on the report dated June 6, 1991 said I was an hourly employee who had been hired as full time. The box was marked "B-work suitable for small stature or lightweight". The remarks read: "As of September 20, 1990-exp '93" and this note was signed by medical representative S.M. The bottom of the form read: "IND REL APR 77. #5150".

I do remember Dr. Care as being a young White doctor who took his medical profession seriously by protecting the body from unnecessary overuse. I know he gave me this restriction as a means of preventing injury because of my height. He was trying to protect his employees from common destruction of the body that could be easily acquired in the plant (which I had no idea existed). I remembered Dr. Care being a physician who cared about his employees with great interest and concern. Looking back at Dr. Care's concern for the employees, he may have just come from medical school—not yet having the chance to be corrupted by the company. It was always a saying among fellow workers in Woodrow Stamping Plant, "Good doctors never stay with the company very long". The company needed doctors who sided with the company. Over the years I slowly understood why the restriction was given and what the company doctor meant. Woodrow Stamping Plant used jobs as the means of retaliation to force employees to comply with their demands.

Dr. Care gave me the bare truth. Of course it didn't take very long for some very inarticulate supervisor to challenge the doctor's authority. I was put on many difficult jobs that my height could not withstand. Fellow co-workers often came to assist me on my job assignment. They wanted to make my job tolerable and less difficult. Some fellow co-workers often traded jobs with me when my height became a factor. There were just as many caring supervisors as there were unscrupulous ones. Some gave me the best jobs they had. But many times they weren't quite good enough because I was still rather short in comparison to the majority of other workers.

After the formalities were completed in the Medical Department, the next phase was to complete my Employment Application. The Personnel Office clerk asked to see my driver's license for I.D. verification. I was told to go across the hall to a room where there were tables positioned in a circle. A group of us were asked to take a seat until it was time for our group, which consisted of fifteen people, to get their medical issues cleared. I was excited when I was told I would be a full-time employee. It was a full-time position available at the time I was hired.

We completed the remainder of the necessary paperwork for the Hourly Health Care Plan and Metro Craft Insurance Company. We weren't just handed the papers to fill out. We were walked through every step to make sure all the forms were filled out correctly. It was almost like we were in elementary school. We followed instructions as we were told. I remember vividly Mr. Stall, a Labor Relations Representative that worked in the front office, assisting in completing the paperwork when the employees were hired. He made a joke when we completed the beneficiary form. He said, "If you want to, you can put my name in the box as the beneficiary". After all forms were completed, we handed the forms in and were called at a later date for orientation (which was September 28, 1990.)

The first day of orientation seemed to be the longest day ever. Although the information was beneficial, it was hard to keep my eyes open. I guess this is why they gave us so many breaks between segments. The orientation lasted for two weeks informing the group of the rules and regulations in the plant. This orientation gave the group extensive information concerning chemicals and policies & concerns regarding Woodrow Stamping Plant. The union's rules and procedures on how to access the union when inquiring for help were also discussed. Job safety was one of the main topics and how the plant could be a dangerous place to work. The plant's motto was: "Leave the plant in the same condition you were in before you started work". This meant to have all body parts in tact-such as arms, fingers, hands etc …

Orientation was on the mezzanine floor of the plant. To get to the mezzanine you had to go in the plant's main entrance and take the escalator to the upper floor. When you reached the top you had to walk about half a mile to get to the orientation room. This was on the west side of the mezzanine. On this floor was the Committee Room for Local 783, the cafeteria, training rooms, and the locker rooms.

When I was hired at Woodrow there were four locker rooms. Three were for the men and one was for the women. The women's locker room was lined with lockers on both sides and there was a long bench that extended the length of the lockers. There were four rows with lockers on both sides. There was a bench handy to sit on between each set of lockers. The lockers were so narrow not much could fit in them. There was an area over the locker that was about the size of a shoebox. This area was used to place small items in. If you put your winter coat in the locker, you would have to put your purse on the floor or in this shoebox-sized compartment above the locker. You could tell the lockers were made for men because the lockers had very little storage space.

There was a shower in the locker room. There were two large round basins that resembled birdbaths with a foot peddle to control the water release. There were two types of soap attached to the basin. One was a green, very gritty soap normally used to remove grease or oil. This soap was very harsh on the hands and arms. The pink soap was softer on the hands and had lotion in it.

The locker room had a small section used as the lavatory. There were three stalls with toilets and a round birdbath basin for washing your face and hands.

There were lounging sofas in the ladies locker room where women would rest during their breaks and sometimes have lunch. The cafeteria was only down the hall. It was a meeting place women gathered to talk during their resting time.

When I first started working at Woodrow Stamping, there were sanitary napkins in the locker room placed on the mirror ledges in each restroom. After about three or four years, the plant stopped putting sanitary napkins in the ladies restroom. Some of the women misused the privilege by taking the sanitary napkins home. I can sometimes be very opinionated, but some people make it awfully hard for others. You would think women who made adequate salaries would pay for such items as sanitary napkins. But I guess thieves were everywhere—in and outside of the plant.

While I was in orientation, each individual table sat about six comfortably. We basically sat at the same table each day throughout the orientation. There were all women at my table. I became friendlier with them each day by sharing stories of family, friends, and prior work experiences. We also had small talk of news worthy current events. It was good to have lunch and keep conversations with my group each day.

Monica was an educated housewife with no children. Her husband was a superintendent at another plant. She wanted something to do other than just stay at home. Monica felt she would start working in the plant and later use her qualifications and education as a means to promote herself to other positions within the plant.

Donna was a young lady that was hired in the 70's. Donna was in great hopes of trying to obtain her back seniority. She had a problem with her attendance prior to being hired this second time around. Donna was a single parent with two children—a girl and a boy. Donna was about 5 feet 9 inches tall and weighed about 165 pounds. Her complexion was dark brown. She had deep holes in her face, which to me indicated a heavy drinker. She always wore her hair in braids. Some of the braided styles were short and other times long. She had extremely large hands for a woman. The rings on her fingers didn't do very much justice for her hands-making them appear much more noticeable.

Donna always seemed to be under the influence of something. She was very fidgety and at times incoherent. Donna was married to a man in his 70's and she was in her 30's. She had many male friends who were happy she was returning. I noticed most of the men attracted to her were somewhat older. I can't say for sure if she was on drugs or had alcohol issues. I can't say anything unethical about her. She was a friendly young lady who always had a smile on her face. Donna had faced many obstacles on her journey in life. She didn't own a car and I'm not sure if she even knew how to drive or not. She always had to get a ride to & from work.

Yvonne Stay was another woman hired with my group employed at Woodrow Stamping Plant in the 70's. She was called back without being given her back seniority. Yvonne was happy to be called back to work. If I can recall correctly, she had six children. Her husband was employed at another Famous Parts Company facility. She said her husband got addicted to drugs and that her rehire couldn't have come at a better time.

Her husband's job was hanging on a thread. Yvonne never complained too much about anything. She didn't want to make waves or jeopardize her job. She didn't want to give Woodrow Stamping Plant any reason for not hiring her full-time. Even though Yvonne was very dissatisfied with what was going on at the plant, she felt she should have gained her seniority back as some of the other employees had.

Karol Henderson another young lady hired in the 70's, never regained her original seniority date. She was married when she started working at Woodrow Stamping Plant in the 70's. Her husband was incarcerated and had apparently spent many years in and out of jail. She told us of how her husband would come to the plant during the 70's and pick her up from work in an angry rage. He had thoughts of catching Karol in some kind of unethical conduct unbecoming of his wife. I really didn't know the exact details of their relationship, but he was in prison. When she was called back to work he had been in prison for quite some time. Later they divorced and she married a man that worked at Woodrow Stamping Plant. She had two children by her first husband and one child by her new husband.

Pam Felson was another woman in our immediate group. Her husband was an inspector on the Assembly Side of the plant. Her plans were to work for ten years and retire when her husband retired. At the time of Pam's hire at Woodrow Stamping Plant, her husband had twenty years of seniority. Pam had one child with her husband.

Mazzie Cane was another story. She was too, hired at Woodrow Stamping in the 70's. At that time she was on medical leave quite often. Mazzie was laid off when Famous Parts Company had a massive layoff in the 70's. Woodrow Stamping actually started recalling employees hired in 1970 back to work in 1988. Woodrow Stamping Plant began hiring once again in 1990. The reason was so that in ten years the majority of the plant would be preparing to retire with 30 plus years of seniority.

When Mazzie Cane was called back she started as a part-time employee. She was never allowed to utilize her seniority recall rights. According to the contract, employees called back were supposed to be hired back before any 'new hires' and their seniority was to be adjusted accordingly. When Mazzie was called back in 1988, she was denied entry to the plant because when she was given a physical, the doctor gave her a lightweight restriction. She went to see her primary physician. He examined Mazzie and found no reason for her to be on a lightweight restriction. A note was written from Mazzie's doctor to Woodrow Stamping Plant's Medical Department to this effect. The letter didn't help Mazzie get her job back.

Mazzie was called back to work in 1990 with the group I was in. Mazzie Cane's husband was a supervisor and also an acting superintendent on the plant's floor. The reason she was called back to work this last time was because her husband did a favor for one of the union members. Once Mazzie was hired back she tried faithfully to obtain her original seniority from 1977. She had no success. She tried talking to Mr. Sophie in Labor Relations and she also contacted Bob Fleetwood, Bargaining Committeeman for Local 783. Mazzie had gone through the appropriate steps to gain her seniority back but all of her attempts were to no avail.

In the last days of orientation the group was notified there was a change in the hiring process. Some of the group would be part-time employees and others would be full-time. This information wasn't given until right before I started on the floor. I was told I would be part-time just before orientation was completed. I had no problem with being part-time. I made more money working part-time than working another full-time job elsewhere. Famous Parts Company's part-time employees started at $14.12 with $0.05 Cost of Living Allowance. I really couldn't complain about this at all.

3

FIRST EXPERIENCE ON THE FLOOR

On the last day of orientation, the group of fifteen people had a walkthrough of the plant. When I went on the floor, I was truly amazed at the size of the machines and the amount of noise produced by them. While touring the plant we had to wear earplugs to protect our ears from the noise. We also had to wear safety glasses to protect our eyes.

On the Press Side of the plant, there were large machines as tall as two-story buildings. These machines were as wide as a large house. I had never seen any-place so large where so many people worked at one time. The front of the line was called the *Draw*. The person running the *Draw* would place a piece of pre-cut steel in the press die using a tong instrument. It had a steel handle with a suction cup that would lift the pre-cut steel from a stack that was place it in front of the operator on a steel pallet. He or she would press the palm button to cycle the press. The press would make a loud booming sound vibrating the floor beneath us.

After the steel was molded and pressed into form, it went to the next station and exited the press from the back. Each part was lifted from the press by a robotic arm. Next the robot placed the pressed steel on a conveyor belt carrying the molded part to the following press station. A robot clamped each part and placed the molded part on the conveyor belt, which carried the steel down the line until each part in the back of the press was completed. In the process, the part passed through each press station until it became a finished product. At the end of the line there was a person who stacked the finished product into a basket/rack. After the part was put in the appropriate basket/rack, the materiel handler removed the part from the line for warehousing.

This was the process with all the lines on the Press Side. The amount of people who worked the line varied depending on the part being made. Each line had a production standard per hour that had to be met. Otherwise the supervisor was held accountable for not getting production quota per hour. This is how the Press Side of the plant worked.

Next, the group walked through the less noisy Assembly Side of the plant. The lines on this side of the plant didn't press parts. This side of the plant completed the unfinished parts by placing on additional parts (i.e. nuts and bolts) so the part could be shipped to its final destination. The Assembly Side of the plant had plenty of smoke and sparks coming from weld guns. It wasn't uncommon for sparks to set an employee's clothes and hair on fire. The sparks were hot and many times they would pierce right through the fabric.

On the majority of the lines on this side of the plant, there were stations where people sat or stood to place parts into a machine to be welded. This process would go down the line until the part was completed. After the product was completed, at the end of the line the material handler would move the basket/rack to a storage area. The parts were later placed in boxcars or trucks for their final destination at the assembly plant.

When the tour was complete our group went back to the mezzanine floor. We were told to make sure we brought back our safety glasses and earplugs. We were also instructed of the proper safety shoes to wear when we came in on Monday. We were told to meet at the Production Office and a supervisor would come get us from there to give us a job assignment.

If you were assigned to work on the Press Side of the plant, you were to stand at the Production Office on the press of the plant. If you were assigned to work on the Assembly Side of the plant, you would stand in front of the Production Office on the Assembly Side of the plant. I remember so very often waiting for a job when I was first hired. It made me think we were picked from a group like we were cattle to be sold. You were looked over very carefully and you were chosen by what they thought you could do—even if you couldn't do a job. The supervisors picked their best workers or their friends and family first.

Some supervisors would pick their workers late and as a result they would get the people no one wanted. Sometimes the employee didn't work fast enough or some were just plain lazy. If you were a good worker, then you were guaranteed a job each day. The word would spread around the plant if you were a good or lazy worker. The Production Office sat in the middle of the plant where supervisors would complete their paperwork on a daily basis. It was divided into many offices handling the process of daily overall production. The superintendent's office was located in the Production Office as well.

The plant was so large it took me a good month or so to become familiar without getting lost. The inside of the plant reminded me of a small city with hundreds of people. Some lines varied in the amount of people needed to run the line. Some lines had ten or more people working. On Line #551, it had 22 people working including the material handlers. When it was time to start work, you really couldn't see how many people worked in the plant because it was a steady stream of people coming through the doors. When it was time to get off work and the whistle blew, there were a thousand or more people in a mad rush going out the plant doors to the parking lot. Each employee was eager to get off work, which caused traffic jams.

On the Press Side there were lines as long as a mile or so. The lines were about 25 to 50 feet apart. Each line ran at least one model part, depending on the size of the product. A line would run a particular amount of parts and after that a changeover would be done. This is when the skilled tradesmen would remove the die from the gigantic machines. These machines held the die that molded the steel parts. The die-Setter replaced all dies down the entire line. When changeover was complete, the skilled tradesmen ran a trial part. If the part came out good according to inspection, the line is ready to run. The line wasn't supposed to run before the inspector checked for all holes, molds, and cutouts being in their proper places on the finished steel part. At that point, the part passes inspection and the line is ready to run. The inspector was to notify the supervisor of his line being prepared for running.

After I completed orientation, I worked on the Press Side of the plant. I was working on Line #25, which ran special parts. The Press Side was the side of the plant that ran at a very fast pace. I worked on many lines on the Press Side of the plant. Many of the jobs I worked were not very accommodating for my short arms and my height-being only 5 feet 1 inch tall. When I would work on the Press Side of the plant, accommodations had to be made by finding or making something called a *man stand* that would assist with me reaching the machines. A *man stand* usually made by the salvage repairmen, was a small ladder with a platform allowing me to stand at a comfortable height to work.

The Press Side was a very dangerous place. Each press had a scrap chute catching the falling pieces of discarded steel scrap. Sometimes the scrap was as sharp as a razor or as fine as a grain of sand. These scrap shoots were open wide enough for a person to fall through. The scrap shoot had a conveyor running to the Baylor House. Here the scrap parts were packaged and later shipped away. There were occasions of workers falling through the scrap shoot. Employees had to be especially careful because it was very easy to lose body parts in the presses. If any part of your hands or arms were caught between the presses, oh well … You can say goodbye to your hands and arms forever. In some cases employees or repairmen working on the dies stuck their heads in to retrieve parts. If the press were to fall at this time, they would die instantly. If your body was crushed or pinned between the die there would be no need for a doctor-only a body bag.

Before I would start work each day, I would have to go to the glove box and obtain gloves, padding, and sleeves to protect my arms. Each supervisor would furnish his employees with the supplies necessary to start a job before the beginning of the shift each day. Each supervisor had his own computer not far from the glove box. The people on the line, who had jobs already assigned on a daily basis, would be on their jobs when the whistle blew and the shift began. The others would wait right next to the computer and the glove box. The supervisor would then assign people to available jobs. If there were no more jobs to work on that day, the supervisor would call other supervisors in the area and tell them how many people needed to be placed. Another supervisor may have been looking for extra people to run their line. The extra employees would then be sent to the alternative line short of workers.

I became very friendly with Mazzie Cane because we were not only in orientation together, but it just so happened we'd be put on many jobs together. Mazzie was a nice person with a very pleasant personality. She always spoke of her husband and how he would always call her "fat". She was always trying to please her husband in any way possible. Mazzie's self esteem was rattled. She was never blessed with any children although she wanted them. Her husband Wayward Cane had two children from a previous marriage. Mazzie always tried to please Wayward's children. This sometimes became a challenge and she would be stressed out at work. Mazzie was about 5 feet 9 inches tall and weighed 170 pounds. Wayward was only about 5 feet 2 inches and weighed about 98 pounds soaking wet. Mazzie was a very attractive Caucasian woman with a Coke-a-Cola bottle shaped body. Though Mazzie suffered with her self-esteem, she was always neat in appearance.

Mazzie's husband Wayward was a supervisor who wasn't very well liked for one reason or the other. Woodrow Stamping Plant as a whole harassed this man on a daily basis. They fired him on numerous occasions and he would be hired back after contacting his lawyer. I later felt sorry for Mr. Cane because he was a nervous wreck. I knew how he felt because I too, had grown to know the feeling of being harassed constantly. It seemed that there was always something. I couldn't understand how these people who brought so much pain in harassing people, slept at night. It would be disgusting to any human being.

Management at Woodrow Stamping Plant was aware some of the lines in the plant didn't work. They always wanted to patch up the lines and never shut them down for the necessary repairs. Repairs were only made if the line broke down to a total stop as to where the line couldn't be forced to run under any circumstances.

When the lines would break down, the superintendent would walk up to Mr. Cane and literally curse him out. Mr. Cane was called every name but the Child of God. Sometimes it depended on how bad the part was needed or if there were any parts in stock. If the line that was no longer running had no available stock, this could cause a plant to shut down and send their employees home. If this happened that particular supervisor was truly in trouble. In this case, it happened to be Mr. Wayward Cane. The company would reprimand Mr. Cane and place him on various shifts. They'd have him working on the day shift one week, afternoon shift another week, and midnights on another. This could happen to Mr. Cane for months at a time. Many occurring events happened at no fault of Mr. Cane, but he was punished anyhow.

Mazzie Cane was a re-hire and should have been hired full-time. When she returned in 1990 she was part-time and it was as though she had never worked for the company before. She was hired in the 70's and laid off in the 80's. Mazzie was re-hired at Woodrow Stamping Plant as a part-time employee. Mazzie should have been full-time long before I was put on full-time status. This plant did exactly what they wanted with no accountability and the union went right along with it. The union gave them the authority to do as they pleased.

Mazzie contacted the union with regards to her hiring status. She became agitated when she saw many new employees hired before her. I felt Mazzie had a valid excuse for being angry because there was no one she could go to for help. The union did as they pleased. Mazzie thought about her husband. She felt if she pressed the issue with regards to her hiring status, Woodrow Stamping Plant might retaliate against Wayward. This is something Woodrow Stamping Plant did on a regular basis if you displeased them.

The more Mazzie Cane brought her situation to Local 783's attention, the more she was dismissed. The contract stated if you were a prior employee laid off and rehired, you should be placed on full-time status before any newly hired employee who had never worked for the company. This was not the case with regards to Mazzie Cane. Many others experienced not getting their seniority back. Nor were they placed on the full-time roster when rehired.

Mazzie and I often had lunch together and she always brought more than enough food to eat. She always tried different types of foods and would say,

"Crista! Here have some. It tastes good". Some things I would try eating, but some of the food that Mazzie tried, I refused to eat. She had all kinds of diet food to help her lose weight. "Wayward told me I had to lose some weight", she'd say. After our breaks were over, we'd go back to work. Mazzie was a good worker. She felt she had to always prove herself. I'm not sure if it was because of her husband's position or not but Mazzie always went that extra mile.

When we would first arrive to begin working, the part-time employees would gather in the groups they were familiar with from orientation. Many of the supervisors were glad to see Mazzie. She and I would always have a job each day. I never had a problem getting a job because I too, was an excellent worker. Mazzie and I always talked about how the part-time employees were treated differently. The majority of the part-time employees would usually stick together to keep up with the latest information regarding part-time employees. We were concerned because we were initially supposed to be full-time and at the last minute they changed plans. (At least that is what we as part-time employees were told.)

My brother-in-law Bob, who married my oldest sister Janet, would often come to my line and greet me. Bob worked a lot of overtime. He was one of the happiest people you could ever meet. He always had a smile on his face. Bob was a person who loved life. He would drink his liquor and he dabbled in just a few other pharmaceuticals as well, but his demeanor never changed whether he was drunk or sober.

Bob was over 6 feet with an oval shaped head. He was very thin weighing about 160 pounds. Bob had a warm and pleasant sense of humor. He had a laugh waiting for anyone who seemed to be depressed or under pressure. He would go that extra mile to find a smile, which meant a lot when one experienced unwanted fate from time to time. He was a gentleman if you ever knew one. He would pull out the chair in the lunchroom for you and open car doors. Anywhere there was a door, he was always ready to hold it open for the women. Bob loved women and gave them the utmost respect.

He would come to my line with a big smile. Bob thought I was a pretty smart person who wasn't afraid to stand up for what I believed in. He would smile and proudly tell his fellow co-workers I was his sister-in-law. Co-workers of Bob would come up to me, as I worked on the line to confirm I was his sister-in-law. Many of these people knew Bob very well because they had worked with him for years. Bob worked as a Die-Setter. His job was to insert the dies in the large presses. He also transported dies from one destination to another using the plant's flatbed truck. He was really proud I was hired at Woodrow Stamping Plant and proud I was an employee who took great pride in whatever I did.

When Bob's co-workers found out I was a hard worker and a smart one too, this gave Bob great pride. He was quite pleased with my work ethic. Word would always spread like a wild fire when you were a good worker, supervisor would talk, and employees would talk. When the word got around to Bob, he was surprised and felt very good that they were talking about me. Some of his co-worker never knew that Bob was married until he told them I was his sister-in-law.

Once I was hired, I found Woodrow Stamping Plant to be one of the most prejudiced places one could ever work. When I started working there in 1990, they had maybe one Black person in management. They had a few Black supervisors, but the way they were talked to was very disrespectful. The plant wasn't a racially friendly place with the exception of some women and some young White men. Most of the young White men were merely sons of supervision or the local union. The Black, Hispanic, and Middle Eastern men had a hard time. The Black supervision was treated with so much disrespect. All upper management was, as I like to call it, "Lily White". I will later explain of how some of the Blacks were treated.

I was so disappointed with Sam, a Black man that worked relief on the line. If Supervisor Joey Nick respectfully asked Sam to pick up paper and gloves under Line #551, he would have done as his supervisor asked anyway. But instead Joey said, "Sam you get down and clean this damn shit up!" It was the tone he used which made me feel he wasn't talking to me in such a belittling manner. Joey Nick was speaking of the area I worked. Under the stand there was a lot of paper, gloves, and other rubbish the afternoon shift hadn't cleaned up. All the people working this job prior had to do, was throw their trash and dirty gloves in the proper containers. The trash cans and glove baskets were only a few feet from every job.

My job was to place a part called an *elbow* on the conveyor. The conveyor would carry the elbow to the robot that dispensed glue. The glue gun would spread the glue along the edge of the part. This was to help the part stick together when the part was welded to the floor plan of the truck. I had to stand on a *man stand* that elevated my body to the conveyor.

The former shift would just leave the gloves and garbage in the small area I worked. I stopped the job I was working and asked Sam, "Why did you allow Joey Nick to talk to you in that manner? I don't see him talking to anyone who is White in that manner. Why are you allowing him to curse you like that?" Sam looked up at me and said, "Joey is my friend. We got hired in together. He didn't mean nothing by what he said."

I replied, "That doesn't give him the right to disrespect you in that way. Friend or no friend—he had no right speaking to you in that manner. I would never speak to my *friend* that way. Maybe you need to re-evaluate who your friends are." I meant what I said to Sam.

The Blacks were always the last hired and the first fired. The plant as a whole was majority Caucasian. It didn't matter which office you walked in at Woodrow Stamping Plant. There might've been one Black, but believe me they weren't going to be there very long.

4

EMPLOYMENT STATUS IN QUESTION

I completed my 90 days of employment at Famous Parts Company—Woodrow Stamping Plant and I started receiving full-time benefits. There was a problem with my employment status. In December 1990, I was paid for Christmas and New Year's Day as a full-time employee. I didn't know at that point that part-time employees weren't supposed to receive holiday pay. To receive this Christmas Bonus, I had to have actually worked 90 workdays as a part-timer. If this had happened it would take six months to be able to receive benefits as a part-time employee. Although I had worked 90 days as a full-time employee under the contract, Famous Parts Company and Local 783 said I was not full-time.

After the Christmas holidays were over and we returned in January 1991, I received holiday pay for Martin Luther King Jr.'s birthday. It was about one week after receiving the money that it was taken back. Our union representative said the money was given in error. When I received the first $600 dollars in December 1990 as my Christmas bonus, I bought a new cooking stove and a used sofa to put in my basement. I looked up the agreement between the Executive Branch of Union and Famous Parts Company—Volume I—Section K, which pertained to part-time employees only. The contract stated part-time employees could not receive holiday pay until 90 actual working days. If this was true, I had to have been full-time.

At this time, I had received a Christmas bonus and Martin Luther King Jr. holiday pay. That's two errors within sixty days. If Woodrow Stamping had corrected the error, it would not have appeared. I was a full-time employee. It wasn't that I wanted to become full-time at any cost. I did feel that since Woodrow Stamping and Local 783 never corrected the error with my hiring status when they first became aware of the so-called error, I deserved to be full-time with all the benefits. I didn't feel the company should keep the money to do as they pleased, when the money should have been directed to the person it was intended for. Woodrow Stamping and Local 783 wanted me to stay full-time so they could continue receiving my money. They didn't want me to be labeled as full-time. I knew it wasn't fair, but at the time there was little I could do about any-thing—but it wasn't because I didn't try.

I was working on the Assembly Side of the plant when I summoned my Union Representative, Billy. I asked him if he was sure I wasn't full-time. I only wanted him to check my employment record to verify this information. He said, "Now Crista you know you're part-time!" I figured he thought this was too much for me to ask of my union representative. Ideally if I had a concern calling for assistance, I was to seek the help of my Local 783 Committeeman. The reason this information was so important to me was because I was to have originally started working full-time in the first place. I knew I was at a full-time status, when all the adjustments and withdrawals kept reoccurring.

I thought there might have been a mistake in paperwork at first. This was my main focus for contacting Billy. I didn't like the idea that money was given and taken away by "error". The company should have kept better records of events such as this because incidents like this should never happen. The union was allowing this to happen with their approval. It was clearly evident the union wasn't representing its union members because I wasn't the only part-time person this happened to. The part-time employees started getting their heads together and I later found out by talking to others, they had in fact experienced the same problem. After a while I put the subject to rest since more than one part-time group had the same problem. I thought this problem could very well have been an error. I had no idea this would become a common problem in the future in which no one wanted to fix.

Billy, the Committeeman said to me, "You are not full-time" and became agi-tated with me inquiring about my employment status. He wanted me to say nothing more on the subject and began walking in the opposite direction, as he was speaking to me. "You are not full-time Crista!" I yelled to him as he kept walking, "Part-time employees don't receive benefits—only medical insurance. Full-time employees receive these benefits. Is that so Billy?" Billy then slowed down and said, "The Company had ten days to clarify an error", and expressed the company was within the ten-day frame of protection. I just stood there for a minute and said to myself, "You lying buzzard". He really thought I was stuck on stupid.

I walked back to my job complaining to Mazzie Cane. Mazzie then told me she talked to Johnny Hail who was Plant Chairman at the time. She said he told her I had no right to complain about my employee status. He said, I was part-time and had no union rights what so ever and if I kept on complaining about this mistake, it could hurt my chance to become full-time. In essence he was telling Mazzie to threaten me to keep my mouth closed. I then told Mazzie sooner or later the truth would come out, even though at the time no one was listening.

I along with some of the other part-time employees began receiving literature intended for full-time employees. Some of the benefits included direct deposit, a credit card application from Union Privilege, information regarding higher learning, not to mention medical insurance benefits from Metro Craft, and full life insurance benefits. I started asking questions. Still, the only answer I received was the company made a mistake and I was not full-time.

In February 1991, I was laid off. This was when the Persian Gulf War was beginning. The new contract was being negotiated and was later ratified in September 1991. I was laid off in February 1991, returned in July 1991, laid off again in December 1991, and called back in April 1992. Woodrow Stamping was flourishing with the money they were pilfering and they didn't just stop there. They became greedier and greedier and started pilfering from more than just Woodrow Stamping Plant's part-time employees. They began pilfering money from people who were obtaining Worker's Compensation benefits. They also pilfered money from employees who were laid off in the 70's. They pilfered from those on long term medical leaves while retiring them. The employees had no knowledge they had a retired status. They thought they were on a long-term medical leave for many years.

The amount of money pilfered was massive. The company pilfered all benefits from part-time employees, who were actually full-time for three years or more. Woodrow Stamping Plant was allowed to get away with what they were doing because of Local 783's participation. I know now what Chairman, John Hail meant when he said, "There will be a time Woodrow Stamping Plant will hire part-time employees only". Their plan was to hire all employees as full-time while paying them part-time wages as they did others and me. I guess people in the groups hired in the 90's were a pilot program. It was successful because they have been pilfering ever since.

I didn't know then I had hit the nail on the head and had figured out what was going on. They decided to get rid of me for learning of their piracy. I became a threat and I didn't understand why until later. I didn't know exactly what it was I knew, but they knew I knew something. I was right they were pilfering. They knew the longer I was at Woodrow Stamping Plant I'd constantly piece together what they were doing.

Mazzie and I were wondering what was going on because according to the contract, we were working many days 32 hours a week. There would be times that we would work 5 days a week. Looking back at what happened, it's quite clear how the company got away with pilfering money from the part-time employees and anyone else they could pilfer from.

While laid off I should have received a vacation check in June 1991. But instead, the company's Controller diverted it to the special account set-up. The checks wouldn't reach the part-time employees by putting us on lay-off. They knew they were safe that way. The checks would have been distributed to us as they were in June 1992. That was assurance the checks wouldn't reach the person they were intended for. When we returned back to work in July 1991 after shut down, there would be no problem regarding employees receiving checks due to them. They collected the checks and laundered the money prior to our return from lay-off.

When I returned in July 1991, I didn't have to take a physical as required by contract for part-timers. I only had to have a hearing test given once a year near my birthday. When I returned, I was working for Mr. Wilmore. He was about 5 feet 9 inches tall and weighed about 140 pounds. Wilmore was an extremely pale Caucasian man. His skin pigment appeared to resist tanning from the sun. He had dark brown hair that was parted on the left side of his head. His mustache curled up reminding me of Adolph Hitler.

Wilmore wasn't a very nice guy either. I worked for him on Line #22. The line ran long thin parts placed in the dashboards of small compact cars. Mr. Wilmore was the type of supervisor who wanted his line running smoothly as most supervisors did. It kept the heat off his behind so management would leave him alone.

Wilmore wasn't afraid to speak about how he felt. He expressed his opinions openly. "Women should not be working in the plant." He didn't feel sorry for women and he would say, "Women should be at home taking care of the children and not working in a plant". He also stated, "If women want to be paid the same as men, they should not complain about the jobs I put them on". I would tell Mr. Wilmore that if the men wouldn't leave the women with the babies and paid the women child support, just maybe the women wouldn't *have* to be working in a plant. I told him it was only fair women had the opportunity to hold a good job in order to support their families just like the men. From what I could see in the plant, a lot of women literally out-worked the men.

When I worked for Mr. Wilmore, I was his shortest person. He would always have to accommodate the jobs I worked because it was quite difficult for me with regards to my height and arms' length. If the accommodations still presented a safety factor, he would just have me stack the finish product into the baskets at the end of the line. I must admit even that was a challenging job at times. I had to bend into the large baskets and stack the parts that had been completed during the stamping process. The parts were ready to be shipped to the Assembly Side of the plant. By the end of the day my back would feel numb. The stacking jobs were considered the best jobs if they were small parts.

I said then, and I will say now, that the plants cater to taller people at least 5 feet 7 inches. There was only one section in the entire plant catering to the smaller stature employees. That was the CT20 area. And I don't want you to think there weren't any short men, because there were. They had the same problems the small stature women faced, even though they may not have complained as much.

5

PROBLEMS WHEN LINES ARE DOWN

Many of the lines on the Press Side were often down because of various problems. Sometimes the line would go down for the total shift and the employees would be placed on another line. If parts were not needed elsewhere in the plant, the supervisor would ask for volunteers to go home. If the supervisor had a line not running because of mechanical problems, the supervisor would start another line up in that department. Sometimes a line was thought to be fixed and when the line was started up for the first trial run, the same problems existed. It was not unusual for employees to go from one line to another in an effort to keep them working. Many days I was shifted from line to line while repairs were being made. After running a few parts and the line breaking down again, I would be transferred to a line where the parts were not needed or I would be asked to clean up around the line.

The supervisor would always try to stay in good standing with the machine repairmen. The repairmen could keep their lines down for long periods of time and keep the supervisor from getting any parts ran. When the line went down, the supervisor would stand right over the repairmen while they were repairing the line although that didn't make them work any faster. Since supervision didn't know how to repair the machine, it was almost a useless act for them to stand over the repairmen. They yet took their time to repair the machines. If the skilled trade's repairman didn't like the supervisor he was working for, the line just might be down all day depending on the repairman's mood. The skilled trade's repairmen threw their weight around Woodrow Stamping Plant. They also stuck together. I witnessed this action taking place for many years. If workers got angry with the supervisor, then everyone would work together in unison until the supervisor changed his attitude and treated his employees with a little more respect.

In many instances Woodrow Stamping Plant didn't maintain the machines properly. When the problem started, it might have taken maybe a half an hour to repair the minor problem. The supervisor would not allow the repairman to stop the line for parts and repairs because he was only interested in getting his quota for the day. When they couldn't get their parts out on time, it would cost the company dearly.

Management's stand was to fix the line enough to run on short terms. Each time the line went down they lost precious time, money, and parts. The idea was not to allow the 'parts plant' to shut down because of having no parts. A machine may have been down because it was off gauge, or it could have a cracked die, electrical malfunction, broken pens, or motor burn out. These are just a few reasons why a machine might break down.

There would be times when the line would break down and the skilled tradesman was repairing the machine while his supervisor, area manager, plant superintendent, and the plant manager all joined him as he worked. They all would be standing around in a group watching him work. I could never understand why all of management would stand around the machine repairmen. None of management knew anything about machinery. If the repairmen were tearing the machine apart under their noses they wouldn't know the difference. I always thought when management stood over employees that it was a form of harassment. I think the moral was that if management stood over the repairmen, they'd fix the machines much faster.

There weren't enough skilled tradesmen in supervision. Therefore Woodrow Stamping Plant placed just about anyone as skill trades supervision. Many times when the lines broke down, the machines needed a miracle. The repairmen weren't miracle workers. Often times this is what was needed because the machines were never allowed to be properly maintained when initially necessary.

Woodrow Stamping Plant would allow minor mechanical problems to become major problems by allowing the machine to continuously run when malfunctions occurred. There were times when a part was a *hot part*. A *hot part* is a part needed desperately in order to keep suppliers facilities stocked with parts supplied by Woodrow Stamping Plant. *Hot parts* had to be well stocked to keep plants from shutting their lines down and sending their employees home for lack of parts. If employees had to go home due to shortage of *hot parts*, Woodrow Stamping the supplier, would have to pay the cost of any losses suffered.

Another heavy expense is the transportation cost to get the part to its destination as quickly as possible. If this were the case, the parts would be shipped by truck if the destination were local. If the destination was at a distance, the parts might be shipped by airplane or helicopter. The train wouldn't be used for hurried situations because they were too slow. They wanted to use whichever transportation was the fastest. It would be very expensive for the company if they couldn't get the parts to their supplier on time. The plant always tried to keep the supplier happy by having their parts at the destination on time. The major problem was faulty machinery, which was the blame for the parts being in high demand. Woodrow Stamping Plant would run the parts around the clock on all three shifts if there were a need for a *hot part*. They would do this even if the machines weren't at one hundred percent.

I would always wonder how a repairman could work when he was stepping on the toes of supervision, managers, superintendents, and sometimes even the plant manager. This was just the way the plant operated. Logic wasn't always an issue. Management had no idea about repairing a machine. This was when the repairmen were important. It was at those times the repairmen gained respect of management.

6

RETURNING TO WORK

Upon returning from lay-off, there was much commotion with the discontent of the employees recalled in April 1992. Local 783 told former employees they were getting their original seniority back. Some employees received their seniority back, but not many. The remainder of the employees was extremely dissatisfied with what the union expressed to them. Local 783 continued telling local union members there were no provisions for them to receive their back seniority. This was to be the bottom line on the subject.

Employees wanting their seniority back, organized for a class-action lawsuit against Woodrow Stamping Plant. They assumed their lawyers were going to take the union to court for breach of contract. Something happened somewhere between their first visit with the lawyer who had agreed to take the case for them, and the last meeting with this lawyer. The lawyers had them thinking they were his potential clients. They had grounds for a lawsuit after conferring with counsel. Three to six months into the case, the lawyers backed out of the lawsuit by stating there were no grounds for a lawsuit.

The employees went back and forth with Local 783 on the subject of why they hadn't received their back seniority and why 'new hires' were being hired before them. This was the issue the part-time employees faced when they returned from layoff. Some people originally hired in the 70's were hired with back seniority. Others were not. Local 783 were unable to come up with any answers and ignored the employees. According to the contract, the former employees should have received their back seniority. They should have been hired full-time before any part-time employee, but this was not the case. Woodrow Stamping Plant hired part-time people before they hired seniority employees whom were laid off during the 70's.

At the same time, the part-time employees had an agenda of their own trying to obtain their full-time status. Mazzie Cane, Karol Henderson, and Yvonne Stay wanted their seniority back and also wanted to be reinstated as full-time employees. The prior employees were upset for losing their seniority. They were dismayed seeing new hires come in the plant as full-time employees while they remained part-time. This was brought to the attention of the union and they were treated as though they didn't exist. The union gave a song and dance of what they were trying to do regarding the subject, knowingly applying stall tactics to keep the employees hopeful for a while. According to Local 783's Plant Chairman John Hail, they were going to meet with the International Union at the Executive Branch on the subject. The answers were never on a positive nature.

Local 783 didn't have to do anything they didn't want to do. Local 783 wasn't being held accountable for the decision they made due to being in the pockets of Woodrow Stamping Plant. Management always seemed to back them up. They also had the Regional Office of the union to assist in backing up Local 783's wrongdoing. This didn't just stop at the Regional Office. The range of dishonesty spread all the way to the Executive Branch of the Union and also to the Executive Branch of Famous Parts Company.

I'm not saying the entire Executive Branch of the Company was involved. However I do believe Local 783 had special individuals such as lawyers and government agencies involved in the cover-up of my grievance never being filed. You will read about this in later chapters. The lawsuit I filed against Famous Parts Company never went any further than the judge's chambers, where it suddenly died. I believe this scheme was so large that the individuals were running a company within a company without some of the Executive Branch of the Company ever being aware of what was transpiring.

I am aware that not every individual involved from the lower level of the union to the Executive Branch of the Union was involved. Local 783's and Woodrow Stamping Plant's actions were condoned by both the Executive Branch of Local 783 and the Executive Branch of Woodrow Stamping Plant. They were well aware I was not being represented by Local 783 as a union member should've been.

For the most part, I paid close attention to what was going on within the plant and kept my mouth shut if it didn't pertain to me. There was a group hired full-time at Woodrow Stamping Plant before the group I was hired in. Although they were hired about a week or so before I was hired, they were allowed to work 89 days. At the last minute, the plant told them they'd have to revert back to part-time. These employees were angry although there was nothing they could do about the situation. That scenario happened on many occasions where employees worked 89 days before they became full-time. The employees were promised they would become full-time but each time this happened, they were reverted back to part-time. All benefits they received as full-time were being pilfered.

I worked through the hunting season, which started in September of 1990. I worked five days a week until December 1990 and was laid off for the Christmas holiday. While off, I came to Woodrow Stamping Plant to pick up my last pay-check of the year 1990. As I stood in line waiting for my check I was asked if I was full or part-time. When I answered part-time, I was then given two checks stapled together. One was for the prior week I had worked. The other check was my Christmas bonus. Of course, I later learned part-time employees didn't receive fringe benefits such as this.

The following year in December 1991, I received a Christmas bonus once again in the amount of $600. According to contract after working 90 days, only full-time employees are entitled to receive these benefits. I later found out if I had received a Christmas bonus as a part-time employee, it would have been in the amount of $300. When I started receiving these benefits, I took my check stub to the union and tried to have them investigate whether I was full-time or part-time. I never received that particular check stub back for the year of the second Christ-mas bonus.

I was later told that Pike Pavis, Union Representative, misplaced my check stub. Since I was paid my Christmas bonus during the second week of December 1990 for $600, my assumption was that I was full-time. (Although neither Woo-drow Stamping Plant nor Local 783 would admit to my full-time status at the time.) It didn't matter because when I did obtain a copy of my employment record, it stated I was full-time at the time, I was complaining about my employ-ment status.

When I returned to work in April 1992, I worked various hours. The majority of the time I worked three to five days a week. According to the contract part-time employees were to only work Monday, Friday, Saturday, Sunday, and holi-days. Many others and I worked days outside the contract. I always felt some-thing was wrong because there was always some kind of error on my paycheck. Whether it was pay shortage, shortage of hours, days worked and not calculated, and of course withdrawals of monies from my pay check each week.

Woodrow Stamping Plant always said money paid by error had to be paid back through adjustments. I never received credit as paying the money back. I was becoming flustered with what was happening and I began complaining. I went to Local 783 and Woodrow Stamping Plant's Labor Relations Supervisor to obtain answers regarding my employee status. No one seemed interested when I said the money taken back wasn't going to the company. I guess no one was interested in knowing where the money was actually going.

I walked into the Labor Relations Office and saw Mr. Doso, the Labor Relations Supervisor, before he passed away. I explained my situation as it occurred and he promised me he would address the matter and eliminate the problem. I asked Mr. Doso how it could be possible that I was receiving the full-time benefit package and being paid part-time pay per hour. I asked him if it was possible to be in the computer system as a full-time employee. His reply was "No! You are not full-time!" Whenever I asked this question, I was looked upon as a person with no sense of intelligence whatsoever.

It was something in the way they always answered "No!" Real snappy and to the point, as to say you're not going to get any further information. I then proceeded to ask Mr. Doso if I could get a copy of my employment record. He said, "No!" He eventually gave me a copy of my payroll record and asked me not to show anyone else. It was only my payroll time sheet. I didn't think much of it then, but there had to have been two sets of records for each part-time employee that Woodrow Stamping Plant pilfered from. Mr. Doso gave me an inaccurate time sheet.

I was receiving full-time benefits although Woodrow Stamping Plant wouldn't admit I was full-time, when I sought clarification on the matter. I was not working the normal hours or overtime hours as a part-time employee. Again part-time employees' regular scheduled days were Monday, Friday, Saturday, Sunday, and holidays. We were forbidden to work Saturday and Sunday because Woodrow Stamping scheduled us to work as full-time on their other separate set of records. Woodrow Stamping Plant should have paid us part-time employees on our regular days of work. Instead, they allowed full-time sets of records to maintain time and a half for Saturday and double time for Sunday. They funneled and laundered the whole week's check including the weekend. Since we were full-time, Woodrow Stamping Plant's records showed we worked those weekends. Therefore we couldn't actually work Saturday and Sunday as part-timers. As part-time employees, we were forbidden to work those days while those days were our normal days of work. The company was pilfering the Saturday and Sunday pay.

I told my co-workers something was wrong with the picture when I returned in April 1992. I told my fellow co-worker in the ladies locker room during our lunch break, "You can't tell me I'm not in the computer as a full-time employee. I think we all are". Everything that happened thus far pointed to me being a full-time employee. I wanted to know why no one wanted to clarify the problem and fix the so-called "error". The company just let the problem go on repeatedly year after year.

During March of 1992, I decided to call Famous Parts Company's Headquarters to gather more information regarding my work status. I wasn't having much luck in terms of obtaining my employment status at Woodrow Stamping Plant. If nothing else, I was in hopes someone outside of Woodrow Stamping Plant and Local 783 would look into the problem and fix it.

Most all employees referred to the World Headquarters of Famous Parts Company as the *Transparent Headquarters*. I wanted to inquire about my work status and my seniority date because I felt I had a right to know. I spoke with a lady named Diane. After I explained to Diane what I wanted, she asked for my social security number and other information to verify my identity. This lady looked up the information and told me my seniority date was September 28, 1990, but there was a problem as to my work status. Diane informed me I would have to speak to Labor Relations at Woodrow Stamping Plant to have them clarify the work status error. She said the error had to be clarified and changed from the plant I was employed. No matter where I went, it appeared no one was willing to help. I was always getting the run-a-around.

After speaking to Diane at the Company's Headquarters, I went back to Woodrow Stamping Plant and spoke to Peter Lett, Labor Relations Supervisor. When I entered his office, his desk was a mess and he looked as though he had been on a drunken stupor before he entered the plant that morning. I remember when I walked in his office the first thing I smelled was the scent of alcohol on his breath. The scent filtered the room with a foul odor and it was only around 8:30 a.m. He has since retired, but he told me not to worry about a thing because I was part-time and nothing was going to change regarding my situation. I started wondering why everyone was so adamant about me not being full-time, but no one wanted to look to find out what was happening. Instead they pretended there were no grounds for any kind of investigation whatsoever. I felt there was a need contrary to what they said. I was willing to prove otherwise, but each time Woodrow Stamping Plant and Local 783 stopped me dead in my tracks.

I had December eligibility and during April of 1992, I started noticing a difference in my paychecks. I had forty hours of vacation time and forty hours of personal time coming. The fifteen people who were reverted back to part-time all experienced the same events. Once again I became puzzled about the reoccurring events. I was constantly told I was not full-time by the union and the company. With all that had transpired, the company still tried to tell me I was part-time status. They couldn't explain how to clear up the misunderstanding. They were aware of the fact they couldn't just tell me anything in order for me to stop fanning the flame. I wanted answers that no one was willing to give. It really didn't matter where I had to go to obtain satisfactory answers—I was willing to go.

In June of 1992, I was prepared for the vacation shut down where the whole plant goes on vacation for two weeks. On the last day of work, the paychecks were distributed and I received my vacation check along with my regular check. I wondered how this could be possible if I was being told I wasn't full-time. I started thinking of the Christmas bonuses, the vacation checks, and the Martin Luther King Jr. holiday pay. There were so many unanswered questions in my head. It weighed heavily on my thoughts.

By this time I was ready to confront Local 783 and Woodrow Stamping Plant. After I received my vacation check in June 1992, I returned the following week to pick up my prior week's paycheck. At that time I was informed I had a hold on my paycheck. To my surprise, I was told by security I had to see someone in Labor Relations. I would be able to have my questions answered upon seeing Mr. Sophie, Labor Relations Supervisor.

Mr. Sophie met me at the Labor Relations Office. I identified myself at the doorway of his office. He then rose from his desk. He looked down on his desk shifting papers around until he picked up a piece of paper and handed it to me. He said I had to sign the paper, which stated I had to pay back the vacation monies given to me, or return the check back to the company. I became furious because Woodrow Stamping Plant knew far enough in advance that they could have stopped the vacation check given to me in June 1992. This information appeared on my weekly pay stub from April until June 1992.

My eligibility was December of each year, therefore giving the company six months to notify me this money wasn't due to me. Instead the company waited *after* I received the check to inform me I had to repay the money. I was so upset I told Mr. Sophie when the government or any other debtor garnishes a person they don't take the whole check without notification. Normally when there is a garnishment, there is always notification given prior to the deduction being withdrawn. Woodrow Stamping Plant knew in advance and did nothing to stop the vacation check to be issued in June. If I weren't part-time, you would assume I was full-time by the repeated occurrences. (Woodrow Stamping Plant later stated I was full-time.)

When Woodrow Stamping Plant withdrew the money from me, they gave me no notification the money was going to be taken. I was steaming with anger. Woodrow Stamping Plant was in error and I took it seriously. I had good reason for concern because all these discrepancies had everything to do with my seniority and whether I was actually full-time or not. Not only that—where was the money going? I had enough inconsistencies concerning my part-time versus full-time status. I decided to get some answers from Local 783 on the matter once again.

I was aware that in December 1990 and 1991 I was under full-time status. In 1992, I was scheduled to receive a check again in December as well, but I had it stopped. In 1993, I did not receive a performance bonus or a Christmas bonus because I'd transferred to Sarrow Stamping Plant in November 1993. Neither did I receive the unused portion of my vacation and personal days. A few of my co-workers received their money and they were all White. There was an explanation given, but Woodrow Stamping always had an excuse for whatever they did regarding Crista Carrie.

When I returned from vacation shut down in mid July 1992, I went straight to the union office on the mezzanine to discuss what happened with Mr. Hame Pate, Committeeman of Local 783. When I came to pick up my last check after shut down, I met with Mr. Pate and I discussed my situation. I wanted firm answers. I didn't want to hear I wasn't full-time any longer. I knew better than to believe anything other than I *was* full-time. Mr. Hame Pate said, "Let's go to Labor Relations". When we reached our destination we met with Labor Relations Supervisor, Mr. Doso and the Union Representative from the day shift. Larry a skilled trade's Union Representative, also attended because he was already in Mr. Doso's office.

While Hame Pate and Larry looked into the computer along with Mr. Doso, they looked at each other and said, "Yes Crista *is* in the computer system as a full-time employee!" However they still insisted it must've been an error. I thought to myself, finally after 2 years this is the first time anyone has come close to admitting I was full-time in the system.

Finally being told it was an error, I decided to continue fighting for my seniority. Woodrow Stamping Plant and Local 783 had always known I was full-time. They thought I would just go away. They wanted to continue doing what they had been doing for the last two years. They were playing mind games. If I was correct, I was determined to know where the money went that I paid back through adjustments.

After returning from vacation, the part-time employees in my group were becoming unsettled as to what was going on. The group kept trying to get a few straight answers from Mr. John Hail of Local 783, who always promised them they were "going to be full-time soon". Each time John Hail was asked the date and time they would become full-time, the date was moved back even further.

Mr. Hail began building false hope in the part-time employees. Hope was what the entire group had to hold on to with regards to becoming full-time. Other part-time employees were experiencing the same problems I experienced, and they wanted answers as well. They started asking questions about their work status and why they had experienced the same issues. It was brought to the attention of Local 783 and management at Woodrow Stamping Plant, but again they avoided giving us any answers regarding our issues we were facing. The least they could have done was not act as though we were transparent or weren't standing there asking questions.

I thought the money, I should have received and had to pay back was being pilfered right before my eyes. At this point years had passed from the time I was told I was full-time in the computer system. I was aware it was no "error" while Woodrow Stamping Plant and Local 783 knew it too. But that didn't stop them from continuing to pilfer money from me. They knew at that point some of us knew the truth about what they were doing, but said nothing. They also knew there was nothing I could do about it since I was the only one aware of this information who'd speak freely about it. They wanted it to stay that way—silent.

The group of fifteen and I realized we were getting the run-a-round from the union representatives and the Union President/Plant Chair, Mr. Hail. The group as a whole wanted to take action but didn't know how. Local 783 was telling some of the part-time employees they had no right to access the union. Some of them were told the union couldn't represent them until they were full-time. I could not believe what I was hearing. Believe it or not, many part-time people believed every word Local 783 told them. I informed many of my part-time co-workers they *did* have union representation from the time the initial fees were taken from their checks. Not to mention the union dues that was being withdrawn from their paychecks each month. They couldn't just take our money and not represent us—so I thought. Many part-time employees weren't ready to challenge what the union said for fear of losing or complicating their jobs. They wanted to be full-time as soon as possible. Therefore they didn't question if they had rights or not as union members. Local 783 were aware there would be no questions asked.

There was a group that worked about 30 days (a little more than our group). Since they hadn't received their 90 days, they were reverted back to part-time. Mr. John Hail told them, their group of part-timers would be the first group to go full-time. Others and I were told the company was going to hire in the order of which groups were hired first. However this wasn't always the case. The young White men were the first to be hired because they were the future of the nearly all-Caucasian dominated management. The union and company wanted to groom these young men for management to help carry on the company tradition in the future.

7

THE DELIBERATE ACT OF DECEPTION

I wanted to file a grievance to obtain my seniority back as of September 28, 1990. It was discovered there was an error in the computer. I was listed in the computer as a full-time employee. I complained about the problem for two years and was totally disregarded. Woodrow Stamping and Local 783 had no answers as to what was going on except to say it was all an error. I wondered how long an "error" could continue being an error. Errors don't last forever. Normally they're corrected when first noticed. No one ever questioned the reoccurring errors regarding part-time employees. It seemed to be a calculated risk that Woodrow Stamping and Local 783 were pilfering money. It was a deliberate act and Local 783 was starting to get a bit nervous since the problems were getting out of hand. Local 783 and Woodrow Stamping didn't know what to tell its members when they ran out of excuses regarding the ongoing errors.

Hame Pate my Committeeman at the time, told me there was another young lady Polly, who filed a grievance for the same problems I experienced. He told me, "We are going to add your name on Polly's grievance". I agreed because Polly's grievance was asking that employees' seniority be restored to September 1990. She also asked for back pay. I didn't know Hame Pate wasn't being candid with me, when he said my name would be placed on Polly's grievance. He deliberately misled me. I had no way of knowing that after a grievance was signed, no one could be added. I had no way of knowing I was lied to. I guess this was their way to keep my mouth closed for a short time. I didn't know this was a rule. I took the union for its word because two union members were representing me. I trusted what they were telling me to be true.

Polly and I worked many jobs together on the same line. Polly was a blond small-framed Caucasian lady about eighteen at the time. She was about 5 feet 5 inches and weighed about 110 pounds. She walked slumped over with a round curve in her spine. Polly was a pleasant and mild mannered young lady. On a warm summer afternoon, Polly and I were working on the same line together on the Press Side of the plant. In the break room, we talked about how we had been treated since our hire. We complained about our seniority and what had happened to us while working at Woodrow Stamping Plant.

Polly expressed her dissatisfaction regarding Local 783 bringing in new hires from other plants in September 1991. I told Polly this full-time/part-time status had to be the biggest joke I'd ever heard. I asked Polly what she thought about Woodrow Stamping Plant not hiring us before bringing in other part-time employees from other plants. The union forgot about the prior full-time employees of Woodrow Stamping Plant labeled as part-time, that should have been hired back with the company before any 'new hires'.

The 'new hires' had never worked for the company before. In fact, some had never stepped foot in a plant and had to be trained. I told Polly since we'd been experiencing all the errors and lies Local 783 told us on a daily basis, they could have just hired us full-time. That would have eliminated all our problems once and for all. This is when I told Polly there was something more than met the eye and that I truly believed money was being pilfered from us. I told her I wasn't sure where it was going, but I would soon find out one way or another. Polly stated how unfair Local 783 and Woodrow Stamping were treating us as part-time employees and how dissatisfied she was. I told Polly I didn't understand why Local 783 and Woodrow Stamping Plant were not hiring their original part-time employees. Since we were deliberately passed over, it indicated something negative.

Employees who signed Polly's grievance petition became furious when they filed their own grievances with the union after shutdown in 1992. The people on Polly's grievance were only a portion of those who received their vacation pay that was taken back by Woodrow Stamping Plant. The money was eventually given back to some of the so-called part-time employees through adjustments on their paychecks.

Some of my Caucasian co-workers received their checks earlier than usual and were excluded from paying their money back because of the ten-day rule. This rule meant the company had up to ten days to correct an overpayment error. They were allowed to keep their money with no complications. They didn't experience the existing problems because they were the sons and daughters of management. I thought since the grievance was in the beginning stages, they would put everyone's money on hold and evaluate the problem. The union said those listed on Polly's grievance were allowed to keep their vacation pay given in error without the grievance procedure being complete. I was one of those who received my vacation pay. I had to pay the money back, when my Caucasian co-workers were allowed to keep theirs. The union told me I would be added to Polly's grievance, but I was not. At that time, I figured out the money was being pilfered from me.

The premise is that big business and union leaders working in unison to bilk employees out of their pay through an elaborate system of separate books and computers. Since Woodrow Stamping finally admitted I was full-time, I really didn't understand what the problem was. All they had to do was give me full-time status. Why should I have to go through a grievance process if everyone knew I was full-time? They made up a big lie that Local 783 was representing me through the grievance procedure. Local 783 knew everything they said and did had been built on lies. The grievance wasn't ever filed and everyone knew that too. There were no fools in this money-laundering scheme. I will later discuss in detail how I was transferred from Woodrow Stamping Plant and Local 783 treated my transfer, as if it was a termination in order to hide the pilfering of my money. They were determined not to give me my money, but if I were Caucasian, I would not be writing this book. It didn't take a brain surgeon or rocket scientist to recognize something was clearly wrong with what they were doing.

I was irritated and disarranged at how the situation was handled. All this was happening and the grievance was a long way before being settled. Part-time employees were told it would take a year and a half before the grievance would be settled. I later found out that was a lie. I thought, "Is this strange or what?" They were putting the cart a long way before the horse. Why did Woodrow Stamping and Local 783 pay the part-time people before the grievance was settled if it was an error they were challenging? The status was confirmed and Local 783 and Woodrow Stamping Plant allowed my Caucasian co-workers to keep their vacation money. I had no doubt the money was due to them and the union knew this as well.

I was supposed to be added to the grievance and receive my money back. The union felt I was causing them problems and they rewarded me for doing so. It's ironic how Woodrow Stamping Plant and Local 783 always saw me as the enemy when they were the ones at fault. They had a "You got me and I'm going to get you back" attitude. And as a result, I was terminated when I was being transferred. They stopped hiring at my name showing me they were going to do whatever they pleased. It was their way of showing me that I wasn't going to get my money back. These people were definitely paying me back.

Woodrow Stamping Plant and Local 783 literally felt I was out of my place asking about my full-time status. I found out the vacation money I paid back didn't go back to Famous Parts Company. The money was taken from me, but my check stub said the overpayment wasn't paid back to Famous Parts Company. I never received my back money, but I did find out I was full-time just as I had suspected for years.

Woodrow Stamping Plant and Local 783 took me through their bribing government agencies to come in the plant and inquire about my status. The agencies found loopholes in the laws without penalizing Woodrow Stamping Plant and Local 783. I went to the National Labor Relations Board (NLRB), the Department of Labor, the Department of Civil Rights, the Executive Branch of the Union, and the Executive Branch of the Company, to expose them as significant parts in this massive cover up. Let me not forget about my local senator who I clearly reached out to. I was denied access to his office, only to receive a letter stating I should contact all of the above institutions which did nothing in my defense. I understood my state senator was working on an investigation on money laundering. He needed to look right in his own backyard to see Local 783 and Woodrow Stamping Plant had been laundering money for years. I wrote him asking him to investigate Woodrow Stamping Plant.

I elaborated on the fact that all the people allowed to keep their money were Caucasian. Of course when I found out about this, it didn't set very well with me. All the circumstances of the part-time employees were the same on Polly's grievance. Polly informed me of this information due to the indifferences discovered. I contacted Mr. John Hail, Plant Chairman of Local 783, to see what could be accomplished. I wasn't satisfied with the involvement at the lower level of Local 783's representation. I had given the union the benefit of a doubt thinking my name would appear on Polly's grievance. I was trying hard to continue trusting the union. I believed Local 783 was strong enough to fight for its members' causes at any particular time. I heard the union was an organization that would fight for members, when companies displayed unfairness by breaking various contract and/or labor laws, which violated the Constitutional rights of employees by their employer. This is why I paid union dues—so I thought.

July 1992 had come and gone and I was still working on the Press Side without resolution. I was allowed to file a grievance on June 3, 1993. The circumstances surrounding my grievance were due to the union's reluctance to file a grievance on my behalf. They continued to tell me I was part-time when I was actually full-time. They wanted to take me through the formalities of filing a grievance, but never intended to follow through. If I had not been persistent, they would have ignored me as they had in the past. If they wanted to give me full-time status, they would have. I was already full-time and there would be no need for a grievance. Why should have I filed a grievance when I was already full-time? That didn't make sense. Woodrow Stamping Plant's intention was to continue taking money from me while not having any shame in what they were doing.

Bob Fleetwood was Woodrow Stamping Plant's Bargaining Committeeman for Local 783. He handed me a form without vital information, to sign as a grievance. On this form the majority of questions were incomplete. It was almost a blank piece of paper except for where I signed. I assumed it would be completed at a later time. This form had blank spaces for my name, social security number, date of hire, what shift I worked, and the department I worked. On the bottom of the form where I signed, it read, "Not necessary to fill in enclosed space when grievance concerns union right only."

After I signed the grievance, I asked Bob Fleetwood for a copy. When the union didn't give me a copy, I knew then the union was up to no good. There was no reason I should have been denied a copy of the grievance I'd just signed. Mr. Fleetwood stated he was unable to give me a copy due to the copy machine being out of order. I asked Bob Fleetwood, if I could go elsewhere in the plant to make a copy and return with the original. The answer to my question was, "No!" I knew he was lying and my inner instinct told me something was very wrong with him not wanting me to have a copy of the grievance. There's no question that when a grievance is filed a copy is to be given to the grievant.

A few months later, I received a piece of paper from Local 783 that had three lines on it. When it was handed to me, I was informed by Bob Fleetwood this was the grievance settlement. This form was just as fraudulent as the grievance itself. I couldn't believe these people thought I wasn't smart enough to know the difference when they handed me this piece of paper. They called it a grievance, but it had no Local 783 logo, no date, and above all, no explanation of the grievance.

I was always full-time and there was no question in reference to that. The question was how long was Woodrow Stamping Plant going to continue pilfering my money? There was no need for a grievance when Woodrow Stamping Plant already established the fact I was full-time in July 1992. When Bob Fleetwood gave me this grievance, I looked at him and said, "Do you really think this is an acceptable decision when there is no Local 783 logo, date, social security number, or explanation of what the grievance is regarding?" It didn't even have where I signed my name to the so-called grievance settlement. It was a plain piece of paper. I told Bob the grievance was unacceptable and he had to come back with a form resembling an actual grievance.

There was no reason why Local 783 should have outright lied to me about filing this grievance. It was their hopes they would not have to file it. Their first attempt failed when they told me my grievance was denied and when the grievance hadn't been processed. This is when Bob came back to me with the form I signed. This time around the information was filled in. They knew I was full-time and it wasn't a secret. Why couldn't I keep my money, if Woodrow Stamping and Local 783 both agreed I was full-time? Why did Polly's group receive vacation pay and bonuses, and I did not? Local 783 knew they weren't going to put me on Polly's grievance. It didn't matter what I knew. They were not going to put me on full-time at Woodrow Stamping Plant knowing I couldn't force them to.

From July 1992 to September 1992, I constantly asked Committeeman Mr. Hame Pate, for an update concerning my grievance. Every time I saw him he told me the grievance was in the second stage. I didn't find out I wasn't on the grievance until September of 1992. This was a deliberate act because they considered me to be a radical and troublemaker. Woodrow Stamping felt my opposing views could cause havoc when part-time employees were dissatisfied with what was transpiring. As a result, I was ignored and never got honest answers. The situation was like a simmering pot ready to boil over into something out of control. Local 783 felt they had to do something with me.

I went back to the union contract book to familiarize myself with the grievance process and procedures. According to the book, the grievance should have lasted no longer than 120 days. This includes the appeal to the umpire level. I was tired of hearing the grievance was in the second stage. I wanted to know what was really happening. It seemed all the part-time employees who were involved in the grievance procedures, started communicating together. They discovered someone wasn't being truthful with them. They didn't know if it was Local 783, Woodrow Stamping, or both.

I called a meeting with someone who was well aware of the facts regarding my grievances and the grievance procedures. This was none other than Mr. John Hail, Plant Chairman of Local 783. This is when Mazzie and I became even closer friends for the common cause. Mazzie and I thought of ways we could obtain information. Both of us were at a virtual stand still as to any enlightening information. The more questions we would ask, the more unanswered questions we received. This is when we decided on getting a petition started to grant part-time employees the opportunity to ask questions about how they were being treated. We needed to be able to ask questions regarding our work status and other issues. I drafted a short letter dated October 19, 1992. The following short letter was addressed to Mr. John Hail:

"The part-time employees would like to meet with you to discuss the grievance filed in June 1993 and why the union will not allow us to work on Saturday and Sunday—our regular scheduled days. It states in the agreement between the Union's Executive Branch and Famous Parts Company that part-timers are allowed to work on premium days."

The company and union stated otherwise and totally disregarded what the contract book stated. This type of action was displayed continuously. Part of the problem was that the contract book was given to employees, but only a few employees took the time to read it or find out what their rights were. They depended on the union to know what their rights were. This is when the new hires were taken advantage of. If you don't know something, you're unable to recognize if you are receiving proper representation or not. I truly feel this is how Woodrow Stamping Plant and Local 783 became so powerful. They assumed if people didn't know the contract book, they could continue taking advantage of employees.

The company and union continued with everything they were doing. Today they are at the point of total corruption. It's awful when a union won't file a grievance against the company. Mazzie and I wrote a petition and had all the part-time employees sign it. Local 783 weren't very happy with it because they were being put in the spotlight. I was a person they didn't want to hear from any further. The memo read:

"We the members of Local 783 believe we deserve answers to our questions concerning the company's part-time employees. We have many questions regarding our work status. Woodrow Stamping can't seem to determine if we are full-time or part-time. We would like to know what rights we have under these circumstances. It seems we are unable to get any concrete truthful answers from Local 783 or Woodrow Stamping Plant."

The note said thank you. Mazzie and I signed our names, we had all the part-time employees to sign the letter, and it was given to Mr. John Hail. The meeting was granted at the Local 783 Union Hall. Chairman John Hail led the conversation as the meeting took place. The entire group of elected representatives sat at the table. Mr. Hail made a statement referencing the part-timers, "They will most likely get their seniority back although they will not be getting their money back". He also stated, "In years to come, no one will be hired in these plants except part-time employees". John Hail meant their plan was to hire full-time employees, pay them part-time wages, and not inform them they were at full-time status. They had it all planned. The last groups hired were never to make full-time. Their plan came to an end when John Hail was indicted for racketeering in 1999.

Someone asked about the employees who were laid off during the 70's. They wanted to know, if they would be obtaining their seniority back. Many complaints mounted regarding this mater. Some employees received their seniority but the majority did not. There were other issues brought up in essence of putting the minds of the part-time employees to rest. However the questions were not answered satisfactorily. Answers were evasive with no complete details. Some employees left with a sense of hope and others with a sense of defeat. The union avoided answering their questions. I was only allowed to ask two questions and was told I had asked enough. They said they wanted someone other than me asking questions. The reason the union did this is because they didn't want the rest of the part-time employees to know as much as I did. This was the real reason I was shipped out of Woodrow Stamping Plant with the help of Local 783.

Our contract book had no meaning because Local 783 didn't follow its guidelines. Not even when the employees found a conflict of interest regarding the company violating labor laws. The contract book was written as a guideline for the union member to know what their rights were. Local 783 and Woodrow Stamping Plant always worked hand in hand. You'd hear the employees complain the union was no good, but that's as far as they went. The employees felt Local 783 and Woodrow Stamping Plant were too big to fight against. It was easier just to succumb to them and say nothing rather than make things more difficult.

The company had a history of retaliating against the 'problem employee.' This was displayed at Woodrow Stamping Plant throughout the years I worked for them. Woodrow Stamping Plant placed fear in the employees so that whatever the company did, employees would be afraid to complain about it. Woodrow Stamping Plant felt I was a bad seed. They needed to do something with me fast. I knew how to read and they feared that. Some employees would rather quit than go against both the union and company—and I understand why. I didn't know then, but I found out later how much pressure both of these entities used to keep their secrets from employees and union members.

I was aware of what they were doing, but they didn't want anyone else aware of what was happening. In my case, Local 783 and Woodrow Stamping both sought to have me moved. I started putting together a vivid picture of the pilfering and deception. I wanted to know where the money was going that was meant for me. The other part-time employees, who didn't have to pay the money back, weren't as inquisitive.

When I filed my grievance I never received a copy. Therefore when I saw Bob Fleetwood in September 1993, I inquired about the grievance and how it was going. He stated he would give me a copy when they met on the grievance. It was about a week later Bob Fleetwood came to my work station on the Assembly Side of the plant and gave me a piece of paper that stated:

"The grievant (Crista Carrie) is a part-time employee and in the absence of any violation of Appendix-K this complaint is without merit and is accordingly denied".

I felt if Local 783 was planning to give me a copy of the grievance, I should have received it when I signed it June 3, 1993. The grievance findings stated the grievance didn't have merit contrary to the facts. I knew it *did* have merit and Local 783 and Woodrow Stamping Plant were aware of the fact as well. They just chose to continue using their power to do anything they pleased.

8

NEW HIRES

In September 1991, Woodrow Stamping brought in new part-time employees from Martin Stamping Plant and Wright Steel Company. These were both subsidiaries of Famous Parts Company who supplied parts to one another. Woodrow Stamping Plant offered the 'new hires' a full-time position if they were willing to change plants. These 'new hires,' were given their seniority going back to their actual date of hire. Both groups were brought to Woodrow Stamping Plant under the same circumstances—being hired to full-time positions. I wasn't quite sure how many people were hired from Martin Assembly Plant or Wright Steel Company. It had to be over one hundred that came from both plants.

Some employees were full-time at the plant they came from, and some had worked a short period of time on the plant floor. The others had no experience working on the floor at all. What I mean by this is the 'new hires' completed all the formalities of being hired, but they were on a waiting list to start work. They never had the opportunity to work on the plant floor. I wondered why Woodrow Stamping Plant wasn't hiring their *own* part-time people first. Their own part-timers were experiencing many complications regarding their full-time verses part-time status. Not to mention grievances were being brought against Woodrow Stamping Plant. I couldn't quite understand what was happening because there wasn't much logic to it. I didn't find out the reasoning for their actions until much later.

The part-time employees asked Plant Chair, John Hail, about becoming full-time since Woodrow Stamping Plant had new employees hired from Wright Steel and Martin Assembly Plants. Woodrow Stamping Plant's part-time employees were aware of the circumstances of the new hires. The original part-time employees became annoyed having to train the employees who had never worked in a plant before. A group of part-timers brought this to John Hail's attention. His reply was, "Don't worry you'll be full-time soon".

I became concerned and asked why the plant would bring in people to full-time positions that were part-time at other institutions. There was obviously space available to hire. This scenario infuriated many part-time employees including me. It left us to wonder why we were being passed over. Here we were part-time employees receiving full-time benefits, such as vacation, personal days, and full insurance. The only thing I could think of was Woodrow Stamping Plant and Local 783 didn't want to stop their flow of money. They were steadily extracting from the part-time employees and the rehires of the 70's. Woodrow Stamping Plant was putting the money to be laundered in special accounts so the money could not be found. I constantly asked questions and no one could answer me, as to why this problem was occurring?

I was telling Mazzie and a few others my perception as to what was happening to us. This of course, was pure speculation at the time. The only thing I had to go on was the experiences of others and me. I wasn't satisfied with the way Woodrow Stamping Plant handled the withdrawals. Both Woodrow Stamping and Local 783 gave the part-time employees flimsy explanations.

I would like you as my reader, to understand I did everything I could to get my problems solved regarding my seniority prior to going outside the plant. I contacted Local 783 and tried to get this settled before I received my vacation check in June 1992, but at first the union wouldn't file a grievance on my behalf. This was when I contacted the Department of Labor and the Department of Civil Rights. I later contacted the CEO of the Executive Branch of the Company and then the Executive Branch of the Union.

I was aware I was receiving part-time pay with full-time benefits, but I wasn't allowed to keep the fringe benefits that came with being full-time. What I *did* receive was part-time pay per-hour and fringe benefits for holiday pay that went in someone else's pocket while the money appeared to be directed to me. These benefits were taken away when I received them from 1990-1993. I knew I would be receiving a vacation check in June 1992 and Woodrow Stamping Plant was aware I would be receiving this check as well. My check stub informed me I would be receiving 40 hours of vacation and 40 hours of excused absences and/or personal days. It was known months in advance by the company that my vacation check would be issued in June 1992. My check stub informed me in advance but they did nothing to stop the vacation pay. When it was first brought to my attention, I had no knowledge of what it meant. I had never received a vacation check from the company before.

Woodrow Stamping Plant and Local 783 constantly told me I was part-time. There seemed to be no question whether I would receive a vacation check in June

1992, because I had December eligibility. Famous Parts Company employees have either June or December eligibility dates. Employees with June eligibility dates were hired from January through June and those people, who were hired from July thru December, have a December eligibility date. These dates tell each employee when his or her vacation days and personal days will be issued. All December eligibility vacation status is given on the first Friday of December. Therefore I was going to be receiving 40 hours vacation pay and I still had 40 hours personal days that had not been used. If I were part time, I would have only received 20 hours as vacation pay and no personal hours. There were so many complex problems regarding this full-time versus part-time situation. It was enough to make me wonder if I were sane or not. This was truly the best mind game a person could play on an individual. These people had no conscience at all. I felt their actions were cruel and unusual punishment.

In December 1993, after the company admitted I was full-time, I once again received full-time status on my check stub. At least my hours re-appeared on my check stub. Each year Famous Parts Company would give each employee these 80 hours paid vacation for the first 5 years of employment. These days were used at the employee's discretion. All days were to be used by the employee's anniversary date/eligibility date (June or December). In June 1993, I did not receive a vacation check, but the hours remained on my check stub as being paid. If an employee didn't receive their vacation check, personal days, or excused absences, it would be given to them on the first Friday after June 1 or after December 1, as in my case.

The company would pay the money to employees for the unused portion of days left, whether it was vacation days or personal days unused. If none were used, the employee would be paid the total amount of vacation, personal, or excused absence days. These days varied depending on the amount of seniority the employee had with the company. I received a check for 80 hours. This appeared on my check under the "regular dues" column in December 1990, 1991, 1992, and again in 1993. The amount always re-appeared, when they would remove the amount from my check stub, as being paid to me for the personal day. The same thing happened in 1992 when I paid back my vacation pay, but it remained on my check stub as being paid to me and not the company for the remained of 1992. The money was repaid back in full in July 1992. I did receive a 40 hour vacation check in June 1993. I took a personal day that my Supervisor, Orlando Martz, paid me for since I had personal and vacation hours in the computer as a full-time employee in February 1993.

Randy Facade, Labor Relations Supervisor, had the audacity to tell me, I should not have taken that day. He was supposed to have fixed the problem in February 1993. Again, we were in November 1993 with the situation yet in existence. I was to be receiving another Christmas bonus in December 1993 and nothing had changed. Everything remained the same. I should have received the days that weren't used throughout the year ending December 1993, but I did not because they were pilfered away from me too.

My check stated how many days I would have been paid for. I had only used one day, which was paid back, and it yet left me with having 32 hours of unused days. I didn't receive payment for those unused days that I should have had coming to me, when I was terminated from Woodrow Stamping Plant November 1993. The office of Labor Relations Supervisor, Randy Facade, had kept the checks. After I was terminated, this meant I would be receiving another 32-hour check for the unused vacation days and/or excused absence days in December 1993. Whether I was re-hired or terminated, what happened to the unused portion of my money? It really didn't matter because I was supposed to have been paid those days and never received payment for them. My questions were: Where was my money and who could account for it?

Woodrow Stamping Plant was yet telling me my full-time status was an error. Local 783 did nothing regarding my grievance and the money I was to receive. There were many occasions my checks were in such a mess due to money being withdrawn or days in which my time wasn't computed correctly. There was always some kind of complication regarding my money and I just wanted them to stop. I became tired of my checks being short and full of adjustments.

After viewing my check stub in November 1992, I went to Labor Relations and spoke with Mr. Randy Facade on the afternoon shift. I expressed how excused absences once again appeared on my paycheck. Mr. Facade took the matter at hand and said, "It's good you notified the company of the error". He also expressed to me he had taken care of the matter and corrected my work status and informed me this kind of problem wouldn't happen again.

How many times have I heard this lie? I didn't receive my unused personal and vacation days for December 1991 through November 1993, but I received a vacation check, which was taken back in 1992. In June 1993, I received full vacation pay under full-time status. I received only holiday pay, vacation pay, a Christmas bonus, and other benefits from September 1990 until year ending November 1993 only. From 1991 through 1993, I was afforded all full-time benefits until I was transferred to Sarrow Stamping. I figured the vacation checks and all other benefits I was to receive, were intercepted, pilfered, and laundered throughout the years from 1990 through 1993 when I was terminated. This included my vacation in June 1991.

I was laid off during vacation time in June 1991. I wasn't off work long enough not to receive my vacation check since I was already full-time on record. I didn't have my employment records then, but I received a copy of them some years later, which proved I was right all along. Woodrow Stamping Plant was able to steal my money because my employment records stated I was full-time.

Local 783's fraud led all the way up to the Executive Branch of the Union's CEO, James York. He stepped down in 1995 and handed down the position of Executive Branch of the Union CEO to Don Hangem. Therefore both men were aware of all the aspects surrounding my situation with Local 783 and Woodrow Plant. The action taken by the Executive Branch of the Union proved they condoned what was going on. They knew of the money being pilfered from the full-time employees, by paying them part-time pay. They pilfered the remaining benefits the employees had coming according to the contract. That should not have been acceptable.

The money Woodrow Stamping and Local 783 pilfered, had to have been diverted to a secret account. If I received my full-time benefits when I returned and never received my personal days, the money had to dwell someplace. What happened to the remainder of my personal days for which I was paid for and had not received? What other alternative can you come up with under these circumstances?

When I transferred from Woodrow Stamping to be rehired at Sarrow Stamping, I had no idea Woodrow Stamping had planned to terminate me. I was told it would be an interplant transfer, since I had been full-time for three years by error. I wanted to know what happened to the last check I should have received after I transferred. It didn't matter if I was terminated or not. I had 80 hours coming to me when I transferred from Woodrow Stamping Plant. I was never paid for the accumulation of hours for that past year. It was November 1993, when I transferred to Sarrow Stamping Plant and I never received a check for those unused days. Where did the money go?

I asked Labor Relations Supervisor, Randy Facade, "Who keeps keying the wrong information in the computer system or verifying information that constantly gives me full-time status?" Mr. Facade came up with some vague answer, although I don't remember exactly what he said. I told him I wanted the headache to stop. In essence, he reiterated the fact I was a part-time employee and not full-time. He wasn't vague at all about that. That came through very clear.

I told my co-workers I felt boxed in due to casuistry. Afterall, who would believe such a place as large as Famous Parts Company would resort to these kinds of fraud tactics? I didn't know where to obtain help under the circumstances. I couldn't prove anything, as of yet. Therefore I could do nothing but sit still and absorb the punishment of harassment and discrimination. You would think a company such as Famous Parts Company, who professed their institutions' diversity, would notice something wrong with all the complaints received from the part-time employees. I felt many knew the situation and just turned their heads. How could Famous Parts Company—Woodrow Stamping Plant ignore something of this magnitude?

Part-time employees were laid off in February 1991 and called back in July 1991 after the vacation shutdown. To me, this meant all of Woodrow Stamping's part-timers were in the computer system incorrectly. This meant there was vacation money issued to the part-timers during the vacation shut down period during the summer of 1991. The part-timers didn't physically receive this money because they were technically on 'layoff.'

The company diverted my money someplace other than in my pocket. My concern was if the company never corrected the so-called errors, where did the money from that June of 1991 go? Not to mention profit sharing and performance bonuses, which I never received. There were no lapses in my employment on record. In 1993 before I transferred, the error was supposed to be fixed. But instead I was terminated when I was transferred to Sarrow Stamping Plant. Their way of finally fixing my problem was to terminate my employment without my knowledge and hire me as a brand new hire. Woodrow Stamping had me on lay-off on one set of records and continued paying me on the other. Woodrow Stamping and Local 783 kept two or more sets of records on employees. I will explain this in further detail in *Part II* of this book.

At this time, I had many questions and hadn't quite figured out the entire scenario. My money was pilfered for at least three years. I wanted to know why Local 783 didn't file this grievance, while telling me I had representation. When I had Mr. Facade intercept my check in November 1993, he assured me it would never happen again. I wasn't terminated until November 13, 1993, which was the last day I worked at Woodrow Stamping in 1993. I had vacation time from that year. If this was so, what happened to the remainder of my vacation and personal days at the end of 1993? I surely didn't receive it.

If I weren't full-time, I would not have received $600 dollars like I received in the first 90 days of employment. Mr. Facade supposedly stopped my $600 dollars and the other unused benefits I wasn't supposed to be receiving, but the money was actually being pilfered. When the money was allocated to me and then taken back because I didn't possess full-time status, where did it go? Why wasn't I credited with paying the personal day back to the company? I wanted answers. That caused me to be labeled as "troublemaker". They had nasty attitudes and gave me disparate treatment quite often. They said all that I experienced, was my fault. A troublemaker is one who makes trouble. I wasn't making trouble—only asking questions Woodrow Stamping Plant and Local 783 didn't want to answer.

I never received my unused personal days for the years 1991, 1992, or 1993. Mr. Facade was aware of the company's pilfering and laundering money in special accounts set-up by the Controller. These events weren't errors at all—just cover-ups in hopes they wouldn't get caught diverting employees' money in these separate accounts. The only thing these thieves thought about was not getting caught, for fear of losing their retirement among other things. It's ironic how management pilfered money from employees in the name of 'the company', but they didn't want anyone hampering them from receiving their own retirement or Worker's Compensation benefits.

Before transferring from Woodrow Stamping Plant, the box on my pay stub was marked "vacation balance". This indicated I would get another vacation check in July 1994. I knew there had to be some kind of mistake or mismanagement on the part of Woodrow Stamping and Local 783. This was the main purpose I spoke to Mr. Facade in November 1993. I was trying to prevent the "error" from re-occurring.

I was discriminated against in a variety of areas—especially in the area of livelihood. Woodrow Stamping Plant felt I became a threat. I will provide further details in later chapters as to the reasons why the company terminated my employment. I talked with a variety of part-time employees, including some relatives of management who indeed verified they didn't have to pay the money back. This was a matter I felt needed handling. Woodrow Stamping knew in advance the money was coming, and could have stopped the payment before it reached me. The stand Local 783 took in supporting the company in the matter left me outraged.

In October 1992, I filed a complaint against Famous Parts Company—Woodrow Stamping Plant and Local 783. I went to the Department of Labor for the state of Michigan. I was angry because I had to pay my money back through adjustments and deductions while others with my same work status, kept their money. I felt this was unfair labor practice and discrimination in every sense of the word. I felt it was illegal for a company to pay me vacation pay and take it back—especially when they knew it was going to be given far in advance.

I didn't understand why Woodrow Stamping refused to clear up the error. Other part-time employees and I were laid off twice. These dates were February 1991 thru April 1991, and December 1991 thru July 1992. The second time we were laid off, Woodrow Stamping Plant never acknowledged the part-time employees were full-time until July 1992. This was no error. It was purely thievery on the behalf of some union and management officials. In many instances, their actions reiterated my suspicions of something being terribly wrong and should have raised a red flag for others as well.

9

TO WHAT EXTENT WILL THEY GO

With all the surrounding circumstances as they were, I felt I had the right to fight for what I believed. I felt I should have been reimbursed. If no one was willing to correct the errors, I surely was not the one to blame. All my conversations and efforts with regards to getting the error corrected were useless. Local 783 and Woodrow Stamping Plant had a plan for me so there wouldn't be questions or mistakes with regards to my seniority any longer.

For this reason in October 1992, I contacted the Michigan Department of Labor to file a complaint against Famous Parts Company—Woodrow Stamping Plant. I went to the Equal Opportunity Employment Commission (EEOC) of the State of Michigan because I felt it was illegal for a company to give me vacation pay and take it back. I really felt my issue would be investigated and that something could come out of it.

It took about six months or so before I received a representative who'd look into the matter. It took so long for the Department of Labor to contact me. That's when I sent them a letter dated February 8, 1993. I was told an investigator had not yet been appointed. When I hadn't heard anything further regarding my complaint, I sent the following letter:

"To whom it may concern:

On October 27, 1992 I sent information in reference to Famous Parts Company and myself. This information was to see if Famous Parts Company—Woodrow Stamping Plant was appropriate in withdrawing my vacation pay issued to me in June 1992. The company said this pay was given to me in error, but I know that is a lie. This problem has been ongoing since I was hired in September 1990. At one point, the company admitted I was full-time but never corrected the errors.

When I would be paid due to an error, the money would be paid back from my paycheck through adjustments. I believe the money was put in a special account for laundering purposes.

I received a card by mail in November 1992 stating Famous Parts Company had been notified and I would be hearing something from them very soon. I called in December 1992 and talked to the receptionist. She said if I hadn't received any money, normally they would send a representative to the employer to verify employment records. She said I should be hearing something during the month of January 1993. I called in February as a follow-up because I still hadn't heard anything and I wanted to know what was happening.

Meanwhile during the month of December 1992, Famous Parts Company—Woodrow Stamping Plant gave me credit for more vacation days and personal days. I hadn't used any of my excused absences days, which I was told were also given to me incorrectly. I am sending copies of my check stubs I've received from December 1990 to February 1992 when I was laid off. As of now it has been 2 years that I've been full-time by "error" according to Woodrow Stamping Plant and Local 783. My name is Crista Carrie and I was hired September 28, 1990 at Famous Parts Company—Woodrow Stamping Plant."

I listed my social security number and said thank you. I signed my name and wrote the word "enclosure" at the bottom of the letter. I enclosed my check stubs, which stated I had vacation pay coming when my eligibility came around. I later retrieved the following letter from my employment record. This was written to Mr. Henry, Supervisor of the Department of Labor, in response to the complaint I filed against Woodrow Stamping Plant. The following is Woodrow Stamping Plant's response to Mr. Henry's letter from the Michigan Department of the Labor. The letter was dated December 2, 1992 from Mr. Sophie, Woodrow Stamping Plant's Labor Relations Supervisor. It read:

"Re: Crista Carrie

In response to your communication of November 23, 1992 you will find enclosed a copy of Appendix K—Memorandum of Understanding Temporary Part-time Employees, which governs the employment status of Ms. Carrie. Paragraph 9 of Appendix K indicates the compensation and benefits provisions of the Master Agreement, which is applied to temporary part-time employees. Vacation pay provided under the Master Agreement and governed by Article IX, Sections 23 through 26, is not extended to temporary part-time employees.

There were seventy-six employees governed by the temporary part-time employment status similar to Ms. Carrie. Through an improper code, twenty-six of these employees including Ms. Carrie, were incorrectly identified as full-time employees in the payroll computer system and had indication of vacation pay eligibility. The vacation paychecks were disbursed prior to the plant vacation shutdown that began on June 29, 1992. The majority of the paychecks were not issued to the part-time employees and were subsequently cancelled. Some of the checks were erroneously distributed to temporary part-time employees working on the afternoon shift.

Deductions were made on the paycheck for the pay period ending June 28, 1992 with deductions from subsequent pay periods for any remaining balance. In the case of Ms. Carrie, the balance of the overpayment was deducted from her paycheck for pay period ending June 26, 1992. The amount of $630.84 is the specific amount Ms. Carrie was overpaid. That amount was deducted from subsequent payment due to Ms. Carrie. Notification was made to employees who had received the erroneous payments on July 2, 1992—the payday for the pay period ending June 28, 1992. Mr. R. Sophie of the Labor Relations Office notified all of the employees affected by the erroneous payment."

This is the letter sent on behalf of Woodrow Stamping Plant. Mr. Sophie forgot to mention all part-time employees didn't have to pay the money back. Nor did he write in this letter that the employer was aware the money was to be given months prior to receiving the checks in June 1992. This was a process clearly thought through in its entirety to hide money paid to presumably part-time employees. This letter was not true. Mr. R. Sophie sent his explanation to the Labor Department. I received a final response in a letter dated May 18, 1993 from Mr. Henry at the Labor Department. The letter stated:

"Crista Carrie vs. Famous Parts Company:

On October 28, 1992 the department received your complaint alleging nonpayment of vacation pay earnings during the period June 21, 1992 thru July 26, 1992 as an employee of Famous Parts Company. An investigation was conducted under the authority of 1978 PA 390. The (state) Payment of Wage and Fringe

Benefits Act has revealed the terms and conditions of what your employment is governed by, the collective bargaining unit and Famous Parts Company covering, the period October 22, 1990 thru September 14, 1993. It has also been determined that the resolution of your claim would require the department to enforce the terms of that agreement, specifically Article IX, Section 17.

Please be advised that the department is prohibited from the administration and enforcement of wage/fringe benefit claims based on a Collective Bargaining Agreement by the provisions of Section 301 (a) of the (federal) Labor Management Relations Act of 1947 which govern employment relations between private sector employers and employees. Section 301 (a) has been interpreted by state and federal court to indicate that the exclusive remedy for violations of a contract between employees and employers represented by a labor organization is a suit to be brought in United States District Court.

The position of the department is supported by the decision of the United States District Court. For this reason the State of Michigan in the matter of Complete Auto Transit v. Elisabeth Howe (Michigan Department of Labor) Civil Action No. 88-CV-70863 and Attorney General Opinion No. 6649 of July 11, 1990, which held that the State's Payment of Wage and Fringe Benefits Act, were preempted by the Federal Labor Management Relation Act where the resolution of a state-law claim is dependent upon the meaning of the collective bargaining agreement.

Accordingly this will inform you that no further action may be taken on your claim and the department's file is being closed. If you have questions regarding this matter please contact the department at the address listed on our letterhead." The letter was signed and dated by the Regional Supervisor of the Wage Hour Division.

I wondered what had Woodrow Stamping offered Mr. Henry to look the other way. There should have been no question as to my status after receiving a 40-hour vacation check. It doesn't take a brain surgeon to recognize only full-timers receive those benefits. What more was it to see? Why was Woodrow Stamping trying so hard not to pay me in order to pilfer money from me? This investigator should have and could have intervened. He knew Woodrow Stamping Plant had me as full-time. Perhaps if Mr. Henry examined the records more carefully, he would have discovered they paid me accordingly. Records would have reflected the personal days given and taken away. In July 1992, the company stated I was full-time. Mr. Henry, Department Supervisor of the Labor Department, stated he couldn't get involved.

I knew Mr. Henry had been bought and paid for. No way could this situation have been an oversight by Woodrow Stamping Plant or the Labor Department for nearly three years. Mr. Henry covered his behind with the laws working in his favor. I began wondering how many people Woodrow Stamping was willing to pay in exchange for favors not to expose them. This investigator didn't say he didn't find anything wrong during his investigation. He turned his head to what was happening to me. This investigator should have known I was covered under the union contract prior to his investigation at Woodrow Stamping Plant. He knew Famous Parts Company was a private company. Why did Mr. Henry even bother going to Woodrow Stamping Plant to investigate? He knew all this information beforehand. This representative could have saved himself the trouble of investigating this claim, knowing there were no questions as to what he could or couldn't find among Woodrow Stamping Plant's records. Again, I was left wondering where I could go for help. It was a known fact that getting help from Local 783 was like representing one's self in a court of law.

I had enough of the run-around and the lies presented to me. I fought against what I believed was unfair treatment. I stood for the truth. By this time I didn't care if I was a thorn in their side, a troublemaker, or whatever else they wanted to label me as. I was tired of the harassment, discrimination, and the many other obstacles I was forced to encounter. In order for Woodrow Stamping and Local 783 to keep their dirty little secrets, they had to find a way to get rid of the one who was causing trouble. I couldn't be selective about who I got to help me. Help was very limited when you opposed the union. I contacted Mr. Jess McGregor, Local 783 President, for assistance. I sent Mr. McGregor a letter dated April 6, 1993. The letter was sent to Local 783 and the Executive Branch of the Union. The letter stated:

"Dear Mr. McGregor:

I have worked at Woodrow Stamping Plant for over two years. I was hired when Woodrow Stamping Plant hired a large volume of employees. The class I was in was told some of us would be hired full-time and others would be on a waiting list after completion of orientation. Prior to taking the test, I was told I would be full-time. But when I started working on the floor, I was told I would be working as part-time. I started in September of 1990 and I worked 90 days and started getting holiday pay for New Year's Day and Martin Luther King Jr.'s birthday. The Martin Luther King Jr. holiday pay was taken back. I was told it was given to me in error.

There were other part-time employees whose pay was also given in error—or so we were told. I talked to our Union Representative, Billy. He informed me the holiday pay was given in error because part-time employees had to work 90 actual workdays, which would amount to working six months. Some weeks we would work 40 hours a week—even through deer season. This was the annual time the majority of men at Woodrow Stamping Plant would go hunting. Woodrow Stamping Plant accommodated the employees wanting to take off work for hunting. The part-time employees filled in for these employees. At that time, we worked four days a week totaling 32 hours a week, which was considered full-time according to contract. The company later informed us we would be working four days a week seven hours a day totaling 28 hours a week. The afternoon shift on the Press Side worked the same amount of hours for three weeks. After that, the hours varied from 16 to 32 hours a week until November 1990 when we were off with our Christmas bonuses.

I came back to work in January 1991, and worked until February 1991. I wasn't called back until after shut down in July 1991. After vacation checks were distributed, we didn't receive any vacation during shut down. The money was already pilfered. If I were full-time when I was hired and when I was transferred to Sarrow Stamping Plant, I could not be transferred because part-time seniority can't be transferred. I'll say I was full-time until 1993. I was labeled as full-time in Woodrow Stamping Plant's computer. My seniority date was September 28, 1990 as I have been professing. This information was left in the computer and I read the information myself. It was no longer hearsay.

If this was the case, why didn't Plant Chairman, John Hail, work to settle this problem a long time ago? Why allow it to carry on for so long? Local 783 is to represent us to insure things like this don't happen. John Hail went as far as threatening some of the part-time employees, saying they would lose their jobs if they signed any more letters. He later apologized for making the threat to them about signing another one of my petitions.

In January 1993, I went to work and my supervisor, Orlando Martz, didn't have a job assignment for me. He asked me if I'd like to go home and I said no. I asked him if he checked everywhere, even on the Assembly Side for work. Martz told me he would check and see if he could find work for me. If not, he would have to send me home. He looked in the computer and verified vacation and excused absence hours. He told me he'd pay me for the day and then asked if I wanted to take a vacation day or a personal day. I replied I'd take a personal day. I signed the appropriate form, received a receipt for my vacation day, and went home. I was paid for that day on the following pay period. If I hadn't any vacation time I wouldn't have gotten paid for that day.

Why I had personal and vacation time when I was to be part-time was beyond my imagination. It doesn't matter what I say to Labor Relations. They continue telling me I'm part-time even as these events occur on a continued basis. Labor Relations constantly enforce all that occur are errors. All of the protesting I did was to no avail. This was all occurring before my grievance was in existence. I tried to obtain a copy of my employee record from Labor Relations and was denied. Mr. Doso, Labor Relations Representative, gave me a copy of my time-keeping report, told me it was my employment record, and asked me not to show anyone.

I'm usually a very compassionate and sympathetic person, but when I heard Mr. Doso had died of a heart attack, all I could say was, "Good for him. He got what he deserved". I do what is required of me and Woodrow Stamping Plant still puts me through Hell. *(I didn't care if they all fell dead at this point.)* The company and the union are victimizing me and no one seems to care.

It was around this time I contacted the Department of Labor and the Department of Civil Rights all to no avail. There seemed to be no justice when I tried to understand what was happening to me and why. I informed John Hail, Local 783's Plant Chairman, about these problems with regards to my part-time/full-time status. He told me Labor Relations told him it was a mistake pertaining to my social security number. I felt this was another insult of my intelligence. I can say I'm experiencing a clear case of embezzlement—plain and simple.

I've protested to Local 783, Woodrow Stamping Plant, and anyone else who would listen to my complaint. Woodrow Stamping Plant and Local 783 are involved in an embezzlement scheme. That is the reason it took them three years to correct these errors. Their solution was to terminate my employment. The error isn't I'm full-time and they're pilfering my money—but the error is my knowing something that I should not know.

Mr. Randy Facade, Labor Relations Supervisor, needed to speak with me on January 18, 1993. He and Pike Pavis, Local 783 Committeeman, informed me my paid personal day in which I was paid for, was being withdrawn. They said I wasn't entitled to receive a paid personal day since I was part-time. My reply to Mr. Facade was if I didn't have the time, I wouldn't have gotten paid for the day. If I wasn't qualified to receive this day why do you think I received payment? If this is not harassment, I certainty would like to know what is.

I took advantage of my situation because it was to my advantage to prove I was full-time with no mistakes. When Mr. Facade and Pike Pavis approached me, Mr. Facade seemed to be annoyed and a bit uncomfortable. He said, "Crista! I know you're smart enough to know better than to take a day you weren't entitled to take by you being a part-time employee". Pike Pavis, my Committeeman, never said a word in my defense when Mr. Facade, the Labor Relations Supervisor, was speaking to me. Mr. Facade was out of place speaking to me on a matter the committeeman should have approached me about. It wasn't management's position to reprimand me. They were aware I was full-time and not by error. They had known since my hiring in 1990 I was full-time, but were reluctant to admit my employment status until July 1992. This is when I was informed I was full-time. If they didn't correct the error, there was nothing I could do about it except allow the error's continuance.

The following week the paid personal day amount was withdrawn from my check. I had the hardest time getting Woodrow Stamping Plant to update my pay stub to state I didn't get paid for my personal day after all. Since the money was paid back, I felt my check stub should reflect it as being paid back. As of November 2, 1993, it was not corrected. I notified the Department of Labor, the Department of Civil Rights, Felix Mann; CEO of Famous Parts Company, and Mr. James York; CEO of the Union, and I could not get anyone to investigate my complaint. I also made complaints to Woodrow Stamping Plant. You would think someone would give me the benefit of a doubt and investigate the company's records. I informed John Hail, Plant Chairman of Local 783, and he set up a meeting and forgot about it. Again, I was given the run around and let down. I also tried to inform Mr. Paul Nashing, Committeeman for the Assembly Side of Woodrow Stamping Plant, on the afternoon shift. He told me it would be taken care of on my following check. If not, Woodrow Stamping Plant would have to re-pay me for that day. I also asked Mr. Nashing about filing a grievance. Again, he said it would be taken care of and a grievance wouldn't be necessary.

Woodrow Stamping eliminated the unused days and excused absences, but my check stub remained with the excused absence as being paid to me. No credit for the repayment was applied. If the money was given to me incorrectly, why was it a problem to have it taken off my check stub? Something's severely wrong with this situation. Is it a cover up between Local 783 and Woodrow Stamping? If so, Local 783 isn't properly representing me as a member. They can't represent me *and* protect the company. It's impossible. Thus far, my problems haven't been taken seriously. I feel if I work for a company, there shouldn't be problem with me getting paid. The union should uphold the contract.

Local 783 and Woodrow Stamping Plant are working hand and hand being unconcerned about the needs of part-time employees who are actually full-time. They continue to lie while they pilfer employees' money—placing it in separate accounts set up by the Controller. These are employees who are paying union dues. As members we should not be discriminated against by not being allowed to file a grievance …" I signed my name and sent Mr. Jess McGregor's letter certified mail, return receipt requested.

10

FORCED TO LOOK FOR ANYONE WHO WILL HELP

I went upstairs to the locker room, found Mazzie Cane, and told her what Mr. Randy Facade had done before I transferred to Sarrow Stamping Plant. I told Mazzie I thought Mr. Facade had fixed my problem once again returning me back to part-time status. I thought the changes were made and the errors were going to be a thing of the past. I had experienced these errors for the last 3 years. I'd been fighting them since 1990. *(My fight finally came to a halt in 2004 when my case was thrown out of court a few months before I was retired.)* I told Mazzie Mr. Facade told me I would be part-time and there would be no more errors occurring. Since I had been lied to for the last 3 years, I wanted to believe this was true. I believed his action to be valid since Mr. Facade was a minority himself. Maybe he understood what I was going through. One thing I did know—I wanted the nightmare to end.

I told Mazzie if I ever had a problem again with my seniority, I would fight until I obtained my original seniority date. I told Mazzie I would get my seniority because Mr. Facade assured me the error was being corrected. Mazzie said not to trust management because all they did was lie. Mazzie had already told me how management was treating her husband, Wayward Cane. She tried to get information from her husband about what was going on with the part-time employees, but Wayward didn't tell her anything. If there were any new information to be found surrounding the part-time employees, she'd let me know from management's point of view.

Mazzie was very resourceful by gathering information from other supervisors about Famous Parts Company employees and their work status. She didn't want to expose her husband to any more trouble than he always found himself in. Mazzie didn't make much noise regarding her situation concerning her own seniority status. Her husband had asked her not to cause any trouble since management was on him like white on rice.

In the locker room, Mazzie talked about her seniority and her concerns on how she could obtain it back while at the same time not jeopardizing her husband's job. After telling her about the meeting with Mr. Facade in Labor Relations, I showed her my check stub. She put her magazine down as we talked, taking my check stub and viewing it. "Crista, you have vacation and personal days coming too", she said as she pulled her check out her purse and opened it. She hadn't looked at her check after her supervisor handed them out that morning. She opened her check and saw her stub had the same information as mine in terms of personal days and vacation time. I told Mazzie I was tired of Woodrow Stamping making adjustments on my checks all of the time.

One week after Mr. Facade allegedly corrected my employment records, I found once again Labor Relations had lied to me. My problems had not been taken care of at all. It seemed my problems concerning my work status were just put on hold for a week. The errors continued as they had previously. Nothing had changed and the union was still of no help. At this point, I was asking Local 783 to do something. But since I was trespassing on forbidden territory, they weren't anxious to do anything. I was trying hard to understand what was transpiring with the part-time employees. I told Mr. Facade if I was part-time to let me maintain a part-time status with part-time benefits, but if I was full-time make me full-time and keep it that way. I asked him to correct my records so I could get on with my job and my life. I asked Mr. Hail, Plant Chairman of Local 783, to intercede for me but the problem went ignored again.

All the company had to do to eliminate these reoccurring problems was give me the full-time status, which was already in existence. If this had happened, a grievance would not have been necessary. I exhausted all means of getting my seniority back. The Department of Labor said their hands were tired and stated I had a union to protect my best interest. If the union was protecting me, this problem would have ended a long time ago.

I wouldn't have to search for outside entities to assist with my problem. How much did Woodrow Stamping Plant pay these people to look the other way? I spoke to Mr. Hdith, the lawyer who took my case before his death. He told me the Department of Labor could have handled the problem. Local 783 didn't look out for my best interest and it was offensive. They continued labeling me as a "troublemaker". Woodrow Stamping Plant and Local 783 began to get nervous in the second quarter of 1993. Prior to my transferring from Woodrow Stamping Plant to Sarrow, I thought my problems were just about over. I thought this especially, when Mr. Facade had supposedly taken care of my problems with the adjustments. The mounded abundance of problems just seemed to be getting started with no end in sight.

I went back to Local 783 once again and the union had nothing to say on the matter. They told me if I wanted things to change, I had to write a resolution stating clearly what I wanted. The union was surprised to find out I took them up on their suggestion. I wanted other people outside of Woodrow Stamping to get involved in the situation. Maybe they could help. I didn't know which way to go. I couldn't go to Local 783 or Woodrow Stamping Plant. They were both of no help. At this point, I told Local 783 I wanted to file a grievance. When I told Committeeman, Paul Nashing, I wanted to file a grievance it was as if I was speaking in a foreign language. Paul was the Committeeman for the Assembly Side of the plant and Mr. Hame Pate was the Committeeman for the Press Side. There was no specific committeeperson who could address my problems, because I worked from the Assembly Side to the Press Side.

When problems arose, I would talk to Committeeman, Hame Pate, who also happened to be an elected union official. I eventually stopped asking him for anything because he was so pitiful. What were the odds of Hame Pate winning the elections by one vote in the last two elections anyway? The union probably gave him that one vote each time he won. I assume Local 783 got tired of giving Hame Pate that one vote. Later he stopped running for any election and Local 783 kept him in the union office shuffling papers, just to keep him from having to go back on the plant floor. I always thought how strange and unlikely this man's fate in the union was—always hanging by a thread in Local 783 elections. In my opinion he was the sorriest committeeman I had ever seen. He never knew anything regarding union business and he'd always give me unreliable information. No matter what I asked him, he didn't know.

The union was shady and corrupt. We wondered if the elections were really elections at all. I felt they were appointing persons to the position of Plant Chairman themselves. It was done on the 'down low'. This meant they went through the formalities of an election, but the winner was known ahead of time. It was a joke in terms of how the company carried out their business. Woodrow Stamping and Famous Parts Company always had someone carrying out their corrupt duties.

I say this because Robert Haste III was elected as Plant Chairman in April 2000. He was not the man Woodrow Stamping wanted holding this position, because he wanted to make a difference. Mr. Robert Haste III only stayed Plant Chairman for about a year. He eventually got the Hell out of there and I can't say

I blame him. Word around the plant was that private meetings were taking place regarding union business, which didn't include the new Plant Chairman, Robert Haste III. I went on medical leave in June 2000 and returned a few months later. Upon my returning, Mr. Robert Haste III was wearing a neck brace due to some sort of accident. He told me he planned on retiring soon. I tell you a man doesn't run for office, then suddenly turn around a few months later and tell you he's going to retire from the company soon to be with his family. In my perspective, Robert Haste was frightened enough to get out of the plant in a hurry. My close friend and co-worker, Andrea, wasn't that lucky before she was hit with a hi-lo in Woodrow Stamping Plant and then terminated.

Frankly speaking, Woodrow Stamping wanted men like Committeeman, Hame Pate, working for the company who had no business being a committee-man in the first place. It appeared Hame Pate had never looked in the contract book or read anything else concerning the contract. It was ironic. As an employee you had to follow rules, but management seemed to be the exception. Hame Pate was a pathetic Uncle Tom Committeeman who was kept to represent the Black minority group in the company. Woodrow Stamping Plant wanted everyone to know they were "diverse". However not one minority had the authority to do anything in terms of decision-making. This was the way Local 783 and Woodrow Stamping Plant wanted it. The majority of Local 783 was Caucasian and they wanted it to stay that way.

Prior to my return to Woodrow Stamping Plant, they had a minority as Plant Manager. He was unable to hold that job because Woodrow Stamping Plant and Local 783 weren't going to have a Black man in noteworthy positioning for too long. They were in control and he seemed not to work out for whatever reason. I can imagine what this poor man experienced while holding that position at Woo-drow Stamping Plant for even a short while. The minorities were holding spaces in the union chairs, being satisfied by the mere fact that they didn't have to work on the floor. This made them feel important, kept them loyal to Local 783, and made them not care what happened to other minorities. Afterall, Woodrow Stamping Plant had to have a minority face someplace so others couldn't say the company wasn't racist or practicing discrimination. But this is exactly what they were doing. The unions were prejudiced and kept the minorities at arm's length.

Woodrow Stamping had a habit of teaching minorities a lesson. To keep them in their places, they would commonly have a minority do the dirty work. It couldn't be called discrimination then. They used Black supervisors to commit discriminatory acts and use unfair labor practices against other Blacks. Woodrow Stamping Plant used unfair labor practices even against other supervisors. The orders always came from upper management or the union, when and how to retaliate against an employee. I would always hear management speaking of the *Good Old Boys Club*. I had no idea of what they were talking about at the time. This was a group of men that had clout and could side with other organizations for a common cause. Everyone in this club could do anything they pleased. The club included doctors, lawyers, lawmakers, lobbyists, and judges. Most—but not all of Woodrow's upper white-collar management belonged to this group. This group did exactly what they wanted and wasn't held accountable.

The *Good Old Boy's Club* was a group of gentlemen that stuck together at any and all costs. They worked together as a totality and were a powerful organization of White men. I guess that's why some lawyers I approached regarding my problems at Woodrow Stamping honored the club's activities. I was told it was hard to win a case against Woodrow Stamping Plant. I also heard someone in management gloating Woodrow Stamping Plant had never been sued for discrimination. They were always able to throw cases out of court through the Summary Judgment because Woodrow Stamping Plant and Local 783 had people in high places. It wasn't that Woodrow Stamping Plant and Local 783 didn't discriminate. They had enough influence in the *Good Old Boys Club* to stop good lawyers in their tracks. I guess it was like a union protecting their own.

I experienced this influence first hand, when my case was dismissed during a Summary Judgment hearing. It wasn't because I didn't have a case, contrary to what Woodrow Stamping Plant wanted everyone to believe. I did have a case and that is the reason I was offered the $7,500 dollars to settle in the first place. I was an exception to the rule because Woodrow Stamping Plant never paid any minority money, even if the ruling was found in their favor. I didn't think the amount was fair. Therefore I didn't take the $7,500 dollars offered. I truly felt after all Woodrow Stamping Plant and Local 783 had done to me, and this amount of money was an insult. If I had accepted this money, I would have enabled them in their wrongdoings against me.

When I refused the money, I asked the judge to give or appoint me a lawyer and he refused. I was denied an attorney by Judge Patrick Turncoat. He stated he felt I didn't need a lawyer and if there were a need, he would grant me one. How could this be? I was denied a lawyer in a court of law, which is contrary to what the United States Constitution said I was entitled to. I surely wasn't a lawyer and didn't have to be one to know the judge clearly overstepped his authority. Did Judge Turncoat think I had a limited thinking capacity or what? Why would the judge deny me an attorney, if he was supposed to be representing the justice system? It truly seemed he was representing 'big corporate business' and gave less than a damn about me as a person of color with no money to fight big business.

In the meantime, I wrote letters to anyone I thought would read them. Not only did I write Mr. Jess McGregor, President of Local 783, I also wrote Mr. Johnny Hilter, Representative at the Executive Branch of the Union. In April 1993, I sent the first letter to Jess McGregor in hopes of getting some help from the Local 783 Executive Branch because the first letter went unnoticed. This was the second letter, which was sent to Mr. McGregor concerning the problems I was experiencing. The letter stated:

"Dear Mr. McGregor:

I am writing this letter due to my concern about the wording in the agreement between the Union's Executive Branch and Famous Parts Company's union contract. I asked many questions in reference to the part-time employees at Woodrow Stamping Plant. I have fully read the text pertaining to part-time employees. The section on part-time employees is very brief. I have asked Local 783 why the part-time employees were not allowed to work any Saturday, Sunday, or holiday, which were our regular days to work. I was never answered adequately.

There is a contradiction between what's written in the contract book and what Local 783 is actually doing. Part-time employees hired by the company are scheduled to work only on Monday and Friday in addition to Saturday, Sunday, and holidays. Part-timers can't work on their regular scheduled days according to Local 783. Other part-time employees and I, were told we could not work any Saturday, Sunday, or holiday unless the plant worked at 100%. Saturday, Sunday, and holidays were our regular workdays. When we were scheduled to work by the supervisor, and the supervisor wasn't aware the part-time employees weren't supposed to be working, he was reprimanded while these were our regular scheduled days. Why won't Woodrow Stamping Plant allow part-time employees to work Saturday, Sunday, or holidays? The contract states part-time employees can work on premium days, just as long as they don't displace regular employees. The company insists we are not allowed to work on these days. However, I have not found it in the local agreement or the international agreement. So please tell me where it is located.

On one occasion I was asked to work overtime. The supervisor needed another person due to a full-time employee going home. The supervisor asked me to work overtime and I agreed to do so. When I informed him I was part-time, he said he would have to withdraw because he *didn't* have enough people to run the job. He knew it would have been clearly overtime for me. On another occasion there was a part-time gentleman who worked overtime because they did not have anyone to work the *Draw*, whom was full-time. (*The Draw was the first station on the line. The operator would place a sheet of steel into the press and press—the palm buttons to cycle the machine. The steel was formed to a mold that made the desired part.*) Weeks later this gentleman's supervisor informed him there was an error regarding his overtime because—part-time employees were not allowed to work overtime.

In recent months, the union had been sticking to the agreement about part-time employees, working only on Mondays and Fridays. In many instances prior, we worked days on Tuesday through Thursday. This is clearly evident the agreement had not been followed. My question is, if we can work Tuesday through Thursday, why can't we work Saturday and Sunday—especially if we are not replacing full-time employees' jobs? Why can't we work our regular scheduled working days—and weekends too?

The way it was stated by Local 783's contract is that part-time employees are nei-ther—allowed to work daily overtime nor weekend overtime, which were our regular scheduled workdays. I interpret this as a breech of contract. As a union member, I feel I deserve some straight answers as to what I can do about this mat-ter. As I understand it, the contract is binding and should go according to the agreement. It is the union's job to oversee the agreement to make sure it goes according to the way it's written. Can you inform me, as to why the union isn't enforcing what's written in the guidelines? Maybe our union representatives don't fully understand, or is it *I* who don't fully understand?

It appears Famous Parts Company and Local 783, at Woodrow Stamping doesn't want part-time employees working overtime, even when there is a shortage of full-time employees. Why haven't these rules been omitted from the contract, if they're not going to be followed? As I see it, the union isn't properly representing me as a part-time *or* full-time employee, on this matter. Please respond."

I also sent this same letter to the Executive Branch of the Union on January 20, 1993. Executive Branch of the Union Representative, Johnny Hilter, informed me I must go through the proper channels. He informed me if the problem still existed, to contact him again. I thanked him in another letter and signed my name.

The above letter dated April 1993, resulted in a meeting with Jess McGregor at Local 783. Those in attendance were Plant Chair, John Hail; Local 783 President, Jess McGregor; and I, Crista Carrie. I explained to Mr. McGregor my situation as it stood and my concerns regarding everything in the letter addressed to him. Our conversation got as far as the Christmas bonuses, and other full-time benefits. I was not allowed to use any full-time benefits, vacation days, bonuses, profit sharing, or personal days (for the exception of 1990 and 1991, when I received my Christmas bonuses only). As I was speaking about the Christmas bonuses and other full-time benefits, the expression on McGregor's face looked rather strange.

"I know Brother John Hail will handle the problem", said Mr. McGregor. Brother Hail told me that someone in the plant had the same social security number as me. This same person was full-time. He was correct about one thing, and that was I was a full-time and a part-time employee, both at the same time. The employee who shared the same social security number with me *was* me. *I* was the person who was full-time and part-time. Plant Chairman, John Hail, had stated that as the reason I was listed as full-time opposed to part-time.

Did they really think I was stuck on stupid? There are no two social security numbers the same. Your social security number is your lifetime identification number according to the Social Security Administration. I wondered just how stupid these people thought I was by them giving me a line like that. They really thought they could tell me anything and expect me to go along with what I *knew* was a lie.

11

CHASING LIES, FINDING RESOLUTIONS

I had an appointment in January 1993 to meet with Labor Relations regarding my full-time/part-time status problems. Plant Chairman, John Hail, told me to come to his office, on the mezzanine floor so he and I could go see Mr. R. Sophie, Labor Relations Supervisor. On the day the meeting was to have taken place, I missed my entire lunch hour going on a wild goose chase around the plant. I first went to Mr. Hail's office where I was to have met with him. From there we were to join Mr. R. Sophie in his office. But when I reached the committee room, I was told Mr. Hail had just left. I thought there might have been some kind of misunderstanding. I headed to the front office to see Mr. Sophie. When I reached the front office, he too was out of his office.

My lunch hour was over and the meeting I was to have had with Labor Relations Supervisor, Mr. Sophie, never took place. The Plant Chairman/President John Hail, was nowhere to be found. The following day I tried reaching Mr. Hail to no avail. It seemed Woodrow Stamping Plant and Local 783 were giving me the run-a-round once again. If not, Mr. Hail was aware of where I worked on the plant floor he could have found me anytime, after the meeting hadn't taken place. Since he put forth no effort finding me on the floor, I concluded there was no intention to meet with me in the first place.

Another red flag sparked my attention in December 1992. I received an unexpected surprise. When I received my W-2 statement at the year ending 1992, I noticed the amount wasn't consistent with my check stub's year-to-date information. My W-2 was overstated along with many other part-time employees', especially those in Polly's group. The question of why this had happened was brought to the union. I soon received a Western Union Mailgram sent from Woodrow Stamping. The mailgram was addressed to me and stated:

"Your 1992 W-2 statement has been found to be incorrect in that certain amounts were overstated. Corrections are in process and an amended W-2 will be mailed to you in the very near future."

I had to gather my thoughts on this new incident. Would this in fact be the money, which was calculated and taken back through adjustments? What else could this overstatement mean? Was it the money pilfered from me that was placed in the secret N file—their money laundering account? I figured this happened in order to keep the plant's doors open, but I could have been wrong. The money could have been going for drugs or weapons of some sort. The pilfered money had to reside someplace. No one ever investigated where any of the money was going—because they were too busy making sure I didn't receive a dime of the money designated to me. Was it inadequate bookkeeping, a case of mismanagement, embezzlement, or fraud? Needless to say, I never received the amended W-2 Form for that year.

I added up all the different mistakes, lies, and contradictories. For one, it took the company two years to admit I was not part-time but full-time. When Local 783 and Woodrow Stamping Plant finally admitted I was full-time, it was said it was an error by both Local 783 and Woodrow Stamping Plant. The union never elaborated on my behalf. Nor did they for any of the others who were supposed to be part-time and were actually full-time. The union didn't help in the matter. They stood by and let Woodrow Stamping Plant—do as they chose to do against its members. My vacation adjustments and the repayment of my holiday pay—were adjusted from my paychecks. The paid personal day I had taken, was withdrawn from my earnings because it was also given in "error". I knew the money wasn't returned to the company. I wanted this amount off my check and re-listed as being returned or paid in full. Since Woodrow Stamping Plant insisted I was not full-time.

The person able to correct the error was out on vacation for a few days. Therefore the money was going to be returned to me if they couldn't contact the Controller. The Controller came back from vacation and corrected the problem in part. The amount of money remained on my check stub as being paid, but my eligibility date was changed from "December" to the letter "S". I wanted my check stub to state the money was paid back. That was my only problem at that point. If my money wasn't pilfered, there wouldn't have been a problem correcting my check stub. I guess I was part-time and full-time too.

I would think the money allocated to me would stay with me. If they can force me to pay the money back, they should have been forced to correct my stub to state the money was returned. I met with Paul Nashing, Local 783 Committee-man for the Assembly Side of the Plant, and Mr. Sophie, Labor Relations Super-visor. We discussed the matter but they didn't know how to fix the problem. They called the Controller from wherever he was vacationing to correct the problem. They didn't know how to change my check stub to reflect my return of the money because of their pilfering. Common sense would tell anyone, if I didn't get the money and the money was never returned to the company, something was wrong. Who pilfered the money? Most importantly, why didn't anyone investigate where it went—especially Local 783? As a result, they terminated my employment from Woodrow Stamping Plant some ten months later.

I started thinking about my problems and concerns. I dared not think too hard. I was already treading on thin ice. I was asking far too many questions in which the union and the company had difficulty answering. I was becoming widely popular in the union and the company's surroundings. There was no one who I could confide in because I was regarded as a "troublemaker". It was basically because I had been treated extremely unfair by—being discriminated against and improperly labeled with no justification on their part.

The resistance basically started when I didn't accept the lies Local 783 and Woodrow Stamping Plant wanted me to go along with. I became their enemy and a threat to them. I was either with them or not. Therefore I became the enemy. At that point, it was all out war between Local 783, Woodrow Stamping Plant, and me. They felt I was someone who they could discredit and take advantage of.

It could have very well been that people were scared to open their mouths about what was happening in terms of the money laundering. Management's relatives weren't going to say very much. They were also receiving benefits and were told to keep their mouths shut. When questioned about the benefits, the union would tell employees that since they had full-time medical benefits, they would be taken away if it were found out. Local 783 advised the part-time employees to say nothing or their medical benefits would be withdrawn. They were blackmailing employees by telling them this to make them think they were getting something for nothing. Employees didn't know they were paying with their silence by having their money pilfered. Woodrow Stamping Plant continued to go along with Local 783 while taking employees' monetary benefit package. Their silence came with a price. Woodrow Stamping Plant felt if I stayed there long enough, the employees would start believing what I had been telling them all along about being full-time. Woodrow Stamping and Local 783 didn't want that.

The more I thought about my situation and asked questions, the more evasive Local 783 and Woodrow Stamping Plant became. I couldn't quite put my finger on whatever it was. There were so many things not adding up. The 'new hires,' from 1991 were gaining seniority while part-time employees were still part-time some 5 years later. Many of the part-time employees worked three or four years before becoming full-time, but this happened because there were more than two set of records on these employees.

Amidst all this confusion, I was prepared to fight for my seniority and back pay. At this point I knew management was seizing funds by labeling part-time employees full-time. However, I wanted to be sure before insinuating such strong allegations. Afterall, who would believe a "troublemaker" sticking her nose where it didn't belong? I felt I was within my boundaries of asking questions because it was my personal days, profit sharing, vacation time, and performance bonuses in question. I never used my personal days, therefore not receiving the money. I didn't use my vacation days I gained through the years, therefore it had to go into another account. My greatest fear was that the Controller had the access to transfer money from one place to another.

Woodrow Stamping Plant was very much aware the money was being taken from the part-time employees, who were actually full-time. This is why the part-time employees weren't allowed to go to another plant for full-time status. I believe it was Tom Hemp, Plant Vice-Chairman for Local 783, who told me if I didn't like the way things were, I should write a resolution. I felt some of the issues I was referring to were already addressed in the union contract book. The union just wasn't following through with what was written. I said to myself the union didn't really want me to write a resolution. They just didn't think I would follow through with writing one. I proved them wrong when I returned to the committee room upstairs on the mezzanine floor. I handed my written resolution to Tom Hemp. He was John Hail's alternate. Tom Hemp told me he didn't see anything in my resolution that would be accepted except for the educational aspect of it. I guess it was too honest. I was only addressing some of the problems that hadn't been addressed while working part-time.

I was having many problems with Woodrow Stamping Plant, but I was always willing to work the hours necessary. While I worked, I was being paid $14.12 and $0.05 Cost of Living Adjustments. I was willing to work as much as I could. I would always have adjustments taken from my paycheck, whether it was for holiday pay or adjustments for a day worked and not paid. I had problems quite often where I'd work and wouldn't get paid. I would have to wait until the following pay period in some cases to get things straightened out. I worked as many hours as I could, so I could make up for some of the shortages and adjustments I received.

There were many instances I was expecting a certain amount of money on my paycheck and was disappointed when I received it. I would not have received payment for the hours actually worked. I worked a week without being paid on a few occasions. I needed to work as many hours and save as much as possible because I couldn't depend on my check being accurate. I fought so hard for change because I never knew what my check was going to look like at the end of the week. The following resolution was written November 10, 1992 and submitted to the union in hopes a change would occur.

"We feel part-time employees are discriminated against as a group at Woodrow Stamping Plant.

1. We have been part-time employees for over two years. We've contributed our best. We work side by side with full-time employees doing the same jobs. Why should full-time employees be granted bonuses and part-time employees who have worked on the same jobs, receive no recognition for their performances taken with great care?

2. We feel if a part-time employee has worked for one year or more, they should be given paid vacation. They have contributed within the year as other full-time employees have. (*This was already in the contract. Part-time people had to work 90 actual days as part-time and they would receive benefits such as holiday pay.*)

    I wrote this resolution because I was in hopes someone other than Local 783 and Woodrow Stamping Plant would see what was happening. I hoped someone would stand up and say, "Why is she writing this information when what she is requesting is already in the contract? But no one caught on to what I was saying, or even questioned my motive for writing the resolution. I stated in the resolution that part-time employees should be allowed to work over-time on a regular basis if it's scheduled. The resolution continued:

3. The part-time employees should be allowed to work Saturdays and Sundays if overtime is scheduled. Since these are the part-time employees' regular days of work. Part-time employees can only work Saturdays, Sundays, and holidays if the plant works at 100%. Part-time employees are not allowed to work daily overtime. Many full-time employees turn down Saturdays and

Sundays, and part-time employees are never placed on the overtime schedule. (*This was already in effect because part-time employees worked Mondays, Fridays, Saturdays, Sundays, and holidays.*)

4. Part-time employees feel Saturdays and Sundays are not taking work from the full-time employees, because working weekends are not mandatory. Weekends are on a volunteered basis unless posted 100%. Why shouldn't overtime be distributed evenly with full and part-time employees? (*This was not enforced because if you were full-time, you would already have the privilege to work Saturdays and Sundays, which was why we couldn't work the weekends. They kept two sets of records—one for the part-time employees and the other files were for the full-time employees. They had to keep their books and records straight.*)

5. After working one year or more, a part-time employee should have a consistent schedule so they'll be able to attend an educational institution. Maybe a person would like to take courses in the area of skilled trades to benefit one's self at Famous Parts Company. What better time to take classes while only working two days a week? (*They used to put some of the skilled trades' sons and daughters in apprentice programs while they were working part-time. I was going to school while part-time and Woodrow Stamping Plant refused to work with me. I tried to coordinate my classes with the shift when I was working. Then Woodrow Stamping plant would change my shift. I actually went around the plant to find anyone willing to change shifts with me until the semester was complete. The union and company accommodated others who were going to school. When I wanted to be accommodated, the union said they couldn't assist in changing anyone's shift any longer.*)

6. After working for Famous Parts Company for a year or more, part-time employees should carry their seniority with them until they become full-time employees. (*This was already in effect, but the union told the part-time people otherwise.*)

7. We also feel part-time employees should have seniority among themselves. As of now, the company can call anyone whom they wish to start work at any given day—leaving the employees with less seniority working and the higher seniority part-time employees laid-off. There should be a seniority system to prevent less confusion among part-time employees. As it stands, we never know what order we are to be called back to work if we are laid off.

It seems as if it makes the company no difference. We feel this should change. (*The company called those whom they chose when they chose to call them to return. There was no definite order in which they called the part-time employees back to work. Even part-time employees were supposed to be called back in the order of their social security number—greatest last four digits first.*)

8. We feel that part-time employees should not be discriminated against as a group at the Woodrow Stamping Plant. (*The company clearly didn't follow rules already in place. They paid some of the part-time employee's full-time benefits and not others.*)

9. We as temporary part-time employees, feel we have no rights as an employee to stand up for what is right according to the contract. Part-time employees working at Famous Parts Company should be given a sense of respect and self worth. Instead we are made to feel that Famous Parts Company doesn't care about its part-time employees as a group. We believe we have to come up with solutions to solve some of the discomfort shared among the employees. Keep in mind we are all human beings with emotions. Please also keep that in mind when discussing these resolutions, we are only asking for fairness and nothing more." I signed my name and stated on behalf of my part-time co-workers.

After I handed the resolution to Tom Hemp, Plant Vice-Chair of Local 783, I left the mezzanine and went back to the floor on the Press Side of the plant. The line I worked that day was Line #52. When I went back, I told the part-time people on the line I had finally handed over the resolution for change regarding the part-time employees. Again Plant Chairman, John Hail, had already threatened some of the part-time people if they participated in any occurrences with regards to me, they would not be hired full-time. The company used their own discretion in placing people full-time when they wanted to. John Hail had the authority to hire as he pleased and there was nothing anyone could do about it. He saw me as a threat because I came too close to the truth regarding the pilfering of money from the part-time employees. I was also informing others of this truth.

I was determined to find out where the money was going. There were about thirty people who I was aware of being incorrectly labeled as part-time, though there may have been more. Some employees, who had relatives in management, quietly received their money. They received bonuses, vacation pay, and profit sharing. I noticed when the checks came in the plant on Tuesday; management pulled their relatives' checks. Some of the employees received their checks on

Tuesday when the checks reached the plant. All other checks were supposed to go directly to the Controller who would then divert the money in the appropriate account. I was aware of the fact but could do nothing. I'd heard there were as many as 300 part-time employees on the employee rosters.

In the year 2003, I received an income tax statement from the State of California saying I didn't file my taxes in the year 1999. I contacted the State of California and told them I had neither visited California, nor had I ever worked or lived in their state. The information came from Famous Parts Plant. I say this because the California tax form had the correct name and social security number on it. Personally, I felt this was the Controller trying to get someone to pay taxes on the money *they'd* pilfered and laundered. As a result, I wasn't forced to pay the taxes to a state I had no affiliation with.

12

ERRORS ARE NORMALLY CORRECTED

I didn't find out I wasn't on Polly's grievance until September 1992. I was told I would be added when Woodrow Stamping finally admitted I was full-time. The union did not do as they had promised. In September when Hame Pate of Local 783 notified me my name wasn't on the full-time list, this was something I really didn't want to hear. I became very angry when I first became aware of this. I was working hard to get this matter resolved regarding my seniority. I evaluated my situation and tried to obtain information from other part-time employees also affected by these unusual events. When I thought about it, I understood what was happening. Woodrow Stamping was trying to teach me a lesson, which meant I had to fight my own battle against Woodrow Stamping and Local 783.

They made it quite clear I was a problem and they were in control of the situation. They had the resources and all I had was a deep-seated sense that someone was misappropriating money from part-time employees. I hadn't quite figured how they were turning this situation into a lucrative business. I asked Woodrow Stamping and Local 783 where the money went and I received no answer. Most times they said just enough to satisfy me for the moment and resumed business as usual.

When all on Polly's grievance were put on full-time as of October 1993, they received their seniority as of October 1990, but received no back pay as stated in the meeting with Chairman, John Hail. The company knew this wasn't fair, but they didn't want me around putting ideas in the employees' minds causing them to also ask questions. My determination wouldn't allow me to just forget what they had done to me as an employee.

From July 1992 to June 1993, I put pressure on the union to file a grievance in my behalf regarding my employment status issues. Local 783 really didn't want to write the grievance. Finally June 3, 1993 the union wanted to give me a piece of paper that would get me out of their hair. The union had no intention of going through with the grievance. I didn't know this was Woodrow Stamping Plant's and Local 783's plan until much later. It appeared Local 783 saw this as a way to prevent me from causing trouble. By their analysis, they needed a peace offering because I was becoming a thorn in their side.

If you recall, when I first signed the grievance, the information wasn't complete in its entirety. It remained incomplete until after I contacted the National Labor Relations Board (NLRB). I tried to get a copy of the grievance, but was denied. They filled in the information when they saw I was serious about this grievance. Bob Fleetwood, Bargaining Committeeman for Local 783, prepared the necessary papers to be signed with a short statement saying:

"(1.) Nature *of Grievance:* Full-time status.
(2.) Violation *of Article:* Appendix K.
(3.) Statement *of Case:* The union and aggrieved
The grievant is protesting that she should be placed on full-time status due to the company working the aggrieved four days a week for more than 90 days straight. *The Adjustment Requested:* The aggrieved demands that the aggrieved be placed on full-time status at once and made whole."

Bob Fleetwood knew the rule was to always give the aggrieved a copy of the grievance once it was signed. There were nine other names on the grievance I signed and there was never any mention of any other persons other then Mazzie and me with reference to this grievance. I was surprised Mr. Fleetwood refused to give me a copy of the grievance I'd just signed. He said he wasn't going to make a copy. When I asked Bob to allow me to make a copy within the plant and bring back the original, since his copying machine was down, his reply was, "No!" He made no effort to obtain a copy for me and I never did receive a copy until the grievance was over. From June 1993 until February 1994, I hadn't received a copy of my grievance. I never stopped trying to obtain a copy of it. I decided to take my complaint to the National Labor Relations Board.

On April 26, 1993 I had it up to my tiny little neck with the lies told by Local 783 and Woodrow Stamping Plant. I figured I would be unsuccessful in getting either party to represent me in a fair and truthful manner. It all boiled down to nothing being accomplished by my complaints. I contacted Local 783 again and they didn't represent me to my satisfaction. I came to the conclusion that just maybe, if I could get Local 783 and Woodrow Stamping Plant together, something could be accomplished. Even that didn't work because the only person who showed up to this scheduled meeting was I.

I became so flustered my blood pressure started to rise. I was working, paying union dues, and couldn't get anyone in the union to represent my cause. I started taking very well to my name as "troublemaker". At this particular time, the word had extended all around the plant. My dissatisfaction was aggravated by the constant shortage of hours and adjustments with my monetary sources. My problems went on for three years until I transferred to Sarrow Stamping Plant. Then I was bombarded with even more complicated issues regarding my pay. I gave the company enough time to correct the problems and they chose not to. This is the reason I was asking for my back pay.

I noticed the first group hired full-time had no minorities. The second group had no minorities and the third consisted of six Caucasian males. The last time, there were four or five Caucasians and they stopped hiring right at my name. This was obviously discrimination. This was a reminder that a minority was to stay in their place and keep their mouth shut.

I had already filed a complaint with the Labor Department for the State of Michigan to no avail. After their investigation, they declined to help recover my vacation pay that was withdrawn in June of 1992. After the Labor Relations Board investigated the allegations, I was informed by the Labor Department I had a union to represent me in this matter and their hands were tied. I was to be represented by Local 783's union. That was a joke.

In April 1993, when I filed a complaint with the Department of Civil Rights and the National Labor Relations Board, I seemed to be running out of steam. But even though nothing seemed to be going my way, I couldn't just sit and do nothing. At one point, I started thinking I was fighting a lost cause. My dear friend and next-door neighbor, Thomas, advised me to hang in there. *(I will give you more details of Thomas at the end of this chapter.)*

I was clearly devastated in what they were doing to me. It just wasn't in me to allow the company to clearly rob me right in front of my face. I can't say they were robbing me blind, because my eyes were wide open. The union allowed the company to abuse me mentally and financially, and did absolutely nothing in my defense. In the meantime while I was waiting between organizations to hear something on a positive note, I was called down to the National Labor Relations Board (NLRB) for a deposition hearing. My deposition read as follows:

"Famous Parts Company at the Woodrow Stamping Plant employed me. I started working for Famous Parts Company on September 28, 1990. I am currently a machine operator. I am a current member of Local 783 while working at Famous Parts Company. When I was hired, I was hired as a full-time employee but then I was told I would be working part-time. I worked from 16 to 32 hours a week from the time I was hired, until sometime in the second half of 1993. I was then put on full-time status at another plant.

In July 1992, a grievance was filed about getting my vacation pay back. Polly Rice was a part-time employee at the same time, I filed the grievance and there were other names on Polly's grievance. My name was supposed to appear on it. Hame Pate the Committeeman, and Larry, Skilled Trades Committeeman, told me my name would be on Polly's grievance. In September 1992, I discovered my name was indeed not on the grievance. I found this out from Hame Pate first, and later from Local 783's Plant Chairman Mr. John Hail. I met with him about the processing of Polly's grievance and he told me I wasn't on the grievance. Bob Fleetwood, Bargaining Committeeman, filed a second grievance on June 3, 1993. This grievance said I was entitled to seniority as a full-time employee.

Though hired as a part-time employee, I received holiday pay and vacation pay from the time I was hired. Each time this happened I notified the company and union that my records said I was full-time. On February 17, 1991 my records were changed on paperwork to show, I was part-time. However the company continued issuing holiday checks and vacation pay as an error. At first I would be paid for various holidays and then they would later deduct the money back. I decided since the company never corrected their records to show, I was part-time instead of full-time, I was entitled to vacation pay and seniority as a full-time employee.

I kept inquiring about the grievance. Mr. Bob Fleetwood told me it was in the second stage. The first stage had been denied. He said it would go to the third step. In the summer of 1993, John Hail informed me they were putting the grievance on hold. I contacted Johnny Hilter at the Executive Branch of the Union. My first contact with the Executive Branch of the Union since filing this grievance was when I sent a letter dated January 20, 1993.

The day I signed the June 3, 1993 grievance, I asked for a copy and Bob Fleetwood said he wasn't going to make me one. I asked him if I could make a copy and return with the original. Again he refused. I was working on the floor when I told him for the second time I wanted a copy of my filed grievance. He said he would give me a copy and that they were going to meet on it. No one else was present during this conversation.

About a week or so later, Fleetwood gave me a paper. I asked Jess McGregor, President of Local 783, for a copy of the grievance sometime in September 1993. I asked him on the telephone and he said John Hail would take care of the matter. Mr. McGregor said I was supposed to have gotten a copy when I signed it. These are the only times I talked with anyone from the upper level of the union about getting a copy of the grievance.

I have read this statement consisting of 4 pages including this page. I fully understand its contents and I certify it is true to the best of my knowledge and belief. I'm also requesting a copy of this affidavit."

I felt much better when I filed this complaint but my situation was far from over. I was tired of all the treatment received while employed at Woodrow Stamping Plant. It seemed as though when I told people of my situation, some considered me as telling the truth, but I had no evidence to prove what I was saying. Employees weren't eager to believe the company was pilfering money from them, and the union would try to make sure what I said wasn't given a second thought. I told friends and family for years the plant I worked for was taking money from me. I knew Woodrow Stamping Plant wasn't paying me as they should have been.

I am a person with character and integrity. Wherever there was a topic of conversation, I would tell of my employment and how I was being treated—whether it was at family functions, picnics, birthday parties, or in grocery lines. It seemed like mental therapy for me. Woodrow Stamping Plant thought if the employees didn't know their money was being pilfered it wouldn't hurt them. They felt what employees didn't know couldn't hurt them. Others told me that a company such as Famous Parts Company wouldn't stoop so low. I was hurting mentally, physically, and financially as a result of the company's treatment.

Working for a company like Famous Parts Company had a reputation of paying and treating their employees with dignity and respect. But the corruption was beyond every employee's imagination. As far as they were concerned, it was their word against mine. The company had an image to protect. This information was to never get out. Local 783 would not tolerate this kind of image even if it were accurate.

It wasn't that I was the type of person that lied and no one believed me, because my character clearly wasn't at state. I am a person of my word. I don't just go around lying on people. It just seemed no one wanted to get involved. When an employee had a conflict of interest, the union was to reflect to the contract guidelines. This is the way I see it, I was paying Local 783 to screw me, and that's exactly what they did.

Before the death of my neighbor and good friend Thomas, he stood in my defense and stated the Executive Branch of the Union and Company was where all the corruption existed. Thomas was also an elected shop steward in his days. He believed in and valued the union. Thomas went strictly by the contract. He wasn't always favorable when union members and/or representatives lazed on their duties. Thomas understood I had a union working against me, opposed to working for me.

It took years for me to gain evidence against Woodrow Stamping Plant. My family and friends grew tried of hearing the same old stories over and over again. My family, and friend Thomas, saw how stressful it was when I came home with a new story of what Local 783 and Woodrow Stamping Plant did to me. I wanted everyone to examine and evaluate for themselves what happened through the years. After contacting the President of the United States, governor of Michigan, government agencies, the local senator, attorney general, Executive Branch of the Union, and company, where else should I have gone for assistance?

Having my best male friend, Thomas, made things a lot easier for me. He was a person anyone would have enjoyed having as a friend. If there was anything he could do to help anyone, it was as good as done. He was always willing to go that extra mile. It was a pleasure to have known him from 1974 until his death in 2004. I lost a good friend indeed when he died. When I moved next door to him, my children were quite small and Thomas was always there for them. He never forgot my children's birthdays. He would have his wife make cakes for them even though he always professed he made the cakes with his own two hands. The children believed Thomas made the cakes because he would always be in his back yard cooking on his grill, or working in his garage, or doing something or the other.

Thomas loved the outdoors. Even in the winter months he would be outside with just a sweater. He loved his "Polish Pop". This is what he called beer. He was an entertainer and loved to host parties year-round. Thomas would always invite me over and introduce me to his family and friends. It was as if he adopted me and I became one of his family members. That's the way he wanted it. When I was in the hospital, he would come in my hospital room with a bunch of flowers. He was thoughtful like that. Thomas became my close friend and an adopted member of my family as well.

Thomas was a tall man who kept his haircut close—somewhat like a brush cut. He was about 6 feet 3 inches tall. Thomas's grandparents migrated from Poland. He was born and raised in Detroit near the area of the old Tiger's Stadium on Michigan Avenue and Trumbull. He spoke his native language often and played his Polish music. He loved to dance.

Thomas's wife, Teresa, and I talked while sitting on our front porches in the evening after work. We would talk across the fence while sitting in our back yards. We discussed many subjects, ideas, issues, and current events. When I would stand next to Thomas while taking a photograph, I was so short that my head only reached his elbows. One thing I can say about Thomas is he did many good things for my family and me. I'm grateful for him in helping me keep my sanity with all I was going through with Woodrow Stamping Plant and Local 783. He kept me in balance in my times of need. Lord knows I was grateful for that.

13

WOODROW STAMPING PLANT'S BLATANT HARASSMENT

Once or twice a year Woodrow Stamping Plant would give all employees an update of how the plant was doing in terms of profits and losses. Even when the plants in general were flourishing in the early 1990's, Woodrow Stamping Plant wasn't having such a profitable time—at least according to management. They've never made a significant profit. Management told employees they were always in the red. They seemed eager to inform the plant of whose fault it was that the plant was in the red. Normally management would say the fault belonged to those who worked on the line. Management never took the blame as to why the plant wasn't making a profit, even though management did all the decision-making.

The employees on the line only did what they were told. Management never took the blame for the bad decisions they made. It was always someone else's fault. Management would always tell us we were producing too much scrap. Much of the scrap the plant produced was at an astronomical cost to the company. We were told we might all be out of a job if we didn't put out a better product.

We were initially told if we saw scrap going down the line, not to run the part. We were to notify the supervisor immediately. They really didn't mean what they said because when scraped parts were running, the most important fact seemed to be producing as many parts for production quota. The need for quality parts was just thrown out the window. It seemed like the main factor was quantity over quality. When we would find something wrong with a part, we were told to still run it. The way I saw it, if management told me to run a part and I knew the part was no good, the only thing I could do was run it just as I was told.

In my opinion the plant was totally mismanaged. Woodrow Stamping produced so much scrap it had to be a joke. Sometimes they would run scrap days at a time. The proper maintenance wasn't performed on the machines. The plant would knowingly send scrapped stock to its suppliers. They would actually pull tags off the scrapped material and send it out as good stock. As a result, when noticed, the stock would be returned at the cost of Woodrow Stamping Plant.

In between bad stock, we had broken down lines that were not maintained properly. Woodrow Stamping Plant expected the lines to run on a continuous basis. The managers pushed the machine repairmen and they become angry because the plant wanted them to half do a job—just to get the line running for the moment. The line would break down so often that the plant would have to almost overhaul the entire line. The lines would shut down to a complete stop and wouldn't move an inch. The line might work around the clock just to get the parts to the original destinations if they were needed once the major overhaul was over. When the parts were *hot,* the plants would ship the parts by air to keep the plant from shutting down. This would keep their suppliers from sending employees home for lack of parts. If this happened, Woodrow Stamping Plant would have to pick up the cost.

I truly understood why Woodrow Stamping Plant never made a profit. The decisions about running the plant would always come from management. It was the worst case of mismanagement on a continued basis. I never understood how a plant was run until I actually started working in one. Each plant is its own entity and absorbs the costs of profits and losses. Each plant has the sole responsibility of keeping their doors open by profit or whatever funds they come up with. And since the plant wasn't making much profit, the doors were always open.

I constantly tried finding some logic as to why Local 783 and Woodrow Stamping Plant would not correct the "errors" as they called them. I sincerely found something wrong with my situation. I was also trying to find out where the flow of money was going. It really took years for me to understand what was happening and why. I always seemed to find myself right back at the mercy of Local 783, who refused to represent me. It seemed like a circle of never-ending situations. I couldn't let go of the fact my fellow Caucasian co-workers didn't have to pay their money back as I did. I really felt defeated because I had nowhere to go for help. I felt like all the odds were stacked against me when it came down to Woodrow Stamping and Local 783. This was the honest to God truth.

Being a minority myself, I started seeing a pattern with the Caucasian employees and how the minorities were treated. I felt degraded in every sense because my problems with the company were real. The union was set on refusing to honor my full-time status. I fought so hard and my opponent felt I was out of my place in acknowledging what was going on. I informed everyone I came in contact with how dissatisfied I was with how the company and the union handled my situation. I needed my job and I needed the money. Yeah, I could have quit, but I *thought* I had a union to protect me! This is what I was paying union dues for, right? They were pilfering my hard earned money and I wasn't supposed to say anything about it.

I had fought many battles and was defeated. I was a woman in a nearly all male dominated plant which was over 90% Caucasian. Upper and middle management were mostly men. I hardly ever saw women of ethnic backgrounds in management. Caucasian women were in the office sector only. There might have only been 3% to 4% minorities in supervision on the floor, all of which were men when I started working on the floor in September 1990. I couldn't quite understand why were there so few Skilled Tradesman after a few years of employment? Why were the Caucasian employees the only people able to pass the skilled trades test? Almost all the skilled trade's people were Caucasian. This wasn't only at Woodrow Stamping. It was the same at Sarrow Stamping too.

Labor Relations Supervisor, Randy Facade, was an exception and the only minority in the front Labor Relations offices. The union had appointed positions that minorities were given to make them look important. I want to express that it was only one or two minorities elected in Local 783 on the first and second shifts. And at that time the upper and middle management had about 1% minorities.

In 2005, my insight on discrimination at Famous Parts Company regarding the irregularities in the hiring practices in the skilled trade's field was proven correct. During my inquiry, I always asked management at Woodrow Stamping and Local 783 about there being little or no minorities in the skilled trade's field. I asked Plant Chairman, John Hail, "You mean to tell me the only people who can pass a skilled trades test are Caucasian people?"

The minorities in skilled trades employed at Woodrow Stamping Plant and Sarrow Stamping Plant could be counted on one hand. At one point of my employment, Woodrow Stamping Plant's census was about 1200 employees per shift. It was impossible for the census of the skilled trade's minority to be so low in both plants. Although there were always more Caucasian workers in both plants than minorities, there were many minorities testing for skilled trades positions. It seemed the minorities could never pass the test according to Local 783, Woodrow Stamping, and Sarrow Stamping Plant.

There was a lawsuit filed which proved they *did* discriminate at Woodrow Stamping Plant, Sarrow Stamping Plant, and at other plants too. This was only the case when outside sources were brought in to get involved, whereas the company was forced to make a change. When Woodrow Stamping Plant started soliciting minorities in the skilled trade's field in April 2002, I knew their decision was made under duress and not by choice.

If Sarrow Stamping Plant had hired with the intent of being diverse from the beginning, they wouldn't have been forced to hire more minority women as they were in 1994. Instead they chose to demonstrate favoritism. Even though the company professed its diversity, it was only a word. As the saying goes, "You can fool some of the people some of the time, but you can't fool all of the people all of the time". If you were to survey minority employees in each of these two plants by asking them if they ever felt Woodrow Stamping Plant discriminated against them, the answers would be surprising. Woodrow and Sarrow Stamping Plants both claimed to be equal opportunity employers with diverse facilities. Someone really needed to survey and find out for themselves, because this wasn't true—at least not while I was there.

Woodrow Stamping Plant and Sarrow Stamping Plant both used racism on a daily basis. Harassment and retaliation activities played a significant part in the employment of minorities. The case *Roberson vs. Famous Parts Company* stemmed from 1997 until 2003. The company was found guilty in discriminating by using unfair labor practices while hiring in the area of skilled trades. If Famous Parts Company was sued for discrimination regarding the skilled trades field, don't you think it's inevitable they discriminated in other departments as well?

Yes! My race played a significant part in how I was treated because if I were Caucasian, my experiences would have been different. Here Woodrow Stamping Plant and Local 783 pilfered from me for many years. When I tried to file a lawsuit it was said, I was trying to get something for nothing. What were they doing when they were pilfering my money? If my money is being pilfered then who's getting something for nothing? Surely it wasn't me. Those who think minorities always want something for nothing need to readjust their way of thinking.

With the women working, the men felt they would no longer remain in control. This kept the men at a disadvantage. The men started to wonder what a man could do for a woman if she was able to be self-sufficient in taking control of her life by being self-supportive. The men felt the women wouldn't have to tolerate their unacceptable behavior, big egos, and in some cases violence. This information came from the men I worked with on the lines at Woodrow and Sarrow Stamping plants.

When women started working and earning as much as men, this played a significant role in how women were treated in the plant. It didn't matter very much whether you were a minority or a Caucasian woman. The men felt women shouldn't be working in a plant—and that was all to it. The men stated the work was too hard for women. Although I thought some of the jobs were difficult for men too, depending on their body stature.

I felt nearly all jobs were structured for persons 5 feet 5 inches and taller. Anyone else had problems. Practically none of the jobs in the plant were ergonomically designed for the smaller stature employees. This was a true fact for men as well. The men were angry because women were coming in the plant taking *their* jobs. Some men felt since women were working, they should be working the exact same jobs as men. When the men made this statement, they weren't referencing the men who worked light jobs in the plant. They weren't referring to the men working hard laborious jobs that even the men complained of working.

Then there were some men who felt they weren't going to work hard. They wanted to do as less work as possible—especially if they were high in seniority. I have to admit when the male supervisors didn't get their way, they knew how to get the attention of the women by putting them on very difficult jobs. This happened until the women submitted or catered to what their supervisor desired.

Randy Facade, Labor Relations Supervisor, did this to Andrea Smith. She continuously refused his flirty advances, so he sought out to destroy her. He finally succeeded in 2003 when she was fired. Randy would order supervisors to put Andrea on jobs so difficult she would have to go home. There were times when Randy Facade followed her out of the plant to the parking lot—just to make sure she didn't go straight to the Medical Department. There were times during the 90's in which Randy Facade told Andrea he was going to fire her. All this occurred because she did the best job possible, which didn't mean lying on her back.

Randy carried much clout at Woodrow Stamping Plant as a minority. Management used him at their convenience to do dirty work. He was the only Black that had clout as a Labor Relations Supervisor. Randy Facade also worked with Local 783 in their scheme of pilfering money from the part-time employees. This was done through employees' retirement funds after experiencing a work-related injury. The Medical Department changed the employees' diagnoses to a personal injury.

Woodrow Stamping Plant paid very few employees Worker's Compensation, if the injury was incurred on the job. If you didn't know about the rights under the Worker's Compensation rules and regulations, you can be assured Woodrow Stamping Plant wasn't going to explain them. Who was it that said, "What you don't know won't hurt you"? That's an understatement because what you don't know *can* certainly hurt you. This pilfered money could've meant the difference between an employee being above the poverty level or below it.

The Medical Department was knowingly changing employees' medical diagnoses from an 'occupational injury' to a 'personal injury'. Woodrow Stamping was robbing Metro Craft Insurance Company by having them pay for an injury that was work-related. There were two sets of records kept between Woodrow Stamping Plant and Local 783. I'm not sure how the files were distributed between both entities. There were files on part-time employees, which listed them as part-time employees. Then there were files that listed these same employees as full-time. In fact, I would not have been surprised if these companies had ghost accounts on employees. If they had two separate accounts one part-time and one full-time, it's possible to have ghost accounts as well.

They did have employees on the floor working full-time and part-time as though they had never worked for the company before. They were pilfering from both employees' files. All I can say is Local 783 had access to personal files and records they should not have had. It was the Controller's job to keep the records, so the money could be transferred into special accounts set-up to launder the money from employees. Woodrow Stamping Plant was paying Worker's Compensation benefits to employees, but the employees never received the money directed to them. I know Woodrow Stamping would tell the employees their Worker's Compensation was denied or closed, which entitled the company to keep every penny of the money.

For the 'occupational injured' employee, Woodrow Stamping was paying them Worker's Compensation while putting that money in the special accounts. In the mean time, the employee is put on a 'no work available' status and awaits payments from Metro Care Insurance Company. Woodrow Stamping Plant had other ideas for the money and it didn't have anything to do with the injured employee's pockets. Woodrow Stamping Plant was keeping the money from the occupational injuries and laundering it.

This was done because employees received more money, when they were out of work for an occupational injury. Woodrow Stamping Plant pilfered from those employees that paid the most money. The employee is paid much less for a personal injury while being on a no work available. The other set of records stated the injured employee was not getting credit for the occupational injury sustained in the plant. Metro Craft was paying the bills as a 'personal injury'. Nurse Tootie, of Woodrow's Medical Department, kept some of those files in her office that were being used and not with the other files until, they could be returned back to the other Famous Parts Company subsidiary in Brownstown where those files were kept. Therefore the employees were out of work attributed to a medical leave from Woodrow Stamping Plant for a personal injury.

There was another dilemma I faced while on medical leave. Why did Woodrow Stamping Plant have me employed while I was on medical leave for a personal injury according to their records? I was on the *drot*, which is the company's time sheet, as working various hours while I was on medical leave. It was almost as though I was working on a part-time basis while, Woodrow Stamping Plant had me on a 'no work available' for purposes of Worker's Compensation.

Since they were receiving employees Worker's Compensation, they had to continue these employees as working unless they retired them. If you're injured while working, it is the company's responsibility to find work for you within the plant. They had already done that on one set of records, but there was more than just that one set of records on employees. While Metro Craft paid me for an occupational injury on medical leave, Woodrow Stamping Plant pilfered the money I should have received for my occupational injury. They were robbing Metro Craft Insurance Company by changing employees' medical diagnoses. Woodrow Stamping Plant should have been paying those benefits from the Worker's Compensation fund.

Woodrow Stamping Plant was pilfering my money when the Medical Department had me off work for an occupational injury on their records. This was for the Worker's Compensation records, but they were yet getting paid for me working when I was not in the plant while on medical leave. Woodrow Stamping Plant made it seem as though I was having problems working 8 hours. According to paperwork I received from Woodrow Stamping Plant, the medical records showed I was unable to work a normal 8 hour shift. I worked hours varying anywhere from 1 to 10 hours, but this report showed I was unable to work a full shift. All this happened while I was on medical leave receiving payment from Metro Craft. This was done because they were ready to start me on long-term medical benefits in an effort to pilfer my retirement.

As I have stated, they had two sets of records on employees. There may have been even more. They changed employees' names, birthdates, and social security by one or two numbers. By changing this kind of information, it can totally change a person's identity. The mere fact that I was on payroll while I was yet on medical leave, was out-right fraud. I reported this to the Public Review Board and they did nothing. I was totally ignored as I had been for the last 14 years while complaining of the mistreatment.

Woodrow Stamping Plant had me working while drawing Worker's Compensation at the same time. I was receiving payments from Metro Craft Insurance

Company. I notified the Medical Department that an error had been made. My Medical Department's timesheet reported I returned to work, while the Medical Department said I was on a 'no work available'. I informed the Medical Department that I wanted the information corrected. I had not been cleared to return back to work through the Medical department or Labor Relations.

I was on medical leave when I was reported as being employed at the same plant I was on medical leave from. This could not happen if there was only one set of records for employees. Woodrow Stamping Plant actually had me 'working.' This happened on a few occasions when I was out of work according to Woodrow Stamping Plant. It was impossible for me to be two places at once. I mentioned this to Nurse Tootie and Committeeman of Local 783, Zeb Star, but no one wanted to investigate my suspicions. Woodrow Stamping Plant never listened to me.

For many years the Medical Department did the same to my friends and co-workers, Andrea Smith and Linda Jackson. Linda Jackson has been off work from 1997 'til at least June 2007. Andrea Smith was off work from 1995 to 1999 and then from 2002 until she was fired in 2003. When she started asking questions, the Social Security Administration told her the company she worked for had her 'retired'. Woodrow Stamping Plant brought her back and she was later fired in February 2003. Both women's retirement was pilfered by the Medical Department at Woodrow.

For this reason, they didn't honor the occupational injuries for the employees who were on restrictions by their medical doctors. The company wanted to get rid of them as soon as possible, so they could receive their retirement money and Worker's Compensation benefits leaving them with nothing. The only thing the employees received was their Social Security benefits. Woodrow Stamping Plant went as far as leaving Andrea Smith with no medical coverage when they knew just how serious her medical condition was. Andrea was suffering from major depression and Degenerative Joint Disease when she was terminated. Nurse Tootie changed Andrea's medical information to fit the Medical Department criteria from an occupation injury to personal injury. They were aware of all aspects of Andrea's medical condition including all medical findings and restrictions by company and personal physicians. Head Nurse Tootie, in the Medical Department, was later fired in August 2004. This happened after I wrote a letter to the Executive Branch of the Company's CEO, Mr. Robert Wart. She was fired for embezzlement, falsifying government documents, and falsifying medical documents.

It didn't matter how Andrea Smith complained about the job she was put on. Once the word was around the plant for all supervisors to get involved in retaliation and harassment, it was as good as done. The supervisors stuck together that way. Supervisor, Joey Nick, told Andrea in the 90's as she was working a hard job, that not even the men wanted to work this particular assignment. Joey Nick, who put Andrea on these jobs daily stated, "Now you know how it feels to be caught in the middle". Andrea had no idea what he was talking about, but she *did* know he could have found other jobs in the department for her to work. This meant his orders came from someone in the higher level of management. He stated he had no choice in the matter of what job to put Andrea on. He was caught in the middle by putting her on the hardest job in his department. This job ultimately caused the Degenerative Joint Disease, Andrea is currently suffering from.

Randy Facade, the Labor Relations Supervisor that often harassed Andrea, fought her from the 90's until she was fired. He was not employed at the plant when she was fired, but he had access to come and go at Woodrow Stamping Plant as he pleased. He even appeared at one of Andrea Smith's Worker's Compensation hearings ready to testify against Andrea. When Andrea informed Referee, Jackie Arnold that Mr. Facade was no longer working at Woodrow Stamping, he was told his testimony was not necessary. There was no need for Randy Facade to be at Andrea's hearings because he had nothing to do with Andrea's Worker's Compensation case.

Randy Facade had a reputation in the plant with the women. He was determined to have Andrea but she repeatedly turned him down. This was something he wasn't quite use to. Andrea embarrassed Randy Facade and his reputation was shuddered. After his advances failed, Andrea's life became a living nightmare. Randy Facade affected her life both inside and outside the plant. Woodrow Stamping Plant and Local 783 had to continue their lying scheme so others wouldn't find out what they were doing in the Medical Department.

There were some women who fought the system and there were those who submitted. Many women worked very hard and earned every dollar they made not trying to beat the system. The men finally realized the women were in the plant to stay and weren't going anywhere. Yet there were those diehard men who wanted to hold on to their sense of control.

Many laws changed in favor of a person's civil rights in the workplace. Management at Woodrow Stamping Plant had to get a handle on their old way of life for fear of being fired, reprimanded, or maybe even sued for discrimination or harassment in the workplace. There were supposed to be many laws protecting employees in the workplace if they were violated.

In July of 1992, I had an experience on the job when I was working on the Press Side of the plant. On this day, I was working a job controlling the foot-peddle of the conveyor belt that carried parts down the line to be put onto a rack. My Caucasian Supervisor, Roger Mailer, had retired from the military before working at Woodrow Stamping Plant. The job I was working was the only job available at that time. I was given this job because they had no jobs to fit my small stature. This line pressed the fender for a small automobile. When the fender came down the conveyor, it was put on the rack. The part itself wasn't heavy at all. The racks sat off the floor about eighteen inches because of the wheels it was on. The racks were lined with padding, giving the rack additional height.

There were two men stacking the fenders on the rack who began to complain. One of the men's fathers worked in upper management. He was Caucasian and the other man was Hispanic. They had decided they wanted to rotate jobs with me because it was said I wasn't doing any work. I was told they wanted to do the same even though these men were much larger than I. It wasn't that I didn't want to work that job. It was clearly a fact the job was hazardous to my health. When those men continued complaining to Roger Mailer, he ultimately agreed with them. These two men wanted to know why I couldn't rotate the job in order to give each person a turn stacking fenders in the rack. They also wanted to control the conveyor belt. Mr. Mailer came to me and stated I had to rotate jobs with the two men. I did as I was told. As I stated prior, the parts weren't heavy. They were just awkward.

I lifted the part from the conveyor belt to put it on the rack. I then turned to the lift with the part in my hand and as I turned to slide the part in its slot, I cut my knee. I then had to be taken to the hospital for stitches. I was angry because anyone with any common sense should have known a short person shouldn't be lifting a part on a rack higher or equivalent to their own height. The reason I worked the rotated job was because I had to at least make an effort before I could say the job was unsafe, or I would have been sited as refusing to do a job.

Of course, everyone realized me working that job was a mistake after the fact. The supervisor didn't use his common sense. He was just trying to satisfy his male co-workers who complained I was doing no work. I was appalled at the fact I had a senseless accident because of the supervisor trying to satisfy a relative of upper management. I felt if I were Caucasian, there wouldn't have been a question about rotating jobs or putting my safety in jeopardy.

I didn't realize until after my accident, Dr. Care would confront me. He told me if I were to get a supervisor who put me on jobs my body could not withstand, have them look in the computer and they would have to find another job assignment for me. I carefully explained how my accident occurred. Dr. Care sincerely cared about his employees' health and welfare. After my physical was complete, I was surprised when he made this statement:

"The reason I gave you the restriction was due to your height. I knew there would be some unscrupulous supervisor who would do as I carefully explained to you when you were first hired."

Dr. Care stated for me to be careful incase this kind of problem presented itself again. He again advised me to have my supervisors look into the computer and see my restriction. He put the restriction in the computer and stated he didn't want to see me in the Medical Department with this same problem again. I saw Dr. Care once or twice more after my injury for follow-up treatments. I left in November 1993 and never saw him again. When I returned in July 1997, he was no longer working for Famous Parts Company—Woodrow Stamping Plant. One could probably guess why. Woodrow Stamping Plant didn't want doctors like him. They only needed doctors who were unconcerned about employees' medical conditions. I assumed they were paid well for being so insensitive.

Needless to say, the restriction was intentionally removed and never put back into to the computer. Woodrow Stamping Plant didn't honor my restrictions because they were too busy trying to get back at me for causing them so many problems. Their action was in retaliation for my action toward them. What would it have cost them to put the restriction back in the computer? It was only for stature. This gave them the opportunity to punish me when they felt I did something wrong.

For instance, Woodrow Stamping Plant became angry with me when I filed charges against Tom Hemp, Local 783's Plant Chairman, and Al Snake, a representative at the Regional 21A. (*The Regional 21A is the middle level of the Executive Branch of the Union.*) The charges stemmed from Tom Hemp and Al Snake working in the best interest of Woodrow Stamping Plant and not the union member. This was a few days before I re-submitted my Article 33 grievance since it was put on hold. The letter regarding the Article 33 was resumed and took effect on May 10, 2002. On May 14, 2002, I was put back on the line, which violated all my restrictions. That following Monday morning is when the plant superintendent told my supervisor while I had braces on my hands, that I had to pick up a rail weighing about 45 pounds. I practically had casts on both hands but they didn't care about my condition. My restriction was "no lifting more than 15 pounds". This was 30 pounds more than my restriction allowed me to lift.

The plant only wanted doctors who would help the plant break down their employees' bodies. The company would then try getting these same employees to quit their jobs. From what I experienced, this may just have been the plan Woodrow Stamping used to extort money from the employees through Worker's Compensation. When the injured employee went to court and was granted a lump sum payment, they never received the money. The money was pilfered from the employees and put back in the plant helping the plant's doors to stay open so I thought. I wondered why a plant would continue losing money as stated during the quarterly meetings, and continue keeping the doors open. What would be the purpose of allowing a plant to stay open if it never made a profit?

Dr. Care was a good doctor concerned about Woodrow Stamping's employees. I'm stressing this fact because from my following experiences, Woodrow Stamping Plant's doctors had a lack of interest in assisting the employees injured in the plant. The Medical Department didn't care about what happened, just as long as it didn't cost the company. I looked at the doctors they hired as rejects of the medical profession who probably lost their license from a malpractice suit. I would be a little sarcastic by saying all they needed was a doctor like the famous Doctor Death (Dr. Kevorkian), and Famous Parts Company would save millions of dollars. It's cheaper to eliminate a person rather than pay the rising cost of medical treatment for an occupational injury, right?

The Medical Department didn't want to own up to the occupational injuries sustained in their plant. The company always stated the injuries were of a personal nature. It was almost like the Medical Department was getting bonuses for keeping the medical census down. That wasn't the only problem with the Medical Department because Woodrow Stamping had another agenda for these injured people. It didn't matter whether you quit or not. They were going to pilfer your retirement money either way. They just preferred you to quit.

This happened to other employees, but I have creditable information from Linda Jackson, Andrea Smith, and myself, Crista Carrie. These documents include information and actual correspondences, court papers, and Worker's Compensation decisions and depositions made by Woodrow Stamping Plant's management's staff.

I truly believe the reason two computers were mysteriously stolen from Woodrow Stamping Plant was because they contained vital illegal information regarding all employees at Woodrow Stamping Plant who were pilfered from. On these computers is where the secret files were kept. This is the information Woodrow Stamping Plant tried to hide. I can almost guarantee these were the computers holding all the information regarding employees' pilfered records and illegal Worker's Compensation and retirement accounts. These computers would have contained information on past and current employees, their social security files, and work status. They had to know this information in order to know whose retirement was to be pilfered from. Woodrow Stamping Plant had only one person handling these files. This was a Labor Relations Supervisor who was never seen very often. This supervisor never had much involvement or interaction with other employees. He always hid in his office with the door closed where he could never been seen. He was the only one handling the files of the pilfered money accounts. What are the odds of only two computers being pilfered in the midst of many investigations?

They didn't have this information on all computers because that would lead to getting caught. I'm sure these two computers had any and everything to do with where the company kept the money and whom they were pilfering from. I truly don't blame the attempt to discard this incriminating evidence because there would be no hope in them being found innocent. Money talks and bullsh*t walks in the corporate business world.

14

GRIEVANCE COMPLICATIONS "THEY STOLE MY MONEY"

After numerous failed attempts to contact the Local 783, I decided to obtain help from other sources. On April 19, 1993 I filed a complaint against Famous Parts Company Woodrow Stamping Plant for discrimination. My complaint to the Department of Civil Rights read:

"On July 2, 1992 I received vacation pay for one week for the vacation shut down period. I was later notified the pay had been given to me in error. On July 10, 1992 the money was taken back out of my check. In January of 1993, I became aware of two Caucasian employees in my same classification that received vacation pay in July of 1992. Unlike me, they were not required to pay it back. On April 23, 1993 I learned of White employees given performance bonuses in September of 1992. I had not received this bonus. I am a Black woman and I believe the respondent has unfairly denied me because of my race."

The complaint was signed and dated on April 23, 1993. There was also a signature of a Notary Public of Wayne County, which was supplied by The Department of Civil Rights. *This complaint was based on the Elliott-Larsen Civil Rights Act—P.A. of 1976 and amended Title VII—U.S., Civil Rights Act of 1964.*

When I filed my claim with the Department of Civil Rights, it was beyond the 180-day limitation. Since 180 days had lapsed before I filed my claim, my case was to be handled by The Equal Employee Opportunity Commission (EEOC). My first complaint was filed with the EEOC in April 1993. I'd heard nothing with regards to their investigation. I left for Sarrow Stamping in November 1993. I called the Department of Civil Rights numerous times and was told they were yet investigating my complaint. As things stood, I was gathering all the information, I could find to prove I was treated unfairly in comparison to my fellow Caucasian co-workers.

In October 1992, I wrote the EEOC. After I filed my initial complaint, I went around the plant asking who'd received performance bonuses. Just through small talk part-time employees usually informed each other of what they heard, received, and so forth. I was surprised to find the people, who I thought were full-time, were actually part-time and in the same classification as I. Co-workers told me they received vacation and performance bonuses. I thought by gathering this information, it would show proof I wasn't lying. I gathered the names and social security numbers of these people who were privileged enough to obtain money when I was not. I sent a letter to the EEOC dated October 10, 1993. It stated:

"I am sending the names of the people who were paid vacation pay and/or performance bonuses when I was told part-time employees didn't qualify for these benefits. *At that time we were all in the same classification.* All the people I'm referencing to are White employees. I have listed their names and social security numbers. I was unable to get all the check numbers of these employees. I was able to obtain the social security numbers and date of their performance bonus given on October 1, 1992. The vacation checks were issued for the week's pay period ending July 21, 1992.

Ave Sophie received his bonus. His name and social security number is as appears on the time sheet. I am aware that Ave Sophie's father is the Labor Relation's Supervisor in Woodrow Stamping Plant's front office. I am giving you this information to substantiate I am telling the truth. When you choose to investigate you'll know where to look. There were three other young Caucasian men whose fathers work in top management's staff. These gentlemen are also on the list as being paid their performance bonuses." The letter said thank you. I signed my name and sent the letter certified mail, return receipt requested.

On January 11, 1994 I was conscious I was getting nowhere with my grievance, so I filed a claim with the National Labor Relations Board after I left Woodrow Stamping Plant. I told them of what I was experiencing at the time and how Local 783, who was representing me, had been of no help. I also explained how I was sent home in January 1993 because of lack of work.

My supervisor informed me I had vacation and excused absence days. I was told I'd be paid because he had no work for me to do. My supervisor looked in the computer to verify this information was correct. He asked me which type of day I wanted to use. I told him I would take the personal day. He then pulled out a form from his desk and completed it, stating I was okay to take the personal day. I signed the form and he gave me a carbon copy. I went home and later found out, I was not allowed to take the personal day because of my work status was part-time. I had never heard of anything so blatant. They were pilfering my money and they considered me to be the feeble one. I said to myself, "They really think I'm stuck on stupid".

I filed a grievance on June 3, 1993 and never received a copy of my grievance. Although the grievance was pending in its third stage, Local 783 continued to refuse me a copy. In October 1993, I asked for a copy again only to receive a letter stating the grievance had no merit. Just before transferring from Woodrow Stamping Plant to Sarrow Stamping Plant, I went to the National Labor Relations Board in September 1993.

Woodrow Stamping Plant received a notice from the National Labor Relations Board stating they had to post a letter saying a union employee had a right to file a grievance and the union had the responsibility to give the union member a copy of the grievance. This paper was supposed to be posted at the plant, but instead it was posted at Local 783's Union Hall, where it could not be seen. I never saw the letter posted at the plant before leaving Woodrow Stamping. After I was transferred to Sarrow Stamping, I asked Mazzie if the letter had been posted. She said no! Woodrow Stamping Plant didn't want the part-time employees to know they could file a grievance. Maybe Local 783 figured since I was gone, they didn't have to worry about any of the part-time employees finding out their rights.

I complained to the man in charge of my claim at the NLRB since the letter had not been posted at the plant. He stated Woodrow Stamping Plant was supposed to have posted the notice. He didn't seem too worried about my complaint though. It was about December 1993 when Mazzie went to a union meeting at the Union Hall and saw the note posted. I complained in vain about where the letter was posted.

Few union members ever went to the union meetings because they felt the meetings were useless. The union was only interested in union dues and catering to Woodrow Stamping Plant. They weren't interested in their union members. Their participation in corruption was totally in favor of the company. The union representation vowed to change things during election time, but after the elections were over everything went back to normal. At any rate, the union didn't want employees to be aware of their union rights as a union member. They didn't want the employees to know their money was being pilfered. Most importantly, they didn't want the union members to educate themselves in knowing the intended purpose of the union. After I complained to the NLRB, I was sent another letter. An appointment was made for a deposition about a week later. On February 16, 1994 I received the following letter from the NLRB regarding Local 783 (Famous Parts Company) Case No. 7-CB-9966.

"... Enclosed you will find a Settlement Agreement and a notice to employees who will settle the above referenced matter in full. Please review the documents and sign in the appropriate area at the bottom of the Settlement Agreement. If you have any questions regarding this matter, you may contact me at the above referenced telephone numbers." I signed this agreement on February 17, 1994.

On March 29, 1994 I received from the National Labor Relations Board, a letter addressed to Beth Angel, the Union-Legal Staff at the Executive Branch of the Union. This letter was regarding Local 783 Case No. 7-CB-9966.

"Dear Ms. Angel,

I am enclosing herewith for your files a confirmed copy of the Settlement Agreement in the above case. The Employer may now undertake the steps necessary to comply with the provisions of the agreement and I am therefore enclosing herewith twelve (12) copies of the Notice to Employees for immediate positing. Also enclosed is a copy of a list of instructions regarding the procedure to be followed with respect to posting of this notice. In the event additional copies of the notice are required, more will be furnished upon request. This office will be pleased to assist you with prompt compliance regarding the Settlement Agreement. I have talked with the Supervisory Compliance Officer. Please return six signed and dated copies of the Notice to Employees to this office. Very truly yours," signed the Regional Director.

There was also a letter that said:

"NOTICE TO EMPLOYEES AND MEMBERS
POSTED PURSUANT TO AGREEMENT APPROVED BY A REGIONAL DIRECTOR OF THE NATIONAL LABOR RELATIONS BOARD, **and Agency of the United States Government.**

We post this Notice to inform you of the rights guaranteed by the National Labor Relations Act as amended and we give you these assurances:

The Act gives all employees these rights:

- To organize themselves

- To form, join, or assist labor organizations

- To bargain as a group through representatives they choose

- To act together for collective bargaining or other mutual aid or protection, and

- To refuse to do any or all of those things.

We will assure our members that we will not refuse to provide any employees whom we represent, upon request with a copy of any grievance filed by the requesting employee or on the behalf of the requesting employee. We will provide employees whom we represent upon request with a copy of any grievance filed by them or on their behalf.

This notice must remain posted for 60 consecutive days from the date of posting and must not be altered, defaced, or covered by any other material. Any questions concerning this notice or compliance with its provisions may be directed to the Board's Office."

In December 1994, the Executive Branch of the Union told me I should have received my first copy ever of the grievance I filed in June 1993. I didn't actually receive the copy until August 9, 1994 which came from Plant Chair, John Hail. In theory I guess the NLRB must have told Local 783 they had already given me a copy of the grievance. The letter came from the Executive Branch of the Union. Famous Parts Company and Local 783 addressed Grievance #H-135381 and Review Board #RB-7210. The letter had my current telephone number and social security number. It stated:

"Enclosed you will find a copy of your grievance and the deposition from the December 15, 1994 Review Board Meeting. This is a final settlement on your grievance ..."

I didn't know at the time, but if my grievance reached the Public Review Board, that was the final stage and it couldn't be appealed. That's when I knew something was wrong with this paper Local 783 gave me. The Public Review Board's decision was made. The date stamped on the decision was December 22, 1993 and the other was dated December 15, 1994. This was impossible when only one grievance was filed. I started to put everything in perspective.

First I didn't receive a signed copy of the grievance and at this point I had received a copy of the decision. I told Plant Chairman for Local 783, John Hail, I wanted a copy of the actual grievance. I needed it for my records. I didn't understand why it was so hard for the union to give me a copy of the grievance and the various stages it went through. I truly didn't know then what I know now with regards to Local 783 and the NLRB. Local 783 had no intention on writing this grievance, although they did it just to satisfy me at the time. I believe when I signed the grievance, they just threw the paper work in the garbage, not really thinking they would ever need it again. At that time, I was at Sarrow Stamping, so I wasn't at the plant to get on their nerves about the grievance and its handling.

Local 783 claimed they took the grievance to the Public Review Board. The grievance decision was made in January 5, 1995 for the last time. I did not receive notification until July 1995. They could have informed me of the outcome but they didn't. If I had not inquired about the outcome it would have been just fine with them. When the grievance was settled I was supposed to be notified by certified mail, and that didn't happen either, seeing that the grievance went to the Public Review Board. The grievance never went through the grievance process. The grievance was only written on paper.

With my persistence, Local 783 had to show something to the NLRB as verification that a grievance was indeed filed. This is the reason there were so many decisions made on one grievance. I didn't find out until later that the grievance went to the Public Review Board, so I was told by Local 783. Local 783 must have made photo copies of a prior case that had already went to the Public Review Board. They then cleared off the information using correction fluid and re-typed my information so it would look as though it was an original page that is fraud by deception.

Woodrow Stamping Plant was satisfied I was working at Sarrow Stamping Plant. They supposedly had it fixed that way. They never dreamed they would ever have anything else to do with me. Local 783 and Woodrow Stamping didn't figure I would continue asking questions. At Woodrow I was a pest who would never go away. At any rate, things didn't work out the way Woodrow Stamping

Plant and Local 783 had planned for things to turn out. When they thought everything was over and forgotten, I always came back wanting answers.

Why was the grievance taking so long? Why couldn't I be included in the meetings regarding the grievance process? Why was the grievance put on hold without me being notified? Why was I hired as a 'new hire' as if I had not worked for the company ever before? Why did it take Local 783 so long to make a decision on this grievance when the facts were already established in my employment records? Why did the union tell me the grievance went to the Public Review Board when in fact it did not? I had all these whys and none of them were ever answered. I was asking questions from the time I was first hired and was totally ignored. They felt they didn't have to hear anything I had to say. There was no one who could make them do otherwise because the corruption was that great at this plant. They just kept doing business as usual because they had the big bad union backing them up in the scheme of thievery and dishonesty. My letter from the Executive Branch of the Union regarding Grievance #135381, closed:

"… If you have any questions, I am also enclosing a copy of the Constitution of the International Union which explains the appeal procedure" signed John Hail, President of Local 783.

I filed a grievance in June 1993. I filed only one grievance and received three different determinations for this one grievance. My concern was that there was no paper trail verifying the grievance was discussed. I wanted to know what was said and who said what. I also wanted to know the purpose of a grievance, when I was already full-time at Woodrow Stamping Plant's own admission. I knew Local 783 was stalling, but I wanted to know what the Public Review Board had to say since Local 783 said it had been to their level. I wanted to know what the empire level had to say, since I was already full-time. Instead, I received nothing of what anyone said in an effort to settle my grievance. The grievance filed against Woodrow Stamping Plant was in June 3, 1993, and the first determination read as follows:

"The grievant is a part-time employee and in the absence of any violation of Appendix-K this complaint is without merit and is accordingly denied."

I was appalled when I received this grievance result. When I first inquired about the grievance I filed on June 3, 1993, I didn't receive a copy of the grievance until after August 1994. I was told this one paragraph on this single sheet of paper was the final result of the grievance I filed. It was a strip of paper that had no date, no Famous Parts Company logo, or union logo. It didn't have anything concerning what the grievance was about or who took part in decision-making. They really thought I was living on a cloud on this one.

I told Local 783 Bargaining Committeeman, Bob Fleetwood, this was unacceptable as a grievance determination. I later received the same paragraph, this time with a cover sheet attached. It stated: "Notice of Appeal to the Umpire" and the cover page had a date stamp of June 25, 1993. Bob Fleetwood was the only signature this time around. It did state I was seeking full-time status because I had worked over 90 days straight. I was told once again, this was the first determination of the grievance out of the three I received. At this point they took the plain piece of paper and put a cover on the first page. It stated it was the grievance form, but the one paragraph above remained the same. This time they thought I was a complete airhead.

I kept pursuing the union for an actual copy of the grievance and the paper trail of the various stages it went through. I only received a blurred copy of the grievance's determination cover sheet. Yes, I wanted a copy of the grievance since I was denied the right to participate in the grievance process. I wanted to know what Local 783 said and did in getting this grievance resolved. Local 783 was forced to send me a copy of the final determination and they refused for the second time.

Local 783 couldn't send something that they didn't have. I guess when they sent this last copy again they figured that I was stuck on stupid. I don't think they understood what I wanted. I wanted more and I wanted the answers they weren't willing to give me. They didn't keep a copy of the determination because they thought I was desperate to get the matter settled and would settle for whatever decision they came up with.

Local 783 always thought short term regarding my grievance. It was apparent the grievance wasn't filed. They had no idea I would come back and ask questions regarding a third time around. When I transferred to Sarrow Stamping Plant in 1993, they thought that was the end of me. They didn't have to pursue the grievance, which was something Woodrow Stamping Plant wasn't going to do anyway. Since I was gone, there was no watchdog looking over their shoulders.

I continued to seek answers while I was at Sarrow Stamping Plant. I waited for results from Local 783 with regards to the grievance I filed. I still occasionally contacted the Department of Civil Rights, the National Labor Relations Board, the state senator, the American Civil Liberties Union (ACLU), and later the President of the United States regarding Andrea Smith. I also wrote Mr. Felix Mann,

President and CEO of the Executive Branch of Famous Parts Company, on July 15, 1995 notifying him of my problems. Felix Mann never responded to my formal letter. Along with the letter, I sent my employment file and check stubs. But I didn't even receive a letter of acknowledgement from Mr. Mann or Famous Parts Company.

Each attorney I contacted stated I had a case, although not one of these entities stepped up to the plate to say they'd help me by taking my case. None of the above organizations did anything in my defense while knowing an injustice had been committed against me. They passed the buck and gave me names of other organizations that might be interested in taking the case.

When I would call the referred number given by one of the above, they too referred me to someone else. It was a game of cat and mouse. Everyone was just passing me to someone else. I became dissatisfied with the system as it stood. The system didn't work for people like me—a minority woman. Woodrow Stamping Plant thought I should have kept my mouth shut. That way, they could do anything they chose with nothing being done about it. Woodrow Stamping Plant was proving my skepticism correct because not one organization I contacted could help me. They just ended up slamming their doors in my face and sending me somewhere else.

They didn't care what happened to the employees because management at Woodrow Stamping Plant and Local 783 had all the resources to fight against anyone, who might want to put up a challenge against them. Woodrow Stamping Plant and Local 783 weren't worried about their pilferage. They had the Controller to launder the money, which covered their asses.

They've often told me to leave well enough alone because I was only causing trouble. Who could I have gotten to represent me? This is one of the reasons I felt, I was falling through the cracks of the system set up to help people just like me. You can very well say with all the secrets and mistreatment that occurred, I was hidden somewhere between the cracks in a system of bureaucracy.

In the meantime, I had been trying to get the union to expedite my grievance. Afterall, a grievance should have been entirely completed within 120 days. It should not have taken any longer according to the agreement between the union and Famous Parts Company. My grievance was filed in June 1993 and as of mid 1994, I still had not received a copy of the grievance I signed. When it came to Local 783, unusual events always occurred. The union representation would make up rules not pertaining to the union contract. New union members had no one to govern the union and if they did, they didn't know where to start. Local

783 would give you a union contract book only upon request. I always had to request a union contract book. It was never voluntarily given out.

15

CONSTANT MEDICAL PROBLEMS

I worked on Line #551 for a few years after my return to Woodrow Stamping in 1997. In 1999, there were some changes made to the line and the job I worked on was eliminated. I worked on the same line but I was put on Station #2 where I placed an elbow in the machine from a rack. The rack sat on a tilted stand and when the basket was full, the parts would fall out of the basket. The parts were so sharp I could have cut my flesh if I was not careful. The tilted stand was too tall and my arms were too short therefore I was later moved.

The location I was moved to was #551-Station #15. Here I had to load two long parts called *seals* into a machine. I was actually too short for that job as well but I worked it just the same. I was stationed on a platform about 15 feet off the floor. The racks with the seals were lifted 15 feet to the platform from the ground floor below. There were two racks I had to pull parts from. I had to pry the parts from the racks before placing the parts in the machine. I had to put the parts in the machine at an angle because of my height. I had to have both *seals* in place when the machine cycled until the parts attached, to another part down the line. The line was making floor pans for large trucks.

I started having problems with my right shoulder, back, and neck from working this new job about three months later. In April 1999 my back was injured from working this job. The bending and prying the *seals* apart took a toll on my body. I went to the Medical Department and reported I hurt my back, shoulder, wrist, and arm. The Medical Department did nothing about my complaints at all in April 1999. They put it on record that I had injured my back and I had them put the incident in the computer for the record. Later the Medical Department denied I ever made a report of an injury to my back, neck, arm and wrist in April 1999.

In April when I reported my back injury, it was clear the Medical Department wasn't going to do anything about my back. I was told the nurse in the Medical Department had made a note of this incident. After x-rays were taken, it was a fact, not a presumption that I suffered with a sprained/strained upper and lower back. I re-injured my back in July 1999 and I was told I needed no restriction. I was allowed to continue to work without a restriction. After many complaints, the Medical Department finally sent me to see Dr. Butt in January 2000. After I re-injured my back, Woodrow Stamping Plant sent me to see Dr. Steeler, another one of Woodrow Stamping Plant's treating doctors.

As a result of my shoulder problems, I was sent to physical therapy for 8 weeks. I was given Worker's Compensation benefits when I was unable to work this time for the period of 8 weeks only. Dr. Steeler treated me for a shoulder injury only. I continued complaining verbally how my back was in such pain when I visited her throughout the 8 weeks she was treating me for my shoulder. It wasn't that Dr. Steeler didn't know about my back, because I brought her the x-rays on my first visit. She would not address my concerns with my back. It didn't matter how much I complained it was as though my words had fallen on deaf ears.

After I was injured, I remembered being given the restriction when I was hired back in 1990. I went to the Medical Department on April 20, 2001 after my back was injured. I asked the Medical Department about the restriction and they acted as though they didn't know what I was talking about. I was inquiring about the restriction of stature. Dr. Care gave me this restriction when I was hired at Woodrow Stamping Plant. It was given for the purpose of stature only. There was a copy of the restriction on file when I left Woodrow Stamping Plant in 1993. I noticed the restriction was not in the computer when I returned. In fact it wasn't in my file in the Medical Department at all. I had a copy at home and I brought it to the plant the following day.

I first took a copy of my restriction to the union and asked the union to have the restriction put back in the computer. The union told me to take the restriction to the Labor Relations Department. I did as I was told and I gave it to Verlinda Moose, the Labor Relations Supervisor. She told me to take it to the Medical Department. I took it to the Medical Department and I was taken to a room. I was then measured and weighed. I was told since I weighed over 120 pounds, I couldn't be put back on a restriction. I told the nurse the restriction had nothing to do with my weight in the first place.

The plant didn't put my restriction back in the computer. That meant I would have to be put on various jobs my height couldn't withstand. This is when

I found out the plant was keeping two sets of medical records. Other information was missing from my medical records as well. Anything to do with my hiring in September 1990 was missing from my current folder.

Having time to evaluate the reason why my restriction was not put back in the computer, I realized the Medical Department didn't want their very best kept secret revealed. If the restriction would have been put back into the computer, it would reveal I was hired September 1990. My copy of the restriction stated exactly that. The restriction noted my date of hire, which they were trying to hide. The restriction was given in September 1990 when I was hired. When Woodrow Stamping Plant terminated me in November 1993, they terminated my restriction given in 1990. Sarrow Stamping Plant wouldn't accept me at their plant with restrictions, but the real reason was that I could not be hired as a new employee with this restriction. Therefore the Medical Department expired my restriction.

How could these people be so cold knowing my height and arms' length was clearly a factor? My height didn't change. Why would they remove my restriction of stature? When I was terminated, the company didn't want anyone to know I was accurate all these years I claimed to be full-time.

After my back injury, I was taken off Line #551—Station #15 and moved to the CT20 area in the #92 Department. That was an area with a variety of small jobs. Many of the short and small stature women worked in this area. I worked various jobs in CT20. Some were a challenge and others were not. The bending was the most difficult because the basket was so large and deep. I had to bend extremely low to put the finished part in the basket.

In June 1999, I was working on Line #484 filling the trays that supplied the robot with parts fed to the main line. There were large baskets sitting on a tilted stand. I had to reach in the basket to get the part out to fill the trays. The basket on the tilted stand was taller than I. Many times when the baskets were filled and placed on a tilt stand, the parts would fall out of the basket to the floor as I reached above my head to retrieve them. The basket wasn't supposed to be filled to its capacity because of the parts being on a tilt stand. Many times I had to duck and dodge falling parts as they fell to the floor from the basket.

I was loading the table that fed the robot when my back went out. My back pains were getting worse and I had pains in my left leg. At the end of the day when I went to the restroom, I literally had to hold both sides of the stall in order to use the toilet because my back ached with such sharp pain. I went home that evening, but not before informing my supervisor I had re-injured my back.

The next day, I started working and the pain in my back worsened. I went to my supervisor and told him I needed to go to the Medical Department. This all happened on the last day before employees were going on vacation for plant shut down. This was when the majority of the plant went on vacation for two weeks. I went to the Medical Department and saw a Dr. Straw regarding my back. He was just going to give me some Motrin for the pain and send me back to work. I became angry and I said to him, "I hurt my back in April and you gave me no follow-up treatment". I sprained/strained both shoulders many times during my employment. I was told by one of the doctors, I would eventually develop arthritis and/or tendonitis in my shoulders because of injuries sustained through the years. "I came in here complaining of my back and you people treated me for my shoulder, ignoring the complaint of my back."

Then Dr. Straw sent me to the hospital for x-rays. When I went to the hospital, Nurse Tootie told me to tell the hospital not to charge this to Worker's Compensation. I really didn't know what that meant at the time. When the results came back, they stated I had a sprained/strained upper and lower back. I thought when Nurse Tootie told me to tell the hospital not to charge my back condition to Worker's Compensation, Worker's Compensation was paying the hospital out of the miscellaneous fund. I really didn't know the implication behind what Nurse Tootie had requested me to tell the hospital.

When I returned to work after shutdown, my back had some pain but not as much as before. The Medical Department sent me to see Dr. Steeler. I went to see her for my shoulder, but I received some treatment for my neck as well. I received heat treatments and massages while in therapy, for my shoulder only. Officially my shoulder treatment lasted until October 1999. This was when I stopped seeing the company doctor for my neck and right shoulder.

This plant harassed me and gave me so many problems with regards to my occupational injuries. In October 1999, my Worker's Compensation case was closed and my restriction was lifted. Woodrow Stamping Plant did not address my back, even when I had the x-rays to prove I had a serious problem with my back. I truly didn't know what the Medical Department had planned, but I did know it was clearly illegal.

At first Dr. Steeler was saying I had *Fibromyalgia*, a (non-occupational) condition in which, a person experiences pain, stiffness, and fatigue throughout the body where there is on specific cause of pain. The company doctors were trying to steer my diagnosis in favor of the company. They knew if the company diagnosed me with Fibromyalgia, the company would not be responsible for my injury. This was what Woodrow Stamping Plant and Dr. Steeler was setting the stage for with regards to my back injury.

I really didn't understand why my restriction with the company was lifted for my right shoulder when I continued to complain about by back. Dr. Steeler stated she could not address my complaints regarding my back without Woodrow Stamping Plant's authorization. I was complaining to Dr. Steeler and the Medical Department as well. I had an issue with my right arm, wrist, and shoulder, but the only problem addressed was my shoulder. They treated me as though my back was never injured. Dr. Steeler's summation of my diagnosis was a lie. She just lied in Woodrow Stamping Plant's favor because they were sending her new clients. In her summation she stated she was going to obtain some x-rays of my lumbar spine to rule out the degenerative arthritic process. Dr. Steeler stated:

"I've known Ms. Carrie for a long time and she tends to have a lot of somatic complaints. At this time her neurological examination is normal in the lower extremities and the primary goal is to rule out a pathologic process. As noted, she has multiple myofascial complaints at different times, perhaps related to Fibromyalgia Syndrome. Fibromyalgia is a diagnosis of exclusion and it is not a work-related condition. At this time she can work without restriction. No medications are recommended and I will see her in approximately a month."

When Dr. Steeler made this summation, she was setting her diagnosis in favor of Woodrow Stamping Plant in hopes the responsibility would fall on me as a personal injury. After Dr. Steeler ordered the x-rays for my back, she refused to treat me any longer. The x-rays were taken and they showed I had a sprained/strained upper and lower back for the second time. There was no change. If anything, I had gotten worse because I was working without restriction. Worker's Compensation addressed the problem on paper but never tried to fix the problem. They never gave me therapy for this problem.

After the x-rays came back, the Medical Department set an appointment for me to see Dr. Butt, the company doctor, in January 2000. This doctor gave me an EMG all over my body from neck to toe. He gave me both parts of this test checking for nerve damage. I kept inquiring about the test results. Dr. Necktie, Woodrow Stamping Plant's physician on staff that day, told me Dr. Butt stated in his report there was nothing wrong with me. He stated there was no need for any restriction. I asked for a copy of the results but the report was only halfway completed. The report Dr. Necktie gave me only had six to eight categories listed that I was tested for. This was incorrect and I told the Medical Department as such. I asked Nurse Tootie where were the rest of the test results.

Nurse Tootie lied to me, saying I only had a test regarding my lower back, when in reality I was tested all over my body. I knew the results were in the hands of Woodrow Stamping Plant's Medical Department. I decided to write the Medical Department a letter of my dissatisfaction and told them I wanted to know about the remaining results. The letter was in regards to a test given on January 17, 2000 by Dr. Butt.

"… I would like to know how Dr. Butt derived his information with regards to the tests given. If he has no print out of the EMG, there has to be some sort of information concerning the places on my body Dr. Butt placed a needle in and the electronic prods produced by this machine. I would like something with the doctor's office logo stating this information came from this office. Since my health depends on this information, I feel entitled to request it …"

The report Dr. Butt sent to Woodrow Stamping Plant on March 22, 2000 was not clear to me. I have to admit I'm not a doctor, but I didn't have to be a doctor to know the facts were not all there. The letter I received from Dr. Butt sent as my final determination stated, "There is no tenderness to palpation about the neck or shoulders".

I told Nurse Tootie I wanted the remainder of the test results Dr. Butt had taken. I wanted information on how he determined the information factual. The information was quite vague on the report. I know he had to have more than six to eight numbers totaling all areas evaluated on my entire body. Nurse Tootie said those were all the tests taken of my lower back. After I asked for the complete test results, Nurse Tootie had the audacity to stand in my face and say, "What test? No such test was given to you". Why did Nurse Tootie question me when she was aware of exactly what I was asking for? Did she think I was foolish? She figured I wouldn't know what kinds of tests were administered to me.

I truly didn't think this game the Medical Department was playing, nor the position they were putting me in was funny. After Dr. Butt evaluated me in January 2000, he stated he performed nerve conduction studies of the bilateral wrist, which were normal. He said there was no reflection of carpal tunnel syndrome. He also stated every test he gave me was fine and he could find nothing wrong with my upper or lower extremities. All the tests given were said to be normal. Nurse Tootie stood in my face and told me the bold-faced lie that Dr. But only tested my back and stated my wrists were normal.

This doctor stated I had no intermittent somatic complaints of the back, legs, neck, and upper back that day, which was an outright lie. He really didn't need to be practicing medicine. Dr. Butt stated there was no relation to any specific incident or event as a precipitating factor. This was a lie too. In essence he was saying my condition was not work-related. He said there was no specific incident that caused my condition. I was telling this man what happened on the job. He saw me dragging my left leg as he asked me to bend and touch my toes, which I could not do. It obviously didn't matter what I said. Dr. Butt's findings were in favor of the company and not in my health's best interest.

Dr. Butt sent me back to work with no restrictions. I was put back on the line and did the best job I could do. I continued to complain about my back and other parts of my body. I worked various jobs in Department #92. I went to the Medical Department on three occasions and was denied the right to see the doctor.

On January 5, 2000 my complaints were of my right hand and arm. On March 22, 2000 my complaints were of pain in my back, right arm, and wrist. On April 19, 2000 I went to the Medical Department and complained of my back neck, shoulder, and forearm. On all three dates the Medical Department denied me the right to see a doctor. I felt like my body was falling apart and there was nothing I could do. On two occasions I went to the Out-Patient Emergency Room and brought the bill to the Medical Department.

According to the contract, when I am injured on the job I have the right to see the doctor on staff in the Medical Department at the time of injury. The Head Nurse, Tootie, denied me that right. She made all the decisions in the Medical Department with regards to medical treatment. In April 2000 I went to the Medical Department and gave them the emergency room bill for a work-related injury. I was told by one of the nurses in the Medical Department not to go to the hospital or an urgent care facility unless I consulted them first. I asked this nurse, "How can I inform you I need to go to urgent care? When I come here to see a doctor, I am denied access. I'm going to the hospital when there is a need and have the Medical Department billed for my medical attention".

I truly don't know why the Medical Department refused to allow me to see a doctor. You would wonder why I was forbidden to see a doctor in the first place when my injuries were incurred in the plant. Nurse Tootie was aware of my true condition. Dr. Butt had run the necessary tests and was also aware of my medical condition. They expressed my condition was caused by my age and not the work I did in the plant. I later found that the Medical Department wanted me out of work because their plan was to retire me for my back injury under Worker's

Compensation. But I fought to return, so they had to bring me back to work. They brought me out of retirement in December 2000 with plans to put me back in retirement.

I became tired of the run around the Medical Department was giving me. Therefore I contacted my primary physician. She evaluated my condition and referred me to Dr. Sonia. An appointment was made and my first visit was on February 14, 2000. Dr. Sonia started out by giving me an examination and had me take an MRI/CAT scan on the first time visit. I also took my x-rays that revealed the strain/sprain to the upper and lower back was taken by Midway Hospital. The Medical Department gave me the x-rays to keep so there would be no records of x-rays taken of my back. I have those same x-rays in my possession today.

I felt free speaking with Dr. Sonia for the first year. I felt real comfort in discussing my medical condition. I felt a sincere sense of care and I knew my body was in good hands. She took time and patience with me and was very understanding of my condition. She sent me to therapy at The Rehabilitation Institute for Physical Therapy on March 24, 2000 for the duration of eight weeks.

At this point I needed someone to talk to about my condition, considering it was worsening and I was depressed. My body's health was falling completely apart. It was as though I had no control of how the Medical Department was treating my condition. Woodrow Stamping was actually causing my condition to go downhill by denying my medical condition even existed. I have to admit I was naive in thinking that since I was injured by the company they would treat me as they should have.

I tried to follow procedures by seeing a company doctor first. I thought they would address the problem when I presented it to them. I followed the contract and I can kick myself in the butt for expecting Woodrow Stamping to do right by me. I didn't know I was dealing with a ring of organized crime. I continued complaining to my primary physician. I had no idea they'd try to say my injuries were something other than what the x-rays had shown. I truly had a rude awakening.

I found out the Medical Department was aware I had Degenerative Joint Disease. I worked on a daily basis with aches and pains. I would take non-prescription medication to carry me through the day since my prescription medication made me drowsy on the line. I had no idea the pain I was experiencing was a disease I would have for the rest of my life.

If I had known the Medical Department wasn't going to honor my medical condition, I would have seen a physician long before I did. I had no idea the company would manipulate my current treating doctors. There was nothing I could do about my health problems. I needed someone to talk to who wasn't biased. My condition became a struggle to deal with. Everyday became a task. That is when I finally decided Woodrow Stamping Plant's Medical Department wasn't concerned about properly treating me. It was hard for me knowing the Medical Department was knowingly destroying me. As much as I complained, no one would come to my defense—absolutely no one.

I needed my doctor at that point. I trusted Dr. Sonia. But she too betrayed me when Woodrow Stamping Plant contacted her and tried to manipulate my medical condition to fit what *they* wanted it to be. After Dr. Sonia started siding with Woodrow Stamping Plant, she no longer wanted to treat me. She couldn't satisfy Woodrow Stamping Plant *and* me too. Therefore I assumed since she sided with them, there was no room left for her to treat me. I decided to stop treating with Dr. Sonia and that was the end of our doctor/patient relationship.

Dr. Sonia had treated me for my back, shoulder, knee, wrist, and hands—all of which should have been covered under Worker's Compensation. There was some treatment paid for by Woodrow Stamping Plant's Worker's Compensation, and others were not. After I started seeing Dr. Sonia as my private physician, I received a letter from Worker's Compensation stating my claim was denied. My claim was denied by Dr. Butt's opinion through a letter stating my injuries were of a personal nature. My diagnosis was Lumbar Spondlylsos, Knee Joint Arthritis, Bilateral Dequorvain's Tenosynositis, and shoulder tendonitis.

The tests taken basically said I had arthritis in many areas of my body. My restrictions at that time were: no repetitive bending over ten times per hour and I had to wear hand braces while on the job. The restrictions by Dr. Sonia recommended limited repetitive movement with my back, hands, and wrists. At one point Dr. Sonia said, "no repetitive twisting" as one of my restrictions. These restrictions stayed with me until I was retired with a medical disability in December 2004.

Before I stopped treatment with Dr. Sonia, she sent me to see Dr. Hammer, a hand surgeon. My restrictions from Dr. Hammer were: no repetitive twisting of the wrist, avoiding air tools, avoiding forceful grasping, and avoiding pushing and pulling with both hands and wrists. The Imaging Center was where Dr. Sonia had me go for imaging of my body. The results of the imagining center report stated:

"… Multiplanar multisequence imaging of the lumbar spine was obtained. The signal intensity within the osseous structure is with normal limits and the alignment is normal. There is anterior disc dessication at T11-12. The conus medullaris is located at L1. From L3 to S1 axial scans reveal no evidence of neurological impingement significant facet arthritis or disc bulge ..."

This paragraph is saying my lumbar disc cushions were narrowing. The disc spacer or cushion separates the spine to keep the bones from rubbing together. This test is saying arthritis affected my back.

At this point I had seen two of the company doctors Woodrow Stamping Plant sent me to. Dr. Butt and Dr. Steeler both stated I did not need restrictions and they gave me no medication for my condition. My Worker's Compensation was turned down since it was said my injuries weren't occupational, but personal. The Medical Department railroaded me. I refused to literally stand by and allow them to treat me in that manner.

They had been taking medical information out of my medical folder and placing it into another file. I finally got them to straighten this problem out in 2000 when Tom Hemp was running for Bargaining Committeemen for Local 783. I told Tom Hemp I wanted my medical information back in my file. All my information was returned (at least for a while). The Medical Department was lying about the tests given to me. My last complaint at that time was the fact the Medical Department denied me the right to see a doctor on company time when I was injured on the job. I went to Local 783 to see my committeeman. I wanted to file a grievance for harassment against the Medical Department.

Tom Hemp wasn't Plant Chairman at that particular time. John Hail was the Plant Chairman when I originally filed the grievance against the Medical Department for harassment. Tom Hemp wanted to win the election so he wanted everyone happy. He wanted every vote he could get. Therefore he fulfilled my request in having my medical information put back in my file. In early spring of 1999, John Hail resigned as Plant Chairman due to racketeering allegations. After he resigned, the Bargaining Committeeman, Bob Fleetwood, who was John Hail's sidekick, got a promotion to the Executive Branch of the Union. His position of Plant Chairman was open and the union had an election. Tom Hemp took the place of Bob Fleetwood as Bargaining Committeeman.

I filed a grievance June 23, 2000 against the Medical Department for harassment, but not before the Medical Department put me on a 'no work available'. I don't have the original grievance written at the time because getting a copy from Local 783 was very difficult. The grievance I filed against the Medical Department addressed the mistreatment and harassment they put me through. The grievance was put on hold. I filed a complaint with the NLRB and was told I had to drop the charges against Local 783 or they would do it themselves. I didn't want to sign off on the complaint because what I said was the truth.

I wrote my withdrawal stating if Local 783 discontinued the grievance process and/or my complaint against the Medical Department that would be the only way I would withdraw. The National Labor Relations Board tried to convince me they were going to drop the charges against Local 783, because they were working to settle this grievance in good faith. If they were working in good faith, I would not have had to file a complaint with the NLRB in the first place. If Local 783 stopped the grievance and they didn't follow through, I stated I'd bring this complaint back to the NLRB's attention—and that is what I did.

The harassment in the Medical Department got worse and I filed another harassment grievance with Local 783 in June 2001. I was pressured by the NLRB to drop charges against the Medical Department and I assumed Local 783 promised they would stop harassing me. I was not allowed to file a grievance at Woodrow Stamping Plant. If I did sign papers to file a grievance, it would never go through the various stages. It would just sit on the desk gathering dust. The National Labor Relations Board was aware Local 783 wasn't filing the grievances because it became a pattern. They would lie and use stall tactics to keep from processing a grievance.

By this time I was very upset with the way the Medical Department was treating me. I was tired of going in circles. It was like having an incision and pouring salt into the open wound. I decided to write an article in the union newspaper since I had written a few letters in the past with regards to my opinions. I wrote an article called Medical Matters and Concerns—My Experiences and Opinion. I took the article to Local 783 at the Union Hall and put the article in the editor's box. It went to the union and I was later told Local 783 refused printing the article because it was a "conflict of interest" between Local 783 and the nurses' union Local 600.

After being put on a 'no work available' my grievance didn't seem to be going anywhere. I couldn't get any information on how it was going and no one claimed to know anything about the grievance. It was now September 2000, and I was inquiring about the fact the union violated my rights as a member by not printing my article in Local 783 newsletter. I thought the paper was for the union members to read. I was never told the union paper had to be censored. What happened to the Freedom of Speech Amendment? You could only write or print information *they* wanted. I told the union the treatment I was receiving from the Medical Department was unacceptable and I was angry. It should not have ended in the Plant Manager's Office where and when they determined the article would not be printed. This was supposed to be a union newspaper.

As stated prior, I felt I should have seen a doctor when Woodrow Stamping Plant first became aware that I had a sprain/strain to the upper and lower back. I truly believe I would not have the problems at the magnitude that I'm suffering from now, if the Medical Department would have acknowledged my disease when they first knew of the problems. If my restrictions were honored by Woodrow Stamping Plant's Medical Department along with therapy for my back and other parts of the body, my occupational medical condition would not have progressed at such a fast pace. The Medical Department could have made things more tolerable for me, but I got worse when they denied I had any problems and when Dr. Butt stated I didn't need restrictions. The Medical Department wanted to harass me until I quit my job. I couldn't quit my job. Who else would hire me with all my (work-related) pre-existing conditions? I knew I couldn't give up. It was too much at state. This was my life and my body. There was one thing I was striving for and that was justice.

16

DIVERSITY WAS CLEARLY AN ISSUE

Caucasians at Woodrow always tried to make the Blacks and other minorities look bad in order to make themselves look good. This was done similar to the way the media reports frequently on minorities in order to spread negative propaganda before the facts are displayed. It's a lot of hype because a thief can be of any race. The Caucasians hold all the money, yet minorities seem to take up all the space in the prison population. Has anyone ever wondered why? The Blacks and other minorities are characterized as criminals who always receive a much harsher sentence from the justice system, in comparison to the Caucasian race even for the same crime.

The media is always used as a means of propaganda to frighten Caucasians of minorities. Meanwhile, the Caucasians are robbing everyone blind while all eyes are focused on the Blacks and other monitories. The amount of money minorities thieve is nothing in comparison to the amount Woodrow Stamping Plant and Local 783 are pilfering. I think it's safe to say these executives were Caucasian. We're talking mega dollars from employees' retirement accounts, back pay, benefit packages, and then some.

I didn't see minorities participating in the Enron scandal, the Kmart scandal, or the Standard Federal Savings & Loan scandal in past years. I did see minorities in the stock market as brokers on Wall Street, but they were few. In my opinion, Martha Stewart was an example of how tough our government is on those who use inside trading information. Martha wasn't a minority but she was a woman handling business as a successful wealthy entrepreneur. My point is it doesn't matter whether you are Black, White, male or female, discrimination is discrimination. It doesn't necessarily have to be a Black and White issue. Discrimination is against the law once it's proven—but who takes discrimination cases anymore? Famous Parts Company was guilty of discrimination in their hiring practices against minorities in the skilled trades department. This was proven because they were sued and lost.

Martha was given stock information as a tip and she pulled her money out of the depreciated stock in an effort not to lose money. Seriously I can't fault her for the information she heard and acted upon. She pulled her stock out of the market because of insider information. What fool wouldn't withdraw their money when they actually knew some trading information prior to the end of the bell? At the time, she just acted on what she heard and if she had not, she would have lost. Then again who's to say that it wasn't a set-up? The government investigated and came down hard on her. She paid a heavy price on the information she received. But she wasn't the only person trading stock by inside trader's information. I'm sure this happens on a daily basis. Wall Street is full of stockbrokers and traders who have access to inside information. She's the only woman who has ever been publicly found guilty for reacting to inside information. Wall Street has majority Caucasian workers, but very few are found guilty of breaking this same law. Obviously Caucasians operate under one set of rules, while Blacks and other minorities are to abide by a totally different set of rules.

I watched as Woodrow Stamping Plant pilfered money from me for years, as well as others, through Worker's Compensation and employees' retirement fund. The pilfering is continuing because they are still trying to cover up the lies they told on employees to acquire their money. It's almost as though nothing can be done about the company pilfering from itself. It's business as usual.

Woodrow Stamping Plant kept two sets of records. One was full-time and the other was part time. They were pilfering from both sets. They pilfered employees' Worker's Compensation settlement by simply not paying the court ordered amount which should have been paid 30 days after the decision was made. They never paid the money to the employees but kept the money and placed it in separate accounts. The Social Security Administration granted both Andrea Smith and Linda Jackson their Social Security benefits for their disability. Their retirement was supposed to have followed due to their injury being of an occupational nature.

To my knowledge, there was only one minority who directly assisted in the pilfering of money at Woodrow Stamping Plant. He was compensated for making sure employees didn't receive money directed to them. Woodrow Stamping Plant pilfered the money allocated Linda Jackson and Andrea Smith. They didn't receive a dime from their Worker's Compensation. Nor did they receive their retirement once their Worker's Compensation was settled.

When money was being pilfered at Woodrow Stamping Plant, the Caucasians didn't normally put Blacks in charge of the pilfered money for fear of Blacks or another minority doing the same thing *they* were doing. It's hard for one thief to trust another. However all minorities aren't thieves even though we're perceived as such because of the color of our skin or lack of education. I couldn't believe Caucasian management at Woodrow Stamping discriminated and thought they were better than minorities when they were the ones pilfering and breaking the law. If caught and found guilty, a Caucasian employee would go to court and receive a slap on the wrist or plea bargain. The crime would be labeled as 'white-collar crime'. The stipulations for a Caucasian committing a 'white-collar crime' carry a much lighter sentence than for a Black or other minority.

If Blacks pilfered the kind of money Woodrow Stamping Plant and Local 783 pilfered, the outcome would be much different. A Black person or another minority would be put in jail for the remainder of their life. It took a long time for the executives at Enron, Kmart, and Standard Federal Savings & Loans to be indicted for the crimes they committed. Yes! They were found guilty, but Enron was "the example" just as Martha Stewart was. Someone had to take the rap.

A jury found two men guilty, but I don't think those were the only two involved in the Enron scandal that made millions. Come on give me a break! The theft was so great they actually needed more participants than just these two people. If they were going to prosecute, why not prosecute all those involved? There were more than two men making profits from all the money pilfered. Why were those two the only one's indicted and tried? It's now 2008 and the Kmart executives are yet in the courts after all these years. No one has been held accountable for their actions. They pilfered many people's life savings and left them wondering, if they'd have enough money to retire and support their families. People now have to work longer and the cost of living is rising out of control. If they are old enough and can't work, the only avenue left is social security.

Minorities aren't always the culprits in crime as the media exploits them to be. This causes people to categorize people of color as being criminals until proven otherwise. The media categorizes Whites as good and minorities as bad. We're trained to see a Caucasian and assume they're less likely to commit a crime. But if you see a minority, it's already assumed they're trouble. The media makes a big issue about minorities in the inner-city committing crimes only to take the focus off more 'well-off' criminals. Big businesses are the biggest thieves of all and they continuously represent the corporate Caucasian businessman. Many Blacks and other minorities don't have access to millions and billions of dollars, in comparison to the Caucasians in businesses who owns ABC, NBC, CBS, and the large newspapers. I would imagine if someone reported a minority company for the things Woodrow Stamping Plant and Local 783 were guilty of doing, they would have been held accountable a long time ago. An investigation would have been brought against the company at first accusation.

Getting back to the skilled trades discussion—if these plants hired minorities in a specialized field, you can bet your bottom dollar the company only hired them because they were forced to do so. The company doesn't want minorities sitting around when the machines aren't in need of repair. If the line ran smoothly all day long, this meant the skilled tradesmen were sitting on their behinds all day. The company always wanted minorities working.

Skilled trade's workers should have been hired according to their test scores in the first place. I have a family member who was compensated for the discrimination act in the field of skilled trades. This occurred during my time of employment with Woodrow Stamping and Local 783. The minorities who took the skilled trades test during this time didn't score high enough to be accepted in the program. The employees were later compensated because the truth of the matter was there were irregularities in the hiring practices. All those who took the test were compensated because of the discrimination existing in the hiring of skilled trades. They were paid for the period of 1997 through 2003. Woodrow Stamping began soliciting minorities in the field of skilled trades in April 2002.

In my opinion if Famous Parts Company was not found guilty, they would have continued to discriminate in the field of skilled trades. Firstly, I'm sincerely surprised by the fact that Robinson, who brought suit against Famous Parts Company for discrimination, was able to obtain an attorney to represent her case. It's ironic because Andrea and I have never been that successful. Every attorney we tried hiring turned us down. When we filed our cases in the 36th District (federal) Court, the presiding judge wouldn't appoint an attorney to our cases. Not even when Andrea and I made our request to the judges presiding over our cases. We had two separate judges. Secondly, I wondered how Robinson was able to get past the Summary Judgment in order to get a trial date. I assume Robinson was a female of Caucasian race because Blacks and minorities were unable to get representation for their claims in a court of law.

If their claim was filed against Famous Parts Company—Woodrow Stamping Plant, Local 783 is guilty as Hell for allowing them to discriminate. What does this say about both entities? It says to me Woodrow Stamping Plant and Local 783 are *both* guilty of discrimination, one can't be guilty and not the other. I haven't heard of anyone suing the union for discrimination in many years. Does that mean discrimination by Local 783 doesn't exist? They discriminate against its union members by race and also in other areas. They often use retaliation and harassment tactics. I saw minorities ready to protest in front of Famous Parts for discrimination in 2006, but I didn't see these same people protesting the Executive Branch of the Union's headquarters. They were involved in discrimination practices too. Can you tell me why this was?

The Executive Branch of the Union was just as guilty of discrimination as Famous Parts Company was. *UnionFacts.com* is a website serving as a watchdog for union misrepresentation and unions are harming the very same people they're supposed to be protecting. According to this website, the government is aware of this negligent activity. The company harassed and retaliated against Andrea and me without a second thought. Nothing has ever been done about Local 783's actions leading all the way from James York, who served as the CEO of the Executive Branch of the Union, to Don Hangem, who came soon after York stepped down. This is why our complaints weren't being heard. These politicians were in the pockets of 'big business' and lobbyists too. Personally I feel one can't be on both sides of the fence. You're either on the right side of the law or not.

Special interest groups and their attorneys were very loyal to Famous Parts Company and the union. This was because the company contributed too many causes and organizations in the community. These organizations and special interest groups knew where their funding was coming from. They dared not cross the free money that supported their cause. Many attorneys could have been afraid to take these cases for fear of retribution from the union, company, or both. These entities are powerful enough to totally shut down a law firm and put them out of business.

Why didn't the lawyer show Robinson the door as they had done Andrea and me? We interviewed with many attorneys. It was clear the contracts were violated and laws had been broken, but there was nothing done in our defense. I had the hardest time getting my case in the courts. The judge who refused to grant me an attorney, knew in advance my case would be thrown out during the Summary Judgment proceeding. We're supposed to have democracy in the United States of America but we didn't have a fair chance of our cases being heard in a court of law. All the people involved in my case, including the judge, were bought and paid for in an effort to make sure my case didn't make it to the jury. I wasn't considered a person of interest in the eyes of those with money and clout paying for justice (or injustice) transpiring at Famous Parts Company. No amount of money could have matched against these entities when they were breaking laws and violating contracts.

It didn't help when the government agencies condoned what Woodrow Stamping Plant and Local 783 were doing. I followed the laws and applied the laws, and can you believe these organizations ignored them. To me this meant these companies were above the law. I'm not a naive person and I am smart enough to know when I have been discriminated against. I had no doubt I was treated differently than my other co-workers in the same classification or job position. The judicial system discriminated against me by not appointing me an attorney. I wrote the directors of the National Labor Relations Board and the Department of Civil Rights, and nothing was ever done on a positive note about Woodrow Stamping Plant and Local 783. They too, never found reason to bring charges against Woodrow Stamping Plant and Local 783.

These big businesses and large private companies paid their way to keep from being sued for unfair labor practices. Even after Andrea and I asked for a trial by a jury, the judges ignored our request. We were simply railroaded by the judges and the justice system. We asked for something and they gave us what they wanted us to have. Our objective was clear in our statement to the court when we filed our cases. We stated what we wanted and why, but instead we were the two invisible individual totally ignored.

In my opinion, racism is running rampant in our society. However for the most part, it's of a silent nature. Although the KKK is quite blatant with their hatred and rallies, they're yet allowed to march under 'freedom of speech' while our government is aware of the disruption and danger it causes. Here I am, not even being able to have a voice through the union newspaper. I was sanctioned and asked to never write another news article. I also found myself in the Plant Manager's Office being called a "radical", and was later retaliated against for my outspokenness. I couldn't even have 'freedom of speech' when my rights were violated regarding publishing an article in the union newspaper. I was censored only being able to write what Woodrow Stamping Plant and Local 783 wanted me to write. If I didn't abide and write a controversial article, I would end up in the Plant Manager's Office and later published.

What Martin Luther King Jr. fought and died for was equality. He fought long and hard in an effort that *minorities* could become equal in our society. Our government is slowly ripping our civil rights away. You can't even go to the Department of Civil Rights, the Department of Labor, or the National Labor Relations Board for assistance in unfair labor practices. When I *did* get a 'right-to-sue' letter, the above institutions were aware that I would not be able to find counsel. They found no reason for charges against Woodrow Stamping Plant or

Local 783. They continued to discriminate, harass, and retaliate against Andrea, me, and others who dared not complain.

I would receive a 'right-to-sue' letter of which no lawyer would honor upon my request. One did take the case in 1994. Attorney James Hdith became ill and was forced to retire. His associate, John Bushe, inherited my case and purposely allowed the statue of limitations to run out. All the above agencies had to do was to investigate and file charges. My charges along with Andrea Smith's charges alone should have been enough to have attorneys lined up ready to take our cases. I have never been compensated for the money Woodrow Stamping Plant pilfered from me. Not even in the harassment grievance I won against Woodrow Stamping Plant in July 2002. Andrea Smith wasn't even compensated after she was hit by a hi-lo truck and later terminated on the lie that she threatened Nurse Tootie and Dr. Slick in Medical Department.

Nurse Tootie and Dr. Slick stated Andrea went to Woodrow Stamping Plant for a medical evaluation concerning the stress leave she was already on medical for. There was a second IME (Independent Medical Evaluation) done by Woodrow Stamping who concurred with Andrea's doctor, Dr. Kindly. When a person is on medical leave for long periods of time by their personal physician, the company will have another evaluation done on that same employee, which causes the employee's medical leave. This is done to make sure the employee is not out of work for reasons other than the claimed sickness.

Both doctors concurred in their findings that Andrea could not return to work. That should have been binding according to contract. The results weren't good enough in the eyes of Woodrow Stamping's Medical Department because they wanted to terminate Andrea. They set up another evaluation, this time administered by Dr. Slick and Nurse Tootie. Andrea was under a great amount of stress from the treatment she received from Woodrow Stamping Plant's Medical Department and Local 783, repeatedly siding with Woodrow Stamping Plant in whatever they did. Dr. Kindly felt Woodrow Stamping Plant and Local 783 caused the pressure Andrea experienced. She saw this as being a cause of her near breakdown.

Andrea was requested to appear in the Medical Department by Nurse Tootie in January 2003. Nurse Tootie and Dr. Slick knew of the company inducing Andrea's stress. They asked her multiple questions such as, "Do you have a gun?" and "Do you know where you can get one?" Shortly after Andrea appeared at Woodrow Stamping Plant's Medical Department, she was fired. They acted as though they were suddenly her psychiatrists.

Andrea was fired while she was on medical leave, which was not in accordance to contract. After being on medical leave over 90 days, you're no longer on active payroll. How Woodrow Stamping Plant pulled this one off is a miracle. Local 783 didn't want her back. This firing was allowed to become final and binding when Andrea had done nothing to be terminated for. Woodrow Stamping Plant and Local 783 did as they pleased and didn't have to be held accountable. Woodrow Stamping Plant sent Andrea Smith a letter stating she was not to come on company property or she would be escorted off by security. Dr. Slick and Nurse Tootie said Andrea came in the Medical Department and threatened someone. It was never clear who exactly was threatened. According to the deposition I've read, it was all hearsay. All this was staged in an effort to terminate Andrea's Smith employment while she was on medical leave.

What makes it so bad is that Andrea found out this type of behavior happened on three different occasions. She actually had no knowledge of these incidents ever happening. They were made-up lies. Woodrow Stamping made these lies stick because they knew there was nothing that Andrea or anyone else could do to get her job back. Local 783 and Woodrow Stamping Plant was successful in pulling this one off.

In 2005 Andrea appealed her complaint with the National Labor Relations Board when they denied the charges she filed against Local 783. Andrea complained about her grievance because she never received a copy of the various stages it went through (from the start 'til its completion in September 2005). Local 783 couldn't provide Andrea with a copy of her grievance stages because they didn't file it. This time when she complained to the National Labor Relations Board, I assume they told Woodrow Stamping Plant to come up with a grievance. That is exactly what they did. This was the only copy of this grievance ever presented to the NLRB, or anyone else from the time Andrea had been requesting a copy of the grievance until she filed it in February 2003. All this time the NLRB never required Local 783 to produce this document. Even when Andrea asked the NLRB to have Local 783 present her grievance information, they were never forced to show a grievance had actually been filed. Woodrow Stamping Plant and Local 783 wouldn't file a grievance—especially if the grievance had merit.

Woodrow Stamping Plant and Local 783 were told Local 783 needed a copy of some kind of grievance. Therefore in the spring of 2006 in a last ditch effort to save themselves, Woodrow Stamping Plant got some papers together and called it a grievance. Prior to this day, they didn't have anything proving a grievance even existed. Andrea asked, but no one had copies of anything regarding the grievance

Local 783 had supposedly filed on her behalf. That's because they didn't file one. This grievance was made up after the fact and not during the process as it occurred. Andrea routinely expressed she wanted to be part of the grievance procedures and was always denied. It was all one big lie. She didn't have rights to the grievance procedure.

Local 783 had my grievance for three years and I was not allowed to participate in the grievance process either. Nor did the grievance leave a paper trail of the various stages it went through. Woodrow Stamping Plant and Local 783 thought Andrea and I both were stuck on stupid and out to lunch on this one. We refused to believe these lies after everything they had done to us. Three years was enough time to produce a grievance. I didn't understand why all the finger pointing was on Andrea. She did everything according to contract and that wasn't good enough to have her grievance investigated.

Andrea and I brainstormed on how we could outline what was in the contract and how it had been violated, but that still wasn't good enough. The National Labor Relations Board was determined not to file charges against Local 783. The Department of Civil Rights wasn't going to file charges against Woodrow Stamping Plant for violation of the contract and/or labor laws. The last and final words came from the National Labor Relations Board that no charges would be brought against Local 783. It didn't matter what was written in the Constitution of the Union regarding contract and labor laws being violated, the government agencies weren't going to file or investigate the charges against Local 783 and Famous Parts Company—Woodrow Stamping Plant.

Local 783 never gave Andrea Smith any verbal or written warnings on any of the supposed three occasions when Andrea allegedly threatened the nurse and doctor in the Medical Department. Andrea had no idea what Nurse Tootie and Dr. Slick was talking about. When she first received her firing she had no idea what it was about at all. She contacted Woodrow Stamping Plant regarding her firing and wanted Local 783, to file a grievance in February 2003. Andrea also expressed her desire to participate in the grievance procedures. Woodrow Stamping Plant noticed that Andrea Smith began hanging around me. They felt I was influencing Andrea's decisions on how to cause trouble. This is something Woodrow Stamping Plant and Local 783 didn't want. If too many people found out what they were doing, it could cause much trouble for them. When Andrea started asking questions about her retirement and her Worker's Compensation money she hadn't received, she was later fired.

Andrea became frightened in her last days of employment at Woodrow Stamping Plant. She was hit in the chest with a large industrial broom and nothing was done about it. Ronald Hatfield, who hit Andrea with the large industrial broom, had cursed at Andrea using vulgarities and obscenities the week prior to him throwing the broom. This caused Andrea to become afraid of him. Ronald never got as much as a reprimand for cursing at her or hitting her with the broom. Andrea clearly stated she wanted him reprimanded so he would at least think about what he had done. Woodrow Stamping Plant would not tolerate this lack of respect toward employees without reprimanding them—so they professed.

When Andrea was hit with the hi-lo truck, it was in an area where the truck didn't belong. When Andrea was hit nothing was ever done. Not even to the driver. The mere fact Woodrow Stamping Plant hid the fact Andrea was struck with the truck, shows it was done maliciously. They got rid of all records and files regarding the incident. I think the only proof the incident happened were the medical bills Andrea received. Woodrow Stamping Plant paid for Andrea's medical bills when she was transported and examined at Midway Hospital in June 2002. Andrea was the only person possessing any paperwork stating she went to the hospital and received treatment.

It didn't make sense for Andrea to threaten Nurse Tootie and Dr. Slick when she was afraid to re-enter Woodrow Stamping Plant for fear of what would happen to her. She was so afraid she called the Executive Branch of the Union's Headquarters and also the Regional 21A—Area Office. They told Andrea a union representative would meet her in the Medical Department. When she arrived, there was not one union representative who showed up. They had no intentions of coming to meet Andrea because their intention was to fire her.

I don't believe she would threaten anyone. She called me crying stating she didn't want to go back in the plant for fear of her life. All this was done to Andrea with intent and she was fired for something she didn't do. Andrea took her husband to the Medical Department and asked Nurse Tootie, if her husband could go back to the examination room with her. She was told no.

If she was so much of a threat on that day she entered Woodrow Stamping Plant, why wasn't security called? Why did Andrea and her husband wait in the waiting room to be discharged for over an hour if she had just threatened Nurse Tootie and Dr. Slick? They said this happened three times, but Andrea wasn't aware of any of these occasions until after she was terminated. If this happened, Andrea should have received a copy of the incident report and the union should have given her a copy of each following occurrence. If this happened, why was Andrea denied participation in the grievance process? I bet they didn't even think that far ahead. They were too busy pilfering employees' money.

Andrea wasn't running from the union. The union was running from her in an effort to get away with how she was fired and why. Why not allow Andrea to appear at the hearings to represent herself? If someone wants to participate in their grievance process, according to contract, they should be allowed to do so. Woodrow Stamping and Local 783 were aware of their wrongdoing.

They also met in secrecy regarding *my* grievance. I'd always wanted to participate in my grievance procedures. I went to the Public Review Board in January 2003 because after I won my harassment grievance against the Medical Department, the Executive Branch of the Company stated there would be no compensation. Mind you, compensation was discussed in November 2000 at Local 783's union hall. I was not going to receive any money from the grievance. I was told the way the grievance was written-up precluded me from being compensated. This was a lie. The money amount was indeed discussed. Why do you think I was forbidden to speak or represent myself at the hearing pertaining to me? I wasn't given the opportunity because I would have been very persuasive. I had the truth on my side. All the union had were lies they didn't want to get caught-up in.

Andrea's experience was the same—even when she tried to speak at my hearings. She was given credit as being there, but Local 783 never included her testimony in the final report. Woodrow Stamping Plant did all their dirty work in secret and it was always against the union member. Why hasn't Andrea ever received any Worker's Compensation? Her injuries went all the way back to 1992. Why did Andrea's Worker's Compensation case stay in the court for 8 years before a settlement was made in July 2002? Why was it that Andrea's doctors were paid and she never received a dime of her Worker's Compensation settlement? Why was Andrea's second claim rejected by Worker's Compensation after she was hit by the hi-lo? The same judge, who presided over Andrea's first Worker's Compensation claim, turned around and filed the second claim. She treated Andrea's claim as though she never had any prior history of injuries in the Worker's Compensation court while employed at Woodrow Stamping Plant. The judge was aware of Andrea's medical condition and denied her Worker's Compensation for being hit by the hi-lo in the plant. This was one of the biggest cases of fraud ever.

Woodrow Stamping Plant had to fire Andrea on ghost charges. She knew she hadn't threatened anyone. Local 783 and Woodrow Stamping Plant knew it too but they allowed Andrea's terminated to stand for over three years. They knew they'd lied on Andrea not allowing her to defend herself. She was deliberately not allowed to be involved in the grievance process. This kind of treatment is a farce and truly cruel, inhumane, and unbecoming of a company and union. They had reason to fire Andrea alright. Can you believe Local 783 and Woodrow Stamping Plant were angry with Andrea when they brought everything on themselves? They were the ones pilfering money. Andrea was fighting Woodrow Stamping Plant and Local 783 because she was fired unjustly.

Andrea never received her job back. She's currently satisfied CEO of the Executive Branch of the Union, Don Hangem, has been indicted and CEO Executive Branch of the Company, Robert Wart, has stepped down. This proves both entities at the Executive Branch of the Union and Company were aware of what happened to Andrea Smith and other employees. They were in hopes Andrea would not have found out they were pilfering her retirement. When she became aware of this information, they set out to destroy her because she'd too learned of what Woodrow Stamping Plant and Local 783 were doing.

She was fired through the mail while on medical leave regarding the incident with Nurse Tootie and Dr. Slick. She never received any verbal warning or reprimand from Woodrow Stamping or Local 783. The union ignored many violations according to the contract. But no one's eyes were on Local 783 in what they failed to do. It didn't matter because their main goal was to fire Andrea and that's exactly what happened. It didn't matter what Local 783 did or didn't do—just as long as their charges stuck against Andrea Smith. It didn't matter what these entities did in a joint venture to violate Andrea's labor laws and contract laws by unjustly terminating her.

It was never enough evidence or documentation she supplied in an effort to bring charges against Woodrow Stamping Plant or Local 783. There should have been red flags when there were no records indicating Andrea's hi-lo accident occurring. I truly find something wrong with these kinds of civil rights. These agencies don't follow through or give less than a damn about how we as minorities are being treated. They continue turning their heads permitting 'big businesses' to remain protected from their discriminatory acts. Until this day, big businesses receive protection by the Department of Civil Rights, the National Labor Relations Board, the Equal Employment Opportunity Commission, and other government agencies.

17

PREPARATION FOR TRANSFER

I contacted Johnny Hilter, Representative of the Executive Branch of the Union who represented Local 783. Shortly I became angry from trying to understand how to handle this situation. I explained everything to Mr. Johnny Hilter. After a few conversations and some investigating, he asked me if I'd consider going to another plant. "Yes", was my response. He informed me he would contact me after he talked to Mr. John Hail, Plant Chairman of Local 783. Mr. Hilter said he would get everything situated. In the meantime, I had filed complaints with the Department of Civil Rights, the Department of Labor, and the National Labor Relations Board.

Prior to my going to the National Labor Relations Board, I sent Mr. Johnny Hilter a letter dated August 10, 1993. I had completed and followed the necessary procedures in trying to obtain my original seniority and back pay. This is when I contacted the Executive Branch of the Union and was forwarded to Mr. Johnny Hilter. The following letter was addressed to the Executive Branch of the Union and it read:

"I signed a grievance dated June 3, 1993. I felt that grievance was something to pacify me for a short while. I feel the union isn't negotiating my grievance properly. When I signed the grievance in Bob Fleetwood's office, I asked for a copy and was denied. He said he wasn't going to make a copy and therefore didn't give me one. I feel the grievance procedure wasn't handled correctly. The contract book states I should be able to obtain a copy of a grievance filed on my behalf.

I'm beginning to feel Local 783 and Woodrow Stamping Plant don't care how their members feel. However, they keep taking our union dues faithfully each month. I feel this is highway robbery. The union is taking my money and not representing me as they should in reference to job security. I couldn't file a griev-ance because the union wouldn't allow me to.

John Hail, Plant Chairman of Local 783, lied to me saying I would be in the next group going to full-time status. This was said in front of my co-worker Mazzie Cane, but Mr. Hail said he didn't make that statement. I can quote him as say-ing, "Crista you will be in the next group that goes full-time. I can't give you a specific date or time but it will be this spring sometime". When the last group went full-time, in the last week of July 1993, I was not in that group. I really wasn't surprised, but I was still disappointed Mr. John Hail lied and had no problem doing so.

Mr. Johnny Hilter, I would like you to answer a few questions for me. Why won't Local 783 allow us the choice to go to another plant? Martin Assembly just hired 400 people off the street—many of which will be obtaining their 90-day probationary period very soon. I have been at Woodrow Stamping Plant for almost three years with the impression I will become full-time. This is not fair because I was hired at Woodrow Stamping Plant as a full-time employee to begin with. The union always tells me it's an error.

John Hail hasn't put pressure on Woodrow Stamping Plant for my full-time sta-tus. While I have been employed at Woodrow Stamping Plant, there have been employees who came into our plant as full-time employees. They were part-time employees at the other plants. Woodrow Stamping has not been following the procedure. There have been so many problems with my employee records regard-ing my full-time versus part-time status. I don't see why John Hail hasn't worked on clearing up this misunderstanding. Please clarify some of my issues and give me some answers, which will satisfy me as a union member. If you can't clarify any of the problems, it only makes me think you are aware of what is happening at Woodrow Stamping Plant. I will not let this issue rest until I get some satisfac-tory answers. I do hope this problem gets solved soon. I will also be sending a copy of this letter to Local 783 President, Mr. Jess McGregor. Please respond."

With all the letters I was writing, Woodrow Stamping was more than ready to get rid of me. I began getting a picture of how Woodrow Stamping Plant and Local 783 were pilfering money. At the moment, I thought it was only from part-time employees. They didn't want to take any chances of someone else finding out what they were doing. At this time John Hail was Plant Chairman of Local

783, but when I was transferred to Sarrow Stamping Plant the positions of President of Local 783 and Plant Chairman became one position. This is the reason I may refer to John Hail as President and at other times Plant Chairman. Woodrow Stamping Plant was aware I was full-time. Because of all this confusion surrounding my work status, I couldn't transfer to another plant as full-time without hassle. It would cause a lot of problems. It was clearly easier for the company to terminate my employment without my knowledge rather than have me causing continuous headaches for them. If I were gone, they could continue pilfering money from employees as they had been doing all along. They were going to fix it so I could never return to Woodrow Stamping Plant again.

This made a lot of sense to Plant Chair, John Hail. He was thrilled I would never be returning to the plant again. There was only one way they could not transfer me and that was by terminating my employment with Woodrow Stamping Plant. After doing so, they could hire me as a full-time employee with no seniority at Sarrow Stamping Plant. This is exactly what they did to hide my seniority as being September 28, 1990. Clearly they were aware they were omitting and violating rules written in the contract, but they didn't care. They had no one to answer to. The Department of Civil Rights and the National Labor Relations Board were clearly going to drop employees' charges when they came down to file with them. Local 783 would make a deal with the Labor Relations Board to get charges dropped. I've never known Local 783 to be honest with anyone. That's why I'm writing this book.

On a few occasions when I went to the National Labor Relations Board they would try to deter me from filing a complaint. They would turn me around and walk me right back to the door. Andrea Smith was also a victim of this treatment regarding the NLRB. There were a few more employees to my knowledge who tried to file complaints and were turned away. They didn't allow the employees to go as far as filing a complaint. There was another young lady I met who experienced the same problem as I with her work status. This was in 2002. Ronda Summers had proper documentation to prove she was full-time and had much trouble filing a complaint.

After I exhausted my rights with the Department of Civil Rights, the Department of Labor, and the National Labor Relations Board, I seemed to be at the same place I'd started in 1990. When I was terminated Woodrow Stamping Plant wasn't held accountable. I couldn't go to court and have my case heard. These two entities had so much clout it was almost impossible to get your case in court. I was *blackballed* or *red-flagged* in the system and no lawyer would take my case. When I use the term *blackballed* or *red-flagged* it means one's name is in a universal computer system. If your name is on this list, there is no lawyer that will take your case. It doesn't matter how much merit your case has, you are unable to obtain an attorney. It wasn't that I didn't have a case. It's just that Woodrow Stamping Plant and Local 783 had enough clout to have cases thrown out of court in a Summary Judgment. A Summary Judgment is simply a bench trail where the judge is supposed to examine, evaluate, and decide upon information by the discovery of evidence.

I believe they thought I was a buffoon fool. It was already established I was full-time. It was also later established I was unfairly terminated when I was supposed to be a re-hire. I was certain they had pilfered all my money for the last three years. Local 783 didn't want me back either and I had no union representation. The Department of Civil Rights did not help me even though they were well aware of Woodrow Stamping Plant's actions. Not even the U.S. District Court would help after I refused to accept the measly $7,500 dollars offered for the discrimination, harassment, and retaliation.

I found out I was going to Sarrow Stamping Plant as a part-time employee not a re-hire as discussed prior. Woodrow Stamping Plant was so blatant. They couldn't deny I was full-time when I reached Sarrow Stamping Plant. Sarrow Stamping agreed to help Local 783. Sarrow Stamping Plant would hire me as a new employee as a favor to Woodrow Stamping Plant. Instead of hiring me as a re-hire, which was what Sarrow Stamping Plant was supposed to do, they hired me as a new employee in hopes I wasn't going to find out. I was surprised Woodrow Stamping Plant terminated me and Sarrow Stamping Plant, hired me as a new employee as though I had never worked for the company before. I had just transferred from Woodrow Stamping Plant on Friday, November 13, 1993 and just over the weekend there became no apparent history of me (as of Monday, November 15, 1993). How did they pull this one off?

I was clearly full-time when I left Woodrow Stamping Plant. Government agencies did nothing for the exception of forcing me to drop charges against Woodrow Stamping Plant and Local 783. The Labor Department told me their hands were tied because of union contract negotiations. I felt the union owed me every dime I paid for representation I didn't receive. This was a breach of contract. They not only pilfered *my* money, they pilfered other employees' money too. They cheated Karol Henderson, Mazzie Cane, and others out of their one-time lump sum payment when they returned back to work. They were the employees hired during the 70's. The majority of these past employees became 'new hires' as though they had never worked for the company before. Some employees got their time back upon retirement, but they never received a dime of the money when they returned from their long layoffs.

Karol Henderson was inquiring about going to another plant to gain her seniority. Plant Chairman, John Hail, told Karol she was not allowed to go to another plant, although she had been employed and laid off in 1977. According to contract, Karol should have been placed full-time even before me. John Hail knew he had no one to challenge his actions once I was gone. He knew he could do anything he wanted to do. He told Karol I was gone and wouldn't be returning. He said he was ecstatic I was gone.

Those hired and called back were supposed to receive their seniority and back pay. They were told they'd receive their plant seniority for time worked as part-time employees and it would go toward their retirement. How could John Hail tell the part-time employees that big lie? Part-time employees couldn't accrue seniority. I found something wrong when he made that statement. When they returned during the late 80's and 90's, they received no back pay nor did they receive their seniority. Woodrow Stamping Plant and Local 783 pilfered it all. Woodrow Stamping Plant was going to keep the employees full-time and part-time at the same time. Woodrow Stamping Plant was pilfering the profit sharing, vacation pay, personal days, excused absence days, and bonuses. Some of the vacation pay would range from three to four weeks pay and Woodrow Stamping Plant would keep these same employees part-time long term.

Woodrow Stamping Plant kept the full-time benefits package for the full-time employees putting that money in separate accounts. They had these same full-time employees working as part-time employees, paying them part-time pay per hour. During the time Woodrow had been pilfering their money as full-time employees, their seniority should have moved forward. This is why Woodrow Stamping Plant and Local 783 wouldn't send these employees to other plants. They would have had to be re-hired and they would carry their seniority with them.

This is how I became a re-hire when I was only supposed to be transferred to Sarrow Stamping Plant. The employees were unaware they were full-time and part-time too. They thought they were part-time only. They had no idea their money was being pilfered from them. They would have never imagined Local 783 being a part of something of this magnitude. Woodrow Stamping Plant was robbing the employees by not notifying them they were full-time.

Remember, there were two separate sets of records I talked about. Woodrow Stamping held one set and Local 783 held the other. The union kept a set of records that stated employees were full-time and part-time too. They kept the full-time records separate from the part-time records. Both sets of records were kept at two separate entities. What would Local 783 need with this kind of information when their only interest was to protect the union members? They had to be very careful because once the money was put in these accounts it was difficult to retrieve.

Karol Henderson asked Plant Chairman John Hail, "Where is Crista going? Is she transferring to another plant?" He said, "Yes, and I'm glad to get rid of that troublemaker". Karol should have been placed full-time and offered a transfer before any new hire. She was unhappy. It was unfair, I was transferring and she wasn't since she was employed long before me. She expressed this to John Hail and he dismissed her inquiries as though the words were never spoken. Karol knew there was virtually nothing she could do. John Hail felt she had no place to question his authority. This was when Local 783's Plant Chairman expressed he wasn't willing to help her acquire full-time status elsewhere and he didn't.

In my opinion, Karol wasn't willing to upset the apple cart in fighting for her rights as I had done. She was willing to talk about her situation and stress how unfair things were. She wasn't ready to fight in fear of not becoming full-time or being retaliated against. The union used full-time status as a means to control what the part-time employees did and said. The part-time employees weren't willing to take any chances.

It was clear John Hail wasn't going to help Karol get hired at any other plant because Woodrow Stamping Plant was making money off her. The newly elected union members weren't going to challenge Hail's decision. Part-time employees who were hired during the 70's never received full-time status until 1994 through 1996. When they were hired at the same plant they were laid-off from during the 70's, many newly hired employees passed them up. All the while the company was pilfering monies and benefits associated with their full-time status, allowing them to remain on the part-time package. Woodrow Stamping Plant was putting that money in separate accounts from 1988 through 1996. That's when I became aware of what Woodrow Stamping Plant was doing.

They were using one set of files in the Worker's Compensation Court having the plaintiff's attorney settle for meager amounts of money. This left the plaintiff with nothing to say in their own defense. At this time, their case becomes a "take it or leave it" offer. It was their first and last chance to accept Woodrow Stamping Plant's offer. If the employee didn't agree with the settlement agreement, they would settle the case just the same and the employee would receive nothing. Then Woodrow Stamping Plant would push the second set of records through the Worker's Compensation Court as though the employee with the occupational injury has never filed a prior claim in the Worker's Compensation Court. Local 783 used the files in their possession for the employees working in the plant. When the employee retired, or was put on a 'no work available' status, Woodrow Stamping Plant continued to make money off these same employees. Worker's Compensation would deny the same claim settled the first time around. When the second claim files, it leaves the employee only social security benefits to live on.

Woodrow Stamping Plant would make sure employees received their social security. Woodrow Stamping Plant and Local 783 thought they had it all worked out. Woodrow Stamping Plant would honor the last decision because they didn't have to pay the employee with the injury sustained in the plant anything at all. Woodrow Stamping Plant would use the same employees from their Worker's Compensation claim and pilfer their retirement money they should be receiving from Metro Craft Insurance Company. Monthly stipend, Worker's Compensation benefits, and their retirement were put in these separate accounts at Woodrow Stamping Plant. Woodrow Stamping Plant, Local 783, judges, and the plaintiff's lawyers all teamed up in order to pilfer these benefits and claims. The ones injured receive nothing on the Worker's Compensation Settlement.

Some employees received 1994 seniority and others received seniority as 1996 with the exception of Mazzie Cane. She received July 15, 1991 seniority along with me. Karol Henderson spoke to John Hail in reference to obtaining her prior seniority status along with her full-time status. She too was part-time upon returning to Woodrow Stamping Plant. Some employees received their seniority and others did not because their money was pilfered. "Some of the prior hourly employees will not get their seniority back until their retirement", John Hail said. After all that was said and done, John Hail proved to be correct because as of January 2004 many did not obtain their back seniority. They would receive their seniority back when they retired because their seniority continued to grow in years.

At retirement, their plan was to somehow combine the two files—employment and retirement. I wasn't sure how they were going to fix that problem. I guess they were leaving that problem to their predecessors since all those involved in the scheme would soon be retiring with thirty years of service to the company.

Many employees who returned from lay-off had not expected to start working for the same plant they were laid off from as 'new hires'—especially at a time Woodrow Stamping Plant were hiring full-time employees. Woodrow Stamping Plant was replenishing their work force. During this time all Woodrow Stamping was interested in was making money off the employees (i.e. profit sharing, performance bonuses, vacation time, excused absences, and personal days). What they were doing was illegal and there was no justification for it. These employees from the 70's should have been the first in line for hire before any new hire was put on the full-time roster.

This is when the two sets of records came into play. One set of records were of the employees hired back from the 70's as full-time and the other set was of the same employees listed as new part-time. Woodrow Stamping Plant worked it out this way because there would be no questions asked. They had to make things appear to be accurate. They didn't want part-timers wondering about all the money they should have received. Can you imagine how much money was being pilfered from these employees? Those who were hired during the 70's and returned received a double whammy. They were victimized three times because Woodrow Stamping Plant pilfered their money and benefit packages too. In 1999 the Collective Bargaining Agreement was ratified. These employees laid off in the 70's were to receive a one-time lump sum payment along with their back seniority. On top of all that they couldn't even get their seniority restored.

The group of employees finally found a lawyer to take their case in a class-action lawsuit. This class-action lawsuit would have consisted of all employees hired in the 70's and returned from 1988 through the 1990's. After the lawyer began his investigation, he too started working for Local 783 and Woodrow Stamping Plant by not pursuing the cases. All of a sudden the lawyer contacted the employees and stated they didn't have a case, even though when originally taking their cases he'd stated otherwise. What changed in a matter of weeks? The lawyers had enough time to evaluate the facts, records, and testimonies with Local 783 union members and employees when they decided to take the case on. The lawyers would have found out through a simple investigation that Woodrow Stamping was indeed pilfering employees' money.

This was similar to when I had a discrimination case and the lawyer representing me didn't file my claim in federal or state court. You can't tell me my lawyer didn't know I was full-time when he had my records in his possession. Mr. John Bushe, my attorney, was supposed to be representing my best interest. He knew Woodrow Stamping Plant terminated my employment on November 13, 1993. He was also aware I received disparate treatment when Woodrow Stamping Plant and Local 783 stopped hiring employee's right at my name. Woodrow Stamping Plant stated they met their quota and could not hire anymore employees. They were already aware I was a full-time employee before the termination of my employment when placing me at Sarrow Stamping Plant. It was established I was full-time in July 1992 with full benefits. This meant Woodrow Stamping terminated me with full intent to hide my real date of hire. This was premeditated and done with intent, which is clearly illegal under the law.

All done to me at this point was done to deceive with intent. Why couldn't I obtain help from the Department of Labor, the Department of Civil Rights, the Equal Employment Opportunity Commission, or the National Labor Relations Board? These organizations were supposed to help the public sector with unlawful acts committed against employees with or without a union. I was the only Black person and the only woman sent to Sarrow when there were others with higher seniority requesting to be transferred.

Attorney Bushe was aware Local 783 didn't file my grievance when I was told it went to the Umpire Level and the Public Review Board. The grievance didn't get that far. Mr. Bushe knew Local 783 and Woodrow Stamping were using unfair labor practices. He was aware they did nothing in my defense to settle the grievance. He did nothing to settle my case.

I received a letter sent to the Attorney Grievance Commission by Mr. Hdith, the original attorney who took my case. He became ill and later died from complications with Prostate Cancer. He stated my case should have been settled out of court. He never completed the case. However there was talk of a settlement before he became ill. It was imminent this was going to happen. In his absence, my case was handed to Mr. Bushe, who then turned his head to all the existing discrimination, retaliation, and harassment charges.

Mr. Bushe had everything to prove I was full-time when hired at Woodrow Stamping Plant. My transfer was disparate treatment when I was terminated. I should have been a 're-hire' when I transferred but instead I was a 'new hire'. Mr. Bushe allowed the statue of limitations to run out saying he had no proof as to my allegations. Mr. Bushe did this as a favor, just as the other attorneys had done when they took the cases of Woodrow Stamping Plant's employees of the 70's.

The 1999 contract stated the employees were to receive their back seniority and back pay from the time they were laid off until the time they returned. Looking back now, how could someone be so cruel to another in such an inhumane manner as I had been treated? My attorney knew what he was doing when he failed to represent me. I saw it then, but after looking back at my situation, it should have been obvious to anyone something was severely wrong. I truly don't think you have to be an attorney to see what Woodrow Stamping Plant and Sarrow Stamping Plant were doing was illegal.

I obtained a copy of the 1999 Famous Parts Company Summary Contract, which gave an overview of what was covered during the contract. It basically stated: employees who had reliable seniority who had at least five years of seniority as of October 1, 1999 and were laid-off from 1979 through 1983, would be credited with 40 hours of seniority with the company. For each completed calendar week while absent the worker had seniority according to the percentage shown below.

- Twenty years or more—100%

- Fifteen years but less than twenty years—75%

- Ten years but less than fifteen years—50% and

- Five years but less than ten—years was to receive 25% of their pay.

I could only dream of what kinds of fees the lawyers would have made on this kind of case in a class-action lawsuit. It's not logical for a lawyer to settle for nothing. Local 783 simply made a deal with the law firm that was to take on these cases. They were bought and paid for by not taking on the cases regarding the employees trying to collect money due to them. This was a massive cover-up that neither Woodrow Stamping Plant nor Local 783 wanted uncovered. Logically speaking, I can't see a lawyer dropping this kind of case and getting nothing when it could have been very profitable for them.

These employees had cases just as Andrea, Mazzie, and I had through our years of lawyers slamming doors in our faces. We weren't crazy or stupid. So why couldn't we receive help while we were seeking it? We learned that just because a lawyer didn't take our case, didn't mean we didn't *have* a case. The question is how much money did the lawyers make by *not* taking these cases? It had to have been a substantial profit.

The plant didn't want any unauthorized persons invading their record keeping. I didn't know at the time, but it all manifested itself in later years. I'm willing to bet Local 783 cut a deal with the lawyers not to take the union members' cases. Can you imagine what kind of havoc this would cause if this information ever got out? We're talking scandals, imprisonment, and firing. We're talking about FBI involvement, courts, family reputations, and so on. It was much easier for the group to allow Plant Chairman, John Hail, and Bargaining Committeeman, Bob Fleetwood, to take the indictment (or wrap) for racketeering in 1999 so the company could continue business as usual.

The government agencies didn't get all the records during the investigation because the other set of records could not easily be found. If I knew this scheme existed, one would figure it would be apparent to the investigators as well. It had everything to do with management. I think the FBI must have been paid not to give out all the information during their investigation. One set of hidden records was in the union's possession. The other set was in the hands of the Medical Department at Woodrow Stamping Plant. Since they had lawyers, doctors, referees, judges, senators, and attorney generals working for them, there was no reason they should be afraid of being caught. They had all areas of their asses covered—even in the media.

Woodrow Stamping carried a lot of weight and no lawyer wanted to stand up to them because of the existing corruption. They believed in putting fear in employees by retaliation. They were very good at this. Even Metro Craft Insurance Company was on Woodrow Stamping Plant's books for payoff. They saved the plant money by helping them avoid lawsuits. The company was self-insured. There was no reason for these lawyers to drop the employees' claims when the employees had valid claims regarding their pilfered money. The employees were unable to get a lawyer to represent their cases so there was no case. Some employees didn't know they were supposed to receive back pay from the time they were laid-off until 1988 or 1990 when they retired. These employees didn't seem to know what was written in the contract book and had no idea they were to receive anything. While those who knew they didn't get a dime when the money became available. The union made up their own rules as they went along anyway. Local 783 made up rules on a daily basis regarding the union contract. Karol Henderson ended up with 1996 seniority. She and others noticed new employees who had not worked for the company being hired as full-time before them. This included me. Mazzie Cane and I received July 1991 seniority. The other people on my grievance didn't receive their seniority back.

I was informed in July 1995 that my grievance was settled after returning from vacation shut down at Sarrow Stamping Plant. Salma Bears, in Labor Relations, informed me I officially received the seniority date of July 15, 1991. I had the same seniority date as I did when I filed and signed my grievance in 1993. As a reminder, I still had not yet received a copy of the various stages the grievance went through. I had to sign a form in order for the union to *start* the grievance process, so why not *after* the grievance was complete? I didn't sign off on this grievance stating that I agreed with the terms of this grievance. When Salma told me the grievance was settled, I was truly surprised because I had no prior notification of it being settled.

When a person files a grievance, they agree a violation has occurred out of context of the contract. When a grievance is settled, one agrees to the terms of the contract by signing off on the grievance that they agree to its terms. This didn't happen. They just shoved this grievance down my throat forcing me to accept their terms. This was a grave injustice to me. The biggest injustice of all was Local 783, Woodrow Stamping Plant, Executive Branch of the Company CEO Robert Wart, and Executive Branch of Union CEO Don Hangem, all knowing they hadn't filed my grievance.

I kept in touch with a few part-time employees from Woodrow Stamping Plant when I transferred to Sarrow Stamping Plant. Mazzie Cane's seniority was adjusted as a result of the grievance I filed. She originally received June 3, 1993 seniority in April 1996 when Woodrow Stamping Plant hired the part-time employees that had been part-time since 1990. When my seniority was adjusted, they gave Mazzie Cane and me the seniority date of July 15, 1990. There were others on my grievance that happened to not receive their seniority dates. They should have fallen in line with Mazzie Cane and me. After the grievance was complete, everyone on the grievance should have received the same seniority date but they did not. We all hired in together. Therefore we should have had the same seniority and job classification.

Prior to being transferred to Sarrow Stamping, I continued trying to obtain a copy of the grievance I filed. I was looking for the paper trail regarding all the stages of what transpired during the grievance process. I requested to take part in the grievance procedure but was denied. I was making more than enough noise regarding this grievance prior to it being settled. They became tired of me, but not enough to grant my original seniority date and back pay. Afterall, I received nothing from the grievance. I received no back pay and my seniority date stayed the same. What was the purpose of the grievance in the first place, if nothing was accomplished and everything stayed the same?

I requested the various stages of my grievance before it went to the Public Review Board in 1993, 1994, and 1995. They didn't have a single piece of paper to show the grievance had ever been to the Public Review Board. I told Local 783 if the grievance had been to the Public Review Board, there should have been a paper trail stating what happened during the process. I never signed off on the grievance saying I agreed or disagreed with its outcome.

At one point Local 783 wanted to start the grievance procedure all over again. Local 783 didn't file the grievance the first time. Therefore they could have treated the second grievance in the same manner. What was the purpose? Who's to say they wouldn't pull the same scheme all over again? Local 783 owed me all the money I paid in the union for no service at all. They allowed Woodrow Stamping Plant to pilfer my money.

What would be the reasoning behind the union not giving me a copy unless they were up to no good? The contract book stated after a grievance is signed, the company, union, and the grievant receive a copy. This was truly not the case. I don't believe the union ever filed the grievance. This was a formality they had to go through for my benefit pretending they were working on my behalf. They had no intention of following through with the grievance because they knew they were going to sweep the issue under the rug. They had already told me I wasn't going to get any money back. They had to be stupid if they thought they couldn't settle this grievance before a two-year period. The grievance should have been completed in its entirety in 120 days unless there was a mutual agreement between both parties to do otherwise. This was not the case, three years was much to long to settle a grievance.

I was already full-time. It was agreed upon by Woodrow Stamping Plant and Local 783 that I was full-time by error. I would have been satisfied if they left me with a part-time status and stopped taking my money. They were greedy and didn't care if I knew what they were doing. They were unfair and unscrupulous. I truly don't think Local 783 filed any grievances on my behalf against Woodrow Stamping Plant. These acts of deception occurred throughout the entire duration of my employment.

18

TERMINATION IN THE PROCESS OF TRANSFERING TO SARROW STAMPING PLANT

In October 1993, six Caucasians were hired before my transfer and I was not put on full-time status. This was the second time I was passed over. I thought John Hail, Local 783's Plant Chairman, was retaliating against me for challenging him. When they stopped hiring at my name and I was outraged! Woodrow Stamping Plant and Local 783 refused to honor my full-time status and they wanted to prove they had the authority to do so. The six Caucasians hired obtained their original seniority as of the year 1990. I couldn't help but notice there were no minorities hired in the last three groups. I took this situation personally.

Johnny Hilter, Executive Branch of the Union Representative, contacted me a few weeks later informing me I would be going to another plant. He stated I would be a rehire at the new place of employment. I asked him how I could be a rehire when I was never officially a full-time hire. He didn't elaborate on the matter and it was as though he didn't hear the question. He informed me I would be going to Sarrow Stamping Plant in the Detroit metro area. I was forced to drive 45 minutes longer from my home to work opposed to a 20-minute drive. Mr. Hilter called me at my home and gave me directions on how to reach Sarrow Stamping Plant. He said everything was all set up and Sarrow Stamping would be expecting me to complete all the necessary paperwork. All I had to do was be at Sarrow Stamping Plant on November 11, 1993. No specific time was given.

Sarrow Stamping was a very old plant. It looked like there were many old buildings put together during the plant's history to accommodate one large building. The owners of the old buildings prior to Famous Parts Company sold the property to them during the 50's. There were many chemicals on the property that seeped in the ground. When I first entered Sarrow Stamping the first thing I could see was a big cloud of smoke. The smoke came from the welding torches, which sent a cloud of smoke bellowing all over the plant.

Soon after I arrived, Sarrow Stamping installed vents inside the building to vacuum the welding fumes and clouds of smoke produced by the weld guns. I was concerned about all the smoke. I wasn't aware of the type of chemical contamination that surrounded Sarrow Stamping Plant. I didn't know the extent of the contamination or the harmful effects. Sarrow Stamping Plant had just signed a contract with a company to come on the premises to clean the chemicals from around plant's grounds. The place was full of toxin contamination in and around the grounds. In November 1993 Sarrow Stamping had the company clean some of the chemicals in the soil around the plant grounds. The men cleaning up the chemicals wore unusual outfits resembling space suits. The football field's soil right across from the plant had to be turned over. They used something called *mesh* to help absorb the chemicals from the ground.

After the chemical clean up was complete, word around the plant was Sarrow Stamping hired a company to remove the hazardous waste from the ground. They didn't have the proper license to transport and dispose of the chemical waste. Therefore hazardous waste stayed on a truck on Famous Parts Company's property for approximately a month until they could find someone licensed to dispose of the waste.

I didn't drink the water at Sarrow Stamping because I suspected the water wasn't fit to drink. Some of the drinking fountains had not only one filter, but two large filters. I stopped drinking the water after an experience with the new fountain placed by the Dantly's Presses at the back of the plant. Three to six months after it was placed there, the water was extremely bitter. I had to spit the water back in the fountain. I noticed the fountain had corroded to the extent the new stainless steel basin and spout had rusted. The company eventually removed that drinking fountain and never replaced it with another—at least not while I was there. The chemical contamination in and outside of Sarrow Stamping Plant was one of my main concerns while being employed there.

The women's locker room was located on the second floor next to the cafeteria. When I entered the plant, I would walk up a set of cemented steps leading through the cafeteria. There was a door at the rear of the cafeteria leading down a hall lined with lockers. This led to the women's locker room where many of the women kept their belongings while working. Many of the women, who worked in the front of the building, would go on their breaks to the locker room through the front entrance. There was comfortable seating in the lounge. This was where

I exchanged many ideas, opinions, and of course gossip with my co-workers. A place like Sarrow Stamping had gossip going around on a regular basis. If you were to tell your secrets in a place of this sort, depending on whom you told, your news would soon become plant news.

When I arrived at Sarrow Stamping Plant on November 11, 1993, I walked from the parking lot past the security guard and down the path until I reached the first building on the left side of street. It said, "Employment Office". I walked through the lobby's first set of doors. This is where the ATM machine and vending machine was located. There was a long counter lining the wall. On the right side of the wall employees could review, apply for, and bid on job openings according to seniority. The application forms were completed in this area.

As I walked a little farther, on the right hand side of the wall there was another office across from the Personnel Office. Sarrow Stamping Plant was separated into two buildings. The Personnel Office and other business offices including the Plant Manager's Office were located in the building just outside the site adjacent to the plant. I walked in and identified myself. I was then asked to go to the office across the hall. There Tarry Johnson, Labor Relations Supervisor, greeted me. He asked for my picture identification. I then reached into my purse, to retrieve my driver's license and social security card and handed both pieces to him.

After I gave Mr. Johnson the information, I was then directed to the Medical Department located inside the plant. Mr. Johnson informed me I had to take a physical. I was a little surprised when he made that statement. I reached the Medical Department with some uncertainty thinking, "If I was to be a rehire, why am I *just* being told to take another physical?" A physical examination wasn't necessary. I was just transferring from one plant to another. I thought maybe the physical consisted of a drug test. I felt something was wrong with the picture. I wasn't supposed to be having a physical when only transferring to another plant.

When I arrived at the Medical Department, my medical records were already there. The nurse in the Medical Department expressed her concerns as to why I was having a complete physical. She stated it was an unusual procedure during a transfer. I explained in some degree my concerns as well and just decided to let the matter rest. After all it was just a physical. This physical could've only helped prove I was in good physical condition. Little did I know what was about to actually happen. I had no idea regarding the extent Woodrow Stamping would go to keep me out of their plant for good. Tarry Johnson, Labor Relations Supervisor, asked me to return to his office after I completed the medical portion of my examination. I walked back across the street and finished completing the remainder of the paperwork for employment.

I returned back to the administration office in the old building at Sarrow Stamping Plant to the Employment Office. After I met with Tarry Johnson, I met with Salma, the Labor Relations Representative. This was to finish the necessary paperwork in a front office across from Tarry Johnson's office. She informed me at that time, I would never be able to return to Woodrow Stamping Plant unless Sarrow Stamping plant burned down. I didn't really quite understand what Salma was saying because I knew Woodrow Stamping was my 'home plant' where my seniority originated. I knew this information was binding if I didn't know anything else. This was something I read in the contract book. When I finished, I left the Employment Office and went home.

When I reached home I received a telephone call from Salma. She informed me I would be starting (as a new hire) part-time on Monday November 15, 1993. I told Salma, "Mr. Hilter told me I would be a rehire". I was supposed to be a rehire and I didn't receive any paperwork from Woodrow Stamping Plant or Sarrow Stamping Plant regarding this transfer. Johnny Hilter told me when I got to Sarrow Plant all I needed to do was identify myself. He said everything would be taken care of and all I needed to do was be present.

I was furious, disappointed, and outraged at the idea of starting part-time at a plant I was to have been full-time at. I thought to myself, "What are they up to now?" I told Salma, with no uncertainty, if I was going to be part-time the deal was off. There was no need for me to leave Woodrow Stamping as being part-time when Woodrow was much closer to my home. I asked Salma, why I should drive 45 minutes further to another job only to remain at the same work status I had prior to leaving Woodrow Stamping Plant. I informed Salma I would be staying at Woodrow Stamping Plant if that were all Sarrow Stamping had to offer.

I ended my conversation with Salma with much dismay. I called Mr. Johnny Hilter, Executive Branch of the Union, and immediately informed him of what Sarrow Stamping told me. I remembered what Mr. Hilter said in our last conversation over the telephone. After speaking with him again, he said he would take care of the matter. He gave no further explanation on the subject except to say he would be getting back with me.

Later that evening on November 11, 1993 I received a telephone call from Salma, informing me I would be starting full-time on Monday November 15, 1993. I then informed Woodrow Stamping Plant my last day with them would be on Friday, November 13, 1993. I was very appreciative of the assistance from Mr. Johnny Hilter who was trying to help—so I thought. Thus far he had been the one and only person who made a step towards solving my problem. Mr. Hilter assisted me in my move to Sarrow Stamping.

I had some issues in terms of the grievance I filed in June of 1993 that needed to be settled. I began contacting the union regarding the status of my grievance. I wanted to know if there had been any progress. When I transferred to Sarrow Stamping Plant, I wasn't given a copy of the grievance I signed. There was much work to be done because it seemed Local 783 wasn't about to move on the matter. It seemed as though a grievance wasn't written at all. This was when I sent Johnny Hilter another letter dated November 26, 1993 addressed to the Executive Branch of the Union. The letter read as follows:

"Mr. Johnny Hilter:

I would like to personally thank you for interceding on my behalf in obtaining my full-time status at Sarrow Stamping Plant. I truly appreciate your patience and understanding. I would like you to inform me as to the status of the grievance I filed in June 1993 in an effort to obtain my seniority along with back pay. When I last spoke to you in reference to the grievance, you informed me that as a part-time employee I didn't have merit in filing a grievance. I then informed you I disagreed by stating, "That isn't what I read in the contract agreement".

If you would turn to page 16 paragraphs 5, it states my claim is correct and I do indeed have a valid right to file a grievance. There has been a violation of my rights and I have notified the union. The company said they had made an error by making me full-time. The supposed error was made from September 1990 through November 1993, the company admitted I was full-time in July 1992, the problem was never fixed. It didn't take three years to correct an error. Therefore they pilfered my money. I notified Labor Relations and Mr. John Hail, Plant Chairman of Local 783. He informed me it was an error due to my social security number being similar to someone else's. I replied by saying, "How could there be a mistake in my social security number when the name and social security number belong to me, Crista Carrie?" I wondered if they really thought I was spaced out on something. If they really thought I would believe something like that.

I noticed my pay stub changed for the first time in a while. Since my checks were being directly deposited into my bank account, I only received a check stub. I would merely glance to see if my hours worked were correct and to verify the amounts were correct going direct deposit. I would like you to look closely at my last check stub. I noticed the amounts in the year-to-date column were incorrect. The numbers are larger than the gross for the year. I've grossed for the current date, X amount of dollars for the total year. Please take it upon yourself and help get my grievance settled because the errors are beginning to add up and take a toll on me. I would like something done about my problem once and for all. This grievance has been going on for much too long.

I'm not trying to be sarcastic or anything. I feel three years has been long enough with Local 783 turning their heads as though nothing happened. It's insulting to be labeled as a "troublemaker" or a "radical" when I'm just trying to get a problem solved. I'm upset at Local 783 and Woodrow Stamping Plant. I don't seem to care what they say about me. I'm just doing the same as anyone else would do in this situation."

I said thank you, enclosed a copy of my check stubs, and a copy of a statement for the year-to-date that differed by a few hundreds dollars. I signed my name and sent the letter off certified mail. My last check of the year and my W-2 were not the same. It was enough that Woodrow Stamping Plant sent a telegram stating the amounts were inconsistent and incorrect. The telegram stated a newly amended W-2 would be sent at a later date. It was never was. Even though I couldn't quite identify what was happening and why, I could feel there were many unethical situations occurring regarding my transfer. Whatever it was I knew all that occurred wasn't in line with normal procedure.

After the holidays, I got acquainted with the new employees at Sarrow Stamping Plant. I shared experiences with my soon-to-be family. I always expressed the anger I had towards Local 783 and Woodrow Stamping Plant because of their unfair treatment. When I started telling my story, the employees were a little surprised. There were a few people that felt they too were treated unfairly, but not nearly to the extent I had been.

I was rather outspoken but stayed to myself minding my own business. I was a loner in every sense but I was friendly each time you saw me. I always had a book to read in my spare time. I tried to mind my own business. Even when I became familiar with my surroundings, I didn't carry gossip. If someone told me something in hopes I would spread information, they were disappointed because I didn't spread the information given. What was told to me as gossip about other people never was repeated.

People knew very little about me outside Sarrow Stamping and I liked it that way. I felt I lived two lives—one outside the plant and the other inside the plant with my fellow co-workers. I felt this was the best way of handling my life. I didn't want every detail of my life floating around as plant gossip. I felt if I didn't separate the two lives, life would be more complicated. I had to be very selective of who I brought home from the plant to keep lies and gossip at a minimum.

When I first transferred from Woodrow Stamping Plant, I really didn't want to go to another plant. I just wanted to obtain my full-time rights. There was a group hired in 1991 and they were put on part-time status. They were hired and received their seniority date going back to the date the company first hired them. I started taking censuses of the minorities hired. I noticed through the plant's hiring practices the minorities were the last to be hired unless they had family or friends in the union and/or the company.

19

FAIRNESS WAS A SERIOUS ISSUE

Sarrow Stamping Plant, like Woodrow Stamping, hired more Caucasians than minorities. They kept control of the minorities in the plant. The minorities who were elected for union offices were few if any in some elections. I guess it would be fair to say that there was one or two more at Woodrow Stamping Plant than Sarrow Stamping Plant. When they did hire minorities, they fired them at an alarming rate. They were the last hired and the first fired. If they hired too many minorities, it would be difficult for Caucasians to win Local elections. They would place one or two minorities in appointed positions in the union so it wouldn't look discriminatory. The company put a cap on the hiring of minorities. This helped the union too, because it would limit minorities running for Plant Chairman. The union felt that Whites were going to vote for Whites. This would make it less likely for a minority to be voted as Plant Chairman. The fewer minorities hired, the less they would be able to hold union positions.

Minorities were unable to hold any position of importance in the union office at either plant for very long. The union and company at Woodrow and Sarrow Stamping were one in the same. When elections occurred in the union, it was almost a guarantee a Caucasian person would be elected. Woodrow Stamping didn't want a minority to be in a position of authority. Woodrow Stamping Plant wanted to keep minorities at arms length.

When I left Woodrow Stamping Plant on a medical leave in May 2002, there must have been a compliant filed against them by the Department of Civil Rights. Both, the union and the plant's Civil Rights Board at Woodrow Stamping Plant went around the plant trying to sign-up these minority women into skilled trades. As long as I'd worked for Woodrow Stamping Plant, they'd never recruited *any* minority for skilled trades. The skilled trades department was 95% men and 5% women. There was 1 Hispanic female machine repairwomen, 2 female Caucasian electricians, and 2 Black machine repairwomen before I left. All the rest were Caucasian. Believe me—minorities could almost be counted on one hand! This went for both Sarrow Stamping Plant and Woodrow Stamping Plants.

Before I transferred from Sarrow Stamping in 1997 to return to Woodrow, my basic unit (the plant where my seniority first started), I overheard one of the union representatives say they didn't care how many people they hired, they were only going to hire 3% minorities and no more. The company would hire 70 people in one group of employees and there would be about three minorities. As it stands now, if you take a plant tour around Sarrow Stamping or Woodrow Stamping, the majority of people seen are Caucasian. The minorities are the last to be hired and the first to be fired.

When I reached Sarrow Stamping, I anticipated problems going to another plant because of my full-time status. At this point my situation seemed like a hot potato and John Hail didn't want very much to do with what was going on. After I finally decided to transfer to another plant, I couldn't change my mind. If I did, according to contract, my option of going to full-time status would be passed over to the next person in line. My records meant nothing regarding my full-time status at Woodrow Stamping Plant. They said I was part-time and that was all that mattered. If Sarrow Stamping would have hired me part-time, I couldn't be penalized for not moving to another plant. Woodrow Stamping said I was part-time because of their pilfering. They would have said I turned down my opportunity for full-time status. I didn't want Woodrow Stamping Plant to pull a rabbit out of their hat. I just wanted it to be acknowledged I was full-time.

When I moved to Sarrow Stamping Plant, Woodrow Stamping Plant took offense by me knowing they were pilfering my money. Therefore rather then give me my seniority, they though it was best to terminate me. They were really vengeful, spiteful to me, and felt I needed to be taught a lesson. If they didn't return my money, it was no danger I would receive my seniority. For them to hire me as a new part-time employee because I was supposed to be a rehire, proved my speculation was correct. When they hired me as though I'd never worked for the company before, it proved they had plans to continue stealing my money.

When I found out I wasn't going to start at Sarrow Stamping Plant as full-time. I decided to go back to Woodrow Stamping Plant. Sarrow wanted me to start as a part-time employee but those weren't the original conditions of my hire. Woodrow Stamping continued receiving my part-time money and benefits package but that wasn't enough. They wanted it all. When I transferred Woodrow

Stamping Plant, Local 783 wanted to get back at me for implying what they were doing. I wasn't totally sure who was doing the pilfering at the time. All I knew was someone was pilfering my money. I didn't know whether it was the employees working for the company or the company itself. I felt something was wrong with all that happened to me. Neither the company nor the union wanted to give me answers. It was my money disappearing not theirs.

Local 783 was being paid to make sure I didn't get what belonged to me. They wanted me to stand around and allow them to do so. Even though I left Woodrow Stamping Plant, they continued to pilfer my money. It just wasn't right in my face. I had been unable to do anything about the thievery. If I had not started working part-time at Sarrow Stamping Plant, they would have continued to pilfer my full-time benefit package as a full-time employee at Woodrow Stamping Plant.

Instead Woodrow Stamping Plant had to settle for the part-time pay per hour. They'd take anything they could. They continued keeping me at part-time status and they continued to pilfer the part-time benefits. Instead of the full benefit package, they settled for less. The separate files of the other employees at Woodrow Stamping Plant remained open when I transferred to Sarrow Stamping Plant. If Sarrow Stamping had honored Mr. Johnny Hitler's recommendation on transferring me as full-time and rehiring me, there could have been less confusion. I could have remained at Woodrow Stamping Plant.

I was already full-time but only Woodrow Stamping Plant and/or Local 783 had the authority to make it official. Woodrow Stamping Plant and Local 783 were in charge of this situation in terms of seniority and everything else. They were in constant denial of the fact that I was full-time. It didn't matter what the record stated. If the company said I was part-time then that meant I was part-time. It didn't matter what I said nor did. They made it as hard for me as they possibly could have. It would be their own decision when and if they offered me full-time status at a later date. If I declined the opportunity, I would be right back where I started.

Woodrow Stamping Plant continued to pilfer my money and the money of others for at least 6 years. They had the audacity to continue pilfering even when the employees were fired. They would continue to keep an employee on file as though the employee were still employed by the company. They used ghost accounts to receive vacation, personal time, and other benefits of the individual no longer working at the plant. There was no shame in their game. It was all about money and they weren't choosey about how they got it. I was put in a no-win situation and I ultimately had to make a choice.

If Sarrow Stamping Plant changed their mind and hired me as part-time instead of full-time, it would be impossible for me to transfer back to Woodrow Stamping Plant. If I had not found out about my termination, I would not have been able to return to Woodrow Stamping Plant. I would have returned back to Woodrow Stamping with no seniority if I had started working at Sarrow Stamping Plant as a part-time employee. I would not have had any recall rights. Woodrow Stamping Plant continued treating me as though I was part-time and they were enforcing the fact. Since this was the case, what else was it for me to say? They already knew the truth of the matter and Local 783 went along with everything that happened at Woodrow Stamping Plant.

The part-time employees, whose family worked in management at Famous Parts Company—Woodrow Stamping Plant or Local 783, didn't have problems with *their* employment status. Management within Woodrow Stamping Plant and Local 783 looked out for their families and friends. The majority of people hired from the management's staff were looked upon as the next generation of young people being groomed as the company's future management. These people were so blatant that they felt Woodrow Stamping Plant belonged to them personally. This is just how much clout they felt they had over everyone else at Woodrow Stamping Plant. Some of the union members whose children were hired at Famous Parts Company were unable to get hired in Woodrow Stamping Plant because of the controversy with the part-time employees. Those family and friends would be tested at Woodrow Stamping Plant. They would have their physicals at Woodrow Stamping, but would be sent to work for Sarrow Stamping and other area plants.

Rob Nashing, one of my co-workers, was hired at Woodrow Stamping Plant and transferred to Sarrow Stamping Plant. As a result, Woodrow Stamping would be Rob's 'home plant'. Rob Nashing was the son of Paul Nashing, Woodrow Stamping Plant's Committeeman for the Assembly Side of the plant. Why was Paul Nashing's son being hired at Sarrow Stamping as a re-hire when there were people who were part-time hired in the 1970's still awaiting to become full-time?

At the time I left Woodrow Stamping in 1993, many recalled employees still hadn't made full-time status. I'm talking about years here. When I first went to Sarrow Stamping Plant I met Rob Nashing in orientation. He explained how he and his sister were hired over others at Woodrow Stamping. Rob stated his sister went to another Famous Parts Company plant. When his name was called, I asked Rob if he was related to Paul Nashing and he said yes. I thought of how unfair Woodrow Stamping Plant had been in terms of hiring practices.

Here I was being transferred to Sarrow Stamping Plant because there was a problem with my work status. Woodrow Stamping hired young Caucasian men and somehow stopped at my name on the list. It didn't matter whether the errors were conflicting or not. The bottom line was I was indeed full-time when I transferred from Woodrow Stamping Plant. When I transferred in November 1993, I was to have been a *rehire* not a *new hire*. As I was being hired Woodrow made it clear to Sarrow Stamping Plant that I was to be hired as if I had never worked for the company before. I had full medical benefits when I left Woodrow, but I later found out I had no insurance benefits when I made the transfer to Sarrow. This was a cruel act by Woodrow Stamping and Sarrow Plant to cover their pilfering plot.

When other co-workers found out I was being transferred to another plant, they became disturbed by the treatment I received. They were under the same circumstances as I, but yet I was the only one leaving. There were a few people who expressed their dissatisfaction to the union. They wanted to move forward in terms of gaining their seniority too. This included Mazzie Cane and Karol Henderson, both hired in the 70's in the same situation. I grew uncertain as to why others weren't allowed to transfer when there were openings at other plants. Woodrow Stamping claimed Sarrow Stamping had no full-time positions open. But they surely made a position for Rob Nashing, the son and daughter of a Woodrow Stamping Plant's Local 783 Committeeman.

Many part-time employees had been part-time for three years when I left Woodrow Stamping Plant and none of them were intended to be hired full-time. When Local 783 and Woodrow Stamping Plant wanted to hire full-time, they did so at other plants. This way no one would know Woodrow Stamping Plant was hiring and sending the new employees elsewhere. They didn't want anyone within the plant knowing they were hiring because of the part-time employees being on their payroll for years. No one noticed this going on but me—and I knew only after I transferred from Woodrow Stamping Plant.

Mazzie Cane, Karol Henderson, and the others should have been hired before Paul Nashing and me. The only reason I was hired was because they thought I knew more about what they were doing. At this time I was unaware of exactly how much I knew, but they weren't willing to allow me to stick around and find out. When Rob Nashing told me he hired in full-time with Sarrow Stamping Plant but had his physical at Woodrow Stamping, this was strange because of the problems the part-time employees had experienced. They wanted to be transferred to Sarrow Stamping too. They were told no openings were available. Sarrow Stamping was willing to start me off part-time when they hired Rob full-time.

I started orientation on November 15, 1993 and was surprised to find other job openings available at Sarrow Stamping Plant. Woodrow Stamping had lied again. Sarrow Stamping Plant had openings for a few part-time employees for one or two years and the rest were new hiring positions like mine. For Rob Nashing there was no waiting period, no mistakes on paychecks or vacation checks, and no hassles about being hired. This allowed Rob to have the 'home plant' advantage if he chose to return to Woodrow Stamping. He was hired in the midst of controversy with regards to other employees being eager to become full-time.

I'm sure there were many part-time employees at Woodrow Stamping willing to go to Sarrow Stamping and become full-time. I saw how unfairly and uncaringly these employees were being treated. They were treated as second-class citizens. Why would Woodrow Stamping bring part-time people to work full-time from two other plants? Woodrow Stamping Plant would not hire their own part-time employees for two and three years while some stayed part-time in error for 6 years. This had everything to do with the hidden secrets between Local 783 and Woodrow Stamping Plant.

Salma Bears, Labor Relations Representative at Sarrow Stamping, informed me for the second time, I could never return to Woodrow Stamping unless Sarrow burned down. I didn't understand the reasoning behind her re-statement that I could not return. She spoke to me as if I didn't hear what she said the first time we spoke. It sounded like there was something she was trying to embed in my subconscious mind. I thought, "This is the second time she has made this statement". Was she really trying to tell me something else? If not, why another reminder? I knew Woodrow Stamping wouldn't accept me back with open arms. Was there a specific point Salma was trying to make? I knew eventually I'd return to Woodrow Stamping Plant. I decided I wasn't going to lose any sleep over the matter. I knew Woodrow Stamping was my 'home plant' according to the contract. I was aware I had 'home plant' advantage even though Sarrow Stamping hired me as a new full-time employee. In essence, I had only transferred from one plant to work at another. What were Woodrow Stamping and Sarrow Stamping trying to hide?

I had peace of mind at Sarrow Stamping for about 13 days before havoc started showing its ugly face. I was shortly confronted with complications regarding my past brought on by my move to Sarrow Stamping Plant. During my first Thanksgiving holiday, I didn't receive my holiday pay that I was entitled to receive under the contract. I informed Sarrow Stamping's Local 873 within the plant, and I was then referred to Salma in Labor Relations. *(I don't want to confuse Local 783, which is Woodrow Stamping Plant's Local. Sarrow Stamping Plant's Local is 873. Very similar and can easily be confused.)*

I handed Salma my check stub in a way both of us could review what appeared on it. I asked Salma why I hadn't received my holiday pay. This is when Salma informed me I didn't have 90 days worked. Therefore I couldn't get paid. I explained to Salma I was receiving holiday pay prior to transferring from Woodrow Stamping Plant. I also explained to Salma since I had worked as a part-time employee for three years, I had actually worked more than 90 working days and was still entitled to my holiday pay according to contract. I told Salma, "If you were part-time, started receiving holiday pay when you're hired full-time, and located in another facility, you are entitled to receive your same benefits. You're not subjected to work another probationary period before receiving your holiday pay".

Salma left the calculating of hours earned up to me to prove I should have been paid Thanksgiving holiday pay. I'm sure the three computers in Labor Relations should have given Salma the information needed to assure her I should have been paid. They counted on me not having the proof to establish my probationary period. One thing is for sure—if I didn't have my check stubs, I would not have been paid.

I reviewed all my check stubs, calculated my hours and days worked, and gave the information to Salma. After careful review, Salma made a statement and then began calculating all hours worked. Labor Relations reviewed it and it was about a week later I was paid for the Thanksgiving holiday. When I received my check, there was a separate check attached to an adjustment shortage form. The form was coded as a day of work but not paid as holiday pay. I was concerned about what had taken place.

I saw this incident as a continuation of a cover up. My payroll record from Woodrow Stamping should have reflected my pay history if Salma obtained it from the computer. All Salma had to do was verify this information at Woodrow Stamping Plant in the computer system. There was no reason why I had to experience more complications. I didn't find out the real reason until much later.

I had actually been terminated after transferring from Woodrow Stamping Plant. I didn't find this piece of information as a true fact until I returned to Woodrow Stamping Plant, my 'home plant', in 1997. I had assumed I was terminated. Reason being—when I talked to the person who restored my health benefits at the Service Center of Famous Parts Company, she stated I was hired at Sarrow Stamping Plant as though I had never worked at any other Famous Parts

Company Plant before. According to her information, I had not even worked at Woodrow Stamping Plant. When I returned to Woodrow Stamping Plant in 1997, the computer was left on when Labor Relations Supervisor, Verlinda Moose, called me to the Labor Relations Office. I read in Woodrow Stamping Plant's computer that I was "terminated" on November 13, 1993. I couldn't believe that Woodrow Stamping Plant had me terminated and hired me as a new employee at Sarrow Stamping Plant when I was supposed to be a rehire. On November 15, 1993 Sarrow Stamping Plant hired me as though I had no prior history working with the company and I had just left Woodrow, the plant in which I had seniority for three years.

20

CRISTA WAS REALLY FIRED

It was in Woodrow Stamping Plant's computer that I had been terminated. I was told I was terminated in November 1993, but in 1997 I actually saw it for myself. I had not worked a month at Sarrow Stamping Pant. I was told by the Employees' Service Center that Famous Parts Company, Woodrow Stamping Plant had terminated me.

Salma, Labor Relations Representative, as well as Local 783, Woodrow Stamping Plant and others, were aware of the circumstances they did nothing to help me. I wasn't to find out about this until after I became officially full-time on Sarrow Stamping Plant's roster. I didn't think it should have been a problem to contact Woodrow Stamping to get the necessary information regarding this matter. I was tired and decided to let Woodrow Stamping Plant and Sarrow Stamping Plant handle the predicament. It didn't matter as long as I received payment for my Thanksgiving holiday. I was tired of the circumstances surrounding my work status. I felt I needed a rest because I knew the fight was just getting started when Sarrow Stamping Plant started my seniority as November 15, 1993.

I had another unexpected surprise when I became the legal guardian of my grandson. I was trying to add him to my medical insurance. I contacted Famous Parts Company's Service Center for Employees to have him added to my medical insurance. The representative I spoke with stated I no longer had medical insurance coverage and my policy expired when I came from Woodrow Stamping Plant. I was told my policy had expired in December 1993. This was cognate to when I was hired at Famous Parts Company—Sarrow Stamping Plant. Woodrow Stamping Plant deliberately sought out to deceive me when they hired me as a new employee as though I'd never worked for the company before. I became very angry and disturbed.

I informed Famous Parts Employees' Company Service Center's Representative that I transferred from Woodrow Stamping on November 13, 1993 and started working at Sarrow Stamping Plant November 15, 1993. How was this possible? I told the representative, "I wasn't hired off the street". I stressed to the representative I was to have been a rehire not a new hire. I became furious at what I was hearing. There weren't any lapses in days worked between the days I transferred from Woodrow Stamping Plant to Sarrow Stamping. The representative I spoke with informed me she would contact both plants and get back with me on the matter.

After I hung up, I called Sarrow Stamping and spoke with Salma, knowing the representative from Famous Parts Employees' Company Service Center would speak to her. I figured this woman would contact me in a few hours and I didn't expect her to contact Salma right away. I told Salma of the incident. She was a bit agitated and had a sense of not knowing what to do. In fact, she didn't even know what to say.

I started wondering what had Sarrow Stamping and Woodrow Stamping gotten me into this time by not admitting I was full-time. They were the reason I was having these complicated problems regarding my work status. I now knew the real reason I was sent to Sarrow Stamping. Woodrow Stamping's sole purpose was to hide my actual seniority date. I recognized this when no one ever wanted to admit my work status. I was considered full-time at Woodrow Stamping Plant and it was no "error". In all actuality I was full-time and the Controller at Woodrow Stamping was transferring the money I didn't receive into their special account.

My seniority status was said to be an "error" for three years without corrections. They took monies that should have been directed to me while paying me part-time pay per hour. I was asking far too many questions and people started believing me. They wanted nothing to do with the consequences of being caught but they didn't have a problem pilfering in the name of Woodrow Stamping Plant. It didn't matter if they received any money personally, directly, or indirectly.

Nurse Tootie had to look at the charges she faced: embezzlement, falsifying government documents, and falsifying medical documents. She was guilty of all the above. It would be a blessing for her to sit in jail and think about how many lies she told on employees and how many diagnoses she changed in the name of Woodrow Stamping. She needed to think of how many people she had unjustly terminated when they became aware of their money being pilfered. There were others involved that lost their jobs too. This is why they became so nervous. They entered this pilfering ring at their own risk. If they were caught pilfering, they would have been terminated just as Nurse Tootie was. The people involved couldn't take the chance of anyone finding out what they were doing. It could be very costly to them as far as their jobs and families were concerned, not to mention jail time.

What other reason could Woodrow Stamping Plant have to allow their part-time employees remain part-time when they actually needed additional manpower? This is when Woodrow Stamping Plant went outside to hire so nothing would be discovered. The union and company thought no one was paying attention to what was happening. The employees were conscious of what was happening but thought they could do nothing in their defense. Many didn't know where to go for help and others thought it wasn't worth their time. They didn't want to interfere with any chance of them not becoming full-time as soon as possible. The many pieces of the puzzle began to fit.

I had a few choice words for Salma when I spoke to her. She was angry insisting on not knowing what was going on at Woodrow Stamping. When I spoke to Salma I also wanted to know why I was hired as a new employee instead of a rehire. Salma then asked me to hold on the telephone line. When Salma returned to the phone she was apparently speaking to someone in the background and hadn't completed her conversation before returning to the phone. I heard Salma say, "I'm not going to lose *my* job". She stated she would take care of the problem with regards to my insurance and that she did! The representative from Famous Parts Employees' Company Service Center contacted me informing me my insurance would resume on December 16, 1993 but my seniority yet stayed November 15, 1993.

I started feeling the stress from the pressure. I had to get a grip on the lies and deceit that apparently both plants were subjecting me to. It wasn't just one plant I was in conflict with. Now there were two plants. I'm not sure if Sarrow Stamping hired me as a favor to Woodrow Stamping Plant. This could have been the case because the lies and deceit didn't end at Woodrow Stamping. They just seemed to follow me to Sarrow Stamping and continued causing more hassles for me.

Shortly after I was transferred to Sarrow Stamping Plant, Tarry Johnson, Labor Relations Supervisor, received a promotion to the Executive Branch of the Company's headquarters. Tarry Johnson became officially involved in the pilfering schemes taking place at the Executive Branch of the Company. Tarry Johnson stayed there for a few years and when he left the headquarters, he was sent to Woodrow Stamping Plant. I'm not sure if this was a step down or not, but he returned to the very same plant having everything to do with his promotion. In 2002, Tarry arrived at Woodrow Stamping Plant as Head of Safety &

Security. It seemed to be a pattern for anyone who handled my case to be deeply involved in this thief scheme.

Sarrow Stamping Plant knew I was full-time but they had to cooperate with Woodrow Stamping. Sarrow Stamping had to have known there was a problem if the Medical Department noticed it was strange I was having a complete physical. My holiday pay was always adjusted for days worked which I wasn't paid for. I had the problem with my medical insurance that had been cancelled and eventually restored. My direct deposits to my bank account suddenly stopped because of my termination. The reasoning behind my direct deposit issue was never explained.

Labor Relations couldn't and didn't answer my questions to my satisfaction. Salma just told me to go to the bank and have my direct deposits started over again. When I asked Salma why this was happening she couldn't explain why. All these incidents were somewhat out of the ordinary, and as a whole should have stuck out like a sore thumb. It really didn't take a brain surgeon to know something rather shady was going on. The time and effort to prove a cover up was truly going to be a challenge. There were so many forces working against me. Local 783, Woodrow Stamping, and Sarrow Stamping all became involved in the mess together.

In December 1993 I encountered another set of circumstances surrounding my Christmas bonus and holiday pay. Salma met with me in regards to me not being paid for the first week of January 1994. She told me I had to apply at the Michigan Employment Security Commissions Office (MESC) to receive my Christmas vacation pay. She told me this after my returning from Christmas vacation, when she should have informed me of this *before* returning.

Something was wrong. I was aware I was to be paid for the holidays leading to the New Year holiday, but I was not. That meant the termination wasn't withdrawn. My insurance was given back, but my hiring was yet November 15, 1993. Now I was being told Sarrow Stamping couldn't pay my Christmas vacation or my first paycheck of the year and I'd have to get them from Woodrow Stamping Plant. I was terminated from Woodrow Stamping Plant and I hadn't received my 90 days as a full-time employee at Sarrow Stamping Plant. Because of this reason, I was told I wasn't entitled to Christmas and New Year pay. If Woodrow Stamping Plant had transferred me instead of terminating me, I wouldn't have been going through these problems.

Salma instructed me on how to apply at the Michigan Employment Security Commission to obtain my pay for the first week of 1994. I filed a claim and was later denied payment. Woodrow Stamping didn't respond to the MESC request.

I explained to the MESC representative how I had transferred from one plant to another and how I was receiving my holiday pay before leaving Woodrow Stamping Plant. I didn't quite understand why I wasn't paid for the first week of the New Year for the Christmas holiday. The MESC representative, who assisted me in trying to obtain my money, stated they received no response once again from Woodrow Stamping. This was the second time she'd tried to contact Woodrow Stamping Plant.

The representative said they were looking back at my payment record. She didn't quite understand why my payments were so low according to the code I was listed under in her computer. Woodrow Stamping Plant never did respond to the MESC. The Michigan Employment Security Commission paid me for the first week of the year 1994 based on payments received. Had I not been working at another plant, maybe Woodrow Stamping and Local 783 would have accomplished what they set out to do—fire me. If I had been terminated, I would not have been paid for that week originally. Woodrow Stamping almost got away with this termination—at least on paper.

With all these problems, I still hadn't heard any information regarding my grievance filed in June 1993. I called Local 783's Committee Room on the mezzanine floor at Woodrow Stamping Plant. The only thing I received was the run around. Local 783 had no intention on settling my grievance. I decided to write Mr. Johnny Hilter at the Executive Branch of the Union. The letter dated December 29, 1993 stated:

"Dear Mr. Hilter:

I am writing this letter because I am in need of some information. I talked to Jess McGregor, Local 783 President, and John Hail, Local 783 Plant Chairman on December 6, 1993. I talked to John Hail first in reference to my grievance filed in June 1993. He informed me it was no longer in McGregor's hands and that my grievance would be heard Wednesday, December 8, 1993. Since I am no longer working at Woodrow Stamping, I expected to receive a phone call or a letter informing me of the outcome. I would have called earlier, but there was a time the union was to have met on this same grievance and the meeting never took place. I haven't received any information. Therefore I called Mr. McGregor on December 13, 1993 and was informed he would not be back in his office until January 3, 1994.

I stated the reason I was calling and expressed my wanting to know where I could obtain information concerning the outcome of the meeting regarding my grievance. The lady on the phone told me to contact John Hail because he would have some answers. I called John Hail because my phone had been ringing constantly with employees at Woodrow Stamping expressing their interest of the outcome. There were nine other people listed on the grievance and they too, were interested in knowing where the grievance stood. They also contacted John Hail and he refused to give them any information regarding this grievance. I informed them I heard nothing of the outcome. I later called John Hail on December 13, 1993 and he informed me the grievance had gone to the next stage and you'd be handling it as of now. He informed me they would be meeting with the company on my behalf.

I truly can understand the many procedures involved, but I haven't been notified by phone or by mail. I have to justly express my anger because this is a business matter and it should be handled as such. Since this matter pertains to me, I feel I shouldn't be kept in the dark with regards to what the results are. John Hail told me you would be contacting me and as of yet I've heard nothing. I'm only seeking information with regards to my grievance filed. I would like this subject matter to come to an end once and for all. If you are in charge as of now, will you please inform me?

I thought coming to Sarrow Stamping would give me a clean slate, only to find errors are still being made beyond my control. I was told the changes would be made when and if the grievance is settled. But until then, holiday pay is restricted to only Monday and Friday until I obtain my 90 days. I would like all this controversy put behind me and this can happen only when the grievance is settled." I said thank you and signed the letter.

21

NEICY'S AND ROSIE'S HELP WAS APPRECIATED

One particular day in December 1993, I had a problem with my car. Although I made it to work, my car died in the parking lot of the plant. When my car didn't start I turned it off and tried to start it once again. I knew I had a serious problem when it still wouldn't start. I went into the plant and informed my supervisor I needed to make some telephone calls to have my car towed. He granted me the privilege. I talked to my co-workers focusing mainly on the people living in Monroe, Michigan where I worked. I asked if they knew anyone in the area who could repair and tow my car. I was in hopes I could get it back that afternoon. I worked the afternoon shift and I figured I would get my car back before leaving work that evening, but it didn't work that way.

My co-worker, Rosie, and I were hired the same day at Sarrow Stamping Plant. She informed me there was a repair shop on Elm Street that did towing and repairing. When I contacted them after the car was towed, they were unable to tell me the problem with my car that same evening. I had to wait until that following day just to get an answer as to what the mechanical problem was. This is when I realized I had to find a way home for the next few days. My co-worker, Barbara, worked on the same line I did. She lived on Wyoming Street in Detroit, not even 10 minutes from my home. I asked Barbara for a ride home and told her I would pay her. She said she'd be glad to take me home. While on my way home, I asked Barbara if I could ride home with her for a few days since we were going the same way. I didn't have a problem getting to work. Barbara agreed to take me home in the evenings but only followed through with taking me home *one* evening.

The evening after my first ride home with Barbara, one hour before it was time to get off work, Barbara told me she could not take me home. I was annoyed because Barbara had seen me on the line all afternoon and didn't say anything to

173

the contrary about being unable to take me home. I became angry. This gave me little or no time to get someone else to take me home that evening. I could have even called home and made arrangements for someone to drive to Monroe, Michigan and pick me up. I could have found someone going my way. There were many people who worked in Monroe, Michigan and lived in Detroit. I didn't know many people personally, at the time because I'd only worked at Sarrow Stamping for less a month. If I had known in time, I wouldn't have had a problem with Barbara's waiting to the last minute. It caused me to have no time to prepare for a ride home.

I decided to ask Neicy, who lived in Monroe if she knew anyone else that might be willing to take me home or near home. All I needed was to be dropped off at the Livernois Avenue exit on Interstate-75. From there I could catch the bus the remainder of the way. Neicy said she would get back with me. Meanwhile, I asked a Caucasian woman named Vickie, who lived in Eastpointe, Michigan, if she would drop me off. Vickie said she'd gladly take me home after work.

When Barbara found out I had a way home, she went out of her way and told Vickie not to take me home. She said I lived in a bad neighborhood. She told Vickie there were people hanging out on the corner selling drugs and that drug addicts were on the corner too. Barbara's lie sounded very persuasive. Barbara told Vickie, "If I were you I wouldn't take her home because of the neighborhood". I understood Vickie not wanting to drop me off in the city of Detroit because of Detroit's bad reputation (especially from Monroe, Michigan's perspective). Barbara scared Vickie by stating how dangerous it was for White women to be in Detroit's Black neighborhoods late at night. Vickie became apprehensive due to what she heard from Barbara. She believed Barbara because she had taken me home the night before.

Neicy said, I'll take you take me home. She said when we get off work she would pick up a friend and then we'd be on our way. I agreed and after work Neicy did as she said. She refused the money I offered her and looked at me like she was rather offended. She said she thought taking me home was the right thing to do. I thanked Neicy for her very unselfish deed because I greatly appreciated it. I became closer to Neicy as a friend after the ride home that winter evening.

I usually drove 90-miles going to and from work each day. I drove 45 minutes or more, depending on the weather conditions. I found myself driving this distance with tired and weary eyes on many occasions. There were many days the miles seemed like I was driving a thousand. The summer months weren't quite as bad unless I worked an 11 or 12-hour shift. I worked at Sarrow Stamping many long hours for three years, not realizing I was away from home quite a bit.

The afternoon following my ride home with Neicy, she informed many employees at work of how Barbara lied in order to keep me from having a way home. Barbara never said much to me after that. Neicy and I discussed why a person would do such a thing and all we could come up with was maybe she was jealous or intimidated for some crazy reason. Barbara's actions were insensitive and spiteful. There was no valid reason why Barbara behaved the way she did. I was only asking a favor, and she agreed because she lived in the same area. I have no explanation as to why she lied to Vicky, the White young lady that agreed to take me home. Afterall I hadn't been at Sarrow long enough to really know this lady. After that, the matter was never spoken of, but I'll never forget it.

One January afternoon in 1994, I was in the locker room. A few women were lounging in the break area when my co-worker Rosie asked me about my experiences at Woodrow Stamping. She was interested in what she had heard and wanted first hand information regarding Local 783 and Woodrow Stamping. Rosie was curious because she was hired full-time when I was hired and heard bits of information regarding my situation. She wanted to know what really happened.

Rosie was good friends with Ima, another one of my co-workers. Rosie and Ima were much older than I. Ima was a Caucasian woman waiting to retire with 30 years of seniority. She only had a few years left to go and I knew she wasn't going to stay any longer than she had to. She had one child and her plans were to move to Florida to be close to her daughter. Rosa, Ima, and I all would meet at the same place on break time for small talk.

One day Ima suggested I wrote a book about my experiences while employed at Famous Parts Company. I told her that was my plan. In fact I had already started organizing notes for this book at that time in 1994. I felt there were many people who had experienced similar unpleasant treatment while employed with Famous Parts Company institutions. I was aware of many persons discussing the discrimination, harassment, pilfering, and retaliation dished out by both plants. I knew as long as there were dishonest people lining their pockets and covering a trail, there were people whom were being taken advantage of.

Ima always said she looked forward to reading my book, and at that time I felt it would only take about two years to complete. Since Ima would be retiring in two years and moving to Florida, Rosie was to have informed Ima when the book was completed. Rosie and Ima stayed in contact after Ima retired. In 1997 when I returned to Woodrow Stamping Plant, I lost touch with both women.

Before our loss of contact, Rosie told me of how she had worked for a company in Monroe, Michigan before working for Woodrow Stamping. This company closed their doors without notice although employees received severance pay. Rosie and a few others forfeited their severance pay, which they had received from the company when they closed their doors. They obtained a lawyer and their plans were to initiate a class-action lawsuit against the company. There were some questions as to whether the union worked along with this company to help close the doors permanently or not.

The union apparently knew the plant was closing and the employees had no idea until they became unemployed. The employees were irritated according to Rosie. She said the people that forfeited their severance pay hired Attorney Hdith to represent them. Mr. Hdith's law firm interceded on their behalf. Rosie told me she was waiting any day for a settlement in her case and asked if I was interested in obtaining a good lawyer. I told Rosie I wasn't quite interested in a lawyer yet. There were still other avenues I wanted to try before doing so. I took Mr. Hdith's business card just incase things didn't work out as planned in the future. I wasn't ready to pay any out of pocket expenses if I didn't have to. *But later down the line, as we know, Mr. Hdith took my case before his death and Mr. John Bushe taking it over.*

The only person who had a sympathetic ear was Mr. Johnny Hilter at the Executive Branch of the Union who represented Local 783. Mr. Hilter later left his position at the Executive Branch of the Union after he helped me transfer to Sarrow Stamping Plant. But before he left, he wished me luck in obtaining my rights as an employee. I'm sure Mr. Hilter knew the problems I was facing. As it stood, I needed all the luck in the world.

22

ALL DECISIONS MADE BY THE NATIONAL LABOR RELATIONS BOARD WERE THE SAME

I went back to the National Labor Relations Board after I transferred to Sarrow Stamping Plant in an effort to receive a true copy of the grievance I filed. I was requesting the grievance in its entirety. They didn't give me a copy before I left and I didn't trust Local 783 and Woodrow Stamping Plant in what they were going to do next. I wanted verification that my grievance had been discussed and how they reached their decision on two occasions before and after transferring from Woodrow Stamping Plant.

I really didn't expect to receive a third determination of the grievance because that wasn't what I wanted. Local 783 knew exactly what I wanted but chose to lie over and over again. I was actually given nothing of what I asked for—not even the right to participate in the grievance procedures. They never seemed to have any information regarding the grievance. Nor did they want my input.

In the file, there was no paperwork regarding the Public Review Board. Nor did it say the grievance had been to the Umpire stage of the grievance procedure. It was a lie when Local 783 stated my grievance went to the Umpire stage in order to get matters resolved. I did not want a couple sentences on a piece of paper. It was impossible for a grievance to be negotiated at the Umpire level and with the Public Review Board with no paper trail.

I and everyone else involved in the grievance process, were aware I was full-time. It was acknowledged in July 1992, but Woodrow Stamping Plant wanted to continue taking the money allocated to me from 1990 until 1993. They continued to pilfer my money as they continued to tell me I was part-time. Woodrow Stamping Plant just terminated me and Sarrow Stamping Plant hired me as though I had never worked for the company. If you say this action wasn't with intent, then I would clearly have to differ. I really couldn't understand the grounds my grievance was denied upon—and this decision was even upheld by the National Labor Relations Board. I was angry at the fact that I was denied access to the grievance procedure each time I would request to take part in the grievance hearings. They didn't want me to participate because I knew the truth. They were aware I knew they were pilfering my money. The procedures that were supposed to have been followed were not.

Local 783 had the audacity to become angry with me. At first I was only asking for my seniority date on record. I expected Local 783 to give me an explanation as to why wouldn't Woodrow Stamping Plant give me my seniority on record. They knew I was full-time. They didn't give me an answer or change my seniority date to my original date of hire. For this reason, Woodrow Stamping Plant and Local 783 weren't willing to give me any paperwork I requested regarding this grievance. Therefore I filed another claim in October 1995. I tried prior to get the copies of the section that Local 783 stated went to the Public Review Board. I wanted to read their decision and opinion surrounding this grievance, but was denied that too. My October 1995 statement was made with the National Labor Relations Board, Case #7-CB 10782:

"I Crista Carrie, being first duly sworn upon my oath hereby state:

I have been given assurances by an agent of the National Labor Relations Board that this affidavit will be considered confidential by the United States Government and will not be disclosed unless it becomes necessary for the government to produce the affidavit in connecting with a formal proceeding.

I reside at 4366 Wills Street, Detroit, Michigan 48210. The Famous Parts Company—Sarrow Stamping Plant in Monroe, Michigan employs me. I have been a member of Local 783 since I've worked for Famous Parts Company. I started with Famous Parts Company on September 28, 1990 at Woodrow Stamping Plant. The initial hire-in records show I was hired as a full-time employee. However while at Woodrow Stamping Plant I only worked as a part-time employee.

What I really sought to grieve was my original seniority date according to record. I had full-time benefits and was paid part-time pay per-hour in an effort to save themselves from the lies. They were obviously getting out of control. I wanted them to stop pilfering my money and allow me to receive the money allocated to me. I received vacation pay and paid personal days while Woodrow Stamping Plant deducted the money from me and put it in separate accounts. While they were taking my money back through adjustments after it was given to me, the money never went back to the company. This is why I was asking for my full-time employment status. My check stub never reflected the money as being paid back to the company, making me believe the money was being pilfered. *I knew part-time employees were not entitled to receive these benefits nor were they entitled to profit sharing and performance bonuses.*

I was transferred to Sarrow Stamping Plant on November 15, 1993. Johnny Hilter, of Woodrow Stamping Plant's Executive Branch of the Union, told me there was a full-time position available in Monroe, Michigan. I accepted the position rather than remain at Woodrow Stamping Plant as a full-time employee without full-time benefits. I would have preferred to stay at Woodrow Stamping Plant if they would have given me full-time pay. I already had full-time benefits. Sarrow Stamping Plant hired me as full-time. I was treated as a new employee with a new seniority date of November 15, 1993. A few weeks later, I found that I had lost all my prior seniority and accumulated benefit rights.

This case arises out of the facts and circumstances involved in case #7-CB-9966. The NLRB's complaint was issued on February 9, 1994 regarding noncompliance. The NLRB approved a settlement in this case on March 7, 1994. I signed that settlement agreement on February 17, 1994. The settlement required the union to provide me with a copy of the grievance filed on my behalf in 1993 ..."

I received a copy of the grievance by letter dated February 7, 1994 prior to signing the settlement. The package of material I received from the union indicated that in December 1993, Woodrow Stamping Plant denied the grievance at the third step on December 22, 1993. The grievance was appealed to the Umpire but there were no facts proving the grievance reached the Umpire. As far as I knew, the grievance was at the Umpire stage of the grievance procedure when I got the materials from the union in February 1994.

I was very clear of what I wanted when I communicated it to Plant Chairman, John Hail, prior to the second complaint being filed when I left Woodrow Stamping Plant. I really didn't have proof I filed a grievance. Local 783 could have said I never filed a grievance at all. This is one of the main concerns I had after transferring to Sarrow Stamping Plant. Each time I would contact the

NLRB, Local 783 would give me another grievance determination. This told me they didn't keep the last decision they sent me. It seemed Local 783 should not have had a problem keeping track of the paperwork regarding my grievance.

I figured the grievance never went to the Umpire Level or the Public Review Board even though the logo stamp stated otherwise. They had no paper trail of the grievance being at any stage. Wouldn't you think if a grievance had gone to the Umpire level someone would have a copy of the results? They would give me no more than three pieces of paper from the first stage and a photocopy cover sheet stating the grievance went to the Public Review Board. I only filed one grievance. Therefore there should only be one determination, not three. Local 783 and Woodrow Stamping Plant never could get the names and dates correct. Woodrow Stamping Plant couldn't get the same person to sign the grievance deposition. Each time the grievance was signed, a new person signed the grievance. There were three different determinations signed by three different people for *one* grievance. This grievance was one big lie. Local 783 never filed this grievance and the Executive Branch of the Company and the Union knowingly stood behind this lie.

If the union didn't file this grievance, why didn't anyone help me? These organizations were aware the grievance wasn't filed and never went to the Public Review Board. All these lies were told in an effort to deceive. Why didn't my attorney help me? When I tried to file suite, why didn't the judge hearing my case appoint me a lawyer when I requested one? Why did he throw my case out of court in a Summary Judgment when my case had merit? He was aware that the CEO's of the Company and the Union didn't represent me and he blocked every effort to keep my case from going forward. Don't you think all these circumstances were very unethical?

I've been speaking of the Umpire who's supposed to serve as a mediator. This is a person who tries to help in making a decision when a grievance can't be settled in the earlier stages. He evaluates the argument and makes recommendations based on the facts surrounding the grievance. If there is something that should have or could have been handled between the local union and the company, then he sends the grievance back to them to settle at the local level. I always had complications with all of the above regarding this grievance. For the most part there was no information stating the grievance went to the Umpire. There were other problems I incurred and couldn't get any straight answers. Explanations of these problems and resolutions will be elaborated on in further chapters.

I want you the reader, to evaluate the circumstances and come to your own conclusion as to what happened with all my complaints against Local 783 and

Woodrow Stamping Plant. How did they work together in a cover-up involving unethical conduct? The last and final copy of the grievance was given to me when I filed the last claim against Local 783 with the National Labor Relations Board in 1995. You will read more on this in later chapters. I went to the National Labor Relations Board and the Department of Civil Rights around April 1993. I tried to file charges against Woodrow Stamping and Local 783. I was later called into the NLRB for a deposition of what happened. I had been working at Sarrow Stamping for two years when I received a certified letter from the U.S. Equal Employment Opportunity Commission stating:

"The Detroit District Office is bringing charges for Crista Carrie (charging party) vs. Famous Parts Company (respondent).

Under the authority vested in me by the Commission, I issue the following determination as to the merits of the subject charge filed under Title VII of the Civil Rights Act of 1964 as amended. All requirements for coverage have been met. The charging party alleges being discriminated against in violation of Title VII and was unfairly denied vacation pay and performance bonuses because of her race: Black.

Examination of the evidence reveals that charging party and 26 other employees in charging party's job classification were improperly paid vacation and/or bonuses. The mistake was found and the vacation pay was deducted from all employees' checks. Both Black and Whites employees were part of the mistake and were required to repay the money they received. Based on this analysis I have determined the evidence obtained during the investigation does not establish a violation of the stature. This determination concludes the processing of this charge. This letter will be the only notice of dismissal and the only notice of the charging party's right to sue that will be sent by the commission.

The charging party may only pursue this matter further by filing suit against the respondent(s) named in the charges in federal district court within 90 days of the charging party's receipt of this letter. Therefore if suit is not filed within this 90-day period the charging party's right to sue will be lost."

There was also an enclosure with the above letter that was an information sheet on 'Filing Suit in Federal District Court". The letter read:

"*Private Suit Right under Title VII and the Americans with Disabilities Act (ADA)*:
The determination and dismissal becomes effective on the date you receive it. To pursue this matter further you must file a lawsuit against the respondent named in the charges in U.S. District Court within 90 days of that date. Once this 90-day period is over, your right to sue will be lost. Filing the notice is not sufficient. A court complaint must contain a short statement of the facts of your case, which shows that you are entitled to relief.

Your lawsuit must be filed in a U.S. District Court. Generally suits are brought in the state where the alleged unlawful practice occurred, but in some cases can be brought where relevant employment would have been or where the respondent has its main office.

Attorney Representation under Title VII and the ADA:
If you cannot afford or have been unable to obtain a lawyer to represent you, the U.S. District Court having jurisdiction in your case may at its discretion assist you in obtaining a lawyer. If you plan to ask the U.S. District Court to help you find a lawyer, you must make this request of the court in the form of manner it requires. You should make this request well before the end of the time period mentioned above. A request for representation does not relieve you of the obligation to file a lawsuit within this 90-day period. You may contact the EEOC if you have any questions about your legal rights including advice on which U.S. District Court can hear your case.

Notification of Suit and Destruction of File:
If you file suit please send a copy of your court complaint to this office. (Generally the EEOC's rules call for your file to be destroyed two years from this date.) By complying with this request you can be assured the file will be retained for the stated period. If you file suit please notify this office when the lawsuit is resolved."

As a result I received a 'right to sue' letter and ultimately I handed the letter over to my lawyer who was supposed to represent me in this case. The National Labor Relations Board (NLRB) had already made their decision as to whether any wrong doing on the behalf of Local 783 and Woodrow Stamping Plant occurred. It's ironic that Woodrow Stamping was not being held accountable for their criminal activity. It didn't matter what documentation you had. Woodrow Stamping ran the plant on total corruption on a daily basis and would pay anyone crossing their path to keep their dirty little secret.

Thus far I have tried to get the Department of Labor involved but they secretly walked into Woodrow Stamping, reviewed the records and took money/favors under the table. If my lawyer and the NLRB found something, I'm sure the Department of Labor found something as well. I know the investigator could have done something but instead he turned his head as though he saw nothing.

The <u>first determination</u> had no date given for Grievance Number H-135381. It stated: "The grievant (Carrie) is a part-time employee and in the absence of any violation of Appendix-K, this complaint is without merit and is accordingly denied". The <u>second determination</u> dated December 20, 1993 and the grievance had the same number RB-7210 H135381, although each had a different determination:

"This instant grievance filed on June 3, 1993 claims for an unspecified period of time employees should somehow be recognized as full-time status to specific part-time employees. The aggrieved has been employed on the customary part-time schedule with other exceptional periods being at the discretion of the parties (e.g. deer season). The grievance has been afforded all rights pursuant to Appendix K of the Master Agreement. The specific adjustment requested is denied. It is further noted that the grievant has transferred to full-time status since the filing of this grievance …" Employee Relations signed and dated this determination December 8, 1993 and John Hail signed on December 20, 1993.

The <u>last and final determination</u> I received stated in regards to Grievance #RB-7210:

"In full and final settlement without prejudice or precedent for any issue, grievance records shall be reviewed by Body and Assembly Operations Labor Relations Office in conjunction with a further review of several employees hired to full-time status on June 20, 1994. Supervisor of Labor Relations and the Local Union President will implement this review. This review shall establish/adjust seniority dates for the grievance. It is further noted that employees in the June 20, 1994 hiring status including some of the specific "grievant" may also become eligible for adjustments in performance bonuses for the year ending in 1994." Attached et.al. This letter was signed by John Hail on January 5, 1995.

The discussion dated December 5, 1995 after my transfer to Sarrow Stamping Plant, had everything to do with the violation of contract laws. When I filed the grievance, Local 783 should have negotiated obtaining all of my back pay and my original seniority date of September 28, 1990. My employment record showed this date as my original seniority date. Why wouldn't Woodrow Stamping Plant give me the date on record? It was already established and substantiated by Woodrow Stamping Plant. They were just being spiteful because I knew what they were doing. They were proving a point that I wasn't going to get anything whether I had it coming or not. They had the power to make the call.

In the last grievance dated January 5, 1995 the grievant should've received a performance bonus going back to year ending 1994. I never received any of this back pay. Nor did I receive my original seniority date. I should have received bonuses and other benefits from 1990 thru 1993 when I was transferred to Sarrow Stamping Plant. But instead Woodrow Stamping Plant terminated me unjustly. Some did eventually receive some of their back pay, but I never did. I guess Woodrow Stamping Plant and Local 783 showed me just how powerful they really were.

23

SUPERVISION IN THE PLANT

There were male minorities and no women in supervision at Woodrow or Sarrow Stamping Plant when I arrived. I would listen to the skilled tradesmen talking and at times I would join in on their conversations. I would talk with them giving my opposing views. They would stress how they didn't want a woman in supervision telling them what to do. It was okay for a man to do so, but not a woman.

I would always tell the men they made it bad for the women by making babies with the women and not taking care of their children. That is the reason some women had to enter the work force. Someone had to care for the children. If the women weren't self-supportive, their children would starve. I would stress there were men who had never even seen their children, less known give the child's mother support. It is only fair that the women got sufficient jobs with sufficient pay to support themselves and their families.

The money at the plant was great and you didn't have to "rob Peter to pay Paul" in order to support your family. More men need to be responsible for their lost and unwanted children, in which they discard as they would a piece of paper in the wastebasket. They no longer want anything to do with their child/ren or child's mother for one reason or another. These men yet have a responsibility for caring for the children they produce. Many of these men fail to pay support for their children, even as they were working a good paying job at Famous Parts Company.

Women's liberation (as they call it) would not have been an issue before the women entered in the workforce full force. Children need food to survive and a place to live. If the men didn't pay to help support their children, women were forced to work. Not all women have children, but even those women need to support themselves when men stop being the sole supporter of the household. Women wanted equal pay for working the same jobs as men in order to support their families. There came a point where women had to take the means necessary to support their family whether a father was involved or not. When women started working in the plant, men felt they should not have been there. Men had to get use to the fact women were in the workplace to stay and nothing could be done to stop the pursuit of their survival.

What I said to them went in one ear and out of the other. These men were from the old school where women stayed at home and the men went out to work. Some men understood, but the majority of them were not pleased. These men always felt they were in control and wanted to control what women did in and out of the workplace. It was beneath them to answer to a woman because some of these men had serious ego problems. They were proud in what they were doing and they weren't losing any sleep at night because of their actions. If they were put in that same position, they wouldn't want to be treated in the way that they treated Ronda Smith, the newly hired Caucasian female supervisor.

This woman was treated so badly by the upper management and the men of skilled trades. When a woman came to supervise them they did nothing in assisting to make her job tolerable. Men running the plant sided with other men. This is the reason the men at Sarrow Stamping were allowed to get away with what they were doing to Ronda, who was in training. After she left Sarrow Stamping they didn't get another woman supervisor until 1996. All this happened from 1993 to 1997 and the men's behavior was accepted the entire time.

Janet, the second woman put in supervision at Sarrow Stamping Plant, had a little easier time since Ronda paved her way. Surprisingly this time the supervisor was a Black woman. The skilled tradesmen didn't like her authority, but they were beginning to be more accepting. These men gave her a hard time, but not to the extent as they did Ronda. I guess the skilled tradesmen accepted women were there to stay so they gave her somewhat of a break. It wasn't because they wanted to accept the women. It was because they were basically forced to.

As a result, Janet got a break from some of the skilled tradesmen but then caught pure *hell* from management. The discrimination was the biggest factor endorsed by management. I saw Janet shed many tears. She was clearly stressed and depressed from the pressure of being a supervisor when she first started. Not only did she have problematic experiences concerning her sex, but because of her race too. She had two strikes against her.

Dave, a young Black male hired in management, also experienced great agony when he first arrived. He thought of leaving to go to another plant in the metro area of Detroit because of the prejudice and harassment. But he decided to stay after he was offered more money and a better work environment. This young gentleman stated things became tolerable because management left him alone in terms of harassment. Don't get me wrong, they didn't stop discriminating against him. They just allowed him to do his job. At this time they did not have a choice with the Department of Civil Rights hanging out at Sarrow Stamping Plant. At one point in time, the Department of Civil Rights were very effective here in the late 80's to this present time, they have not been so effective in following the law.

Mr. Jessie, a Black supervisor at Sarrow Stamping, was harder on his own race than he was on anyone else. The company used him to practice reverse discrimination. They used him as they saw fit and the big dummy had no idea he was being used, to do the company's dirty work. He was known not to back down. He was a very intimidating man and he carried this fault with pride. It was almost like giving honor to a sergeant in the army. He didn't like me very much. I called him "Uncle Tom". Maybe he felt I would be a threat to him in the future. Little did he know there wouldn't be enough money in the world causing me to lose sight of who I was as a person.

Mr. Jessie was about 6 feet 2 inches tall. He was very dark brown, only a few shades off from being the color black. He kept his haircut short and lined very neatly. He had a round face and kept a close shave. He had brown eyes and the white in his eyes was very bright. He also had very bright white teeth. Mr. Jessie had some gray hair and walked as though he didn't bend his knees. He weighed at least 200 pounds and had a very deep-based voice.

When I started working at Sarrow Stamping in 1993, Mr. Jessie was a man appreciated by the all-Caucasian management staff. The company put him and other minorities up to doing their discriminating favors. Sarrow Stamping and Woodrow Stamping Plant retaliated and discriminated using minorities to do their unjust treatment against other minorities. If the company wanted to fire a minority or teach them a lesson, they would get a Black supervisor to do the job. This way it wouldn't be viewed as harassment or discrimination.

The end result of all Mr. Jessie's doings for the company made him look as stupid as he really was. You can never change the color of your skin, but you can have character and respect for yourself in whatever you say or do. This clearly shows what you stand for. The position you take in life should reflect what position you take with regards to your character. You should take great care of your character where and when it counts.

It was degrading how Mr. Jessie looked upon himself. I don't know how this man slept at night because I'm sure *he* didn't want to be treated in the same manner he was treating the other Black employees. It was as though they were beneath him in rank, but in actuality he had no rank. Jessie didn't have any more authority than any other person in supervision, but he was a man clearly beside himself. If he had any more authority, he would be so tickled feeling like a king and knowing he was on a special pedestal. He truly felt he was in the royal family, not knowing the company would give him the shaft just as they did the other minorities in the plant. I suppose Mr. Jessie passed all his colleagues up by stepping on them on his way up to the top. When Mr. Jessie finally took a tumble, it was said to be over the harassment of a White woman. He never survived this fall and was quickly put back where he belonged. The last I heard, he was eventually let go and no longer worked for the company.

Mr. Jessie was the type of man in management who would never move up in position at the plant. They gave him just enough authority and would pull it right back when he got comfortable. The big dummy didn't have sense enough to know he was being used. This man wasn't the brightest person you'd want to work for. He was so comfortable with the young White women who gathered around him daily. They were in hopes they could use him in exchange for making their work load a little lighter.

Things got so great at one point that he would hang out at the bar with these young White women. There was a White woman named Marva, who came to Sarrow Stamping Plant in early to mid 1994. She was hired in the last group before I left Sarrow Stamping Plant. She didn't want to work and she didn't like the kind of work she was doing. She would always say that she hated "this place".

Mr. Jessie thought she was fresh meat. He thought she was a beautiful Caucasian woman and took a liking to her. She would sometimes go to the bar with the group on Friday and Saturday nights to party after work. Marva might have flirted with the idea of getting next to Mr. Jessie in hopes of obtaining the best job possible doing little work. As she played with the idea, Mr. Jessie was determined Marva was going to be his woman in the plant for a little while. I'm not sure what transpired between them but as a result, Mr. Jessie found out where she lived in Monroe, Michigan. According to Marva, he began stalking her and waited outside her home watching her movement.

At one point things were going well, but all of a sudden things turned for the worst. She was put on the most difficult jobs in the plant. It wasn't long that the word got around to the other supervisors in the plant. The supervisors stuck together. If the word got out that you wronged a supervisor, it meant you would be taught a lesson by *all* the supervisors. They would participate in group retaliation after the word spread around the plant. This is what happened to Marva. She would literally cry daily from the treatment in the plant. She left Sarrow Stamping Plant due to the last job they put her on—never looking back.

Marva was forced out of the plant and she eventually sued for sexual harassment. The amount of money was undisclosed. She never returned to Sarrow Stamping Plant but that was because she chose not to. She didn't want or like the type of talk going around about her. Mr. Jessie's actions worked out to her advantage. She received enough money that she didn't have to worry about coming back to a job she hated. I would guess she thanked God for Mr. Jessie.

Though Mr. Jessie wasn't fired, he could never advance in the company. He was allowed to keep his position as supervisor at Sarrow Stamping. The plant as a whole condoned this kind of action. The supervisors were the only ones who could harass and discriminate (especially against women). They had the power to do so and the company and the union took all the slack. When people like Marva sued or raised attention to a controversial situation, they would normally send the accused to another plant for whatever reason. Mr. Jessie stayed at Sarrow Stamping Plant, but things were never the same for him from that point on.

Although Mr. Jessie never said very much to me anyway, I never gave him any reason to say anything inappropriate to me. I always stayed to myself reading books, magazines, or playing computer games in my spare time on my breaks. I would stay to myself unless I was in one of the break rooms; even though, I was very well liked and respected by the majority of the plant. I gave respect and I usually received respect in return when it came to my co-workers. I really didn't have a problem with anyone I worked with on the plant floor. After a year or so, the company started hiring more women and minorities in supervision. The plant was basically forced to do this. But no matter the position of the minority, they always experienced the pressures of racism and discrimination by the company.

24

FEMALE SUPERVISOR

The first woman supervisor *had* to be a strong woman or she could not have made it at Woodrow Stamping Plant. Caucasian women also had a devastating job due to working in an all-Caucasian all-male dominated institution. The men felt the women in the plant, whether minority or Caucasian, were trying to take their jobs. The men's mindsets were if women made as much money as they did, the women would no longer need them. This would cause the men to lose their superiority and domination over the women in the plant and in every day life.

You would be surprised how many men were stuck on the fact that women shouldn't be working in the plant. I'm talking about in the year 1990 here. Men were intimidated by the fact they could no longer dominate women by making them do what they wanted at will. Prior to women's liberation, men felt they were in total control. They were the only ones who had monetary resources for the household. This carried a lot of weight with the men in terms of having a big ego.

The skilled trade's people were majority made up of Caucasian men. There were only five minorities total from 1990-1997 in each plant where I'd worked. They had just enough minority skilled trades employees to say the company didn't discriminate. Woodrow Stamping Plant gave their first female Caucasian supervisor, Ronda Smith, such a hard time. It took pure perseverance for her not to quit. In fact she started her internship at Sarrow Stamping Plant but she wasn't readily accepted there. The men at Sarrow Stamping Plant weren't ready for a woman supervisor. As a result they gave Ronda a miserable time. The skilled tradesmen at Sarrow Stamping Plant expressed how they weren't willing to assist the new female supervisor. She struggled to survive and keep her head above water in a nearly all-male Caucasian management sector. To them, it was a man's world and she was trespassing on their territory.

They took offense to Ronda's job position when she gave them job assignments. She was later transferred to Woodrow Stamping Plant but the staff members at Woodrow Stamping Plant weren't any better. She'd be literally in tears and her face would be as red as a ripe tomato. This was a game of power—so they thought. The men felt she shouldn't have taken the job if she couldn't handle the pressure. They didn't have sense enough to know *they* were the ones putting the unnecessary pressure on Ronda. The male workers did many things to make her job difficult. They felt Ronda's delegation wasn't the same as a man supervising them. They were male chauvinists and as long as they were the kings of the plant, women were going to have to stand up to the pressure.

Accepting a woman supervisor was a very difficult task for the men. They laughed in their groups making their opinions known. They tried to make a mockery out of a situation, only showing how ignorant they were. If the tables were turned and a man was in training to become supervisor, the treatment would have been different. Woodrow Stamping Plant came a long way since the 90's, but Ronda paved a way for the other women in supervision at the plant.

Gradually management and supervision became a little conscience of what they were doing and how they were doing it. They'd band together and take their own time to repair Ronda's machines properly. She was unable to reach her production many days. When this happened she would really be disrespected. When Ronda first started, the men she had to work with were spiteful. They treated her in a manner unbecoming to any human being. It would have made her job easier if they only worked with her and helped her. They didn't realize they were harassing this woman.

Ronda withstood all the punishment through tears, pain, and perseverance, by being a strong determined young woman. I gave her the utmost respect because she was able to handle her business when things were rough. I give her the greatest credit for withstanding what Woodrow Stamping Plant and Sarrow Stamping Plant did to her by making her job more difficult. They wanted a man for a supervisor not a woman. They weren't quite ready for change at this magnitude. It was only a few years ago those women were allowed to invade the men's workspaces, in the plant and now these same women were handing out their job assignments.

The company hired Janet in supervision a year or two later at Sarrow Stamping Plant. Ronda had a very hard time at Woodrow Stamping, but Janet experienced nothing in comparison to what Ronda had since she was the first Caucasian supervisor. Since then, women have become more accepted in supervision at Sarrow Stamping Plant and Woodrow Stamping Plant. Ronda continued to work as supervisor on the Press Side of the plant before I retired.

25

WORKPLACE DISCRIMINATION

I was a minority expressing my concerns on how racism, harassment, and discrimination played a significant role in the plant. I became extremely observant of my surroundings, especially when I noticed very few minorities working at Sarrow Stamping Plant. I always felt uncomfortable working and living in an area of any one specific ethnic group. I would walk from one end of the plant to the other during my lunch hour for exercise and I'd find little or no variety of ethnicity. The total plant population was approximately 2,100 including part-time employees. There were 136 part-time employees. About 97 percent of these were Caucasian. 1511 were production employees. About 85 percent of these were Caucasian. 453 were skilled trades. They were Caucasian with the exception of about two in 1993. By 1997 there were about five total.

I thought Woodrow Stamping Plant was racist and I could not imagine other plants being as racist as Woodrow Stamping. I felt since many civil rights laws had been implemented, racism wouldn't be so prevalent in a large institution like Famous Parts Company. This kind of company was supposed to be a diverse place of employment but the bold signs of racism still existed. Discrimination should not have been allowed to progress as it had in the plant.

I felt the overseers were the roots of the discrimination. They were causing the issues regarding discrimination. Who's going to admit in a group of Caucasians they were discriminating against minorities? Even those Caucasians who disagreed with the practices stood by and said nothing. Management had control with their discrimination practices and could have halted it when it was noticed. Discrimination was the plant's hidden agenda. It was like they acted on the rule "Don't ask and don't tell". This statement meant Caucasians were to cater to *their* ethnic group. Don't get me wrong, some management and employees would give respect as long as that imaginary line of a minority 'staying in their place' wasn't crossed.

Some minorities stated many of the employees belonged to the Klu Klux Klan. Word around the plant was Sarrow Stamping was where many Klan members worked and lived. As of today, not much has changed because the Caucasian employees wanted it to stay that way. The union assisted the company with keeping the discrimination and thievery alive. For years Woodrow Stamping Plant and Local 783 worked together for a common cause of discriminating. These two entities had many resources outside the plant aiding what they were doing.

Woodrow had a reputation that many lawyers didn't want to touch. The plant managed to pay off any person that came through their doors to investigate. If they were not paid money, a favor was done for them instead. Although I've never seen money change hands with my own eyes, I knew favors and promotions were granted for those working on my complaint I filed against Woodrow Stamping and Local 783. I am aware these promotions are not given at any cost. I knew of one lady (with an organization handling my case) who received such a promotion from the Department of Civil Rights in 1997.

The Department of Civil Rights, National Labor Relations Board, Equal Employment Opportunity Commission, Department of Labor, and other organizations were granted favors from Woodrow Stamping Plant and Local 783 for protecting disclosure of their illegal activities. I had questions regarding the NAACP because each time I called on them, they were uninterested. Woodrow Stamping had just the type of access to do what they pleased. Two women told me they were receiving a promotion during the same time I was asked to withdraw my complaint. Why did their promotions (on two occasions) come when they were handling my case and as I was asked to withdraw my claim with the Department of Civil Rights? After the second time this happened, I assumed their promotions came with a price. That price was to see that my case was withdrawn.

This complaint was withdrawn in 1997 under the condition that I brought in official documentation of my original seniority date. When I did receive this information to have my claim resubmitted, I was told the claim was too old and the statue of limitations had run out. I had been assured there was no statue of limitations regarding this claim. I granted them a favor in good cause only to prove I was telling the truth, but in the end the Department of Civil Rights refused to file the same charges against Woodrow Stamping Plant for wrongful termination and unequal pay.

I did drop the charges in August 1997 and December 2000 as requested in hopes I would receive justice. But as a result, I received many injustices. I became aware of what Woodrow Stamping and Local 387 were doing. Therefore I became a threat to them. When lawyers asked where I worked, I would say Woodrow Stamping Plant. They just didn't want to take on the case plain and simple. They would say the plant was very uncooperative.

When I arrived at Sarrow Stamping Plant, Mr. Stevens was the Plant Manger (*no affiliation to Pedro Stevens, who was Bargaining Committeeman.*) Plant Manager Stevens retired soon after I arrived. Racism appeared in its truest form with Mr. Andrews, the incoming plant manager after Mr. Stevens retired in 1994 from Sarrow. After Mr. Stevens retired, word around the plant was there was going to be a new manager who was Black. This didn't set well with management and some of the employees on the floor. They let it be known that this is the first time a minority and/or Black man has ever hired to maintain the daily operations of Sarrow Stamping. Can you imagine working among a specific ethnic group and they felt you were beneath them because of the color of your skin on the plant floor? They never once thought this man was being paid to keep the plant afloat. It really didn't matter to them at all.

Some Caucasian employees felt if it meant the plant would have to close its doors then so be it—just as long as a minority wouldn't tell them what to do. This showed the extent, of superiority with regards to the discrimination and how they felt they had all the control of Sarrow Stamping and Woodrow Stamping plants. They felt they were within their right by being Caucasian to say what they weren't going to do. At least this is what I heard some say who were very close to management.

The skilled trade's workers, along with other employees, talked amongst each other. They were going around the plant saying they weren't going to take orders from a Black person. The new plant manager hadn't even arrived at Sarrow Stamping Plant and the survey of many wasn't very good. This Black plant manager was put in charge of an almost all-Caucasian upper management. Even the uneducated employees who couldn't so much as write their name felt the same. I know it had to be a difficult task being a Black employee with Caucasian employees on every level (whether on the floor or in management) being more superior than you. It's ironic working in a place where you see almost all of management of one race, but they brag about company diversity. It was a joke with a capital letter J'.

They actually felt Blacks and minorities were beneath them. It didn't matter that Mr. Andrews was a qualified Black Plant Manger. He was the only Black in upper management. In fact Mr. Andrews was the first Black in the plant's history who totally ran the plant's daily operations. Some employees didn't hide the fact they didn't like the idea of having an African-American plant manager. If they'd band together as a whole, they could have made it difficult for Mr. Andrews to perform his work properly. I assumed this is what was going to happen to Mr. Andrews once he arrived.

He was in essence a tall, thin, Black man, with short black hair that receded a little. He was in his late forties to early fifties. If he was any older, he looked excellent for his age. He was a very soft-spoken man. There was talk upon his arrival at the plant, but little was said after his arrival. Mr. Andrews spoke with due respect but said very little as he walked in observance of his new job position. He was very business oriented—no small talk. I could have imagined what his job was like stepping on a bed of hot coals.

As I recall there was only one Black woman working in the plant's offices permanently in the plant. She worked in Employee Relations. She calculated the time and handed out shift preference cards or layoff cards. Her name was Ms. Deloris. I couldn't recall any other minorities working in the offices unless they were restricted from working on the plant floor. If I may reiterate, all office personnel was Caucasian and this was normal at Sarrow Stamping Plant.

The minorities were not going to get any further in management unless the Department of Civil Rights came in the plant and told the company otherwise. This happened at Sarrow Stamping in the early part of 1994. Sarrow Stamping Plant was forced to make a change. Sarrow Stamping was forced to hire more "minority women" because the census was too low. Management went around the plant personally asking Black and Hispanic employees, if they knew anyone interested in working at the plant. That was all they hired when they were solicited. The plant's theory was if they didn't hire very many minorities, the minorities couldn't take control of the plant. It didn't matter if you were a qualified worker or not.

When Sarrow Stamping Plant did solicit minorities around the plant, the daughter of Carol Bail (my co-worker on the line) was hired under those circumstances. Her son was never called to work after he passed the test—at least not while I was there. When I was hired at Sarrow Stamping Plant there weren't many minorities hired per group of about thirty. I was the only minority in my hiring group following my acceptance at Sarrow Stamping Plant. Soon after that, there were many groups hired because of employees retiring. It didn't matter how many people were hired, you'd see no more than three minority faces at a time.

I noticed that Sarrow would hire Hispanics before they would hire Blacks. Sometimes they would hire one Black, one Hispanic, and one other (maybe Arab-American.) The remainder of the large group would be Caucasian. I thought the plant was supposed to be diverse and an equal opportunity employer. It didn't look that way once you entered the plant's doors. There was only one Black electrician out of 100 at Sarrow Stamping Plant. It wasn't much difference at Woodrow Stamping Plant.

Something was wrong with the type of diversity the plant proclaimed. They went as far as having classes on diversity for employees and that was in name only. It only told management how far they could go before they crossed the line of discrimination. They didn't practice what they preached. It was all a facade because when the Black plant manager came, Caucasian employees began showing their true colors. You can ask any minority that has worked at either of these two plants. Anyone can detect an atmosphere where there is tension as thick as it was. "You can fool some of the people some of the time, but you can't fool all of the people all of the time."

I was trying to get my daughter hired at Sarrow Stamping Plant near the winter of 1995. Word around the plant was that they were going to be hiring soon. I received this information by word of mouth first. Later the bulletin board had a memo posted in the plant. But the memos were never posted in the section of the plant where minorities were working. I know this because during lunch each day, I walked around the plant for exercise in hopes of losing a pound or two.

As I walked I would look at the various bulletin boards to see if there was anything new or of my interest. Surprisingly the bulletin boards didn't have the same information. If I didn't check all the boards, there were many things I would have missed out on. As time went on, I noticed information was posted in certain areas and not others. I felt the plant had specific reasons for posting information in areas where minorities were less likely to read the information. They made the information privileged to some and not others. Most employees wouldn't read the bulletin board if the information was posted in their area.

Anyway I spoke with Mr. Fairfield who was taking names for new hires in the front office across the street. I desired to inquire about the hiring information. I was asking with regards to Kathy, a friend of the family, and also my daughter, Cella. Mr. Fairfield then informed me I needed their names and social security numbers. He explained their names would be added to the list and they would be tested in the next group. After I presented the information needed to qualify them for testing, Mr. Fairfield told me to have them go to Sarrow Stamping's

Employment Office and fill out an application. He said their names would be pulled from the applications.

I followed his instructions and a few weeks later they both were tested. Soon after the testing, my daughter received a letter stating she didn't pass the test. The test was a basic skills test that wasn't very difficult to pass at all. My daughter was an honor student before graduating from high school and the idea of her not passing this test was beyond something I could imagine. I didn't feel so bad after other minorities with college degrees were informed by the company they hadn't passed the test either. The other young lady, Kathy, was hired in the next part-time group.

I couldn't believe both plants I'd worked for claimed they were diverse. I was apprehensive about the plant's testing strategy because I was basically being told minorities couldn't pass a simple skilled trades test. My leeriness served me correct. Someone filed suit against Famous Parts Company as a whole and it was discovered the company's skilled trades testing strategy in 2005 was flawed. My niece, who applied for a skilled trade's position, was also told she did not pass the test. It was revealed there wasn't just a problem in their skilled trades testing, but in their hiring practices as well.

Woodrow Stamping Plant or Sarrow Stamping Plant didn't want minorities in skilled trades because they felt Caucasians were the superior ones. They wanted minorities to work the most difficult job assignments leaving the *gravy* jobs for Caucasians. They were limiting the amounts of Blacks hired in the plant as they limited the amount of skilled trade's positions.

I talked to many fellow employees who had years of seniority (anywhere from twenty to thirty years.) They were very disappointed because of all the people hired. They weren't able to get any of their friends and family hired during this time. When the plant started hiring new employees, many minorities weren't ever considered. Many employees tried long and hard to no avail. They stopped trying just as I did at one point. Then after that I became very persistent. I felt there were some underlying reasons as to why the groups hired weren't diverse. The hiring test qualification was basically on an eighth-grade level. The skilled trades test may have been a little harder but not much. I'd heard from some, you had to have known some algebra. Others stated the test didn't seem too difficult. I didn't know because I never tried taking that test.

Some employees were never persistent enough with getting their friends and family hired. Many were told the way to be hired was to enter their name in the plant's lottery. While I worked at Sarrow Stamping, only one or two names were ever pulled from the lottery and the winners were Black. I felt Sarrow Stamping

Plant's saying they were drawing from this *lottery*, was a way of keeping employees' inquires at a minimum.

If you were close to a member of the union or knew who was taking names, you had a better chance of getting a minority hired in. One thing I always noticed was that it was very hard being a minority to gain rank in upper management unless the company was forced to. Sarrow Stamping increased population of Black women when they didn't meet the quota required. When these women were hired, they didn't have to play the wait & see game as other minorities did. They were hired and they didn't even have to be tested.

I overheard the Union Committeeman say Sarrow Stamping Plant was only going to hire 3% minorities. When Sarrow Stamping Plant did hire new employees, a walk-through of the plant, reviled how many minorities were hired which proved this to be true statement. When I heard the union representative say this after my daughter was denied the opportunity of being hired, I decided to contact Mr. Andrews, the new Plant Manager. Though Mr. Andrews was Black, I would have done the same thing if he were a White plant manager. This information was important about the hiring quotas. The plant was supposed to be an equal opportunity employer, but it couldn't be if there was a hiring quota for some and not others. When I looked around, I couldn't help but believe what this committeeman said. When I was hired at Sarrow Stamping Plant, I was the only Black and the only minority hired from a group of about 30.

I sent Mr. Andrews a letter regarding the matter. I had never met this plant manager before, but I had seen him walking through the plant on official business. One afternoon I saw Mr. Andrews walking into Sarrow Stamping Plant from across the street where his office resided. I introduced myself and stated I had sent a letter to the plant via certified mail concerning the plant's hiring practices. Mr. Andrews extended his hand to meet mine and gave me a gentle handshake. I informed him how concerned I had become in hearing the statement the union representative made. I wanted to see if it was cause to worry. He assured me the matter would be investigated. About a week later, I received a response from Sarrow Stamping Plant stating that my allegation would be investigated.

Months later I received another letter from Sarrow Stamping Plant stating they thoroughly investigated all aspects of their hiring practices and found there was no wrongdoing. Under the circumstances, I expected to hear this kind of result. Afterall from my perspective, the manager didn't want any negative labels on his term in the plant such as unfair hiring practices or discrimination. Remember Mr. Andrews was a minority among an all-Caucasian upper management.

In 1996, I was working in the wheel-room checking rims that came down a line on hooks. The wheels had to be checked for cracks and splits. My co-worker, Carol Bail, and I were in conversation. Mr. Andrews came through and spoke to us. He wanted to know how things were going generally on the job. After his greeting, he seemed to be in a very pleasant mood for talking. He didn't normally come to the wheel-room unless there was a problem. On this day, all seemed to be in order. Carol took the opportunity to ask Mr. Andrews why her son hadn't been called to work after he had passed his test some time ago. Mr. Andrews told Carol he would check into the matter. When he was finished talking to Carol, I inquired about my daughter Cella. I informed him my daughter had taken the test and was told she didn't pass it. I went on to tell him I thought there was some kind of mistake. I expressed how she was an honor student and so forth. I said the test was basically on an eighth-grade level and I wanted her to have an opportunity to be hired just as any other person would.

He then told me to write down my daughter's name and social security number and give it to his secretary. He said Cella's name would be entered on the list to be re-tested. But this didn't happen before Mr. Winski, in the Labor Relations Office, accused me of going over *his* head. Mr. Winski was very angry with me for going to the plant manager regarding the matter. It wasn't as though I went *looking* for the plant manager when I inquired about employment for my daughter. I had the opportunity to ask the plant manager about a job opening and I took advantage of the opportunity I didn't feel any guilt whatsoever.

My daughter was tested again, and this time I went to the union office to find out if Cella had indeed passed the test. At that time the union would give this information to the parent regarding their family member's test scores. I did this because she hadn't received her test scores and two weeks had already passed. Mr. Louis, Sarrow Stamping Plant's Chairman of Local 387, looked up my daughter's scores and I was told she had passed the test this time.

I started to become concerned due to Cella not receiving a formal letter as of yet. I went to see Salma Bears, in Labor Relations. I was told not to worry because if she hadn't received a letter that meant Cella passed. We're now in the fourth week and Salma said, "No news is good news. If you haven't heard anything as of now, assume she has passed". A few more weeks passed and once again I went to talk to Salma. I stated my daughter hadn't received an appointment for her physical. She had yet to receive a formal letter or phone call stating she had passed the test.

A few more days passed from the last time I had spoken with Salma regarding Cella, who later received a letter stating she did <u>*not*</u> pass the test. Of course by this time, I became very angry and went to see Mr. Louis, Plant Chairman of Local 387. I was asking for answers because I had seen the list that stated my daughter _did_ pass the test. Mr. Louis, of Sarrow Stamping, told me he would check into the matter and as a result, he informed me Cella would be called in the next group. This ended up being two long years later.

I was full of frustration because I knew my daughter had passed the test the first time. Having to take the test a second time with the same results was wrong. I started thinking about what I'd overheard the union representative say regarding the plant hiring only 3% minorities. I began to think maybe something was true to his statement afterall.

I became so flustered I contacted Plant Manager, Mr. Andrews, again and expressed to him what had happened. Mr. Andrews told me to bring the letter I received stating Cella had not passed the test. I assumed he may have looked her score up himself. This letter was to be given to the Human Resources Office located in the same office building as Mr. Andrews. Mr. Roberts was the Human Resources Supervisor located down the hall from Mr. Andrews. Mr. Roberts was absent the first time I went to see him. I was told to try contacting Mr. Roberts the following day because he hadn't come to work due to a doctor's appointment.

The following day, I was working my job on the floor and I saw Mr. Andrews walking down the aisle looking for someone. I had no idea he was looking for me when I saw him walking in my direction. When he reached me, he asked if I could see Mr. Roberts in his office today. I replied, "Yes!" On my first break of the morning I went to see Mr. Roberts and I took with me the denial letter Cella had received. When I met with Mr. Roberts, he gave me a long song and dance scenario about "parents getting their children jobs and the children not being interested in working ..." True that was, but this had absolutely nothing to do with why I was there to see him. I asked Mr. Roberts why I was given the run-around in reference to my daughter being hired at Sarrow Stamping. The only thing he could say was they were sorry for any inconsistencies. He said Cella would be brought in for her physical exanimation in the next group, but not before there was some kind of investigation in the office.

Until this day I can't explain, but all I know is the next day three people in the plant's front office were fired. Word around the plant was they were fired because of unfair hiring practices. It was found out that Salma, of Labor Relations, was selling jobs. She had hired too many people and was unable to obtain jobs for everyone—especially some of the people who had already paid for their jobs. If this was the case, I'm hopeful Salma returned the money. I figured whoever turned her in to the plant manager must have been very angry with her. My complaint didn't help much because afterall, I had been twice unfairly disappointed.

I can clearly say something was going on with the hiring practices and the one's involved lost their jobs in the process. However, it didn't matter what the Caucasian employees did to get fired. If they had the time accrued, they were always allowed to retire. I assumed they didn't have to pay the money back. This is something I never understood. It didn't matter how much money they made in the process. They were allowed to keep their money and their retirement as well. It was almost as if they were rewarded for the unlawful action that had taken place on the job.

It was eventually found that many groups had actually passed their tests. My daughter still had not been called and I became concerned once again. I decided to talk to Mr. Winski in Labor Relations. Previously he felt I should not have bypassed him when I inquired about getting my daughter tested. I stated to him I felt the reason behind my daughter not being hired had something to do with the firing dispute.

Cella had nothing to do with them selling jobs or their unfair labor practices. Therefore she should not have been punished. Why did she stick out like a sore thumb? They had been using these practices for years and we had nothing to do with what they were doing. We couldn't take the blame for their unfair labor practices. It was all of their own doing but my daughter and I became the villains.

I felt many management employees and some union employees sided with management. The union and upper management always played politics when it came down to getting something accomplished. I told Mr. Winski I wasn't interested in anything but giving my daughter a fair chance in employment whether she was Black or White. I expressed how neither my daughter nor I were looking for special treatment. Thus far Cella hadn't received any favors.

I guess Mr. Winski must have given some thought to what I said because after our conversation, Cella was called. I'm not sure if Mr. Winski was going against all odds in bringing my daughter in to work or not. When she was called, he didn't notify anyone in management she was coming in for her physical to start work. She was the only one called and the only one that had a physical on that Saturday morning with no other personnel around. Mr. Winski seemed to have had a change of heart and from that point, I had an official gain of respect for him as he did me. He gave my daughter a fair chance. Not as 'my daughter' but as a person who was interested in obtaining a job. That was all I had been asking for the entire time.

Cella began working part-time in spring 1997, some two years later. After Cella arrived at the plant, Bonnie, who replaced Salma in Labor Relations, was the one who met Cella first when she arrived. Bonnie's prior job was with Employee Relations in the plant's Production Office. Bonnie was the only person who was aware of Cella's arrival. When Bonnie introduced herself to Cella upon her entry, she informed Cella that she made the call for her appearance to come for her physical. Cella started working part-time one week following her physical.

I would like to thank Mr. Winski; not for giving Cella the job she should have obtained prior, but for going against the odds with no strings attached. Almost ten years later, Cella is still working with a very good work ethic. Since then, Cella says she's seen so many people come and go. I am very proud of my daughter's accomplishments. She proved she was willing and able to do her duties as an employee. I couldn't have asked for any more and I must say that Kathy, the friend who originally tested with Cella, is yet working—also with a very good work ethic. It was well worth the effort in fighting the best I knew how for a job opportunity for someone who was willing and able to work.

26

STOLEN IDEA

Most of the skilled tradesmen were the laziest people in the plant. This is one reason there were so few minorities in the plant with that kind of job. The company couldn't see a minority sitting down and not doing any work. It was too much down time when the plant ran with no problems. During these times, skilled tradesmen did with their time as they chose with the exception of leaving the plant. There had been so many times my machine broke down. I had to often go get a repairman to fix the machine in order to make my production quota.

The majority of the time, skilled tradesmen would be sitting behind the lines asleep or reading magazines. Sometimes there would be days they didn't have to work on a machine all day. There would be times when they would show *you* how to fix the machine so you wouldn't disturb them again. I would become so disturbed because these skilled tradesmen would become angry when called to a job they were paid to fix. I didn't have the luxury to sit as the repairmen did. These were considered 'gravy' jobs. So the skilled trade's positions were saved for the Caucasian men

One day my line broke down and we had to transfer to another line that wasn't working as well. I thought perhaps if the skilled tradesmen would not be sitting on their behinds all day, they could work on the lines that needed repairing while they were down. I felt this was a good time for the skilled tradesmen to do any maintenance on a machine that had reported mechanical problems. There was no reason for these men to be sitting down all day and when you'd look for them to repair a machine, they couldn't be found. At times they would hide behind the machines when they saw you coming.

This was why I came up with an idea in April 20, 1997 while on a broken line. This line had baskets stacked near the machine I was working on. I would stare at the men working on the line who were in no hurry to fix the machine. I started pulling product tags off the empty baskets and started writing down my idea to keep these men working.

Maybe the lines wouldn't be in such bad shape if the repairmen were aware of what the problems were on the line. If it was noted, it could be fixed in a timely manner. I sat on the line and wrote my idea on the product tags that came off the baskets. I then went to the Plant Production Office and inquired if anyone had ever come up with an idea with regards to the skilled tradesmen and how the machines were being repaired. I was told no and that the machine repairmen would truly be angry with me for my idea. I said I really didn't care about them being angry with me because when I ask them to fix my machine, they're angry just the same.

I had a job to do and for me to complete my job I needed them to fix the machine when it broke down. I couldn't do the job I was being paid to do on a broken machine. I spent more time looking for the repairmen and having them hide from me than you could imagine. After I verified there were no plans for such a program, I went to the Recognition Program Office. The women who took the information couldn't wait for me to transfer the idea from the card tags to the proper paper. The idea specialist took the idea and typed it directly from the cards. The number on the original form was N673891-00. On it was my social security number and the department I worked.

My idea was for each machine to have a completed checklist. This would be a list of things that needed fixing. This form will give the operator the date the problem is spotted. It will also give the date and time the machine was repaired, and by whom. My idea was submitted and accepted in April 1997 and it was written as follows:

"Machine repairmen when not on assignment, should start checking the Operator Checklist for minor repairs needed which are supplied by the operators in their department. If the repairs only take a few minutes he can be repairing the machine while the operator is on lunch break. One repairman's breaks should not be with the other repairmen.

I think a checklist might work because the maintenance persons would come every now and then to check for any specific problem listed. The repairmen don't normally come unless they are asked to do so. They may not know exactly what a problem is unless it is noted. If the problem is noted and placed in view on the machines, the repair process can be started as quickly as possible.

I think we sometimes have problems with our repairmen because they are so lazy. I had the opportunity to experience a problem on a Saturday when my conveyer belt stopped. It was toward the end of the shift and I had about 45 minutes remaining. I called our repairman and he couldn't fix the problem because he had to call a millwright person. I also contacted my supervisor and was told it wouldn't be fixed right away. The machine was not fixed until Monday of that following week. I came in on overtime that Monday and the machine was down for at least 45 more minutes. It shouldn't have taken so long to get things repaired. The millwrights worked that weekend.

I didn't come to work just to sit down. The line was scheduled to run that day and it was still was out of order. The work hadn't been completed from the business day prior. There was no reason the job shouldn't have been in working order when the repairmen was notified the prior workday there was a problem. The work could have been completed on another shift if the line was scheduled to run on overtime.

This seems to be a problem on this line (check notes). We have gone for months with complaints of minor repairs not being done. Check February thru May notes thus far. I think if everyone takes responsibility for their job, we can put out better products. This is when I came up with the idea of having an Operator Checklist.

It wouldn't be a bad idea to have the repairmen keep track of hours worked on a job, how many jobs are completed in a shift, what the repair issues are, date repair is completed, and the time it takes to complete. His form would show all the proper elements in completing a job. If skilled tradesmen are going to be paid, they must put the books and newspapers down and do some actual work. Don't get me wrong, we have a lot of good repairmen who care about their work. But most of them don't care how the machines are handled mainly because management doesn't seem to care unless the machine breaks down. I have noticed that sometimes the problem may start off small with a lose bolt or something of that nature, but the problem goes without being fixed. This becomes a much greater problem sometimes taking up to an hour or even days to fix.

THIS IS HOW IT *SHOULD* WORK.

Each repairperson should fill out a form each day, which would calculate time worked for the day. The form should be called 'The Repairman's Worksheet.' The form would detail what job or machine they're working on, the machine's problem, how much time is spent on a particular job, date, and the number of the machines repaired. If on any given day all machines are working well, the repairman would have time to check the Operator's Checklist in the area. This would tell the repairman the minor or major problems that needed addressing. The Operator Checklist should be put on every machine so the operator can explain the machine's problems. Who knows when a machine is having problems better than the operator? Repairmen may say they don't have the time to complete a job, but later another repairman on the following shift may be able to complete the job.

1.   Minor repairs should be done during the machine operator's break. Things that can be done in 15 or 20 minutes should be completed at this time. If repairs seem to be a major problem then the problem should be completed on the following shift or on the weekend. By no means should a problem be left undone for weeks if there is a repair tag on the machine. If there are two or more repairmen in a department they should have alternate breaks unless working on one particular job together.

2.   If all repairs are completed in one department, the repairmen should be able to cross the aisle to complete other minor repairs from the Operator's Checklist just as long as he/she can account for the work and repairs completed for that day.

3.   Each repairman should be required to work at least 6 to 7 hours a day, depending on how many hours worked and how many machines worked on.

4.   All jobs that are not completed on the spot should be finished at a week's end. The repairmen should go to the next job if supplies aren't available. This goes for jobs such as pipe fitters and tool & die. No matter how small or how large the job is the repairmen have to account for their time.

5.   There should be a specific work form requesting repairs needing to be done by importance. A request for work should be made and dropped in the appropriate box.

6.   During a shift, there may be a machine idled for whatever reason. While doing nothing for 3 to 4 hours or sometimes all day, repairmen would be able to keep notes of what they've done for the day. If the jobs were not completed, the notes would explain time spent, everything repaired, and what needs to be completed."

After this part of the idea was expressed, there was another form called a Cost Summary Worksheet. This sheet explained how much money the company would save if the idea were implemented. There were also a few other processes of information needed for the line. There were other necessary forms that needed completing. There was an Idea Development Worksheet that needed to be completed before I could go any further. There was a form requesting information on the line I worked. I needed to request information concerning how much the plant lost in the last 12 months in down time. When I completed the form, my request was as follows:

"I would like the total scrap count for the past 12 months. I would like to know in terms of dollars and units where there was a loss or profit. At this time I'm only asking for Line #24's cost sheet."

According to my paperwork, the date on this form was June 4, 1997 and I needed a response by June 10, 1997. After I completed this information, I needed to complete a cost analysis of the line. I used the pay scale on page 3 of the plant's report of tool and die. I based my calculation of $22.55 per hour at the time. The number of skilled tradesmen came from the Chairman's Report in the local news.

"The repairman calculations are as follows:
    $22.55 x 8hrs. a day = $180.40
    $22.55 x 40hrs. a week = $902.00

    Saturday would be as follows:
    $22.55 x 48 hrs. = $1082.40
    + 4hrs. O.T. $90.20 = $1172.60

Sunday would be as follows:
    $22.55 x 56 hrs. = 1262.80
    + 8 hrs. O.T. $180.40 = $1443.20

The rate information may not be exact but is a round about figure. There are 480 skilled tradesmen who cost the company when they work four out of eight hours per day. My calculation of 480 skilled trades is costing the company approximately $2,251,895 a year. If on average, the skilled tradesmen work four hours out of eight per day the company is losing at least $11,259,465 for work not performed. My idea would keep skilled tradesmen working for a full shift. This could call for less skilled trade's people in a department. The machine repairmen are assigned to specific lines to work on and it would help skilled tradesmen account for time worked.

One skilled trade's employee would cost the company nearly $46,414 a year. But if the employee only works an actual 4 hours, the company is losing approximately $23,457 a year, which is a substantial loss not including overtime. One skilled trade's employee works 7 days a week for 52 weeks. It would cost the company about $84,427 if they only worked 4 hours out of their entire shift. On average the company is losing $42,023 for work not performed.

I feel the company will save by repairmen working on machines within the department or machines that are to run on the next shift. If the skilled trades department is utilizing time properly, this idea can be rewarding for the company. Many times when machines are working properly skilled tradesmen have nothing to do while being paid top dollar. My idea doesn't just save in maintenance. It also saves in quality and production. Therefore the company has everything to gain by implementing my idea. This idea will save on down time. The time sheet should be kept and computed as time actually worked. Additional information can be used to see if there is a constant problem with a certain machine or if it's a manufacturer's error."

Shortly after completing the final stages of the implementation of my idea, I received a call from my home stating I had a house fire. When I heard this news, I froze and my heart seemed to have skipped a few beats. I really didn't know the details surrounding the fire. I was only told that everyone was fine and no one was hurt. This was the only information given over the telephone. As I was driving home, I only wondered what happened and how the fire started in the first place. I became frightened as I was driving, not really knowing what to expect when I pulled in the driveway. I sat in the car for just a few minutes viewing the outside of the house which didn't look too bad.

When I got home, the fire had been extinguished and the fire trucks had gone. I walked into the house to evaluate the damage the fire had caused. There was more smoke damage than anything and my bedroom, which was locked, received no damage at all. I really didn't know what to do next. I called the insurance company and inquired about the necessary procedure for getting my house boarded up. I took a few days off work and found someplace to stay until the house was finished. I found that my daughter, who suffers from ADHD and Bi-Polarism, set the house fire. I had been in the process of trying to get my daughter the help she needed because her medication just didn't seem to be working. I was very distraught because among being under mental pressure due to having a job that was robbing me blind. I now had fire damage to attend to.

I did receive a bit of good news as I was walking out of Sarrow Stamping Plant on the day of the fire. I was told to stop at the Labor Relations Office before I left the building because they wanted to see me. When I answered the call to the Labor Relations Office, I was told my transfer back to Woodrow Stamping Plant was granted. I was surprised when I was given this news since I had been told I could "*never*" return back to Woodrow Stamping Plant.

I felt my idea was secure at that time. Even though I was leaving behind my idea, I had been through the necessary steps and the paperwork was complete. I really didn't worry about the idea because from my understanding, it was no way anyone could steal it. I truly thought Sarrow Stamping would contact me when payment was due, but that never happened. Since I didn't receive payment I wondered if this move was a planned effort on the part of Sarrow Stamping Plant, to pilfer my idea and money because my signature was the only thing needed and they could have cut me a check before I left. I was to be paid for my idea. But as a result of leaving for my home plant/basic unit, I was never paid. They pilfered that money too.

At the time I transferred back to Woodrow Stamping Plant, I was in the final stages of my idea (at Sarrow). I had already signed papers and completed the Level 2 Award Form, which was the last step. I never received credit for my idea. I was told the idea had been given to a young Caucasian male. It was said *he* came up with the economical idea regarding skilled trade's workers *first*.

I transferred back to Woodrow Stamping Plant in June 1997 and was denied entry, but was called back after shut-down in July. The idea was in the final stages when I left Sarrow going back to Woodrow Stamping Plant. I was certain I would be contacted at Woodrow Stamping Plant regarding implementation of my idea, so I didn't inquire about it at this time. When I returned to Sarrow Stamping Plant, I figured the process wasn't fully complete since I hadn't been contacted.

In November 1997, I contacted the coordinator of the Continuous Improvement Recognition System (CIRS) at Woodrow Stamping Plant about my idea. The coordinator contacted Sarrow Stamping Plant and they weren't cooperative with allowing the information to be obtained. About a month later, I was told the Caucasian gentleman had come up with my idea first. That was a lie because before submitting my idea I went through the company's necessary procedures, which included researching if my idea had ever been submitted. I was again out-done because they lied. It seemed the lies and pilfering was done on a regular basis. Famous Parts was a company I could never trust again. I must have been crazy thinking an idea couldn't be pilfered. I thought there were safeguards to keep that from happening. I guess I was wrong.

The company implemented my idea and saved them money, but I didn't get credit for it. What happened to the reward money I should have been granted? I didn't know and Sarrow Stamping didn't want me to know either. They are still using my idea until this day. I have kept and always will keep the idea's serial number and all the necessary papers regarding it. Not one person ever asked to see any of the information concerning my claim. No one even questioned me in reference to what happened with the company pilfering my idea.

27

"MISSING CHAPTER" NO REASON FOR A GRIEVANCE

Note to Reader: This is <u>one of three chapters to follow</u> which were deleted from my original transcript. I honestly can't say at what point they were lost, but I decided to add them in the final stages of the book anyway. (The three chapters are 27, 32, & 35.)

I filed a charge with the Department of Civil Rights on September 26, 2000 and I also wrote the Executive Branch of Famous Parts Company, asking the company to work around my restriction. This letter was sent to the Executive Branch of the Company's CEO, Mr. Donald Nelson. The letter read as follows:

"I'm writing this letter because I'm quite concerned with my health and trying to make a living for my family and myself. I have been diagnosed with repetitive sprain/strain injuries to both my elbows, hands, cervical spine, both wrists, shoulder, and upper & lower back. I was appalled when the company put me on a 'no work available' and informed me my injuries were of a "personal" nature.

To my dismay, the Medical Department has failed to look into prior medical records verifying my sprains/strains sustained repeatedly during the past years. When I had an injury in the past, I would always bounce back. I wasn't as fortunate this time. The sprains/strains recently incurred have been much harder on the body than in the past. Each injury I incurred was due to not being ergonomically fitted for various jobs, yet I was required to work.

I truly have a problem with Labor Relations and how they handled the problems, which shouldn't have been problem whatsoever, in terms of preventing injuries in my work environment. There have been times that I was denied medical treatment. This was when I decided to write the article, *Medical Matters—My Experiences and Opinion*, which never went too printed, at the union digression. The finial decision whether to print the article in the union paper was left up to Woodrow Stamping Plant's Manager—not union Local 783. This is what angered me because I thought the union newspaper had the approval of Local 783 and its members. From my understanding I assumed this was a union newspaper.

I was simply denied my freedom of speech when I was denied medical treatment in the Medical Department. If the union members can't print about their experiences, within the plant whether positive or negative I should have had that right. I thought the newspaper was for those who have something to say. Local 783 were knowledgeable of everything that went on in the Medical Department. The union newspaper might as well belong to Woodrow Stamping Plant. This first Article was called medical Matters My Experiences and Opinions. I gave this article to the union to be printed in the union newspaper, but instead I was told that the union couldn't print the article because it was a conflict of interest. The article was regarding the Medical Department, since they belonged to Local 600. If that's the case Local 783 shouldn't put them-selves in such a compromising position. It didn't matter if the Medical Department and the nurses, who were involved, in violating contract and labor laws. It shouldn't have been a problem at all to file a grievance and/or complaint against Woodrow Stamping Plant and the Medical Department because they were wrong. I felt that employees in the union have a right to their opinion and if they want to voice their opinion in the union newspaper, the union had no right to involve Woodrow Stamping Plant's Management staff. If they were not going to print the article then so be it, they could have returned the article back to me? I filed a complaint with the National Labor Relation Board and they did nothing regarding the Medical Department, and they didn't file a report.

The article that I really got in trouble about was called Safety this article was taken to the Plant Manger office from the editor box. My article was unwelcome for the second time in a row. As far as I was concerned, my unfair treatment was purely retaliation for the article, *Safety—My Experiences and Opinion*. I myself thought that the article was informative and true. For the first time I notice the newspaper was censored and I couldn't write what I wanted to write. I wasn't defaming anyone or telling lies on anyone, everything I was writing about could be verified. I had to print what they wanted to print and not what I wanted to print. The treatment that I received after Jack Snow the Plant Manager didn't allow my article to print. I found myself in the Plant Manager's Office and the article was never printed, although it wasn't what they did, it was how they did it. In the past, I have written articles on what I thought were interesting topics in hopes union members would read with enthusiasm.

After I had written this article, I found myself on the Press Side of the plant, where I normally don't work because of my seniority. The job required a lot of repetitive movement with my right arm, should and wrist. On this particular occasion, I was sent home and given the balance of the shift off, because I refused to do a job which was a lie. I felt I couldn't do the job because I'd just finished working a line before lunch and my shoulder was in great pain. I told the supervisor I worked for on this day, that I didn't think I could do the job but would try. As a result I could not. I ran four parts and it became too painful for my shoulder. I turned the line off after asking to go to Medical and being ignored. Later, the supervisor said he didn't hear me when I asked to go to medical. The supervisor became furious with me and asked why I cut his line off. I explained it was for safety reasons. If I had not stopped the line, the parts were so long they would have fallen at an angle which could have cut me or my co-worker, Marie Wills. This job called for *two* people to stack the fenders of a large SUV.

I told Labor Relations it would have clearly been a safety issue if I had not stopped the line. Another one of my concerns was that the conveyor in which the part came down was so high it reached my neck from the floor. If I were not careful I could have cut my neck clean off my shoulders. The conveyor was too high. I can truly understand why this info was missing from my first transcript of this book. I had to find this information stored in an old computer from when I first began this book. I <u>know</u> it was in my book originally, and this is the reason I am replacing it after the chapter in which it should've been.

I could have cut my neck clean off because the steel is so sharp going down the conveyor belt. I don't think the company was trying to kill me, but their main focus was to retaliate against me. I'm considered to be a "short" person, but I had to reach up higher than the average person of average height would. The job was unbearable. My co-worker, Marie Wills, couldn't run the job alone—therefore I turned it off. They knew what they were doing, because they had a young lady waiting in the aisle to work the line right after I went to the Medical Department.

It was later determined this incident shouldn't have come to the attention of Labor Relations. After careful review, I was paid for being sent home. Even my union representative told me my experience was done out of retaliation because I wrote the article. I had not been on the Press Side for years, and for me to be handling large truck fenders was just a bit much. The parts were taller than I, and were very long and awkward to handle. Peter Nashing, my union representative, informed me that this supervisor got in a bit of trouble because of the Safety Article. Everything I complained about in the article was addressed and fixed. Plant Chairman, John Hail, asked me not to write anymore articles such as the one on safety. If I ever had a problem again, I was to contact him and *he* would make sure the problem were fixed immediately. I guess if I were to let them know, I wouldn't get punished and the supervisor in charge won't get in trouble either. That's a bunch of bullsh*t.

I was unhappy with how the union betrayed me and set me up for the 'final kill' when the article was written. The day after the article was written I was working on the floor and I was just coming off my break, when the cart Wayward Cain was driving stopped right in front of me. The Superintendent, Wayward Cane, escorted me to the front office. The cart he was driving was provided by the company, as I ascended from the cart. Wayward asked me did I know what Plant Manager, Mr. Jack Snow, wanted with me. I told him that I didn't know. As I was walking into the office, I saw every management official standing outside the Plant Manager's doorway. I had no idea they were waiting for my appearance. As I walked into the Plant Manager's Office, I was greeted and asked if I wanted a beverage. I stated no. As I looked around the office's large table, I saw my article on every place-setting.

After everyone walked in the office and sat down, the meeting started with Jack Snow, Woodrow Stamping Plant's Manager, explaining if he allowed my article to be printed he would have every entity knocking at his door. He meant the board of health and MOHSA (Michigan Occupational Health and Safety Administration). Those people he didn't want coming inside the plant to investigate anything. He didn't allow the article to be printed. I then found myself in a compromising position of being retaliated against. As I was in this meeting, I was called a "radical" in front of everyone by the Local 783 Plant Chairman. I didn't like that one bit. There was a problem, and as far as I was concerned the problems were fixed immediately after my article got to the hands of the Plant Manager. This happened around April 2000.

They were the ones who professed safety. These problems would not have been addressed, if I had not written the article. Because of this, they decided to unrightfully punish me. They became that much angrier with me, and there was nothing I could do about it. I had already been to Local 783's Plant Chairman. I later went to the Executive Brach of the Union at the Regional 21A Office and met with Innocent George after I was told, I could not file a grievance against the Medical Department. A grievance was written but Local 783 settled my grievance a few weeks after I was put on a 'no work available'. I couldn't even complain about how I was being treated after I completed the article. I was informed by the union that my complaint was a conflict of interest between Local 783 and me and that he couldn't go forward with this grievance. The name of the article that caused so much trouble was _Safety—My Experiences and Opinion by Crista Carrie_ but the article before that was called _Medical Matters—My Experiences and Opinion by Crista Carrie_. This grievance didn't cause as much trouble for me because I was put on a 'no work available' soon after it was written in June 29, 2001. When I return the grievance was agreed upon, but local 783 forgot to inform me of the information, when I return back to work in October 2001. I had no knowledge that the grievance was settled on July 30, 2001. The article on Safety that caused so much trouble for me reads as follows:

"I have received many letters from Woodrow Stamping Plant regarding safety in the workplace. I've received mail on how important safety practices are in the plant. We are told if we see a safety problem to report it immediately. When we return from short vacations, we receive leaflets reminding us of how to work safely. Safety talks are given on the plant floor and we have to sign statements as to what we've been told. Safety is often spoken of however the standards are not always followed.

Safety isn't a top priority in our plant as far as I'm concerned. It is said to always practice safety. Is this a true statement, or just something to keep us satisfied for the moment? If you have a safety concern that hasn't been addressed in a timely manner or if the concern has been forgotten, it's a dead subject. What do you think? How committed is management to safety issues if the union has to be called to correct the safety problem? Majority of times the union sides with the company.

Oftentimes the restrooms are filthy. Some have no hot running water to wash your hands. The restrooms are not cleaned daily. Grease and water puddles are left on the plant's floor. Our machines leak fluids having foul smells. Unknown strong-smelling fumes were coming from machines on Line #484. I know of one person who got sick to their stomach. The Line Leader couldn't get a simple straight answer on what we were breathing from the machine, even though he tried. Many jobs do not have proper floor matting. People are working on the floor doing jobs their body stature doesn't permit. Where is the safety team? In many cases, the safety team is not on the floor identifying these problems? What about ergonomics? People are supposed to be in proper alignment to do their jobs. Are these people sitting in their offices ignoring the health and safety issues on the floor? Could the union be using safety issues on the floor as a bargaining factor for various causes?

The job I normally work was a health hazard prior to my working it. The mating was cut, slit, bubbled up, and uneven. When I'm working, I'm constantly tripping over the mats on the floor. I complained during the summer and the issue has long been forgotten. I work the side job adjacent to Line #484.

Many times the issue has been brought to management's attention. Our Line Leader complained about the lack of response she was getting from management, as far as matting is concerned for Line #484. Our Line Leader received promises but no cooperation. She was told a few months ago that matting had come in for our line, but all of a sudden, we were told the matting disappeared. I truly have a problem comprehending how matting repeatedly disappears.

If the matting is disappearing on a regular basis, shouldn't management or the safety team investigate where the stolen matting is going to? Who was in attendance when the mats disappeared? Floor matting is very expensive. It doesn't just disappear into thin air. Someone should be held accountable for the mats, since this is the second time they have disappeared. No one seems to know where the mats are that were scheduled for Line #484. The first time the matting was said to be stolen was in fall of 1999. The second time the matting was said to be stolen was on January 29, 2000.

Our Line Leader was told the matting would be laid on Friday, January 29, 1999. Friday when the line leader met with management, she was informed once again the matting had been taken. If stealing matting seems to be a common problem, why not place the matting on the floor the minute the matting comes in? Line #441 had this same problem about a year ago with disappearing matting—at least this is what the line was told. Does anyone care where the floor matting is disappearing to? Or maybe the matting has never been ordered for Line #484 to begin with. This is another way to tell us what they want us to adhere to. It prolongs the fact that management isn't taking care of business. If this is the case where is management? Where is the union?

The matting was taken from the floor on January 14, 2000. I feel the condition of the floor should've been cased before allowing us to start work. Working long hours, walking on hard wood, cracked blocks, and uneven floors can cause serious back problems. Tripping and falling on the uneven wood blocks or working in a too congested area could cost someone their life. If a person were to fall and hit their head on a steel item, whether it's the machine itself or the basket containing the steel parts, it's dangerous.

"Safety" should be protecting the employees from potential injuries. The floor is in such havoc condition, that walking without matting with large holes, is as hazardous as not initially having matting at all. It doesn't matter how you look at it! The safety of the people on the line isn't always a main concern.

As of February 2, 2000 our union representative has been working diligently to change our working condition on Line #484. He has been on the line on numerous occasions checking to see what has been completed. Thus far the lights have been fixed and I was told the matting will be here no later than the beginning of February. When and if the matting arrives, I would truly like to thank everyone involved in making our work area a safer place to work."

This is what all the commotion was all about. I didn't feel the union had the right to take what I gave them to print for their newspaper, and put me on Front Street so everyone in management who felt that they wanted to retaliate against me, could do so. They thought I was a "radical" because I always stood up for what was right. I spoke up if I saw our contract being violated. I actually saw no big issue about the article. If the mats were stolen, they should have found out where the mats went. If Safety and Ergonomics weren't doing their jobs, then they should have been held accountable. In some of the bathrooms they had no hot running water when there should have been. There was no valid reason for the treatment I received because of this article. The article was true. It wasn't like I was lying—but I paid consequences for writing it—just the same.

When I was hired in 1990, the plant doctor gave me Ability to Work Status of B. This is a restriction for lightweight work or work suitable for small stature employees. The restriction had expired in 1993 by someone in the Medical Department. I'm not very tall and I'm ergonomically unfit for many jobs due to my being too short or my arms not being long enough. After my restriction was retired, I had no choice but to do the painstaking jobs I was assigned. I don't understand how someone can cancel this kind of restriction when I'll always be the height of 5'-1". My height will never change. I went through Labor Relations and the union to get this restriction back into the computer, but all I received is the run around. I also sent a copy of this information to Donald Nelson, President and CEO of Famous Parts Company, in 2000. It was around the same time it was announced that the Controller and Verlinda Moose, Labor Relations Supervisor, were leaving.

Now I'm suffering from a variety of strains and sprains. For Woodrow Stamping Plant to refuse me treatment or not acknowledge my injuries occurred on the job, really angers me. I was told I could not return to work with restrictions. I truly feel this was cruel and unusual punishment with all the history of sprains/strains I've incurred while working for the company through the years. Earlier on, the Medical Department gave me the opportunity to drop my restriction, but I refused. I guess since I didn't drop it myself, they were going to drop it for me. They did this to other employees quite often.

I have actually heard the Nurse ask employees to drop their restrictions in order to return to work. Employees' medical benefits would be held up until they became destitute and would do anything to return to work. When the employees dropped the medical restriction, it only caused their medical condition to worsen. When the Medical Department urged the employee to drop the restriction, they were doing so at their own risk. This takes the blame off the employer and puts the blame on the employee since the Medical Department just says the decision was made at the employee's own discretion. When I witnessed this happening, I would say to the employee that these people didn't give a damn about their health. I would tell them how they shouldn't take the blame off the company, when the company caused the problems.

Since Woodrow Stamping Plant was going to receive the employees' Worker's Compensation that was meant for the employee's occupational injuries were soon going to be personal. If the employee followed their doctor's recommendations under the personal injury, they couldn't hold the company responsible. When you volunteer to drop a restriction, the company won't be liable, and if you leave the company, you won't be able to sue the company when and if the occasion were to arise. The Medical Department made them sign when they dripped their restrictions. What makes it so bad was that all the restriction was for the occupational injuries sustained in the plant, which was soon to become a personal injury.

Having no money for a long period of time causes problems for an employee who is unable to work or who is on a 'no work available'. When they're money is held up by the Medical Department and they have no money saved. The employee will do anything to get back to work, this includes dropping their restrictions. This is why some employees dropped their restrictions. I know it was none of my business, but after they dropped their restriction I would advise them not to do so, because in the end they will pay the price. I would tell them when their condition worsened, the Medical Department will only say, "Oh well! You should not have dropped your restriction". When employees would drop their restrictions at the Medical Department's request, the Medical Department would have the employee sign a paper stating the employees is disregarding their doctor's restriction and won't hold the Medical Department accountable.

The company will send employees out as fast as they can, so they can make money through their Worker's Compensation and retirement plan. The employees won't see a dime of that money. I asked the employees if they thought the people working in the Medical Department were going to help them. I can answer that question—hell no! If the Medical Department were to look in the employee's file and discover their restriction were dropped, the company would not lift a finger to help them with their condition because they knew the company wasn't held responsible. The dropped restriction takes the blame off the company. They would not have been asking the employee to drop their restriction in the first place without a motive. Some employees can't afford not to be working. They can't afford to miss any additional days of work by the company not honoring their restrictions and not sending their Sick & Accident payments in a timely manner. In my case if I voluntarily dropped my restriction, it would do even more damage to the injuries I've already sustained.

I have dedicated the last ten years working for Famous Parts Company six days a week (sometimes seven), many of which I work ten to twelve hours a day. I worked for Woodrow Stamping Plant for three years, from September 1990 thru November 1993. I was then transferred to Sarrow Stamping for three years, from November 1993 thru July 1997, when I then returned to my basic unit—Woodrow Stamping Plant.

The reason I'm writing this letter is because I feel Labor Relations and the Medical Department are playing politics with me. I see no reason why I should be on a 'no work available' when I qualify for various other jobs in the plant. There are appointed positions and there are bid positions, which are given to the Caucasian women with restrictions. On some occasions, co-workers at Woodrow Stamping would tell me when there was to be a vacancy, because of someone retiring with a restrictive appointment. Other Caucasians, who had less seniority, were placed or given appointed positions because of their restrictions. Why can't I receive an appointed position? I have the seniority, educational background, and could do the job well.

I am a minority and I was denied many of the appointed positions by the company and the union as well. Woodrow Stamping Plant doesn't respect the minorities as they do their own kind. They discriminate on a regular basis and they don't care who objects. They have the power to do as they please and there is nothing I can do about it. If I were given the opportunity, I could be very beneficial in any area of the work force. I am a minority and a very outspoken woman. The company seems to have a problem with this.

I'm complaining because Woodrow Stamping's Medical Department has totally been harassing me, and Local 783 allows them to do so. I brought the problem to Woodrow Stamping Plant's Manager, Jack Snow's attention. The company began giving me inaccurate medical information when I requested material regarding my medical condition from my file. They ran specific tests that weren't authorized and I wanted that information in my medical file. I received Worker's Compensation for my back and on one occasion for my shoulder at the same time. Woodrow Stamping Plant had me on their set of files, not to receive payment for my occupational injury. They used the first injury (for my back) to keep for themselves. The way they saw it, we *both* couldn't receive my Worker's Compensation. They kept that occupational injury, pulling money out of the

Worker's Compensation fund at Woodrow Stamping Plant, and set up a retirement account. I kept the personal injury, which paid less—and that was all I was going to get.

Remember when I was on a full-time and part-time status at the same time, they were using both of these files at this time? This is why Dr. Butt was able to continuously deny my injury as being occupational. They didn't want the flow of money going to me when it was quite profitable to them. That is when the two sets of records came into play. Their file stated my medical condition was of a personal nature. This is why my Worker's Compensation had been denied. The Medical Department would not release any medical information regarding my condition to my personal physician, Dr. Sonia, after I signed for a release of medical information. They kept this Worker's Compensation file at the Brownstown facility, another subsidiary of Famous Parts Company.

The file with the personal injuries were kept at Woodrow Stamping Plant and when I would bring medical information to the Medical Department, it would eventually be put in the Worker's Compensation file folder in Brownstown. This is when Dr. Sonia filed for payment through Worker's Compensation and was denied by Woodrow Stamping Plant. Since they were pilfering my Worker's Compensation from the file in Brownstown, Woodrow Stamping Plant only kept information at Woodrow Stamping Plant regarding the personal injury. I continued to treat with Dr. Sonia at that point. She returned me back to work in October 2001. It wasn't Dr. Sonia that took me out of the plant it was the Medial Department, only to have found out that I had already returned back to work according to Woodrow Stamping Plant's records pertaining to Worker's Compensation. They stated I returned to work according to Woodrow Stamping Plant's Worker's Compensation file. I was brought back to work on the file with the personal injury for those eight weeks when they opened my Worker's Compensation file.

They turned around and closed that Worker's Compensation case, allowing me to be put on a 'no work available' for a long while in order to continue receiving my Worker's Compensation. They would receive my retirement for the first time in 2000. They had no plans of me ever returning. I was actually retired when I received my retirement news letter in September 2000, but I fought back to return to work and I was brought back in December 2000. As they closed one file they re-opened the other. They closed my Worker's Compensation file for the second time when I started seeing Dr. Sonia in February 2001. They were going to make sure she and I didn't receive any money regarding my Worker's Compensation claim and I didn't either.

The Medical Department wasn't very kind to me by allowing me to receive my Worker's Compensation for eight weeks and pilfering the remainder of my money. They paid doctors to say there was no problem with my health and caused me to work without restrictions. Because of their lies, my condition deteriorated at a faster pace. They knowingly kept the proper diagnosis of my occupational injuries at the Brownstown Plant. The doctors Woodrow Stamping Plant sent me to see always stated that nothing was wrong with me. This was done to hurry me out of the plant so they could start receiving my retirement benefits in February 2002. I am now receiving medical benefits from Metro Craft. I received nothing covering my medical cost from February 2000, when I had my first medical visit with Dr. Sonia, until I received Worker's Compensation in February 2002 in a settlement.

I feel Woodrow Stamping Plant—Famous Parts Company should take responsibility of my medical costs knowing my condition was caused from a sprain/strain to the upper and lower back. That would be the correct thing to do. If I would have gotten the proper medical treatment and my restrictions were honor, I probably wouldn't be in such bad shape as I am today. It's quite hard to manage on the insurance benefits I now receive when I have to see doctors at least twice a month. I feel the company is at fault because I worked in good faith and was injured through other individual's shortcomings. As a result, my family and I are paying the ultimate price.

I am now aware of legislation to prevent these kinds of injuries, but for now I must deal with my injuries the best I can. All my injuries are repetitive sprain/strain injuries and I'm asking for your help if you will. The injuries sustained in the past ten years are quite unethical. I am a person who values her job, but I feel I'm not getting any compensation for the work I've done.

If you could assist in this scenario, it would be greatly appreciated. My name is Crista Carrie and my seniority date is September 28, 1990. I will be awaiting your response in one form or another. I know you are very busy person, but I feel only you can help by looking into this matter for me. Please respond."

I wrote this letter in September 2000 and as a result of this letter, in November 2000, I was asked to appear at Local 783's Union Hall to discuss Grievance # L-5962-LB-710. I met with Plant Chairman, Robert Haste III, and Albert Snake, Regional 21A Representative, concerning the grievance. We also discussed an amount of money to be paid out if the plant was found to have harassed me and pilfered my money, as claimed in my grievance.

Albert Snake asked me how much money I was asking for with regards to the harassment I had received. I told Mr. Snake I didn't know how much money to ask for because I wasn't a lawyer. Mr. Snake asked me to come up with a number. The first number that came to my head was $85,000 (eighty five thousand dollars). After I gave Mr. Snake the amount of $85,000, he explained to me this money would be taxed. I then said $100,000 and that is the amount of money Mr. Snake put on paper. After that, I don't know where this paperwork went to. After the meeting, Local 783 seemed to have lost this information. As a result, it was as though the meeting had never taken place.

I remember so clearly the day I was called to the Union Hall. I remember seeing a copy of the union newspaper sitting on a table, next to where I was sitting. It stated the Labor Relations Representative at Woodrow Stamping Plant, Verlinda Moose, and the Controller was leaving Woodrow Stamping Plant in January 2001. This was very important to me because I had written the Executive Branch of the Company CEO, Mr. Donald Nelson, in September 2000. I talked about how I was treated in the Medical Department. I told him of how I had been sent to Sarrow Stamping, and of what part Verlinda played in telling me I had to return to Sarrow Stamping Plant. I also expressed to him about how money was being pilfered, and how Woodrow Stamping Plant had me on full-time status, as I continued to receive part-time pay per hour. How could this have happened for the period of three years? I had personal days, yet when I took one personal day, Woodrow Stamping said I should not have taken it because I was part-time. I couldn't have received that personal day as a part-time employee in the first place.

Mr. Facade, Labor Relations Supervisor, told me I was not entitled to that personal day and expressed I'd have to pay the money back. Labor Relations and my union representative from Local 783 stood by and said nothing in my defense. It was as though I didn't know any better. I responded by telling Mr. Facade that if I didn't have the time, then I would not have received the personal day in the first place. By the way, the company admitted I was full-time by error in 1992, and it was never corrected. Here we were in February 1993, and the error still had not been corrected. There was an error indeed, but it had nothing to do with me or giving the money back to those who it belongs too.

In actually, I had been full-time all along. They'd been lying ever since I first started complaining about my employment status. They were paying me part-time pay per hour when I was full-time. I told Mr. Donald Nelson, CEO of the Executive Branch of the Company, how I had paid the money back through adjustments from vacation checks and holidays, such as on the Martin Luther King Jr. holiday. My check stub never stated the money went back to the company. I expressed how my W-2 dollar amount didn't match my "year-to-date" amounts at the end of the year.

I told him of how I was terminated when I transferred from one plant to another with no lapses in time worked. I told of how I was denied the right to re-enter the plant after I used my recall rights to return back to my basic unit. I inquired about where the money went that was stolen from me from 1990 to 1993. I told him the Controller had to be a part of this scheme, which was pilfering money from me and others. I know the money was being stolen because when the company made the adjustments, the money never went back into the company. After I explained all this information, the very two people who were involved were leaving the plant. Prior to this letter, I sent another letter to Felix Mann in 1995 expressing the problems with my part-time full-time status. I also sent along with the letter an audio tape explaining what I was going through, but I never received a response.

This was very important to me because I knew I was full-time for three years and the company said otherwise. They were pilfering my profit sharing, performance bonuses, vacation pay, and personal days for those three years. I even found out that the money was hidden in an account called the N file. The union had a set of their own files too. There was no reason Local 783 should have had access to the files of employees working in Woodrow Stamping Plant at that magnitude. Sarrow Stamping Plant's Local 873 wasn't even privileged to this information in 1993. The money was diverted with the help of the Controller using employees' files, such as Linda Jackson's and Andrea Smith's. There was another letter addressed to Felix Mann, President and CEO of Famous Parts Company's, which preceded Donald Nelson's in 1993, but I didn't get a response.

When I heard that Verlinda Moose and the Controller were leaving, it only made sense because the Controller was placing the stolen money into special accounts. The main two people involved were now leaving their jobs at Woodrow Stamping Plant. At that time, the Medical Department's implementation was not mentioned. Nurse Tootie was saved even though Plant Chairman, John Hail, and Bargaining Committeeman, Bob Fleetwood was not. To me this was a signal I was on the right track. I knew the money was being pilfered, but at the time this was all I knew. Woodrow Stamping Plant didn't know how much I knew but they were aware I knew something was wrong. They didn't want to take a chance of this information getting out at any cost. I was very glad I was called to the union on that day, because I had learned there was some truth to what I was saying.

Robert Haste III was the newly elected Plant Chairman, but was never around after the elections. Word around the plant was that Woodrow Stamping Plant and Local 783 didn't want Mr. Haste III as Plant Chairman, therefore blocking him at any and every meeting having anything to do with union business in the plant. You would see him at large union events, but as far as union business went, Plant Vice-Chairman, Mr. Tom Hemp attended in Mr. Haste's place. Woodrow Stamping wanted Tom as the Plant Chairman since he was Vice-Chairman when John Hail was Plant Chairmen. Hemp was aware of the pilfering and the manner in which the company was using to keep the thief scheme alive. Woodrow wanted someone as Plant Chairman who would adhere to their illegal demands and unfair labor practices. Robert Haste III wasn't who Woodrow Stamping Plant and Local 783 wanted as a leader.

Mr. Robert Haste III was never in his office at the union hall nor was he in his office on the mezzanine's committee room on the second floor. I would always ask where he was because I had problems needing to be cleared up—one of which was Grievance #L2695 filed against the Medical Department and Woodrow Stamping Plant. When I went to see Mr. Robert Haste III in July 2001, he was in his office. I was on a medical leave, but I came into his office to discuss my grievance, the harassment I was experiencing, and issues regarding the Medical Department. I also wanted to discuss the union's refusal to print my article, *Medical Matters and Concerns*. I wanted to know why there was a "conflict of interest", which is the reason Local 783 gave me. They could not file a grievance against the nurses in the Medical Department because they were also in the union, Local 600.

When I needed a union representative, I didn't want just anyone. I wanted someone who could help me and had knowledge to make a judgment call right away. Local 783 sent me a replacement representative who had no clue or no knowledge of the shady matter needing addressed. This only wasted my time. Many times, after I would question their lies and cloudy tactics, they didn't know what to say to me. I would distinctly ask for someone who knew the union contract. I didn't mean any offense. As far as I was concerned, it didn't matter if they were representing a union or a company, what they were doing was clearly illegal. Both Woodrow Stamping Plant and Local 783 were using unfair labor practices and violated contract and labor laws against me. I wanted it to stop.

One day I saw Plant Chairman, Robert Haste III, wearing a neck brace. I inquired about what happened, and said he'd been in an accident and would be retiring in a few months. This didn't sound like the man who was running for office of Plant Chairman just one year ago. He sounded like a man that was loosing hope. He didn't look as if he was a happy camper at all. I could tell by the way he spoke to me, he felt his health and family were the most important things in his life, and he was retiring to be with his family. I wished him well as I left the mezzanine committee room.

After filing charges with the Department of Civil Rights and the National Labor Relations Board, in December 2000 I was called back to work. I received a letter from the Department of Civil Rights stating:

"RE: #252194 v. Famous Parts Company

Dear Ms. Carrie,

This letter is to confirm our telephone conversation of November 30, 2000. As we discussed at the time you contacted the department, you had not yet filed a written accommodation request with your employer. As a result, we could not take a formal complaint. On September 25, 2000, you did make a written accommodations request. Under the *Persons with Disabilities Civil Rights Act,* your employer has a reasonable time period to respond to your request. We believe that time period should be no more than 15 days.

If your employer rejects your request or has taken no action after 15 days of your request, please contact the department so we can determine if their actions violated the Persons *with Disabilities Civil Rights Act.*

At this time, we are going to cease the processing of your reconsideration request of the above captioned statement of concern. If you have any questions, please contact me at the telephone number below."

I was called back to work at Woodrow Stamping Plant on December 8, 2000. Woodrow Stamping was angry with me for returning to work. The harassment started again when I returned back from my medical leave. I had applied for a variety of bid jobs and union-appointed positions, but all that was to no avail. When I returned, I was yet-working in area CT20. I mainly worked small jobs. I was normally on clean-up detail. The line I worked moved to Mexico in spring of 2001. After the line moved out of the plant, I was sent to the Medical Department because my supervisor said he had no work for me at that time.

While I was on medical leave, Metro Craft, the insurance company for Famous Parts Company, sent me for an evaluation on January 29, 2000 and Woodrow Stamping Plant sent me to an independent evaluation by Dr. Butt on January 17, 2000. This was my first evaluation.

My supervisor told me to go to the Medical Department because he had nothing for me to do. When I reached the Medical Department, they in return sent me to Labor Relations. There was a new Black woman who was the Labor Relations Supervisor. Her name was Ann Spivey. She took the place of Ms. Money, who was also Black. Neither woman stayed in Labor Relations very long. The company got rid of both Black women who had degrees in their field. They were ultimately replaced by Silly Sally, who didn't know her left hand from her right. She had no degree and to make matters worse, she hadn't even completed her high school requirements. I guess all she had to be was Caucasian for Woodrow Stamping Plant to hire her as Labor Relation Supervisor.

Anyhow, my supervisor sent me to see Ann in Labor Relations. She asked me why I was sent there. I told her I really didn't know, but I had been told there was no work for me. Ann called the Medical Department and spoke to Nurse Tootie. Nurse Tootie told Ann they'd sent me to two doctors who found nothing to be wrong with me. I then told Ann that my injuries were incurred in the plant and they were just telling me nothing was found wrong concerning my health. In essence, Nurse Tootie was telling Ann to send me home but she didn't. I told Ann that I had hurt my back, had x-rays taken, and had many other medical problems. I told her of my restrictions that the Medical Department refused to honor.

The Medical Department was angry with me because I stated my condition derived from the work I did. The Medical Department wanted to say they had nothing to do with my occupational injuries. Nurse Tootie thought Ann was going to send me home, but instead Ann sent me right back to the Medical Department for Nurse Tootie to straighten things out. I didn't like the fact that Nurse Tootie said I had received two medical evaluations, which stated nothing was wrong with me. Nurse Tootie lied when she made that statement. However, Dr. Black, the doctor Metro Craft sent me to, opinion was contrary to what was

Dr. Butt's diagnosis which stated I had repetitive sprains/strains and that the company was at fault. Dr. Black didn't send me right back to work because I was unable to return at the time. Dr. Necktie was to have set up an appointment so Dr. Black could confer with the difference in diagnoses, but the Medical Department never set up the meeting.

Not long after that, the nurse in the Medical Department told me to see Worker's Compensation Representative, Mr. Allen Red. Each time I went to see him he was never in his office. When I finally caught up with Mr. Red, he asked me what I needed. I told him I didn't know, but I was told to come see him. I stated to Mr. Red that the only reason I could think of was the difference of opinion between Dr. Black and Dr. Butt.

I told the Worker's Compensation Representative, Mr. Red that my Worker's Compensation settlement was resolved in February 2002 and he told me he hadn't seen the paperwork. I told Mr. Red that I had the paperwork in my locker. But before I left headed upstairs to my locker, I told Mr. Red I had brought a medical document and handed it to the Medical Department to substantiate my medical condition. He had my medical files in his hand, and looked for tests I'd taken, which weren't in my file. I was really upset when he said my tests were not in my folder. I asked Mr. Red to allow me to see since I knew what I turned in to the Medical Department.

I had always run into problems with the Medical Department with regards to, testing that was done, which they always took medical information from my medical file. I even brought it to the attention of the union, on a few occasions the information was put back into my file. But that didn't last for long because they went right back and took it out. The time they put the information back in my medical file was when Tom Hemp was running for Plant Chairman. He was trying to please everyone because he wanted to win this election.

Mr. Red allowed me to see my file folder. After glancing through, I could not find this one particular test result, but I didn't see any of the information that I gave to the Medical Department. I was outraged! I went upstairs and brought back my Worker's Compensation settlement letter with me. I was going to give it to Mr. Red, but when I returned, his demeanor went from an all-time high to an all-time low. I knew something was wrong. The young man stood all red in the face and told me he couldn't do anything until he received the papers from Worker's Compensation.

I asked Dr. Necktie about the meeting that was supposed to have taken place between Dr. Black and Dr. Butt. He said there was no such meeting. I asked about the note Dr. Necktie, put in the computer in my presence. Then Nurse

Ruth More came and handed Mr. Red a piece of paper. I glanced at it and asked for a copy for myself. Mr. Red then told me I could not see it because my medical condition was not occupational, but personal. I was so outraged at the Medical Department I could have screamed. Mr. Allen Red, the Worker's Compensation Representative, had the nerve to tell me I could not have a copy. I told him I would not allow him to withhold this information pertaining to me. I took it upon myself to slide the paper out of his hands. I told him I was going across the hall to make a copy and would bring him back the original. The young Caucasian man turned as red as a ripe tomato.

As I walked to the door of the Medical Department, Nurse Tootie called me back and stated *she* would make a copy of the piece of paper, but she lied. She also called Labor Relations and the union to tell them of the incident. As a result, Mr. Red winded up losing his job because he should not have allowed me to look in the file folder. This incident only proved to me that there were two sets of records.

I was called in the Labor Relations Office and admitted I took the paper out of the representative's hands. They wanted to reprimand me, but they didn't reprimand Diane, the Worker's Compensation Representative, when she snatched the payroll deduction sheet from me because wasn't planning to pay me. It was almost like she would receive a pay loss if she paid me. I truly think bonuses were given, when they successfully pilfered money from employees with occupational injuries. She was giving me difficulty regarding my lost check stub. She told me if I'd ever lost my check stub again, I would not be paid and it didn't matter how high I went. I then told Diane I hoped I never lost my check stub again, but in the event I did, I *would* get paid. She had a lot of nerve, it sounded as thought she had a lot of pull someplace. That is when I first noticed the Medical Department was pilfering from Worker's Compensation. How could they take my money and keep it just because I lost my check stub? I then asked Diane if I didn't get my money back, where was it going. Diane had no answer to my question.

As I was being written-up for taking the paper out the representative's hands, it was noticed that I hadn't any blemishes on my employment record. The incident winded up being classified as a verbal reprimand. It was three weeks later I received the piece of paper I shouldn't have had access to. The Medical Department should've given me a copy on the day they called Labor Relations, but they didn't. I guess they had to regroup because they didn't know what else I was capable of doing at that point. I knew and they knew there was another set of records.

I was so feed up the Local 783 and the Medical Department in the year 2000. It wasn't just the Medical Department it was Woodrow Stamping Plant. They were pilfering my money telling me, I was part time when I was actually full time. They pilfered my money for three years and I was so tired of these two entities railroading me and everyone that came down their path, so I wrote this grievance thinking that I would be heard. I wasn't choosy who was listening as I was reaching out to anyone and there was no one reaching, back to help me so wrote this grievance. This is the letter handed to Tom Hemp as my grievance but he never acknowledge it, but is in my files if he didn't keep his copy.

This was the grievance that I filed in December 18, 2000 but there was another grievance filed in June 12, 2001 right before I was put on a 'no work available' by the Medical Department. The grievance explained what kind of treatment that I received by the Medical Department. I had written this grievance because I was continuing to have problems with the Medical Department, I thought if I could write my own grievance then there would be no problems with comprehending what had transpired against me and the Medical Department in my own words and the grievance reads as follows.

"I, Crista Carrie, received 120 hours of vacation pay for June 2001. I had Paul Nashing to review why my vacation pay hours were shorted by 40 hours. I was due to receive 160 hours in total this year. 2001 Paul Nashing stated he would get back with me with this information because he had to look the information up in the computer.

In the latter part of the afternoon, Paul informed me the reason I only received 140 hours was because I was penalized for being on medical leave for six months.

My grievance with the company is because I was recently put on a, 'no work available' at the Medical Department's discretion by not allowing me to work. My doctor never ordered any kind of medical leave—only a restriction, which cut my work capacity by 25% due to my wrists and hands. The restriction stated "no repetitive lifting over 10 pounds, no pushing or pulling over 15 pounds, and limited use of both hands". The restriction also requests, "Crista must wear braces on the job".

The following document was taken from the 5166 medical form completed by Dr. Sonia.

"The Medical Department wouldn't allow Crista Carrie to return to work although her doctor stated that she could. The company doctor also stated Crista could return to work. Crista had no problems complying with her work duties. What was the purpose of the Medical Departments action? I truly don't understand, but it seems to be a common practice.

The aggrieved, Crista Carrie is challenging the decision to withdraw 40 hours of vacation pay. Crista had no choice but to take a 'no work available' by the Medical Department, who would not allow her to work when she was willing and available to work. Her doctor had no recommendation for the aggrieved to be put on medical leave therefore she can't be held responsible.

The aggrieved has a grievance pending in reference to the Medical Department for harassment and the grievance is pending."

I found out this week there's a person who is on medical and has been every since the beginning of the year—yet received all his vacation pay. I can't give this person's name, but it will be a clear case of discrimination by this being a person of the Caucasian race.

I returned to work December 8, 2000, which was with regards to a decision made between Famous Parts Company and the Department of Civil Rights. (Case #SOC252194—Carrie v. Famous Parts Company)

Comment:
I have worked for this company for ten years and I have been discriminated against for the entire duration of my employment. I must say this facility is one plant that practices discrimination against minorities. A person really doesn't have to look very hard to see that racism is alive and well at this plant. Woodrow Stamping states it is a diverse institution. I as a minority, feel this company doesn't practice what it preaches in terms of diversity. This plant seems to be just as blatant on how they feel about minorities, and the Caucasians don't seem to mind in terms of job preferences. I feel the union is working along with management and allowing this practice to continue. Famous Parts Company as a whole doesn't tolerate this kind of practice—although I don't think this company as a whole has any idea on how the plant is run in terms of diversity ..."

After I left the Medical Department, I went straight to the committee room and asked Committeeman, Zeb Star, about filing a grievance against the Medical Department. I wrote my own grievance stating what the Medical Department had done to me. This grievance was dated June12, 2001. In this grievance, I also stated I wanted to be compensated for all the harassment I'd endured. Committeeman, Zeb Star, didn't accept my written grievance, but wrote a grievance which stated in partial:

"Since this is the second harassment statement I've made in the last year, I feel I must fully explain what harassment really means to someone how has been harassed on numerous occasions. The first harassment case was dropped under pressure, but my stipulation, was that if the harassment resumed I would file again.

The Medical Department is yet taking information out of my medical folder. They are constantly giving me the run-around about getting information regarding my health care and as a result, I was written up because the information that should have been in my folder wasn't there. I truly don't like mind games which the medical department plays on myself, and others employees who have work related injuries on the job and treated in this manner on a daily basis at this plant. This medical department is not interested in the employee's health and safety. The only thing they are interested in is keeping the census down in regards to work related injuries. I guess Woodrow Stamping Plant bought and paid for the safety award because they're too busy sending employees home with personal injuries which originally happened on the job, or taking people off their restriction between doctor's visits. I would like you to know how these injuries have affected my medical condition today.

The company is not interested in the employee's well being, it doesn't matter how they profess safety and health issues it's all a lie. Can you tell me why there is no information or literature informing the employees of their right under the worker's compensation laws in the state of Michigan? Employees need to know which rules and regulation effect their situation regarding work place injuries and not just having the company words on how worker's compensation works. There have been many employees who are injured or have been injured and didn't know they were to be compensated for lost work time. There was a time I lost my check stub and was told I could not get paid for that week because the lady stated I had to have my original pay stub which was impossible, before I could get paid.

I went to payroll and obtained a copy and she said she couldn't accept the copy from payroll because she couldn't read the various codes. After given the run around for a week or so I contracted Mr. Money the women in labor relation and the matter was settled. Although Dian Pest who was the worker's compensation representative in the early part of last year told me, if I lost my check stub again I would not get paid. I would like to see some of these rules in writing, stating you can't get paid if you loose our paperwork or if you make too much money you're not eligible to receive Worker Compensation for work related injuries, this is what has been told to some injured in the workplace. Why can't employees know what their right are if they are injured in the workplace.

I saw Dr. Necktie in March when he was ready and willing to discuss the report, which Dr. Butt had completed on January 25, 2001, stating I needed no restriction. He stated I could complete a normal day of repetitive work with braces on both hands. I thought something was wrong with the man's logic because working with braces on both hands is almost like working with a cast on both hands. You can't tell me I can complete a normal day's work with no full use of my hands. Working with limited use can result in a serious health hazard to others and me. My grips in my hands are weak sometimes. I have dropped two hot cups of tea, which just dropped out of my hands in the break area. If perhaps I weren't at the table I would have wasted the hot tea in my lap, which could have caused serious burns not to mention I could have accidentally waste the hot tea on someone in the break area.

My back is a different scenario altogether. This time a year ago, I walked with a limp on occasion, now it seem as though I have a permanent limp, with constant back pain. I have problems with my knees, back, and foot. I have to rest at the stairs landings before reaching to the top. I must say watching me work or just looking at me with all my added devices you would say it is impossible to accomplish a normal day's work as though I was going on a football field. The remarks are made daily.

At this doctor's assessment with Dr. Butt, in the month of March I gave him a copy of a report by Dr. Black. This report was given by Metro Care Insurance Company on January 29, 2001. Dr. Necktie stated their opinion were similar. In my opinion they were not the same, it doesn't matter how he looked at this situation because my hands are a very important factor when I'm always in constant pain from the Dequvain's disease. How can this factor be overlooked and seen as nothing is wrong. Dr. Necktie made it a point to say Dr. Black was a M.D. and my reply was, Dr. Black and Dr. Sonia came with the same diagnosis and Dr. Butt is a specialty in his field and he stated I had nothing wrong with me that an aspirin wouldn't cure.

Dr. Necktie noted after receiving Mr. Black's report that both doctors, Dr. Butt and Dr. Black both needs to come together to reach some kind of agreement as to what kind of restriction that is needed regarding my injuries. The medical department at Woodrow Stamping Plant was to have contacted me on this matter, although they did not. I constantly inquired and received no result.

In April I saw Dr. Necktie once again although not before the medical department sent me to labor relation because I wanted something in writing, stating that they were aware I was working on the plant floor in my condition, working without any restriction. They knew they were wrong since no one wrote anything stating that I could work without restrictions, while wearing braces on both hands. I talked to Candice Clark in Labor Relation and she informed me, she had talked to Nurse Tootie. She said she had sent me on two occasions, to see an Independent Medical Examination paid by the Medical Department. I was told by Dr. Butt there was nothing wrong with me, as I sat in Labor Relation talking to Mr. Clark with braces on both hands. Dr. Butt stated I needed no restriction, and my injuries were of a personal nature. If that was the case the Medical Department should not have ignored my doctor's restrictions.

I said to Ms. Clark I was sent to the same consulting physician on two occasions which stated I needed no restriction. The physician I saw the first time was the same physician I say on the second consultation. I explained to Ms. Clark in Labor relations how I was injured in 1999 working on line 441 stations 15. I complained about my back for 10 months before I decided to talk to my family doctor and she made an appointment for me to see Dr. Sonia. I stated I didn't quite understand why they sent me to Dr. Butt on two occasions, when the first time the Medical Department had him to complete and EMG (Electrophysico-loic, which test the activity of the muscles) on my whole body. When I started asking about the results they always had to have the information faxed, never having the information at hand. Nurse Tootie made it seem as though I was asking Labor relations for a restriction, which I was not, quiet as it's kept, I had no business in the Labor Relation regarding my medical a condition.

When I received Dr. Butt first report it was incomplete because it didn't cover all the areas which I was tested. When I contacted the plant manager Mr. Snow regarding this matter he contacted Verlinda Moose to intervene. When I returned to medical with Ms. Moose, Nurse Tootie lied and said I didn't have this type of test done. I became furious because I'm the one who was stuck with needles all over my body and as it stood it was for nothing, not to mention making it look as though I was the unstable one. I resented this fact dearly. The medical department made my appointment on Martin Luther King's Birthday and I was never compensated for this day. I should have been celebrating this holiday as other Famous Motor Company employees were. After discussing the matter with Labor Relation Ms. Clark sent me back to medical to settle the matter with Nurse Tootie and she was fuming with anger when Ms. Clark did this. I spoke to Nurse Tootie she set up another appointment to see Dr. Butt once again.

On my first appointment with Dr. But she stated my back was fine, two month later I received a MRI (Magnetic Resonance Imaging) test which stated I had degenerative disk disease. I have never seen a worker's Compensation doctor, regarding my back even though I complained daily. The medical department knew about my strain/sprain in my upper and lower back. When worker's Compenstion finally set up an appointment to see Dr. Steeler and she order more x-rays and examined my reflexes she made no follow up appointment. After the x-rays were taken an appointment was made to see Dr. Steeler by the medical department for December 21, 1999, which Dr. Steeler canceled this appointment with prior notice. When I reached the office of Dr. Steeler on the 21 day of December her nurse informed me that she couldn't see me. I asked could I speak with her and her answer was no. I feel it is truly a problem when a doctor you're supposed to be seeing can't answer your medical questions. This was Woodrow Stamping Plant's Independent Medical Examination.

The Medial Department had all the information regarding my back, because I had x-rays taken at Midway Hospital in August and at that time I had a sprain/strain upper and lower back. I was given Worker's compensation for my back and the medical department only addressed my shoulder for (Rotator Cuff Tendinitis) and arthritis is my cervical spine. Dr. Steeler sent me to therapy three days a week for about eight weeks.

In June of 2000 I was put on a 'no work available' and was out of work for six months until I contacted the department of Civil Rights regarding this matter. I was called back to work in December and was told by Dr. Necktie that I needed to see a doctor regarding restriction once again. My appointment was made for January 25, 2001 with Dr. Butt for the second time.

I didn't tell Woodrow Stamping medical department I had already seen by Dr. Black because I didn't feel it was necessary at the time. After I saw Dr. Necktie in March, I felt this information was important because my court date had been constantly set back, and my condition wasn't getting any better. I brought a copy of my MRI report and a copy of the hand x-ray upon Dr. Necktie's request. On this day I gave Dr. Necktie a copy of Dr. Black report and his findings.

One of my main conception is the medical department had taken no further responsibility for the occupational injury to my right should and cervical spine. This department has done nothing in terms of responsibility, since I obtained my own physician. As of now the Medical Department is accepting no responsibility for anything what so ever regarding these injuries and the medical department, took it upon them-selves to make my condition a personal injury as well? Not looking in the medical archives to obtain information on how many times I have been injured for the same injuries during these past years.

I'm always having spasms in my neck, back, legs, my hands, arms elbow are cramped and in pain after each day of work on various days, some pain is greater then others. By the medical department not responding to the injuries, which were incurred on the job sending me to a consulting physician on two separate occasions, not acknowledging or taking responsibility of my condition. Giving me the run around to the point I'm asking for copies of information which was stated I couldn't have regarding myself. I was written up for taking the paper and going to make copies. I admit I acted in a negative manner by taking the paper from Mr. Allen Red hands that was the worker's compensation representative hand, but under the circumstances. The medical department has taken information from my medical file and I'm having, to run all over the plant in my condition trying to gather information that should have been in my medical records. I myself brought the information into the medical department. I have never been written up for anything since working at this institution that I can remember. Harassment is not supposed to be tolerated in any institution.

I asked Mr. Red to check Dr. Black's report and a copy of a letter of reconsideration, where the Medical Department had agreed to work around my restrictions, but this letter wasn't put into the file either. He said the information wasn't in the file and I disagreed with hem, because I told him I brought the medical information into the medical department myself. I asked Mr. Red to let me see, and he handed me the file and I myself looked in the file and didn't see the report form Dr. Black or the worker's compensation reconsideration note which was brought in on July 13, 2001. I then told Mr. Red I had a copy in my purse in the locker upstairs and he then asked me to obtain the letter, which I did. I told Mr. Red my case was yet in litigation and he stated when I returned with the paper from upstairs in my locker, that he could do nothing until he received paperwork from the court. I said to Mr. Red, why was the Medical department giving me the run-around when they know they weren't going to do anything with the request Dr. Necktie made in reference to my restrictions.

I asked Nurse Ruth Moore to obtain a copy of this statement, which was made by Dr. Necktie. After I had returned with the paper Mr. Red's attitude seemed to have changed. He became very impatient with me. After Ruth More brought the paper to Red he said to me, your medical condition is a personal injury and he could do nothing. I asked to see the copy, which he allowed me to see. I then asked him for a copy and he said no, because it was personal. I then slipped the paper out of his hands to go and make copies. I walked around to the front of the medical and met Nurse Tootie and she asked for the papers and I handed them to her and she said she would make me a copy. I did receive a copy two weeks later, although I looked at the information, although I became so upset I actually forgot what was on the paper, but I'm sure the paper I received was the one Red had. I do remember the paragraph wasn't as long as it seemed on the paper I first looked at. In my opinion all this could have been prevented and I'm truly sorry this medical department forced me to act in a manner that was unprofessional to me. This harassment has and is continuing from a year ago.

In April Dr. Butt wanted to read over Dr. Black's report once again and I waited in the office about twenty minutes before Dr. Necktie came to me and said, they couldn't find Dr. Black's report. I waited about another ten minutes and the report arrived. Dr. Butt stated once again that a decision had to be made as to a restriction in regards to my condition. When I saw Mr. Red he stated he knew nothing about my condition and or my case. Dr. Necktie stated he notified Mr. Red in worker's compensation of my situation. After three weeks of getting the run around, I just had enough of the lies and misconception. I don't understand why medical information just disappears out of the medical folder.

I asked Dr. Black how Dr. But in his January 25 report could make a determination without the release of the bone scan not taken under consideration since he is after all a consulting physician. I signed an authorization for release of information from Harper Hospital, were a bone scan was done. By this doctor being a consulting physical, how can he come to a decision without all the facts, I truly have a problem with this kind of diagnosis he gives.

On two other occasions information has been missing from my medial folder. In April 1999, I requested a copy of a restriction, which was given to me in 1990. I inquired about this restriction and was told I had no restriction. This restriction was for structure and lightweight work. The Medical Department didn't have a copy of this restriction in the file, after giving me the run-around from the union and labor relation. They didn't want the restriction, they didn't want to know about the restriction, and they surely weren't going to put this restriction back my file. After all—they were the one's who took my restriction out of my file folder. I gave a copy to labor relations supervisor Verlinda Moose, she told me to take the paper with my restriction to the Medical Department. My weight and height was taken once again, I was told by the nurse on the midnight shift I was yet five feet tall, but I weighted over 120 pounds therefore my restriction didn't apply. The ability to work report said nothing about weight. I'm not sure how or why this restriction was expired in 1993. The information was put back in the file during Tom Hemp run for bargaining committeemen. I told him about the missing information and he saw that my information was returned.

The last time I found information missing from my file was when the nurse in the medical department kept telling me, I needed to see Mr. Red who is from Worker's Compensation. He was to have informed me as to what kind of restriction that I should have been given. When I saw him it was as though, he knew nothing about what I was talking about. The nurses kept telling me I needed to see Mr. Red. On the day Mr. Red came back to the plant no one seemed to have remembered, or could even recollect why I should be seeing or talking to Worker's Compensation. I asked Mr. Red, why am I getting the run-around and he said, he received nothing across his desk stating he should do anything. I asked who is it I should be contacting in a mile manner voice, if I may ask. At this point and time he started getting rather uneasy. I expressed to him I meant no harm, I was just trying to get some straight answers.

I asked Mr. Red about my complaints with regards to working and furthering my injuries, or causing my injuries to worsen. I was told if it's an old injury, it can't be addressed because the injuries are not new injuries. I stated, you mean you're telling me I can't complain about getting worse because I have an old injury. I feel just as long as I'm working and my injuries worsen nothing can be done. It shouldn't matter whether it's an old injury or not, because if I'm hurt on the job or my injury is further aggravated caused by the work I'm doing it should be covered. Mr. Red stated it's not covered by Worker's Compensation. This is an understatement and it's untrue and unsafe. Especially, when the company tells you it's a personal injury after their efficient (safety first) scenario. I would like a full understanding of how these rules or laws applies.

Its bad enough I have to work all day with pain along with braces and being constantly harassed and given the run-around by the Medical Department stating, my medical condition is personal and due to my age, and not acknowledging the injuries which they know are a fact. Have anyone cared to look into the medical history, for the last ten years and ten months to see how many times my body had been strained or strained or injured while on the job. I truly don't think so, I truly think the people in the medical Department only cares about saving the company money not caring about their employees. I'm a human being with feeling, there is no need for the Medical Department to put me through the mental and physical abuse, this is truly cruel and unusual punishment. I want to be compensated by the harassment that the Medical Department continue to display against me.

"… The aggrieved is protesting the harassment and lack of cooperation that is received by Woodrow Stamping Plant's Medical Department. The union and the aggrieved demand that this harassment stops and cooperation be put in place …" This was written on June 27, 2001. This is the response the company gave the union when they met on my behalf. This was the company's response giving reference to grievance (L425) which stated:

"The protested employee has not harassed or been harassed and has been uncooperative with the aggrieved. The protested and their supervisor are willing to discuss any pertinent issues with the aggrieved to resolve any questions on the subject of the Medical Department."

I went on a 'no work available' medical leave and when I returned, the union told me we would be discussing this grievance. They lied to me for two weeks when they knew the grievance had been settled all along. I was really angry with Local 783 and Woodrow Stamping Plant for lying and deceiving me. They wanted to make me think the grievance was yet in existence when the grievance was settled in favor of Woodrow Stamping Plant and the Medical Department. At the same moment they were telling me that they were going to meet on the grievance, knowing full well the grievance had already been settled, in July 2001 thirty days after the grievance was filed.

Everything the Medical Department said was a lie, and Local 783 was a liar just the same. I filed a complaint with the Department of Civil Rights and the National Labor Relations Board (NLRB). As a result, they didn't investigate my complaint. I was forced to drop charges against the union by the National Labor Relations Board, and the Department of Civil Rights sent a letter requesting Woodrow Stamping Plant brought me back. Woodrow Stamping Plant and Local 783 did as they pleased, because there was no accountability for their actions. They continued to violate contract and labor laws. Woodrow Stamping Plant and Local 783 were some dirty sons of b*tches.

Soon after I was called back to work from my 'no work available' in December 2000 after the grievance was filed. I received a telephone call from Mrs. Sharon Stench of the National Labor Relations Board. She told me Local 783 and Woodrow Stamping Plant were working in good faith regarding my grievance, and that she felt I should drop my grievance against them both. I felt that this lady wasn't giving me much of a choice in whether to drop my grievance or not. She stated if I didn't drop the charges, she would drop them for me. I truly felt pressured in making a choice because my complaint wasn't complete.

I felt I was within my rights to write an article in the union newspaper. I wanted to know why this woman was forcing me to drop my charges. I told her I'd think about it and get back with her in a few days. She couldn't wait a few days because she called me back and asked me what my plans were. I told her I would drop the charges. I stressed to Mrs. Stench I was working a lot of overtime and had forgotten to do so. I received another call on December 20, 2000 asking if I had written a withdrawal letter. I told Mrs. Stench I would fax the letter on the following day, after I came home from work. At that point and time, I thought I was dropping my charges against the union and company for the "conflict of interest" article. This is what I *thought* I was doing, but that was not the case. I didn't want to drop the charges, but I did so because I felt forced to.

On December 21, 2000 I faxed Mrs. Sharon Stench, from the National Labor Relations Board, in a statement that said:

"I Crista Carrie would like to drop the charges against Local 783. They have been working in good faith since my contact with them. If the union fails to complete their obligation, I will contact this office once again."

Since I was forced to drop the charges, I felt I might have a chance to raise my complaint once again. If Local 783 didn't follow through with the grievance procedure as they should have, I would have the opportunity to bring my grievance back to the National Labor Relations Board's attention. I didn't want to withdraw, I was forced to. I could bring this same grievance to their attention—and this is what I did. At that point the Department of Civil Rights began forcing me to withdraw my complaints each and every time I filed one. It seemed like the more I appealed, the more they denied investigating—so I was forced to do what they asked. I had no idea they would totally stop working on the grievance altogether, but that is exactly what Woodrow Stamping and Local 783 did.

They stopped working on the grievance on the same day I faxed the withdrawal letter, according to paperwork I received from Tom Hemp, who was currently Bargaining Committeeman. At that time, I requested the paperwork on the grievance even though I had no idea they had stopped working on it the day, I faxed the withdrawal to the National Labor Relational Board. I actually didn't find this out until I filed the second grievance against the Medical Department on June 26, 2001. I filed the second grievance with the National Labor Relations Board in 2001 because I had filed another grievance regarding the Medical Department at Woodrow Stamping Plant. Each time I would file a complaint with the Department of Civil Rights, I always filed a claim with the National Labor Relations Board regarding Local 783 was giving me a problem.

The first doctor I saw was Doctor Butt the Independent Medical Examiner third-party doctor for Woodrow Stamping Plant. They sent me to see Dr. Butt on Martin Luther King Junior's birthday. I didn't get paid for going to see the company doctor on a holiday, but I should have. I guess Woodrow Stamping withdrew triple-time from their Worker's Compensation fund. I know I should have been paid and they knew it too. There was nothing I could do about it because the money was put in special accounts. The Medical Department would do things like this in order not to reward me for my occupational injury. The doctor's appointment should have been made on an alternate day on company time—not mine.

Anyhow at my visit with Dr. Butt, I brought my x-rays and MRI which had been taken by Dr. Sonia. This is the day Dr. Butt ran more tests than recommended by the Medical Department. However, Nurse Tootie stated they did not run more specific tests than recommended. She wouldn't even give me the results. Nurse Tootie had stated in a referral what kind of tests she wanted done. The referral was to see Dr. Steeler first, but she refused to treat me any longer in a manner that I would be comfortable with. She allowed me to go so long without examining my back, when I complain she finally decided I was more trouble than she wanted to deal with, so the Medical Department sent me to see Dr. Butt instead. If I would not continue to treat with her, I would have held her accountable for my back. She treated my neck and shoulder but she did nothing to evaluate the pain in my back while I treated with her and I complained for months. This was for an evaluation of the lumbar/sacral spine, but Dr. Steeler never once touched my back, even though I complained constantly about my back. Nurse Tootie's referral to Dr. Butt for the back injury read: "Please identify any physical limitations. There were no specific incident, injury, or trauma to 4s spine." Nurse Tootie lied as usual when she stated no specific injury or trauma occurred. I had taken x-rays by the Medical Department which revealed I suffered with a strained/sprain my upper and lower back. This meant Woodrow Stamping Plant sent me to see Dr. Butt for something other than an occupational injury. I thought the only reason an employee would see a company doctor was, if they had an occupational injury only.

I had been complaining about my back since April 1999 when Nurse Tootie made this statement. My back was the specific cause why I was seeing the doctor in the first place. If you really think about it, what reason would I go to see a company doctor? It had to have been due to the company's insistence. I would go to see my *own* doctor. All the Medical Department did since my injury was to interfere with my doctor/patient relationships. They lied about medical findings, falsified medical records, and even had me on payroll while I was on medical leave. Dr. Butt's first evaluation was on January 17, 2000 and his decision read as follows:

"Ms. Carrie is a 49-year-old woman who has multiple symptomatic complaints worsening over the course of time. Today's clinical assessment is normal from a neurological perspective. The asymmetry to sensation does not conform to an anatomic distribution. There is a non-physiologic gait pattern and non-physiological sensory asymmetry. She is reporting complaint to palpation, but it is no localizing in any landmarks through the upper and lower extremities or back structures ...

If I had multiple symptomatic complaints, why would my neurological assessment be normal? I had "many complaints", but that was "normal" and I was sent back to work without restrictions. Even if Dr. Butt wasn't sure of the diagnosis, he should not have sent me back to work without restrictions because he couldn't find the source of pain. I was yet in pain. My God! He was the doctor.

The report continued:
... In summary, musculoskeletal and neurological examination failed to identify any objective abnormalities. There are other diffused pain complaints and these do not appear to be reflective of discreet musculoskeletal or neurological pathology. Nerve conduction studies today were normal. Other studies available are not productive in explaining her symptoms ...

Where did they find Dr. Butt, in one of the old Frankenstein *movies? Evidently he didn't know how to read the test results—especially when it came down to me. He had the x-rays in his possession for my back, as I continued complaining about my back, being in so much pain while in his office. My complaints were a useless waste of breath because he didn't hear a word I was saying nor did Dr. Steeler. He said there was nothing wrong with my back or any other parts of my body and that I didn't need any restrictions. Dr. Butt did nothing.*

... In summary, I am not able to identify a physical indication for limitations or restrictions. It would not be anticipated that further attempts at physical interventions would positively impact the complaints. I appreciate the opportunity of having assessed Ms. Carrie today. Should you have additional questions or concerns, please do not hesitate to advise me."

This man had me return to work with no restrictions. When I did see another doctor, the Medical Department wasn't corporative in handing over medical results to her. I signed a release of information with Dr. Sonia, but they didn't send her anything regarding my medical condition. When Dr. Butt gave me an EMG on his office machine, he kept playing with the knobs. I assumed he was adjusting the machine to obtain a favorable reading. With all my complaints of pain in his office, I could not understand why he stated I could work without restrictions. At that point and time, I had previously received injections in both hands and my right shoulder, which helped a lot. Dr. Butt was aware I was wearing forearm bands and wrist braces. Under these circumstances, Dr. Butt still felt I needed no restrictions.

After being on my feet for so long, I would loose steam. By the end of the day, I had to walk even slower than usual because I had to drag my leg. I was in a lot of pain. I would also have muscle spasms on a regular basis. Those spasms were painful and left my leg very sore the next day. When I went to work each day, employees would laugh and make fun of me, saying I looked as though I was going on a football field. Labor Relations Supervisor, Mr. Tarry Johnson, in particular teased me about this.

I guess seeing I was very different from seeing any other employee. I didn't see anyone in the plant having to wear all this equipment just to get a job done on a daily basis. Management and co-workers all made fun of the way I walked, and looked with my braces and padding. I remember once I went into the Medical Department and the nurses gathered in a group to stare at me as I signed in. I asked, "Is there a problem?" They had a lot of nerve talking about me as though I was not there. The group broke up and one of the nurses stated, "They weren't talking about you". This was a lie because they were all huddled and giggling while looking at me. I became angry, got loud, and stated, "He who laughs last, has the best laugh". After that, they never disrespected me in that manner again. I think they were more afraid of me because I had no problem challenge them. They knew I was aware of what they were doing in the Medical Department and it was all illegal and wrong.

This following is another medical report. It was done by Dr. Black, IME's doctor, on January 17, 2002—only seven days after Dr. Butt's evaluation. Metro Craft Insurance Company wanted to set up an appointment to see their doctor for an evaluation. Dr. Black's report was contrary to Dr. Butt's. You would wonder how Dr. Butt could just look over these important facts regarding my health. Dr. Butt's license needed to be revoked—never allowing him to practice medicine again. It didn't matter what any other doctor stated about my diagnosis, Dr. Butt was never in line with them. Woodrow Stamping Plant only took Dr. Butt's findings as final, and his diagnoses were always wrong. Dr. Butt was paid by the Medical Department to give insufficient results. He kept the money-laundering schemes alive. Dr. Butt played a massive part in falsely diagnosing employees in order for the Medical Department to keep their flow of illegal money.

Dr. Butt would administer all these tests to employees, but never found anything wrong—even when other doctors stated different. This doctor, who I gave the name "Quack-Quack", had no business practicing medicine and giving patients this kind of treatment. His medical findings and lack of giving me a restriction caused my body to actually worsen. I couldn't believe this doctor took an oath to save lives, but was killing employees slowly. I will have <u>Degenerative Joint Disease</u> for the remainder of my life. All the medication I take on a daily basis causes long lasting side-effects on the body and the heart.

The following report was written by Dr. Black, for Metro Craft Insurance Company's doctor. The succeeding information is in partial:

"… The positive findings were relative to the 1st dorsal compartment in both wrists. The right shoulder has suggestion of impingement syndrome, and in the right elbow there is a suggestion of possible ulnar nerve entrapment. She may have some DeQuervain's Disease.

With regards to her neck, back and shoulder, I feel she has Degenerative Disease related to her age and genetics—which is not work-related. I have requested her diagnostic studies and will issue a supplemental report once those studies have been received.

She is currently working and can continue to do so. However, restriction to power-gripping with the hands may be needed when she is symptomatic relative to the 1st dorsal compartment of both wrists. She did not have findings of Carpal Tunnel Syndrome, but she does have findings of a possible ulnar nerve entrapment at the right elbow. This is a peripheral neuropathic process and she should follow with an orthopedic surgeon regarding that. A simple injection and/or surgery may be required down the road if those symptoms persist. I would also recommend home exercise. I do not see the need for physical therapy, manipulations, casting, or other treatment at this time …"

At this point I have seen three doctors (Dr. Butt, Dr. Black, and Dr. Steeler), two of which the company sent me to see. Dr. Butt was the only one who felt there was no need for any type of restrictions. Dr. Steeler gave me a restriction for a short time for my shoulder with therapy, but when she released me, I continued complaints about my back. I went back to work as though I had made no complaints of back pain or any other pain. Dr. Black diagnosis was to the contrary of Dr. Butt's and he was from Famous Parts Company's insurance company, Metro Craft. Dr. Black felt there should have been a restriction with my hands and arms. You would think Dr. Butt would've been smart enough to know I needed restrictions. He noticed I had a serious problem with my hands, wrists, and arms, but still favored the company by stating I needed no restrictions. If Dr. Butt didn't see anything wrong with my hands and arms, he would definitely not see anything wrong with my lower back. If I was just fine, Dr. Black would have cleared me to return back to work. This proved that my medical condition was something that should not be ignored. I started seeing Dr. Sonia, when my primary physician referred me to see her and an appointment was made, for February 14, 2000. Her finding after careful examination of my neck was:

"… neck and range of motion is close to full limits. Spurling's test is negative for radicular symptoms. Mild tenderness is present over the lower cervical spine midline …"

Even in September 2002 on my final day of work (before I was put on my final 'no work available'). Woodrow Stamping Plant Superintendent put me back on the line when he knew there was a problem with my back. I had to constantly bend up and down. I returned to work after that and worked two weeks before Nurse Tootie put me back out on a 'no work available'. Dave Dickey the plant Superintendent asked me to lift a 45-pound rail while I had braces on both hands. It was as though they were either stupid as hell or harassing me. I wasn't going to allow this treatment, and I was trying to find Local 783 so I could file a grievance against the Medical Department and the nurses too. Management at Woodrow Stamping Plant allowed the Medical Department to treat me in this manner, so I planned to file the third grievance with Woodrow Stamping Plant and Local 783. In September 28, 2002 was the last day that I worked in the plant before my retirement.

Nurse Tootie eventually sent me for another IME (Independent Medical Examination) on January 17, 2000. The following document contains the results from Dr. Steeler.

"… She reports she asked to be returned to work with restrictions. She further reports Dr. Steeler secondary to no referral did not treat her back pain. A referral was then obtained by the patient for her low back and tailbone pain. She was then told she had Fibromyalgia. No follow up appointment was given.

Examination of the left shoulder: shows full elevation and internal rotation. Mild pain is present at the limits of movements. Impingement test is negative. Motor power in the supraspinatus muscle is 5/5.

Examination of hands: Tine's test is negative. Motor testing is 5/5. Sensation is altered in the median distribution—right greater than the left. Reflexes are 2+ and symmetrical.

Examination of the back: shows flexion at 80-90 degrees. Patient is noted to bend her left knee during movement and complains of lower back pain. Extension is 0-5 degrees. Rotation and extension movements are mildly restricted bilaterally. Straight leg rising elicits back and left leg pain to the foot at 80 degrees of left hip flexion. Motor testing is 5/5. Reflexes are 2+ in the knees and are difficult to elicit in the ankles bilaterally. Sensation is altered 20-30% in the left L5-s1 area. Patrick's test elicits significant left hip pain.

Impression of (1) Back pain with left leg redicular symptoms, rule our lumbar radiculopathy, (2) Left rotator cuff tendonitis, and (3) Probable Carpal Tunnel Syndrome …"

Dr. Sonia stated my diagnoses were "bilateral DeQuervain tendonitis, lumbar spondalosis, elbow tendonitis, and shoulder tendonitis". As you can see, Dr. Butt was the only person who stated there was no restriction needed, which caused my condition to eventually worsen. All of the above complaints were work-related injuries. Nurse Tootie advised the Worker's Compensation representative to close my case after it was re-opened February 16, 2000 (for the second time) after seeing Dr. Sonia. On March 28, 2000, Worker's Compensation sent me a letter of dispute stating my injuries were not work-related. This stemmed from Dr. Butts decision on January 17, 2000. It stated, "As of January 17, 2000, patient does not need restriction. Etiolog of pain is unknown". Woodrow Stamping Plant had Dr. Butt to lie and tamper with test results to accommodate the company in making false medical diagnoses. This enabled them to pilfer my Worker's Compensation and retirement benefits. On July 31, 2000 Dr. Sonia sent me to see Dr. Hubert, who is a hand surgeon. Dr. Hubert's findings were after Dr. Butt's examination. The following was the medical finding of Dr. Hubert's regarding my hands.

"On examination the previous tenderness over the first dorsal extensor compartment is resolved. Finkelstein maneuver is negative. Tingles at the elbow and flexion are also negative today for any complaints of parestheisas into the ulnar nerve distribution. She does have decreased sensation to pinwheel in the ulnar nerve distribution. Ulnar motor function is intact. Carpometacarpal grind test is negative on the right and positive on the left.

Impression: (1) Resolved bilateral de Quervain tendinitis, right greater than left. (2) Bilateral trapeziometacarpal arthritis, (3) Question of subclinical bilateral cubital Tunnel Syndrome, and (4) Asymptomatic benign appearing left scaphoid cryst."

This is when my medical condition got even worse, and I became unable to work as I had before. After my body was all used up, the company had no further use for me—other than continuing to take my money leaving me with nothing. This is when the countdown of getting me out of the plant's doors began. They didn't want to pay me for the injuries or illnesses brought on by the constant mistreatment I endured on the job. I had to often come to my own defense, and this is something the company didn't like. They were in charge and had no fear of breaking the law. They felt they *were* the law. It didn't matter how low they stooped, Woodrow Stamping Plant and Local 783 were a powerful entity together. I have seen cruel and unjustly acts committed with both organized groups working together. Woodrow Stamping Plant and Local 783 seemed to be able to move mountains that definitely shouldn't have been moved.

28

WHEN CRISTA FIRST FILED SUIT

One afternoon during lunch in September 1994, I was talking to Rosie and Ima in Sarrow Stamping Plant's break room. Rosie had earlier given me a business card for her lawyer, Mr. Hdith. I decided to contact him once I got home that evening. I called Mr. Hdith and gave him an overview of my case. He set up an appointment for me to come in his office for further information.

After I talked with Mr. Hdith, I informed Rosie I felt comfortable with Mr. Hdith's expectations of my case's outcome. I told her Mr. Hdith said I had a clear case of discrimination. I met with Mr. Hdith the following Saturday morning. Rosie said she had to speak to Mr. Hdith because he had informed her they would be settling her case very soon. Rosie also felt rather comfortable about the way things transpired with Mr. Hdith's handling of her case. We discussed some plant gossip for the remainder of our lunch hour before it was time to return to work.

I had an early class at Wayne County Community College on the Saturday morning of September 3, 1994. After my class was over, I kept my appointment with Mr. Hdith. When I reached his office, the doors were locked and the hallways seemed deserted. I sat on the floor waiting for Mr. Hdith to arrive. After all I was a half-hour early. When Mr. Hdith arrived at his office, I picked my up body from the floor as he approached me and extended his hand with his formal introduction. He then unlocked the door to his office and reached his hand inside the door to turn the lights on. It was quiet enough to hear a pin drop. The room was well lit as we walked down a long hall to his office. There was no secretary in the office on this early Saturday morning upon my arrival.

Mr. Hdith asked me very politely if he could get me a cup of coffee. I declined very politely because I didn't drink coffee. Most offices didn't offer tea and I was definitely a tea drinker. Mr. Hdith stepped out of his office to the coffee maker, changed the prior day's coffee filter, and replaced a new filter for fresh coffee. In just a few minutes the aroma filled his large beautiful office.

While Mr. Hdith was making coffee, I couldn't help but to notice the beautiful view from his office window. It was one of the most beautiful sights you would ever want to see. I was looking out of this large picture window viewing Southwest and Downtown Detroit below. I saw all the beautiful buildings from his office located on nine-mile road near Northland Mall, not far from the John C. Lodge Freeway. From his office I saw the freeways and how they looped around the city. The sun illuminated with a beautiful glow coming from the east. The powder-blue sky with no clouds gave this picture window the most amazing early morning view.

Mr. Hdith soon returned to the room where I sat. He sat his cup of coffee on his desk as he was just getting his day started. He grabbed his yellow legal pad and jotted notes as I spoke giving further information regarding my hiring issues. In detail I gave him the aspects surrounding my complaint and reiterated the information I expressed over the telephone. After completing my explanation, he told me he would take the case with an up front payment of $1,000 dollars for him to get started. I was aware I'd have to pay something although I wasn't sure just how much. I wrote him a check for the amount of $600. Since this was a Saturday, the banks were closed. The drive thru was open but I needed a casher's check, which could only be purchased inside the bank. I completed the transaction on the inside of the bank that following Monday.

Not long after my initial visit with Mr. Hdith, he started working on my case. He wrote Famous Parts Company requesting my employment file to be sent from Woodrow Stamping Plant and also Sarrow Stamping Plant. Mr. Hdith's main focus was on the racial discrimination and unfair labor practices I experiences. The 15 other employees who filed a grievance concerning their full-time status were for the most part Caucasian. As a result of the grievance, the matter was settled by awarding them full-time status. Even though I had identical circumstances, I was not given similar treatment. I complained of unequal treatment and pointed out cases where sons and daughters of Famous Parts Company's management were treated more favorably. I told him how I was accused of being a "troublemaker" and later, a "radical".

They were calling me names because I was aware they were pilfering my money and wouldn't give it back. When I confronted them, I was retaliated against by being transferred to another plant as a new employee. They terminated me to hide my original date of hire. All I asked for was my seniority back at first and it seemed as though I was asking them to give me my back pay as well. It took them three years to terminate me after they stole my benefits package from 1990-1993. I guess I was supposed to be grateful that they pilfered my money. They had already admitted I was full-time so what was the real issue here? I was the only Black person sent to Sarrow Stamping Plant, even though there were others who had more seniority than I who wanted to be transferred.

There were employees bypassed just to get me out of Woodrow Stamping Plant. And they didn't waste any time telling me I could never return. I was told the only condition permitting my return would be if Sarrow Stamping burned down. When I received the seniority date of November 13, 1993, I was very upset because I was told I would be a rehire when I transferred. They were showing me they didn't have to hire me if they didn't want to. I wondered how many people worked for a company and had three seniority dates.

Sarrow Stamping Plant took part in the desperate treatment I received. They agreed to go along with Woodrow Stamping Plant knowing they were breaking the laws and violating the contract. Everything that took place was all intentional. This left me no alternative other to say it was discrimination and retaliation. When I was seeking help there was no one willing to help me in my quest for justice. One of the reasons I returned to Woodrow Stamping Plant among many, was to hold them and Local 783 accountable for what they did to me. I wanted my seniority back with back pay. When I returned, nothing was going according to plan and I had no corporation from anyone.

This letter is a letter Attorney, James Hdith, sent Woodrow Stamping Plant September 5, 1994 before he became ill:

"Shortly after Crista transferred from Woodrow Stamping Plant to Sarrow Stamping Plant on November 15, 1993, she was given full-time status. She was given the above seniority date and no recognition was given to her previous seniority earned from 1990 through 1993. Crista discovered she was considered a new hire at Sarrow Stamping's Facility and that even the hospitalization insurance she previously carried had been canceled. As a resolution of her racial discrimination claims, the demand is made that her seniority date be adjusted appropriately and that she be made whole for such past discriminatory practices."

Mr. Hdith further requested a copy of my personal file pursuant to the Bullard-Plawecki Employee Right to Know Act—ACLA 423.501 Seq., which states:

"This act permits employees to review personal records to provide criteria for the review to prescribe information which may be contained in personnel records and to provide penalties."

Mr. Hdith enclosed a form executed by me authorizing the release of information. He also stated if they should have any questions concerning this matter to contact him at any time. After the letter was sent to Sarrow and Woodrow Stamping, I thought my case was in the appropriate hands and my problems would soon be solved. I assumed I would be receiving my seniority and back pay shortly. Mr. Hdith asked me if I knew anyone else treated unfairly or in the same manner. I told him I knew many people although I didn't have any way of contacting them at the time, for the exception of Mazzie Cane. After I officially hired Mr. Hdith, I was eager to contact Mazzie Cane and ask her if there were others who were treated in the same unjust manner at Woodrow Stamping Plant. Mr. Hdith wanted to know if they were interested in joining a class-action lawsuit. Mazzie said her co-workers didn't seem to want to join her in an attempt to obtain their back pay or their seniority.

Mazzie said she was going to follow through with contacting Mr. Hdith. I gave Mazzie his telephone number. It was a few weeks later Mazzie spoke with Mr. Hdith, and as a result of her conversation, she met him on November 7, 1994. She paid him $1,000 dollars retainer fee for him to be her lawyer. Mazzie tried unsuccessfully to get people aboard in a class-action lawsuit. Mazzie decided to join me in a lawsuit. Although Mr. Hdith represented my case separate from Mazzie Cane's, they were similar in many instances.

Mazzie informed some of the part-time employees about our plans. They felt they would jeopardize being hired full-time if they made Local 783 or Woodrow Stamping angry. Don't get me wrong, some wanted to speak up, but the part-time employees were afraid to speak in their own defense not knowing at the time they were full-time anyway. Plant Chairman, John Hail, told the part-time people there was going to be a time the plant would hire only part-time employees. John Hail stated if the part-time people participated in any of my meetings, their jobs would be on the line. He also told them part-time employees couldn't receive union representation until they became full-time. I tried acquiring answers about what benefits I should be receiving as a part-time employee. The benefits I was receiving were under the guidelines of a person who was full-time. The union became angry with me and told part-time employees they would be fired if they went along with anymore of my plots or plans. It didn't matter at the time if I were full-time or part-time. I only wanted what I was paying for and that was representation from the union collecting my dues monthly.

Plant Chairman, John Hail, had enough power to do what was right in terms of fair employment but instead he sided with the company to do what they wanted. John Hail wanted the part-time employees to be aware he had the option to do as he pleased. I guess that was correct but I thought the contract was binding and the union had the power to enforce what was written in the contract. I thought the contract was as binding as the United States Constitution. I later found out the laws weren't carved in stone as I thought. Even though the laws were written on paper it didn't matter if they were broken because money is power. Woodrow Stamping Plant and Local 783 brought new meaning to the word laws. They didn't follow laws. They were above the law and they made a mockery of the justice system.

The part-time employees were also aware that if Woodrow Stamping Plant wanted to hire new employees, they would be hired from the part-time pool according to John Hail. They didn't have to hire in the order of which they became part-time. Local 783 stressed Woodrow Stamping Plant could hire as they pleased, to whom they pleased, and when they pleased. I later found out the company was supposed to hire employees in accordance to the date they were hired into the plant. The first hired part-time employees should have been the first to become full-time.

They didn't even hire the employees full-time that were laid off during the 70's and rehired from 1988 thru the 1990's at Woodrow Stamping Plant. They should have hired those employees first before any part-time person who had no prior history at the plant. They left them part-time as though they had never worked for the company before. Local 783 being able to hire in any order they pleased was untrue.

On November 8, 1994 Attorney Hdith sent Woodrow Stamping Plant a letter in regards to Mazzie Cane. He stated he represented her claims of being denied seniority and other benefits afforded to full-time employees. He understood a grievance had been filed with Local 783 concerning contract violations but no relief had been granted to Mazzie. He specifically stated he understood Ms. Cane was a full-time employee with a seniority date of August 27, 1977 and that she was laid off in the 1970's. Mazzie Cane was recalled in 1988 but was denied re-employment due to the plant physician's erroneous insistence that she should be placed on restrictive work.

She was recalled in 1990 and was promised full-time employment although she was told she would have to start as a part-time employee. During her employment as a part-time employee Mazzie was also informed she received paid hospital insurance, a Christmas bonus, and holiday pay, which were normally paid only to full-time employees.

It is my understanding that she was finally put on as a full-time employee on May 22, 1994 but that no provisions had been made to adjust her seniority. She identified six employees who had less time than she that were put on a full-time status as of September 27, 1993. Mr. Hdith continued his letter further explaining Mazzie Cane's problems regarding Woodrow Stamping Plant.

"… My client contends the reason from the delay in placing Mazzie on full-time status was due to the erroneous belief that she had back problems. The company doctor stated she had to return back to work with a restriction. To assist us in evaluating my client's claims I am requesting a complete copy of her personal file pursuant to the Bullard-Plawecki Employee's Right to Know Act—MXLA 432.501 Et. Seq. and I'm also enclosing an authorization executed by my client authorizing the release of this information. Should you have any questions concerning this mater, please feel free to contact me at any time."

As a result of Mr. Hdith's letter, Woodrow Stamping and Sarrow Stamping forwarded the information to Mr. Hdith regarding me. This was the information needed to confirm my repetitive statements of being full-time all along. Mazzie wasn't that fortunate because Woodrow Stamping wasn't as cooperative in sending her employment records, or at least that's what Mr. Hdith stated before he became ill. My case was a little different because my employment file came with the information needed to support my claim. After Attorney Hdith fell ill and sold his practice, Mr. Bushe was to take over. Attorney Hdith stated in one of the letters destroyed in my house fire, my case was to have been settled out of court.

Mr. Bushe decided at one point he was going to give his partner my case, but then decided to take my case himself. I gave him all the information needed to file the 90-day right to suit letter in court. It didn't matter whether it was going to be in the federal or state courts. All I wanted him to do was file my case. Mr. Bushe stopped returning my telephone calls and he stopped representing me.

After a short period of time I contacted Mr. Bushe regarding the 90-day 'right to sue' letter. At this point Mr. Bushe had no reason not to contact me as he waited for the 90 days to expire. He had no plans to file my complaint in the federal or state court. First he tried to convince me I didn't have a case, but he knew I wasn't a foolish person and was aware there were many violations of contract and labor laws. Mr. Bushe finally told me the 90-day 'right to sue' letter wasn't filed in court. He had 2 additional years to file the claim in federal or state court. He allowed that time to expire, leaving me with no rights to suit in any court. Then Mr. Bushe decided to lie by telling me he had indeed filed the case in court. I became angry and took my grievance with him to the Attorney's Grievance Commission. By that time I had already received a letter from the Equal Employment Opportunity Commission, I contacted Mr. Bushe regarding the discriminatory practices Woodrow Stamping Plant brought against me. They never stopped their discriminating practices and they never paid me according to contract or under the labor laws of Michigan.

In November 1994, I received a call from the EEOC in reference to my discrimination charge filed in April 1993. Mr. Lance, of the EEOC, called and asked me about the case. He stated he'd just received my case and wanted information regarding my statement. I informed him I had obtained a lawyer handling my interest as of that point. That's what Mr. Bushe told me to say when asked about the case. Mr. Lance gave me his telephone number and asked me to have my lawyer contact him. I assured him my lawyer would contact him soon. I called Mr. Hdith's law office the same day informing the receptionist to contact Mr. Lance at the EEOC and left the telephone number. On several occasions I called and was assured Mr. Hdith got my message. This was before he turned his law firm over to Attorney Bushe.

A month or so after I received the 'right to sue' letter, I called to see if Mr. Hdith had received my messages or had responded to Mr. Lance of the EEOC on my behalf. It was then I was informed Mr. Hdith would no longer be representing me because he would not be practicing law due to him having Prostate Cancer. He had been hospitalized but his clients weren't notified.

I became very upset because not one person from Mr. Hdith's office informed me by telephone or other correspondence that Mr. Hdith would no longer be my attorney. The receptionist said she put all the messages on someone's desk. I'm not sure if it was the desk of Mr. Hdith or Mr. Bushe. I called the attorney's office once again. This time I was asking for the telephone number so I could contact Mr. Lance myself. I had misplaced the number due to thinking the business had been taken care of earlier in November 1994.

Once again on December 26, 1994 I called the law office for information concerning my case. I talked to Don Brown, who informed me he would be taking my case. We discussed my case over the phone for about an hour and a half. He said he'd contact me after further investigation. I called the law office January 9, 1995 due to receiving a 'right to sue' letter that came by certified mail. I called

Attorney Don Brown, who at that time informed me he was not my lawyer. He said Mr. Bushe was my lawyer and would be representing my case.

By then I was in total dismay. As you can imagine I became upset being given the run around. The lawyers didn't know which lawyer was going to handle the cases within the office. My theory was Mr. Bushe wanted to handle the case because he was compromising my case in favor of Woodrow Stamping Plant and Local 783. Mr. Brown on the other hand, wanted to handle the case on the merits. But Mr. Brown lost the argument due to Mr. Hdith's illness, when he left his practice to Mr. Bushe. Mr. Brown's opinion did not carry much weight in this decision. I was assured by Mr. Don Brown from the attorney's office and later by the receptionist, that someone would contact the EEOC on my behalf.

I was not given any satisfactory answers when I asked the receptionist if it would be possible to talk to Mr. Bushe. She told me he was in a conference and would get back with me. He had to go over the case since Mr. Hdith would not be returning back to work. Mr. Bushe set an appointment for January 15, 1995 to meet with me for an overview. From November 1994 until January 1995, Mr. Bushe was using stall tactics by whatever means necessary to keep my case out of court.

At the meeting I had with Mr. Bushe on January 15, 1995, I gave him the certified letter I received from the EEOC and he said he would take care of the matter. I called Mr. Bushe again on Saturday March 4, 1995 and left a message on his answering machine inquiring about my case. After I had not heard anything from Mr. Bushe, I called once again on March 7, 1995 and he informed me he had received my calls. He said he had my file on his desk along with Mazzie Cane's and had to confer with Mr. James Hdith. I asked if Mr. Bushe had received my file from the EEOC. I realized time was running out to file the 'right to sue' letter with the courts. I just wanted assurance that the case got filed before the April 7, 1995 deadline due to feeling a bit uncomfortable. The time was growing closer to the 90-days and Mr. Bushe had to enter the suit.

At the same time, I was trying to handle the grievance with Local 783 myself since Mr. Hdith became ill and had retired. Mr. Bushe wasn't working on my case from that point on. When Mr. Hdith was working on my case, I received some results. The only treatment received from Mr. Bushe was the silent treatment. My attorney Mr. Bushe didn't answer my questions and didn't answer my telephone calls. He forgot he was working for me. When he started working for Woodrow Stamping Plant and Local 783, my case suddenly stopped having merit. I truly think Mr. Bushe received a better deal from Woodrow Stamping and Local 783. I'm not a naive person. I was aware Woodrow Stamping was pilfering money from me and then fired me to hide the very claim I was full-time. I was the only person sent to Sarrow Stamping Plant, which further upheld my claim I was discriminated against.

When I returned in 1997 to Woodrow Stamping Plant, I was denied the right to re-enter to my home plant. There was no reason for this type of treatment. When I was denied entry, I was forced to go back to Sarrow Stamping Plant until all the dust settled. Mr. Bushe knew of the truth and that was the reason he was bribed in an effort not to allow my case to enter into the courts at any level. This was the reason Mr. Bushe didn't return my telephone calls. He had nothing to say on a positive note because he already had enough facts to file my 90-day 'right to sue' letter in the courts in 1994. Things seemed to be falling apart. Each day I went to work not knowing what to look forward to in terms of what Woodrow Stamping and Local 783 were cooking up. Apparently Mr. Bushe just wasn't interested and I was clearly disappointed.

Mr. Hdith would not have taken our cases regarding Woodrow Stamping and Sarrow Stamping Plant if he saw no grounds. Mr. Bushe was just a money hungry character that took payoffs under the table to disregard our cases. I can't see how a lawyer who was trying to stay in business would throw their commission away. Mr. Hdith expressed I had a case and the information he obtained was definitely prevalent to my case. I'm not a lawyer and even I was aware of this fact. Mr. Bushe was aware that an injustice was committed against me, so I don't understand why Mr. Bushe wouldn't represent me. He had a copy of my employment records in his possession stating I was hired on September 28, 1990. What more did he need?

Mr. Bushe was aware I was full-time for three years prior to my filing a grievance against Woodrow Stamping Plant that Local 783 never filed on my behalf. Mr. Bushe would have known a grievance was not necessary because I was already full-time and the grievance was only a stall tactic. Why was I sent to Sarrow Stamping Plant when I was already full-time? Why terminate me just to start my seniority all over again as November 15, 1993? This was what I'd call desperate treatment. Mr. Bushe sided with Woodrow Stamping Plant, Local 783, and the Executive Branch of the Union, the Executive Branch of the Company, the Department of Civil Rights, and the Labor Relations Board.

It didn't matter what Woodrow Stamping Plant did to violate contract and labor laws, you couldn't get anyone to hear your case in a court of law. There were many involved in this illegal activity. The courts were tainted with corruption and it was impossible to file a lawsuit with the judge in favor of Famous Parts Company.

With Mr. Hdith out of the way, Woodrow Stamping Plant and Sarrow Stamping Plant had one idea in mind and that was to make sure Mazzie and I didn't receive a dime. It didn't matter how many lawyers' offices we entered. Mazzie Cane worked at Woodrow Stamping at that point. On September 21, 1995 Mr. Bushe sent Woodrow Stamping Plant's Labor Relations Department on behalf of Mazzie Cane and me. It stated:

"My last correspondence to you was on May 30, 1995 in which you responded by telephone addressing the information contained in that letter, and more specifically the newly adjusted seniority dates for the aforementioned individuals. You indicated the NLRB recently gave the authorization with regards to the adjusted seniority date, but that Mr. Hail, Plant Chairman, published the early posting prematurely. My clients have indicated Mr. Hail indicated to them much earlier their new seniority dates. He also mentioned my client's benefits, specifically vacation days, personal time, Christmas bonuses, and any other benefits with regards to the profit sharing plan, would be adjusted accordingly.

My clients still do not understand why they cannot receive those benefits, yet their seniority has been adjusted. They were not new hires. Therefore their seniority dates should not have been affected. This is true in Ms. Cane's case, which has been with the plant and with Famous Parts Company a lot longer. Her properly adjusted seniority date should go much further back.

There is also the continuing issue as to my client, Crista Carrie, who is looking for a promotion or movement within the company. She was promoted or moved over to the Sarrow facility, which is causing her to endure longer driving distances to and from her home. These occurrences seem to be more retaliation and possibly racially motivated in my clients' cases.

Again I would appreciate a response from your office with regards to this letter. I am also contacting Mr. Hail or Local 783 with regards to his comments, some of which differ from our representation. If you will kindly respond back to my letter, it would further clarify and confer with information I have in reference to Mazzie Cane and Crista Carrie, and it would be greatly appreciated. Both of my clients at this point are very unhappy and if this office does not receive the proper response with regard to their matters, they will have no other choice but to pursue this matter through the courts. Both individuals have exhausted their remedies with the union and have come up empty both with the union and Famous Parts Company. Until next time, I remain."

Attorney John Bushe informed me he had filed the lawsuit with the courts at one point and in the same sentence he went on to ask me if I wanted to file my lawsuit with the state court or federal courts. He stated it would be more feasible to file with the federal courts. He stated the state courts would be more lenient regarding awards against companies who are found in violation of the law, and the federal courts were just the opposite. The judges normally ruled in favor of the big companies and were not as harsh on companies found guilty in violation of the laws. Federal courts normally swayed in favor of big businesses with their decisions.

There was no need to adjust the grievance because Mazzie and I was given the seniority date as of July 15, 1991. The date we received was incorrect because Mazzie should have received her seniority going all the way back to 1977 and I should have received my seniority as far back as 1990. Why would Mr. Bushe threaten Woodrow Stamping Plant and Local 783 of court action if there were no cases? Why would the National Labor Relations Board need to authorize the seniority dates when the dates were already active and in existence? They were yet pilfering our money and weren't planning on giving it back.

Mr. Bushe signed the letter representing both Mazzie Cane and myself, Crista Carrie. Mr. Bush sent this letter two months prior to my receiving the 'right to sue' letter from the EEOC. Mr. Bushe was such a liar. Why he hadn't filed my case in the courts is beyond me. Still he did not return my phone calls and later informed me I didn't have a case after he'd stated otherwise on earlier occasions. This was clearly a case of retaliation from the very beginning. Mr. Bushe was aware an injustice had occurred and he didn't throw my case out for lack of merit. I can't say what he received for throwing my case out, but there was no logic to what he was doing. Woodrow Stamping Plant and Local 783 paid him in an effort that my case didn't make it in front of a judge or jury.

I can say Mr. Bushe received a new, gold, Town Car while he was working on our cases. I hadn't noticed the car until later. To be honest he could have purchased the car on his own, but Woodrow Stamping would always have raffles giving away cars n' such. Looking back at Mr. Bushe's actions, he could have received the car through Woodrow Stamping Plant's raffle not to pursue our cases inherited from Attorney Hdith.

After that conversation with Mr. Bushe, I had some questions regarding my case and I constantly tried contacting him. It was nearing the 90-day period with only a few days remaining. After my lawyer hadn't contacted me, I spoke to a lawyer friend of the family. He was in a different field of law but he told me to contact my lawyer by certified mail, which I did, and then received a response. I didn't know then but I know our family friend could have done more but I guess he didn't want to go against Famous Parts Company either.

This family friend worked for a law firm and tried to get his law firm's assistance in pursuing my claim. The law firm decided against taking my case. Every law firm I walked in knew I had a case, but refused to take it because they didn't want to get involved. Some attorneys wanted to know which plant I worked for. When I told them, they just showed me the door stating Woodrow Stamping Plant was hard to sue. Since I had no contact with Mr. Bushe, I sent him the following letter dated March 20, 1995.

"Dear Mr. Bushe,

I'm not trying to tell you how to run your office. All I'm asking is for a little of your time to inform me as to what is happening with my case. I paid Mr. James Hdith the amount of $1,000 dollars for services. I do not know what kind of arrangements Mr. Hdith made with respect to my case. The only thing I am asking is if you are taking my case please contact me as to what is happening to this date. I am writing this letter to inform you how disappointed I am with how things have gone. Our communication has turned to almost no communication at all.

I want to inform you the grievance was settled. I asked Labor Relations about going back to my 'home plant' or 'basic unit.' I was informed Woodrow Stamping Plant did not want me back at that location. Local 783 and Woodrow Stamping were to notify me by letter stating the grievance had been settled since I no longer worked at Woodrow Stamping.

Mr. Bushe I would like to ask you a question. If you were the client would you be satisfied with the way this case has been handled? Would you be satisfied with the communication that has transpired between our client/lawyer relationship? How would you feel not knowing who's representing you and not knowing what's going on at any given time in reference to your case? Can you honestly say your office has been doing the best of their ability in handling my case? Mr. Bushe if you truly don't understand where these questions come from, I feel you need to give up your law license."

When I left Woodrow Stamping there was a long period in which everything seemed to have been at a stand still. I had not heard anything about the grievance. The 90-days had expired and Mr. Bushe had not filed the charges in neither federal court nor state court. I didn't give up trying to get a lawyer to represent Mazzie and myself. She and I took days off work trying to obtain a lawyer to help us in our fight for what we felt was correct. I'm not sure how many lawyers we saw on our own time or spoke with over the telephone trying to get them to represent us. I yet had a two-year statue of limitation left on my lawsuit and I was trying to find someone else to represent us. Mazzie was doing the same.

In late May of 1995 Mr. Bushe sent Mr. R. Sophie, the Labor Relations Supervisor at Woodrow Stamping Plant, the following letter:

"… I have enclosed a copy accordingly stating her seniority date is June 20, 1994. There was an adjustment, which addressed to all employees stating her new adjusted seniority date was July 15, 1991. No one received this seniority date except Mazzie and Crista Carrie.

My client has also informed me nothing has been done to effectuate such a seniority date. This includes repayment of any and all of benefits that should have been received during that period of time such as seniority, vacation days, personal time, Christmas bonuses, and any benefits through the profit sharing plan.

I would appreciate a response from you as soon as possible with respect to status of implementing the new seniority date for my client. Thank you for your anticipated cooperation and if you have any further questions please do not hesitate contacting my office."

I thought if I would write the CEO at the Executive Branch of Famous Parts Company, maybe I might get some answers. I felt I had a right to fight if I was treated unfairly. I really didn't know what to do. I was let down and I had not one person at Woodrow Stamping helping me. I was only asking for fairness and I was still trying to get my seniority back along with the money Woodrow Stamping and Local 783 took from me. I had a lawyer prior to that point, although I did all the work Mr. Bushe should have done to represent me. For this reason, I needed to get this problem solved. I had three seniority dates. I sent the proceeding letter certified mail just to make sure it reached its destination. Letters dated July 15, 1995 were sent to Mr. James York, President of the Executive

Branch of the Union, and also to Felex Mann, CEO of the Executive Branch of Famous Parts Company. The letters stated:

"First I would like to introduce myself as a Famous Parts Company—Woodrow Stamping Plant employee. I started working at Woodrow Stamping plant in September 1990. I am sending this letter along with a cassette tape in hopes of getting help with a situation that has been going on since my employment started. I am truly not sure if I have stumbled upon something or not, but Woodrow Stamping and Local 783 have treated me in a manner I'm unhappy with. I have only tried to get answers as to what was happening, but management has done everything to discourage me. It has begun to take its toll on me.

I had been denied full-time status until November 15, 1993. On record it clearly stated my seniority date was September 28, 1990. I was separated from my work colleagues and sent to another plant. Labor Relations at Sarrow Stamping Plant told me Woodrow Stamping did not want me back and they could make it quite difficult for me to return. This was told to me when I arrived at Sarrow Stamping Plant and inquired about going back to Woodrow Stamping Plant. I was informed my grievance was settled. At this point I should have been given my original seniority date, but instead Woodrow Stamping Plant and Local 783 decided not to give me what was rightfully mine. They gave me the date *they* wanted me to have.

I have to explain to the best of my knowledge what has happened. I'll leave some details out to shorten my experiences occurring in the past four years, soon to be five. I received a response from the union who was ultimately passing my complaint from one person to another. I never received a response from Felex Mann, the CEO of Famous Parts Company's Executive Branch. I didn't even receive an acknowledgement of them receiving the letter, which is customary when you write a formal letter. I have kept the return receipts through the years stating they did in fact receive my letters ..."

After thirty days from sending my letter and receiving no response, I felt that either one of two things happened. One was that the letter was intercepted by someone working under Felex Mann, the CEO of Famous Parts Company, and the other could ultimately have been he was already aware of what Woodrow Stamping Plant was doing. I sincerely believed this group was well organized and that they had offices at the Executive Branch of the Company. I also believed this group was running a company within a company. When I sent this letter and didn't receive a response, I found it rather unusual for a company of this magnitude not to acknowledge a letter of complaint.

I was really excited when I wrote this letter because I knew I would expose the union and company in what they were doing as far as pilfering money from part-time employees. I really thought there was going to be an investigation of what was happening at Woodrow Stamping Plant. As time went on and I hadn't received so much as a letter or phone call, I became very disappointed. It was as though Woodrow Stamping Plant was laughing in my face … as usual.

29

IT WAS JUST A MISCOMMUNICATION

I had many transactions going on with Woodrow Stamping, Sarrow Stamping, Local 783, Attorney Bushe, and now the NLRB. As far as my grievance was concerned, it was yet on hold. No one ever gave me a reason why it was on hold. I started getting a bit uncomfortable and continued thinking my grievance was never filed officially. I heard the grievance had been finalized but when I wanted to obtain a copy of the final decision from Local 783, they were totally uncooperative.

I couldn't get a copy of the decision made with regards to the grievance I initiated. They didn't have a paper trail of the various stages of the grievance. This is what I was asking of John Hail, Plant Chairman of Local 783. I felt I should have received a copy of the decision as soon as the decision was made, but I did not. I was tired of getting the run around. I decided to file a complaint with the National Labor Relations Board (NLRB) on October 31, 1995 while employed at Sarrow Stamping Plant. The deposition stated:

"I have been given assurances by an agent of the National Labor Relations Board that this affidavit will be considered confidential by the United States government. It will not be disclosed unless it becomes necessary for the government to produce the affidavit in connection with a formal proceeding.

Famous Parts Company employs me. I have been a member of Local 783 since I've worked for Famous Parts Company. I started with this company on September 28, 1990 at its Woodrow Stamping Plant. The initial hire-in records reflect I was hired as a full-time employee on that day. However while at Woodrow Stamping, I only worked as a part-time employee.

I have really sought to question and solve the issue of the company refusing me full-time employment. According to records my full-time benefits were granted and then taken back by deducting monies through my paycheck. Part-time employees are not entitled to these benefits, nor are they entitled to profit sharing and performance bonuses. This is what I was told and also what I read in the contract book. I was transferred to the Sarrow Stamping Plant on November 15, 1993 ..."

Johnny Hilter, International Representative for the Executive Branch of the Union, told me there was a full-time job available at Sarrow Stamping. I accepted that job rather than remain at Woodrow Stamping as a part-timer while they were pilfering my money. I would have preferred to stay at Woodrow Stamping if they had given me full-time benefits. My records at the time said I was full-time. Why should I have to fight so hard for something already granted through the contract negotiations? Woodrow Stamping Plant with the help of Local 783, were taking those benefits and not paying me the amount allotted per hour. It was not until then that I was granted full-time benefits. At Sarrow Stamping Plant I started out as full-time, but Woodrow Stamping Plant had terminated me during the transfer. I was treated as a new employee with a new seniority date. I lost all my prior seniority and accumulated benefits.

This case arose out of the facts and circumstances involved in case #7-CB-9966. In this case the NLRB approved a settlement in March of 1994. The settlement required the union to provide me with a copy of the grievance filed on my behalf in 1993. I received a copy of the grievance by letter dated March 7, 1994 prior to signing this settlement, but it still was not the information I was requesting. The package of materials I received from the Local 783 indicated that on December 20, 1993 Woodrow Stamping denied the grievance. As far as I know, the grievance was at the Umpire stage of the grievance procedure when I got the materials from the union in February 1994.

From the time I received the materials from the union in February 1995 and entered into the settlement, I had no further communication with any union representatives until the grievance was settled in 1995. In July 1995, I was called to the Personnel Office at Sarrow Stamping Plant. Salma, of Labor Relations, told me I had won my grievance and would receive my company seniority going back to July 15, 1991. She said Woodrow Stamping Plant was my home plant and that if there were a layoff at Sarrow Stamping, Woodrow Stamping would have to pick me back up.

The first time I talked to any union representative about my grievance was after January 1994, and again in July 1995. I called John Hail, Plant Chairman, and spoke with him on January 12, 1995. I told him I heard my grievance was settled and I wanted to inquire about back pay. He said there would be no back pay. He also said he'd done his best in settling this case but wasn't able to get any money back. He told me to take that up with Sarrow Stamping Plant. But Sarrow didn't pilfer my back pay. Woodrow Stamping Plant did with the help of Local 783.

In a letter dated July 15, 1995 I communicated with the International Executive Branch. I told them I wanted a copy of the final grievance decision and wanted to know why I had not been involved in the grievance settlement meetings after asking to do so. I received a letter from Mr. Hail in August 1995 enclosing what he said was the final settlement of my grievance. Then a letter dated August 11, 1995 from the International Union advised me there had been a miscommunication with the local union. I was then referred back to Mr. Hail.

John Hail informed me on July 12, 1995 he didn't have to give me a copy of the final decision on the grievance. After all that happened, how was I supposed to know the decision made when I was at another plant? It was obvious I should have received a written copy of what transpired and how the decision was made on the grievance. Without the decision in writing, I clearly had nothing to base my grievance upon. I asked how I could not be receiving any back pay when my grievance clearly stated what I deserved and should have received in writing. I wanted to know how the grievance became half settled. I informed Famous Parts Company's Executive Branch of the Union and Local 783's Plant Chairman, John Hail, by word of mouth and by phone that I wanted to attend the meeting in regards to my grievance. I wanted to express my thoughts and opinions with regards to what happened and I was totally ignored.

I received a letter from Mr. James York, President and CEO of the Executive Branch Union, in August 1995 stating:

"Upon my investigation, I have discovered there has been an apparent miscommunication between you and Local 783 Plant Chairman, John Hail. At this time I must refer you back to Chairman Hail for further clarification of what you are requesting. If I can be of further assistance please contact me." The International Representative of the Union's Executive Branch (who negotiated on the company's part) signed the letter.

At this point I contacted Robert Rocker, Representative at the Executive Branch of the Union. Mr. Rocker was of no help either. When I sent another letter to Mr. James York, the President and CEO of the Executive Branch of the Union, I was referred to Mr. Robert Rocker for the second time. Mr. Rocker then sent me back to Local 783's John Hail. This was what I called the runaround. John Hail and now The Executive Branch of the Union wanted to call it a miscommunication between John Hail and myself. As I saw it, they knew exactly what they were doing. They were passing me from one person to the other and I began to get completely stressed over it. Attorney John Bushe wrote another letter regarding Mazzie Cane and myself.

I was trying to contact Mr. Johnny Hitler, Representative of the Executive Branch of the Union, and later found out he was no longer representing Woodrow Stamping Plant. I sent another letter to James York, the CEO of the Executive Branch of the Union, and he in return passed the letter to Mr. Rocker *again*. Then on October 15, 1995 I sent a letter to Executive Branch of the Union Representative, Mr. Rocker. It stated:

"Mr. Rocker,

The President of the Executive Branch of the Union assured me there would be an investigation in reference to a letter I sent to his office in July 1995. He stated the information I sent would be turned over to the Executive Branch of Famous Parts Company. Upon receiving your letter dated August 11, 1995 I disagreed with the assessment of the investigation stating it was only a miscommunication between John Hail and me. That was truly not the case. If you thoroughly investigated the information provided, it would be quite clear it wasn't just a misunderstanding.

I called Mr. Hail soon after receiving your letter and as far as I am concerned, nothing was resolved. I never received the final decision in reference to the grievance I asked for prior because he refused to grant my request. He finally sent me a letter certified mail, which was senseless. He sent a paper from the third stage decision. I now have two papers from the third stage stating two different solutions. He also sent me a book of The Constitution of the Union, but nothing in the letter explained why it was sent. I assumed it was for the appeal procedures which are all used up if the decision has already been to the Review Board …"

The Executive Branch of the Union Representative, Mr. Robert Rocker, knew this grievance never went to the Public Review Board. He also was aware the grievance wasn't filed. He became concerned when I wrote him a letter notifying him of the pilfering involving Woodrow Stamping Plant and Local 783. There were some questions that desperately needed answering. My letter continued:

"... Since this matter has been to the Public Review Board, I would like to know why I wasn't notified. I'd like to be informed as to what happened and why? I thought this was my right as an employee and union member being represented by the union. There should not have been any reason I wasn't allowed to participate in the grievance procedures ..."

I wanted everyone to know the grievance procedures were unfair and unjust. I always begged to question whom better than I would be able to explain the facts. After all I had the documents that would have questioned my employment status. According to the contract, I have a right to participate in the grievance process. As far as I was concerned, Local 783 prevented me from doing so. I could have explained why I should have received all of my back pay. I would have explained what I went through to get this problem resolved.

I was under the impression after you've completed all the stages of the grievance at the local level, the grievant and the representative sign the grievance. I never signed off on a grievance filed against Woodrow Stamping Plant. It didn't matter when my grievance went to the Public Review Board because the decision was already final. No matter what stages the grievance was in when completed, a call should have been placed for me to signoff the grievance. That never happened. I didn't receive a letter certified mail, which according to contract, Local 783 should have sent. This alone proved the grievance never went through the complete process. The contract explained the various stages of the grievance process. The union didn't follow the process and the appropriate procedures were not used. I guess this was how Woodrow Stamping Plant and Local 783 did their transactions regarding grievances they cared not to process. They just never filed any grievances on paper. I informed Mr. Robert Rocker:

"... I wanted and had a right to have a copy of the outcome. Grievance #H-183531 was filed June 6, 1993. As of yet I have not received a copy. I have to admit I'm growing a little impatient with regards to this grievance situation. It is as though I'm playing tug of war in order to get information that should be given without any hassle. From the start I've had to take Local 783 to the National

Labor Relations Board, just to obtain a copy of the grievance the union refused to give me. *It was a year before I received a copy of this document and it wasn't complete. I received a total of 3 pages. If a grievance has been through all stages, there would be more then 3 pieces of paper as to what transpired during the entire grievance process from start to finish.*

Comment: You claim you investigated the problem during the summer of 1993. I truly have a few questions on your ability if you found nothing wrong other than a misunderstanding. I am appalled. In my opinion, you just took John Hail's word for what happened and called it quits regarding the issue.

Sarrow Stamping's Labor Relations Supervisor, Salma, informed me I had won my grievance and I received my seniority back. This was in June of 1995, although Salma stated she had not received any formal notification of the settlement. They had the authority to correct the seniority date. Before Tarry Johnson, who is now Head of Safety at Woodrow Stamping Plant, left Sarrow Stamping, he asked me if I received a formal letter of response from Local 783. My reply was no. Tarry Johnson told me someone should have sent me a copy. After the discussion with Mr. Hail in July 1996, I decided to let my lawyer handle the matter. At that point I didn't know how useless he would be, but it didn't take long to find out. My lawyer stated he was having a hard time obtaining information from Woodrow Stamping Plant and Local 783. Therefore I'm asking you to send Mr. Bushe, my attorney and Counselor at Law, a copy. I would greatly appreciate it.

I wanted to read the final decision since this grievance had been through all stages and decided upon. I would receive a seniority date, which is obsolete to my date of hire. This date has no significance, except I came back from layoff July 15, 1991. In my grievance I asked for back seniority and back money which Ave Sophie, son of R. Sopie the Labor Relations Supervisor, received and kept along with a few other elites in the group. When we were working part-time together, Ave's father seemed to treat his family and other White co-workers just fine, but left the other employees to fend for themselves. Ave Sophie, son of Labor Relation Supervisor, and a few others received their vacation checks, performance bonus, and weren't forced to pay the money back while we were in the same job classification. The monies of all the other part-time employees who paid these benefits back were pilfered. Mr. R. Sopie stated he had the authority to do as he pleased. I'm truly not asking very much for the NLRB's final decision. I don't trust John Hail or his colleagues with good reason. I would like to know where all the lies stop and the truth begins to come to light.

I'm not quite sure if this is a conspiracy or if it's just everyone turning heads at what's going on. All in all, it's not proper treatment for the people who signed the grievance or me. We are union members that pay for representation when there's a problem between union and company. In my opinion this is why the union as a whole is losing ground. Unions can't work for the company *and* for the union members at the same time. It's either or. They are paid to protect and represent the union member. There is no room in between, or any question as to who the union is being paid to represent. Until something is done about this problem, it's only going to get worse ..."

Even a blind person could see there was a problem with the grievance procedures. When the Review Board made a decision in December 1994 and didn't follow through until June 1995, I was told only half the grievance was negotiated. But I didn't have any of the paperwork to show the union negotiated the grievance in good faith. If this was the case, how could these lies and conspiracies go on? Why wasn't I allowed to receive a copy of the decision rendered December 1994? Why did I not receive papers from the Public Review Board? Why I was never considered a person of interest to be part of the grievance or the Public Review Board's decision?

I received a denial of the complaint I filed against Woodrow Stamping in October 1995. The NLRB stated they would go no further in the investigations against Woodrow Stamping and Local 783. Of course I was very upset with the outcome. I knew then the grievance hadn't been filed. Even the lawyer, who took the deposition at the NLRB, said to me it looked like the grievance wasn't filed. If so why did the constant lies and cover-ups continue to exist? There was no explanation of why I was full-time. The NLRB gave no reason as to why I was allowed to receive the full-time benefit package.

I found that the grievance never went to the Public Review Board. Even after filing a complaint with the NLRB in 1995, they sided with Woodrow Stamping Plant in knowing nothing was filed at the Public Review Board until 2003. It was quite evident the grievance never went to the Review Board in 1995. Because of this, I ended up back where I started. From day one I was only asking for everyone involved in this lie to give me what was owed to me. It was a crucial part of providing the information in my possession. I had substantial facts to prove I was full-time and Local 783 didn't file my grievance. I proceeded to prove my claim.

I sought out to find the truth and to prove my claim true. Upon the denial I tried to appeal the decision. This was the letter written to the Department of Labor in October 1995 in reference to my complaint:

"I spoke to Mr. Henry, who took my complaint at the National Labor Relations Board, on October 25, 1995. This was regarding how I could obtain a copy of the final decision rendered by the National Labor Relations Board regarding the grievance filed in June1993. I received a letter from the President of the Executive Branch of the Union stating he was sending me a copy of the final decision regarding the outcome of my June 1993 grievance. He said the National Labor Relations Board (NLRB) heard my grievance on December 15, 1995. In reality, he sent me a copy of the unadjusted grievance's third stage. Now I have two papers from the third stage stating two different matters altogether.

When I filed a complaint in February 17, 1993 against Local 783 and Famous Parts Company in order to obtain a copy of the grievance, my case was #7-CB-9966. The grievance I am inquiring about is #H-183531. This grievance was stamped and dated on June 24, 1993. I would appreciate if you could help me in this mater since I have been trying to obtain a copy since June 1993 of this year."

This letter was sent regarding the decision made by the NLRB stating they were no longer going to investigate my claim. I was appalled at the fact the lawyer who took the deposition stated it looked as though a grievance was never filed. I kept appealing my decision because from my understanding, I had a right to know why the National Labor Relations Board denied my claim. I was extremely upset because I had a valid claim and was unable to make any sense out of what was happening. The first question I asked myself was "How much money was paid for my complaint to be denied?" I had been dealing with Woodrow Stamping for years at this point. I was aware Woodrow Stamping and the Local always paid people and institutions to rule in their favor. I kept exploring avenues of finding justice.

Woodrow Stamping worked very hard to silence me. I was doing everything I could to expose my situation in an effort to obtain help with my problems. I vowed to myself to attain some kind of justice. Woodrow Stamping and Local 783 literally pilfered my money in a bold manner. They had the audacity to tell me I would never see the money taken back through adjustments. They were right. I never did see the money that was pilfered from me. Where was the remainder of the money taken? Where were the performances bonuses, the profit sharing, vacation pay, and paid personal days?

30

THE EXECUTIVE BRANCH OF THE COMPANY'S COVER-UP

In order to appeal the National Labor Relation Board's decision to investigate Local 783 and Woodrow Stamping Plant, I had to send copies of my appeal letter to the lawyer for Local 783, Famous Parts Company, and the National Labor Relations Board. The letter sent to each person was the same. It wasn't long after I sent the letter of appeal that I received a response letter dated November 6, 1995. The letter was addressed to my lawyer, Mr. Bushe, from Ms. Beth Angel of the Executive Branch of the Union Headquarters. She was the lawyer representing Local 783.

"Enclosed please find a copy of a grievance filed by my client and the deposition of the grievance Local 783 previously provided to Ms. Carrie. In addition I am enclosing copies of Articles 32 and 33 of the Constitution of the International Union which explains the appeal procedure."

I was aware Woodrow Stamping didn't want me to return to their institution. I became a "troublemaker" and a "radical" because I was aware of my money being pilfered. I went to government agencies, I wrote to my state senator and anyone else that would listen to my claim. I had something to say but no one was willing to hear what I had to say. I was determined and wasn't going to give up.

This saga started in 1990 and didn't end until December 2004 when I retired. I had to write a book before someone would listen to what I had to say about Woodrow Stamping and Local 783. I felt the treatment I received was unwarranted and unjust. I had been denied rights by Local 783 and harassed by Woodrow Stamping Plant. They breeched the contract and didn't give it a second thought. They felt whatever I came up with in terms of getting my story heard, could be stopped in its tracks.

I was an excellent worker. I came to work everyday and I worked overtime whenever asked. I did whatever I was asked with regards to my job since I really appreciated my job. I was very dependable. When the company wasn't able to get anyone to work, supervision always found me. I was dedicated to my job and took pride in whatever job I worked even though some of the jobs were quite difficult. I truly felt I owed the company nothing because I worked hard and earned every penny I received. I felt good after receiving my check each week for a job well done. This was part of the reason I was fighting so hard for justice.

In November 1996 I sent a letter to Mr. Rocker, Representative of the Executive Branch of the Union, informing him I wanted to return to my home plant. I continued to hold my seniority date of July 15, 1991 officially. I felt I had to do everything 'officially' because I didn't trust Local 783 or Woodrow Stamping. The letter I sent Mr. Rocker stated:

"Mr. Rocker,

When I spoke to you in July 1996, I informed you I wanted to return to my home plant. Some employee's who work at Woodrow Stamping Plant has told me five new employees were hired in the last few weeks. I would like to utilize my recall rights at Woodrow Stamping Plant being that it is my home plant. I spoke to you by phone when I told you I wanted to return. Now I am putting it in writing informing you once again that I would like to return. I would appreciate a response regarding this matter."

I needed to return to Woodrow Stamping Plant so I could complete unfinished business regarding my seniority and the grievance. I was told the grievance was settled prior to my transferring back to Woodrow Stamping Plant, but it seemed that nothing was settled or completed. When I was transferred to Sarrow Stamping, I was so unhappy with how my grievance was handled. Unfortunately I was located where there was nothing I could do about it. Attorney Bushe allowed all my statue of limitations to run out, but he told me there were other grounds on which he could bring the case back to court. I sent Mr. Rocker a letter dated November 15, 1995. I also received a letter from Attorney Bushe. This is when Mr. Bushe received a letter from Attorney Wanda Scorn, of the Executive Branch of the Company for Famous Parts Company's Headquarters. The letter pertained to both Mazzie Cane and me, Crista Carrie:

"Dear Mr. Bushe,

Your letter dated September 21, 1995 was forwarded to me. As you are aware Ms. Cane and Ms. Carrie are hourly employees whose seniority and benefits are governed by a collective bargaining agreement between the company and the union. You are also aware of a grievance regarding seniority and benefits were filed on behalf of these clients and other employees. That grievance was resolved in accordance with the procedure specified in the collective bargaining agreement. The grievance resolution provided for seniority-dated adjustments, but no benefit adjustments for Mazzie Cane or Crista Carrie. In that resolution, all employees affected by the grievance were treated in the same way. Thus there is no basis for any claim that Ms. Cane and/or Ms. Carrie should now be treated differently. In fact the National Labor Relations Act prohibits the company from unilaterally changing either employees' seniority or benefits.

With respect to Crista Carrie, she was hired as a full-time employee at the company's Sarrow Stamping facility rather than the Woodrow Stamping facility because she wanted a full-time position (instead of part-time.) There were no full-time positions available at Woodrow at that time. Ms. Carrie could have stayed at Woodrow but chose to accept the position at Sarrow Stamping. This was an opportunity not made available to other part—time employees …"

Discrimination! The reason they didn't give other part-timers the same opportunity was because we all were full-time and Woodrow Stamping Plant had to keep all the employees they were pilfering from at *that* plant. They didn't want to stop this flow of money. If they sent the part-time employees to other plants, they would be presented with many questions they weren't ready to answer. Their seniority would have to pick-up where it left off and they would take their seniority with them. It would be found out they were full-time and the company would face being sued for unequal pay and back seniority. Questions would also arise of where the money was going they were pilfering from the employees. The letter from Famous Parts Company's Headquarters continued:

"… Please note the Sarrow Stamping position was neither a promotion nor a transfer. The two facilities are separate bargaining units and the collective bargaining agreement does not make provisions for inter-unit promotions or transfers except in certain layoff/return to work situations. Thus the Sarrow Stamping position was not retaliatory or discriminatory. To the contrary Ms. Carrie was afforded better treatment than other employees were. (*Discrimination!*) In short there is no basis for modifying the status of seniority and/or benefits of either Ms. Carrie or Ms. Cane. While your clients may disagree with the resolution of the grievance, the resolution was negotiated in good faith to provide a resolution as quickly as possible for a significant number of employees."

The first question is why would Woodrow Stamping Plant and Local 783 treat me better than the other part-time employees? That clearly shows *discrimination*. First of all they didn't like me that well. Secondly to give me such 'superb' treatment is clearly *discrimination*. This was a retaliatory move because of what I found out. They were greedy and didn't leave a stone unturned if they thought a dime was under it. I was the only one to transfer to another plant even though others requested doing so and was denied. They would have to terminate them as they did me because their records would show they were full-time.

In the letter (to Mr. Sophie and sent to Attorney Bushe) dated September 21, 1995, Mr. Sophie, Labor Relations Supervisor, stated the NLRB has just recently given authorization for the seniority date to be changed. In this same letter dated October 21, 1995, it stated the National Labor Relations Act prohibited the company from unilaterally changing either employees' seniority or benefits.

Wanda Scorn, Attorney for Famous Parts Company, stated "Ms. Carrie was treated more favorable than the others" and it was also stated my move was "neither a promotion nor a transfer". This was *discrimination*. I guess at this point I couldn't tell who was out right lying. Local 783 and Woodrow Stamping Plant put together a well thought out plan to deceive me with the help of the Executive Branch of the Union, by deliberately lying and giving me the run around to get rid of me. They knew all along they were discriminating. It didn't matter whom I spoke to, the information I obtained from Local 783 and Woodrow Stamping Plant was always inconsistent. The union had their story and the company had theirs. Attorney Wanda Scorn even had hers.

I say this so-called "favorable treatment" was blatant *discrimination* & *retaliation*. I was the only person who received "favorable treatment" in being moved and passed up before many people working for the company prior in the 70's. Come on! Give me a break! Famous Parts Company didn't like Blacks or women that well. As I stated in the past, racism is yet alive and well in the top level at Famous Parts Company—Woodrow Stamping Plant. The company professed diversity, but as you can see for yourself, that was one big lie. It's an even bigger joke to tell this lie to the employees while putting them through *Hell*. Actions speak louder than words. You don't have to profess diversity because it will show in the work environment. Racism was definitely an issue at Woodrow Stamping Plant.

If I received "favorable treatment" then I wouldn't be complaining right now. It is impossible to say I was treated favorably when I never received the money pilfered from me, and my fellow Caucasian employees received theirs. There was clearly a contradiction. Were they were forbidden to change employees' seniority dates by treating me more "favorable" than other employees? It was *discrimination* by their own words. I should have been treated just as everyone else and given no special privileges.

To be honest, I wouldn't treat my worst enemy as Woodrow Stamping treated me. It's was like they were always casting stones and hiding their hands saying they did nothing wrong. I would like you to ask yourself if you would have liked receiving the same treatment I received. Would you say I received "favorable treatment"? Would you have liked going through the same things I've experienced so far? This is only the tip of the iceberg. Just wait until Part 2 of this book. If we were all treated fairly regarding our seniority date, Mazzie and I would not have held a seniority date of July 15, 1991. I would have received September 1990 and Mazzie would have received 1977.

After reading the previous letter from Attorney Wanda Scorn, I would like to express my thoughts concerning the grievance I filed. Wanda Scorn represented Famous Parts Company and the letter was of double standard. I'm not sure if she was aware of all the facts surrounding my situation. If she was, then she should have noticed something wrong in what she was saying to Attorney Bushe, who supposedly worked in my best interest.

First she stated the grievance was resolved through the collective bargaining agreement. She said our grievances were adjusted although she stated the law prohibited change of employee seniority dates or benefits. My argument is our seniority didn't need to be adjusted because they were already in existence. Another fact omitted was that I didn't receive a "transfer". My records clearly stated I was indeed a "rehire" but I received neither a transfer nor a rehire. I was terminated. The grievance I filed stated I wanted to receive my back pay. I was aware of the conditions made with regards to my transfer.

I have never received a dime of the performance bonus taken away from me. Yet in the grievance it states I should have received my back pay. I never received any benefits and I am the one who filed the grievance. Woodrow Stamping Plant hired one or two groups of part-time employees to full-time before my transfer. They thought I was causing problems and they were showing me they didn't have to hire me if they chose not to. They cut off hiring full-time right before my name I was the next to hire. They said they could not hire anyone else full-time at that point. This forced me to complain and accept the transfer because they stated they didn't want me at Woodrow Stamping Plant any longer. On November 25, 1995, I sent another letter to the National Labor Relations Board appealing their decision and the reason for such dismay. It read as follows:

"Dear Sir or Madam:

I feel there is reason for an appeal, being that my seniority date wasn't restored to its original date. The seniority date should have been September 28, 1990. This was the reason I filed the grievance in the first place. There were others that retained their 1990 seniority date. The Employee Relations Manager's son and a few elites within the group all retained their 1990 seniority, yet I was denied. They received the monies while mine were taken back. This is why I was asking for back pay and your help to investigate. I would like to stress I had an attorney working for me at the time. He should have handled all of my appeals, but he sat back and allowed me to represent myself. I am uncertain as to how far this grievance has progressed.

According to the contract between Union and Famous Parts Company: *The purpose of filing a grievance is to show intent and show cause to assure there will be full discussion and consideration of all issues regarding the pending issues. The basis of the full disclosure is to bring out the facts and to show what happened throughout the various stages of the grievance.*

Woodrow Stamping Plant never gave me any facts of any grievance I ever filed. As far as I am concerned, these steps were never followed. I have asked for a transcript from the union and company discussing this grievance or anything stating what happened on my behalf. Thus far the union hasn't answered any questions to my satisfaction. All I'm asking for is something concrete stating the union represented my grievance fairly. I know there should be a statement of facts and position, at least according to the agreement between the Union and Famous Parts Company.

In the contract book between the company and the union it states there should be a Statement of Fact and Position: *Every person's grievance should be in detailed form with the facts and the reason for the grievance. The issues regarding the grievance and the facts that support the grievance should be available to support the claim for filing a grievance. It should also state the company's position on the grievance.*

Thus far these measures have not been met. I don't know what the union agreed upon on my behalf pro or con. I can't get information regarding these events. The union has not represented me fairly and this is why I am appealing. There has to be a transcript or something submitted to both parties as to what was said. I really don't understand why this has been such a problem. I have asked Local 783's President, John Hail, and Mr. Rocker, at the Executive Branch of the Union, for a copy and I haven't received anything.

I really want to know if the union ever discussed the back pay issue or if it was omitted from the discussion. Why wasn't my seniority restored to its original date? All I'm hearing at this time is that the union has done all they could to represent me. If so, please provide me with the information I'm asking for. I informed the union I wanted to attend the Review Board's hearing to help represent my grievance, but my request was denied …"

After I sent the letter dated November 25, 1995, I received a letter from the National Labor Relations Board. This was the response:

"The above captioned case sharing violations under Section 8 of the National Labor Relations Act as amended, has been carefully investigated and considered. As a result of the investigation, it appears further proceedings are not warranted at this time. I am therefore refusing to issue a complaint. A written summary report of the basis for my conclusion is attached. Please refer to the enclosed NLRB form as to the procedure and deadline for filing an appeal of your dismissal action."

I clearly wanted things to make sense but I was unsuccessful in getting the NLRB to back me up or further investigate Local 783 and Woodrow Stamping. The Summary Report from National Labor Relations Board said:

"The charges in the captioned matter filed alleges during the six month period prior to the filing of the charges, Local 783—International Union failed to fairly properly represent her. In the processing of a grievance Crista Carrie had filed and was refused to be provided with a copy of the final settlement of the grievance. She was not provided information regarding what transpired during the grievance for arbitrary, invidious, and capricious reasons.

The investigation disclosed that on June 3, 1993 Crista Carrie filed a grievance against Famous Parts Company seeking to be appointed to full-time employment status and to be compensated full-time benefits previously denied. The union processed the grievance on Carrie's behalf however subsequent to the filing of the grievance, the union declined to provide Crista Carrie with a copy of the grievance. The union did not provide Ms. Carrie with a copy of the grievance until after she filed a charge against the union in case #7-CB-9966. Upon the settlement of that charge, the union continued to pursue her grievance.

On December 15, 1994 the union and Famous Parts Company entered into a final settlement of the grievance. They were providing Ms. Carrie seniority and status as a full-time employee would be evaluated and adjusted. However the settlement did not provide for back pay. In the latter part of June 1995, Famous Parts Company advised her of the actual seniority adjustment determined pursuant to the grievance settlement. Ms. Carrie had her first communication with a representative of the union during the six months preceding the filing of the instant charge. Crista had no communication with Local 783 from the time she transferred from Woodrow Stamping in November 1993 until January 1995.

This letter was sent to Ms. Carrie as a response to the National Labor Relations Board's decision that she continued to challenge because it was as though nothing was done to Local 783 for violating contract laws and allowing the discrimination to progress. Again Ms. Carrie was advised of the settlement terms while the union had not achieved a change in her seniority date and was unsuccessful in its efforts to obtain back pay adjustment. Thereafter in early August 1995, the union provided her with a copy of the grievance settlement, which it had initially declined to provide her in mid July 1995. In summary, the evidence failed to show the union failed to fairly represent her or failed to provide her with a copy of her grievance settlement during Section 10(b) period for arbitrary, invidious, or capricious reasons."

This was my statement from Grievance No. 135381—LB-7210 and what happened with regards to Local 783 and Woodrow Stamping Plant after I filed the charges. The charges were later dropped. I was furious and wanted to appeal the decision. I appealed the decision and that too was denied. The short note read:

"Accordingly based upon the foregoing and the evidence disclosed by the investigation considered as a whole, I am refusing to issue a complaint and the charges are dismissed."

I couldn't get the NLRB to file charges against Local 783. The NLRB decided not to investigate and I decided to appeal again. There was another note attached to the Summary Report stating:

"Pursuant to the National Labor Relations Board Rules and Regulations, you may obtain a review of this action by filing an appeal with the General Counsel of the National Labor Relations Board in Washington D.C. This appeal must contain a complete statement setting forth the facts and reason upon which it is based. The General Counsel in Washington D.C. must receive the appeal by the close of business at 5:00 p.m. EST on December 4, 1995. Upon good cause shown, the copy of any such request for extension of time should be submitted to Ms. Carrie."

If you file an appeal, please complete the notice forms enclosed with the attached letter and send one copy of the form to each of the other parties whose names and addresses are listed. The notice forms should be mailed at the same time you file the appeal but mailing the notice forms does not relieve you of the necessity for filing the appeal itself with the General Counsel and a copy of the appeal to Ms. Carrie within the time stated above."

On December 14, 1995 I received a letter from the Regional Director of the National Labor Relations Board. Again they refused to issue a complaint that was carefully considered. The Regional Director's letter on November 20, 1995 stated, "... Accordingly further proceedings herein were deemed unwarranted ..."

Copies were sent to the Union Executive Board, Local 783, and Famous Parts Company. The first denial was to have had a summary of the why, although it did not. I wanted to know how and why the charges were unwarranted. I never received why the NLRB decided not to go forward with the investigation.

I truly believe Local 783 and Woodrow Stamping Plant thought I would not appeal. I did appeal because I felt an injustice was brought upon me. I couldn't just stand still and be taken advantage of. I filed the appeal along with its copies with the General Counsel within the allotted time stated. Upon the response to the notice from the NLRB on December 14, 1995, I decided to appeal the decision once again on January 17, 1996.

"Dear Counsel:

I am requesting for consideration in the case filed October 27, 1995. I once again received a letter dated November 20, 1995 refusing to issue a complaint against Local 783—International Union and Woodrow Stamping Plant.

What I want to know from the NLRB's investigation is how they determined Local 783 wasn't guilty enough to warrant an investigation. I wanted to know the merits determining Local 783 and Woodrow Stamping Plant did not fail me when they failed to give me the appropriate paperwork regarding what transpired during each stage of my grievance. They knew exactly what I was asking for but denied my complaint. In the grievance filed in 1993, it was to have been to the Public Review Board. Local 783 lied about that too. Everything they did was a lie. I'm not sure why my claim was denied in the mist of all their lies.

I received a letter in November 1995, not fully explaining how this decision came about. I'd like to know on what grounds the National Labor Relations Board based their decision. I had facts no one cared to read or look over. I have nothing to base the decision upon in reference to the matter. Though I know who was there, I don't know what was said. I don't know if the facts were stated or not. I am asking the counsel to give this case more consideration and fully give me an explanation as to why I was denied.

Since the union lied, this was the reason I asked the NLRB for help. In return, I know no more now than when I filed this case in October of 1995. I'm asking for reconsideration. Please see what the union and company have done on my behalf and why."

When I appealed the decision of the National Labor Relations Board, I had to send notification to each party involved in the complaint. I was to inform them I was appealing and bringing charges against Local 783 and Woodrow Stamping Plant. I had written another letter dated November 15, 1995. This letter was sent to Robert Rocker, Representative of the Executive Branch of the Union. He replaced Johnny Hilter after he left his position.

Plant Chairman, John Hail, corresponded with Ms. Beth Angel, Attorney for the International Executive Branch of the Union. I was asking that they revise their decision not to file charges against Famous Parts Company—Woodrow Stamping Plant and Local 783. The NLRB may not have thought anything of this complaint even though it was a big issue to me personally.

After the decision to further investigate, my claim was denied. My lawyer Mr. Bushe, informed me he spoke with Wanda Scorn, Attorney at the Executive Branch of Famous Parts Company. She said the grievance never got that far. If the grievance never got that far, why did the union send papers stating this was a decision made by the Public Review Board? I was correct all this time when I told the NLRB and the others the grievance was never filed. They tried to tell me an outright lie and go against the law. The union's lie was even upheld by the National Labor Relations Board.

After inquiring about the Review Board's decision, my lawyer informed me I might have to file a grievance all over again. If the grievance was half settled, why file over again? Everything they did was misleading. This was the reason I requested a copy of the decision. I was sure the company hadn't negotiated my back pay that I asked for in my grievance. I wanted straight answers. It was clear to me there was corruption amidst everything happening. Woodrow and Local 783 were paying under the table. After I had written the NLRB in January 1996, I received a short and sweet responding letter on January 30, 1996 stating:

"This letter is in reply to your letter dated January 17, 1996 regarding the captioned matter. Again we reviewed this matter and found no basis for the issuance of a complaint. Consequently this matter is closed. Accordingly further proceedings herein were deemed unwarranted."

It didn't matter what I said or did. They were determined they weren't going to file charges against Local 783 or Woodrow Stamping Plant. I was positive they knew what I knew. They just weren't going to do anything about it. I never received any information stating to the contrary that an investigation was ever filed.

31

IS ANYONE WILLING TO HELP ME

I finally decided the government agencies weren't going to represent me properly. I felt I needed someone to represent me in what I called breech of contract and wrongful termination lawsuit. At that time I found I was actually full-time. Woodrow Stamping Plant was aware that I was full-time too. Mr. Hdith (before his death) was also looking into my termination and the desperate treatment I received from Woodrow Stamping Plant and Local 783. I hired Mr. Hdith in September 1994 and this was one of the letters he sent to Woodrow Stamping and Sarrow Stamping Plant:

"Crista Carrie apparently started working at the Woodrow Stamping Plant facility on September 28, 1990. Although there was a desire to transfer her to full-time, such full time employment did not occur until November 15, 1993—at least this is what I was told. Famous Parts Company's records will show full-time employment began September 28, 1990. When Crista requested "official" full-time employment at the Woodrow Stamping facility, she was accommodated in such a way that she was transferred or moved to Sarrow Stamping Plant (since there were no full-time positions available at Woodrow Stamping) when she was already full-time.

Both men Mr. Sophie, Woodrow Stamping Plant Labor Relations Supervisor, and John Hail, Local 783's Plant Chairman, indicated this to my office with regards to the union. Notwithstanding some of Local 783's and Famous Parts Company's procedures are contained in your letter. Ms. Carrie still has a problem accepting the fact that her seniority adjustment date has been rolled up to July 15, 1991. In regards to her grievance, official records indicated she had been working since September 28, 1990 as a full-time employee. She disagrees with the arbitrary manner at which the union eventually adjusted the seniority dates without observing or researching the proper records.

The union indicated they accommodated her by transferring her seniority, which is not in conformity with union rules. I won't comment as to why this may have happened in her favor, but it seems as though the accommodation was based on the fact there was desperate treatment. In addition, she has lost her vacation time and performance bonuses during the period from 1990 to the present. She was promised her seniority was to be restored by Local 783 and Woodrow Stamping Plant's Personnel Department after the grievance was settled.

As I indicated in my past telephone conversations with your office, this is the information Ms. Carrie would like to pass on to Famous Parts Company so that Famous Parts Company can look into it. She firmly believes she has been treated desperately. If your office can fill the holes in or enlighten me with regards to any additional information that I do not have in my files, it would be greatly appreciated. I will be looking forward to your anticipated response."

When I transferred to Sarrow Stamping Plant, there was nothing in writing to state this was an official transfer. There was no paper trail regarding this transfer because it was clearly illegal, though I didn't know it at the time. The attorney for Famous Parts Company stated they didn't transfer employees under the circumstances I was transferred in November 1993. If they told my attorney they didn't give unilateral transfers and they did, that makes the attorney for Famous Parts Company a liar.

Soon after this letter was sent out to Wanda Scorn, Attorney for the Executive Branch of the Company, I guess that's when Mr. Bushe decided to come aboard and work with my opponents Local 783 and Woodrow Stamping Plant. The grievance I filed didn't go as far as the union claimed it did. In fact the grievance was never filed officially. It never left Woodrow Stamping Plant. When I finally had the opportunity to file a complaint with the Public Review Board in 2002, I realized the papers attached to the grievance in 1994 were only copies of someone else's cover page that went to the Public Review Board. What they did was took information from someone else's case and used correction fluid to make a blank copy. After they made a xeroxed copy, all they needed to do was fill-in the blank spaces—making the page look as though it was an original. This was done to make me believe the grievance went to the Public Review Board.

I realized it was impossible to successfully file a grievance with the Review Board because the appeal process would constantly be denied. I was active in my defense in 2002 regarding the Article 33 I filed against Tom Hemp, Local 783 Plant Chairman, and Al Snake, Union Representative at the middle level of the Executive Branch of the Union's Regional 21A Office. Since the company and union lied, they had to try to cover the mess they found themselves in. It seemed they were digging themselves into a deeper hole and they didn't know how to get themselves out. Instead of just giving me what was rightfully mine, they became angry because I was causing them so many problems.

As I saw it, they had no right to be angry with me because I was defending my seniority. If it were they, they would have done the same. There was another reason they didn't want their secret to come the surface. They were afraid all the money they were pilfering from those employees hired in the 70's would be found out. These people were to receive a one-time lump sum payment when they returned from their layoff that they never received.

When they returned, there should not have been a waiting period for them to start receiving their vacation pay or performance bonuses. They were already full-time when they were laid off. If they had been re-hired, they should have been hired full-time before any other employees who had never worked for the company. When they returned instead of placing them full-time, Woodrow Stamping Plant and Local 783 pilfered their entire full-time benefits package. When they started back to work, many started working as part-time employees and they were actually full-time. Woodrow Stamping Plant didn't inform them of this information because there were two or more records on some employees being paid part-time pay while their benefit package was being pilfered. If my theories were correct, I couldn't understand why I couldn't get anyone to investigate my claim and the filing of my grievance. Everyone told me off the record my grievance wasn't filed, but for the record no one told the truth about anything.

In February 1996, I sent a letter to the American Civil Liberties Union, my state senator in Michigan, and to the CEO's of the Executive Branch of the Union and Company. I sent a letter to the local news station and as a result I found myself back in the same situation as before. I was flustered because I couldn't get anyone to listen to what was happening. Therefore I sent this letter to the ACLU stating:

"American Civil Liberties Union,

I am writing this letter pleading for your help. I have run out of options in fighting my cause. This problem has been going on for the last five years. I have worked at Woodrow Stamping Plant for over two years. I was hired when Woodrow hired a large volume of employees. We were told some of us would be hired full-time and some would be on a waiting list after orientation.

When I started working on the plant floor I was told I would be working as a part-time employee. I was told prior that I would be full-time when I started in September of 1990. I worked 90 days and started getting holiday pay for New Year's Day that year and the Martin Luther King Jr. holiday in the following year. The Martin Luther King Jr. holiday was taken back because I was told it was given to others and me in error. How can I have received holiday pay if I wasn't full-time with benefits? ..."

I talked to our Union Representative, Bob Fleetwood, who was the Bargaining Committeeman for Local 783. He informed me the money *was* given in error. Part-time employees have to work 90 actual days, which would amount to six months. If I was paid as a part-time employee, I hadn't work enough time to receive full-time benefits. I was laid off in February of 1991 and rehired in July of the same year. I worked four days a week, 32 hours, clearly against the contract for a part-timer. The company later informed us we would be working four days a week at seven hours a day totaling 28 hours a week. The afternoon shift on the Press Side worked those hours for three weeks. After that, the hours varied from 16 to 32 hours a week until November 1992 when we were off with our Christmas bonuses.

We were called back to work April 4, 1992. When we returned in April, there were two part-time employees that noticed a change on their checks in the vacation hour's section. Our checks said we had 40 hours of vacation pay coming three months in advance. This small bit of information was omitted because the union and company were aware some of us were actually full-time. As a part-time employee I was receiving full-time benefits, but I should not have been receiving a 40-hour vacation pay because I wasn't working full-time. I did have 90 days of actual days worked at that time I received 40-hour vacation. As a part-time employee, I should have received 20 hours of vacation pay. Only full-time employees should have received 40 hours vacation pay. In June 1992, we received our vacation checks and cashed them—or at least I did. The following week others and I on the afternoon shift went to pick up our checks and received a note saying:

"As a TPT (temporary part-time) employee in 0700 you were incorrectly credited with and paid vacation pay. This overpayment will be deducted from future payments unless you are able to return the vacation check for cancellation." The note was dated July 2, 1992 and was signed R. Sophie, of the Labor Relations Department.

I went to Labor Relations and spoke to Mr. Sophie. He stated there was nothing he could do. I asked, "Why did they take the whole check?" He then told me, "In the near future arrangements will be made incase this happens again". After our vacation check was withdrawn, Polly Rice, another part-time employee *(as discussed in earlier chapters)*, filed a grievance with the union to get her vacation check back. The list consisted of fifteen people who had worked two weeks as full-time employees. My name was added to the list because Mr. Doso, Labor Relations Supervisor, and two union representatives, Hame Pate and Larry of Local 783, looked in the computer and noticed I was a full-time employee. I had been telling them this all along. I was told my name would be added to Polly's grievance. I believed this to be true since the words came from union officials.

In September 1992, I asked the union representatives if they had heard anything about the grievance. The others and I were told it could take up to a year and a half before the grievance was settled. In October 1992, I drafted a letter to John Hail, Plant Chair/President of our Local 783. I later contacted the Michigan Department of Labor's Office because I felt the company was in error by withdrawing our vacation check they knew we'd be receiving in June 1992.

I had informed John Hail of Local 783 and he was to set up a meeting with Mr. R. Sophie, Woodrow Stamping Plant's Labor Relations Supervisor. Somehow they must have forgotten a meeting was to have taken place. I had been given the run around by the union and the company once again. I also told Paul Nashing, Local 783 Committeeman for the Assembly Side of the plant, I wanted to file a grievance. His reply was, "It will be taken care of on your check. A grievance will not be necessary".

I felt something was severely wrong. It could've just been a cover up between Local 783 and Woodrow Stamping Plant. If that was the case the union wasn't representing me as a union member. This clearly was a breech of contract and no one was willing to help. I felt if I had an unresolved issue and wanted to file a grievance, it should not have been a problem. My problems weren't taken seriously as a part-time employee and I wanted it to stop. I felt if I worked, there shouldn't have been a problem with me getting paid. I've always had a problem with my check as far as shortages or withdrawals in one form or another since my date of hire.

The union didn't allow me to file a grievance until June 1993. If I felt there was a problem the union was supposed to be there representing my problem. Local 783 and Woodrow Stamping Plant seemed to be working hand in hand not caring for the needs of their part-time employees. I felt since we paid union dues, we should not have been discriminated against just because we were part-timers. I was told I had to go through the necessary steps before I went any further with taking action on my behalf against the union. At one point I went to the Regional Office and voiced what was happening. Again nothing was ever done about it. In June 1993, I was allowed to file a grievance in response to obtaining my back pay and seniority. I asked for a copy of the grievance and was denied. I asked Bob Fleetwood, Bargaining Committeeman for Local 783, to "give me the grievance and I will make copies of them". Again I was denied.

I was informed in July 1995 the grievance I had filed had been won. My seniority date at Woodrow was changed from November 15, 1993 to July 15, 1991. Labor Relations at Sarrow Stamping Plant informed me Woodrow would be my home plant in the event of Sarrow laying workers off. I would have the opportunity to return back to Woodrow Stamping Plant. Salma Bears, Labor Relations Representative at Sarrow Stamping, said she never received the formal papers pertaining to the grievance, but she had the authority to change the information.

At this point I was wondering if my seniority was just on paper. Had it actually been changed? I knew my seniority started on September 28, 1990 at Woodrow, but the union made it a problem for me because I spoke up for what I felt was right. Employees at Sarrow told me Woodrow didn't want me back. This was indeed the case because I had great difficulty getting back to my home plant. The Executive Branch of the Company had been siding with Chairman, John Hail, and not working to assist my problem.

Again in October 1995, I filed with the National Labor Relations Board, claiming arbitrary, invidious, and capricious treatment by the company. I filed this due to the union giving me no back pay when other employees I worked with received this money and was allowed to keep it. I wanted to know why the union gave no mention of the back money at the Review Board meeting. My original seniority date was September 28, 1990 and the union gave me July 15, 1991. My fellow workers received October 1 and October 5, 1990. I wanted to know how this could be.

The National Labor Relations Board sent me a letter dated November 20, 1995 stating they were refusing to issue the complaint followed by a summary from which the conclusion occurred. I didn't feel the union represented me properly. I wanted the final decision of the Public Review Board and got no response. I sent Famous Parts Company's Attorney, Ms. Angel, a letter requesting a copy of the Review Board's decision and she hasn't responded to me as of yet. I later found out by my lawyer, the matter had never reached the Public Review Board. If this was the case, why did the National Labor Relations Board decline to further investigate the matter? After filing this charge with the NLRB, I didn't know any more than I knew before I filed charges.

The National Labor Relations Board gave me until December 4, 1995 to appeal, in which I did. I referenced the contract and found where the union failed to appeal my grievance, which meant the union failed to represent me. The appeal was denied the second time and I still don't know why. Clearly breaking the contract and also the labor laws, no one ever lifted a finger to help when I was crying out for it.

I had a problem with the National Labor Relations Board failing to press for further information. When there was cause, the union refused to give me a copy of the grievance. I refused to file another grievance when all this time the union should have taken every step to represent me and did not. It was apparent there were many issues serving as a red flag to the National Labor Relations Board. I sent this letter to the National Labor Relations Board regarding this decision. I kept on appealing their decision using the guidelines according to the contract book. The NLRB never found grounds to investigate Woodrow Stamping Plant and Local 783. It didn't matter how much proof you had against both entities, the General Counsel of the NLRB was never going to find reason to bring charges against them. This is one of the letters that I was appealing to the General Counsel of the NLRB trying to get them to change their minds. The letter read:

"… I had a problem as to whom my lawyer was working for. He never returned my calls, lied to me constantly, and never did what he said he was going to do. I have a case where no one will help. I'm writing you in hopes you won't turn me down.

The grievance I am inquiring about is #H-183531. This grievance was written and filed June 3, 1993. I would appreciate if you helped me with this matter."

I sent another letter dated January 17, 1996 asking the National Labor Relations Board Office of General Counsel to reconsider my claim. I felt the union didn't represent me fairly. I also stated I wanted to know the reason why my case showed no cause for an investigation. I don't know why it was denied when I found out the union neither filed the grievance nor argued my case. The letter read:

"Dear Counsel:

I am requesting for reconsideration in the case #7-CB-10728 filed September 27, 1995. I received a letter dated November 20, 1995 refusing to issue an investigation against Local 783—International Union (Famous Parts Company).

I'm not sure why my claim was denied. I received a letter in November 1995. I don't fully understand your explanation, as to how your decision came about. What was the National Labor Relations Board's decision based on? I have nothing to base the decision upon in reference to the above matter. I know who was there, but since I don't know what was said, I don't know if they told the truth or not. Apparently they did not.

I am asking the counsel to give this case more consideration and fully give me an explanation as to why I was denied. What was said at the hearing determining there would be no further need to investigate? I don't quite understand how the counsel looked over the matter where the union failed to give me a copy of the Public Review Board's decision. I have sent correspondences to Ms. Beth Angel, Attorney for Famous International Executive Branch of the Union; Robert Rocker, Representative at the Executive Branch of the Union who represented Local 783; and John Hail, Local 783 President/Plant Chairman. I was asking for the decision the Public Review Board made in reference to the grievance I filed in June 1993.

After the decision to further investigate my claim, my lawyer Mr. John Bushe, informed me he spoke with Wanda Scorn, Famous Parts Company's Attorney, and she said, "The grievance never got that far". If the grievance never got that far, why did the union send papers stating this was a decision made by the Public Review Board? After inquiring about the Review Board's decision, my lawyer informed me I might have to file a grievance all over again. If the Public Review Board half settled the grievance, why file over again?

The reason I requested a copy of the decision is because I was sure the company didn't negotiate my back pay. I'm asking for back pay because many of my fellow employees working under the same classification as I, received bonuses, vacation pay, and were allowed to keep their pay while receiving their original seniority date. My original seniority date was September 28, 1990 and I'm asking the union to represent me in this matter.

Since the union only told untruths, this is the reason I'm asking this agency for help. I know more now than I knew when I filed this complaint in October of last year. I'm asking you to please reconsider and see what the union and company has done on my behalf and why."

In the meantime I was waiting for a reply from the state senator and also the American Civil Liberties Union of Michigan. I really didn't anticipate how difficult it would be to obtain help. I had all the proof needed to substantiate my money being pilfered. I truly felt since I was under Local 783, I would get some kind of justice with regards to myself and the others that signed my grievance. I really didn't focus much on the others as much as I did with my own problems. I figured maybe it would help some people if I got my problems solved with regards to my part-time/full-time status. All the negativity and lying resulting from what happened made me think this was some kind of conspiracy.

Upon my dissatisfaction with what I was experiencing at Woodrow Stamping Plant, I often talked to my family and friends concerning my situation. I was so disappointed and depressed. I constantly brought my problems home with me. I always tried to keep my employment life separate from my private life. I wanted to leave the plant life in the plant.

I complained for years about my status as a part-time employee and how I was receiving full-time benefits. The adjustments continued. My money kept being given to me and taken back later. I was trying to get someone to listen to me. I could understand if the company was unaware a problem existed and corrected it, but this wasn't the case. At this point it had been six years the problem was still being quietly skimmed over. I was pretty sure they wanted it to stay that way too.

After years of the same complaints about my employer and the local union, eventually some people started making sense out of what I was saying. My story never changed but they began listening. For years my situation seemed to differ at times, but the accusations stayed the same. I had proof and I had kept information throughout the years to substantiate what I was saying. Larry Jackson, one of

Famous Parts Company's attorneys, once told me the type of proof I had to substantiate my findings wouldn't make a difference in the end. From my experiences, I found that to be true.

In the first part of 1994, I heard the local news station was going to have a forum for people having continued problems in a variety of areas. I left work and went to the Fisher Building, in Detroit's New Center Area, where a major local channel sponsored a gathering to help consumers with their problems. I had with me copies of information to prove there was some kind of conspiracy with reference to my employer. I used the cover letter I sent to my state representative and the American Civil Liberties Union (ACLU) as a cover story. I had everything needed to prove I had a serious problem.

When I was called up, I was told they couldn't help me with my problem. Here I was with a detailed statement of what I was going through, and this was yet another let down. I was so disappointed. It was almost as though I had a contagious disease and when they saw me coming, they slammed the doors in my face before I could even reach it. As I was walking away, a lawyer called me back and asked me if she could have my cover story to keep. Some weeks later, there were some changes in the front offices of Woodrow Stamping. There was some kind of investigation taking place. This is when the various investigations first started at Woodrow. I personally, had no results as far as getting my seniority back or my back money, but there were some changes made within the plant as a whole.

While I was awaiting the answer from the ACLU, I received a letter written by Wanda Scorn, Lawyer for Famous Parts Company forwarded by my lawyer, Mr. John Bushe. The statue of limitations had not yet run out on my case at this point. The letter stated:

"... I have received your letter of January 17, 1996 which details two issues. First Ms. Carrie continues to disagree with her adjusted seniority date (and the other items such as vacation eligibility and performance bonuses which are related to seniority). As indicated in earlier correspondences, those issues were resolved by disposition of a grievance filed on behalf of a significant number of employees.

While Ms. Carrie may not agree with the grievance disposition, her disposition was agreed to by her collective bargaining representative acting on behalf of all the employees affected by the grievance. Federal law (the National Labor Relations Act) prohibits the company from making unilateral changes in matters covered by the collective bargaining agreement. Thus the issue related to Ms. Carrie's seniority will not be reviewed again.

Secondly, Ms. Carrie contends that 16 employees were given full-time positions at Woodrow Stamping and that she should have been given full-time status at the facility at the same time as, or before those individuals. Before addressing specifics related to the employees identified in your letter, some background on hiring protocol is necessary. Temporary part-time (TPT) employees are chosen for full-time positions based on service date by the earliest first. Among employees with the same service date (which is common when groups of employees are hired), the tiebreaker is the last four digits of the social security number—highest number first. (The same tiebreaker is used for promotions, transfers, layoffs, recalls, etc.——any issue to be determined by service date or seniority) …"

If this was true, why weren't Mazzie Cane, Karol Henderson, and many others able to transfer to another plant since there were no placements occurring at Woodrow Stamping Plant? Their service date was far before mine. They had years in comparison to mine. The other employees were hired before me in the October 1993 group of Caucasians. They stopped at my name and sent me to Sarrow Stamping Plant. Attorney Wanda Scorn lied. I know this wasn't the case from my experiences or according to those who had prior seniority with the company.

Woodrow Stamping and Local 783 gave seniority back to only some employees, but none were given their seniority back in the group I was hired in. Some received 1994 seniority and others received 1996. Those were the ones in the group I was hired in (September 1990). They should have received back pay with seniority when they returned back to work. All that money was pilfered from those employees. I always thought the money was being diverted to keep the plant's doors open because the plant never legally made a profit.

Hypothetically, the money Local 783 was pilfering from employees could have gone many places. This money could have been used for drugs, arms, militia groups, and etcetera. But at any rate, the money was being laundered and these government agencies allowed Local 783 and Woodrow Stamping to continue taking money from their employees. Attorney Wanda Scorn's letter was an outright lie and my lawyer chose not to believe me when I told him so. Again I became an invisible person. Even Mazzie Cane had problems getting her story heard. She was one of the people hired in the 70's, but even with her attorney Mr. Bushe, she could not get her money or seniority back when she rightfully should have. Woodrow Stamping Plant never released Mazzie Cane's file. Mr. Bushe stated Woodrow Stamping Plant wouldn't cooperate by sending him her file.

Attorney Wanda Scorn's letter continued:
"… With respect to the 16 individuals identified in your letter, some of the information Ms. Carrie gave you was inaccurate. With the exception of one person, there are basically three groups of individuals:

Group A:

- 9 individuals who were initially hired as TPT's (temporary part-time) on September 21, 1990 and as full-time on October 1, 1990

Group B:

- 3 who were hired as TPTs on September 21, 1990 and were full-time on October 5, 1990

Group C:

- 6 who were hired as TPTs on September 28, 1990 and was full-time on September 24, 1993.

- All hired as TPTs September 28, 1990 hired as full–time on September 24, 1993

- All with adjusted seniority of July 15, 1991 (the same as Ms. Carrie's)

- All with the last four digits were higher than Ms. Carrie whose last four are 3554.

As shown below, all 16 individuals were properly hired to full-time positions before Ms. Carrie. This may have been because of their social security number tiebreaker. *Clearly forgetting the employees were laid off during the 70's and hired back.*

Everyone in Groups A and B had earlier TPT hire than Ms. Carrie and thus were properly hired before her. Everyone in Group C had the same TPT hire date as Ms. Carrie. They also had higher tiebreakers than Ms. Carrie (last four), and thus were properly hired before her. It appears that one was placed early. With his service date as August 28, 1990 and last four as 6214, he should have been placed on full-time after the three employees in Group B (who have earlier dates of TPT hire) and after the six employees in Group C (who have higher last four). However all 16 of the individuals identified in your letter were properly given full-time status before Ms. Carrie.

In summary, despite Ms. Carrie's belief she was somehow treated desperately, the facts do not support that belief. As detailed in earlier correspondences, Ms. Carrie was actually treated *better* than others. She was given a full-time position at Sarrow Stamping with adjusted seniority (pursuant to the grievance disposition) based on TPT work at Woodrow Stamping."

I was treated better than the rest, but the rest received their original seniority date. They also received vacation pay and other benefits I didn't receive. These people forgot about the fact I was full-time when hired. (Even by the admission of Woodrow Stamping Plant and Local 783.) Both were aware of this information. I didn't understand why the established facts were ignored. My attorney Mr. Bushe was aware of this because he had copies of my employment records in his possession.

Mazzie Cane, Karol Henderson, Donna Smith, and Yvonne Stay all worked for Woodrow Stamping Plant in the 70's and were laid off. When they were rehired they tried to gain their seniority status but failed. They saw new hires placed before them in many instances. This proved Attorney Wanda Scorn a lie once again. They weren't hired full-time because Woodrow Stamping Plant was pilfering their money and benefits under full-time status while paying them part-time pay per hour. If they had me full-time and part-time at the same time, I can say there was more than one set of records on some employees? I was one of those people Local 783 and Woodrow Stamping Plant both, had a second set of records for.

32

"MISSING CHAPTER" THEY WEREN'T VERY SYMPATHIC

Note to Reader: This is <u>the second of three chapters</u> which were deleted from my original transcript. I honestly can't say at what point they were lost, but I decided to add them in the final stages of the book anyway. (The three chapters are 27, 32, & 35.)

Each and every lawyer Mazzie Cane and I tried obtaining for representation worked in unison with the company in a joint venture. We walked in and out of various law offices, only to find we couldn't get any lawyer to represent us. Mazzie and I knew we both had cases, and the lawyers who viewed them knew we had cases too. Some lawyers had sympathy, but they weren't sympathetic enough to take our cases.

Attorney Hdith made a statement to the Attorney Grievance Commission, which was included in the documents I received from Mazzie Cane. This letter was included in Attorney Bushe's paperwork with regards to Mazzie. It mentions how Mr. Bushe and Mr. Hdith discussed occurring events before taking her case. It also explains how Mr. Hdith felt when taking on the cases of Mazzie and me. Mr. Hdith's April, 1996 letter to the Attorney Grievance Commission stated:

"… Mr. Bushe advised me of the call indicating that Mazzie Cane was coming in my office, and he wanted me present for the interview with Ms. Cane. Mazzie Cane, as I recall, was a pleasant lady and articulated her claims well. Her claim, as I recall, was that she was improperly recalled after lay-off and was discriminated against on the basis that males with the same or less seniority than her were called back before her following lay off. She was able to identify the males involved. At the conclusion of the interview with Mr. Bushe and me, we were of the opinion that this was a valid claim and indicated to her that on the basis of what she represented to us we would take the case on a contingency basis. I do recall sending a letter to Famous Parts Company advising them of Ms. Cane's claim and requesting a copy of her personnel file.

Mr. Bushe also stated Crista Carrie's case was in the midst of an out of court settlement. From his recollection of what occurred in 1994, Mazzie Cane discussed her case with Mr. Bushe by phone first. Ms. Cane contacted our firm because she became aware that we were pursuing a matter on behalf of Crista Carrie (also a Famous Parts Company employee). They most frequently made good faith settlements in employee complaint cases so as to preserve employee morale.

I tend to agree with Mazzie Cane as to her belief that the contract was breached. Some of the correspondence suggested that a suit would be filed and clearly it was not. It appears there were satisfactory reasons why this suit was not filed, but Ms. Cane wanted to have her day in court and believed that was what she was paying for. Fortunately Ms. Cane has until September 23, 1996 before the statute of limitation has run and therefore, she can obtain another opinion on the case. I nevertheless feel badly when clients perceive they have not been treated fairly by their attorney."

On March 7, 1996 in response to the letter I sent my State Senator on January 17, 1996. I received the following:

"Thank you for contacting my office regarding the problem you are experiencing with your employer. I can understand your concerns. However it appears the resolution to your problem lies within the judicial rather than the legislative branch of the government. Since law precludes me from becoming involved in judicial matters, it would be appropriate for you to seek the advice of counsel. If you are not pleased with your present attorney, you may contact the Attorney Referral Service (number listed). I appreciate you sharing your concerns with me and regret I cannot be of more direct assistance."

I spent hours on the phone explaining what my problems were and had been in and out of attorneys' offices, but couldn't get lawyers to take my case for whatever reasons. Oddly enough—it wasn't because I *didn't* have a case. No lawyer would touch our cases with a ten foot pole. I can't imagine why. There was a lawyer's *code of ethics* which prevented lawyers from taking our cases. It was a few days later after I received the response from my State Senator, that I received a response the American Civil Liberties Union of Michigan. This was in response to my January 1996 letter sent to solicit their assistance. The response read:

"The American Civil Liberties Union is a private, non-profit membership organization, which seeks to preserve and extend constitutional rights and civil liberties through participation in legislation, litigation, and community education. Since the Constitution is designed to protect citizens from government, private individuals, or employers, the ACLU is generally involved in cases in which there is action of government, rather than action of private institutions.

From what you have provided, it does not appear your case is one for which we can provide assistance. This is not to say that you do not have a legitimate claim, but simply that it does not fall within the scope of our organization and limited resources.

If you believe you have been a victim of unlawful discrimination, you may wish to contact the Michigan Department of Civil Rights or Equal Employment Opportunity Commission. You should also consider consulting with private counsel. Your Local Bar Association can help you locate an attorney. Again, we regret that the ACLU is not in a position to assist you. We wish you the best of luck."

At that point I had "been there and done that". It was as though these lawyers saw me coming and closed their doors as if I had the plague. After I received both responses, I contacted Attorney Susan White. Ms. White was going to refer my case to another lawyer. I called lawyers upon lawyers and had appointments setup, only to be told they could not take my case after viewing my material. I did lawyer searches on my lunch break at work, and I would visit law offices after work, but it was all done to no avail. Mazzie Cane's experience has been just the same. I knew I had a case because I could read the contract and comprehend what mistreatments occurred.

I often used Wayne State University's Law Library (in Detroit, Michigan) for much of my research, but it was not helpful enough—especially when it came to biased judges refusing to appoint counsel. I requested an assigned attorney because I couldn't find one to take my case. I was able to find more than enough information regarding discrimination, harassment, retaliation, and labor laws violated by Famous Parts Company—Woodrow Stamping Plant and Local 783. As a result of my research, I knew I had a case. There was also contract violation and it was a shame that we could not find counsel.

Just because an attorney won't take your case, doesn't mean you don't have one. And just because an attorney says your case doesn't have merit, doesn't mean it's the truth. Don't be fooled by lies and rejection. Most likely if you know in your heart you're within your rights, you probably are. Take it upon yourself to research laws applying to your treatment. If a judge doesn't appoint you counsel when you clearly need it, this could mean you have been *red-flagged* or *black-balled*. At that point, you have to be ready to fight because the odds are really against you. There is one thing to remember: if you find fraud was involved in your court case, you can bring your case back in a court of law. You can take an attorney to the Attorney Grievance Commission if you've discussed your case with a lawyer and they state you don't have a case when you really do. You can actually sue them. I think lawyers would prefer fighting cases against other lawyers, opposed to fighting Famous Parts Company or the Union.

I learned about suing lawyers after the fact. I could have been a wealthy woman. I will never give up until I receive justice because Woodrow Stamping Plant—Famous Parts Company was wrong. I truly believe if I were Caucasian, I would not have been treated in the manner I was. It was always said at Woodrow Stamping Plant that minorities want to constantly sue someone—only to get something for nothing. With all the money that has been pilfered from me—who *really* wants something for nothing? It's clearly not me.

The way things are setup, the media puts fear in Caucasians by labeling Black and other minorities as purse snatchers, unarmed robbers, and burglarizes. Caucasian women are told to hold onto their purses when a minority is within their distance. All this is a myth because every minority isn't going to rob you. Minorities aren't the only one's committing crimes. Caucasian people commit them too—they just get lighter sentences. Good and bad are found in all ethnicities—not just in the Black and Hispanic decent.

The law is not as harsh Caucasians involved in white-collar crimes (or any other crime for that matter). They usually receive a slap on the wrist in comparison to Blacks. Minorities are judged much harsher, sometimes for the same crime. There is a two-tier justice system when it comes to the minorities and Caucasians. The corporate crooks always give minorities a bad rep, while they give pilfering a different meaning altogether. The ones pilfering from me were common cut throats in the name of Famous Parts Company. They stole from me and employees like me who could least afford the thievery. They pilfered my idea and had been pilfering money ever since I started working for them. So who are the true thieves?

In my case, corporate fraud was going on and Local 783 always covered for Famous Part's Company—Woodrow Stamping Plant. The Company was guilty of insurance fraud and money-laundering, among many things. It was the corporate Caucasian at Woodrow Stamping Plant who took advantage of the poorest people. They ripped off the ones how worked for a living, many of whom were living from pay check to paycheck. This elaborate thief ring has been in operation for many years. They pilfer money by the billions and when there're caught, they only receive a slap on the wrist—such as in the cases of Plant Chairman, John Hail, and Bargaining Committeeman, Bob Fleetwood.

Woodrow Stamping Plant's Plant Chairman Hail, and Bargaining Committeeman Bob Fleetwood, both were guilty of racketeering. They only received three to five years in a federal prison. If they were Black, they would have received life in prison for these same crimes. Woodrow Stamping Plant and Local 783 were committing corporate fraud. The crimes they committed were through Worker's Compensation, retirement, and the employees' insurance fund. This scheme was one big lie. What makes Nurse Tootie, Dr. Butt, John Hail, and Tom Hemp so different? They committed crimes, which were kept low-key. The media doesn't cover those kinds of stories. They're hushed up. Since Famous Parts Company insures their self, that makes it a lot easier to commit fraud. When no one saw what they did, or when everyone looked the other way, they continued business as usual.

All the events transpired during my employment at Woodrow Stamping Plant—Famous Parts Company combine to be a case of corruption. When my grievances weren't filed there was so much fraud going on, but they had all their areas covered. The fraud extended to the Department of Labor, National Labor Relations Board, the Department of Civil Rights, and the EEOC. After trying to get them to investigate, I became aware of all the government agencies participating in the conspiracy to cover the asses of Woodrow Stamping Plant and Local 783. I had great difficulty trying to get my case heard in a court of law, even though I knew I had a case. I read the law and had to take it upon myself to bring my case back to courts. It's a shame that I won a grievance and received no punitive damages because of the way the grievance was written up. It was all done for the hell of it, according to Woodrow Stamping Plant and Local 783. This grievance reached the Executive Branch of the Union CEO, Mr. Don Hangem. He did nothing to settle this grievance in a way that I would be compensated.

This following letter is from one of the several attorneys I contacted for assistance with my case. The July 12, 1996 letter read:

"Thank you for providing me the opportunity to review the information you gave my secretary by telephone. Unfortunately, I will not be able to handle your case. However, you may very well have a case against your former/current employer. Should you want to pursue this matter, you should immediately contact another attorney. The Detroit Bar Association Attorney Referral Service can provide you with name of other attorneys.

I spoke with lawyers from the referral service, and the results were the same. I tried contacting other lawyers, but that too was of no avail. Mazzie didn't have much success either. This is when we finally realized that we both were Black-Balled.

The letter continued:

You should know that (with cases of this type) if you are considering filing this case against your former/current employer, you must do so in a certain time. These types of cases are subjected to strict and short statute of limitation periods, beyond which time you will be forever precluded from filing a lawsuit against your former/current employer.

State and Federal law has a three-year statute of limitation for discrimination claims, which commence at the time of the discrimination for Federal law rights. You must file an EEOC charge within 300 days of the discriminatory action and then you must file a lawsuit within 90 days from the date of receipt of a 'right to sue letter'. Breach of contract cases (non-union) must be filed in court within 6 years from the date of any breach of contract. If you are a union employee, you must immediately take appropriate action as called for under your particular collective bargaining agreement. Whistleblowers claims must be filed within 90 days of any wrongdoing or adverse employment action, and defamation/slander cases have a 1 year statute of limitation from the defaming act. There are other very strict and short statutes of limitations, depending on the nature of the claim you wish to bring forth, so you must act immediately to preserve your rights. If you have any questions, please do not hesitate to contact me."

This man has just told me he couldn't take my case, when I knew I had a case. There weren't just a *few* laws violated between Woodrow Stamping Plant and

Local 783. Now there were many. I couldn't even get my day in court after a serious wrong had been committed against me and others. Mazzie Cane and I had to seek outside help because we weren't getting any help from Woodrow Stamping Plant or Local 783. This was a conspiracy.

Another lawyer I contacted for help addressed the following letter to Attorney Bushe in July 1995. This was a family friend who was aware of my conflict with my employer. Looking back, he advised me on some matters, but did nothing to help me challenge Famous Parts Company or Local 783. The law firm he worked for at the time, refused to take my case. This friend of the family was in Maritime Law (from my understanding dealing in ship and cargo). I believe he could have done more to assist me, but maybe he too was afraid of The Big Three and the Union. His letter read:

"... I am the family's personal attorney. On September 8, 1994, Ms. Carrie executed a Contingency Fee Agreement with Attorney John Hdith to represent her in her cause of action against Famous Parts Company and/or Local 783. A $1,000 (one-thousand dollar) retainer fee was paid. Attorney Hdith sent a letter on September 5, 1994 to Famous Parts Company. After a good deal of time passed without any word from her attorney as to efforts being made on her behalf, Ms. Carrie attempted to contact attorney Hdith. She was eventually informed Mr. Hdith had been ill and her case was handed to Mr. Bushe.

As such, please provide the undersigned at the earliest possible date a status report on Ms. Carrie's file. Have any other actions besides your letter of May 30, 1995, to Mr. Sophie of Famous Parts Company, been taken on Ms. Carrie's behalf? Please also include your plan as to filing an action against Famous Parts Company and/or Local 783. I would note that Ms. Carrie still has not obtained any reimbursement for back pay. Further, apparently the grievance she filed has culminated in a decision, but her union is not allowing her to obtain a copy of it. Please assure that a copy of the decision is obtained at the earliest possible date. Thank you for your attention to this matter. I look forward to hearing from you."

There was no response from Mr. Bushe to the family friend. This showed that Mr. Bushe must have been assured by Local 783 that there would be no repercussions for his failure to represent me as a client. If not he would have gotten on the ball, for fear of being sued for failure to represent. There was another letter dated September 18, 1996 from another prospect lawyer. She wrote:

"Per our meeting on September 16, this is to confirm that I will not be filing a complaint or any other legal papers on your behalf, relative to your ongoing dispute with Famous Parts Company and the Local 783.

In our meeting, you provided documents that show a statute of limitations date as identified by your previous attorney of September 28, 1996. Please note that I have not replied or indicated to you in any way that I am going to attempt to refer this matter before that date. If you wish to attempt legal action before that date, you will have to find your own attorney.

The phrase, "statute of limitations" (a certain time frame) means that you cannot file a lawsuit against Famous Parts Company or the Executive Branch of the Union after September 28, 1996. Therefore, if you continue to believe, after our discussion that you have a good cause of action against Famous Parts Company and your Local 783, you must get something filed no later than 4 p.m. on September 30, 1996. (The court rules give you until the following work day when a court date occurs on a weekend or holiday.) In the meantime, I will review the documents you have left relative to your concerns about attorney malpractice. I will be in touch with you in the next few weeks."

The following letter is from the above lawyer. I call it a "Cover Your Behind" letter because she was aware I had a valid case and did nothing to assist me. She didn't want me to bring charges against her before the Attorney Grievance Commission. Her second letter was dated February 3, 1997 and stated:

"I am sorry it has taken me so long to get back to you, but since we last met I have had nothing but health problems. Is there a jinx on this file? (*That was a very unusual statement to make, wouldn't you think?*) I have reviewed your file and I am not persuaded that you have a malpractice case against your former attorney. Your statute of limitations, as you already know, is two years from the last date he provided legal services to you, or six months from the date you first discovered the alleged error—whichever is latter.

I will not make a referral in this matter, nor will I be filing anything on your behalf. Please call my office to make arrangements to pick up your file as soon as possible. I am sorry I could not be of more assistance in this matter. There is a labor lawyer downtown, (number listed) who you might want to call and talk to about your situation regarding Famous Parts Company—Woodrow Stamping

Plant and the Executive Branch of the Union. Please tell this person I referred you to him."

It so happened that he never returned my attempts to contact him on the matter, but that was to be expected. I was so frustrated with Attorney Bushe and how he was handling my discrimination case against Woodrow Stamping Plant and Local 783. I told Mr. Bushe I was going to take him to the Attorney Grievance Commission. When Mr. Hdith took my case before his retirement, I consulted with him and he stated I had a case. After he received my employee records, he stated I was not being properly paid. This information only substantiated the truth as I had stated prior. I was full-time when I was first hired at Woodrow Stamping Plant, and I was terminated when I transferred to another plant unlawfully. Even Wanda Scorn, Attorney for Famous Parts Company, admitted this in correspondence to my attorney, Mr. Bushe. <u>Upon taking Attorney Bushe to the Attorney Grievance Commission, Attorney Wanda Scorn admitted the grievance never went as far as to reach her desk.</u> That's when she stated I had been treated better than the other employees. Why was I singled out to receive "better treatment" than anyone, and why was I yet complaining about this "better treatment"? If I was complaining, that meant I wasn't satisfied. It really didn't take much to satisfy me. I was only asking for the money they pilfered from me for three years and my seniority for those three years. I only asked because the company knew of the error for three years—never correcting it. Why shouldn't I have received my back pay?

As far as the transfer is concerned, it was very unethical. I was the only one who was sent to Sarrow Stamping Plant when there were others who had higher seniority than I, including Mazzie Cane. This was in violation of labor and contract laws. Mr. Hilter, International Representative of the Executive Branch of the Union, informed me I was going to be a rehire. I was glad to go! But still no one, and I mean no one, came to my defense when I was terminated in the process instead of "rehired". I was terminated at Woodrow Stamping before being hired at Sarrow Stamping Plant. When I was hired at Sarrow Stamping, I was hired as a new employee. They did the same to Andrea, my friend and co-worker, who was wrongfully terminated. Woodrow Stamping or Local 783 never came to her defense either. There was no help to be found on any level inside or outside of the plant.

What happened between Mr. Hdith saying Mazzie Cane and I had cases and all of a sudden we were being told we didn't? What would constitute such change? Again, the same thing happened when the people who where hired during the 70's were called back to work. They didn't get their seniority back, nor did they receive their back pay. The company was first hiring new people who'd never worked the company before—when according to contract, if an employee had worked for the company before, *they* should have been the ones to hire full time first. Local 783 allowed other new hires to become full-time before those who were hired during the 70's. When they were hired back, there were no questions or concerns as far as being full time was concerned, because they worked for the company before and there were prevision made for them to receive the back seniority and back pay. Instead Woodrow Stamping Plant hired these employees as new employees as though they had never worked for the company ever.

Woodrow Stamping Plant with the help of Local 783 pilfered their money which the employees should have received upon their return. So the employees hired a lawyer to represent them. They too, went from having a case to not having a case in a matter of a month or two. What transpired that caused such a significant change? Mazzie Cane and I both went from having a case, to not having a case. This significant change was beyond our comprehension. In a letter to the Attorney Grievance Commission regarding Mr. Bushe, Mr. Hdith stated, "There were provisions made" and my case should have been settled out of court. These provisions were made by Mr. Hdith.

We *all* knew Mazzie and I had cases. We were just waiting for them to be heard in court. Woodrow Stamping Plant and Local 783 were in violation when they hired me full-time before Mazzie Cane. I was under the assumption that this is what Mr. Hdith discussed with Mr. Bushe, when Hdith left the practice to him. But instead, Mr. Bushe chose not to pursue our cases. Mr. Bushe sold himself to the highest bidder in order not to pursue our claims in court. Mr. Bushe then asked me to give him another chance in handling my case, before I went to the Attorney Grievance Commission. I was so angry that I just couldn't. Through the entire events, he only wanted to help himself and I wanted to make him accountable for doing nothing with my case. I did the work, with the exception for the responses Mr. Hdith sent to Woodrow Stamping Plant and the two or three letters Bushe sent on my behalf.

If you recall, I was recommended to Mr. Hdith by my co-worker, Rosie, who'd worked for a unionized company prior to coming to Sarrow Stamping. Rosie and the other employees were one day told they didn't have a job any longer since the business was folding. They were given severance pay, but Rosie and a few others didn't take it. They contacted Mr. Hdith for advice and he recommended they did not cash their checks. Whether this was a subsidiary of

Famous Parts Company or not, the union allowed the company to close their doors unlawfully—and I'm sure it was for profit for the union members.

Mr. Hdith was almost ready to settle Rosie's case on any day, in an out of court settlement. She was only waiting for the word. Then Mr. Hdith became ill and everything changed. Her case went without justice. Rosie became appalled and angry because Mr. Bushe told her at this late date that she didn't have a case either. This seemed to have become a problem with lawyers admitting you have a case and weeks later the clients are informed that they don't have a case. This seemed to be a common pattern. The other women that refused the severance pay lost their money when Mr. Bushe sold their cases to the highest bidder. Mr. Hdith had made promises to them that Mr. Bushe could not fulfill because of his greed.

I told Rosie she and the other women affected including myself should take Attorney Bushe to the Attorney Grievance Commission, because he should have been representing us as his clients more sufficiently. We all gathered together and took him to the Attorney Grievance Commission separately. He took the responsibility of our cases before Mr. Hdith became ill. I know there were at least 5 complaints filed against Mr. Bushe, but the Executive Branch of the Union helped him out on this unequal justice, because he did them a favor. When we all decided to file a complaint against him this was something that he hadn't anticipated on us doing. He got himself, into serious trouble while representing 'big businesses'. There was no way 5 people making claims against him wouldn't leave a mark on his record someplace. The union carries much clout and corruption within every organization in the state of Michigan. The union is a large group of organized crime figures that buy and sell favors—even in the court of law. They allowed Mr. Bushe's continuance of practicing law in the state of Michigan. As a result he was scared for the decision he made to work for Woodrow Stamping and Local 783 and Rosie's group turned around and filed a complaint against him too.

I was so angry I called Mr. Bushe and told him I was very dissatisfied in how he was handling my case. I was doing all the legwork filing charges with the National Labor Relations Board and inquiring about the grievance. I informed him every step of the way of everything I was doing or going to do. He didn't return my phone calls unless I sent letters certified mail, but that wasn't enough to persuade him to start working for me and Mazzie. He didn't tell the whole truth when he stated that I was keeping important information form him. He failed to divulge the fact that he was holding in his possession valuable information to substantiate Woodrow Stamping Plant and Local 783 violated contract and labor laws too. He was informing Local 783 and Woodrow Stamping what my next move was. As a result, they were always one step ahead of me, waiting for me to approach the subject. I had become so fed up with his behavior I could have screamed.

When I told Mr. Bushe I would be taking him to the Attorney's Grievance Commission, I told him I would be coming to his office to pick-up my file. He was trying to explain something as to how he would get down to business on my case at this late date after all the statute of limitations had run out. He asked me to give him one more chance, and I told him *NO!* I also told him that he may have gotten off with me, but he wouldn't get off so easy with the Attorney Grievance Commission.

Attorney Bushe was willing to continue my case if I didn't take him to the Attorney Grievance Commission, but he wanted nothing to do with Mazzie Cane's case since he claimed she didn't have one. Mr. Bushe betrayed me once by holding my case for two years while knowing I had a case and not filing it in federal or state court. It was only when I told him I was taking action against him that all of a sudden he wanted to sit down and discuss my case. Mr. Bushe was a man I could no longer trust. He knew Mazzie had a case and two years later he wanted *me* to tell her that she didn't have one. He couldn't even look her in the face and tell her himself. That was his job—not mines. I told him, he really thought I was stuck on stupid. I told him what I *would* do was inform her to file a complaint against him at the Attorney Grievance Commission.

The company and the union worked miracles with the two sets of files kept on employees, and Mr. Bushe knew this as well. For this reason, he wasn't working on Mazzie Cane's case. When he looked in her filed, he noticed what Woodrow Stamping Plant was doing. I'd heard Mr. Bushe say Woodrow Stamping Plant wouldn't send him information, he requested regarding Mazzie. If Woodrow Stamping Plant wouldn't cooperate, then he should have taken them to court. The judge could sanction Woodrow Stamping Plant and make them turn over information, if this was honestly the problem. The judge could have held Woodrow Stamping Plant in contempt for nondisclosure. There were other alternatives Mr. Bushe could have used to force Woodrow Stamping Plant to comply. He just chose not to.

It is ironic that through all these years, not one attorney, or judge, the Department of Civil Rights, the Equal Employment Opportunity Commission, or the National Labor Relations Board, ever investigated Woodrow Stamping Plant or Local 783. No one suggested filing suit against the union. I thought that was rather unique.

When I released Mr. Bushe, I then realized I was in the same shape I was in before. I had no lawyer and the odds were very slim that I would find one. But I'd much rather an attorney working for me opposed to my opponent. I never did get a lawyer to represent me, even though I'd tried on numerous occasions obtaining one. I was aware of how hard it was to get a lawyer—and who's to say they'd even take my case seriously at such a late date. I was better off representing myself, which I ultimately did. There is more elaboration concerning that in Part II of this book.

Mazzie and I were set up to fail—and that is exactly what happened with the help of Woodrow Stamping Plant, Local 783, and above all my attorney Mr. Bushe. I had been with him from 1994 until 1996, and he had literally done nothing on the case—even by his own admission. Why would I give Attorney Bushe another chance to help Famous Parts Company and Local 783? All they had to do was promise him enough money and he would betray me again. Why did he, all of a sudden want to work on my case when I had been calling all along and he wasn't returning my calls? This is what lawyers do when they don't want to talk to you. They say "silence is golden", but is it really?

Mr. Bushe was even slow about answering my letters. He just wanted to make himself look good. He didn't care about me as a client. Yes! I was angry with Mr. Bushe because I gave him all the information and opportunity he needed in representing me, and he chose not to do so. I gave him all the information that he had in his files. I went to the National Labor Relations Board myself because he wasn't doing his job. He could have looked into my allegations and requested records for Mazzie and me.

I am aware Famous Parts Company didn't have a 'user friendly' reputation when it came to obtaining information. But at that time Mr. Bushe had enough evidence to file my 90-day 'right to suit' letter in the state or federal courts. My employment record from Woodrow Stamping Plant and Sarrow Stamping Plant was in his possession. Those were the official documents from when I was hired. Why was everyone looking the other way, was beyond my comprehension. When all the government agencies got involved or (didn't get involved), the pilfering scheme became a cover-up. This was fraud by deception. Famous Parts Company has *deep-pockets*, which means they can pay anyone any price for whatever they want accomplished. This includes the union.

What more files did Mr. Bushe need? I was, as the saying goes, "too through" with Mr. Bushe. He screwed up and I wasn't going to let him get away worry-free. I had worked for Famous Parts Company four years at the time I received my 'right to suit' letter. After I filed the charges against Mr. Bushe, I went to his office, picked up my file, and started going through the information. Mazzie's case was lost in the midst of all the cover-ups going on at Woodrow Stamping. What good is information if it not used when needed? I knew he threw my case out for a profit, and the profit didn't come from *my* pockets.

I tried to get the Department of Labor to look into the reason behind, my holiday pay being withdrawn from my funds. I was aware the company was pilfering from the full-time employees, because what I was experiencing just didn't make since. I didn't want to think Famous Parts Company—Woodrow Stamping Plant was pilfering money from employees. Not until after the company admitted I was full-time in July 1992, when I received my vacation pay. This should not have happened if I was part-time. I brought this to the attention of management at Woodrow Stamping, when Donald Nelson was the CEO of Famous Parts Company. The company was paying me for holiday pay 90 days after I started working. I started receiving full-time benefits and part-time pay, but my records stated I was full-time.

At Woodrow Stamping Plant you could find out anything through plant gossip. I had the reputation as a "troublemaker," because I was constantly on Local 783's and Woodrow Stamping Plant's backs asking questions. I knew they were up to no good, but they didn't care because they had no fear of getting caught. They were appalled when I got all the part-time employees to sign a petition for a meeting with Local 783 to find out why they were hiring new employees from other plants. Why was it that Woodrow Stamping Plant would not give there own part-time employees that worked at Woodrow Stamping Plant full-time status first? Many of these employees had been part-time for two years or more. I started informing the part-time people there was a reason, the company was passing us over and hiring people from other plants first. I told my co-workers we were full-time and the company was taking our money. I winded up being correct.

After Mazzie Cane and I started asking the union to meet with us regarding our concerns, Plant Chairman, Johnny Hail, told the part-time employees if they signed any more petitions, they would not be given a full-time status. I told Mr. Hail he had no right telling the part-time people they would not be hired, if they signed another petition that Mazzie and I came up with. Why did he tell the employees this? The meeting was for one reason only, and that was to gather information about our employment status, in which they were not telling us. Those who were hired during the 70's wanted to know when they were going to receive their seniority and back pay, but the union strayed away from that subject. These employees were angry because Local 783 always eluded questions employees would ask, the elected officials who refused to answers our questions to our satisfaction. Chairman Hail later apologized for making that statement, but he had already made a statement to me without, having to say a word. The main reason Woodrow Stamping Plant terminated me when I left for transfer to Sarrow Stamping Plant was because I knew too much.

I learned that for every action I took with Woodrow Stamping Plant, I always received a reaction in return. This taught me a lot, with regards to how Woodrow Stamping Plant and Local 783 did business. If I did something to prove the plant's guilt of my accusations, they would try to prove me wrong and retaliate against me. This type of treatment was a characteristic, trait of Woodrow Stamping Plant and Local 783. They were use to treating employees in a retaliatory manner, when the company was displeased. Local 783 backed the retaliatory action because of what they were doing. They did this so their actions wouldn't be construed as discrimination. I think all The Big Three are involved in that aspect.

Remember in Chapter 23—Supervision in the Plant, when Marva sued Sarrow Stamping Plant for an undisclosed amount of money, when she didn't heed to what Mr. Jessie, her supervisor wanted? Remember how all the supervisors stuck together in her punishment by putting her on the hardest and most difficult jobs they could find for her?.

Their reactions told me I was right all along. I didn't have to be in the plant to know when there was some type of investigation occurring, but they always assumed it was, I at the bottom of the investigation. I'm sure I wasn't the only person who knew Woodrow Stamping Plant and Local 783 were pilfering money, from employees and treating them unjustly. I just didn't keep my mouth shut, like everyone else. They took a disliking to me because I stood up for what I believe in. Nevertheless, I had something to say, but no one was willing to listen. So I decided to write a book to tell my side of the story uninterruptedly. Its bad one has to write a book to defend oneself. My obstacles just made me that much more determined to get my story heard. I knew what I was saying had merit. Woodrow Stamping Plant and Local 783 were as wrong as "two left shoes," while they tried to make it seem as though I was mentally imbalanced.

All this was done to hide my full-time status because I was complaining of all the adjustment being made on my checks. I thought I would get some kind of justice when I filed my grievance. Attorney Bushe simply sold me to the highest bidder. He did what he felt he had to do. As a result, I did what I had to do as well. I was going to get back at him in whatever way possible. His law license should have a few stars because of the choices he made, not to represent Rosie's group consisting of five more women. When we all filed complaints against Mr. Bushe, it should've been noted that his practice was a fiasco. It was a cover-up right from the beginning, amidst a bunch of lies and contradictories regarding, the actions of Woodrow Stamping and Local 783. Through all of this, the only ones who profited were Famous Parts Company—Woodrow Stamping Plant and Local 783.

I asked the Department of Labor to look into whether, I should have been paid holiday pay and vacation pay. With all that was happening to me, I thought the gentleman from the Department of Labor would find something wrong for sure—but again I was wrong. It took a while for him to come, but when the representative came to the plant, he claimed I had the union to represent me on the matter. There must have been some kind of payoff, because the information was the same then, as it was in July 1992 when the company admitted an error was made. When the man came from the Department of Labor, he had the opportunity to look at the employee file. When he read the file, it stated I was a full-time employee and was entitled to the vacation pay withdrawn from my paycheck. If I was full-time when the company found me to be full-time, then I had to have been full-time when the gentleman from the Michigan Department of Labor, came to the plant to verify my employment records. He viewed the same files in which I have in my possession until this day. That is the reason Woodrow Stamping Plant, would never give me a copy of my employment file upon my request. I tried on numerous occasions, but was denied.

When the grievance didn't seem to be working in my favor in July 1996, my lawyer Mr. Bushe seemed to have switched sides by working for my opponents, Woodrow Stamping Plant and Local 783. I had been appealing my decision with the National Labor Relations Board until they told me, flat out do, not to write back because my case was closed. They weren't going to investigate my complaint and they were tired of me. I thought I would try in a last ditch effort to make the wrong brought against me, made right. So I sent this letter to the attorney for the Executive Branch of the Union, Beth Angel. I also sent this same letter to Director of the Regional 21A Office, Nosy Nort. I felt Angel Stone and Nosy Nort may have had enough clout to investigate the happenings at Woodrow Stamping Plant and Local 783. They were over Local 783 and could've investigated, but did not. They weren't receiving proper feedback from Regional Director Nosey Nort and Beth Angel. When I didn't receive any help at the Regional Office, I was aware I was in trouble. The following letter was dated July 19, 1995.

"My name is Crista Carrie. I am writing this letter trying to get some answers. I recently talked to an attorney about my problems and he told me I should contact you. The story has been going on for so long it's hard to know where to even start. Please see the attached 'cover story', which summarizes what has occurred and why I'm fighting so hard for fairness. In my heart I know I am right. I'm not asking for anything I don't think I deserve.

I originally contacted an attorney, because of the actions of Local 783 and Woodrow Stamping. I seem to be getting nowhere and always ending up back where I started. The only things, I receive are lies and contradictions, which only make me more determined. I have many questions and no answers. This is the reason I am writing this letter. I hope this letter will be self-explanatory, with enough detail for you to get a clear picture of what has occurred.

When I sent this letter to Beth Angel, she advised me to contact Nosy Nort, and he didn't have the dignity or respect to reply. I know he received the letter because all my letters were sent, certified mail-return receipt. I did receive my receipt signed.

I filed Grievance #H135381 on June 3, 1993. Building: Woodrow Stamping Plant, and Local 783, who was representing my grievance. You will find both copies enclosed along with a few other papers you should find important. I have a variety of questions, which I feel, need to be answered. Maybe you can shed some light as to the answers:

1. Why are there two decisions both signed by Plant Chairmen, Jim Hall and L.F. Norman, Manager of Employment Relations, when only one grievance was signed and dated? (Grievance dispositions dated January 5, 1995 and December 8, 1993.)

2. I was told by John Hail, Plant Chairman at Local 783, after a grievance was signed, no one can be added to the grievance. I would like to know how twenty-five people were added. The nine people that were on the original grievance (see attached sheet) didn't receive anything through this same grievance. These nine people didn't receive the same day as Mazzie and I, and they should have. They were on my grievance too and they were the forgotten few. The people, who were added after I signed the grievance, should not have been added. Especially when the nine people who were on the grievance, didn't get their seniority or back pay. These nine people, who signed my grievance, received nothing, while at the same time, those who

were added after the grievance was singed, received something. Those employees are also on this attached sheet. I would like to stress there is no reason this grievance should have taken from June 3, 1993 to July 1995, when it was supposed to be settled.

3. When and if the grievance ever reached the Public Review Board, why wasn't I allowed to attend the meeting? I went out of my way to inform, Mr. Rocker (at the Executive Branch of the Union), John Hail (Plant Chairman), and Mr. McGregor (President of Local 783) before he retired. I wanted to argue my case, before the Public Review Board and I was denied that right. According to the contract, I have that right. I felt I had enough evidence to prove, what I said was true. Not allowing me to say a word only silenced me. That sends the message to say I'm the guilty one, while everyone is speaking on my behalf except me. They lied and I couldn't argue the truth regarding my grievance. They didn't file my grievance. This was a witch-hunt because after all that transpired, Local 783 never filed the grievance. They just lied and everyone lied for them. This includes the government agencies, who allowed them to keep me in silence.

I sought help from all these agencies and they knew this grievance was never filed. Local 783 and Executive Branch of the Union's CEO, Don Hangem, was aware of this fact too. So was his predecessor, James York. This grievance never went to the Public Review Board, or the Umpire stage, and everyone knew it—including the National Labor Relations Board, the Department of Labor, the Department of Civil Rights, and the Equal Employment Opportunity Commission. They all lied for Famous Parts Company-Woodrow Stamping Plant and Local 783 to keep this money-laundering scheme alive and well.

4. Why wasn't I notified of the decision which was supposedly made, December 15, 1994? According to the contract, I should have been informed of every step made regarding the grievance I filed. I wasn't notified until July of 1995 that the grievance was settled. One grievance states one date, and the other grievance was settled on another date, all together (December 8, 1993). Clearly something is wrong when I received two grievances, when only one was file.

Not to mention the piece of paper that Bargaining Committeeman, Bob Fleetwood, handed me with no logo or anything referencing a grievance on it. However, he told me this was my grievance determination. This grievance paper had three typed lines on it. If I were to count that as a grievance, it would now be *three* determinations when only one grievance was filed. I'm not sure, which date the grievance was settled. Can you explain this matter to help me understand? This grievance couldn't have been settled on all these different dates.

5. Why has this grievance taken so long, when a grievance should have exhausted all procedures in a 90-day period of time? It should have been no more than 120 days, unless, I've misread the contract.

6. Why didn't any of the nine grievant receive the same seniority date, when we all started the same day except for two people? Karol Patton, Mazzie Cane, and Donna More, were hired with the company, long before I had been.

7. Why didn't I receive my original seniority date of September 28, 1990? I have check stubs confirming, I worked in January of 1991 and received my first Christmas bonus. This is what the grievance, was all about in the first place? I did receive July 15, 1991 seniority, which is ten months short of what I was asking for in this grievance. I didn't receive my original seniority date, and I would like to know why.

8. Why were Local 783 and Woodrow Stamping Plant trying to cover this matter up when the computer and my employment records stated my date of hire as September 28, 1990? I was told this was a "figment of my imagination". Thus far I have proven it was not just my imagination. (Please see attached documents.)

9. I have asked for documentation which states this grievance did in fact go to the Public Review board, and no one has been able to prove my grievance has been there. I would like to know why my back pay was not restored and why the seniority date only goes back to July 15, 1991. Who made the decision to settle this grievance in part and not in its entirety? All I'm asking for is some valid answers as to what happened and why. I was paid vacation pay and a personal day, which I had to pay back. Since the decision was rendered in my favor, why didn't I receive my back pay and original seniority?

When I was hired at Sarrow Stamping Plant, Tarry Johnson, Head of Labor Relations, told me that after the grievance was settled I would receive my

Christmas bonus and all my back pay. I didn't receive anything during my first years of employment at Sarrow Stamping Plant. I never received a dime. I will enclose my first vacation check stub. I was told by John Hail, Plant Chairman of Local 783, that I may get my seniority back but that I wouldn't receive any money. I would like to know why. I'm wondering if this is a conspiracy. Everyone is turning their heads away and not wanting to get involved. It's not fair for me as a union member who pays for representation not to be represented. Again, there is no reason this grievance should have taken from June 3, 1993 to July 1995 for me to be notified.

I left Woodrow Stamping Plant after I was told there were no openings for new hires. However, they told me there was an opening at Sarrow Stamping Plant. It was offered as an option, but it was indicated that if I chose not to accept it, I would waive my rights for full-time employment (even though I was already full-time on records). There were about six people hired on a full-time status at Woodrow Stamping Plant before me in October 1993. I don't believe the company didn't have enough room for one additional employee (who was already full-time on file). I was totally passed over for a position at Woodrow Stamping Plant. They didn't want me there because I was considered a "troublemaker". Woodrow Stamping Plant reviled this information to my attorney, as well as Mr. Tarry Johnson, Labor Relations Supervisor, that they didn't want me back at Woodrow Stamping Plant. I always wondered how they could admit, to the Department of Civil Rights and the National Labor Relations Board these derogatory and discriminatory statements, without anything being done about it.

After leaving Woodrow Stamping, I was appalled to find out that on record I was actually terminated, not transferred. I lost all my insurance benefits, which were later reinstated. I was to have been a rehire, but I found out I was a new hire. I found this out through Famous Part's Employees Service Center (NESC). This could not have been a mistake. This was something I wasn't supposed to find out.

After working at Sarrow Stamping, my checks stopped being directly deposited into my bank account and I wanted to know why. This is when I called the Transparent House Headquarters of Famous Parts Company and was told part-time employees can't have their checks directly deposited. This is the point in which I discovered Woodrow Stamping had been trying to conceal this matter by saying I was terminated. I could tell anyone because there was anyone willing to help me at all. All the doors for any opportunity of help were closed tight and I was looked upon as the feeble one. Woodrow Stamping Plant and Local 783 thought there was no need for help because there was none to be found anywhere.

I feel Woodrow Stamping Plant has discriminated against me. I was terminated and sent to another plant when no one in the same classification, as I was allowed to transfer—including those with more seniority than I. The ones that stayed behind never regained their seniority except Mazzie Cane. My seniority stayed the same. Some of the employees were allowed to keep their vacation pay and bonuses, yet I was not. To make matters worse, my desire to return to Woodrow Stamping Could or would never be acknowledge. I will never be able to return. I never returned and I wanted to know the reason. It's ironic how the union can fix a situation to comply with whatever they want at any given time. I was told since Woodrow was my home plant, I could return in the event of a lay-off or Sarrow Stamping Plant burning down.

My ex-attorney, Mr. Bushe, spoke with Wanda Scorn, Attorney for Famous Parts Company. He was told my grievance had never gone to the grievance stage. If this is true, please inform me what the union has done for me while I've been paying for the assurance that nothing like this would happen. I have the union "on my side". I thought union officials' best interest was to protect the best interest of their sisters and brothers. I feel this is why the unions are growing weaker with each passing day. Are the elected officials not working for their sisters and brothers, but only for themselves? As I consider this matter of great importance, please respond as soon as possible."

I guess it goes without saying that my questions were never answered by anyone, and my condition stayed the same. If it were not for the union supported by The Big Three, the union's doors would be closed. 'Big Business' is what they do for their sisters and brothers. If you have been mistreated, write letters to any and everyone. If you can't write letters, have someone write them for you. Letters are binding. Let your voice be heard so your congressperson, senator, governor, or even the President of the United States can address your problem. Wake them up so this kind of treatment can stop!

Michigan got rid of the Affirmative Action program so discrimination can continue. Companies are going to do as they please until companies like The Big Three get disciplined for their illegal behavior. The company should not have been stealing employees' retirement and Worker's Compensation. They were never held accountable for treating employees unjustly for the color of their skin. Discrimination is alive, well, and growing in the state of Michigan. To only think, it doesn't make a difference ...

33

ATTORNEY GRIEVANCE COMMISSION

I received a letter from the Department of Labor in the spring of 1993. It stated I had the Collective Bargaining Unit to represent me, which precluded the Labor Department from intervening on my behalf. This was a lie. The Labor Representative could have done something but he chose not to. I wrote a letter to the Attorney Grievance Commission summarizing the events regarding the illegal malpractices of my case and the misrepresentation by attorneys, Bushe and Hdith.

Before Mr. Hdith retired and passed away, he assured me I had completed all the necessary steps before contacting him to get my grievance solved. He said I had a valid claim. After I talked to my co-worker, Mazzie Cane, she decided to take Mr. Hdith as her lawyer too. Our cases were similar because she was also having the same problem as I in obtaining information from Woodrow Stamping Plant. It seems as a result, the law firm was $2000 dollars richer from supposedly handling our cases, while nothing was actually being done.

Due to lack of response to a letter I sent the law firm, I gave the office a follow-up call inquiring about my case. I was told at that time Mr. Hdith was ill. After my case was passed on to Mr. Bushe I found that he wasn't representing me properly. He didn't give the necessary attention to my case. Often times he wasn't even available in the office and neglected to return my calls.

When I finally was able to contact Attorney Bushe, I inquired about my case. He never seemed to have much to say. I then proposed to Mr. Bushe, "Since Famous Parts Company—Woodrow Stamping Plant and the Local 783 are not cooperating with you, why don't we go to court to obtain the information which is needed?" He said he didn't want to go to court and get egg on his face because he didn't have enough information regarding my case. He said he didn't want to get laughed out of court. But the truth of the matter was he did absolutely noth-

319

ing with regards to my case. Mr. Bushe only stalled, which allowed the statue of limitations to expire. He was well aware of what he was doing.

I couldn't understand what Mr. Bushe was saying. I was sure he knew what the word *sanction* meant when the defendant wasn't cooperating in giving information. So I wasn't sure what Mr. Bushe was talking about when he said he didn't want to go to court and get "egg on his face". Mr. Bushe waited until March 1996, almost two years later to tell me time had lapsed on my case. He told me the statue of limitations ran out and nothing could be done about filing a lawsuit against Woodrow Stamping and Local 783.

At one point Mr. Bushe told me the union wanted me to file the grievance over again. I informed him I wasn't going to file another grievance when they didn't file the first one. Mr. Bushe said the grievance wasn't filed because the attorney for Famous Parts Company told him as such. I felt he was giving me bad advice and stalling on many matters pertaining to my case. When speaking to Mr. Bushe in January 1996, he told me (on one hand) he didn't believe in a union. Then he told me in the following sentences that he was going to a union party to obtain information with respect to my case. I didn't like Mr. Bushe's idea of fraternizing with the enemy. One doesn't socialize at a union gathering unless they are invited. Hmmm … I wonder why he was invited.

After the party, I called Attorney Bushe and there was no further information given to me. Mazzie Cane and I met with Mr. Bushe. He reiterated he was working on our cases the best he could. He told me he couldn't do much for Mazzie Cane's case and wanted me to relay the message to her. I told him this wasn't what he told Mazzie in September 1995. When we both met in his office, Bushe said he would have to take Famous Parts Company—Woodrow and Sarrow Stamping to court. Mazzie and I were satisfied with his message and we contacted him once again asking him to go ahead and take them to court. From the time Mr. Hdith handed Mr. Bushe the case, nothing was done for the exception of the two or three letters he sent on our behalf. My case was virtually at a stand still and he did nothing to change that fact.

Also in January 1996, Mr. Bushe informed me he would not be handling the case with Local 783. He informed me no other lawyer would take my case due to me being *blackballed* with Local 783. He said the courts would almost always side with the union. I wanted to know why he didn't tell me this before now. I was aware he never once sent Local 783 any correspondence with regards to my case. He only contacted Famous Parts Company.

I felt Mr. Bushe was biased but there was nothing I could do at the time. Therefore I started trying to obtain more information to help me. Mr. Bushe informed me my case didn't have much hope. Famous Parts Company and the union said they were in the right. I had a lawyer who had done nothing to help my case, which only discouraged me at this late date. He said the company and union felt they did all they could to satisfy me. Mr. Bushe said they had bent over backwards to give me what I wanted.

In your opinion, does this sound like a person being represented by a lawyer who knows what he's doing? He truly didn't give a damn about me as his client. After I filed charges with the Attorney Grievance Commission, Mr. Bushe sent a reply in response of the charges. The charges were brought because Mr. Bushe had information in his possession constituting I'd experienced desperate treatment, harassment, and retaliation. I experienced this treatment because of the pilfered money allocated to me of which I had to pay back to the company. Mr. Bushe wrote the following letter to the Attorney Grievance Commission defending his reputation in April 1995 and his action while representing me in the desperate treatment by Woodrow Stamping Plant and Local 783. The letter read:

"Crista Carrie first retained an attorney by the name of James Hdith. Currently he is retired or on an indefinite medical leave. He is no longer a licensed attorney in this state due to his failure to pay his annual dues. He was retained on September 3, 1994. Ms. Carrie never met me (*Mr. Bushe*) until much later although I was informed by Mr. Hdith I was to be co-counsel on the case. According to records, Mr. Hdith left me with the responsibility of continuing representation of Ms. Carrie's and Mrs. Cane's cases. Ms. Carrie did in fact pay a non-refundable investigation fee of $1,000.00. *According to Mr. Hdith my case was ready for an out-of-court settlement. This information was in a letter responding to the Attorney Grievance Commission when they contacted Attorney Hdith.*

To set the record straight, I have not received any economic benefit from the monies paid by Ms. Carrie. Further I did not even share the fee with Mr. Hdith. When he went on leave, no bank accounts were transferred to me. Contrary to statements contained in the grievance by Ms. Carrie, no promises were made guaranteeing her return to Woodrow Stamping Plant or to get her back pay and benefits returned. Besides, I was never present when she retained Mr. Hdith. I have never made such promises to her.

Initially my role was to act strictly as co-counsel to Mr. Hdith, not to spearhead efforts in moving the file forward. My role became more supervisory when Mr. Hdith went on an indefinite medical leave in late December of 1994. He left to recover from complications following his Prostate Cancer surgery. We were expecting his return at least five to six months later. This of course did not happen and he has been away ever since. He has since retired.

At the same time, I more than doubled my workload in an instant, being forced to familiarize myself with all these new files including Ms. Carrie's. I continued handling and managing the cases of Ms. Carrie and Ms. Cane. Also my associate, Mr. Don Brown, who worked at the law firm of Mr. Hdith, was interested in taking over my case. It was already established that Mr. Hdith would not be returning. Attorney Don Brown who worked at the law firm prior of Mr. Hdith leaving, he wanted to familiarize himself with the files so he could answer proposed questions from the clients. Mr. Hdith had first sent a letter out to Famous Parts Company on September 5, 1994. He received a delayed response with regards to retrieving the files of Ms. Carrie. Such files were received and reviewed by myself through the consultation of Mr. Hdith. In the meantime, Ms. Carrie filed a complaint with the Equal Employment Opportunity Commission (EEOC) and the Michigan Department of Civil Rights (MDCR) on April of 1993.

Ms. Carrie received an answer following an investigation by the EEOC and the MDCR in December of 1994. The investigation concluded there was no desperate treatment or racial discrimination by Famous Parts Company and Local 783. This claim has yet to establish a *prima facie* case even after my investigators' efforts. As with any conclusion of an investigation at the EEOC, a 90-day 'right to sue' letter was given to the complaint. This letter has been explained to Ms. Carrie in a one-on-one consultation. What Ms. Carrie does not seem to comprehend is that a 90-day right to sue letter does not mean you have provided a *prima facie* case to start a suit in the U.S. District Court, but rather you disagree with the findings of the investigation. You have the authority to go ahead and file, but you do so at your own risk (subject to Rule #11 'Sanctions for Filing a Frivolous Complaint') unless you can establish a *prima facie* case.

I am continually reminding Ms. Carrie of what a proper investigation involves and what this 90-day 'right to sue' letter means. After consulting with Mr. Hdith and my associate Mr. Brown, it was agreed this office would not proceed to the U.S. District Court for a number of reasons. This is a collective bargaining case which means Ms. Carrie needed to exhaust her union remedies. Ms. Carrie did not like this because she felt she was doing the entire running around while I did nothing. But the documents we needed were mostly in her possession.

Establishing a case of racial discrimination in the workplace is difficult through the courts and further without solid statistics, a *prima facie* case could not be established with a common element set out by leading federal case laws. It would be difficult to investigate this case within a 90-day period and further, the union grievance was still on the table.

The Labor Relations Management Act would kick out the case alone as prematurely filed. It was best to seek out preemption under Sec. #301 with a state claim of racial discrimination with a three-year statue of limitations, which would expire in late September of 1996.

Ms. Carrie agreed, somewhat disheartened but understanding the strategy. At any time subsequent to that, Ms. Carrie could seek other legal advice and did so on numerous times. Prior to my wedding in early April of 1995, it was already known by Ms. Carrie there was no intent to file in a federal court. Although I was busy at this time of year due to certain events, it had nothing to do with letting the 90-day deadline pass. Ms. Carrie just did not like my reasoning according to her grievance.

In May of 1995, Mazzie Cane another client and co-worker of Ms. Carrie, brought in a new listing of an adjusted rollback of seniority for certain Woodrow Stamping Plant employees. Ms. Carrie and Ms. Cane were upset that although their seniority was pushed back in time, it was not pushed back far enough. Further they were bothered it was not officially on their paychecks or company documents. I then wrote a letter to Mr. Sophie, Plant Labor Relations Supervisor at Woodrow, on May 30, 1995 inquiring about the delays in implementing this rollback along with other matters. I eventually received return telephone calls from Mr. Sophie. I was informed their back pay and benefits would follow later, which Mr. Sophie later denied. Hearing this, I contacted Mr. John Hail, Plant Chairman of Local 783, to make further inquiries.

At this point I thought we were getting somewhere. This thrilled both Ms. Carrie and Ms. Cane. Mr. Hail did not return my phone calls and I finally caught-up with him from my car phone one day late last summer. He was familiar with Cane and Carrie and stated both he and the union bent over backwards for them.

He stated they had been ungrateful. He was upset Mr. Sophie was informing me both women along with others, were to receive back pay and back benefits, which was not part of the deal approved by the company or sanctioned by the National Labor Relations Board.

Mr. Sophie later confirmed this and admitted he was originally incorrect. I also asked him for the copy of the opinion on the grievance and the paper trail following each stage of the grievance. I inquired as to why Ms. Carrie did not receive the copies. He stated she did receive them, but somehow she thought there should've been more. Mr. John Hail said whatever copies I had in my possession was all of the opinion. Ms. Carrie of course disagrees but has absolutely no information to suggest otherwise.

Going back to earlier chapters:
The last grievance determination I received stated all employees would receive their adjusted seniority dates and profit sharing going back to 1990-1993. Maybe Mr. Bushe just got his lies mixed up.

Ms Carrie continued from that time on to work out a crusade of letter writing to anyone who would hear her story. She also filed numerous grievances with the Local 783 and the NLRB. I was not aware of these because they were independently filed and not through my office. When I did find out, it was through correspondence with legal counsel at Famous Parts Company.

In fact by Carrie's own admission, she continues to possess documents she claims are important, but has not shown me for my review. Most of those complaints to the NLRB, DOCR, and EEOC have been denied. This includes claims made to the ACLU and her state senator. Especially with the NLRB, there were no violations of her union representation and no need to further investigate or complain additionally. She even appealed this decision although I was not aware of this until mid-November of 1995.

Once again Mr. Bushe lied. He knew every aspect of what I was doing. Because I accused him of sitting on his behind doing nothing, Mr. Bushe allowed me to take the lead in trying to get my problem solved.

The appeal was denied. Knowing these events, I decided a suit against Local 783 for failure to provide fair representation to her, would be unsuccessful and futile as it almost always is. She did in fact get her seniority rolled back to July 15, 1991. However she did not start an official full-time position at Sarrow Stamping until November of 1993. She was also allowed to keep her seniority when she arrived at the Sarrow facility instead of starting with "day one" plant seniority, which usually only occurs on an interplant transfer. This was not an interplant lateral transfer but an interplant promotion. This is totally unheard of and almost never occurs. I have never seen this occur in my career in dealing with labor unions. It could have also started an uprising by other union employees at the Sarrow Stamping facility. This is indicative of the treatment the union has given to Ms. Carrie.

There is no court that would line up against the union when they rolled back her seniority and gave her a full-time position. That actually violated other collective bargaining agreements and that was the reason for not pursuing a lawsuit against the union. Ms. Carrie was fully informed of this decision much earlier than January 1996 of this year as stated in her grievance. I have to continually bang things into her head.

What did happen in January 1996 was a follow up investigation to what I felt was the only case Ms. Carrie had left. This started back on September 21, 1995 when I sent another letter to Mr. Sophie to get more information on this issue and clear up some confusion as to any remaining matters. I was trying to help her with getting to the bottom of her grievance (which was already decided). She neglected to tell me the outcome of her grievance and establish a *prima facie* case of racial discrimination.

In response to the September letter, I finally got somewhere and received a letter from Attorney Wanda Scorn, in the Corporate Legal Department at Famous Parts Company. The letter explained a few things I was not aware of and the letter spoke for itself. I sent this letter to both Carrie and Cane. Both women responded and disagreed. I then decided to have the women come into my office—but separately. I'll discuss Ms. Carrie since she is the focus here.

I again informed her of the difficulty in proving and prevailing in a racial discrimination claim and what was required, and that somehow we needed substantially more information to establish a *prima facie* case. For the first time, she finally began to think and focus my way. I informed her I needed names, dates, and social security numbers for employees at Famous Parts Company to investigate and to dig up such information to establish desperate treatment. She was upset because she had to do all the groundwork. I informed her that Famous Parts Company would not release such information without authorization from those individuals. So therefore *she* is the only one that could put it together. She left and came back with the information. I then wrote a letter again to Attorney Wanda Scorn on January 17, 1996. I also withheld additional damaging information from Ms. Carrie with her knowledge in order to see how well Famous Parts Company's legal department would conduct their investigation and she was fully aware of this.

He lied.

Soon after sending out this letter, I saw Ms. Carrie in my office and she had the opportunity to review the same letter since most of the content related to her case. As she read it, she began to notice half the information contained in the letter was false. This information involved gender identities and dates of hire. At this point I was not very happy and Ms. Carrie did not seem to care. In fact she claimed she was still correct.

When I received Ms. Scorn's letter dated February 16, 1996, my worst nightmare after a year and a half was realized. There was no *prima facie* case of racial discrimination that would preempt the National Labor Relations Act and allow the court claim to move forward. Not only did Ms. Carrie's discovery get printed out regarding gender identity and incorrect dates of hire, but additional information such as tiebreaker procedures in promoting people to full-time status were discovered. These discoveries revealed to me that Ms. Carrie had nothing to dispute the procedure. Again the letter spoke for itself.

This letter was again forwarded to Ms. Carrie to review and she called twice and left messages with my secretary. I returned her telephone call and spent an hour and fifteen minutes with her on the phone around 9:30 to 11:15 p.m. in late February. Every time she tried to persuade me that she believed she had a case, I would play devil's advocate to test her. I was successful every time. She then said I did not have everything in her file and she had more at home with her. She did raise her voice that evening because after over a year of investigating, she informed me that I did not have it all. I was upset because I felt that she needed to bring something into my office immediately.

In fact it was a Friday night and I told her to schedule an appointment the following week. I wanted to spend at least three hours with her if I had to. She laid out all the documents she had and I laid out what I had in order to make a last stand to find a case to go forward with. If we were not successful, then at least I would give up the fight and she could go elsewhere while she still had time to pursue her case with another attorney. She never made that appointment and after one month, before I called her to check on the status of the meeting, I received this grievance she chose to file instead of meeting with me.

It seems as though Ms. Carrie is on a crusade to nail Famous Parts Company and Local 783 and will take this case to anyone with a mailbox. She does not like to hear the fact she may not have a case strong enough to move forward into the judicial system. Therefore since I am the bearer of bad news, she has now taken up the call to file a grievance against *me*. I firmly believe I have done everything possible for Ms. Carrie without getting as Ms. Carrie alleges "egg on my face," meaning I will not file a frivolous lawsuit to satisfy one's crusade to get even with someone or something. I believe this grievance should be dismissed since there has been no unethical behavior on my part except for the diligent investigation of a case that didn't turn up a positive result.

At the time I would like to challenge some of the absolutely false allegations contained in Ms. Carrie's grievance.

1. I personally have not received $2,000 dollars from Ms. Cane or Ms. Carrie, since Mr. Hdith has kept that money and I have I have not received any money from Mr. Hdith.

2. I never promised or guaranteed Crista's return to a full-time position at Woodrow Plant. That would be against union rules as detailed in a Local 783 correspondence to her unless there is a layoff at Sarrow Stamping Plant and a position at Woodrow Stamping became available.

3. No excuses were ever given to Ms. Carrie as reason for the delay in the pursuit of her case except that more information was needed to investigate her case and that it was not as clear-cut as she thought.

4. Before any possible deadline or statue of limitation expired, Ms. Carrie was fully informed with details, case law, union procedures, and court procedures for not pursuing certain actions. Furthermore, Ms. Carrie always con-

sulted other attorneys, including a family attorney who also contacted my office at one time by correspondence. She always made available other sources for second opinions, but always seemed to come back to my office. I gave her a listening ear and decided to give her every last chance to succeed.

5. Her claim of being forced to go to Sarrow Stamping because they did not want her at Woodrow Stamping Plant is untrue. She wanted a full-time position so bad with all the benefits Sarrow Stamping offered to her, she took it and then later complained that someone put a gun to her head.

6. Ms. Carrie complains in the first paragraph of the second page of her grievance that I didn't investigate information about her benefits and seniority when moving from Woodrow Stamping Plant to Sarrow Stamping Plant. This is a complete falsehood and my letter of correspondence between Famous Parts Company and my office speak for themselves. In fact her representations do not match up with actual documents and statistics which was a common occurrence dealing with Ms. Carrie.

7. Ms. Carrie continues about her grievance that she did all the groundwork in gathering information, but the plain fact is that she had the access to key information and continued to withhold it from me even until the end of this attorney-client relationship. Further, Famous Parts Company was not initially cooperating in turning over information that would satisfy Ms. Carrie and without solid documentation there's no way a lawsuit can be filed.

8. On page two she had a hard time grasping the concepts of establishing a *prima facie* case of racial discrimination. When it did not satisfy my expectation, she got frustrated. A race discrimination claim has never been proven on mere conjecture and speculation and if it has, then it is likely to fail during summary proceedings.

9. Although Famous Parts Company would like to help her with her back pay, they can't because of other collective bargaining units that will want equal treatment and further the NLRB, when discovered, would strike it down. To do so would be a violation of the collective bargaining agreements of different units. Ms. Carrie is also aware of this.

10. In the fourth paragraph on page two, I have always had a plan and that was to properly investigate a case before filing a complaint. If *prima facie* ele-

ments cannot be established, then I do not file a complaint. I believe that this is a disservice to a client and a waste of their time and money.

11. In the paragraph from page two to page three, Ms. Carrie's seniority was rolled back because of the grievance that included her name among others. Complete information on these grievances did not come to me at once but in a piecemeal basis. Union guidelines and rules prevent her from returning to Woodrow Stamping Plant except in a layoff/rehire situation. To do so at whim will sacrifice her *plant* seniority, not her Famous Parts Company seniority. What is unusual is that she kept her plant seniority on a lateral transfer/promotion and jumped ahead of people who started at Sarrow Stamping before she even arrived at that plant!

12. On that same page with regards to her NLRB appeal, she lost both times against the union and Famous Parts Company. Local 783 did represent her properly. Especially, when she won her grievance, but didn't get back benefits that were not part of the deal confirmed by Famous Parts Company in subsequent letters. There is no known success in suing the union when you win your grievance. I tell every client this fact.

13. I did in fact, tape conversations of Mr. Sophie and Mr. John Hail, to show inconsistencies. At that time I thought I was on to something but eventually hit a brick wall. This happened and I had to face this reality, but Ms. Carrie didn't want to.

14. I never felt she was "rushing" me at any time except that she wanted to jump the gun and file a lawsuit that had no element to establish a claim.

15. On page three it is true that I told her of the success rate of union cases and told her there aren't many attorneys that would take her case. I even tried to find one by calling someone I knew on the inside of the union who could anonymously help me locate an attorney I could refer Ms. Carrie to, but I had no success with doing so.

16. The facts surrounding Plant Chairman, Mr. John Hail, is total "junk" and quite frankly, I can't follow the basis of that allegation.

17. I want to clear up something. Ms. Carrie seems to write very affirmatively such as her calling me the "sorriest attorney she ever met" or how "dissatisfied" she was with me. The plain fact is that when she is in my office and on

the telephone, she is quite subdue, quiet, and pleasant. She usually listens without many questions and when you read her letters you would think quite differently about her. She is quite an enigma.

The plain fact is that she does not like to hear bad news and the bad news here is that she does not have a case to pursue. What's even more interesting is that she still holds on to what she considers important documents. I sincerely wish her the best."

Mr. Bushe lied and the excuses he gave can't cover the reason he decided to represent big businesses. He took this case for a mere profit after he inherited the cases of both Mazzie Cane and I. Mr. Hdith was able to retrieve my plant records from Woodrow Stamping Plant and Sarrow Stamping Plant. They were in Mr. Bushe's possession. However he was unable to retrieve the files for Mazzie Cane. Woodrow Stamping Plant wouldn't cooperate by sending Mr. Bushe the information requested. This is how Woodrow Stamping Plant and Local 783 did business. The problems were quite small and could have easily been corrected. The treatment was just down right harassment. What I went through just to get someone to listen to me was ridiculous.

My lawyer Mr. Bushe had a duty to see that my money was paid back to me from the unfair labor practices that occurred but instead he worked with them. He had all the facts and evidence needed to go forward with my case, but instead he chose to work for 'big business' and allowed Famous Parts Company to win. I felt Mr. Bushe would protect my best interest. I was very disappointed when he allowed Woodrow Stamping Plant and Local 783 to treat me as they saw fit. I was full-time when I was transferred from Woodrow Stamping Plant according to records.

There was clearly a difference of opinion when I went to the National Labor Relations Board. Mr. Bushe did absolutely nothing while handling my case. Nothing! He was aware of every aspect of my case. I made him aware of what I was going to do prior to my pursuing the truth and he commended me for doing so. He sat on all the information needed to pursue this case. Mr. Bushe gave me nothing but excuses. I know Woodrow Stamping Plant and Local 783 violated laws, but there was nothing I could do. No one would listen and if they did, they chose not to get involved.

I could not get Mr. Bushe to return my phone calls let alone meet in his office. I met with him twice regarding my case. The first was when I gave him the 90-day 'right to sue' letter. The second time was when Mazzie and I met at his office together though our cases were separate. The last time I saw Mr. Bushe was when I went to his office to pick-up my files and release him as my attorney. This man plain and simply stonewalled Mazzie Cane and me. This was just the beginning of the saga Mr. Bushe left me facing by falsely misleading me and leaving me with no representation. This cover-up lasted from September 28, 1990 until September 15, 2002 when I was put on a 'no work available'. The harassment didn't stop there. It lasted until December 2004 when I was given a medical retirement.

The last grievance of the three different decisions stated I should have received back pay. This grievance was completed in December 1995, long before I had filed my complaint with the Attorney Grievance Commission in March 1996. Mr. Bushe forgot to mention my alleged termination from Woodrow Stamping Plant by them hiring me as though I had never worked for Famous Parts Company. All my benefits were lost, but were later restored in December 1993. This was after I started working at Sarrow Stamping Plant and noticed my medical benefits were taken away.

Since Woodrow Stamping treated me with such great care, why do you think they allowed my seniority to remain at July 15, 1991 and my records proved my seniority date was September 28, 1990? Why didn't it revert back to September 28, 1990, as it should have? If my employment records stated I was full-time and I was constantly being paid full-time benefits, one would assume I was full-time. Woodrow Stamping Plant stated they were doing me a favor or giving me special treatment. That's something they didn't do because they didn't like me that well.

When I started working at Sarrow Stamping Plant I started at day one with the seniority date of November 15, 1993. This is why I fought with these people. Attorney Wanda Scorn said it was not an inter-plant lateral transfer in one of her letters addressed to Mr. Bushe. I was not an inter-plant transfer, nor was I a promotional hire. I was a new hire in Sarrow's system. I don't know how Bushe fixed his lips to tell that lie because I was terminated when I was transferred. FIRED! Mr. Bushe stated it was a transfer/promotion and that they were doing me a favor. Yeah! I received special treatment alright. Mr. Bushe stated I was promoted. It was something "totally unheard of" because that was the truth.

Woodrow Stamping Plant knew my move to Sarrow Stamping Plant was neither a transfer nor a promotion and according to contract, it was clearly illegal. They knew my transfer and/or promotion was a termination and Mr. Bushe my attorney knew it as well. I was already full-time on record contrary to what Woodrow Stamping Plant, Local 783, and Mr. Bushe said. What did I need with a grievance when everyone was aware I was already full-time? They didn't want me to know they were pilfering money from employees under several files kept by

Woodrow Stamping and Local 783. The Department of Civil Rights, the National Labor Relations Board, and the Department of Labor knew it as well. But not one agency tried to help in the matter including my lawyer Mr. Bushe.

They transferred me while firing me at the same time. The grievance stated I should have received back pay. Woodrow Stamping Plant had plans for the money they were pilfering from me and it had nothing to do with paying me back my own money. They successfully stole my money for three years and nothing was ever done about it. Woodrow Stamping Plant just said it was an error and they kept pilfering.

1996 and 1997 were very changeling years for me with all that was happening at home with my seven-year-old daughter diagnosed with ADHD (Attention Deficit Hyperactive Disorder) and Bi-Polarism. She needed plenty attention and I had much more than I could handle at the time. I really didn't want to go to Sarrow Stamping because it was farther than I wanted to travel. The school that my youngest daughter attended would call me at work. I would have to leave work to pick her up from school. Kameica was such a problem that when I went to register her for the upcoming school semester, the school told me to keep my money because they had enough of her hyperactivity in the classroom. Her condition was more than they could handle. She'd always caused some kind of disruption or another.

Kameica wouldn't listen to the sisters/nuns teaching her. She had to be watched at all times and the school decided they wanted no more to do with my child. There were times when as a parent I didn't know what to do. I had to leave work to go to her school because of all her disruptions in the class and I had to make a living for my family and myself.

Kameica was sent home one afternoon and I had to leave work to pick her up. She decided to stand on a chair and jump on the nun's back for a piggyback ride as she walked past. It may sound funny, but this nun had no idea she would be carrying any unwanted weight of a child. She was truly caught by surprise and I was too when I heard of what Kameica had done. This is just one among many things I had to deal with concerning Kameica on a daily basis. I think it's purely an act of God that I have kept my sanity over the years.

I came home from work one afternoon and put my key in the front door to find the lock falling off from the inside. Kameica had taken all the screws out of every doorknob in the house with a screwdriver. She even went under the kitchen table and took all of its screws out. When I went to sit at the table, it fell to the floor.

I had Kameica in a day treatment program and I was eventually told they didn't want her there either. I asked the hospital treating her why they were turning her away. Her hyperactivity was more than even *they* wanted to handle. I then asked the administrator how they could put my daughter out of a day treatment program specifically set up to help children with her disability. They ended up keeping Kameica in the program until I was able to find another program suiting her needs.

Along with a disruptive home, it seemed I was experiencing problems with Woodrow Stamping Plant, Local 783, and the government agencies still not coming to my defense. Mentally I was at the point of not knowing if I was coming or going. I didn't want to hear any more lies these people were trying to push down my throat.

Mr. Bushe was telling me he was trying to get to the bottom of the problem. All Mr. Bushe was doing was adding to my problems because he was aware I had been mistreated. If Wanda Scorn, Lawyer for Famous Parts Company, told Mr. Bushe the grievance never made it across her desk, this meant exactly what she said. The grievance never got out of the plant and it was never filed!

It is clearly a violation and illegal to change anyone's date of hire unless there was a valid reason. In my case, I was full-time and all who were involved were aware of that fact. How could anyone deny what was on my employment record? My record spoke for itself. That was one thing that always stayed the same no matter what anyone said. They were trying to make me look as though I had a few screws loose but I guess that was what they were supposed to do. They were the ones breaking every law conceivable.

I never knew Woodrow Stamping Plant and Local 783 were able to tell the lawyer for the plaintiff that they weren't going to comply when requested to hand over the plaintiff's employment records. Of course this was according to Mr. Bushe. Woodrow Stamping Plant was to provide and hand over any and all information regarding the interested party who had a signed release document from the client. If Woodrow Stamping Plant refused the attorney's request, the representing attorney could go to court and ask a judge to sanction the non-complying party. There were certain means that Mr. Bushe could have used but chose not to.

It is impossible for an employee to have three seniority dates. My three seniority dates were September 28, 1990, July 15, 1991, and November 15, 1993. Since Woodrow Stamping Plant fired me, that severed all ties with Famous Parts Company. I completed an application and went through the formalities of a new hire. If I was a re-hire, why was it a formality for the plant to take another application and physical? There was clearly a *prima facie* case but Mr. Bushe couldn't get Woodrow Stamping Plant to comply by giving him the information needed to pursue it. That shouldn't have been an issue because Mr. Bushe was supposed to be an expert on the case.

I returned back to Woodrow Stamping Plant because I wanted what belonged to me. They owed me money and they terminated me for no reason. I was even forbidden to step foot back on Woodrow Stamping Plant's property. For what reason would I be forbidden to return? How did I win a grievance when the outcome was that I retained the same seniority I had when I first filed the grievance? I believed in the system of democracy and justice. I felt the laws would prevail. Boy was I wrong!

34

RETURNING TO MY HOME PLANT

After the new contract was ratified in September 1996, is when I decided to apply for returning to my home plant at Woodrow Stamping. I read the contract book I received from the union and found the section stating, I could return to the home plant at the beginning of a new contract. I could do this only if my home plant was hiring and they were at this time. I would have the first option to return before any new hires were added to the roster at Woodrow Stamping Plant, since this was my home plant. This could only be done at the beginning of the new contract year.

I completed the necessary forms to return to my basic unit. The confirmation came later when I was called to the Labor Relations Office on May 20, 1997 at Sarrow Stamping Plant. Both, I and the Employee Relations Supervisor at Sarrow Stamping signed the necessary paperwork. I heard from Mazzie Cane that Woodrow Stamping Plant was going to hire the part-time people who had been part time since 1990.

As you can imagine, there were many unresolved issues regarding the grievance filed in June 1993. In 1997, I wasn't happy I received a seniority date of July 15, 1991. I was still seeking answers as to why I hadn't received my back pay. Many of the employees hired that were supposed to be on my grievance were to receive their adjusted seniority along with their back money from Woodrow Stamping Plant, but did not. Out of the nine people, Mazzie and my seniority were the only ones changed. It seemed as though the remainder of the employees were never on the grievance. I was at Sarrow Stamping Plant and I didn't receive any money at all from any grievance settlement. The grievance was yet an issue and I sent a letter to the President of the Executive Branch of the Union in January 1997 addressing my concerns. On March 26, 1997 I received a response from

Mr. Robert Rocker, Representative at the Executive Branch of the Union representing Local 783. It said:

"Dear Sister Carrie:

Your letter dated January 1, 1997 to the Executive Branch of the Union's President, James York, has been referred to me for reply. Your letter addresses concerns over procedure specifically with respect to the resolving of Grievance #H-135381 protesting your date of hire and plant seniority date. It is the responsibility of the union exclusively to represent its members relative to conditions of employment including the grievance procedure.

The grievance was settled December 8, 1993 in the second stage of the grievance procedure, changing your service date from November 15, 1993 to July 15, 1991. While establishing basic unit seniority in Woodrow Stamping Plant, you were subsequently hired at Sarrow Stamping Plant on November 15, 1993 after you applied to return to your basic unit. You are to be placed at Woodrow Stamping Plant as soon as possible in accordance with the 1997 agreement. Woodrow Stamping has employees on layoff at this time." The letter was signed, Mr. Robert Rocker.

For years I have professed Woodrow Stamping Plant and Local 783 were involved in a criminal enterprise built on lies and deceit. Woodrow Stamping Plant told so many lies that one entity never knew what the other entity was doing. As far as Mr. Rocker was concerned, he was going on information given to him. Most likely it was by telephone because there was no verification of the grievance he used as a reference. Mr. Rocker stated in his letter that the grievance was settled on December 8, 1993 while in the second stage. I don't know whether anyone knows the exact date of the grievance being settled according to records because they didn't keep accurate records. There were three different determinations when only one grievance was filed at that time.

The grievance was said to be settled but it was never officially filed. I guess Mr. Rocker really thought about my accusation and decided to send me this letter in May 1997. In his letter he tells me my seniority date is November 15, 1993. Did anyone know anything about this grievance? If the records were accurate everyone would have the same date of hire. That's what I meant when I said the grievance never made it out of the plant.

Woodrow Stamping Plant and Local 783 lied all through the grievance procedure. That is why there was no paper trail of the various stages the grievance went through. I wanted to take part in the grievance procedure and was denied by the union when according to the contract I should have been able to do so. I have documents stating the grievance went as far as the Public Review Board and that was a lie too. It never went there either. If the grievance was never filed, how could it have gone to the Public Review Board with Grievance #H135381—Review Board # 7210?

There were three dates given on which I received regarding the determination filed on June 3, 1993. The first decision was written on a piece of paper with three lines on it. Local 783 couldn't get by me with the pretense of a piece of paper with three lines as being a final grievance dated June 25, 1993. They came to me the second time around with a decision made on December 8, 1993, and again on January 5, 1995. Mr. Rocker was referring to the letter dated December 8, 1993 stating my idea of money being pilfered was preposterous and something of my imagination.

I can only wonder how the government agencies condoned what Woodrow Stamping Plant and Local 783 were doing. They were guilty as hell of money laundering, breech of contract, falsifying medical records, and God knows what else. I don't know how they were justified and received all the help needed to pull this act of deception off. The NLRB and all those involved put me through such headaches each time I would appeal their decision. I used quotes from the contract word-for-word to prove my case and they told me they weren't going to investigate.

I received a letter from the NLRB saying they weren't going to appeal the decision because the case was closed. I was within my rights and I really became frustrated at the fact they were guilty of every thing I accused them of. They put me out of the plant, terminated me unjustly, and sent me to another plant because I found out what they were doing.

The Attorney Grievance Commission didn't file charges against this lawyer when he told me the Attorney for Famous Parts Company stated the grievance was never filed. Mr. Bushe's letter to the Attorney Grievance Commission was full of lies and contradictories. He was also guilty as hell for not representing me. It didn't take a rocket scientist to know Local 783 breached the contract and discriminated against me by terminating me when I was told I'd be a rehire. Woodrow Stamping Plant violated my rights; these people just ganged up on me and threw me to the wolves. A person at the Department of Civil Rights office told me all of management agreed they didn't want me back at Woodrow Stamping Plant. Everyone just turned their heads as though nothing even happened.

For this reason, Andrea Smith and I tried to band together to become stronger as a unit. But everyone we were fighting started fighting us even harder—especially in the courts. I experienced the biggest case of fraud with the justice system. I would have never imagined the hypocrisy that existed in the justice system. I really believed in the justice system. This was until I needed justice to help me but was failed. In Mr. Rocker's second letter he wrote:

"Dear Sister Carrie:

Regarding any allegations of converting monies from part time employees for personal gain, it is unclear where you derive such notions or allegations. You may be assured that no pilfering occurs from part-time employees.

Unless you have additional information, there is no need for further communication from this office regarding your participation in Grievance #H135381, your employment status (originally recorded at Sarrow Stamping November 15, 1993), or the issue of allegation of pilfering from part-time employees."

I had to take orientation classes in order to return to Woodrow Stamping Plant. On the second day I was sitting in class at about 9:30 in the morning. The class was interrupted to inform the instructor that Labor Relations wanted to see me. I got up and walked across the hall to the Labor Relations Office. I told the clerk I was asked to come in to see the Labor Relations Representative. I was then told to have a seat and someone would be with me shortly.

I had no idea of the reason I was summoned to this office. As I was sitting in the Labor Relations Office, I saw John Hail, Plant Chairman, coming out of Verlinda's office closing the door behind him. Verlinda was the new Labor Relations Supervisor who replaced Mr. Sophie. When I was transferred to Sarrow Stamping Plant, Mr. Sopie was the Labor Relations Supervisor there. I wondered what Woodrow Stamping was up to now.

I sat there about five minutes when I was called into Verlinda's office. She seemed very nervous and asked me to have a seat and I accommodated her request. Verlinda said she was sorry but I had to return to Sarrow Stamping Plant because I didn't belong at Woodrow Stamping Plant. I told Verlinda I did have the right to come back. She then told me I was hired at Sarrow Stamping Plant and *that* was my home plant. I stated since I won my grievance, which gave me seniority as July 15, 1991, it made Woodrow Stamping Plant my home plant. Verlinda didn't want to hear what I had to say pro or con. She just told me I had to leave Woodrow Stamping and go back to Sarrow.

I told Verlinda Sarrow Stamping Plant had released me from their payroll roster. I asked her what I was supposed to do. She then told me to go back to Sarrow Stamping Plant and that was what I did. After Verlinda gave me the news, I was told to have a seat in the lobby. As I went back into the lobby, I noticed my name was on the computer screen. I guess Woodrow Stamping Plant had accessed my records and left the screen up in the Labor Relations Office. As I was reading the information on the computer, I noticed it had my original seniority date as September 28, 1990. It also stated I was terminated on November 13, 1993 which was the last day I worked at Woodrow Stamping before being hired at Sarrow.

I have to admit I was very upset being refused entry in my basic unit. They didn't want me there and they were afraid to admit that fact to anyone. Their thoughts were if I was allowed to stay I would be able to find out just what was happening and why. I would know they were using dirty tricks to keep my hire a secret. When the termination was lifted, the seniority had to continue where it was because there were no lapses of time in my employment status.

I left out of Woodrow Stamping Plant's doors and went back to Sarrow Stamping Plant. I went to the Labor Relations Office and spoke with Mr. Winski, the Labor Relations Supervisor at Sarrow Stamping Plant. I told him I was informed I could not return to Woodrow. The expression on his face was very surprising and he asked the reason why I was denied admission. He stated he had never heard of anything such as that in all his working history in the plant.

Mr. Winski asked me if I had contacted the union. He stated he would discuss the matter after my leaving his office with Mr. Louis, Plant Chairman at Sarrow. Mr. Winski told me he had taken me off Sarrow's payroll and he would have to return me to payroll until he got this situation cleared up. He also said I was an excellent worker and he was going to get to the bottom of the situation.

After completing the information to get my name back on the payroll, I clearly had a bone to pick with Woodrow Stamping Plant and Local 783. They must have become very uneasy with my return for them to do something like this because this was a desperate act. They were aware I was returning back to Woodrow Stamping because Mr. Rocker, at the Executive Branch of the Union, informed them I would be returning prior to June 27, 1997. Not to mention Woodrow Stamping Plant had already received my application to return and my response, which gave me the date of return as of June 27, 1997.

I went and talked to Mr. Louis, Plant Chairman at Sarrow Stamping Plant. I was sure Plant Chairman, John Hail, had already informed Mr. Louis I would be returning because that was the way they stuck together. I informed Mr. Louis I wanted to file a grievance against Local 783 and he said he would let Woodrow Stamping Plant handle the problem. I guess Mr. Louis didn't want to get involved in a messy situation. After seeing Mr. Louis and Mr. Winski, I went back to work at Sarrow Stamping Plant for just a short period of time.

When I retuned back on the plant floor at Sarrow Stamping, my former co-workers were very surprised to see I had returned and wanted to know what happened. I simply stated I wasn't wanted back at Woodrow Stamping Plant. My co-workers were glad to see me back. I told them I would be returning back to Woo-drow Stamping sooner or later because they had no right to send me back to Sar-row Stamping Plant when Woodrow was my home plant.

On July 1, 1997 I filed a complaint with the Department of Civil Rights. My complaint was for racial discrimination and retaliation. The complaint stated I began my employment with the respondent in September 1990. I worked as a machine operator and since November 1993, I worked at the Sarrow Stamping Plant. In about 1993, I filed a civil rights complaint against the respondent alleg-ing racially discriminatory pay.

I was made an offer to return to the Woodrow Plant, which I accepted. On or about June 27, 1997, personnel at the Woodrow Stamping Plant told me I could not return because management agreed I couldn't do so. Caucasian managers at Woodrow involved in my prior civil rights complaint were also involved in the issue regarding my return to Woodrow Stamping Plant.

I am a Black woman who filed a prior civil rights complaint and I felt I was being denied recall rights because of my race. I was called back to start working at Woodrow Stamping Plant in the second week of July 1997 after shut down. I was required to attend orientation the first week I returned. After orientation I actually started working on the Press Side of the plant. I worked on the Press Side for two weeks and while working there my seniority was reinstated to September 28, 1990. After a two-week period, I transferred to the Assembly Side of the plant.

I had worked about a month and I called the Department of Civil Rights to inform them I hadn't received any back money due to me. The representative handling my claim told me Woodrow Stamping Plant had taken me back. That was all good because she said they were trying to make amends for what they had done. I called this same woman one summer afternoon and expressed Woodrow had indeed not kept their end of the bargain.

The woman later called me after work hours. I really didn't understand why she called so late. I told her I wanted my seniority date to go back to September 28, 1990 and I wanted my back pay as well. I was concerned about my seniority not being returned to my original date of hire and Woodrow Stamping Plant turned back around and gave me a secondary date. When all this was happening where was Local 783? I told her I always found information within the plant stating my seniority's original date. She said since Woodrow Stamping Plant was putting forth an effort to make amends I should be satisfied they accepted me back. She stated she was going to receive a promotion and asked me to drop the charges against Woodrow Stamping.

The woman told me if at any time I accessed anything with Woodrow Stamping's logo and my original seniority date listed as September 28, 1990, that I would be able to reopen my claim. She said she would note this information in the computer to that effect. I agreed because I knew I was full-time and it was only a matter of time I would receive some kind of correspondence with my original seniority date on it. I told her there was no question what my seniority date was and it was truly going to surface sooner or later. She convinced me to drop the charges against the company. I agreed to her arrangement and therefore, I received a letter from the Department of Civil Rights on August 8, 1997 stating:

"This complaint alleges the respondent discriminated against the claimant in violation of civil rights laws. The claimant submitted a written request for withdrawal of the complaint because the claimant is no longer interested in pursuing the matter since the respondent has taken action."

On this letter the boxes were marked "withdrawn" and "adjusted". The circumstances under which I withdrew this claim were due to an adjustment. I did not submit a written letter as the withdrawal stated. I signed under the assumption the Department of Civil Rights would make good on their promise that I could bring my charge back to the attention of the Department of Civil Rights. If I received any paperwork with the company's logo stating my original seniority date. I always kept copies of any formal complaint. I didn't know at the time this was a common tactic Woodrow Stamping Plant and these government agencies used in order to get employees to drop charges against them. The intent was only to get the charges dropped and it didn't matter how it was done, just as long as they were dropped.

They would get employees who worked at the Department of Civil Rights and other government agencies, to get plant's employees to drop the charges in a good faith effort. I am aware I made the decision to drop the charge, but it was made under false pretenses. Woodrow Stamping had no intentions of honoring the message they were conveying through this Department of Civil Rights representative. If I could have derailed some of the conflict in an effort to cause fewer problems between Woodrow Stamping Plant and myself, I would have done so but the company just took advantage of my situation. The woman received the promotion in an effort to get me to drop the charges. I didn't know at the time I was being lied to but I was neither pleased nor surprised when I found out.

My problem was rather low-key from the time I agreed to drop the charges until November 21, 2000. This is when I finally received the information I had been waiting for since the time I returned back to Woodrow Stamping Plant. In spring of 1999, I received a reprimand for not coming in to work on overtime. This was the first reprimand I'd ever received with regards to the company. I was told this reprimand wasn't going on my record since it was just an informal written warning.

My supervisor put my seniority date on the letter of reprimand stating my seniority date as September 28, 1990. I didn't take the letter back to the Department of Civil Rights right then because I was aware there was no time limit. My understanding was all I had to do was show proof of my original seniority date with Famous Parts Company's logo. I wanted more evidence.

I was allowed to leave the plant on a medical leave. For years the Medical Department harassed me by putting me on medical leave 'no work available' when there *was* work in the plant that I could do. I would turn my medical forms in to the Medical Department sometimes weeks before they were due. The Medical Department would tell me they didn't receive the fax from the doctor's office. After I was injured on the job, they would refuse to allow me to see the doctor for an occupational injury. I would have to leave work to go through the Urgent Care Clinic for treatment and restrictions.

There was one time they wouldn't pay me Worker's Compensation because I had I lost my weekly pay stub for that week. The Worker's Compensation Clerk told me if I didn't have my original check stub, I would not be paid Worker's Compensation for that week. I received a payroll deduction sheet from the Payroll Department and was told by the Worker's Compensation Representative she couldn't accept it since it wasn't the original check stub.

They knew of my medical conditions and the Medical Department allowed me to work without restrictions, causing my ailments to worsen at a faster pace. The company sent me to a company doctor who stated nothing was wrong with me that an aspirin wouldn't heal. They had me on payroll as "employed" when I was on medical leave and being paid by Metro Craft Insurance Company. They tried to force me to complete a medical form stating I was on medical leave in October 2001 after I had already returned back to work. I was told I had to commit fraud by the Medical Department. Even Local 783 enforced the fact that I had to do as the Medical Department requested. I told them that if I did that, I would be defrauding the company and I should not be forced to break the law. No one should be forced to break the law in order to keep their jobs.

I was frightened for my job when I was told it wasn't an option. I had to complete the medical form while working 40 hours a week as though I was on medical leave. I reported this incident to the Department of Civil Rights. After that, I was no longer forced to complete the forms. I knew what they were forcing me to do was wrong, but the harassment continued in various other forms from 1999 until I retired in December 2004.

In April 2000, I was working for Supervisor, Wayward Cane (Mazzie's husband), in the CT20 area in Department #96. I had started going to physical therapy at the Rehabilitation Institute in Detroit's Medical Center in downtown Detroit. The Medical Department wouldn't honor my back injury as an 'occupational injury' because they were planning on pilfering and receiving my Worker's Compensation and retirement payments for my back injury, with the intention of putting that money in special accounts. They decided to pilfer my Worker's Compensation first when they first found out that I had a back injury. Dr. Butt, the company doctor, continued to say there was nothing wrong with me, but I was suffering and even my x-rays stated otherwise contrary to his findings. The Medical Department told me to take the x-rays home. They didn't want any evidence lying around which stated they were aware of my back injury. They did nothing but work me without restrictions, which made my medical problems deteriorate at a much faster pace.

As a result, when I received my Worker's Compensation it was said that I received Worker's Compensation *and* insurance benefits from Metro Craft Insurance Company. This was called double-dipping. I was forced to pay money back in which I never received. Dr. Sonia, my primary physician at the time, even told me I needed physical therapy for the same back injury the Medical Department and Dr. Butt said didn't exist.

I notified the Medical Department to inform them I would be going straight to physical therapy after work. The Medical Department made a copy of the prescription and stated it was okay if I left work. I took the therapist's last appointment of the day, which was 4:00 p.m. I had to leave work at 3:00 p.m. three times a week in order to get there on time Mondays, Wednesdays, and Fridays.

Wayward Cane, my supervisor, was aware I would be leaving the plant early on the days I was scheduled for physical therapy. He was in agreement with my leaving the plant until around the last two sessions. He informed me I could no longer leave early for physical therapy because other employees would start wanting to leave work early too. I told Wayward I was on my own time and off the clock when I was leaving for therapy for my occupational injury. I wanted to know why I couldn't complete the last two sessions.

I knew the Medical Department was behind Mr. Cane's decision because he was only a supervisor. He would not have taken it upon himself to stop me from going to physical therapy. I was aware the Medical Department made the call for me not to complete my therapy even on my own time. The Medical Department would do things like that just to harass me. As I have stated, the Medical Department and management at Woodrow Stamping Plant and Local 783 didn't like me at all. They made anything I did that much harder to accomplish.

35

"MISSING CHAPTER" DEPARTMENT OF CIVIL RIGHTS

Note to Reader: This is <u>the last of three chapters</u> which were deleted from my original transcript. I honestly can't say at what point they were lost, but I decided to add them in the final stages of the book anyway. (The three chapters are 27, 32, & 35.)

I never knew exactly when the grievance was settled or which grievance was accurate and final. I assumed the last grievance which was dated in 1993, was the last until I received the final grievance again in 1995. This grievance stated I was supposed to receive my back pay and my seniority adjusted to July 15, 1991. I couldn't tell you 'til this day how Local 783 and Woodrow Stamping Plant arrived at this date. I was aware that Woodrow Stamping Plant and Local 783 was so angry with me that they were determined not to give me my original date of hire, or anything else for that matter.

If the Department of Civil Rights, the National Labor Relations Board, and the Department of Labor would not have covered for Woodrow Stamping Plant and Local 783, employees like me would not have had to worry about discrimination. If these organizations would have done their jobs, Local 783 and Woodrow Stamping Plant could not have advanced their scheme into a large-scaled cover-up. The Department of Civil Rights, the National Labor Relations Board, and the Department of Labor could have investigated Local 783 and Woodrow Stamping Plant, which would have prevented their money-laundering scheme from growing to the magnitude it, has today. They first started pilfering hourly pay and then advanced to pilfering Worker's Compensation then went on to pilfering employee's retirement.

They were very angry with me for the changes I took them through to get my money and seniority restored. I was told it didn't matter how long the gathering of proof took, I would yet be able to pursue my claim against Woodrow Stamping Plant and Local 783 according to the Department of Civil Rights. If I could prove I was full-time through documentation, my case would be re-opened. I had no idea I had to experience the things I've experienced to prove something everyone knew and that was I was full time when I was first hired at Woodrow Stamping Plant. The problems I encountered to get charges filed against Woodrow Stamping Plant to get the money back that was stolen form me. My first reaction was to notify the Department of Civil Rights by a letter dated November 27, 2000.

I never received a response to the November 27, 2000 letter, which I had sent certified mail—return receipt. On February 28, 2001, I went to the Department of Civil Rights office inquiring about the reason I had not gotten a response from the letter I sent. I was told they had no record of ever receiving any information from me with regards to my original seniority date. I was supposed to bring verification of my original seniority date on paper with the logo of Famous Parts Company—Woodrow Stamping Plant. I then gave them a copy of the return receipt that one of their clerks signed. The Department of Civil Rights finally admitted they received my letter. However, the statute of limitations had run out, but this was not before I sent the letter to the Department of Civil Rights Director at the Detroit office. The letter sent November 21, 2000 read:

"To whom it may concern:

RE: Claim #R77160—156345—EM 10

I filed a claim July 1, 1977 alleging racially discriminatory pay. I was also denied the right to return to my basic unit, Woodrow Stamping Plant. The company refuses to honor my original seniority date as September 28, 1990. I contacted this office because I was terminated in 1993. I was supposed to be a rehire, but as a result they hired me as a new employee who had never worked for the company ever.

A few weeks after my transfer to Sarrow Stamping Plant, I found out I was a new hire instead of a re-hire which was what I was to be. When I was transferred I was terminated by Woodrow Stamping Plant in the process when I was supposed to be a re-hire at Monroe Stamping Plant. I received no warning or notification of being terminated. This is the reason I contacted this office in July of 1997. I have insisted on my full-time status when Woodrow Stamping Plant and Local 783 fought against my seniority date from the beginning. This has made me angry for many years. I am sending copies of my employment record to prove I was correct, because my retirement may be hanging in the balance. I need ten years of seniority in order to obtain my medical retirement. If I didn't have an exact seniority date, can you tell me how I could be terminated in the first place?

Part-time employees don't have a service date because they don't accrue seniority. The mere fact is there had to be a service date early than 1991, because my date of hire was said to be July 15, 1991, long before this grievance was filed. This is the reason I'm asking you to evaluate this mater. In 1995 I received the seniority date of July 15, 1991 as a result of the grievance process. I've always wondered how I could have won the grievance when nothing changed and everything stayed the same. I received the same seniority date through the grievance process that I had prior to filing my grievance. I received no money through the grievance procedure. So what did I win? This is a clear indication that the grievance was never filed in 1993. So if what I say is true, why hasn't anyone with the Department of Labor, the Department of Civil Rights, the National Labor Relations Board, or the Equal Employment Opportunity Commission helped me? When I came through the doors of these organizations, no one found anything wrong because they didn't investigate. If you don't look for anything, then you won't find anything. How can Local 783 reward me with something I already had in 1993? They didn't give me the seniority date I had on record which Woodrow Stamping Plant terminated me under in 1993, the date on record was September 28, 1990.

I withdrew my July 2, 1997 complaint on August 8, 1997 (Claim #EEOC-156345, EM10-23A977160) because Woodrow Stamping Plant decided not to reinstate me at my home plant after first being denied entry. I was supposed to receive my back pay and my seniority date reinstated as September 28, 1990. I even went through the grievance procedure, but never signed the grievance after it was completed under these circumstances. I had to sign in order to file this grievance, so I should have had to sign when the grievance was complete. I was to have received a letter certified mail after the decision was made, according to contract. I was told this grievance went to the Umpire stage and to the Public Review Board, where I was not allowed to take part in the hearings. If the grievance went through all these changes, according to contract I was to have signed off on it.

I had been terminated when I wasn't even full-time according to Woodrow Stamping Plant and Local 783. Why was I in the computer as terminated in 1993? Woodrow Stamping Plant, Local 783, the Labor Department, and the National Labor Relations Board overlooked everything. They all stated Woodrow Stamping was in their rights to withdraw money directed to me, in the name of an error. Because of the error in my seniority, I was full-time. But that was never corrected to part-time. They just terminated me and sent me on my way.

About a month or so after I'd protested not receiving any back pay and my seniority date changed from September 28, 1990 to July 15, 1991 once again. I returned back to Woodrow Stamping Plant in July 1997. I changed departments from the Press Side to the Assembly side of the plant. I contacted the Department of Civil Rights representative by phone who was handling my case. She reiterated the fact I was accepted back at the plant in a good will effort on the company's part. She stated, after all Woodrow Stamping Plant had employed me back and that was the most important thing they did. I expressed my apprehension and told her, how errors had always emerged with my original seniority date on it. She then said if this ever happened again, she would put a note in the computer and this would be reason enough to reopen the complaint. She also said she was getting a promotion and if I ever received any information with my original seniority date, with Famous Parts Company logo, just ask for her and she would reopen my case.

I don't remember her name, but she worked in the Civil Rights area during July of 1997. I really think they could have found the information I was claiming through names, dates, complaint numbers, and who the complaint was filed against. They could have also found what representative handled this complaint. They could have looked in the computer and found the circumstances in which the complaint was dismissed upon. They could have done many things to view the information in the computer. Since this was 1997, they could have looked up how many times I had filed complaints with them regarding Woodrow Stamping Plant and Local 783, but they did not.

When this letter was written, the complaint number was given and they yet could comprehend what I was talking about. This deal was a lie from start to finish, by allowing me to drop my case under false pretenses. This was fraud by deception. The Detroit Branch of the Department of Civil Rights always said when I dropped the charge by writing a letter. That is not a true statement, and those who made this state-

ment, outright lied. Many of these employees needed to be investigated—including the one's taking the complaints. I never wrote a letter, contrary to what their letter stated.

I received a disciplinary action slip in May 21, 1999. I tried to contact a lawyer and was told the statute of limitations had run out. I was told there was nothing that could be done with the charges I brought upon Woodrow Stamping Plant concerning the promises I made when I withdrew my complaint. I decided to leave well enough alone on this matter until I was injured on the job in July 1999. The company put me on a 'no work available' and I wasn't able to work at that time. I was told my injuries didn't happen on the job, even though my doctor doesn't quite agree. On September 13, 1999, I was to return to work. The doctor in the Medical Department said I could return to work. I asked him if I needed to go to Labor Relations and his reply was no. At this point I had not been off work 90 days, therefore I didn't need a clearance from Labor Relations. I went to work and worked all that day. At the end of the day I was called back to the Medical Department and was informed I could no longer work. I have tried on many occasions to obtain other positions through job bids and placements. I didn't receive any job placements, but my Caucasian co-worker, with less seniority than I, did. I've written the company with regards to working around my restriction and I haven't heard anything as of this day November 2000. My doctor has since lifted my restriction, although I must work with a wrist brace. I'm yet on a 'no work available'.

The main purpose of my writing this letter now is because I received a letter from Metro Craft Insurance Company informing me I have to apply for a medical disability with the Social Security Administration after I have been off for more than six months ..."

When I received my Social Security Disability only, I should have been paid Worker's Compensation according to Woodrow Stamping Plant's records, but they were keeping this money for themselves. Woodrow Stamping Plant didn't want the employees to know that the occupational injury will pay money for their injuries until the restrictions are lifted, but the money was being pilfered and placed in separate accounts set up by the Controller (the accountant). Woodrow Stamping Plant's plan was to put me out on a 'no work available' permanently before I reached my ten years of seniority with the company. If that happened, Woodrow Stamping Plant and Local 783 would have pilfered my retirement as they did Andrea Smith's and Linda Jackson's. If I had failed to reach ten years of service with the company, they would retire me after four years of seniority and keep the retirement and the Worker's Compensation money too. The company attempted this with many employees. They wanted to leave the employee with the Social Security Disability benefits while the rest of the money went back to the company. All this would be done in the name of the employee who had an occupational injury, and the company stated it was personal. This greed was a form of modern day slavery—clearly inexcusable.

Since my injuries were occupational, I should not have been on a 'no work available' in the first place. Linda Jackson, Andrea Smith, and employees like them received Worker's Compensation and Retirement Benefits. I would have been unable to receive my retirement and Woodrow Stamping would have pilfered the remaining money. When everything was all said and done, I would have to pay money back for *double-dipping* (receiving payment twice) from Metro Craft Insurance Company, which I never received.

The company received the Worker's Compensation and retirement, which would leave the employee living on Social Security Disability for the remainder of their life or until they became 62 years old. When the employee tries to receive payment through retirement, they are denied because Woodrow Stamping Plant and Local 783 were already pilfering their money. It didn't matter the way this medical scheme was set up, it was for the mere profit of the company. The employees were in a no-win situation.

Worker's Compensation should have paid all medical costs in my case, but they didn't. After my Worker's Compensation settlement was over, I still had to pay all the 'sick and accident' money back to Metro Craft Insurance Company from being on my 'no work available', when it should've been paid by Worker's Compensation. All outstanding medical costs for treatment incurred during occupational injuries were their responsibility.

Woodrow Stamping Plant and Local 783 have been treating employees in this manner for so long that it's time for this pilfering to stop. It's wrong and unfair. God doesn't like his children treated in this manner and he's made a way to stop this pilfering by these modern-day Robin Hoods characters. The rich is pilfering from the poorest of the poor, and it's fixed so that no one can ever challenge this scheme's setup. The courts were bought and paid for, so Linda Jackson and Andrea Smith could never receive justice in the Worker's Compensation Court or the United States District Court.

If I had my ten years of company service, I could apply for my Social Security Disability and for disability retirement with the company for an occupational injury. I could retire after four years but Woodrow Stamping Plant wants all this money. There was no chance that they were going to give me something that they had been pilfering from me and other employee's who suffer from occupational injuries. The company pilfered so much from me during my years of employment. They were pilfering my money from the time I was hired until the time I retired and they continue to pilfer from me now. They even pilfered from me after my retirement too. All these years, I was yelling from the roof top for someone to hear what I had to say. All I wanted was for someone to help me. It was admitted by the company in 1992 that I was full-time. So what was the problem? I was in a total no-win situation when it came to Woodrow Stamping Plant and Local 783.

Dr. Butt and other doctors from Famous Parts Company falsely denied employees Worker's Compensation and retirement monthly benefits in order to pilfer money from the employees and put that money in special accounts. Really Famous Parts Company-Woodrow Stamping Plant and Local 783 should have commended me for what I found out, but instead I became the enemy. They tried hard not to let me know Nurse Tootie was fired for embezzlement and falsifying medical and government documents. So was John Hail, Plant Chairman of Local 783, and Bob Fleetwood, Bargaining Committeeman. They both were charged with racketeering. I guess silence was golden—at least when it came to their pilfering. This is information that 'big business' doesn't want anyone to know. But when found out, corporate punishment is light. A person will go to jail for a couple years and be right back out to business as usual after serving their time.

Metro Craft Insurance Company was aware of what Woodrow Stamping Plant was doing since they insured themselves. It's hard for Metro Craft not to have known what Woodrow Stamping Plant was doing. 30 days after my retirement in December 2004, I received a letter from Metro Craft Insurance Company stating I owed them no money. My medical bills were paid in full. This is how it should have been because I had an occupational injury. Worker's Compensation should have paid all my medical expenses incurred while employed at Woodrow Stamping Plant.

After the court proceedings were over and done with, Famous Parts Company-Woodrow Stamping Plant began to work fast. On the second set of files, my injuries were personal. This was the file upon which I was paying Metro Craft back since records indicated I was paid twice. I was paid once by Worker's Compensation and also from Metro Craft Insurance Company, when I had only received 'sick & accident' benefits. I never received any weekly Worker's Compensation benefits because Famous Parts Company—Woodrow Stamping Plant pilfered that money and put in separate files located at the Brownstown Plant.

I am now paying Metro Craft Insurance Company back the money I received during my occupation injury, which was pilfered from me. I am not supposed to pay my medical expenses if my medical leave was occupational—yet as of today I am. The Worker's Compensation case is closed because I retired with a medical disability for an occupational injury. Who's going to step up and question what Woodrow Stamping Plant and Local 783 is doing?

I never received any of the money Woodrow Stamping pilfered. Woodrow Stamping Plant and Local 783 had been getting away with what they were doing for many years. They had special employees at Metro Craft Insurance Company handling those claims that weren't of the norm. About 4 months after I retired, I received a letter stating Metro Craft Insurance was paid in full. Then I received a letter stating I owed Metro Craft Insurance $32,301.85 (thirty-two thousand three-hundred & one dollar & eighty five cents) for over payment. Just when I thought all these lies were behind me, here came another set of circumstances I had to face. I thought to myself, why is it I owe Metro Craft this amount of money when my Worker's Compensation should have paid all my medical expenses. Now Metro Craft Insurance Company is saying I owed them. I was furious and called Mr. Mark Hess, my final attorney who represented my claim against Famous Parts Company—Woodrow Stamping Plant. I asked him why I was paying money back. I was told I had *double-dipped* or had been paid twice. This was a lie.

I then wrote Woodrow Stamping Plant and it took them four days to respond. They stated the information in my case didn't say I should not have to pay the money back. At this point, I decided to leave well enough alone for a while. I knew I would again challenge why the court was not forcing Woodrow Stamping Plant to pay me what is owed to me.

The letter I'd received from Metro Craft Insurance Company meant I received nothing for occupational injuries and the other illnesses I suffer from. With everything said and done, I only received $19,000 from the settlement with Famous Parts Company—Woodrow Stamping Plant. They pilfered the remainder of the money. I received $56,000 when I settled, and I've been paying Metro Craft $534.99 each month. I never *double—dipped* and I only received Metro Craft 'sick and accident' benefits. I didn't receive Worker's Compensation, so where was the *double-dipping*?

I'm paying Metro Craft Insurance Company $534.99 a month.

This is $6,419.88 a year.

I have been retired for 3 years (36 months).

I have paid $19,259.64 to Metro Craft Insurance Company since my retirement.

If I live until age 62 (eight years), I will have paid for 96 months totaling $51,359.04.

This means I received nothing for my occupational injuries. It seems I'm paying them for my injuries sustained while working for this company. In the long run, I'm paying all the money back that I received from them. They are making a profit because the total amount I received was $58,359.04 plus the settlement I received, which was $3,000 in the 2003 out of court settlement. I would have received $7,000 overall from Worker's Compensation for my occupational injuries. That is an unfair labor practice for me and business for them.

Local 783 allowed Famous Parts Company—Woodrow Stamping Plant to treat employees in this inhumane manner, only raising their profit margin. It seems I'm paying the amount "owed" including court costs, and the company is making a profit in the long run. I'm scheduled to pay back $51,359.04 and I would like to know if that is fair or not. This isn't the way Worker's Compensation was setup to work. Famous Parts Company and the Union made up this scheme to take back all they were given back in the court settlements. This was a well thought out plan by Woodrow Stamping Plant and Local 783 to pilfer from the poor employees subjected to occupational injuries.

My Social Security didn't come until months after I retired. So where was the *double-dipping*? I brought these facts to the attention of the State of Michigan Worker's Compensation Bureau, Metro Craft Insurance Company, CEO of Famous Parts Company, Robert Wart, and the lawyer who settled my Worker's Compensation Claim, Mark Hess. From that point, I didn't receive a monthly receipt stating what I was paid each month. I only received them about twice a year—one around the first of the year and one at the end of the year (tax time). The tax papers I receive are so vague that they weren't even accepted by my accountant, because this money hasn't been reported to the Internal Revenue Service as an overpayment. Every year since I've been retired, this money had gone unreported to the appropriate parties.

First, Metro Craft Insurance Company sent a letter, which was written in ink, stating how much I paid on taxes. It wasn't a formal tax form. After I contacted Metro Craft, in February 2007 they turned around and sent my W-2 form without the amount that was paid in taxes. This form was just a waste of time and cost of the postage to send it. I can't claim a tax if they only send me forms with blank boxes. This meant I paid taxes on the overpayment. So in that case, why can't I file the overpayment money at the end of the year on my taxes as overpayment from the IRS? Are they paying taxes on this money somehow? This is a scam that Famous Parts Company—Woodrow Stamping Plant and Local 783 thought up to make sure employees don't receive a dime of what's owed to them.

Why don't I receive a statement including the tax amount on the overpayment since its taxable income? I am yet paying money back each month that I did not receive, and I will be paying this money back until I am 62 years old. According to documents, Worker's Compensation should have paid me weekly benefits just as long as I was disabled, but they didn't do that either. The money I should've been receiving from Metro Craft Insurance is being kept by them. They said I was paid twice, but no one can answer me as who paid me twice. No one is listening to my complaints because I don't have enough money or enough clout with people in high places.

I have been retired since December 9, 2004 and I have paid $534.99 back to Metro Craft Insurance for money that I did not receive. I now owe $17,788.69. On each statement I receive, the amount of overpayment decreases. The actual amount I owed Metro Craft Insurance Company was from the time I retired with a medical disability. Retirement was $32,301.85. If I had not acknowledged what they were doing, they would have continued taking advantage of me.

I told Robert Wart, President and CEO of Famous Parts Company, about this money-laundering scheme. For Woodrow Stamping Plant to be disbanded, they would have to close the plant's doors since they have been pilfering from employees for so many years. It would be nice if the money went back to the people it was intended for. I have a feeling it won't because that's too much like right.

With me being the skeptic I've become, it wouldn't surprise me if the reason the union's handling of the VIBA retirement program has a lot to do with the union keeping illegal files of employees. Isn't it ironic that after helping Woodrow Stamping Plant pilfer employees' money through their retirement, they're now handling the retirement program? When employees are found to have a disease that prevents them from working and when their settlement is agreed upon, they should not have to pay any money back to the company. I don't care how you put it, money is being pilfered without employees' knowledge and Famous Parts Company—Woodrow Stamping Plant and Local 783 should be made to re-pay that money back.

Worker's Compensation should have paid Metro Craft all monies in full, but they didn't do this for me after I retired in 2004. Anyone can check my statements going back for years and they will see I received no money constituting *double-dipping.* So really, they owed *me* money. Now I understand why no one took my case and why the President of the United States didn't respond when I asked his office to investigate Woodrow Stamping Plant and Local 783. Not even the Executive Branches of the Company and Union helped me. The Department of Labor, the Department of Civil Rights, the National Labor Board, the Attorney General, and the Governor all took part in the scheme by keeping their silence. Looking back at the treatment of Linda Jackson, Andrea Smith, and other employees, it clearly looks as though this has been a conspiracy for many years. I truly hope that it's stopped in its tracks because it's wrong. Woodrow Stamping Plant and Local 783 aren't part of the solution. They are the problem.

The following letter was sent to the Department of Civil Rights in February 1991 regarding Woodrow Stamping Plant. The letter read:

"To whom it may concern:

RE: Charge #156315 EM10—EEOC 23A97716

I filed a case against Famous Parts Company at Woodrow Stamping Plant in 1997 for retaliation in the company by not allowing me to use my recall rights under the Union Bargaining Agreement. I agree to dismiss the case because the company allowed me to return and receive my original seniority date. As I understood, I was to receive the money owed to me before I agreed to specifics. I called and asked the Department of Civil Rights Representative handling my claim when I would receive my seniority, and I was informed it would roll back to September 28, 1990 ..."

I originally only asked for the money due to me through that so-called grievance. They went through the motions and everyone sided with leaving me with no protection at all. This allowed Woodrow Stamping Plant and Local 783 to do as they wished in harassing me, discriminating against me, and pilfering my money. The only thing they didn't do was to kill me. But they almost succeeded, leaving me with Degenerative Joint Disease, a disease I will have the rest of my life. I have to take medication for the rest of my life. This medication causes side-effects and as a result, can cause damage to my liver, kidney, and heart in the long run. What I'm suffering from is causing a slow death of pain and agony.

When I think about Andrea Smith, I guess I can say that I came out good considering I didn't get fired (even though they tried). I too, was frightened. There were times before I retired that I thought they would succeed in terminating me too. When I was terminated, I was allowed to go back. I think it was an act of God that I was not fired like Andrea. I can't say I got hit with a broom or a hi-lo truck. So maybe I did come out just a little better than Andrea Smith.

I later went into the Labor Relation Office to inquire about a job bid and saw Bargaining Committeeman, Bob Fleetwood. He asked me if I knew what my seniority data was. I told him I didn't know exactly. I'm not sure if telling him I didn't know my seniority date would have made a difference or not, but I know what it should have been. I was terminated November 13, 1993 and my seniority date was September 28, 1990. When I returned back to Woodrow Stamping Plant after returning, my seniority should have remained the same when the termination was lifted. My seniority remained September 28, 1990.

When I first hired back at Woodrow Stamping Plant from Sarrow Stamping Plant, I worked on the Press Side of the plant. My seniority date was restored as it should have been. When I changed from the Press Side of the plant to the Assembly Side of the plant, it should not have made a difference with regards to my seniority date. However when I changed departments, my seniority was changed from September 28, 1990 back to July 15, 1991. I didn't say anything because I thought it was an error on the company's part that they would correct later—but that didn't happen. If you really think about it, if I was officially terminated on November 13, 1993 and hired back July 1997, I wouldn't be hired back with a July 15, 1991 seniority date. The seniority date would return back to the date of seniority when I was terminated.

These people thought I was the stupid one. But as it turned out, who's really the stupid one? I have known for many years what Woodrow Stamping Plant and Local 783 were doing, but could do nothing in my own defense—just as Mazzie Cane, Andrea Smith, and Linda Jackson. The union and company tried for many years to keep me quiet and they were successful for a while. But I was determined since I didn't receive my day in court. I'm going to tell my story just the same in my own words, in my own time, and in my own way. I can tell my story the way it actually happened.

The February 1991 letter to the Department of Civil Rights continued:
"… Before I was transferred from the Press Side of the plant to the Assembly Side, my seniority date was September 28, 1990, which is what my seniority should have been. But when I went to the Assembly Side of the plant, my seniority date changed back to July 15, 1991. I have received no money of which I

asked for while I was supposed to have been compensated through the phony grievance procedure. I thought the matter was settled but I see that it's not. Since, I don't have my seniority date as it should be, they didn't keep their promise as far as I'm concerned.

I made no mention to anyone because I didn't negotiate with Labor Relations to settle this problem. The representative spoke on my behalf and I agreed because I was under the assumption I would receive my original seniority date, which is in the computer. I'm not concerned about the bogus date they gave me by someone else. I only asked about the money which was given to me and taken back that didn't go back to the company. They were allowing me to return to my basic unit, and I was given my recall rights and my seniority date back as of 1991. As far as I am concerned, it was a breach of contract on their part.

I don't remember what my representative's name was that made the deal with me, but that information is easily accessible in the computer. It wouldn't be hard to find the representative which advised me to drop the charges under false pretenses. It took time to get the information to prove what my seniority date was as stated on record. After proving this, I didn't expect to hear the words "the statute of limitations has run out". The letter ended at this point.

The last and final letter I wrote the Director of the Department of Civil Rights was in April 2001. I wrote this after I was told my November 2000 letter was lost. I was very upset. The information sent was straight to the Director of the Department of Civil Rights in order to acquire answers. This was yet another let down after I thought this government agency would help me. The following April 2000 letter touches on subjects included in the "lost" November 2000 letter:

"I am sending this letter with a copy of the information I sent in November 2000. The letter was indeed received because the returned receipt from the United States Post Office was dated November 27, 2000.

I came in the office on February 28, 2001 inquiring about and looking for information regarding this case, only to find out all the information was lost and could not be found. I spoke to a representative and we discussed my situation. I was informed to contact you, the Director of the Department of Civil Rights, because they had the authority to investigate what's happening to me and why. I am sending another set of all the information to your office, which I sent in my November 2000 package.

I truly hope this information doesn't get lost as did the previous package. One of my concerns is I have my 10 years of employment for my retirement from Famous Parts Company—Woodrow Stamping Plant. The company that employ's me put me on a 'no work available' medical leave because of medical reasons brought on by occupational injuries. Since my seniority date has not been changed, I have to go to work each day with severe pain in my legs, hands, arms, back, and in all my joints. I endured this pain just to make the July 15, 2002 deadline to be eligible for retirement with my 10 years of service …"

The Medical Department was trying to make sure I was near retirement, but they wanted my retirement themselves. That is the reason they started putting me on a 'no work available' in 2000 when I didn't quite have my 10 years, but was close. When they put me on a 'no work available' I was able to continue working, but the Medical Department stated they had no work for me to do. This was untrue and that is why I fought to stay working. There were jobs I could have worked in the plant, but they refused to put me on them. I didn't have my 10 years of service and they had me apply for Social Security benefits because that was all I was going to get. While I was in the process of retiring from Woodrow Stamping Plant in 2000, I complained to the Department of Civil Rights about my concerns regarding my return. I was allowed to return. Woodrow Stamping Plant had 15 days to return me to work. I really didn't work out like they wanted me to, so my Social Security was canceled. If I'm able to work then I didn't need Social Security, right?

Their plan was to start this process before I had enough time to retire. That way they would not only have my Worker's Compensation, but my retirement too. Woodrow Stamping Plant would allow some employees to stay off work for 9 years, as they did in Linda Jackson's case. She had to complete a medical form #5166. If I allowed this to happen to me, then I would not have enough time to receive my retirement package. Since I was receiving 'sick and accident' benefits, it made it seem as though my injuries were personal and not occupational. My medical leave was a personal injury on one set of their records—not occupational. When I was applying for Social Security benefits, I found out I was 'working' at the same time I was 'on medical leave'. I complained to the Medical Department and asked them to correct my record to state I was on a medical leave. I informed Metro Craft Insurance Company that Woodrow Stamping Plant had me working while I was supposed to be on medical.

I wrote the Social Security Administration and anyone else I thought could help, but no one would listen to what I had to say. I was able to continue working. The more I found out in the Medical Department, the more they didn't want me around anymore. There was a saying before I left Woodrow Stamping that anyone who worked in the front office had to sign a statement saying they wouldn't discuss anything that went on. I had to ask around my workplace about subjects pertaining to me, finding much information from co-workers. I began putting a picture together from my experiences and those of others.

The letter to the Director of the Department of Civil Rights continued:

"... I also sent the Department of Civil Rights a letter concerning the unjust treatment I received at the time as well, but nothing was ever done about my complaint. I sent this to anyone on my list including my State Senator, Attorney General, FBI, and Governor. That's as high as I could go to get someone to investigate what was happening to me. I sent letters to anyone that would read them in order to tell my story of what they had done to me, but it was all to no avail.

I have been employed at Famous Parts Company for 12 years, and I have endured harassment and unjust treatment each and every one of these years. I began my career at Famous Parts Company—Woodrow Stamping Plant on September 28, 1990 as a full-time employee. The company has on record three different seniority dates September 28, 1990; July 15, 1991; and November 15, 1993. I have been stripped of vacation pay and other monetary benefits from 1990 until 1993. My performance bonus and excused absence days were often granted to me and then taken back because of all the confusion with my seniority date and a wrong assessment that I was a part-time employee. I was singled out in November 1993, and was sent from Woodrow Stamping to Sarrow Stamping. I was given no option and I was the only minority who was sent while others were denied.

This was because I started asking questions regarding my employment status and money that was unaccounted for and had to be paid back to the company through adjustments. I was never credited when the money was paid back to Woodrow Stamping Plant. Since I was asking the questions they couldn't seem to answer, I was viewed as a "troublemaker". After I reached Sarrow Stamping, I lost all my benefit coverage. When I was hired at Sarrow Stamping on November

15, 1993, I had no idea I was hired as though I had never worked for Woodrow Stamping Plant, or any other Famous Parts Company institutions prior. In 1997 when I returned back to Woodrow Stamping Plant, my basic unit, I was told I could never return to Woodrow Stamping Plant. This message was relayed to me by the Department of Civil Rights—the one's that were supposed to be representing me. Why would Labor Relations at Woodrow Stamping Plant tell the Department of Civil Rights to relay this message? It clearly shows how bold and blatant this company is and that they have no worries of being caught while using discriminatory practices ...”

The Department of Civil Rights and the Equal Employment Opportunity Commission could have taken into consideration that no lawyer would accept this unjust charge to court or trial. Instead they gave me a 'right to sue letter'. They weren't that busy that they couldn't try a claim in court. Andrea and I have filed many complaints against the same company for the same reasons and the same agencies could never file anything against the company or union for cause of an investigation. Andrea and I alone, filed nearly 15 complaints between the both of us. Common sense would tell these people if I continued filing the same complaint with the same company, there had to be a problem. Andrea filed eight times for retaliation, harassment, discrimination, and unfair labor practices. It's been seven times for me. This should've said there was a serious problem that needed to be addressed. Woodrow Stamping Plant and Local 783 were guilty as hell of every charge we brought against them.

I don't think the Department of Civil Rights', Equal Employment Opportunity Commission's, or the National Labor Relations Board's dockets aren't full nowadays, because discrimination cases for unjust treatment in the workplace is somewhat almost unheard of these days. Lawyers don't take these cases anymore because there is no money involved. Discrimination is a silent killer and this is the reason Michigan has voted to abolish the Affirmative Action laws in this state. It's not that discrimination doesn't exist. It's just that they are not going to allow minorities to get rich because of discrimination. They have found a loop-hole in the laws. If no lawyer will take your case, then you have one option left—to take a crash course in law to represent yourself. In my experience, I was given a bench trail when I asked for a trail by jury. The judge refused to appoint Andrea and myself a lawyer as we requested.

Racial Discrimination cases aren't being tried—at least in the state of Michigan. The Department of Civil Rights and the Equal Employment Opportunity Commission can try their own cases, but I never knew of a case they tried. Why would the Department of Civil Rights or the Equal Employment Opportunity Commission issue a 90-day 'right to sue letter' when they were aware that even if the case was filed in court, the case would never make it to trial?

What good is a 90-day 'right to sue' letter given by the Department of Civil Rights or the Equal Employment Opportunity Commission when no attorney would honor the letter? If you are able to obtain an attorney, the attorney soon starts working for the opposing party. They do this because the opponent can offer more money or other fringe benefits that the person whom they're supposed to be representing can't offer. The 'right to sue' letter is a worthless piece of paper and a waist of everyone's time producing this worthless piece of paper. The Department of Civil Rights and the Equal Employment Opportunity Commission knows this when they issue the letter to the complainant.

The letter continued:

"… These organizations are supposed to represent civil issues. The Department of Civil Rights is funded by the state of Michigan, and the Equal Employment Opportunity Commission (E.E.O.C.) is funded by the federal government. The only reason Woodrow Stamping Plant didn't want me back was because I found out they were pilfering employees' money and benefits and wanted mine back. This is when I saw on the computer in June 1997 that I was terminated on November 13, 1993. This happened amidst a transfer when I was supposed to be a rehire while transferring from Woodrow Stamping Plant to Sarrow Stamping Plant."

I really don't understand why I had to experience what I did at the hands of Woodrow Stamping Plant and Local 783. My experiences has taught me a lesson and opened my eyes to the realization of what the real world is like. It also showed me how people who have money are treated in the business world. I had my own vision as to what is written in our constitution and how it's applied in our every day life and in our justice system. Through my experience I have learned that justice is how much you can pay for it. If you have the right amount of money the remainder of the laws is just something written on paper which doesn't have any significance.

Discrimination is discrimination no matter how it's presented and it is yet a violation of the law. I found that if no one is held accountable for violations of the civil laws, regarding discrimination. Then discrimination doesn't exist to them. I think it's deplorable for a company to take from employees, who help's the company's profit margin, grow into millions and billions of dollars each year, while at the same time we are doing the actual hard labor. Much of the time the jobs are done with much enthusiasm of what is required by employees to put out the best product possible until management comes down on the floor and bend all the rules. By not caring what kind of product the employee puts out in order to meet product demands.

We as employees try to put out what the company says to put out, but it's not always an option. The vast majority of employees really care about their jobs. They want to put the product together to see a good finished product, because we were paid well to do so.

The scenario changes when an employee is injured on the job, as they were working hard doing their jobs for the company. The moral changes and I'm sure it's because they can always get someone else in your place when the employee is injured on the job. There are previsions made for employees who is working on the job, they should be looked upon as a valuable asset for the company. The employee should not have a problem being paid by their employer, nor should the employer make a profit through their employee's accident or injuries. The employer Worker's Compensation fund takes care of those employees when they are injured, or had reinjured a pre-existing medical condition. That employee should be paid according to the Worker's Compensation fund at the company's expense. Employers are finding ways to get away with paying those who had been injured on the job and the company stated profiting from their injuries. Then the company wants to sever their ties with the employees and keep the money that the employee should have received while injured on the job is wrong.

I followed the laws, rules, and various regulations and in the process, I received unjust treatment in terms of discrimination, retaliation, harassment, while at the same time the company is violating every law possible to keep from paying the employees. They were pilfering what was negotiated in the contract and Local 783 helped the company pilfer from it own members, which is really a sad scenario. When we are given benefits and the company turns around and pilfer the money back without your knowledge. When there is nothing we can say or do, to relieve the harsh treatment that one has received at the hands of their employer. I found that my money was being pilfered and they wouldn't give the money back. I was treated with desperate treatment because I found out what the company had done and what they were doing. I informed the company's CEO thinking that it would make a difference. I was dumbfounded later when I found that nothing was done and the employees involved were move from one plant location, to another and it was business as usual. I reported this pilfering because it was the right thing to do and everyone treated me in an unjust manner because I knew.

It is truly sad to say that discrimination is the silent killer that is/or has destroyed all those, who take part in the harsh treatment for the asking. Simply because they feel people of color should apply to a different beat because their skin is different. As I was experiencing all that was brought upon me and everyone that took part in the unjust treatment for no other reason, for the exception that I found out that my money and benefit package was being pilfered from me.

There was no where I could go for help so that tells me what the justice system stands for. What good are the Department of Civil Rights, Equal Employee Opportunity Commission, National Labor Relation Board, and the Department of Labor, if they won't help a sister when there is a need? What good is the organization and or agencies that are set-up to help employees, when their employer bring unfair labor practices against the employee. Especially, when there are violations of contract and labor laws that have been violated, whether black or white, rich or poor. We all are supposed to have due process of the law and we all wanted to be treated with dignity and respect. Most of all we would like to be able to be heard, and according to the United States constitution, which states if you can't get, or don't have an attorney the judge will appoint you one, upon your request and that didn't happen either. It's not fair when I have a grievance and can't get a lawyer and I can't get the judge to appoint me one. That is truly and injustice to me and others like me. We should not be barred from the justice system because we are Black Balled or Red Flagg, where our claims can't be heard and all I'm saying, is this should not happened here in the United States.

I found out that the justice system does treat minorities in the State of Michigan differently. It is a conspiracy in the State of Michigan that if you're black or a minority it's much harder to have your case heard, whether or not the minority has a claim. If they do have a claim, trying to sue is a thing of the past. This is the reason that the Affirmative Actions Program was voted against in the state of Michigan. They are trying to keep the minorities from suing and next, it will be the poor white that will be forbidden from filing a claim in a court of law. The justice system is suppose to respect all those who have a valid claim, when and employee feel their rights were violated they should be able to take their violators claims to court.

The violators if found guilty should have to pay but they want to discriminate but the company's don't want to pay. The only reason they don't want to pay is because they knowingly discriminate against minorities. The company knows they are guilty, so if no one will take there cases, they have nothing to worry about and the treatment continues and the company knows it's wrong. I feel if they are guilty of breaking the law they should pay. It doesn't take much to treat people the way you want to be treated. Just as long as there are those company's that can pay for justice and keep their dirty laundry covered-up, to make sure that the dirt doesn't make it to the press, then these people are smooth sailing, in whatever they do, whether its wrong or not.

It's always said silence is golden but not to the ones who are treated in an unjust manner. It just gives the ones who want to keep hidden the use of discriminatory practices against employees. Famous Parts Company—Woodrow Stamping Plant and the Executive Branch of the Union know its wrong but they did it just the same. The company will only allow the treatment to continue using the unjust treatment, while it's kept in silence. There is nothing anyone can and will do about what they want to be kept in silence. What they are doing is so graphic they want no one to hear about what Woodrow Stamping Plant and Local 783 was doing and that is the truth. Take a look at what they have done to Andrea Smith she was hit with a broom by a co-worker who cursed at her prior to throwing the broom, which landed in her chest. After the broom landed in her chest Andrea Smith reported both incidents to labor relation while they stood by and did nothing. They turned around and forced her to work side by side this same man, knowing she was terrified of him since they didn't so much as reprimand this employee.

Andrea was also hit with a hi-lo within the plant, Woodrow Stamping Plant and Local 783 cover-up these incidents as though it never happened. Then they turned around and lied on her so that she could be fired. Everyone from the bottom to the top of the Executive Branch of the Company and Union was aware of every aspect of what happened to Andrea Smith. This is one reason the Executive Branch of the Company's CEO stepped down in the summer of 2006. The Executive Branch of Union CEO Don Hangem also stepped down through the investigation. The President of our United States suddenly went to a NAACP meeting unexpected. They all were aware of this book was coming out regarding Famous Parts Company—Woodrow Stamping Plant and Local 783 was aware of the contents of my book but didn't exactly know if they were successful in sabotaging my book. I must say they were successful but I'm coming out again this time being more careful this time around and I've learned to trust no one. All this occurred because of the investigation in the state of Washington D.C. with regards to Andrea's Smith and what had occurred to her.

The Judge who handled her case was aware of all facts and what occurred but instead of helping Andrea Smith she was railroaded and he did nothing to help her. He wouldn't even give her an attorney to represent her case in a court of law. Famous Parts Company Woodrow Stamping Plant and Local 783 wanted to keep this kind of unjust treatment kept silent and they did. This book will bring this treatment out into the open because it's unfair and against the law.

They took and oath and they are not to speak of anything of what they know was going on. That is what has happened to Andrea and me, we were not given the opportunity to have our voices heard we were silenced in the court of law, by the judge who gave us both a bench trial when we asked for a trial by jury. The Federal Court in Cincinnati sided with the judge in my claim, wasn't heard by the higher courts and the company paid the judge well I'm sure. I am aware since fraud was involved and I can prove it, I can bring my claim back to court.

Each time I second guess myself. I always go back to the beginning and look at my employment record and that sends me back to reality. When for three years I was full time and they put me part time and kept my full time benefit package. They did this for three years and terminated me unjustly when I should have been a rehire. They had me going through the grievance process knowing that it was never officially filed and that was fraud too. There was no grievance actually filed on this matter, but they lied and said that one was filed and had everyone to uphold them in their lies. There should not have been any reason for a grievance, because I was already full time but they were adamant that they were not going to pay me the money that was allocated to me and they pilfered it from Andrea Smith as well.

36

LINE LEADER

In the spring of 2000, the position of Line Leader became available when Lorrie Snort no longer wanted it. I worked on the line and since no one wanted the job I decided to take it. I took the Line Leader position only because the line had to have one according to Supervisor, Joey Nick. I decided to take the job only because *someone* had to do it. Plus, I was supposed to be paid more money per hour. After I became the line leader, I first noticed the line leader wasn't being paid the additional seventy or eighty cents per hour. Since no one told me anything about the line leader position, I had to find out this information on my own. When I did find out this information, Woodrow Stamping Plant wasn't very pleased. I sought a pay increase. I didn't stay line leader long enough to receive the pay adjustment, but I made it possible for other line leaders to receive theirs.

I was clearly involved in a conspiracy by Wayward Cane and Mr. James Collen regarding my holding the position of line leader. Both men were supposedly the Superintendents on the Assembly Side of the plant. Actually, they were just fill-ins when the company wanted them to do something other management staff wouldn't. They were puppets for Woodrow Stamping Plant. I don't think Wayward had much education. He also drank too much. Wayward and Collen were normally found working together. I'm not sure if the company had anything against Collen or not, but he was treated somewhat better than Wayward Cane.

At the time, Collen was acting Superintendent. I had been working for Joey Nick, my Supervisor on Line #551, when he was sent to the other side of the plant. I attained the position of line leader and began asking many questions which couldn't be explained regarding my supposed duties. Lorrie, the prior line leader withdrew because the job wasn't quite interesting enough—so she said.

Joey Nick often sent my co-worker, Ray, out of the plant on line business for the company, but Ray didn't once say he wanted to be the Line leader. He wanted to go out of the plant on line business but he didn't want to be the Line leader. I didn't find this out until much later. I had nothing but my imagination to go by when it concerned my new duties. Joey Nick gave me a sheet of paper and said it was all the information he had regarding the line leader's duties. There were supposed to be three sheets of rules and responsibilities. I was only given one of the three pages. I asked Joey Nick who was my supervisor at Woodrow Stamping Plant on the Assemble Side of the plant. How could I be an efficient leader when I had no guidelines to follow? He told me to do the best job I could with the information I had. That's what I did to make the line a success.

I was to have had help from the Production System's team members, but they were little or no help. I worked hard gathering bits and pieces of information on the rules and regulations concerning how to be an effective line leader. I completed weekly reports regarding the line's problems and solutions to help make the entire line more productive. I had the repairmen on the line attending line meetings when other leaders couldn't get them to participate. I invited anyone and everyone to assist in helping line #551 run smoothly. Things needed to be fixed on the line. With very little help the meetings were starting to get some order and the workers became very efficient. We were actually getting things done on this line now.

At first, I had a problem electing officers on the line. There were about 18 people working on Line #551. After the line started taking form, gradually the people participated more. They volunteered for various positions until all positions were filled—with the exception of the secretary. No one wanted that position. That is when Wanda Brooks, an older Caucasian woman on our line, decided she would try for the position as secretary. However she stated she knew nothing about the computer.

After Wanda accepted the position of secretary, all the positions on the line were filled. While I was Line leader, there were various duties calling for me to leave the plant on business and training. I was never told or asked to participate in these trainings regarding plant business. My supervisor, Joey Nick, had always picked Ray, the Caucasian gentleman, to represent Line #551 on plant business. The line workers asked me why I wasn't attending the line business or leadership trainings. I told them I didn't know why my supervisor was sending someone else when I should have been attending the out of plant business meetings regarding the line. I really wasn't aware I had those options since Joey Nick didn't convey information to me as to what my duties were as line leader.

Joey Nick never planed on informing me about the out of plant meetings or training. He had no intentions of telling me because the only thing he wanted me to do was work. To Joey Nick this was a privileged position and I was the wrong color to receive privileges outside the plant. My position only went as far as inside the plant. It didn't matter how smart I was. I wasn't smart enough to leave the plant on leadership business because I was the wrong color. As soon as line workers, Jack and Lorrie, became line leaders, they too were leaving out of state on line business. Yet as far as I went was to the nearby restaurant to have lunch on my own time.

When it was time for Wanda Brooks to be trained as secretary, I took her upstairs to the mezzanine floor. We went to a room with computers where we would use graphs to gather information regarding our line. We kept up with down time, scrap products, machine parts and services, and problems with the line that needed to be addressed. Line production and the product we provided was always discussed at the line meeting each week. I have to admit I had to teach Wanda from the beginning since she had never worked on a computer. I must say she became an efficient alternate. I wanted to teach her everything I could so that in case of my absence, she would be adequate enough to take my place. She would know how to do the necessary procedures for running our meetings. I needed to educate Wanda Brooks of the duties of a facilitator and/or secretary.

The first problem among many was when it became time for Wanda and me to go upstairs to the training room. That's when the rules suddenly changed and only *one* of us would be allowed in the training room at a time each week. Wanda and I were told we had to alternate weeks. I informed Wayward Cane because Joey Nick was no longer our supervisor. This was very unfair because Line #183 (the door line) constantly kept sending both of their line leaders and the alternate to train together and nothing was ever said. I felt they were setting me up to fail at becoming effective at my new position. I was more determined to make the line a success because I had no help from management regarding my duties. I wanted everything to run smoothly. I actually went into the manuals in the computer room upstairs and gathered the information on what it was that I was supposed to be doing.

Wanda tried hard to gain information regarding our line with no help. Wanda was completely computer illiterate. I had to start from ground zero when helping my alternate. I informed my supervisors of the handicap we were faced with. I let them know Wanda needed help but they refused to give it to her. I felt management didn't want my line to succeed because I was a minority. The line had become very popular and well-organized.

There were many line leaders that had run their lines much longer than I, but my line was more productive. Other Line leaders inquired about what I was doing to run such efficient line meetings. I sought information in the plant on the ins and outs and much of the information I gathered was in the manuals in the training rooms.

In December 1998, I became ill at Woodrow Stamping and had to be transported to the hospital by ambulance because I couldn't breathe. I stayed in the hospital for 24 hours with an irregular heartbeat. Before leaving the hospital, I had a stress test to see if there were any irregular problems with my heart. I was off work for four weeks. There was clearly something in the plant I breathed which caused the symptoms. I haven't had that problem since, but many other employees had to be rushed to the hospital for the same symptoms I had.

When I returned to Woodrow Stamping from my medical leave, Wanda Brooks told me the line wanted to elect another line leader while I was gone. They were going to vote me out of office until Wanda and William, the hi-lo driver on the end of the line, stood up in my defense. Lorrie Snort, the former line leader who no longer wanted the job, suddenly decided she wanted to be the line leader again. She somehow came alive while I was away and stated she wanted the position back. I guess I had groomed the position to be more exciting than it was before. Lorrie read a three-paged letter to the line in reference to my incompetence for the job.

I did an excellent job and they were allowed to take that away from me. It just goes to show how envy and discrimination can become a factor against a person who has done a very good job. Sometimes others wanted to gain all the credit of my having a successful line. There were only three minorities who worked on the line. They were William, Casie, and I. While I was out I was very disappointed to hear Casie was one of the persons who voted against me. William was also very disappointed with Casie's action. Not because I was Black, but because I was doing an excellent job as line leader.

When I returned, the line seemed normal as though nothing crazy happened while I was away. Neither Jack nor Lorrie contacted me or tried to face me regarding the overtaking of the line. Lorrie and Jack wanted the job themselves. When I returned, I asked Lorrie if she had read a three-paged letter in regards to my inadequacy as line leader. She said yes. I then asked her to bring a copy of the letter she read in my absence. She said she would do so but never did. After that I decided to let the matter rest.

There was a need for a line leader when I took the job. I took the line from nothing and made it into something of value. I was proud of that fact if nothing else. Management had to play a significant role in what happened. The company didn't stand up in my defense. I can say when Lorrie and Jack took over as line leaders, they both were going out of the plant on line business. They were also traveling out of state with regards to company matters. After I stepped down, I never looked back because it was just part of the job. I didn't agree with how the situation was handled, but I harbored no hard feelings. I would like to thank you Wanda and William for working in good faith, coming to my defense, and sticking up for what was right.

37

MISSING CHEMICAL DATA SHEETS

All plants using a variety of chemicals have to keep records of any and all chemicals used. Each container has to be visibly labeled with its name and contents. The chemical has to have the ingredients noted and the harm that could be caused if it is inhaled, ingested, touches the skin, etc. The plant had Chemical Data Books in designated areas of the plant. One was located in the front of the Committee Room on the mezzanine floor, another was in the Medical Department, and one sat as you'd walk in the main entrance in front of the Security Office.

When I returned from medical leave due to my inhalation incident, I talked to the Plant Chairman and informed him there was something in the plant people were breathing and sending them to the hospital. He looked at me very strangely as if my statement had some merit. I told him I really thought he was already aware of the problems in the plant. There were 9 people rushed out of the plant for the same symptoms I had, but I can't address their names for fear of reprisal. I did send the names to the Michigan Occupational Safety Health Administration (OSHA) and received not so much as a response stating they received my letter. I know they received the letter because I sent the letter certified mail—return receipt requested.

There were many concerns I had with Woodrow Stamping Plant taking the Chemical Data Sheets out of the plant. I felt they had something to hide by taking this action. The majority of the employees didn't notice the books weren't there anymore since the majority of employees didn't look in the book for references anyway. There were few who even cared about the Chemical Data Sheets being removed. I can honestly say the company was using chemicals in the plant that should not have been used. When someone would notice, the company would seal off the section of the plant and take the chemical out.

Mary, a co-worker of mine, was sent to work on the Press Side of the plant. She was instructed to spray a certain chemical on various automobile parts. As Mary was spraying, the residue from the spray was lingering in the air. She wanted to know what she was breathing and became concerned. This is when the Medical Department looked up the chemical number in the computer and as a result the chemical was taken out of the plant. This was the same chemical and chemical number I was using when I worked that job and I was unable to get any information on it. I was trying to obtain any and all information regarding this chemical.

I asked Mary to see if she could find any information about the chemical. The Medical Department also reported the chemical should not be used in the plant. Mary received information regarding the chemical but said she wouldn't be able to transfer the information to me or anyone else. The person who gave her the information was afraid of being fired if Woodrow Stamping Plant was aware the information got out. I respected her promise because I wouldn't want to put anyone's job in jeopardy.

Soon Woodrow Stamping Plant sealed the area off and removed the chemical after the chemical was reported being used in the plant. Local 783 eventually looked up the chemical's data information I requested in the Chemical Data System, but by then I was told they didn't have the chemical in their system at all. It was at that time the chemical was taken out of the plant. Knowing Woodrow Stamping Plant as I do, they probably brought the chemical right back in the plant after I was put on medical leave.

Employees trusted Woodrow Stamping Plant with their lives and felt they were in good hands. As a result, Woodrow Stamping didn't give a damn about them whatsoever. It all added up to dollars and cents. They weren't smart enough to even make a dollar because they never learned by their mistakes. This is the reason they never made a profit on their own. They sought to pilfer every penny they could from the employees. I guess the chemicals they were using were much cheaper in cost and they used whatever they could to get the product out and meet quota.

Who's to know what Woodrow Stamping Plant brought in the plant when they removed the Chemical Data Sheets? They didn't care if the chemicals were inhaled or not. This is a grave statement to make, but people have died at the hands of Famous Parts Company due to chemical poisoning. I'll bet if their bodies were exhumed there'd be some kind of chemical residue in their bodies from a chemical that should not have been in the plant. Even as of October 17, 2006, I was told employees were dropping dead at an alarming rate at Woodrow Stamping Plant.

It wouldn't surprise me if Woodrow Stamping Plant took out an extra insurance policy on employees so they could benefit. Who's to stop them? I feel there isn't much that they wouldn't do. They made an effort to insure themselves, but never made a legal profit as long as I worked there. What kept Famous Parts Company investing in a plant that never made a profit? I don't know but I can truly say it wasn't legal.

Obtaining information about these chemicals was like trying to get into Fort Knox without identification. Chemical data information should be accessible to those who care to view it. They didn't care because the majority of the cleaning crew was made up of people of color when I left Woodrow Stamping Plant. They cleaned up toxic chemicals leaking from the presses to the basement. Prior to Woodrow Stamping Plant taking the Chemical Data Sheets out of the plant, the majority of cleaning crew was primarily Caucasian. When all the Blacks became cleaners, the Chemical Data Books were no longer in the plant.

When I went on medical leave, there was another co-worker that cleaned chemicals in the basement who became ill. All she could do was inform her chemical specialist of the chemicals she worked around. She had some kind of toxic poisoning and they were running specialized tests. They needed to know what kind of chemicals she worked around. I saw her husband the last time I visited the Medical Department. He said his wife was yet on medical leave. I would always tell his wife to keep track of the chemicals she worked around. She did not at the time, but I bet she wished she had.

This plant took out the entire selection of Chemical Data Sheets at Woodrow Stamping Plant. The plant told me all the information I needed was transferred to the computer. I was informed I could get the information by accessing the chemical number in the computer. The information would give me what I wanted regarding the chemicals. I followed the instructions given and the computer stated I needed an access code to get the chemical data information. I was outright lied to. The chemical specialist knew I didn't have the code.

The information wasn't available to regular employees. For me to go in the computer and access information I would need the intervention of management. I was told I could use the Chemical Data Sheets in Woodrow Stamping Plant's Medical Department. When I went to use the Chemical Data Sheets in the Medical Department, there were pages missing from the book regarding the information I needed. I notified the Medical Department about the problem I was having. I wanted to look up this vital information because I was working around chemicals in which I wanted to understand the warnings on. Would you believe the Medical Department's nurse didn't even ask or volunteer to look-up the chemical information for me? This is when I decided to write the Michigan Occupational Health and Safety Administration (OHSA) about my concerns. I wrote them on November 17, 2001.

"To whom it may concern:

My name is Crista Carrie and I am employed at Famous Parts Company Woodrow Stamping Plant. I am very concerned about the Chemical Data Sheets I thought were supposed to be available at the employee's discretion. The Chemical Data Sheets have a listing of all chemicals used in the plant. I'm disappointed with what I was told when I spoke to one of the environmental personnel at the plant. The union was informed the company removed the Chemical Data Sheets to be updated. I have come in contact with some chemicals doing my work and wanted to inquire about the side effects with each of the specific chemicals.

A woman in the Environment Department at the plant told me the Chemical Data Sheets would no longer be displayed because of the constant problem with updating the information. She said everyone would have the opportunity to use the computer to access all chemical information. She failed to tell me I needed a password to access the chemical data file. I asked her how I could access the information on the computer. She wrote incorrect information on a piece of paper, knowing it wouldn't get me in the file. The information was totally misleading and the next day in the lunchroom I told her so. She stated I could bring the chemical numbers to her office and she would show me how to get in the computer. I could tell all she wanted to know was what chemical I was looking up in the computer, so I declined to offer her that information.

When she first told me there would be no more books inquiring about chemicals on the plant floor, my first response was, "You can't do that!" What about the people who are computer illiterate? How were they to access the information if they were in question of a specific chemical or if they needed specific instructions? Precautions were needed to be able to be taken at all times so the employees' knowledge wouldn't be limited.

I've always been told these books would be available to the employees at all times if they chose to use them. How would we know if we were working in hazardous conditions when many containers were not labeled properly labeled (if they were labeled at all)? I'm not sure how this plant gets safety awards each year because there are many things in plain sight that are not acceptable in terms of chemical safety standards. What harm would it have been by leaving the books in the plant's designated areas?

The toxin number of the glue being used was #WSKM2G3841Al. When my supervisor would spray that chemical, it literally took my breath away. I would always breathe in the mist being sprayed. This chemical was used on many occasions. In 1988, I had apparently inhaled something in the plant and had to be rushed to the hospital by ambulance. The symptoms were thought to be that of a heart attack. I had pain in my left arm. At the time it seemed as though the muscles were pulling. It was painful to stretch my arm and my muscles wouldn't extend. I experienced shortness of breath and dizziness. The Medical Department of Famous Parts Company described me as having unstable angina, which is a heart condition. I was transferred to Midway Hospital.

I had been treated for hypertension and hyper cholesterol, but had never experienced anything such as this. My blood pressure had been stable since I began taking prescribed medication by my primary physician. I had to take a stress test prior to being discharged from the hospital. I was advised to have follow-up treatment with my regular physician. I followed the hospital's recommendations and my doctor informed me my condition was indeed an environmental issue due to something I had ingested. The hospital treated me accordingly for a heart condition.

I had worked with the highly toxin chemical #008681 without the use of mask and gloves. At the time, my job was to wipe excess glue from the car doors at the end of the door line. This line needed the use of a mask on many occasions, but I was not made aware of that. I worked on the floor, Line #551. The chemical used to un-stick the conveyor belt was an unknown substance, but I couldn't stand the smell. The smell of the chemical literally took my breath away. Each time the chemical was used, the supervisor went to get it from an unlabeled container. I thought all chemicals were supposed to be labeled. A line repairman told me any chemical that removed glue from parts, should not be used in the plant. This is when I began searching for the Chemical Data Sheets and found they were no longer in existence.

When I worked on the Press Side, my job was to spray a chemical that kept steel from cracking or splitting at the front of the line Mary worked. The chemical toxin #030993 was used and employees were exposed without the use of masks, gloves, or the knowledge of what chemical lingered in the air. I later found out the chemical wasn't supposed to be in the plant period. The company closed a portion of the area and moved the chemical off the plant floor immediately. Of course, this was *after* the fact.

I worked in CT20, which is an area where they had a variety of side jobs that weren't too strenuous on the body. *(CT20 made the dashboards of one of the small cars.)* This was an area where many small stature women and men worked. I worked for two years or more on one job that used copper welded caps in this area. This assignment ejected much smoke and many odd smelling fumes (especially when the fans weren't in working order). I worked the end-plate job on a regular basis for about two years.

When one of the two fans weren't working, I had a serious problem with the fumes—so I called safety. The fan was eventually replaced but not before I went to the Medical Department and asked for a mask. I was not given a mask but I was told to see the company doctor to obtain one. When the fans weren't working correctly, the smoke resembled thick fog. I would start coughing because the smoke left a bad taste in my mouth.

I'm concerned about my health because I've been diagnosed with Asthma. At the time, I was taking Floven every 12 hours to assist my breathing. I was interested in knowing if the chemicals were responsible for my breathing problems and the cause of me having problems with my muscles. I couldn't check for information unless I had access to the chemical data information. I've complained to Stanly Ball, President of Local 783; Tom Hemp, Plant Chairman of Local 783; and Pedro Stevens, Bargaining Committeeman (*no affiliation to retired Plant Manager, Mr. Stevens, at Sarrow Stamping Plant*). I've also complained to the Medical Department's Head Nurse, Tootie, and one of the Environmental Specialists at the plant.

Neither the Plant Chairman nor the Bargaining Committeeman tried to obtain information on this matter. The Bargaining Committeeman told me the Chemical Data Sheets were being updated. This is why the sheets were moved from the security office and in front of Local 783's office on the mezzanine floor of the plant. I then talked to the Union President to inquire about the sheets and was told he would check into the matter. I later contacted other union personnel on the matter and was told there was to be a meeting held regarding the missing Chemical Data Sheets. I then went to the Medical Department and asked one of the nurses why the Chemical Data Sheets were missing. She stated there was a Chemical Data Sheet Book in the next room and I was welcomed to use it if I chose. On this day I didn't have the toxin number with me, but a few days later I took her up on the offer and used the Chemical Data Sheet information in the Medical Department.

All the information on chemicals I was looking for was missing from the book in the Medical Department. This left me still searching for the information I was in need of. It was almost like not having the Chemical Data Book at all. On the morning of November 16, 2001, I went back to see the Plant Chairman of Local 783, Tom Hemp. As I was walking in the plant, I met Carol Downing who was the alternate fill-in for addressing Local 783's union members. We were walking in the same direction going up the escalator when she asked how I was feeling. I said fine. I told her of my concerns surrounding the missing chemical data sheets and the number of people who had fallen-out in the plant needing to be rushed to Midway Hospital. I was included in those nine employees. I informed Carol something in the plant is causing employees to be rushed to the hospital.

Carol then told me Local 783 was keeping track of all those employees who had been transported to Midway Hospital from Woodrow Stamping Plant. I asked Carol why they were keeping track of people being taken to the hospital. I continued to say I thought this was quite strange because if they were keeping track of how many employees were being transported to the hospital, there had to be a reason. Carol volunteered to get me a copy of the list and she went in the committee room while I waited outside.

I assumed Plant Vice-Chairman of Local 783, Tom Hemp, wanted to know who was inquiring about the list. When he saw it was I, he said immediately, "Crista there will no longer be any Chemical Data Books". I then replied, "I still don't have the chemical numbers I want to look-up". From my perspective, it seemed as though it was something many people was aware of or had easy access to, but when Tom Hemp saw it was I waiting for the list, he seemed relieved that he took the time to find out. From that point on there was never any further discussion because Tom Hemp wasn't going to give me any information. He knew I would use it. He was certainly right.

Tom Hemp said all the chemical data information will be on computer. I then asked him to give me the access number and he said he would do so at the end of the day. After work, I stopped in his office and asked him for the access number. Tom Hemp walked in his office as I walked behind him. He sat down in his chair and dialed a number on his phone, but there was no answer. He said he would still get the information for me. I seemed to be getting the run around about the Chemical Data Sheets. I started seeking help in getting chemical data information on November 6, 2001 and it is currently November 17, 2001. I have no more information now than I did on November 6, 2001.

I'm very concerned about my health issues. I may not be so lucky the next time I'm rushed to the hospital. The company isn't taking proper precautions to keep employees healthy. The company's responsibility is to provide this information to employees and it's the union's responsibility to make sure the information is in place. These issues need immediate attention because it's a serious matter. Some-one should check with Midway Hospital and survey just how many employees were carried out on a stretcher with breathing disorders or symptoms of heart conditions. I have a few names of employees who became ill at the plant with breathing problems.

In June 2000, I told the Plant Chairman there were too many people falling-out in the plant and having to be hospitalized. I felt something was very wrong with this picture. I thought the situation would eventually cause a casualty and it may have when one of the female hi-lo drivers, Bertha, suddenly died in the early part of 2005. I met Bertha before her death at a theater function. "We checked the air", Tom Hemp said with a weird look on his face before I left on medical leave in May 2002. I stressed we were breathing something unhealthy. Nine people were rushed to the hospital in the same department. One young lady who worked on the Press Side miscarried, loosing two children. She miscarried the first child one year, and a year later she lost her second. The second baby only lived one hour. I know the same toxin chemical #030993 was used in the area where this young lady worked. Did it have any effect on her losing her baby? We will never know.

If someone looked into this matter, it could keep employees healthy. The plant is using chemicals that aren't supposed to be in the plant at all. I personally saw unlabeled chemicals used on the door line. There was a tag that said "empty" but the container was full of glue with no lid. There was some writing on the drum which read, "LA2/y2. 2/100 Attention: (name) 01/usa/m 4655R1 Livingston". There was no other information on the drum. No labels or safety precautions were visible on the drums.

I am enclosing five copies of documentation. I'm sending a copy of medical forms, my discharged instruction form, a copy of my Woodrow patient information sheet, and my cardiology report & stress test."

I signed my name and I never heard any response from the Occupational Safety and Health Administration (OSHA). Not even the information regarding the chemicals was addressed. I assumed Famous Parts Company—Woodrow Stamping Plant may have paid the Occupational Safety and Health Administration agent off not to investigate because the Chemical Data Sheets should not have been removed. Again, what would it have hurt Woodrow Stamping Plant to leave the Chemical Data Sheets in the designated area? They didn't want employees looking up chemicals in the plant unless they went through management. This letter should have been enough to send someone out to investigate if nothing else. I never received any correspondence regarding the complaint. It's usually customary to respond to a formal letter within thirty days. I know they received the letter because I sent it certified mail—return receipt.

38

TREATMENT BY THE MEDICAL DEPARTMENT

I felt I was wasting my time with the Medical Department. Therefore I needed to see a doctor who was going to help me and not constantly tell me I had no problem. I needed to know the truth about my condition. I was aware I wasn't going to get this information from Woodrow Stamping Plant's Medical Department. I went to see my primary physician and she referred me to see Dr. Sonia. I waited so long to get treatment at Woodrow Stamping Plant because I truly believed my condition would be treated with dignity and respect. I eventually saw I was wrong.

I started seeing Dr. Sonia for the first time in February 2001. I had used all avenues I knew in obtaining treatment for my back, which the Medical Department refused to treat. It really took me a while to understand that what's written on paper as protocol is not always followed. I was trying to follow the proper procedures in terms of what should have been followed regarding an occupational injury. Whether I had to face the doctors who were appointed by Woodrow Stamping Plant's Medical Department or my personal physician, my main concern was my health.

Management at Woodrow Stamping and Local 783 made up their own rules as they went along. It didn't matter who I contacted, there was no help to be found. I wanted to do the right thing by following all the rules but rules didn't seem to be in the equation. The rules didn't make a difference in the end. I was aware my body was falling apart so I decided to seek help outside the plant. The company doctors always told me I was just fine and needed no restrictions. I continued to work without restrictions, which further caused deterioration of my body. My symptoms began to expand when I was working without restrictions.

The first injury to my back occurred in April 1999. About three months later, I re-injured my back in July 1999. I injured my back, neck, right shoulder, and right wrist. This injury could have been prevented if the Medical Department would not have taken away my restriction for a small stature.

I had no idea how serious my back problem had become by not getting immediate attention. Three months later my back injury became very severe. I had never experienced such pain. I would literally have pain in my rectum causing me to curl up as a fetus inside the womb. I could not even bend to tie my shoes.

I told Dr. Straw, Woodrow Stamping Plant's physician, something was wrong with my back. On our original encounter, he sent me back to work my job as though I was complaining of nothing. He was going to send me back to work on the floor as he did before, until I told him my back had been injured twice in three months.

Dr. Straw sent me to the hospital for x-rays which showed I had a sprained/strained upper and lower back. They sent me to see Dr. Steeler to treat my right shoulder. However my back wasn't given a second thought and that was my biggest problem at that time. I started having numbness and tingling radiating from my neck and from down my shoulder to my arm. Dr. Steeler made an assessment of my medical condition. I would like you to keep in mind there were x-rays taken prior to my seeing Dr. Steeler, who also noted I had a sprained/strained upper and lower back.

Dr. Steeler stated she was going to obtain some x-rays of my lumbar spine to rule out Degenerative Arthritis. She stated in her report that she knew me for a long time. I didn't really consider 3 months to be a long time and I never saw her again. She said I had many "somatic complaints" within a 3-month period. Dr. Steelers's neurological examination said "normal" in the lower extremities and she never touched my back. Her primary goal was to "rule out the pathologic process", so she said—but that was a lie too.

Dr. Steeler never touched my back but stated my diagnosis was excluded from being work-related. How could she even know when she didn't examine me? She said I could work without restrictions even with all my complaints. I clearly saw something wrong with what she was saying. No medication was recommended and I was to see her in a week after a second set of x-rays were complete. This was when Woodrow Stamping was setting up the stage for my condition to become a personal injury. From that point my condition became a personal injury according to the Medical Department and they weren't going to pay a cent.

Woodrow Stamping would say the condition was personal and wouldn't take any responsibility. They did not want to take responsibility for an actual injury sustained in the plant. If you have a personal injury which was caused and/or aggravated by your employer then the employer is yet liable, but Woodrow

Stamping Plant didn't see it that way. This is what Dr. Steeler was trying to say when she said I had *Fibromyalgia*. This is a condition that has no specific origin of pain and can't be pinpointed to a specific cause.

Dr. Steeler was aware of my medical condition. When I arrived at her office the first time, I carried the x-rays along with me that were taken in July 1999. It was already established I had a sprained/strained upper and lower back. Woodrow Stamping Plant's Worker's Compensation Representative was telling Dr. Steeler what to treat and how to treat it. The Medical Department wasted valuable time by not honoring any restrictions. They had me work without restrictions when they knew there were many problems after I was tested. Dr. Steeler tested other parts of my body and found there was nerve damage in my shoulder, hands, wrists, and elbows.

I kept telling her my back was the problem that no one addressed. Even during my last visit, she continued to say I needed no restriction while I was still complaining about my back. Dr. Steeler told me she couldn't treat my back because the Medical Department didn't authorize her to do so. The more I complained, the more my complaints went unheard. Why did they not allow me to be treated when they knew my x-ray results by the first hospital?

In my initial visit with Dr. Steeler, she was supposed to be treating me for my back—so I thought. I strained both shoulders many times with the company on various jobs from 1992 until May 2002 when I was put on a 'no work available' status. I did tell Dr. Steeler I was having spasms in my neck occurring on a regular basis. She knew from x-rays I was telling the truth, but did nothing to help relieve the pain I was suffering from. All Woodrow Stamping Plant and Dr. Steeler wanted to do was take the blame off themselves and put it on a similar medical condition by definition while they continued to pilfer my money.

If Dr. Steeler was only authorized to treat me for my shoulder, why was she testing both hands, both wrists, and my neck? If she wasn't authorized to test my hands, neck, and wrists, then why should she need to be authorized to treat my back? Dr. Steeler never touched my back while I treated with her even though she stated my condition was *Fibromyalgia* because of my symptomatic complaints.

I had many complaints. Dr. Steeler wanted to say my health problems had nothing to do with work on the job. On the record she said my "age" was the cause of my medical condition. I was in pain, so why do you think this woman sent me back to work without giving me any restrictions? I had to work as though I had no pain at all. That was the last time I saw Dr. Steeler. After that, the Medical Department sent me to see Dr. Butt.

Dr. Butt did exactly what Dr. Steeler had done. He totally ignored what the x-rays said. He said what I was suffering from was nothing an aspirin wouldn't heal. I was suffering from many conditions needing far more than aspirin. He was aware there was a problem with my hands, wrists, elbows, and back. He still said nothing was wrong with me and that I needed no restrictions, medication, or anything else. There was a second set of tests taken by Dr. Butt that showed the same problems.

During plant shut down my back felt somewhat better after a two-week period. When I returned to work from vacation, the pain became worse and I began walking with a limp. I was having severe pain in both legs and began having muscle spasms at night. I was using heating pads every night before going to bed. Woodrow Stamping Plant was aware my back was injured in the plant. I truly thought I would get the necessary treatment the Caucasian employees always seemed to receive. Why not me? Our circumstances were the same. We were all suffering from 'occupational' injuries sustained in the plant.

I know my body could have been spared if Woodrow Stamping Plant would have given me the necessary treatment and time to allow my body's healing. Instead they wanted me to continue working without restrictions, which only aggravated my condition only to send me out on medical leave. It was like assaulting an already injured body. Boy, I was truly mistaken to believe in the system and how it worked. There were so many double standards at Woodrow Stamping Plant regarding the Caucasian employees and the minorities. An injury is an injury and we should have been treated accordingly, not favored or disfavored.

Five months had passed and my back problem still hadn't been addressed. Woodrow Stamping Plant's Medical Department said I didn't have any problems with my back, wrists, hands, or neck. Therefore they attended to my shoulder only. At this point it was up to me to see another doctor because I was still working without restrictions. Dr. Butt knew what my diagnosis was just as Dr. Steeler and Dr. Straw did. When Dr. Steeler received the results of the x-rays, she chose to totally ignore the report's findings. The Medical Department had plans for me and they were setting me up for the right moment. They wanted to unofficially retire me and take my retirement so I would only be receiving my Social Security. They would help me get my Social Security and they would keep the entire amount of the Worker's Compensation money granted by the court before and after the Worker's Compensation hearing. How could they get away with that? This had to be a powerfully organized group.

In the case of Famous Parts Company Employee, Linda Jackson, she only received her Social Security and never Worker's Compensation benefits. She didn't receive any money from Metro Craft Insurance Company. Linda received her letter from Worker's Compensation the second time around in 2004, when the first claim hadn't been paid. It's unusual for the court to change their decision without justification. The only thing Linda didn't agree on was the amount of money she was being paid after five years of being on a 'no work available' status. The amount she was offered was $10,000 dollars for the period of five years. The amount was so small because Woodrow Stamping Plant had already been reported paying continuous Worker's Compensation to employees since their injuries occurred in the plant. It only makes since, why else would the court agree to a settlements so low for a life time disability?

The court didn't retract their decision made in December 2002. This was another decision all together. Woodrow Stamping just didn't pay Linda the money owed to her. Some two years later, she received a letter stating she was receiving no money when a decision was already made in 2002. She should have been paid 30 days from the decision. They were supposed to subsidize a monthly amount to compensate for her occupational injury, but they did not.

Andrea Smith's Worker's Compensation was pilfered from her in 2002 without her knowledge. She was fighting her claim at the Appellate Court level because she never received any money from her claim. Andrea thought she was yet settling the same old case in 2002 because she had no idea her case was settled earlier. She didn't know she was representing a new claim when she hadn't even received compensation for the first. This claim had to have been a new claim because the old claim dated back to 1995. The new claim had a 2002 date of injury.

According to court papers, Andrea's court case was introduced to Worker's Compensation in 2002. It didn't mention anything regarding the 1992 claim, when it started, or where it originated. It was as though her old occupational injury had no history. The way the courts saw it, Andrea's case started in 2002 and not 1995. The court wasn't expecting the new claim. Therefore the claim was denied. This is the only way Woodrow Stamping Plant couldn't have used the previous claim that occurred in 1992. In Andrea's case, she was trying to represent a claim she was unaware no longer existed. She was not informed the old claim was settled.

Andrea was standing in the court reporting the occurrence with the hi-lo, and her referee, Jackie Arnold, wasn't listening. Andrea was standing directly in front of Jackie Arnold and she made no mention of Andrea's case being settled. She didn't address the hi-lo truck hitting Andrea while she was on the job. Jackie Arnold denied Andrea's claim saying she didn't report the incident. This wasn't true. The only way Andrea's doctor could have been paid for treating Andrea for eight years was if there was a settlement in her case. Referee Jackie Arnold never included in her 2004 report that Andrea was hit by the broom or by the hi-lo truck. When Andrea's doctors were paid, she should have been paid as well. Andrea's new injury with the truck in the plant was swept under the rug as though it never happened. It was hard to conceive this kind of treatment occurred not just to Andrea but also to others.

Andrea has been retired for many years according to Woodrow Stamping Plant's records. A retired person doesn't file Worker's Compensation claims. Only working people can file a claim with the company for Worker's Compensation and Andrea wasn't working, according to Woodrow Stamping Plant's records. Woodrow Stamping Plant and Local 783 needed to get rid of Andrea in a hurry. Referee Jackie Arnold and Arnold Stanford (the attorney representing Famous Parts Company—Woodrow Stamping Plant) became fearful when the truck hit Andrea. They knew someone would not only find out Andrea was not retired, but they would find out Andrea wasn't getting the money the company was supposed to be paying her. Since Andrea was 'working' *and* 'retired', there had to be more than one set of records for Andrea Smith.

Both, Worker's Compensation and Retirement Benefits were pilfered from Famous Part's employees, Andrea Smith and Linda Jackson. Woodrow Stamping Plant kept all Andrea's money when her Worker's Compensation settlement was agreed upon between Referee Jackie Arnold and Attorney Arnold Stanford. Andrea didn't agree to the amount of money Woodrow Stamping Plant's Worker's Compensation was offering. That was no reason to deny her any money at all, then turn around and terminate her employment. Famous Parts Company was known for their "all or nothing" concept. They receive it all and you receive nothing.

Andrea Smith and Linda Jackson disagreed with the settlement amount. This also happened to me in another case regarding Woodrow Stamping Plant. I didn't accept Woodrow Stamping Plant's offer of a measly $7,500 dollars as compensation for their discrimination, harassment, retaliation, and theft of my skilled trade's idea.

If you didn't accept their offer, they would withdraw the offer from the table completely. This meant you received nothing. Woodrow Stamping Plant didn't have to pay Worker's Compensation benefits to neither Andrea nor Linda. The women were living under poverty level when the very company they worked for was pilfering their money. Worker's Compensation claims were granted by the Worker's Compensation court. Since Woodrow Stamping Plant paid the premium, they could take as much money as they wanted to. Sometimes they took it all—as they did in Andrea's and Linda's cases. It was all for Woodrow Stamping and nothing for Andrea Smith or Linda Jackson.

It took a lot of audacity to run this kind of scheme and it took much involvement from other entities. This was not just a one-person scheme. It involved local government agencies, elected officials, lawyers, referees, judges, and of course, the insurance company Metro Craft, who paid weekly and monthly benefits to employees. Woodrow Stamping Plant took care of the Caucasians while the minorities suffered. All these entities played a significant role in keeping this scheme alive.

Woodrow Stamping Plant felt they didn't have much of a choice in firing Andrea. No one would know the difference if an already retired person were fired, right? After Andrea was fired, Woodrow Stamping thought she couldn't cause any more trouble. They felt since she was *blackballed* or *red flagged,* her case wouldn't last in court. The court didn't give Andrea the benefit of doubt because she had been representing herself through the courts. After her failed attempts with two law firms, she had been standing on her own grounds without help from anyone.

They didn't have to report the hit by the truck while she was working because she wasn't supposed to be working in the first place. Andrea's 'sick & accident' benefits were stopped when she was terminated, which left her with no money and no insurance from Metro Craft. The first set of records Andrea was retired. Woodrow Stamping Plant was paying Andrea sick and accident benefits from the second set of records when she was terminated in February 2003. This shows how expendable a person was on the job. When Andrea was terminated, the company and union didn't try to get her back because she had some knowledge that she was already retired. She never received any money for her injuries sustained in the plant. The only income Andrea is receiving as of February 2008 is her Social Security.

Linda Jackson's seniority was growing and she had been on a medical leave since 1997. She returned to work for two days in 2002 and was still on medical leave as of September 2006. She's been completing her #5166 medical forms every six months for ten years now. How can a person be on a continuous medical leave for over 10 years? Occasionally Linda Jackson receives retirement information or handbills regarding retirement through the mail. This is what

Woodrow Stamping Plant had planned for me, but something happened and they closed my retirement account on two occasions.

I had to file for retirement over again. I received no back money during my waiting for it to come through in December 2004. I received no back pay because of what Woodrow Stamping Plant did with the help of Local 783. They brought me back to work on paper, only by Woodrow Stamping Plant's account. I returned and was unable to work without complications and I had to return back on retirement. Therefore there was a six-month waiting period before I could resume my retirement. My retirement was stopped, and resumed when I went on my official medical retirement in 2002. I could actually retire in December 2004.

My first money was going into the special accounts. I should have received money while waiting for my retirement to be accepted. Not to mention on one set of records Woodrow Stamping Plant had me on a retired status. However, it looked as though I took the 'buy-out' in July 2004 on the other set of records. I think the amount Famous Parts Company was offering in my category was $30,000 dollars. I'm sure they collected and laundered that money too.

Woodrow Stamping Plant and Local 783 were working miracles with all these records they had on employees they were pilfering from. I ask you again, to remember there were two sets of records kept on employees. Woodrow Stamping Plant had one and the union had the other. This is how they could retire an employee and have the very same employee as working. This is how they could have someone on medical leave and working at the same time. This is how they could pilfer employees' Worker's Compensation settlements and file another claim in the same court without arousing suspicion.

It seemed they didn't get a chance to treat me as cruel as they did Linda Jackson and Andrea Smith. If something wasn't right on my paperwork, I'd challenge it. I questioned how could I be on medical leave and be in the plant working at the same time I was receiving 'sick & accident' payments from Metro Craft Insurance Company. The real reason Woodrow Stamping Plant overstated their earnings was because they were pilfering from the employees and putting the money back in the company to elevate the company's profit margin. The pilfering from employees became a profitable business for the company. However it left the employees in poverty and ill health. I didn't think Woodrow Stamping Plant was pilfering alone since the Executive Branch of the Union and Don Hangem, the Union CEO, played a significant role in the demise of Andrea Smith. This told me other companies were able to conduct similar pilfering schemes. I believe the other auto and manufacturing companies would have been able to run this same scheme because of the union's involvement or lack of it.

The company wasn't sure how much I knew since Nurse Tootie was arrested on multiple charges. She was the only one arrested in August 2004, but the FBI was in search of Tom Hemp, Plant Vice-Chairman of Local 783. In March 2003, there was a raid in the Medical Department at Woodrow Stamping Plant in which they took files of employees. There were quite a few employees escorted out of the plant in March 2003, and from my understanding only two returned. The scheme still went on although they had gotten rid of Nurse Tootie. They just put someone else in her place and it was business as usual. This was how and why Worker's Compensation didn't work for Andrea and Linda. This kind of treatment could happen to anyone—not just Andrea or Linda.

Their intentions for me didn't work as planned. When they put me on my first 'no work available' I was never to return back to Woodrow Stamping Plant. My Social Security was being processed and when I returned they could no longer say I was disabled. I felt I didn't need to be retired, but I did need restrictions. When I contacted the Department of Civil Rights, Woodrow Stamping Plant had 15 days to return me to work. This was the first time Woodrow Stamping Plant retired me but they didn't stop there. I received my first retirement newsletter in September 2000 when I was put on a 'no work available' in June 2000.

The Medical Department sent me to see Dr. Butt in January 2000. When the test results came back there were eight numbers on the piece of paper representing the examined areas he tested. I asked for the additional test results and Nurse Tootie told me there were no more. The eight numbers on the paper I received didn't reflect all areas tested on my body. I told Nurse Tootie the doctor tested me all over my body with electronic prods followed by placing needles all over my flesh. I was treated as though I didn't have the knowledge of what this doctor did to me in the examination room.

The test that should have been administered was for the lower spine only, but instead I was being tested all over my body. As he was giving me an EMG (Electromyogram), it recorded electrical activity of my muscles. Dr. Butt was playing with the knobs as no other doctors had ever done while I took the EMG. They finally sent me to see Dr. Butt on Martin Luther King Jr.'s birthday for the second time in 2000. I was not paid overtime for seeing him on a paid holiday. After Dr. Butt had completed his testing, he stated there was nothing wrong with me.

Dr. Butt gave me both parts of a nerve test, which revealed I had Degenerative Joint Disease. This wasn't information I was privileged to know by the Medical Department at that time. They kept this medical information from me and constantly had me work without restrictions. I couldn't believe them—especially when Dr. Butt gave me the nerve test. I wanted the complete test results.

When the Medical Department denied they gave me an EMG, I knew that meant one thing—TROUBLE! It only added to the feud between Woodrow Stamping Plant's Medical Department and me. The Medical Department and I had a prior history because they were always taking my medical information out of my medical folder trying to hide the fact I had been full-time since 1990. These files also contained the actual information of doctor's reports and medical tests about my condition that Woodrow Stamping Plant sent me to see. The Medical Department took medical tests and reports out of my file in which I would bring them. They would have that information placed in my folder at Brownstown, another one of Famous Parts Company facilities. The files the Medical Department kept at Brownstown were of those employees who they had retired and/or should have been receiving Worker's Compensation payment from Woodrow Stamping Plant. These were the employees they were pilfering from.

When Woodrow Stamping Plant needed the Brownstown files, they would send for them or pick them up. The files would stay in Nurse Tootie's office until they were returned back to the Brownstown location. They were very careful not to get the files mixed up. I don't know what the Union used their set of records for, but they had a set too. They may have used their files as ghost accounts at another plant, but there was no reason they should've had access to that kind of personal information.

The Medical Department knew Dr. Butt was taking the EMG. Dr. Butt knew through his testing there was something seriously wrong with me that would take more than aspirin to relieve the pain. The Medical Department also knew, but appeared to give less than a damn. The Medical Department had the x-rays of my back verifying my condition. The people who called themselves doctors and nurses needed their medical licenses revoked. Dr. Straw, Dr. Butt, and Nurse Tootie, all were incompetent. Looking at the manner in which they were practicing medicine, they all should have been fired.

In January 2000, Metro Craft Insurance Company sent me to their doctor for an evaluation. This doctor found problems with my back and other parts of my body that Dr. Butt didn't find. The testing was given just two weeks from Dr. Black's determination, but the findings were like night and day. I didn't tell the Medical Department about the second test results at that time. Woodrow Stamping Plant and Metro Craft Insurance Company were supposed to be working for the same company. Woodrow Stamping Plant needed to be held accountable for the corruption they were always partaking in …"

Dr. Black and his report were somehow deleted from the original manuscript and I can't tell anyone how much information was deleted from this book. This may have been the reason Part I was doubled space in order for me not to know exactly how much was missing from my book. I would not have never known the information was missing until this last transcript I sent to the company I'm now publishing with. It seemed to have a few paragraph not published the last transcript that put on disk because the publishing had kept my manuscript for such a long period of time. I read the manuscript and made mention to the Attorney General and the Governor and those two were not in the final proof. The State Senator was left to mention.

This was the time that the Mayor of the City of Detroit lost his Whistle Blowers lawsuit for which two officers that were terminated for investigating a party at the Mayor Mansion. I added a paragraph on how Andrea and I were treated similar to those two police officers. The original man Mr. Wilson who was assigned to my book who edited my book was no longer with the company. I was given Mr. Almost as my new contact person when he notified me by e-mail stating that he would be my new contact person handling my manuscript. I informed him that the original transcript I sent don't use, use the new transcript. When I spoke to Mr. Almost we went over the work count which to use. The transcript that was to have been used was 209.010 word counts and he could have not used that transcript because the added edits were not placed in my proof. So I assumed the transcripts were mixed up.

When I received my proof I know there were a few thing that I had added, but I assumed that the transcript must have gotten mixed up, and they used not the last transcript that I requested him to use but the first one sent. I recommended that Mr. Almost use the last transcript with the work counts at 209.010 because the book had not been in production. That paragraph being missing from the proof stated my searching for information I thought I put in the book that I couldn't find. I had many issue with the back cover of the book because I was given by Mr. Wilson the black space on the back cover to be 2.3"x by 6 inches, which was to big and they want to send my book into production they were aware that the box was too large, so I had my designer to correct the size of the box. Mr. Wilson sent me an e-mail on September 24, 2007stating:

"The design team is currently working on the cover design for your book. We found the back cover graphic (300TIFF Format 8.5x11 Back.tiff) did not leave enough space for the bar code, price, or iUniverse logo. We can overlay the bar code, price, and iUniverse logo, but part of the back cover graphic will be covered. If you do not mind covering the graphic in the lower portion of the back cover, please notify Author Services authorservices@iuniverse.com or your PSA as soon as possible."

After I gave my designer the numbers that iUniverse wanted she asked how big was the iUniverse logo for such a large box for a small book. The size of the box was so big that I took a great portion of the back cover, and it took a great deal of white space that was left that made the book very unattractive. They didn't need a block that large I simply couldn't leave that box at the size that they wanted.

I'm not sure if my computer was hacked and information taken from there because while working on the book, I didn't shut down my computer so I would know what I was working on and I could start from there. I later noticed that much information was missing information. The information that was omitted went unnoticed, until I accessed information from an old computer when I first started writing my book.

It seems that all the notes and letters were taken out of the book that was incrimination to the company and union. I won't be able to exactly know all that was taken out because after I changed computer, I couldn't find some of the letters that were sent to the company CEO's, and the Union's CEO's and doctors reports including the one from Dr. Black who was a company doctor that disagreed with Dr. Butt findings.

I first thought that I had put the information in Part II because I had many characters names in my book of characters who I couldn't account for. The chapter's No Reason of a Grievance, They weren't very sympathetic and Department of Civil Rights was deleted from Part I. There were people and events mention in the book, in various chapters that were deleted. This book has been through many hands and I don't' know where the information was missing or deleted. I'm very glad that I didn't get rid of the old computer.

After carefully reviewing the information I found in the old computer there information that was taken out of Part I of Somewhere Hidden the Cracks. I have only returned three chapters in part I and placed them in back of the chapter where it belonged, instead of inserting the information where it was intended.

".… I can't express what a rude awakening I received from Woodrow Stamping Plant. I would have never thought that I would be harassed or denied medical treatment. I left with no other option than to go to the emergency room for help. This happened on three occasions January 5, 2000, February 7, 2000, March 22, 2002 and April 19, 2000. Woodrow Stamping Plant taught me not to trust anyone with my life and health but myself. Others didn't seem to care about my medical condition. Oops, I forgot! I'm a minority. I bet if the tables were turned, they wouldn't be so happy.

Woodrow Stamping Plant and Local 783 were able to run this scheme after an employee was put on a 'no work available' and was out on medical leave for six months or more. The employees were required to file for Social Security. Many times the company would even help them obtain their Social Security benefits. The company would evaluate the employee after being off on medical leave for a year or more. The insurance company would pay the 'sick & accident' benefits. (In my case, it was Metro Craft who took a great part in this scheme.) Metro Craft had special people to handle the claim of those employees on long-term medical leaves at Woodrow Stamping Plant. If you'd call to inquire about your claim, Metro Craft would tell you whose handling your claim personally. They actually didn't have anyone handling those claims. I'm not sure if long term medical leaves were coded or not, but they didn't have just anybody handling those claims.

Woodrow Stamping Plant had employees on payroll that were not working in the plant. When they returned, that same employee would be put on medical leave and Woodrow Stamping Plant would receive those benefits. That was when the money was being transferred into the special accounts. The company doctor evaluated the employees, and at the employees' retirement, the doctor would find the employees weren't totally disabled. If Woodrow Stamping Plant was unable to find work for the employee after the evaluation from the Retirement Board, they had no other recourse but to retire that employee.

Woodrow Stamping Plant received a copy of the report that had all patient/employee information. They set up separate accounts to electronically receive deposits of the retirement money each month. This was how a person could be retired and not be aware of this fact. I don't know how many people they treated in this manner, but I personally knew of quite a few. This was how Woodrow Stamping Plant and Local 783 worked in unison to take employees' money.

I wrote this book for employees who have been treated like Andrea, Linda, Mazzie, and I—and also for those who weren't able to express the wrongful treatment they too received. This book is for those employees who fought hard for fairness in an effort to gain what belonged to them. For we did nothing but come to work and do the job we were paid to do. When we were injured on the job, Woodrow Stamping Plant should have been responsible for the injuries sustained. Not paying employees Worker's Compensation, and leaving them to survive on Social Security and living under the poverty level, should not be acceptable.

39

CRISTA'S FINAL MEDICAL LEAVE

I guess the Medical Department called my treating physician, Dr. Sonia, and began harassing her by interfering with my medical treatment. She seemed to be expecting me on my last day of work before my final medical leave. I informed her that management had became angry with me, put me back on the assembly line, and that my back was causing me much pain in May 2002. While Dr. Sonia was examining my hands and arms, I told her I was there for my back this time.

Dr. Sonia said, "I heard you were hanging out in the break-room". I didn't come to see her for small talk since I was truly in pain. She could have only heard that information from someone in the Medical Department, and it wasn't true. I was fuming with anger because my being in the break room had nothing to do with my being in her office. I told her I didn't have the privilege to hang out in the break-room, but the Caucasians did. Woodrow Stamping Plant's management had me where they could see me at all times. If they couldn't pinpoint my whereabouts, they would come looking for me until they found me. I was told I had to be where I could be found. I wasn't even allowed to talk to other co-workers on the line. I was so angry with my doctor because she was hired to work for *me*. I was paying her to protect the best interest of my body. When she stopped working in my best interest and started working for Woodrow Stamping Plant, it was time for us to part.

I'm a person with character and integrity and I expect others to treat me with those standards. I decided not to see Dr. Sonia any longer because she began communicating with Woodrow Stamping Plant. As far as I was concerned, she was a trader. One thing I learned was these people stuck together as an entity. If an employee did something unbecoming, the word would spread all over the plant so all of supervision would become involved in the employee's punishment.

This happened to me in 2000 when I wrote the article for the union newspaper on safety. I was punished since a supervisor got in trouble because of my article. Everything I said in the article was true. This was the reason the supervisor got into trouble. I should have not been penalized when safety was supposed to be thrived upon. Safety in the plant was one big lie because they thrived only on the dollar signs. Woodrow Stamping Plant decided to get back at me with the help of lower management. The supervisors were on the lookout, if I was working in their department. This meant I was to suffer on whatever job I worked on.

A perfect example is when I tried working on the fender line. When I began having difficulty placing the parts in designated stacks, I told the supervisor I needed to go to the Medical Department because I was having pain in my hands and shoulders. He would not allow me to go so I turned the line off for safety reasons. Management didn't care if the destruction they were doing to my body was causing medical problems for me. The only thing on their minds was getting even with me. This plant had that much control over employees and many were frightened.

The supervisor wasn't very happy for what I had done. I had to turn the line off because the conveyor belt was too high for me and I could no longer stack the part. The parts were sharp enough to cut my neck off if they weren't handled properly. I couldn't do the job because my safety was jeopardized as well as the safety of my co-workers. When I went to the Committee Room upstairs that day, I could find no union representation. That meant I was in "TROUBLE". The union office was completely deserted. Therefore I went to the Production Office in the Team Office on the mezzanine and contacted Toby, a union member in an appointed position given by Local 783. I explained what happened and he called Labor Relations. Somehow they were already informed of what happened. The following day I contacted Paul Nashing, Local 783 Committeeman for the Assembly Side of the plant, to represent me when I went to Labor Relations.

I found out at the meeting in Labor Relations that the action displayed was planned. The supervisor took part in retaliation as payback. A gentleman at the meeting in Labor Relations asked me to dismiss the incident as a misunderstanding. I told him I could not because the incident was highly unethical. As a result, I was paid for the remainder of the day when I was originally sent home without pay. All who participated in this incident should have been fired on the spot, but as I said before management always stuck together—right or wrong. This plant believed in getting even with anyone that defied them. I always had faith justice would prevail, but I found out there was no such thing as justice. They broke every law with regards to the contract and labor laws, not to mention civil rights laws as well. Justice was for the people who could pay enough money to by-pass the laws like in the case of Famous Parts Company—Woodrow Stamping Plant.

I tried to press charges against Plant Chairman, Tom Hemp, and his sidekick Al Snake, who was a Representative of the Mid-Level of the Executive Branch of the Union. This was the first time my grievance actually went to the Public Review Board, so at this point Woodrow Stamping Plant and Local 783 had been lying to me for years. Everybody lied to me including the lawyer who was supposed to have been representing me when he failed to file my lawsuit in the court after I received a 90-day 'right to sue' letter. I knew the grievance I filed against the company in 1993 never went to the Public Review Board. They all lied and of course, again there was no paper trail acknowledging my grievance had been there. Local 783 was so full of lies and cover-ups that there was no chance of fairness. Tom Hemp and Al Snake worked to solve my grievance in the best interest of the company—plain and simple.

My restrictions at the time were: no pushing and/or pulling with both hands and wrists, no repetitive bending or twisting, and I was to wear braces on both hands while on the job. Woodrow Stamping put me on a job violating all my restrictions, which sent me out of the plant never to return again. They actually assigned me to a job where I had to put parts in a machine allowing my braces to get stuck. My supervisor became angry because my braces wouldn't fit in the machine correctly. I was eventually put back on the assembly line.

One of the salvage repairmen in my area had heard I was causing trouble again. He said, "Crista are you causing trouble again?" I really didn't know what he was talking about and I said, "I never caused anyone any trouble". He stated he heard someone was planning something to get back at me. It must have been about an hour later the Plant Superintendent, Mr. Dickey, who was also Black, came up to me. He asked me what my restrictions were and I told him. He then went to the Medical Department, came back, and said he had a job for me.

I had the option to be an inspector or work two other jobs offered on one of the main lines in Department #92 near the front door. When he returned from the Medical Department, I was told to work the job on the main line until the doctor came to evaluate the other job. The job was against my restriction, but I worked it anyway. A few days later the Plant Superintendent, Mr. Dickey, asked me to lift a rail-bar weighing at least forty-five pounds. I told him I could not pick up the rail because it was too heavy. Mr. Dickey told me I had to pick up this rail, but Tembro, my Supervisor wanted me to know it wasn't his idea.

When I went to the Medical Department, I asked why the doctor didn't come to evaluate the job I was to be working. I told the nurse in the Medical Department the jobs were against my restrictions. The nurse said they knew nothing about the doctor being requested to evaluate a job. I called my personal doctor because when I left out of the plant that 21st day of May, I needed to see a doctor very soon. When I called my doctor, I was given an appointment for the next week. I didn't think I could wait until the next week so Dr. Sonia made time to see me the following day.

On the day of the appointment my hands weren't the problem. My back was hurting so bad I didn't know if I could make it home that evening from work. I would actually have cramps and muscle spasms while driving and would have to pull to the side of the road. There were times I would have to get out of the car to stretch and walk the spasms away. I thought I would never get home this particular evening because I had to stop so many times.

Soon after I went to Woodrow Stamping Plant's Medical Department, Nurse Tootie asked why I stopped seeing Dr. Sonia. I told her Dr. Sonia didn't want to treat me any longer. It was none of the Medical Department's business why I stopped seeing Dr. Sonia. After I left the Medical Department, I assumed Nurse Tootie contacted Dr. Sonia because I received phone calls from Dr. Sonia setting up appointments without conformation for me to come and see her. It was as though I had no control over who was treating me or why. I was determined that I was finished with her because I really felt she betrayed me for 'big businesses'. To hell with me! I walked into her office for my back and I left with a restriction for my hands. I was so fed up and in much pain. Tampering with my doctor/patient relationship somehow just added fuel to the fire between Woodrow Stamping Plant and me. They were furious with me since I refused to see Dr. Sonia any longer.

It wouldn't surprise me if the company is paying the union to take over the retirees benefit program in order to help justify why the union has files of hourly employees. The company continues to pay the retiree's medical benefits, so this won't cause uneasiness as to the files the union has in their possession. This goes for all of the 'big three'. I believe they are all doing the same thing that Woodrow Stamping Plant did for years. Of course this is my opinion.

The Union couldn't follow a simple grievance procedure, such as with Andrea and me. I'm sure there were others treated in this same manner. The union needed to stick with union business because they barely could take care of the grievance process & procedures. Why would they be handling the retiree's benefit program? From what I've seen and experienced, they never followed the grievance processes and/or procedures correctly, so why would anyone think they would be able to handle the retiree's benefits correctly?

From 1993 to at least 1997, Woodrow Stamping Plant received an honor of recognition for having the least number of injuries in the plant. I guess so—especially if Metro Craft was paying for the occupational injuries that occurred in the plant. This was because they weren't reporting injuries. Each time I saw the letter of recognition posted on the bulletin board, I always wondered how much they paid for that piece of paper. I felt they paid to keep the census down. Many injuries that occurred in the plant were always of a "personal nature". They supposedly had nothing to do with the company itself.

The Medical Department would attribute the occupational injuries to employees. The Medical Department tampered with my medical information and they also interfered with my doctor/patient relationships. Woodrow Stamping Plant called my doctors and told them how to treat me. My doctors were told to follow Woodrow Stamping's instructions. The Medical Department also tampered with Andrea's file changing her diagnosis <u>from</u>: (I) CTC Fibromyositis, (II) Reactive Depression, and (III) Lumbar Strain—<u>To</u>: Acute flare-up lumbar fibromyositis from a fall at home.

I was working on a line in the CT20 area on the Assembly Side of the plant. This Station #252 was the nut machine which welded nuts onto the part. The machine was broken and the repairman needed a part for the machine. The part was ordered for the machine's repair. Until they fixed my machine, I had to put the nuts on by hand. During one of those days, my finger became irritated and inflamed. My finger was sore to the touch and I went to the Medical Department after a day or so. The nurse in the Medical Department told me I had a cuticle infection. I told her I didn't have an infection and that I had a piece of steel in my finger. The doctor agreed along with the nurse, saying there wasn't any steel fragment in my finger. I told them of the job I was working and how I was putting the nuts on by hand. I asked Dr. Straw if he could guarantee me my cuticle was the problem and not a fragment of steel in my finger. He said he couldn't. You don't just get an infection in your cuticle. There has to be a cause.

I saw my primary physician. She drew the bruised blood out of my finger and gave me an antibiotic for the infection. After a few days the swelling went down. There was still a snag in my finger everything my finger touched, it snagged. Something was sticking out of my cuticle. I got a pair of tweezers and pulled a small piece of steel out of my finger. The small piece of steel fell from the tweezers as I reached for a piece of white paper to lay it on. My plan was to take the small piece of steel to the Medical Department and prove what they already knew but didn't say. There was no use trying to find the tiny piece of steel because it was the size of a needle's head. I knew the truth and I wanted to show Dr. Straw he and the nurse in the Medical Department were wrong. I really wanted to see the expression on their faces when I showed them I was telling the truth. When I talked to Dr. Straw, he knew I was no fool and he stated his points carefully when I asked questions. Sometimes he wouldn't even answer at all.

The Medical Department had their own schemes to obtain money illegally. When I went on medical leave, the doctor returned me back to work with restrictions in August 2002. After I returned from the Medical Department, Woodrow Stamping Plant put me on another 'no work available' that following September 2002. As I was on the 'no work available' I was put on the active employee log as though I was physically in the plant working. *I really didn't mean to go on to the extent I have thus far. There will be more detailed events regarding my experiences with the Medical Department in later chapters and in part two of this book.*

The company was not interested in their employees' well-being. No matter how they professed health and safety issues, that wasn't their main concern. Can you tell me why there was no informing the employees of their rights when injured on the job under the Workman's Compensation laws in the state of Michigan? I had a problem with the company's evasiveness. Employees needed to know which rules and regulations effected their situation regarding workplace injuries. When employees were injured on the job, the Medical Department would change their diagnoses. The Medical Department didn't inform employees they were to be compensated for lost work time after being injured on the job. They kept the money instead. If the money wasn't going to the employees, where was it going? This plant had a lucrative business of pilfering money from its own employees.

I overheard one of the nurses in the Medical Department tell someone injured on the job there was a stipulation stating if an employee makes too much money they're not eligible to receive Worker's Compensation benefits. I know it's not a logical statement to say the amount of money you make determines if you are entitled to receive Worker's Compensation. The company should have supplied literature properly informing an employee regarding being injured on the job. If you were injured on the job, just as long as it wasn't horseplay, the company's responsibility is to accommodate the employee according to the Worker's Compensation laws. If an employee's prior condition is aggravated by the work they're doing, then the company is responsible for re-aggravating that injury. That's the law appearing in the Worker's Compensation manual. Many employees didn't know this, which allowed Woodrow Stamping Plant to continue business as usual in pilfering money intended for employees suffering from occupational injuries.

40

ANDREA'S WORKING CONDITIONS

I have chosen to devote a significant portion of the remaining chapters to my dear friend and former co-worker, Andrea Smith. Andrea experienced the same harassment, retaliation, and other unfair treatment in which I experienced while working at Woodrow Stamping Plant. While Local 783 took part in, oppose to representing Andrea when she requested help. I personally believe Andrea's story deserves to be shared with the readers of this book because her voice deserves to be herd as well. I first thought Andrea's experiences were equivalent to my horrific treatment at the hands of Woodrow Stamping Plant and Local 783, which we both experienced. After evaluating the events that took place I have to admit Andrea's horrific treatment is an understatement in comparison. The treatment she received was much harsher then what I experienced.

I was not assaulted with a broom and I wasn't hit-by a hi-lo, during which time Andrea was forbidden to speak of neither incident to anyone in the plant. She was told by management both incidents never occurred. While at the same time they covered every trail that would lead up to these incidents ever occurring. Even though depositions were taken regarding these incidents, which were denied by Woodrow Stamping Plant. Local 783 was never questioned on any matter that occurred in this book they seemed to be the silent partner. The representative of Woodrow Stamping Plant continued to support that these incidents never happened and Local 783 sided with this denial. This was relayed to Andrea by the Detroit Branch of the Department of Civil Rights and they were aware of every aspect of what was going on at Woodrow Stamping Plant. While all this was happening Local 783 never lifted a finger to stop the rain of terror that was dispensed by Woodrow Stamping Plant.

After the incident with the hi-lo, Andrea was sent to the nearby hospital. She was treated and released but very shaken up by what occurred. At this point

Andrea was afraid for her life at Woodrow Stamping Plant. To me this was the most extreme hostel treatment I have ever seen or heard of. When Andrea sought help from anyone and everyone only to be harassed by the same company that she just filed a complaint against, only to receive more harsh treatment when she return from filing a complaint. If I had not seen for myself I would have never believed this kind of treatment would have occurred in the 20th Century. I would have not believed a company would be able to violate labor laws, contract laws and Civil laws at this magnitude that Andrea had received in the workplace. Everything they professed about safety and how this plant was a *no tolerance* plant was proven to be a lie. For the first time in my life I realized that we don't have any rights, when those who have money can pay to cover-up any unjust act such as this.

When this treatment was happening to Andrea she couldn't go anyplace to seek help because the company and union had deep pockets to buy and pay any-one who opposes them. They do whatever they can to change what someone has seen or to change their minds of having knowledge of, what they didn't want known, and it is soon forgotten. They wanted Andrea to quit because she was getting to close for comfort. When she found out through the Social Security Administration that the company she worked for had retired her. When Andrea started inquiring about this information they no longer wanted Andrea in the plant, so when she didn't take heed to the warning to quit they were forced to motivate her in doing so. She continued to withstand the harsh treatment because she didn't have much choice, she was forced to stay so ... Instead she would try to file grievances which she was aware that Local 783 would not file. She tried to file charge with the National Labor Relation Board but they wouldn't file any charges, against Local 783. Andrea also tried to file charges with the Department of civil Rights and they wouldn't file charges, then she filed charges with the Michigan Labor Department and they couldn't or wouldn't file charges against Woodrow Stamping Plant or Local 783 for breech of contract, civil, and labor laws violations.

Woodrow Stamping Plant and Local 783 only wanted Andrea to disappear and go away but each time they did something Andrea would file a complaint against Woodrow Stamping Plant, nothing would ever happen on a positive note. This went on until Andrea was terminated in February 2003. Andrea wasn't going to quit her job because the first question she would ask was who's going to hire me with my medical condition being so sever, not to mention that she was a walking medical bill. No company would hire her with all her pre exist-ing medical conditions because the insurance would soar at an astronomical rate.

When you get a job they want you to be healthy and Andrea was a long way from being healthy. For this reason Andrea had to stand her grounds because her life depended on what she was forced to do, to protect her job and her health benefits. In the meantime Woodrow Stamping Plant along with the help of Local 783 worked diligently by covering to eliminate all paperwork stating that both incidents with the broom and the hi-lo never happened.

I believe that Local 783 and Woodrow Stamping didn't start out to actually cause harm to Andrea but they desperately wanted her to quit and go away, so they could continue pilfering her Worker's Compensation and Retirement Benefit package. Things became quite difficult when Andrea would not quit. Andrea wasn't about to quit because her injuries and illness were brought on by Woodrow Stamping Plant in a conspiracy, by forcing her to work various jobs that were against her restrictions so … Woodrow Stamping Plant could send her out on a 'no work available' for a personal injury and make a profit from her injuries sustained in the plant. When at the same time they were aware that her injuries were occupational injuries. They had plans on pilfering her money that she should have received from weekly Worker's Compensation. Instead they decided to pilfer the money directed to Andrea for mere profit for the company. They started out with the Worker's Compensation and finished with the Retirement she was supposed to receive. Woodrow Stamping Plant made sure Andrea wouldn't receive any of the money that was directed to her for, the injuries sustained in Woodrow Stamping Plant while she was employed.

The Medical Department was aware that Andrea Medical condition was occupational because they took part in the deterioration of her body, by the jobs she was forced to work. There plan was inhumane by treating anyone in this barbaric manner that Famous Parts Company Woodrow Stamping Plant and Local 783 were sending Andrea through. I feel it was inhumane because working Andrea until sever pain emerges and when her medical condition was bad enough she could no longer work. They then continue to put Andrea on even more hard jobs making sure that there is no doubt that she would ever return back to work, once she's put on a 'no work available' their job was complete. When the money started to flow it was *smooth sailing* through the special account set up for this reason. This was done because Woodrow Stamping Plant and Local 783 had an ulterior motive to what they were doing. What they were doing was a well thought out plant to deceive Andrea and employees like her, of their Workers Compensation and Retirements Benefits. Once Andrea could no longer work the Medical Department put her on a Medical leave first which lasted over six months. The second time Andrea was put on a long term medical leave in hopes that she would never return. They have Andrea and employees like her on long term medical leave while Famous Parts Company Woodrow Stamping Plant received their entire benefit package. It's a case that they receive it all and you receive nothing.

Andrea never received any Worker's Compensation inside or outside of Woodrow Stamping Plant. They would see to that happening, because they were acting as though the Worker's Compensation belonged to them personally. So with the help and corporation of Andrea Attorneys that was representing her, they were compensated only when they make sure that Andrea received no money from her Worker's Compensation settlement. The attorney's for Andrea were paid well, and as a result she who was injured in the plant receives nothing at all. This is why Andrea Smith's Worker's Compensation case was never settled from 1995 until 2002. Woodrow Stamping Plant felt there was no rush because they were being paid and have been since 1995 with Andrea's money.

If Andrea would not have gotten an attorney to file Worker's Compensation Woodrow Stamping Plant would have been clear sailing with her money. Those employees like Andrea Smith and Linda Jackson who also filed Worker's Compensation claims against Famous Parts Company Woodrow Stamping Plant. They would keep the entire amount of Andrea's Worker's Compensation package that was granted by the Worker's Compensation Court. It didn't matter that she received not a dime. The Medical Department was aware that Andrea knew to file for Worker's Compensation if she didn't the odds of their receiving payment is zero to none. Well, she filed for Worker's Compensation and yet she never received a dime of her Worker's Compensation settlement and it's now been 12 years.

In Andrea's case they had a vendetta against her, evidently. The treatment she received from them showed that they were angry with her for some reason. They decided to retaliate against her only to make sure she would receive nothing, there wasn't any room for a fair compromise, when Andrea decided to cut her losses and get something rather then nothing. Famous Parts Company didn't want to do that but instead they wanted her to receive nothing and nothing is what she received. These are the employee's that's not going to be paid Worker's Compensation by the company because they were going to pilfer their money. Andrea was an exception to the rule knowing what she knew and yet she never received nothing was as far as I am concerned a vendetta.

Most cases if the employee's were aware they should be receiving Worker's Compensation the odds of receiving something from Worker's Compensation was much greater. Most of the time, it would be the least possible amount they thought they could get away with paying. Woodrow Stamping Plant wasn't and didn't inform other employees that they were to be compensated for their occupational injuries. Instead the Medical Department forced employees to believe that the company had nothing to do with their medical condition. They didn't divulge medical information and test results when seen by company doctors, regarding their medical condition unless the employee was forceful. The less the employee knew the more the Medical Department is going to pilfer from them. They really made employees think that their injuries were personal finding diagnosis that was similar to another diagnosis that was not work related, to the actual medical condition calling it a personal injury, instead of a occupational injury in order to pilfer their money. I myself was fooled by them at first, but later understood what they were doing in the Medical Department.

Woodrow Stamping Plant Medical Department was aware that they would have to give some employees, who were knowledgeable about Worker's Compensation, something. After everything is all said and done the employee that received payment through Worker's Compensation benefits. Woodrow Stamping Plant would turn around and make them pay the money back after the settlement was granted by the court. They would tell the employee that they received payment from Worker's Compensation and Metro Craft Sick & Accident payments provided by Famous Parts Company at the same time. While at the same time they were the ones who were pilfering the Worker's Compensation without the employee's knowledge. Woodrow Stamping Plant was going to make the employee who received payment under Worker's Compensation repay the money back long term.

From my experience I incurred an occupational injury with the company and I received a medical retirement from Famous Parts Company, for injuries sustained in the plant. Metro Craft was supposed to compensate me a certain amount of money per month that would accommodate a certain amount of my pay wages that is consistent with my retirement. This includes my social security disability and a monthly stipend from Metro Craft Insurance Company. Since I knew they were using the file that was for my personal injury. Instead of me receiving the monthly stipend Metro Craft is keeping that money. They continue to say that the amount of money I received is owed to them. For this reason, the amount of $534.99 is subtracted from my allowance each month for the said amount of overpayment I received from them. The way it is calculated when I am 62 I will have paid $32,301.00 and that is quite a profit for the company.

In my opinion those CEO's need to be paid less because it is the laborer who is actually doing the work and can't seem to be paid the money that should have been paid to them such as the Andrea Smith's and the Linda Jackson's.

Therefore I receive no money from Metro Craft each month, and they don't send me a monthly statement informing me how much I own each month nor do they send me a W2 form that I could claim the overpayment on my taxes each year. I can't even collect that money on my income taxes as overpayment. In essence I am not supposed to be paying this money back. I have written letters asking Famous Parts Company CEO, Michigan Bureau of Worker's Compensation, Famous Parts Company—Metro Craft Insurance Company, and the lawyer Mr. Stan Hess who handled my Worker's Compensation case. Stan Hess was the one that told me that I was paying Metro Craft Insurance Company for money received for Worker's Compensation. He said I received payment from both entities before I retired.

If I had been paid twice you better believe they would have caught that error long before I retired. If this kind of error wasn't caught it could bankrupt the company, but instead this gave Woodrow Stamping Plant the opportunity to keep this kind of money, knowing the Medical Department had more than one set of records on employees. They know they were taking employee's money keeping it for Famous Parts Company. If they didn't fix the error that occurred to me in 1990's when they found out that I was full time receiving part time pay per hour and the loss of all my benefit package. They were aware that they were pilfering from me, if not when they found the error they would have given my money back. I would not have had to file a grievance to get the money back because my employee's record stated I was full time. When they found the error they never corrected the error which lasted three years total. I was terminated when I transferred to Sarrow stamping Plant's process, when I was supposed to be a re-hire. Woodrow Stamping Plant pilfered my benefit package for all those years. I would always tell them errors don't last forever. Now I assume they used the same concept when pilfering money through the Worker's Compensation and Metro Craft Insurance Company.

All those who were involved should have seen a problem, with what's was going on so, if you are not part of the solution then you have to be part of the problem. This is why this pilfering has gotten so big that they just couldn't stop it at a moment notice because too many people are involved and too many organizations and agencies are involved so they just can't close shop and call it a day. If they are defrauding me then they are defrauding the Federal and State Government.

In my opinion I truly think that "God" has gotten tired of his children suffering from the hands of those who are ready and willing to pilfer from the ones that can least afford it.

It was Andrea and I who were the one who they were treated desperately and decided to fight back against all odds and we were able to put this whole pilfering scheme in perspective. It was the fact that when we had written to the heads of the company's to inform them of what has happened they would make changes and it was business as usual. They only put a band—aid on the problems because they were going to do nothing to stop the flow of money that was going to the company's bottom line. The mere fact that the Famous Parts Company's CEO's and the Union's CEO's never wanted to meet and discuss the problems we were facing, and to see what could be done to correct the problem. Again, I go back to the phrase if you are not part of the solution then you have to be part of the problem. They never wanted to know what I had to substantiate, what I said was the truth. Instead they stone-wall us and made it almost impossible to get this book to print. This is when Andrea and I know the company and the union was working together in there money laundering schemes and used a well thought out plan to defraud their own company and the State and Federal Government.

This organization is big and I really mean big when you can persuade the Michigan Supreme Court not to hear a case. It is big when no newspaper would carry the story. When you can't receive help in the State of Michigan or out of the State of Michigan that means that you are on to something that many people want to stay covered. If it stays covered then they continue business a usual and the ones that can least afford to loose, are the one's who's loosing.

Metro Craft is so bold and blatant that they won't even send me proof as to what would constitute that I have been paid twice, returned check stub or anything they have to prove that I cashed checks from Worker's Compensation during the same time I received Sick & Accident benefits. I doesn't matter after all my protesting that I didn't receive money from Worker's Compensation and money from Metro Craft Insurance Company at the same time. I don't care what they tell me because all they have ever done for me was to lie to me and pilfer my money, while there is nothing I can do about getting it back. This pilfering has been going on since I first hired with Famous Parts Company Woodrow Stamping Plant and I have never thus far found anyone that could help get my money back. Well, even if I have to re-pay the money back to Metro Craft Insurance for payment from Sick & accident overpayment I never received. This was a very elaborate scheme that the Medical Department had going on. According to them I won't finish paying this money back until I'm 62, and they will no longer have to pay me. I will be the official age to retire with my regular Social Security benefits, which was once called old age pension.

They will allow some employees like me to receive my retirement even if they turn around and take it back. Woodrow Stamping Plant was in a position to make a choice a choice of either take a chance to boost the money to their bottom line, or getting caught by allowing employees holding the bag as thought they were pilfering money, or they could take a chance of their whole scheme being revealed. I had already put the scheme out in the open when I contacted Robert Wart President and CEO of Famous Parts Company in 2002, and again in 2004. Woodrow Stamping Plant didn't want Andrea and me to put anymore facts together that would expose what was going on, in Woodrow Stamping Plant's Medical Department.

Some employee's like me are paying the money back long term. I was one of those employees that received something but nothing in comparison to what Famous Parts Company Woodrow Stamping Plant had been receiving back from me. This scheme was set up from another of the set of records which was from the personal injury where I received Metro Craft Sick and Accident payment. This made it look as though I had received Worker's Compensation and Sick & Accident benefits at the same time. Woodrow Stamping Plant was paying me Worker's Compensation that I had never received and I'm paying that money back as of this day, because I *double dipped* meaning that I was paid twice. This is the money Woodrow Stamping Plant pilfered from Andrea Smith, Linda Jackson, and me and others like us.

Andrea being on a medical disability was paid according to the files set up by the Woodrow Stamping Plant Medical Department, which they kept the file that showed Andrea received Worker's Compensation keeping that money for themselves. On the other set of files she would receive payment from Metro Craft Sick & Accident payments, she will be forced to pay the money back that she received because according to their records you were receiving Worker's Compensation at the same time you were receiving Sick & Accident and this was kind of like a no win situation.

Andrea was supposed to receive her Worker's Compensation and her retirement as well. Woodrow Stamping Plant reported that they paid Andrea weekly Worker's Compensation from the time her injuries became an occupational injuries. For this reason Andrea would receive nothing in the end. Although she was never given any monetary compensation from 1995 until thus far we're in January 2008.

If you know about Worker's Compensation they had a fight on their hands because they were going to fight to keep Andrea's money at any cost, this happened to others employees such as Linda Jackson. What reason would Andrea complain in Worker's Compensation Court if she was receiving payment? Woodrow Stamping Plant was stating that Andrea Smith was receiving her Worker's Compensation and her retirement too. If Andrea was receiving her Worker's Compensation for what reason would Andrea be appealing the fact that she never received anything, even though her settlement was decided in June 2002? There would be no way Andrea could bring her case to court if she was actually paid. Her claim had to have really looks as though Andrea was paid when she wasn't because Woodrow Stamping Plant records states she was being paid, so they needed her case thrown out of court or dismissed for this reason.

Woodrow Stamping Plant wasn't going to produce any records because they know what they did to Andrea's money and mine too. So why has it looked as though Andrea had been paid to those that they had pilfered from when Andrea say that she received nothing when they say she did. This kind of information could be verified but Woodrow Stamping Plant didn't want to be in the position that had to challenge anything. I can't see anyone challenging a court decision made by the courts if they had been paid by the company that employees them. Why would Andrea's be in court appearing the court's findings and claiming to the Worker's Compensation Court if she had received payment as Woodrow Stamping Plant states.

Woodrow Stamping Plant had employees on long term medical leave and they were receiving Worker's Compensation under an occupational injury and they also received their Retirement benefit. At the same time the employees are also retired from another set of record under a personal injury. The company has already retired them under the occupational injury. While the employee who is on long term medical leave receiving payment form Metro Craft Insurance Company for a personal injury, and the employee who is on the long term medical leave had no knowledge that he was retired. When the employees, who is on medical leave decides they want to take the buy-out. The employee has to come out of retirement before they could take the buy-out.

Now why would a person on long term medical leave come out of retirement for an occupational injury and opt to take the buy-out. If they were receiving payment from Metro Craft Insurance that was granted by Worker's Compensation, and retirement benefits and social security disability benefits. Why would a person opt to come out of retirement unless they were not receiving all that they should be receiving according to contract? I have heard when employee's who was on a long term medical leave, wanting to take the buy-out the company was offering employees. Some had to come out of retirement and then they would be able to file the appropriate paperwork to retire. Woodrow Stamping Plant's employee's had no knowledge that they were retired until they requested to take the company's buy-out.

Linda Jackson was one of those employees who would not be allowed to take the buy-out because her insurance she receives through Famous Parts Company part B is covered by Woodrow Stamping Plant. There would be a problem because Famous Parts Company is pilfering her Worker's Compensation and Retirement and if Linda Jackson would take the option if they were to allow her to have it. Woodrow Stamping Plant would loose money, unless they allowed her to retire on another set of records. I don't know if she had inquired about retiring yet but when I last spoke to her, she was planning to contact Local 783 to see, if they would allow her to take a but-out.

Logically speaking it wouldn't be feasible for an employee to take a buy-out when they are already retired. While receiving Worker's Compensation monthly benefits from Metro Craft Insurance Company, once a month and receiving their Medical Retirement package. What reason would that person want to take a company's buy-out that would be idiotic to say the least?

When Andrea filed her claim in the Worker's Compensation Court first in 1995 and that is where it stayed. Each lawyer she had sold her case to the highest bidder and the lawyers walk off with the money. While, Andrea was working in the plant she was injured while doing so. As it turns out everyone is paid for the exception of Andrea, when she was the one injured. No one is experiencing the pain she suffers from the injuries she sustained, while she lives only on the little money she receives from her social security because they pilfered their money.

If the Worker's Compensation Court settles a claim, Woodrow Stamping Plant is so greedy that a few months later after the employee's cases are completed. The employee receives a letter from Metro Craft Insurance Company stating that I have to pay the money back that I received from Metro Craft Insurance Company. They said I received through their Sick & Accident benefits that I never received before I received my Worker's Compensation Settlement. They turn right back around before the ink was dry on the paper before they start taking the money I receives through Worker's Compensation back. The employees are not going to challenge this information at first, because in my case I thought it was an error. Until, I spoke to Mr. Hess my attorney who worked on my Worker's Compensation case. I'm sure he knew what was going on and what

Famous Parts Company was doing. I know this because I sent Andrea to him to retain him as a lawyer and he refused to take her case.

Andrea was only receiving Sick & Accident benefits an since she was injured on the job she was entitled to receive weekly compensation benefits. So Andrea hired an attorney to obtain a settlement because she continued on medical leave and was never compensated through Workers Compensation for eight years before any decision was ever made on her behalf. The attorney's who were representing Andrea was being paid by Woodrow Stamping Plant. This was a very lucrative scam that they were involved in. The reason they were allowed to run this scam because Famous Parts Company insures themselves and those state regulator's who are suppose to oversee these private company's who insures themselves helped to defraud the company, because the way this scheme was set-up nobody benefitted by this scheme but Famous Parts Company Woodrow Stamping Plant.

The company helped to defraud its own company. Woodrow Stamping Plant benefitted by this scheme because it all added to the profit line of the company. Those who did so also benefitted at the expense of the injured employees without a second thought. They were the one's who suffered by the insurance regulators who had fallen asleep on the job or were willing to take part in this scheme to pilfer which is fraud by deception.

This group thieves is quite large and have been in existence for quite some time, my guess would be around twenty five years because of the participation of all entities involved. They have gotten so big with pay offs that they believe that this is normal procedure when it is not, they can pay anyone any price for what they want. This includes doctors, lawyers, Metro Craft Insurance Company CEO's for Famous Parts Company, judges, the union, directors of the National Labor Relation Board, the Directors of the Department of Civil Rights who were suppose to oversee Woodrow Stamping Plant and be the watch dog group or agencies that makes sure that people like Andrea is not taken advantage of in this manner.

The Department of Labor is supposed to come to the rescue when labor laws have been violated but that did not happen. The next step was to bring the complaint to our elected official or politician but that wasn't an option either. This is because they favored big business who can add money to their campaign fun's bottom line. It is sad when seeking out help you come across lawyer and/or attorneys and they tell you that Woodrow Stamping Plant—Famous Parts Company doesn't corporate, which means only one thing. That is that they don't think they can win in certain cases so they decline to take on Woodrow Stamping Plant when the lawyer asked where you work. We were told by them that this plant doesn't corporate. Woodrow Stamping Plant is aware that Andrea would ultimately submit to their will, by not being able to represent herself in a court of law, but she had no other choice other than to represent herself.

Woodrow Stamping Plant automatically wins when Andrea and others like her can't find an attorney because she is less likely to win, especially representing herself in her own case knowing nothing about the law. This is what Woodrow Stamping Plant and Local 783 counted on, but they had no idea that Andrea would represent herself so well. Famous Parts Company hired an outside law firm to handle their case against her. This is something that Andrea did when she couldn't receive counsel, but Andrea wasn't going to allow Woodrow Stamping Plant to get off that easy, so ultimately she represented her-self pro per. The case should have been if Andrea couldn't find counsel then the judge should have appointed her counsel. This is a right of a citizen of the United States that we be represented in a court of law to represent a claim. The Judge even took it upon himself to give her a bench trial although she asked for a trial by jury. I will go in more detail in Part II. Andrea couldn't do that because all the odds were stacked up against her and Woodrow Stamping Plant and Local 783 has enough clout that in the end they are going to win.

I met Andrea Smith between 1990 through 1993 but we normally kept our conversation at a minimum to the hellos and how are you feeling, it was simply small talk. When I returned in 1997 I didn't see her, until she returned it was 1999 when I spoke to her once again. I asked her how she was feeling and she replied that she had just returned back to work. She stated that she had been on medical leave since 1995. I would see Andrea working from time to time on the plant floor or walking very slowly as though she was having a very difficult time. From then I would see her working various jobs in the department. Andrea worked #318 right on the isle this is one of the lines I would see her working, as I passed by the job she was working. Andrea normally worked around the door line or some small jobs in that department. She would be working very slowly. One day I walked past the job she was working and I saw that she was having a very difficult time while working and she was in tears. I truly didn't know what she was experiencing and sometime she would say she was sick. I really felt sorry for her because she would always work as though she was in pain. There were other times I would see her in the plant, I would ask how she was feeling and she would respond she was fine and continued to work her job the best she could.

I tried not to ask too many question for fear of her telling me it was none of my business. So I would ask Andrea was there anything that I could do to help and she said no and slowly walked away as though she was having a hard time making it each day. I had not experienced any of what Andrea was experienced at the time. I really didn't understand until 1999 when I injured my back. I wondered why she was yet working in the plant in so much pain. She looked to be having a very difficult time every time I would see her. It was ironic that I didn't see Caucasians working in our condition.

It was in the early part of 2001 when I saw Andrea in my department and my Supervisor Tommy told Andrea to work with me for a few days. Andrea sometimes says that Tommy put her to work with me, because of the treatment she was receiving by Woodrow Stamping Plant. Tommy knew if anyone could help Andrea it was me because I wasn't afraid to challenge the things, Woodrow Stamping Plant and Local 783 did to me, he knew Andrea was receiving unjust treatment. He once went through a devastating time with Woodrow Stamping Plant before his heart attach, but they were treating her so bad he felt that I could help Andrea in some way.

He thought this because I was able to help him out of something and he felt that maybe, I could help Andrea in some way, according to Andrea. Andrea did question at first why Tommy put us to work together. He would tell Andrea, I want you to know that I had nothing to do with the unjust treatment that she sometimes received in his presents.

After he did this Andrea said at first she thought I was a spy with the company, and she didn't accept any help from me, she kept saying that I was too good to be true. She thought that she was the only one who Woodrow Stamping Plant was harassing, she told me. When we were working I would tell her of the experiences with Woodrow Stamping Plant, and how Local 783 was never of any help. She told me the union has never filed any grievance on her behalf. Andrea later told me that what I was saying and doing was authentic but she could trust no one because of the spies Woodrow Stamping Plant, had around the plant. Andrea thought I was seeking out information from her to go back to management to tell of what she said. Woodrow Stamping Plant had many spies working among each other and you never knew who you were talking to. So when speaking to others in the plant if you didn't want anything you said spread around the plant. It was always best to keep your mouth shut and stay to yourself.

While Andrea and I was working line #252 we were talking as we worked and I was telling her more of how I was being treated by Woodrow Stamping Plant and Local 783, allowed them to treat me in this manner. I told Andrea of the many times I tried to file grievances and complaints at the various government agencies and how everything that I did was all to no avail but I wasn't about to give up. Andrea in return told me of how she was working on a line and toxic chemical was left above her head and as the machine vibrated the bucket of cancer causing chemicals fell on her and she was drenched to the point that she had to go home shower and returned back to work.

Andrea told me she thought that she was the only one fighting Local 783 and Woodrow Stamping Plant. I in return told Andrea how Local 783 allowed Woodrow Stamping Plant to pilfer my money for three years saying, I was part time when I was full time. I explained how they treated me during this time. I explained to Andrea why I was treated in the manner that I was treated. I also told Andrea of the many correspondences, I sent to the CEO's of the Company and of the union with no results. I told Andrea I had written numerous correspondences to the senator and to anyone who would listen and no one listen or tried to help me. I told her that I had no plans to stop writing letter until someone took the time to listen to what I had to say. That never happened while I was employed at Woodrow Stamping Plant, soon after I retired I continued to write my side of the story on how I was treated and all of the organizations that was set up to help me turned their backs on me forcing me to drop charges, against the company or the union. They never once tried to investigate what was happening to me but they did know why. Looking back now with respect to what was happened to the both of us and every outside organization we contact or agencies did nothing to help, so the conspiracy was in effect going back to the early 1990 when I was hired.

I then asked Andrea to work with me in writing correspondence to the heads of the Company's CEO and the CEO'S of the Union to try to get some of our problems solve. I asked Andrea to come and joint me because I wasn't going to allow Woodrow Stamping Plant continue to treat me in the manner, which I had been treated and that I wasn't going to give up without a fight. I told Andrea if we worked together we could become a stronger entity together oppose to working separately doing the same things in order to receive just cause for a serious wrong that had been committed against me and at that point there was a serious wrong brought upon her too.

All this occurred for no other reason other then they were pilfering money from me and I was aware of it and I wanted it back and they refused. I left my job at the end of each day, going to the Medical Department for heat treatments before I left work. I gave Andrea my telephone number and asked her to call me and we can put our heads together in order to get someone to listen to the unjust treatment that we were receiving. I never received that call from Andrea and I continued writing letters on my own. I wasn't having much success because I really had no where to go for help because I had been there and done that without any results with the company and the Union. I wasn't about to give up and be defeated when I know that I was within my rights at least according to the union contract and the Michigan labor Laws which were being violated, and at the same time they were mistreating me. I really needed to re-group and think of something that I could do to get the company and union's attention.

It was in 2002 when I wrote a letter to the Washington Branch of the National Labor Relation Board in an appeal, I spoke of the pilfering in the Medical Department and it was March 9, 2003. When the Medical Department was raided and files and records were taken out of the plant. I was told that there were about 14 employees in the front offices that were arrested but only one or two people returned the others were gone for good. I was called into the Medical Department in February 2003 to bring a copy of my ID. I thought it was rather strange this was all they wanted and I had a current copy of my driver's license on record and they had a copy of my social security number and I wondered why, I was really called in the plant for this only. It could have been because Woodrow Stamping Plant though I was behind the investigation that was going on in the plant by the questions that Blare Underwood had asked, while I went to Labor Relation Department on that day.

As I walked in the Labor Relations Office I spoke do Blare Underwood who was a employee who was always working with either the union or the company but she hardly ever worked on the plant floor even thought she was an hourly employee. On this day when I went in the Labor Relations Office I really didn't see anyone there but Ms. Underwood, while she was making copies of my information. She turned and asked me did I have anything to do with the investigation going on, and I looked into her eyes and said. I hope and pray that all those thieves who were involved in the pilfering of money that was going on. I hope that the State Police come in the plant and hand cuff them all, and take them and haul them all off to jail and then turned around and walked out of the door of the Labor relation office. I made that statement but I had no idea at the time that this was really what was going to happen. I know that Blare Underwood went back and gave management the message that I gave to her about the investigation and what I was hoping for because they were so bold and blatant.

I had been on medical leave since September 2002, and they had no plans to bring me back from the 'no work available, medical leave no time soon. I didn't see Andrea in the plant and she hadn't called me. So I went on my way to business as usual going back home. I continue alone trying to find some kind of justice, which I didn't' see no where in sight. I only found doom and gloom, but I wasn't about to quit because that would mean that they win and they were wrong, just because I could not find no one to help me and it wasn't that I didn't have a valid complaint. I was in hopes that someone will hear me sooner or later and if I quit then everything I have fought for would have been done for nothing.

I was called back to the medical doctor for an evaluation and as I was leaving I went to the ladies rest room in the front of the building. Andrea was sitting there crying because she was so ill. I then asked again did she want to join forces with me in trying to uncover what Woodrow Stamping Plant and Local 783 were doing. I told her that we must start with a letter campaign but this time we would send our letters around the same time. She called and we discussed the how's and what's we were going to do regarding Woodrow Stamping Plant and the Medical Department. It seemed that the grievance hearing was where we first saw a little movement but that didn't last to long either. Andrea really realized that I was sincere in what I was doing and she was glad that I came into the restroom on that day. Andrea says that she just felt that we could help each other so when she called and we have been working for our cause every since. We also discussed going on a letter writing campaign. I was discussing on the many times I was denied seeing a doctor on the job for an occupation injury in a letter dated May 2002.

I had a hearing pending at the Regional 21A Office regarding the grievance filed in 2001 and how the grievance was handled by Tom Hemp and Al Snake. The grievance I filed L4521 was for, when I was written up in June 2001 for in subornation when I took a piece of paper out of the hands of Allen Red. Since Mr. Red refused to give me the copy of the medical document regarding my medical diagnosis from the company doctor in the Medical Department. He told me since my medical condition was personal I could not see the information. They had already settled this grievance without my knowledge but they continue to lie to me. This was the grievance that disappeared somehow when I brought charges against the Plant Chairman and the Regional 21A Director. I meant what I said and I was going after Tom Hemp and Al Snake with their thieving behinds. I was very unhappy and dissatisfied with how they handled grievance number L4521 and wanted someone to be responsible. I went directly to Tom Hemp and Al Snake because those were the ones who had the authority to deceive me in this manner, what they did could not have been done without the authority of these head Honcho's. I filed a complaint and Local 783 sent me a letter stating that they could handle one grievance at a time.

So they put the Article 33 against Tom Hemp and Al Snake grievance had to wait so it was put on hold. In the meantime Local 783 went back and reopened the grievance number L-2659 filed in 2000 against Woodrow Stamping Plant and the Medical Department. After everyone saw how unhappy I was with this grievance they never brought me back. I was put back on a 'no work available.' Through it all, it wasn't what Local 783 did to me it was how they did it seriously thinking that I was stuck on stupid and I didn't like it one bit. *They wanted to deal with me on a professional level, and I gave them the authority to do so, but when the heat was to hot in the oven they decided to get the hell out of Dodge.* The Executive Branch of the Union did everything they could to save Tom Hemp Job, anyone and everyone located at Local 783 wanted to get away from all the illegal activities that was going on at Woodrow Stamping Plant. So the Executive Branch of the Union shielded Tom Hemp especially when I filed the Article 33 against him and Al Snake. Woodrow Stamping Plant saw that I was really going after these two men so when I was put back out on medical leave on September 28, 2002 it was for me to never return.

I wanted Tom Hemp and Al Snake to take accountability because they mishandled my grievance and lied to me knowing the grievance was settled, and telling me that the grievance was yet in existence. Since Al Snake and Tom Hemp were in charge this could not have happened without their knowledge. I asked about the grievance filed in 2000 regarding the Medical Department and Woodrow Stamping Plant, since my grievance was on hold in 2000 and now resurrected. I asked Andrea Smith and Linda Jackson to appear at the hearing to substantiate what I was saying was true regarding the Medical Department.

I met Linda Jackson in the Medical Department when I returned back to Woodrow Stamping Plant from medical leave. She was coming into the Medical Department to see the doctor. Linda Jackson and I worked some of the same jobs together when we were first hired at Woodrow Stamping Plant. She was telling me that she had been on Medical leave for a 'no work available' since 1997 and she stated that she wanted to return back to work. Linda Jackson didn't think that she could return. She was telling me of her medical nightmare at Woodrow Stamping and how she was treated. It seemed that there were a lot of employees who were having a medical nightmare. While there was nothing anyone could or would do to ease the pressure of these employees, who was treated unfairly. I told Linda that she could return back to work if she wrote a letter to the company and request that they work around her restrictions. *Since I know what I know I am willing to bet the Woodrow Stamping Plant is paying retirement payments to people who are deceased.*

This was something that Woodrow Stamping Plant didn't want to do because they were already pilfering Andrea money through Worker's Compensation and

Retirement. They did have another file on Andrea Smith and Linda Jackson too, so they had a plan when she returned. Their plan was to send her right back out of the plant. They were aware that if they didn't honor her restrictions that would send her packing never to return again. Andrea's body couldn't withstand the normal everyday workload. So this is exactly what they did. They brought her back on another set of records while continuing to receive her retirement, with her name on it but Linda Jackson only worked two days.

Actually this is what they had planed for Andrea but she put up a fight and caused them so many problems, they had to fire her under false circumstances which they knew was a lie. Since she didn't go on her own they had to use force physically and mentally and again there was nothing anyone could do because she was never to return back to Woodrow Stamping Plant and they made sure of that.

All that which was stated in the opinion order of Linda Jackson, she has never received a dime of her Worker's Compensation, during her employment nor did she receive any compensation after her opinion order from Worker's Compensation settlement was granted. So all this was a lie with the fraud that existed between Woodrow Stamping Plant and Local 783 leading all the way the company and union's headquarters. Since this was an occupational injury she should have received her retirement after four years of employment, instead her money was stolen. As of this day she only receives Social Security just as Andrea Smith is receiving. Linda Jackson sick and accident benefits ran out in 2003. In my opinion this is a crime against humanity when a company is allowed to pilfer money from employees in this manner. I do hope that Linda Jackson eventually receives what belongs to her because she has a right to received what the court ordered her to have and Famous Parts Company needs to be held accountable for what they have done to Andrea Smith, Linda Jackson, me and all the others that Woodrow Stamping was pilfering their money for mere profit.

Anyway Linda Jackson only worked two days because the Medical Department had her working without restrictions for those two days after she returned her hands had swollen twice the size of her normal hand size and on the second day she went back to her treating physician and he pulled her back out of work and he stated that she could never return back to Woodrow Stamping Plant. The Medical Department was aware of Linda Jackson's restrictions were and they didn't follow any of them. Linda Jackson Worker's Compensation findings were made and finalized and as a result she received no compensation at all.

The finding was in her favor and it was found that Famous Parts Company and Woodrow Stamping Plant did cause and aggravated her medical condition.

She too never received a dime and Woodrow Stamping Plant pilfered the money that should have been allocated to Linda Jackson in her report and she never received. That money should have been paid thirty day after the decision was made but the Lawyer that handled her case should be sued for making sure that his client Linda Jackson never received a dime that should have been paid to her. But instead Woodrow Stamping Plant—Famous Parts Company pilfered her money as they did many others employees who trusted their attorneys.

Actually Linda Jackson never did receive her Worker's Compensation nor did she receive her retirement but the company had diverted he money back to the company. Linda Jackson continues to complete a 5166 medical form every six months and she will never return back to work. She does receive her medical insurance paid by Woodrow Stamping Plant, so what is the purpose of this. She should be receiving her Worker's Compensation and her Retirement each month that is cruel an unusual punishment alone. Linda Jackson settlement in December 2002 and she never received any compensation for her occupational injuries according to Linda Jackson. Only to be left with is a broken down body and no compensation at all except for her social security monthly benefits. Local 783 allowed this to happen to the union members because they had a set of files and they could have been keeping the grievance settlements making sure that the grievance settlement never went to the person who the money was intended for, when they filed the grievances. Linda Jackson may not have had enough time to retire with 10 years of service but she had enough time to retire under Worker's Compensation, she would have received her Retirement under an occupational injury after four years of employment for the company.

Woodrow Stamping Plant Famous Parts Company didn't want Linda back in the plant just as they didn't want Andrea Smith back in the plant, because they were pilfering her retirement too. Through their Worker's Compensation weekly payments that as going into separate accounts set up by the controller and Woodrow Stamping Plant's Medical Department is the plant that all plants used to funnel money through.

There was something seriously wrong with what they were doing and every entity that was set up to help the employees from unfair labor practices, all those doors was closed. Employees who needed them were turned away while they all stood by. They all did nothing to help these employees, and they all were aware of what Famous Parts Company-Woodrow Stamping Plant was doing was wrong. There is one thing that I can contest to, which is that if those who took part in or turned their heads to what they saw, if the tables were turned and they themselves were put in the same situation. I would assure you they wouldn't like it at all. So why send other through something that you know you would not want to go through? In the Medical Department at Woodrow Stamping Plant, Department of civil Rights, the Equal Employment Opportunity Commission, and the National Labor Relation Board did nothing but force those employees to drop charges and they had it fixed that Woodrow Stamping and Local 783 both were assured that charges would not be brought against them. This tells me that there was a conspiracy against blacks and other minorities.

This money laundering scheme brought Famous Parts Company millions to the profit margin. This is one reason that these companies can over inflate their profitability and no one questions why. Famous Parts Company doesn't want the word discrimination used, so we won't use it, but it continue to be unfair labor practices against Black Women and other minority's with regards to violations of the labor and contract laws but it seemed that we were all the same color. As stated prior I know of 'no' Caucasians being treated in this manner and I won't use the word Discrimination because I read an article in the local newspaper last year so ..., I will honor the company's wishes out of Respect. So I will use the word SEGREGATION because they prefer us not to use the word DISCRIMI-NATION. I will bet that this same company rallied to get rid of the affirmative action laws in the state of Michigan. What does it matter who the company seg-regates against if the actions they are in compliance with discrimination because it's not equal with the majority and that is against the law. I wasn't aware of any Caucasian and there may have been some but I never saw any.

What the Medical Department and Local 783 would do is to keep the employee off work for the length of their seniority and tell that person that they received time for time for a personal injury. This simply means the employee has been off work on a personal medical leave for the equivalent of years of their seniority for an injury or illness. The only thing that the employee's is to receive is their Social Security. The employee receives nothing more from the company and as a result that employee's no longer has any job. It's hard to believe Famous Parts Company had someone that is on the inside the Social Security Administra-tion that would grant the employees Social Security Disability. They would receive nothing else from Famous Parts Company but the insurance, and no monetary payments from the company that caused her medical condition and she receives nothing.

Employees such as Linda Jackson and Andrea Smith really do have a legiti-mate disability and they are truly disabled but Famous Parts Company made sure that they did received their Social Security. Andrea treating doctor had her to file of Social Security Disability not Woodrow Stamping Plant and when Woodrow

Stamping Plant found this out they were outraged and I don't know for what, because that was all that Woodrow Stamping Plant—Famous Parts Company was going to receive this money only and it didn't matter what was allocated to them both. They were not going to receive any Worker's Compensation and retirement ever. This was what they were left with because the attorneys and/or lawyer helped Woodrow Stamping Plant keeps the money themselves, while Andrea Smith and Linda Jackson both brought there valid claims to the Worker's Compensation Court and received nothing.

Famous Parts Company—Woodrow Stamping Plant made mention around the plant the minorities mainly Blacks were lazy soles and that we wanted something for nothing. They were the ones taking and pilfering from the very one's that they said, we wanted something or nothing. As it stands now, who's keeping this money for themselves that they have pilfered from those same employees that it was meant for. They just wanted money and didn't was to work for it, and they were thinking that they were doing us a favor. They were taking our money and keeping it for themselves and saying that we were sue happy and didn't want to work. What makes Famous Farts Company so different then the common thief right off the street? This is their justification for pilfering money that belongs to someone else. If Linda Jackson and Andrea Smith sue under these circumstances, would they continue to say that they are sue happy and wanted something for nothing? Now I would like to know who wants something for nothing. I truly can't say it was the one Woodrow Stamping Plant was pilfering from for many years, because of how well the money launder scheme has worked. They had no fear of ever getting caught because they had all the area's covered.

I was beginning to see a pattern of abuse of the Medical Department and I was going to fight all the way if I had to. I have caused much disarray and we have been mistreated but in the end we all plan to win this include Andrea Smith. We all will win in the end but when you are fighting a giant such as Woodrow Stamping Plant—Famous Part's Company and Local 783 both the odds are very slim. Your situation is kind of like David and Gallia in the bible. Famous Parts is Gallia and Andrea and I am David. This is the reason I have written this book because Andrea Smith, Linda Jackson, and me all received unequal justice and I wanted not only my story told but I also wanted their stories told from their perspective. I was forced to write a book because I don't have a lot of money, nor do I have people in high places.

This is the only way that I could tell my story without any interruptions. I can say that they have hindered me in every way possible to keep my book from making a complete product. Information has been taken out of this Part I and the only way I can think this happened is through hacking my computer. I would always keep my computer at all times because it was easier to know what I was working on when I would quit for the evening. I no longer keep my computer on at all times any longer. All letters that were incriminating was taken out of this book but I will return them in Part II of this book. I wanted to tell my story the way things really happened with no interruptions and all those who took part in the money laundering schemes should all be held accountable for their activities because it was illegal and wrong. Even those employees who decided to retire because they too took part in the money laundering schemes by pilfering employees Worker's Compensation and Retirement. If you were aware of the money laundering scheme and did nothing or said nothing you are guilty by association. This was an elaborated scheme that was going on at Woodrow Stamping Plant with the help of Local 783 for decades. This includes the politician and local judges who sided with Famous Parts Company to keep this lucrative preferring scheme alive that they were running inside of Woodrow Stamping Plant.

I took bits of information supplied by Andrea Smith from letters she supplied me. Andrea's injury first started in December 1992. She explained what happened regarding her injuries firsthand, beginning while she was working on Line #318, a job women hardly ever worked.

On November 28, 1992 after approximately three weeks of working on jobs #318 and #307, Andrea started experiencing pain in her upper back and hands. Job #318 and #307 were one in the same, but the job had two positions a right-hand side and left-hand side. Andrea's pain became unbearable working this same job. She could no longer pick-up the parts. Andrea went down to Woodrow Stamping Plant's Medical Department to see the doctor. The nurse on duty examined her and the nurse in the Medical Department said she felt something in Andrea's back. She suggested Andrea see the company doctor, and as a result x-rays of her upper and lower back were taken. Andrea was then given pain pills and sent back to work.

The foreman tried to put Andrea back on the same job #318, but she told him the job was making her sick. Andrea continued to have pain working this job while taking painkillers. After her injury Joey Nick, her Supervisor, began shipping her out to other areas in the plant. She called Committeeman/Union Representative, Pike Pavis, and asked him if he could find her another job. There were a lot of workers with less seniority than she had who worked jobs not so hard on the body. Sometimes Andrea would work ten different jobs in one day. One time she just stood in one spot and laughed to keep from crying because of how she was being treated in one of the most demeaning manner. In January 1992,

Andrea started to feel stiffness in her neck. She would go to the Medical Department and get pills for what she thought was a cold. She thought it was the draft in the plant causing cold in her neck.

On November 28, 1992 Joey Nick took a young Caucasian man off his job and told Andrea to take the job on Line #318. She had to lift a heavy part with her left hand and use the weight on her left side to place the long part on the press. She had a partner assisting her on the opposite side. After working a day or two, Andrea asked her partner, Mike, if they could switch sides since his side was lighter. Mike told her no. Later that day another co-worker came and asked Mike to switch sides with Andrea, seeing that she was having great difficulty working this job. Again he said he was not going to do that because her side was too heavy. On another occasion Andrea asked another one of her co-workers, Willie, (*no affiliation with the hi-lo driver, William*) for the same favor. He too told Andrea he was not going to switch jobs with her.

One day when working on #318, Sam Daws, Andrea's Supervisor asked, "What's wrong Andrea?" in a teasing, whining, intimidating voice. This caused Andrea to explode with anger because he knew exactly what was wrong with her. When Andrea worked on a small job near #318, Sam Daws always came on her job to ask her out on dates or to visit her home. Sam Daws would tell my co-worker, Sylvia, he thought Andrea was finally "coming around", meaning she was willing to talk to him on a romantic level. Andrea was clearly not interested in talking to him on *any* level. All she wanted was to come to work and do her job. She didn't come to work looking for a husband or romance—especially with her supervisor. Joey Nick was normally Andrea's supervisor, but sometimes she worked for Sam Daws.

One day Andrea was on her way to the job Sam Daws has assigned her. It was in front of #318, but she believed it was Line #317, a smaller job. Joey Nick asked her where she was going and Andrea told him Sam Daws had sent her on a job. Joey asked Andrea, "Who's your Supervisor?" Andrea replied, "*You* Joey". Joey Nick said, "Then why are you going on that job?" He continued, "Now you know what it's like being caught in the middle". This meant Joey Nick was only doing as he was told. He claimed he felt caught in the middle (since he was told to put her on the hardest jobs). Joey Nick and Sam Daws laughed after Joey made that comment. This made Andrea feel less than a person, but it was nothing she could do.

41

ANDREA'S WORKER'S COMPENSATION DENIED

Andrea's Worker's Compensation claim had been in court since 1995. Her first injury was reported on December 3, 1992 with a sprained/strained upper and lower back. Her next injury was reported on November 28, 1994 and as a result of the first injury, a re-injury occurred on December 3, 1994. When she had her surgery she was yet employed at Woodrow Stamping Plant. According to Woodrow Stamping Plant's records there were restrictions that led up to the Carpal Tunnel surgery dated August 1, 1994.

This information came from Woodrow Stamping Plant's own medical records. I received other information and material directly from Andrea Smith. She felt Woodrow Stamping Plant and Local 783 had tormented her while everyone stood by and watched. What I mean by this is the organizations she went to for help left her to fend for herself with no job and no money. They also made sure all her avenues were sealed tight so she could receive no money or compensation for her injuries sustained in the plant.

This treatment was a forethought. They planned this type of harassment to see what it would accomplish. If you hide information on employees from their doctors and don't honor their doctor's restrictions, that is harassment. If the company makes that employee work outside of their restrictions, it is breaking the law whether it's for retaliatory or discriminatory purposes. This action falls under the category of discrimination under the Americans with Disabilities Act (ADA). Since Andrea was having trouble getting proper restrictions from the company's doctor, she proceeded to get restrictions from her own doctor. Her restriction read:

"No extreme lifting with elbow, no air tools should be used, no vibrating tools, limited and/or no squeezing of the right hand, and limited grasping and squeezing of left hand."

Woodrow Stamping Plant seemed not to have any record of Andrea's last injury on the job occurring June 26, 2002. This report stated a truck carrying a rack, bumped Andrea from behind. It was the pole end of the rack. According to Woodrow Stamping Plant, the hi-lo driver stated he did not see her behind his rack. The truck pushed her on the left side of her upper back while the truck moved away slowly. She did not fall down. Andrea was able to walk away but complained of pain in her neck, chest, upper arm, and lower back. The clinic admitted Andrea had a long history of low back pain. Andrea was transported to the area hospital. Andrea's clinical observation stated she was:

"… an obese female with no respiratory distress ambulating without difficulty. Hard c-collar in place 1-space, 1-posterior chest, 1-shoulder and 1-upper arm and lungs clear with equal bilateral neuro intact …"

The reason I'm making a point of all the details is because after all these years, in 2002 Andrea was denied Worker's Compensation. The findings show Andrea had Arthritis in her back and vertebrae. There were many issues regarding Andrea's Worker's Compensation case causing her not to be granted compensation for her occupational injury. Woodrow Stamping denied Andrea had ever been hit by the hi-lo. It seemed nothing was on record regarding the hi-lo hit. Why didn't the Medical Department address the hit? The Medical Department covered this incident up because it *was* done with intent. All Andrea had to do was prove to the courts the incident did happen, but Woodrow Stamping was making this hard for her.

Andrea's Worker's Compensation decision was reached by Referee Jackie Arnold. Andrea mentioned the truck hit in the records, but she was never compensated for it. The company denied they had anything to do with Andrea needing Carpal Tunnel surgery. With all her medical restrictions, how could Woodrow Stamping Plant deny Andrea compensation for her occupational injury? How could this incident be totally erased when it was a part of Andrea's medical deterioration brought by an occupational injury?

I had the pleasure of obtaining a copy of Dr. Thomas Right's report. He was a doctor who worked for Famous Parts Company—Woodrow Stamping Plant. But his report was overlooked and didn't give any credence to the outcome of

Andrea's Worker's Compensation decision. Andrea had been railroaded since the beginning of her Worker's Compensation case. Dr. Thomas Right's report on Andrea Smith was clear and credible, but was denied as evidence.

I'm bringing this information to the surface because all the information pertinent to Andrea's case was dismissed or denied. Even though all Andrea's medical bills were paid in 2002 by Worker's Compensation, she never received a dime on her claim. Andrea objected to the minute amount of money they were going to give her for eight years of waiting for her case to end. In their final decision, they ultimately denied her *any* Worker's Compensation disability benefits whatsoever.

Woodrow Stamping Plant sent Andrea to see Dr. Right in June 2002. The following report shows clearly that Woodrow Stamping was aware of Andrea's health complaints. Dr. Right, who saw and evaluated Andrea Smith in 1992, wrote the following letter when she was injured at Woodrow Stamping Plant. The date of injury on Andrea's report was January 10, 2002. I don't know all the medical terms, but I can name a few to assist with a better understanding of Andrea's condition. L= lumbar spine, C= cervical spine, T= theistic spine, and S= sacrum spine. The report stated:

"I had the opportunity today to do an independent medical re-evaluation on Andrea Smith. The history portion of this examination was again dictated directly in front of Ms. Smith and she had every opportunity to make any changes in the history that she saw fit.

As you know I originally saw Ms. Smith at your request October 30, 2001 in reference to a work injury dating back to approximately 1993. At that time I did an EMG and nerve conduction velocities of her bilateral upper extremities. This showed no evidence of radiculopathy, plexopathy, or mononeuropathy. I did send you a supplemental report November 29, 2001 after I reviewed further information on the patient.

I received reports including a CT report of the lumbar spine from September 12, 1997 from Botsford Hospital (Farmington, MI) and a bone scan from Harper Hospital (Detroit, MI) dated September 6, 1994. This report suggested arthritic change in her elbows and spine. I also reviewed a September 1, 1994 x-ray of the cervical spine. This showed hypertrophic spurring at C5-6 and minimal narrowing of the interspaces. I also reviewed a July 11, 1997 MRI of the cervical spine, which showed degenerative changes and osteophytic formation with minimal effacement of the-cal sac. I also reviewed a lumbar MRI done the same day. This was considered to be a limited study with no abnormalities seen. I did review an EMG test done by Dr. Cannon from August 15, 1997 which showed nerve rod compassion at C3 to T1 bilaterally as well as L5-S1 on the right. (*Dr. Cannon was an independent medical doctor that Woodrow Stamping Plant sent Andrea to see for an evaluation of her medical condition.*) There was also the suggestion of <u>severe carpal tunnel</u>-right greater than left.

At that time I requested to review the patient's films if they were available. I again saw this patient at the request of Woodrow Stamping Plant on January 14, 2002. At the time I did an EMG and nerve conduction velocities of the bilateral lower extremities. This showed no evidence of radiculopathy, plexopathy, or mononeuropathy. She had gone back to work without restrictions as of February 19, 2002 and was still working at the time I saw her without any restrictions. She stated it was difficult for her to drive to work because of her pain episodes.

At that time she told me she was having pain in the left knee. She told me this would occur on several occasions when she did some twisting. There was no swelling or trauma to the knee. She also had swelling in her right ankle although she had no trauma with that. She was still having pain in both arms, her low back, and both legs. We discussed this prior to her starting a job where she was working with the computer. When I last saw Ms. Smith in March 2002, she continued to treat with Dr. Cannon. She was taking Motrin, Flexeril, Prozac, and occasionally, Valium. She had taken Motrin several hours prior to my seeing her that day. At that time I felt she might have some degenerative changes in her knee. I did review x-rays of her left knee.

Since I have seen the patient last, she has continued to follow with Dr. Cannon. She has continued in therapy there going approximately once a week or as frequently as possible, although apparently she does not always get there. In therapy, she has hot packs to her neck, electro-muscular stimulation to her shoulder and low back, and hot packs to her low back. Exercises are not being done in therapy. She has had neither exercise in therapy nor any further testing since I saw her last.

<u>She is currently working without restrictions</u> although she has been on restrictions intermittently since I saw her last. She is currently doing a job involving sweeping. She is on her feet all day while doing this. She states she does not do much bending on the job. She does not do much lifting either. She is currently taking Prozac, Valium, Flexeril, and Restroil at bedtime, Motrin, and occasion-

ally, Tylenol #3. The patient's last Motrin was taken eight hours ago. Her last Valium was taken six hours ago. She has not taken any other medications today. The patient did work today leaving work after six hours today, so she could come here to see me. The patient states she has not done a lot of repetitive work lately. She has not used power tools for a year.

Currently the patient states that she has <u>pain in both hands more the left than right. The right hand goes numb intermittently which affects the entire hand.</u> The patient states the left hand also goes numb on occasions, although this is not as frequent or severe as the right. She also has complaints of pain in her bilateral lower legs. She states both legs swell and there is pain in the lower leg where they are swollen. The patient states all of her symptoms have gotten somewhat worse since I saw her last. She stated she is swelling more now than she used to. She states she has more stiffness in both hands and feet.

PAST MEDICAL HISTORY: The patient denies any significant changes in her medical history since I saw her last.
SOCIAL HISTORY: The patient denies any significant changes in her social history since I saw her last.
PHYSICAL EXAMINATION: The patient is a 45-year old, right-handed, Black female. She has a height of 5'-5" and she weighs more than 200 pounds. She appears to be awake, alert, and oriented to time, place, and person. Short-term memory, insight, and judgment appear to be intact.

I would suggest that she have a sit/stand option related to her left knee complaints although she has never had an injury to her left knee at work. Her swelling is certainly not work-related nor should it be considered disabling at this time. She does have symptoms, which may be consistent with a right Carpal Tunnel Syndrome. I do feel she could work with the right hand but would suggest against power tools or highly repetitive activities with the right hand. Again, I do not find this Carpal Tunnel problem to be work-related. I hope this helps you to understand this patient's status further. Thank you for allowing me to re-evaluate this patient." Dr. Right signed the letter.

I'm only using Andrea's entire report because it was a known fact Woodrow Stamping Plant was aware of her occupational injuries sustained which agitated her medical condition while working without restrictions. Andrea had to have surgery as a result of her Carpal Tunnel Syndrome when her left hand became worse, which was not only aggravated but *caused* by the job. If a person has Carpal Tunnel Syndrome, using their hands to work repetitive jobs would only aggravate the condition. This was according to one of the doctor's notes. Andrea's condition didn't mysteriously appear. She didn't have it when she was hired and now she has it. How do you think she acquired it? Do you think the job had no part of the demise of the tissues in her hands?

There were many injuries Woodrow Stamping stated were personal. The Medical Department refused to pay Andrea any Worker's Compensation from 1995 until present. Andrea's injuries go all the way back to December 1992. Her injuries have been on record and as of September 2006, she still had received no money when her doctors were even paid. Woodrow Stamping paid the referee with the help of the lawyers representing Famous Parts Company. This was in order for Woodrow to help extort money from Andrea.

After Andrea was denied Worker's Compensation, it didn't matter that the hi-lo hit her in the plant. Woodrow Stamping Plant tried to deny the incident ever happened. Andrea became very concerned about her Worker's Compensation and the lies and underhanded tactics used against her. Woodrow Stamping was planning on not giving Andrea Smith a dime. The same thing happened in Linda Jackson's case. These cases were too old, and questions would arise regarding what happened to the money the two women were to receive; when their retirements were pilfered from them without their knowledge? If Andrea were to receive the back money they were pilfering, someone in management would have to be held accountable. They wanted to pilfer money but they didn't want to get caught. These people were truly pathetic.

No one person ever wondered why Andrea's Worker's Compensation was settled and she never received any money for her work-related injury. This went as far back as 1991 and 1992. There were documents proving Andrea had degenerative changes in her upper and lower back. This was according to x-rays taken for Woodrow Stamping Plant at Midway Hospital in 1991 and 1992, as well as x-rays from her personal doctor. Did Woodrow Stamping Plant think Andrea's Arthritis came on its own? Did they think Andrea's body would work its own miracle and her medical condition would just go away? Everyone who suffers from Degenerative Joint Disease has the disease for life. Woodrow Stamping Plant's Medical Department allowed Andrea to work without restrictions which proves they were guilty of harassment and worsening her medical condition.

Why were these employees retired through Woodrow Stamping Plant and their Worker's Compensation was in the court for the period of 7-10 years. How could this happen and the employee never receive compensation? My theory is when Woodrow Stamping Plant put an employee on a 'no work available,' which had a serious medical condition they were setting the stage for their retirement. When their injury first occurs, Woodrow Stamping Plant keeps their Worker's Compensation benefits instead of passing the money to the injured employee who should've received the money. When the employee is put on a 'no work available', Woodrow Stamping starts their preparation for retirement.

The injured employee files for Worker's Compensation after obtaining a lawyer because their Worker's Compensation is denied by Woodrow Stamping Plant. Woodrow Stamping is aware their injury is occupational, therefore making a settlement on the Worker's Compensation claim. The only parties involved are Woodrow Stamping Plant, the employee's lawyer, and the judge hearing the case. A settlement is already made on the Worker's Compensation case, but the lawyer's responsibility is to make sure the employee never receives compensation and to make sure the case is never brought back to the court's attention. Lawyers do this by not returning the phone calls and by not informing, the client when a court date is on the docket, coming to court unprepared in hopes of getting the case thrown out of court, and by allowing the statue of limitations to run its course.

Woodrow Stamping Plant keeps the remaining settlement from the Worker's Compensation case, which should be paid by Woodrow Stamping Plant Worker's Compensation fund. The lawyers have to do whatever they can to make sure another decision isn't made on the case. When the settlement is made, the Retirement Board is notified and files are then put in place. The Medical Retirement is to follow the Worker's Compensation settlement, where Medicare pays a portion of the employee's medical coverage and the employer pays the remainder of the medical cost not covered by Medicare. The company also pays additional benefits (from Metro Craft Insurance Company) to make-up 100% of the employee's earnings. An employee has to have at least 4 years of employment with Famous Parts Company to receive a Medical Disability Retirement for an occupational injury. At this point Woodrow Stamping Plant acknowledges the occupational injury.

Worker's Compensation is to injury, as Social Security Disability benefits is to medical retirement. If employees are found to be disabled by definition and if the employer is not liable, then the employee can retire after 10 years with a medical disability. The employer would not have to contribute to the employee's disability. An employee can receive retirement benefits and Social Security. If not, the employee will receive Social Security Disability benefits only.

If the employee receives 'Part A' of Medicare, the company has the employee retired without their knowledge. If the employee is yet completing medical forms and only receiving Social Security, that employee has already received a settlement even though they never received payment from Worker's Compensation. Their settlement was pilfered.

Linda Jackson and Andrea Smith were both retired by Woodrow Stamping Plant. They were both retired when put on a 'no work available' (1997 for Linda Jackson & 1995 for Andrea Smith). Both women decided to hire lawyers to represent their claim because there was no question whether their injuries were occupational or not. But could it have been that a settlement was made on their claim without their knowledge? Could it have been that the lawyer and Woodrow Stamping Plant kept the money? Was it possible that Woodrow Stamping Plant paid the lawyer for his services?

It didn't make much sense for Famous Parts Company to pay an outside law firm to represent themselves in an effort that the Michigan Appellate Court and the Michigan Supreme Court wouldn't hear Andrea's case. If Woodrow Stamping Plant had both Linda Jackson and Andrea Smith retired, it only makes sense that their Worker's Compensation cases were settled. <u>Medical retirement is to occupational. But injury, as Worker's Compensation is to Social Security</u>. You have to have all these elements in order to have a medical retirement and/or medical disability. If you're retired without the employee's knowledge, chances are it would be because Woodrow Stamping Plant was pilfering the money allocated to Andrea's Smith and Linda Jackson.

This is why employees are told they have to pay money back to Metro Craft Insurance Company. After their Social Security is granted, it is said they were *"double-dipping"*. This is suggesting they were paid twice since the employees is credited as receiving both Worker's Compensation and Metro Craft Insurance. But in actuality, the employee never saw their Worker's Compensation. Woodrow Stamping Plant never paid the injured worker. Worker's Compensation kept that money by putting it in special accounts set up by the Controller. *Someone* had to pay the money back since the money was being paid out twice but not to the injured employee, but they had to pay it back just the same.

This is why Dr. Butt continued to say I didn't need restrictions. With restrictions, the company couldn't receive my Worker's Compensation. Therefore, my occupational injury became a personal injury which is not acceptable because their definition of personal injure wouldn't count. In reality if it is found that a medical condition is aggravated by the work the employee performs then the company is yet liable, but not in Woodrow Stamping Plant view. This means that you are going to receive nothing and it doesn't matter what the law says. Now if Dr. Butt gave me restrictions, I would receive Worker's Compensation for the occupational injury. This is the reason my occupational injury had to become personal. All they did was assist in aggravating the employees' injuries in order to get the employees out of the plant as fast as they could, so Woodrow Stamping Plant could collect from them. No lawyer could legitimately take the Worker's Compensation cases because the cases were already settled. After Woodrow Stamping Plant settles the employee case in the court there is nothing more left to settle and the employee is left with any compensation at all.

Andrea's disease has consumed all her main body functions where she no longer has a normal life. All these years of pain and suffering are by the hands of the thieves who left her with nothing. Woodrow Stamping Plant and Local 783 weren't satisfied with taking her money. They came back and took her job leaving her defenseless. When I was terminated unjustly by Woodrow Stamping Plant, I couldn't believe they had the audacity to pilfer my money for all those years with my knowledge. I wanted to keep my own money. They felt if *they* couldn't keep my money, then *I* surely wasn't going to keep the money either.

They pilfered money from employees hired during the 70's, who returned in 1988 through 1990, hiring them as new employees with new seniority. Something should have been done to protect those who Woodrow Stamping Plant pilfered from. Local 783 protected the thieves and helped them hide in their thief scheme. Outside entities such as the NLRB and the Labor Department all aided and abetted each other. They didn't care what happened to employees such as Andrea and me, who were traumatized by Famous Parts Company—Woodrow Stamping Plant. I'm sure if Woodrow Stamping Plant were treating employees in this manner, other plants were doing the same. Local 783 were no better than the Mafia or Al Capone's feisty gang. Both Woodrow Stamping Plant and Local 783 were crooks. They had no place for honesty.

42

ANDREA'S FIRING

Woodrow Stamping Plant fired Andrea Smith soon after the hi-lo truck hit her. A Caucasian worker had cursed her only one-week prior before he threw a broom and hit Andrea in the chest. There was no action taken by Woodrow Stamping Plant or Local 783. Woodrow Stamping Plant was supposedly a 'no tolerance' company. Andrea was hit with the broom and *she* was the one fired. Woodrow Stamping Plant swept these incidents underneath the rug as though they never happened.

Andrea couldn't get anyone to help her when she was fired. Not even Local 783 would help because they were involved in her firing. It was Local 783 who sent Andrea the letter when she was told not to return on company property. This was done upon the request of the Medical Department. She was forced to return with much skepticism. Both, the company doctor at Woodrow Stamping Plant and her treating physician agreed she should not be at work. Andrea was fired by a letter through the mail while she was on medical leave with major depression attributed to the treatment she received at Woodrow Stamping Plant. She was called to the Medical Department at Woodrow Stamping Plant with a premeditated plan of firing her. Andrea was afraid of returning back to the plant. Therefore she took her husband with her to the medical appointment. She asked Nurse Tootie, in the Medical Department, if her husband could go back to the examination room with her and Nurse Tootie said no.

There was supposed to have been a union representative to meet Andrea in the Medical Department when she arrived. This was needless because the union always sided with the Medical Department anyway. The union representative should have arrived as instructed by the Executive Branch of the Union's Office. Andrea had no idea while sitting in the Medical Department that she was being set up to be fired. The union would have been of no use to the union member seeking help.

Andrea was not a violent person. In fact she was very passive. You would have to wonder why Local 783 hadn't heard her grievance as of this date. Maybe they didn't know what to do with her. Woodrow Stamping didn't want her back but she too, kept sending letters to anyone who would listen to her cry for help. Unfortunately that was to no avail.

Woodrow Stamping felt time would prevail prior to Andrea's being injured on the job. They had to figure out what to do with her because they had already retired Andrea many years ago. They knew Andrea would be on medical leave again because all they had to do was not honor her medical restrictions. They were definitely going to send her back out of the plant on medical leave. Andrea suffered from Degenerative Joint Disease and her health problems were ongoing. Woodrow Stamping Plant's problems became out of their control when Andrea was injured. They were tying to fix the problem before more problems occurred. They felt no one would notice if Andrea was fired. She was officially retired already and her retirement was being diverted into the separate accounts. Woodrow Stamping Plant had already pilfered her Worker's Compensation money. They wouldn't have much to worry about if she were fired opposed to things surfacing and someone finding out about their schemes.

Woodrow Stamping and Local 783 had a lot at stake here and they felt they had to be very careful. One of the reasons they wanted to fire Andrea was because after returning from being injured in the plant, she asked for Worker's Compensation due to the hit by the truck. How can the plant compensate a person who is supposed to be retired for injuries sustained on the job? Andrea wasn't receiving her retirement money because the Controller was diverting it into Woodrow Stamping Plant's account set up to launder money. They just wanted Andrea to go away and leave them alone, but she wouldn't. Woodrow Stamping Plant was able to fix Andrea's Worker's Compensation where they didn't have to pay her, she was already a retired person already receiving benefits. How could Woodrow Stamping Plant and Local 783 explain Andrea's retirement being sent to a special account and the Retirement Board not being notified she'd returned to work?

I don't care how many courts Andrea entered, they didn't want to expose themselves. Woodrow Stamping Plant planned to manipulate the court system to make decisions in favor of Woodrow Stamping Plant. If this was done, they didn't have to pay Worker's Compensation to an already retired employee who should not have been working in the first place. They only brought Andrea back because the Social Security Administration told Andrea Woodrow Stamping Plant had her in the system as being retired. She was fired in February 2003. Here we were in September 2006, and Andrea is yet fired, out of work and living on Social Security benefits only.

Woodrow Stamping Plant and Local 783 violated the discrimination laws, which stated one couldn't be discriminated against because of race, religion, color, age, sex, sexual orientation, union activity, national origin, or disability. Woodrow Stamping and Local 783 condoned Andrea Smith's illegal termination. Andrea had not been off work for the period of 18 consecutive months before being evaluated again. The contract stated Famous Parts Company was to:

"… refrain from scheduling an employee for another (IME) Independent Medical Examination who has not filed a claim for 'sick & accident' benefits for a period of 18 consecutive months immediately prior to the disability absence".

Andrea went on medical leave on August 5, 2002 for major depression. The contract specifically stated all employees had to go through the proper procedures. According to the contract, that didn't happen. Why was Andrea singled out, when she was scheduled for another IME appointment just one month later. This was in violation of the contract between company and union. Woodrow Stamping Plant and Local 783 proved they were in control in whatever they did. They didn't have to be held accountable because they had the courts on their sides in making favorable decisions—even in Washington D.C. where all the appeals are made final.

Local 783 tried to hide the fact they didn't file Andrea's grievance. The company and union wanted Andrea to agree to a stipulation stating she was guilty of threatening the medical staff at Woodrow Stamping Plant. If Andrea would have agreed to the stipulation, she could have been fired at anytime without notice. She would be unable to file a grievance or question Local 783's and Woodrow Stamping Plant's tactics used. This would make her firing binding and as illegal as it was; they went that extra mile to have Andrea Smith agree to this stipulation. I truly don't know how Local 783 was allowed to draw up an agreement making it binding, while the agreement was against the union contract. I don't know how they got away with what they were doing, but they did.

Woodrow Stamping Plant used a waiver consistent with a person disciplined for using illegal contrabands. If a person is caught using drugs while at work or on company premises, they are usually terminated. There is a standard waiver that must be signed and agreed upon if the company and union agree to save the employee's job. The employee goes into a drug treatment facility and becomes drug-free. When the employee returns to work after becoming drug-free, the company can randomly call the employee into the Medical Department for drug testing. The employee will be terminated if illegal drugs are found in their system and there is nothing the union can do to save their job since they signed a waiver agreeing to become drug fee.

Woodrow Stamping Plant and Local 783 used this kind of waiver stating Andrea could not receive any assistance from the union once she returned back to work. They used this part of the drug-waiver and left out the part after "discharge" which states, "… as the result of a positive test for illegal drugs or unauthorized prescription drugs during a twelve-month period …" They made this grievance up just for her to have no access to protest the reasonableness of any penalty. This would leave an opening to discharge her at will. Again they could not follow the Union Collective Bargaining Agreement. They made up a new rule for her out of retaliation.

The purpose of this waiver was to enable them to terminate Andrea upon a positive drug test result. When she received a positive drug test after she returned, that would give them reason to terminate Andrea on the spot. Mind you the company was aware of Andrea taking psychotropic drugs for her depression, which would prove positive on a random drug test. They planned to leave out much of the information that would work in Andrea's favor. They did the same thing when they illegally put together this waiver. She wouldn't even be able to obtain union representative. These were some dirty and low-down people. When Larry Mean, Plant Chairman of Local 783 at the time, found out about Andrea's waiver, he didn't want to have anything to do with it. He knew it was wrong. He even told Andrea the waiver wasn't a stander waiver, but he wanted no part of it. They had every intention of calling Andrea for a random drug screening sometime during the 24-months so she would test positive.

This would be "reason" to terminate her for a just cause. If this happened, Local 783 *really* couldn't help her then. This is what Woodrow Stamping Plant and Local 783 had planned for Andrea Smith. She wouldn't corporate by signing the waiver. The wording stated she would have no access to the grievance procedure to protest the reasonableness of any penalty, including discharge as the result of a positive test for illegal drug or unauthorized prescription drugs during the 12-month period. The waiver should not have applied to her because it was for drug abusers. This was just another pre-meditated set-up to discharge Andrea.

Andrea wondered why she should agree to a lie just to get her job back and the only ones to gain by her decision would be the Executive Branch of the Company and the Union. If she did return, they were going to fire her just the same. If they terminated her unjustly once, what were the odds of them doing it again, especially since they felt she was a threat to them? Local 783 gave Andrea no other options, but she was still hopeful something would happen that would justify these actions. As a result of Andrea's unjust firing, many union members left their posts and retired. The President and CEO of the Executive Branch of the Company stepped down, allowing a temporary person to take over the daily operation of the company. He regained his position about a month later.

Nosy Nort was the Director at the Regional 21-A level of the union, which was part of the Executive Branch of the Union. He had strong ties with Local 783 and is currently speaking on behalf of Don Hangem, CEO of the Executive Branch, in newspaper articles and news conferences. Don Hangem was the silent one. Hangem was only there because the transition wasn't complete with him stepping down and the National Labor Relations Board in Washington decided to save his job. Some local news stations noted Nosy Nort as the new CEO of the Executive Branch of the Union. Although Don Hangem stepped down, he was voted to continue as the Executive Branch of the Union's CEO in July 2006. Mr. Hangem stepped down because of the investigation, while Andrea Smith had been trying to contact him regarding her Article 33 grievance. She requested help on two occasions and Don Hangem stated he never received the Article 33 until it was too late.

They didn't want anyone to know this information—especially Andrea. They didn't want her to know how much she accomplished when she asked the Washington Branch of the National Labor Relations Board to investigate, though they did reluctantly. Don Hangem was forbidden to conduct any union business until the investigation was over. This left him no other choice but to step down from his position and criminal enterprise that he was involved in. He had to take responsibility for stating he didn't get Andrea Smith's Article 33 in a timely manner regarding her firing.

When Andrea was asking Local 783 to pursue the Article 33 for her firing, she wanted them to investigate all lies told on her by Nurse Tootie and Dr. Slick. She wanted them to be held accountable for their involvement in her firing and in the trail of wrongdoings that followed. I can say Don Hangem, his secretary, and the other vice-presidents all retired because they knew what Woodrow Stamping Plant was doing when Don Hangem was indicted. Everyone involved became frightened after they suspected the lies they'd been telling regarding filing Andrea's grievance were going to be discovered. There was never a grievance filed and each time they tried to cover up what they did, the lies became totally out of control. The Executive Branch of the Union went back and pulled Nosy Nort of out of the woodworks because he was also tied into the thief schemes involving

Woodrow Stamping Plant and Local 783. He was aware the company was pilfering money from me dating back to 1993. I contacted him about Woodrow Stamping Plant's pilfering of money while he was Regional 21A Director, and he never responded.

Nosy Nort was appointed the President and CEO of the Executive Branch of the Union since he was already aware of the criminal enterprise, which had the last 5 out of the 8 union presidents under indictment. Nosy Nort, another criminal, was handed the post. What ever happened to voting for union representatives? I haven't heard of any union campaigned funds since Jimmy Hoffa? The unions don't campaign to elect any longer. They just remove one crook and put another in their place. Nosy Nort knew the ropes of all the illegal activities going on at Woodrow Stamping Plant and Local 783. They knew what they were doing when they appointed Nosy Nort. They wanted someone they could call to assist with the pilfering after the dust settled from the investigations.

Dr. Slick and Nurse Tootie were on staff at Woodrow Stamping Plant on the day Andrea was fired. They both asked Andrea a battery of questions while she was in the examination room. She was asked, "Do you have a gun and if not, do you know where you can get one?" I can only think they called Andrea into the Medical Department for harassment purposes. All her medical papers were in order and the company doctor had concurred with the same diagnosis as Andrea's personal physician. There was no need for Andrea to be called in the Medical Department on that day. They brought Andrea into the plant only to stage her termination and they knew this was wrong. Woodrow Stamping Plant and Local 783 brought Andrea back in the plant in a joint venture. They figured no one was going to find out what they were doing. They knew even if they were found out, there was nothing anyone could do about it. For this reason, they illegally terminated Andrea while she was on medical leave by bringing her into the plant to terminate her employment. They put her under so much pressure they expected some kind of reprisal or negative response. Lord knows when Andrea was hit with the hi-lo truck and when the Caucasian man threw a broom hitting her in the chest, it should have sent a red flag. All this was purposely done to Andrea to get her back out of the plant on medical leave. Since Andrea wouldn't quit on her own, they decided to expedite the matter and terminate her employment—even if it was illegal. It really didn't matter much because they did exactly what they wanted with the law on there side.

Since Andrea's firing, Woodrow Stamping Plant has kept all her money. Her retirement and her Worker's Compensation benefits are being directed into Woodrow Stamping's special accounts. The amount of Worker's Compensation she should have received would have been a durable amount of income per month for her occupational injury sustained at Woodrow Stamping Plant.

When Andrea was hit in the chest with the broom and when she was hit with the hi-lo, neither incident ever went noted as occurring. If Woodrow Stamping was up to any good, why did Andrea have such difficulty getting these incidents documented? The company wanted to act as though they never happened. They were punishing her as they did me. They weren't going to let a Black woman, fighting to survive in a highly discriminated environment, take them down. Woodrow Stamping Plant and Local 783 all the way to the top of the Executive Branch of the Company and Union were fighting against Andrea. Had Andrea and I been Caucasian, she would have found a lawyer someplace in the big city of Detroit. Instead she was *blackballed* or *red flagged*, causing the harassment to continue.

Andrea's response to Nurse Tootie and Dr. Slick was, "I'm not just going to let someone hurt me without defending myself. I'm not a violent person but if I felt someone was trying to hurt or harm me, I'd protect myself if necessary". Andrea has had Cancer-causing chemicals poured on her head. She has been hit by a hi-lo truck and by a broom in the chest. Nothing was ever done to the Caucasian men that hit her on the two separate occasions. Woodrow Stamping Plant turned around and made her work side-by-side of the same man. Andrea reported both incidents to Labor Relations. Andrea was so frightened that she called the union, whom she knew would be of no help. Not having much choice, frightened Andrea was driven to the point of panicking. Woodrow Stamping Plant and Local 783 were aware they put Andrea in a hostile working environment. At the time Andrea was willing to take any kind of help because she was desperate.

When Andrea's examination was complete with Woodrow Stamping's Medical Department, she was told to wait in the waiting room for release. Andrea had already completed an evaluation from her treating doctor and with Dr. Cho, the doctor Woodrow Stamping Plant sent her to see for an Independent Medical Examination. Both doctors agreed Andrea should not return back to work. So why was Andrea brought back in the plant for a medical examination? After her Q&A examination period was over, Andrea sat in the Medical Department's lobby for about half an hour before she was released. If Andrea were such a threat why would they have Andrea and her husband waiting to be released in the lobby? Why didn't the Medical Department call security to escort her off Woodrow Stamping Plant's property if she was such a threat? The Medial Department didn't call security because there *was* no threat.

Each time Andrea would complain to the Labor Department, National Labor Relations Board, and the Department of Civil Rights, the company would retaliate against her when she returned back to work. In October 2005, Local 783 said Andrea could come back to work under the condition she signed the waiver stating she could not file a complaint against Woodrow Stamping Plant and Local 783 for the period of one year. I would like to stress the grievance was settled in September 2005, but Andrea wasn't notified by certified mail when the grievance was settled as stated in accordance with the Constitution of the Union. The grievance was settled in September 2005 according to paperwork, so why wasn't Andrea notified until October 2005? That was unmistakably a violation against Andrea's union and civil rights. For a union to recommend that kind of sanction on another union member, it says to me they all need to give-up their union positions. The union representatives evidently didn't know the definition of union representation.

Andrea even filed an Article 33 under the Constitution of the Union with the CEO of the Executive Branch of the Union. Andrea hadn't received a response as of December 10, 2005. From February 2000 to December 2003 is a long time to be ignored by the Executive Branch of the Union. Her letter was sent in October 2005 through certified mail and was later faxed. She received no response from the Executive Branch of the Union. There was not even a letter of recognition as of September 2006. Andrea had all of her certified cards returned by the post office after the Executive Branch of the Union signed for her letters, but not one person ever asked Andrea questions as to what happened before, during, and after she was terminated.

There should have been an investigation at least according to contract, if there had been a violation of union contract laws. Those involved in the Article 33 should have been relieved of their duties until an investigation was complete. This did not happen and Andrea was a paying union member. She couldn't get anyone to represent her grievance regarding her termination within Local 783, not even the Executive Branch of the Union's CEO Office, who refused to help when she reached out for assistance. Her illegal firing had no merit but they were allowed to make it stick. When she started asking questions, she was terminated. If they wanted to get involved regarding the Article 33 at the Union's Executive Branch, they could have done so.

Andrea's grievance against Local 783 and its members seemed to be a conflict of interest with the Executive Branch of the Union. Andrea contacted the Executive Branch of the Union's CEO, Don Hangem. She still wasn't heard and no one stepped forward to help her with her Article 33. She also faxed her Article 33 grievance to every level of the Executive Branch of the Union. The union was clearly not representing Andrea because they were trying to cover their butts. The union had a binding contract with the employees but that didn't seem to be the case regarding Andrea's firing. For the union not to represent a union member is breech of contract. Of course in my opinion, the way Andrea and I had been treated was a modern-day lynching.

If Andrea had agreed to what the company wanted, she would have been on probation for one year for something she didn't do. They were forcing her to agree to this unfair stipulation. Woodrow Stamping Plant and Local 783 were so bold they didn't care about anything for the exception of saving *their* jobs. Local 783 decided to use Andrea's job as bait, forcing her to lie in poverty. They lied on her when she found out her retirement was being pilfered. This was a criminal offense. They decided "If we give her the job back, we can fire her at a later date". If they were bold enough to pilfer my money for three years and do nothing about it, I knew they were also bold enough to fabricate and pilfer Andrea's money too. Who was going to second-guess their decision? It's unimaginable how cruel people are to others while having no sympathy and focusing on their own criminal activity.

The letter said Andrea was guilty of her firing and the union would bring her back if she agreed to this lie. If Andrea would sign the 'page of guilt', as I call it, Woodrow Stamping Plant would clear their rusty butts of trouble. They wanted Andrea to experience pain and suffering, but didn't want to experience the same bad fate in getting caught for illegally firing Andrea. While they were in the driver's seat causing themselves problems, they became angry and blamed Andrea for putting them in a position too close for comfort. Those who participated ran scared because there were some who lost their jobs in this scheme of pilfering money in 2003. I can say there were many who played a part in the act of deception and I'm in hopes that "what goes around comes around". I hope they get a chance to experience what they did to Andrea, I and the others unable to challenge Woodrow Stamping Plant and Local 783.

They knew what they were doing was wrong and the union just stood by while the Medical Department was setting Andrea up to be fired. They thought it was better not to meet Andrea in the Medical Department on the day they should have been there representing her medical leave. Local 783, Woodrow Stamping Plant, and all who participated were just as guilty by them knowingly participating in the firing of Andrea Smith—innocent of the charges. If not, why wasn't she allowed to speak about the events leading up to her firing?

The way I see it, the people standing by and watching a crime being committed are just as guilty as the one who actually commits the crime. This rule should apply to those who turned their heads as though they didn't see what happened. It is inhumane for anyone to go through the unjust treatment Andrea Smith and I went through in our years of employment at Woodrow Stamping Plant. The judges and referees who sided with 'big business' needed to experience the same fate. I feel since they got away with that kind of treatment, they will be punished in other areas of their lives. I believe "you reap what you sow" in your lifetime, and not after you die.

I really have to make you aware of the pressures Woodrow Stamping and Local 783 put upon Andrea. What she experienced with Woodrow Stamping Plant sent her into a deeper depression. "When is the nightmare going to end", Andrea would ask? I guess they thought Andrea was stuck on stupid too. They thought if she became desperate enough, they would have her right where they wanted her. They knew she needed the money and her job. They knew she had no income with the exception of Social Security. They decided to dangle her job on a string as bait in hopes to get *them* off the hook. If they could get Andrea to agree to this stipulation, they would be vindicated for every illegal thing they did to her since her employment.

They weren't offering Andrea anything at all. They wanted to give her the opportunity to walk back in the doors of the plant, only to be fired once again. She was willing to go back to work even though her doctors advised against it. She suffered for years while Woodrow Stamping Plant played getting even. She was willing to return back to work, but she refused to sign their stipulations. There was no benefit of doubt by Local 783 for them to sit down at the table and discuss the grievance and its merits. Maybe a compromise could have been worked out. Since Andrea was unjustly terminated, she wanted every penny of her back pay but they weren't willing to pay for the unjustified termination. It seemed everyone was standing by yelling "Guilty!" in fear of putting their own jobs in jeopardy. Andrea had nothing to do with the scheme they thought up, but they were blaming Andrea for their bad fate. Andrea was the wrong person to be angry with.

Since Andrea didn't agree to their stipulation, she certainly didn't get her job back. Local 783 never once suggested going back to the table and negotiating or discussing the issue of her firing. Andrea has always asked to be involved in the grievance process and was denied her right to do so. I would think since Andrea's grievance was so harsh and severe, they would allow her participation step by step.

The Medical Department knew they lied on Andrea with the help of Local 783. Why were they having court without Andrea and not allowing her to defend herself? Everything was based on what someone else said, and not what Andrea said. The essence of it all was there was no concept of "innocent until proven guilty". If these entities had nothing to hide, I believe Andrea Smith would have been able to come to her own defense. Andrea was forced to defend herself in silence. Whatever the opponent said, was thought to be valid because there was no opposition. This is what was planned for every employee filing a grievance with merit.

I personally think the courts should stop the union procedures and allow employees to file lawsuits when there is a violation, because the union is so corrupt the grievance never makes it to completion. When valid claims were filed, the union fought so hard not to file the grievance due to cover-ups within the company. The union was the biggest culprit. Employees' complaints rarely made it in front of a judge or a jury. The union was corrupt, the lawyers were corrupt, and the judges were corrupt too. So where is it people can go when they have been treated like Andrea Smith and I?

Andrea asked Local 783 in a request to the Executive Branch of the Union, to follow the paper trial concerning the various stages her grievance went through. Why was it a problem for the union to show Andrea any paperwork in reference to her own grievance or the settlement offer discussed? Andrea wanted to know how they came about this settlement agreement or if the grievance had ever been negotiated on her behalf at all. It seemed as though there was no one representing her from the union, but that wasn't surprising. Andrea had to choose the better of two evils. If Andrea came back to work with no compensation or back pay for her illegal firing, she would come back paying a very high price. This grievance was two-sided and Andrea had nothing to do with either of the two sides. The sides were Woodrow Stamping Plant and Local 783. Andrea didn't have a choice or voice.

Andrea couldn't return back to work if she didn't sign a blackmailing affidavit—plain and simple. Why should she have to plead guilty for something she didn't do in an effort to keep her job? There would be no guarantee they wouldn't fire her once she returned. If she returned, she wouldn't have one leg to stand on. That's what they wanted. Andrea would not be able to complain of anything if she signed the 'letter of guilt—a stipulation for firing'. They should have paid her salary for the last three years because they owed her that much. I truly pray things go much better for Andrea than they have in the past. These thieves needed to be forced out in the open where they couldn't take advantage of anyone ever. Until this day, I have no sympathy for them because they helped none for us. I'm sure there were many others who were "innocent until proven guilty", but weren't treated as such.

Woodrow Stamping Plant and the Retirement Board went as far as hiring an outside attorney for me so they could get my Social Security. Woodrow Stamping Plant interfered in the process of my being denied Social Security before my retirement, so they could pilfer my retirement money before my retirement became official. They were successful for a short period of time. I had already been turned down and my case was being appealed. They assisted in getting my Social Security since they fixed it so I could not get an attorney on my own.

When they decided they didn't want me around any longer, they told me to tell the Retirement Board to help get my Social Security benefits. But until then I could not get a lawyer, not only pertaining to my Social Security but regarding anything relating to Woodrow Stamping Plant or Local 783. I was completely cut off from obtaining a lawyer. However, I was able to get an attorney regarding my medical retirement (for whatever reason). I can't believe I was able to obtain an attorney when I couldn't prior.

After our last day of court, my attorney told me to reapply for my retirement. It was just that simple when they wanted something done, it was done. I'm sure many of those aiding Woodrow Stamping Plant and Local 783 in their illegal scheme expected they would not be punished for their actions. There were a wide range of participants such as government officials, judges, and lawyers. There weren't enough prison cells for all those involved—but that's where they belonged.

The waiver Woodrow Stamping Plant wanted Andrea to sign was a set-up. It basically stated if Andrea walked back in the plant, they controlled her. They could hit her with a truck or pour chemicals on her all over her again. Andrea said she was "a slave at Woodrow Stamping Plant". She couldn't protect herself after all they had done to her. Andrea had no protection before. Can you imagine what she would have to endure if she signed that waiver?

It was clearly illegal and unrealistic not to mention Woodrow Stamping Plant was underpaying Andrea and ignoring her medical restrictions. Before she went on a medical leave, she had just started investigating the issues regarding her back pay, but they couldn't adjust her pay because she was retired. She wasn't making the same amount of money as her co-workers in the same classification. There was a difference between her check each week with one dependent and her co-workers' with the same number of dependents (about a hundred dollar difference).

She appealed the decision with the NLRB in Washington D.C. because the Local Branch of the NLRB sided with Local 783 regarding Andrea's unjust treatment. Andrea wasn't finished with the NLRB because she went back and filed another claim with them for violating her rights as a union member. In my view, Woodrow Stamping Plant and Local 783 held all the cards to her financial well-being. Woodrow Stamping Plant and Local 783 gave Andrea an ultimatum to either take the stipulations they gave her or leave them. Woodrow Stamping Plant wasn't going to budge on the matter until she pled guilty like they wanted. The Plant Chairman sent Andrea a letter by mail in November 2005 stating he had nothing to do with the decision or the outcome of her grievance regarding her firing.

The truth of the matter is Woodrow Stamping plant discriminated against her. They didn't want to give a Black person any compensation for discrimination. They often used ethnic intimidation towards Blacks. They were very good at Black on Black discrimination. The company often got management of Black ethnicity to discriminate against their own so it couldn't be called "discrimination". As you saw in previous chapters, it worked.

The perpetrators felt they shouldn't be punished or lose their jobs for what they did. They didn't feel Blacks or any minority should be compensated. A minority was less than a person to them. Some people allowed their superiority to give them the authority to think this. Woodrow Stamping Plant didn't pay claims to minorities for discrimination settlements. At one point they even gloated at the fact they had never been sued for discrimination or had to pay compensation for discrimination. It wasn't that they didn't discriminate. They just never had to pay on a discrimination claim. Woodrow Stamping Plant always made sure the discrimination claim never made it to court or in front of a jury. Blacks wouldn't receive any payment for wrongful discrimination or termination. Andrea and I fought for years in the court systems. We had to represent ourselves because we were unable to obtain an attorney. It's not that we weren't fighting the system. We just fell through the cracks of the system of bureaucracy.

The bluntness of discrimination was maintained with Caucasian employees not caring who knew how they felt. Working in two large companies, I saw immeasurable discrimination being displayed and nothing being done about it. Discrimination is a powerful word. If we're not careful, minorities will lose all civil rights our predecessors fought for gaining through the years. Discrimination can easily become as outright ruthless as it once was in the past. If the government agencies continue condoning the actions of these entities, minorities are in trouble.

If I walk into a company and the majority of management or employees are of one race, I would assume this company discriminated—no matter what they claimed. Detroit, Michigan and its metro vicinity hosts a large variety of minorities. These backgrounds vary from many parts of the country. There is no shortage of minorities. If I see a local company hiring just enough minorities to say they don't discriminate, this gives me a picture of what this company is *really* about. I would then assume the company is very selective in their hiring practices. When I see a rainbow of colors working together as a totality for a common goal, that's what I would call diverse.

By no means am I saying all Caucasians discriminate. Nor am I saying all large companies discriminate. I'm only speaking of those who practice discrimination and ignore looking at people for the qualifications they possess. How hard is it to treat others as you want to be treated? If we all practiced this, we would have a better environment in and outside of work. Everyone has a right to work and support his or her family without the added pressures Andrea and I faced.

43

WHAT'S WITH THESE LAWYERS

Andrea Smith was having many problems with her lawyers. It seemed each lawyer only represented corruption. She put her trust in two law firms before she started representing herself. Each lawyer she had only exploited her. Andrea's attorney, Mr. David Seamen, told her if she kept treating with Dr. Cannon he would have absorbed all the money from her Worker's Compensation settlement. This was the reason Andrea stopped treating with him for a while and started treating with Dr. Craft.

Mr. David Seamen had been to Worker's Compensation on several occasions representing Andrea and she was never informed of the hearing dates. She only knew of three dates while Mr. David Seamen had attended hearings on her behalf on numerous occasions. Mr. Seamen never gave Andrea Smith any updated information on the status regarding her case. It wasn't that Andrea wasn't contacting Mr. Seamen to inquire about her case. He didn't even return her telephone calls. There were no preparations or any efforts taken to make any type of settlement.

Attorney David Seamen sent Andrea a letter saying Famous Parts Company was offering her $1,500 dollars and that she could continue receiving her disability insurance. Andrea told Mr. Seamen she would not accept this amount of money because it was an unfair amount. After this conversation, he sent her a letter stating he needed a total of $1,500 dollars to obtain her medical records from all her doctors. When Mr. David Seamen took Andrea's case, it was on a contingency basis. Contingency means the lawyer takes the case on his own without any money down or up front fees. If and when a settlement is made, the lawyer will then be paid. He will take his commission and his expenses right off the top and you receive the remainder of the settlement. Andrea told Mr. Seamen she didn't have $1,500 dollars. She then sent Mr. David Seamen a letter telling him she was releasing him as her attorney.

Andrea then went to the offices of attorneys, Mr. Dumb Diddly and Mike Bully. Mr. Dumb Diddly accepted Andrea's case. She later contacted Worker's Compensation informing the court she had changed attorneys. This would give the new lawyer a chance to prepare for her case. Mr. Dumb Diddly contacted Mr. Seamen's office only to find out David Seamen showed up in court to represent Andrea even though she had fired him.

At that time Referee Jackie Arnold threw Andrea's case out of court. Andrea called Worker's Compensation and asked to speak to the referee's clerk. They wouldn't allow Andrea to talk to Jackie Arnold, who was hearing her case in chambers. Mr. Seamen had Andrea's case thrown out of court because he came to court unprepared and with no paperwork pertaining to Andrea's case. Andrea talked to the clerk and explained she had a new attorney.

Andrea went to the office of her new attorney, Mr. Dumb Diddly. He seemed to be a nice person and he assured Andrea it all was some kind of mix-up. Mr. Dumb Diddly told Andrea she could sue Mr. Seamen's office for his actions. Mr. Dumb Diddly would try getting her case re-instated. He did as promised and her case was reinstated. Andrea had been to Worker's Compensation twice since then but she had not seen anyone there representing her.

This was December 16, 1998 and they gave her a new date of March 1999. Andrea's new lawyer turned out to be as bad as the first. His firm literally did nothing and Andrea was forced to represent herself. Andrea ended up firing this last lawyer too. After Andrea started representing herself in court she found that she personally didn't receive a dime from her Worker's Compensation claim. But for some reason, all her medical bills were paid in 2002 and her Worker's Compensation claim was settled.

I read Jackie Arnold's denial from June 24, 2004. I could not understand how Jackie Arnold came to the conclusion that Famous Parts Company played no part in the demise of Andrea Smith's body. The evidence would have proven Woodrow Stamping Plant was guilty of causing Andrea's medical condition. They not only caused Andrea's medical condition. They also aggravated her condition by ignoring her restriction and denying she was hit by a hi-lo in the plant.

After reading Andrea's decision, I couldn't believe how someone could be so cruel. I went through a similar situation, but they finally got tired of me. For many years Local 783 and Woodrow Stamping Plant worked in unison. You will later find to what extent they went through to keep from paying Andrea Smith's and Linda Jackson's retirement and Worker's Compensation. If the company were blameless, why would they pay all of Andrea's lagging medical bills? Considering they were paid in full, I would assure you Andrea's condition was caused and aggravated by the jobs she worked in the plant. Andrea's decision read as follows:

"Petition filed April 29, 2002:

Plaintiff alleged a December 1993 work-related injury. Lifting heavy parts on machine she couldn't get a man to trade. The job was too hard. She had to use the left part of her body. Andrea's now suffers with problems with the left side of body. Her knee catches. Left arm goes out. Left leg and hand goes out too. Plaintiff also suffers from major depression …"

Jackie Arnold also stated Andrea's condition was caused by the harassment she received at work from being sick and having to work. Jackie Arnold acknowledged Andrea's medical condition. So why was her first Worker's Compensation decision settled without her knowledge and she received no Worker's Compensation? Andrea's case was first filed in the Worker's Compensation Court in 1995, even though Jackie Arnold only spoke of the April 22, 2002 claim. Andrea couldn't understand what happened in those ten years. She wanted to know what happened to the years prior to being in the Worker's Compensation court with her two failed attorneys. We knew her case had not been thrown out of court because it was "reinstated".

Referee Jackie Arnold dismissed Andrea's accident in the plant as though it never happened. Jackie Arnold didn't even want to know what happened to Andrea. Andrea never received any notification or money from her Worker's Compensation settlement. Did Woodrow Stamping Plant pilfer Andrea Smith's money? Who were the major players involved in Attorney Arnold Stanford's demise of Andrea's case? Where was Andrea's money and why was it a cover-up? Why weren't Andrea's issues addressed and why didn't anyone tell of the decision already made by Jackie Arnold in 2002 in the same court?

Andrea didn't understand why her medical bills were paid and she didn't receive any money. When she started asking questions, she was only stonewalled and dismissed because they felt they didn't owe her any compensation or explanation. Afterall, Andrea wasn't a lawyer. She was only acting as one and that didn't count toward Andrea's defense. She was never to find out what they had done and they had to fix that in a hurry.

In 2002, Andrea referred to the table in the back of the State of Michigan Worker's Disability Compensation Act of 1969 and Administrative Rules. This manual calculated the amount owed to her. The amount came to $300,000 dollars but Arnold Stanford wanted to offer Andrea $10,000 dollars in Jackie Arnold's courtroom. This was a long way from the amount offered to her. They were $290,000 dollars short. Famous Parts Company became furious at the amount of money Andrea was requesting for her damages. They felt she was asking for far too much. They felt Andrea had been off from 1995 to 1999 on medical leave. When she returned to Woodrow Stamping, they stated they had a job for her within her restrictions. She was later fired while on medical leave for major depression in February 2003.

Referee Jackie Arnold told both parties (Andrea and Famous Parts Company Attorney, Arnold Stanford) they needed to come to a settlement agreement. At that point Mr. Stanford went on a vendetta against Andrea because *he* was being investigated which ultimately lead to his firing. He couldn't explain what actually happened in Andrea's case. The company later got rid of Attorney Arnold Stanford in June 2004. But even after all that investigating, Andrea still received no compensation at all. Jackie Arnold began siding with the attorneys representing Famous Parts Company. She was aware Andrea's case was settled in 2002 and she became an accomplice when she didn't inform Andrea of this small detail regarding her claim.

Woodrow Stamping Plant, Referee Jackie Arnold, and Attorney Arnold Stanford needed to hide the truth about Andrea's case. Jackie Arnold was aware Andrea's case was settled in 2002 and kept it from her. She would be in trouble if anyone found out what she had done by not exposing the fraud that had occurred. She too was later released from her duties as a Referee for her action in Andrea's case.

There were things Jackie Arnold could have done to set the matter straight but she chose not to. When Andrea appeared again before Jackie Arnold regarding the hit by the truck and broom, she seemed to be surprised. I guess Arnold Stanford wasn't completely honest with her either. She didn't expect Andrea would be filing another claim. She could do nothing but note the incident in her decision to address Andrea's claim.

Andrea was supposed to be retired and they brought her back. Andrea was supposed to have been on retirement and not in the plant. Referee Jackie Arnold was not aware of those facts. This is why she didn't address Andrea Smith's hit by the broom and truck, which resulted in Andrea being transported to Midway Hospital. Andrea was on Woodrow Stamping Plant's retirement roster and she was getting too close for comfort. In my opinion, Andrea's lawyers were misfits and this was no longer a case of fraud. Andrea's claim became a massive cover-up.

Andrea had no business working. This is one fact that Attorney Arnold Stanford wanted to keep secret. Referee Jackie Arnold became involved when Andrea was aware her case had already been decided upon without her knowledge. She stated Andrea was only working on the computer for two months. What about the months previous to her injuries? Had that been forgotten? It wasn't as though Andrea was new to the Worker's Compensation courts. Her injuries went back to 1992, according to one of Andrea's medical records.

Jackie Arnold denied Andrea's Worker's Compensation claim stating Andrea did not claim benefits for the hi-lo incident. Jackie Arnold had to cover her behind because she didn't have much of a choice. She needed to prove Andrea received no compensation for this hit. She was saying the job Andrea was working (on the computer) couldn't cause the kind of damages presented to the courts. The referee acted as though Andrea had no prior history of a medical condition going back before 2002, and she settled the case. Jackie Arnold found out this was the only way she could get out of the mess she found herself in and she didn't want to be exposed. Jackie Arnold's stipulation read:

"... In December 1993 the parties were subject to the act. Defendant carried the risk and plaintiff was in its employment. It was denied a work-related injury when it was received. Whether there was a timely notice of the claim was left to proof. The average weekly wage value of fringe benefits and the date were discontinued. The appropriate rates were left to proof. There was no concurrent employment. Alternate benefits were paid but no Worker's Compensation was paid. Woodrow Stamping Plant denied her disability. Filing status was single. Dependency was left to proof ..."

My question is: what was Andrea's source of income when her injury occurred because her Worker's Compensation was denied? Why wasn't it written in her decision? Why didn't Jackie Arnold mention in her findings that Andrea was receiving Metro Craft Insurance benefits from Famous Parts Company before Andrea was terminated in February 2003? Jackie Arnold was hiding where Andrea's money was coming from in her report. "The average weekly wage" did not state a rated amount. Andrea's report didn't show how much money she was making per hour. The report didn't elaborate on her current employment because she was retired on Woodrow Stamping Plants records. Why would benefits be given to someone who was not employed? The alternate benefits were her

Social Security and retirement benefits. But this was not mentioned in the report because it would prove there were more than one set of records for Andrea Smith. It would also prove they were pilfering money from her.

Jackie Arnold accepted no proof from Andrea, Dr. Cannon (her attending doctor), or Dr. Thomas Right (the company doctor for Famous Parts Company). She only wanted to accept lies and what she wanted to hear, which was provided by Dr. Butt and Dr. Slick, Woodrow Stamping Plant doctors. These were doctors defrauding by deception and manipulation in order to deceive Worker's Compensation so they could continue pilfering money.

Referee Jackie Arnold stated she could not accept Dr. Cannon's opinion regarding Andrea's sprained/strained upper and lower back or Carpal Tunnel Syndrome. These are health problems that don't go away. They last a lifetime if the conditions aren't addressed shortly after the injury occurs. Working with no restrictions was clearly devastating to Andrea's body. Restrictions help to protect the body from destruction, and damage to the joints and muscles when one suffers from a condition such as Degenerative Joint Disease.

When the truck hit Andrea, it should have been considered Jackie Arnold's immediate concern. First of all, if Andrea was complaining about being hit by a truck, Jackie Arnold should have investigated through gathering necessary information. Jackie Arnold made her decision without ever giving Andrea the benefit of a doubt by analyzing the allegation. Instead, she made a decision denying Andrea's injury ever happened.

Dr. Right first saw Andrea Smith on October 30, 2001, which meant Andrea, had a work-related injury prior to 1992. In fact, there was more than one injury. Dr. Right worked for Famous Parts Company. Jackie Arnold saw Andrea's 1993 injury was consistent with the stipulation. Jackie Arnold should have taken Andrea's doctor's opinion because Dr. Right did acknowledge Andrea's condition in his report (as you saw in the previous chapter). Jackie only took Dr. Butt's deposition. Dr. Butt only saw Andrea on two occasions. Jackie Arnold and Famous Parts Company's accepted information with no substantiating, relative, or current medical information. Dr. Butt never put any information in his medical file that Andrea brought him to validate her medical condition.

Dr. Cannon had been treating her for years and she is still treating with him even though she treated with Dr. Tango for a short period of time. Dr. Tango was a doctor she sought on her own to continue treating with, since her attorney stated Dr. Cannon was going to receive all her Worker's Compensation. It was proven Dr. Cannon had the necessary information and test results that would substantiate Andrea's true condition. It was established earlier that Andrea's condition was caused and aggravated by the work provided by Woodrow Stamping Plant because they put her on jobs not suited for her body.

Andrea had depositions taken that were very important regarding her medical condition. The depositions could have caused Referee Jackie Arnold to be fired by her actions. Woodrow Stamping was already under the same suspicions when Nurse Tootie and Dr. Slick were fired. Dr. Slick later returned, but he was just as guilty as Nurse Tootie. It could have been they received a commission for each person retired. The majority of the people they pilfered from were minorities. From what I could see, there was only one Caucasian treated in the same manner. There may have been more, but I surely wasn't aware of who they were.

They worked eagerly in an effort not to pay any compensation to the employees. Andrea thought $2,500 dollars was a bit much to have to pay the dictating firm she hired, for two depositions that didn't even make sense. Andrea trusted these people like she would trust a starving dog to watch over food. There was nothing Woodrow Stamping Plant and Local 783 wouldn't do considering what I witnessed through the years.

Jackie Arnold deliberately botched up Andrea's Worker's Compensation case in favor of Attorney Arnold Stanford before his firing in June 2004. Andrea had depositions taken by Dr. Cannon and Dr. Kindly, her psychiatrist. Jackie Arnold dismissed these opinions regarding her medical and mental conditions. In her opinion, Referee Jackie Arnold stated:

"... I don't think there was anything that seemed to be work-related to it. It could have been developed from a number of reasons. Before she didn't have it—and now the second time she does. So it does not appear to be a work phenomenon. She was just doing some computer work in the interim not likely to cause those problems ..."

Being hit by a truck wasn't even considered in Jackie Arnold's equation when she made her final decision. Andrea told Jackie Arnold she was never informed a decision was made on her case in seven years. Jackie Arnold didn't elaborate on Andrea's prior claim at all. It was as though the prior claim didn't exist or as if they used the separate sets of records that kept employees both part-time and full-time. This would explain why there was no prior history of Andrea's claim filed in the Worker's Compensation Court. It seemed Andrea Smith and Jackie Arnold weren't on the same page. Andrea was making a point from 1995 and Jackie Arnold didn't want to go back that far. She wanted to start Andrea's claim from April 2002. Jackie Arnold only wanted to mention the computer job.

Andrea only worked that job two months. She worked many other jobs for the company prior to that one.

Dr. Cannon stated he evaluated Andrea in 1991 and in 1993 for a work-related injury. The damage was already done in 1991. Even way back then, Andrea had problems with sprains/strains of the upper and lower back, shoulders, wrists, hands, and elbows. Working on a computer for two months would not cause all these injuries. Jackie Arnold's decision was flawed. It seems to me they were adding to Andrea's clinical depression she suffered from.

When Andrea was taken from Woodrow Stamping to the hospital by ambulance, that doctor also said the hit by the truck aggravated her condition. Andrea wasn't allowed on the plant's premises and was fired soon after the hit with the truck. This happened so she wouldn't file any more claims with the Worker's Compensation Court because of her retirement and of course the non-payment of her 1995 claim. This incident should have been an eye-opener especially if there were no records kept on the end of Woodrow Stamping Plant. It could have been construed that the hit was done purposely. I wouldn't rule out anything these people might do. They got away with this criminal activity for so many years they felt they were immune from penalization. The courts just continued to aid and abet the corruption and the criminal activities by granting decisions in favor of 'big businesses'. We really need to re-evaluate our state and government agencies. There is plenty of fraud to go around in the business sector and justice system.

While in court, Andrea gave Jackie Arnold authority to obtain medical records from the Medical Department at Woodrow Stamping Plant, with respect to her being hit with the hi-lo in the plant, but she did not. I wondered what reason Jackie Arnold had not to pursue the gathering of more information regarding Andrea's medical condition when she was hit with the hi-lo.

In Jackie Arnold's conclusion, she stated Andrea was hit by a broom in the chest, and also stated Andrea claimed no injury from being hit with the hi-lo. What was Andrea doing when she told the referee what had occurred? Was that not a complaint the referee should have taken into consideration? Andrea was off work as a result of her joint disease for the first few months of 2002. When she returned, she was injured by a broom and hit with the hi-lo. This was prior to her last medical leave for major depression brought on by the harassment of Woodrow Stamping Plant. Andrea wondered how she could get someone to listen to her. With all the correspondences Andrea sent out regarding her work-related issues, she received no responses. When she did receive a response, it was to inform her whoever it was did not want to get involved.

Andrea later found a report regarding payment of her hospital bill from Worker's Compensation. The report explained Woodrow Stamping Plant paid approximately $139 dollars for the injury date June 26, 2002. The date paid was November 2002. (The NAIC/self-insured number was 274F0000A23. The patient's account number was 0001062830.)

With this information, Jackie Arnold excluded all injuries and allowed Andrea to receive nothing. None of the company doctors took tests such as an MRI (Magnetic Resonance Imaging), bone scan, or CAT scan, which would all substantiate Andrea's medical condition. Andrea gave the company doctors her medical information although it didn't make a difference in Dr. Butt's, Dr. Dusty's, or Dr. Slick's opinions.

I want you to remember Andrea's case was in the Worker's Compensation court since 1995 and even at that time there was much more damage to her body than what we've discussed. Some ten years later, she still has not been compensated. When the case was settled in 2002, it was the eighth year. As far as Andrea was concerned, the claim wasn't settled because she didn't receive any compensation. She received no money in 2002, although all her medical bills were paid in the settlement. It clearly doesn't count if everyone got paid but Andrea. In their opinion, she was not important enough. Above all else, she has no money and Woodrow Stamping Plant had no plan of her receiving any. It was supposed to have been *her* case, but she was the one suffering on a daily basis due to medical, mental, and financial problems. She received nothing while the company continued their cover-up.

44

HARASSMENT IS HORRIFIC

Andrea couldn't help that the court hadn't made a decision regarding her Worker's Compensation until years later in 2002. Worker's Compensation and all those who allowed Woodrow Stamping to extort money from Andrea needed to be held accountable. I didn't care who was involved. I had seen more than enough of how Woodrow Stamping Plant and Local 783 treated employees less than human. Andre's medical condition has been overlooked because the court hadn't made a decision or compensated her? Should she not be able to speak on her own behalf? Should she not be able to challenge her claim in a higher court without pay-offs when her case has been denied? Why should Andrea not be granted the right to challenge her case because they pilfered her money?

Woodrow Stamping Plant, Local 783, Worker's Compensation Referee Jackie Arnold, the Executive Branch of the Company, and the Executive Branch of the Union all tried to cover up what they did. Jackie Arnold tried to justify her point of view and wasn't truthful with the facts. She was aware that Andrea's Worker's Compensation complaint went further back than 2002. She was aware she was filing Andrea a new claim in the Worker's Compensation court. She stripped Andrea of everything including her life in a decision made in the summer of 2004, which left Andrea with no job, money, or health benefits. These issues ate away at Andrea's physical and mental health conditions.

Why did Referee Jackie Arnold base Andrea's Worker's Compensation case on the last few days of Andrea's job working on a computer? The damage was already done to her physically and mentally before this job. If Jackie Arnold looked at the situation more carefully, she would've seen Andrea's condition was too extensive to be attributed to a job she worked only two months. The Medical Department never counted on Andrea returning back to work. They brought her back not planning on her staying. The longer she stayed, the more concerned they became. The more trouble Andrea caused, the harder it was to keep a lid on the cover-up.

Woodrow Stamping Plant wanted to work Andrea so hard that she would return on medical leave, but Andrea fought back. They were harassing her by stripping away her restrictions. She would file charges with the Department of Civil Rights and the National Labor Relations Board causing problems for Woodrow Stamping and Local 783. All Andrea wanted was the horrific treatment to stop. Each government agency sided with Woodrow Stamping Plant leaving them to do whatever they chose to do.

What makes this situation so outstanding is with all that happened, the NLRB never filed charges against Local 783 and the Department of Civil Rights never filed charges with Woodrow Stamping Plant. It seemed to be a problem when none of the complaints I filed from 1990 until 2003 were ever investigated by the government agencies. These agencies were just going through the motions of filing complaints, just as Local 783 did with grievances that were never officially filed. It was ironic that Andrea Smith's experiences weren't found to have reason for investigation either. This was our experience with the Department of Labor, the National Labor Relations Board, and the Equal Employment Opportunity Commission. All of these entities would first try to have you withdraw your claim. If you refused, they'd find no reason for investigating, forcing you to appeal. If perhaps your condition was at a point the agencies sent you a right-to-sue letter, it probably meant you'd been *red-flagged* or *blackballed*. No lawyer in or out of state would take your case.

If you or anyone you know has been treated in this matter, please call or e-mail your local mayor, congressperson, governor, or senator to voice your opinion and to put a stop to this kind of treatment. I would like you to report this treatment, and not be a victim or stand by and watch. We are supposed to be a society of fairness. Let's try to get something done about this. If your retirement was pilfered, or if you have experienced harassment of another kind in the workplace, please report it. Tell someone about it and call to see what you can do to be a part of prevention.

If you cry long enough and work hard enough, eventually someone will hear you. I had to write a book to finally be heard. Their determination was so great to silence me in what they were doing, but my determination was much greater. I was in hopes Woodrow Stamping Plant's and Local 783's schemes were brought to the open because others were suffering mentally, physically, and financially with no one protecting us. We were the forgotten few that no one was willing to help—even when everyone knew we were being wronged. All those involved in Woodrow Stamping's money laundering scheme did so by choice. This scheme went on for many years causing many employees to be lied on and to lose their livelihood. This was wrong and they needed to be held accountable for their actions in a court of law.

Andrea wasn't the only person who had retired and didn't know they were retired. If you recall, Linda Jackson faced the very same problem regarding her Worker's Compensation case. She was also retired unofficially and received none of her retirement benefits because the money was being diverted into Woodrow Stamping Plant's and Local 783's miscellaneous accounts. It was ironic how both women experienced the same fate with the company while enduring serious work-related medical conditions going back to the 90's. Do you think it was right they couldn't receive Worker's Compensation for their injuries?

Andrea Smith's Worker's Compensation case was screwed up from the beginning. After firing all her lawyers who weren't working in her best interest, she was not supposed to be working at all. She was supposed to be sitting at home drawing her retirement and Social Security benefits. She shouldn't be receiving one without the other since her injury was occupational. It is impossible to be in the plant working and receiving Worker's Compensation and retirement benefits too. It's either one or the other. Woodrow Stamping Plant wanted it to go both ways so they could continue stealing Andrea's money.

When Woodrow Stamping brought Andrea back, they didn't work around her restriction. They didn't want her to stay in the plant for too long—for they would be found out. This is when Jackie Arnold's decision came into play. The company didn't want to take the chance of their scheme of embezzling being blown out of the water. Andrea continued to work while injured in 1992, 1993, 1994, and then went on a medical leave in 1995. It was in 1995 that Woodrow Stamping Plant retired Andrea.

They thought at least if they fired her they wouldn't have to worry about her ever again. They could continue receiving not part, but all of her benefits. They would receive her retirement until she died. They had enough nerve to collect even from a dead person. Money is power, which is exactly what Woodrow Stamping Plant had. They were full of power and corruption for years, and I told Famous Parts Company CEO, Robert Wart, as much in 2005. I indeed wanted this scheme to surface so others could be free. Andrea Smith and Linda Jackson should have gotten what belonged to them. Others should not have been benefiting from their loss of work.

They had already retired me in 2000 and 2002. They started running scared because they thought there was an investigation in the plant. They felt I was bad news to them and it was only a matter of time before I figured out what happened. When they finalized my retirement, it was clear they didn't want me back. I agreed to terminate my employment because I was tired of them just as they were tired of me. I didn't lose as much as Andrea Smith or Linda Jackson, but the money I should have received during the waiting period for my retirement to be granted was pilfered when I first filed my original claim.

These two women lost it all—their seniority, retirement and their health. I don't know why Linda Jackson didn't fight Woodrow Stamping Plant as Andrea did. She decided not to fight for what was rightfully hers according to contract. Seeing what Andrea and I went through the likelihood would have resulted in defeat. It was a fight that she couldn't or wouldn't win, because the odds were so great in favor of Woodrow Stamping Plant and Local 783. Andrea lost much more through fraud and deception by Woodrow Stamping Plant and Local 783. She fought the corruption and cover-ups that followed, which prevented Andrea from taking her cases to court in an effort that a judge and/or jury would decide her claim on its merits. Only to find the lawyers were corrupt and the judge was corrupt too. Andrea Smith and Linda Jackson were two women that lost everything with the exception of the shirts on their backs, and their creditors were trying to take that too.

As a result of the last investigation I sought in March 2003, some were fired. The person I felt was the ringleader was escorted out of the plant August 17, 2004. I had sent the CEO of Famous Parts Company another letter, and my complaining all these years finally paid off. The state police finally escorted Nurse Tootie out of Woodrow Stamping Plant. This was the same person that lied on Andrea Smith and had her fired. Thank God!

As of November 2005, Andrea's Worker's Compensation case was denied for the second time in the Appellate Court. The courts were bought and paid for. The three of us were constantly railroaded. They wanted everything swept under the rug as though the incidents never happened. Woodrow Stamping Plant knew people in high places and could get away with murder if they wanted to. Andrea added an amendment to her case before the Appellate Court in hopes her case would be heard for the second time. Andrea had plans on taking her case to the Michigan Supreme Court if she couldn't get the lower court to recognize an error had taken place when her Worker's Compensation claim was denied.

Andrea had nothing to lose. No employee should have been treated in the manner she had been treated throughout her employment at Woodrow Stamping Plant. She experienced inhumane treatment while at the same time suffering from Degenerative Joint Disease and major depression. Woodrow Stamping Plant and Local 783 were aware Andrea Smith's medical condition was brought on by many occupational injuries. They knew the major depression became worse when she was terminated while on medical leave. Her life started falling completely apart when she was forced to live in poverty due to her unjust termination. This happened in an effort for Woodrow Stamping to continue pilfering her retirement benefits since she refused to accept the $10,000 dollar settlement they offered her for being out of work for almost 8 years with an occupational injury.

Andrea received a reconsideration decision on November 15, 2005. The Appellate Court denied her reconsideration. The motion to supplement the motion for reconsideration was granted. Andrea submitted documents reporting how Woodrow Stamping Plant paid for her treatment when she was hit with the truck in the plant. Andrea entered information regarding her injuries that happened prior in the plant. These were the injuries the company said didn't exist. At least at this point, maybe Andrea could find a glimmer of hope in a tunnel of dark hidden secrets.

Andrea and Linda both went through the lies and deception Woodrow Stamping Plant and Local 783 took many of the union members through. I said then and I will say now, the union needs to pay every penny they took from us for representation when we had to represent ourselves. Andrea was going through the same experiences I had with Local 783. How could the union get away with so much deception? Andrea was hanging on a thread regarding how she had been treated. I couldn't believe the conditions on which Local 783 brought her back under when she was fired unjustly. What really mattered was Woodrow Stamping Plant wouldn't accept her back unless she signed their outrageous stipulation. It was a known fact Andrea wasn't able to work. She's been fired for years and still hadn't received a dime. It is now 2008.

The union and Woodrow Stamping Plant were guilty of harassment. They were trying to force Andrea to sign an illegal statement in which she couldn't file a grievance against the company or the union for a year. This was after all they had done to her throughout the years. The letter Local 783 bargained in Andrea's "good faith" stated:

"Dear Andrea Smith:

In full complete settlement of this grievance and with precedent to any other issues, the aggrieved employee (Smith) will be reinstated with full seniority and without back pay under the terms of a twelve-month waiver. Ms. Smith will be regarded for disciplinary purposes as being on probation for a period of twelve months with the understanding that she will not have access to the grievance process the reasonableness of any penalty including discharge which she may receive during this probation period for any infractions of company rules. However Ms.

Smith will be prohibited from processing a grievance bearing on the question of guilt or innocence if she believes she is innocent of the charge.

It is understood that time not at work while on any construct leave will not count toward completion of the ream statement waiver period. During the waiver period Ms. Smith is also required to meet on at least a monthly basis with the plant employee support service program. The purpose of these meetings is to discuss if there are services available for an employee assistance plan that may be beneficial for Ms. Smith. In order to be reinstated, the aggrieved must submit up to date medical information from a board of certified psychiatrists indicating she does not pose a threat to co-workers. Then this information must be provided within thirty calendar days of notification of this deposition. She must also submit to a fitness physical at Woodrow Stamping Plant prior to being reinstated."

The union should not have allowed anyone to negotiate a grievance to the degree that a person is forbidden to have access to the grievance procedure. If and when a grievance is needed, the employee is yet paying her union dues. This is a violation of the union contract if Andrea could not challenge a dispute with the company. This is the exact same thing that happened to me when Local 783 didn't file my grievance. They didn't file Andrea's grievance then, and they wouldn't file a grievance in the future. What was Woodrow Stamping Plant so afraid of? Andrea is in the position she's in now because she had no union representation in her disputes with Woodrow Stamping Plant and Local 783. I tell you I'd never heard of anything like this in my entire life. The contract was not worth the paper it was printed on.

Andrea contacted Local 783 and Larry Mean, the current Plant Chairman who stated he had nothing to do with settling Andrea's grievance. He stated he didn't want his name tied anywhere near the settlement agreement under those conditions and mailed Andrea a letter stating that fact. He knew they wanted Andrea to sign an illegal statement and he stated as much. The settlement of Andrea's grievance on September 21, 2005 was in an unethical manner by the union's standards. It went against the union contract and the organization as a whole for what they represented to the employees and union members.

Andrea filed an Article 33 of the Constitution of the Union and months passed before she even received a response. Andrea knew they received the letters because they were sent certified mail. This meant Andrea's Article 33 was ignored. She filed charges against all involved in her grievance in February 2003. This wasn't the first time Andrea's Article 33 under the Constitution of the

Union was disregarded. She experienced this same treatment for each grievance she filed. Why wasn't the union working for Andrea? When I was employed at Woodrow Stamping Plant, they didn't want to accept my Article 33 either. I experienced the same treatment. It wasn't fair. These people didn't need a union if they continuously took employees' civil rights away contrary to the contract. Andrea sent the following affidavit of clarification, on October 18, 2005 regarding the filing of the Article 33 of the Constitution of the Union:

"Re: The settlement agreement of Andrea Smith, Grievance #H121867—Umpire Case #51552.

Do you agree the settlement of Grievance #H121867—Umpire Case #51252 is constitutional under the contract of the union with stipulations that:

1. I would be on probation for a period of twelve months with the understanding that I would not have access to the grievance procedure to protest the reasonableness of any penalty.

2. Time not at work while on any contractual leave will not count toward completion of the reinstatement waiver period.

3. During the waiver period I am required to meet on at least a monthly basis with the plant's Employee Support Services Program Representative.

If you agree with the settlement agreement, please contact me …" signed Andrea Smith.

No one at the Executive Branch of the Union wanted their name involved with this affidavit that was supposed to be a grievance settlement. It was clearly an illegal document. Everyone passed the blame onto someone else, but no one was making any resolutions to correct the problems this grievance caused.

If Andrea signed this acquisition it would become legally binding (even if it was illegal). Therefore Woodrow Stamping Plant could and would enforce the document if Andrea signed it. It's ironic how people can be railroaded so easily and to have absolutely no one standing up against injustice, discrimination, retaliation, or harassment. Andrea was punished because she wouldn't agree to what they did to her. It's simply a plea bargain when you know you're innocent and they know you're innocent too, yet you're forced to take the wrap in an effort to hide what they've done. They blackmailed Andrea using her job as a condition. There was no excuse for what they did to Andrea and me.

Andrea went to the local union hall first and then to the Regional Branch of the Union's Executive Branch. She hand delivered both of them a copy of her Article 33. Andrea gave each level of the union a letter of acknowledgement to sign stating the Article 33 was received. Andrea tried to give the document to the recording sectary at Local 783. She refused to accept the Article 33 although the recording sectary directed Andrea to the Vice-President of Local 783 who did sign for the Article 33.

It was the recording secretary's duty to handle the Article 33 at the local level according to the Constitution of the Union. The NLRB was saying Andrea's Article 33 was inadmissible because she didn't send a copy in ample time to the Executive Branch of the Union. This was a lie. The NLRB dropped all charges against Local 783 and the Department of Civil Rights dropped the charges against Woodrow Stamping Plant after all Andrea had been through. Andrea had information and documents substantiating the various contract violations but there was no one willing to file charges against Woodrow Stamping and Local 783 on the merits of the charges. Instead they made such a big issue about Andrea's Article 33 not being in on time. Local 783 needed someone to keep the lid on their thief ring. I'm sure they were paying very well because Andrea's case had merit. How long did they think their secret would stay a secret? If this information leaked, it would be one of the biggest corruption scandals covering a wide variety of co-conspirators.

No grievance Andrea wrote was ever addressed. Not because she didn't do her part in trying to get matters solved. Andrea's grievances had always been ignored at the Executive Branch of the Union. Woodrow Stamping Plant continued the harassment not caring what happened to Andrea. Can you believe with all this information supplied to the NLLRB, they still wouldn't investigate Local 783 or Woodrow Stamping Plant? Woodrow Stamping Plant and Local 783 were hoping Andrea Smith would just go away. When Andrea hand delivered her Article 33 to Local 783 Union President Stanly Ball's office, he wasn't there. However the Vice-President signed for the Article 33 in October 2003 to assure they received it in a timely manner.

Soon after that happened Andrea received her grievance settlement dated September 21, 2005 although she didn't receive it until October 2005. The grievance stated she was to return back to work only after she signed the waiver. When Andrea read the condition of the grievance she was appalled because this grievance wasn't legal at all. Woodrow Stamping Plant and Local 783 took the standard waiver, reworded the condition, and put their own conditions, which made it no longer a standard waiver. Andrea then sent another Article 33 to President and CEO, Don Hangem, at the Executive Branch of the Union's Headquarters, only to receive no response. She sent another Article 33 certified mail—return receipt, but when she called to inquire about the letter, no one seemed to know anything about it. The woman she spoke with over the telephone wouldn't even give her name as the contact person. She didn't want her name involved in what was going on.

Andrea went down to the Union's Headquarters trying to get answers regarding this grievance and how it was handled. No one addressed her Article 33 on any level of the union from the Local, Regional, or Executive Branch. All she wanted was some straightforward answers regarding this grievance and to hear what the Executive Branch had to say. When Andrea arrived at the union's headquarters and explained why she was there, she was told everyone was out to lunch. I had heard that one before too. Can you believe no one was willing to speak to Andrea about this grievance at the Executive Branch of the Union?

When this kind of discrimination and harassment happened to an employee, there should not be a statue of limitation. The judge threw my case out in a summary judgment in favor of Woodrow Stamping Plant and Local 783. The judge knew they were guilty as hell. He stated if there were a need for a lawyer he would have appointed me one. I also had a 'right-to-sue' letter for discrimination under the Americans with Disabilities Act (ADA), but this judge told me I didn't have a case of discrimination. Andrea filed her case in the court and her judge stated he was going to give her a lawyer after she requested one, but she never received the attorney. Contrary to what I've read, discrimination is discrimination no matter how you look at it. I'm not a lawyer, but I know discrimination is a civil rights violation. The judge knew he was going to throw my case out of court. Therefore I didn't need a lawyer. I wasn't a lawyer, but I knew my rights were violated.

According to the Constitution, everyone has a right to have representation in a court of law. The Constitution also states we as citizens have a right in a democratic society to have representation in a court of law. When the judges refused to appoint us lawyers, it proved the law pertained to some and not others. Andrea and I had clear cases. It was unfair for the lawyers and judges to keep our cases from entering the judicial system. Those cases should not have had a statue of limitation.

I couldn't understand why no one heard the complaints in Andrea's correspondences or why no one got back with her after many years of complaining. No one seemed to care because number one—she's Black, and number two she's a woman. I haven't seen any Caucasians getting treated unjustly to this magnitude. Somehow they seemed to be above the law. I am only speaking from experience. I have seen and experienced the mistreatment for myself. The more I fought, the more they made sure nothing became of my claim. When the courts sided with the company, my claim didn't have a chance even though the accusations were valid. The case was always thrown out of court in a Summary Judgment. It didn't matter how much proof Andrea and I had, we received a bench trial and the judge used his own discretion to silence us and leaving us "up a creek without a paddle".

45

IT'S NOT WHAT THEY DID,
IT'S HOW THEY DID IT

I said then and I will say now, Woodrow Stamping Plant needed a woman to run the plant. In my opinion, the men seemed to make the same mistakes because they didn't learn by their failures. They had their own way of running the plant and didn't want to learn how to run the plant more efficiently. I'm not saying they weren't smart enough. They just didn't accept outside corrective advice.

They were pilfering to the point that waste didn't seem to be a concern. They were thriving on the money pilfered from employees who worked at the plant. Woodrow Stamping Plant's management staff and Local 783 were powerful as an entity. This is the reason Woodrow Stamping Plant was guarded and they couldn't be touched. They didn't need to be concerned about ever getting caught. They were the Robin-Hoods of the future. The pilferage was a waste.

Finding better ways to be efficient was mandatory in a plant the size of Woodrow Stamping. If the plant was constantly losing money, common sense should have told them they needed to do something different. The only way this could happen was by finding a better solution to the problems at hand. When employees pointed out a more efficient way, management didn't value their input. They were a bunch of stuffed-nosed know-it-alls that didn't have sense enough to get the company's numbers in the black.

The plant was losing money when the plants in general were making record profits during the 90's. There was a lot of favoritism, which was another one of Woodrow Stamping Plant's downfalls among many. I truly understood why Woodrow Stamping Plant never made a profit while I worked there. Management would tell us the employees were the cause of the plant's losses—not the company's bad-decision making. They also told us that scrap production was one of their biggest losses. It was always easier to blame someone else for bad decisions.

This is one of the reasons they were pilfering money from employees and taking money from retirees while keeping employees on long medical leaves. Many of those who were retired in the system never knew of their retirement. Woodrow Stamping Plant wasn't paying the money or benefits granted through Worker's Compensation courts. Woodrow Stamping Plant made deals with lawyers in an effort not to relinquish money granted to the injured employee. These lawyers were lying and using stall tactics. Some lawyers didn't even report to court on appointment dates. Sometimes if they did, they'd come unprepared with little or no information to represent their client. They also ignored their client by not returning telephone calls or keeping the client informed of their claim's status. I had to later fire Attorney Silverman, who I hired to obtain my Worker's Compensation since Woodrow Stamping Plant kept denying my injuries were work-related. I fired him for working in the best interest of Woodrow Stamping Plant and Local 783. He assisted in making their pilfering schemes profitable and successful.

If you are on medical leave for two years or more, you should be deemed disabled according to contract. Metro Craft Insurance Company wasn't set up for employees to be paid 'sick & accident' benefits for years at a time as in Andrea Smith's and Linda Jackson's cases. Andrea received 'sick & accident' benefits from 1995 until 1999 and from 2002 until February 2003—when she was fired. This was when medical disability was supposed to come into the equation. Andrea came out of retirement from her long-term disability according to Woodrow Stamping Plant's records in 1999.

Woodrow Stamping Plant called Andrea out of retirement when the Social Security Administration told her Woodrow Stamping Plant had her "retired" according to their records. When Andrea started investigating, that's when she was called back to work. She received a letter from Woodrow Stamping Plant stating she was to return back to work because they had a job for her. This was untrue because the line she was told she'd be working never ran. This left her with no job.

From that point everything started going downhill. Andrea was under paid because when she went out on medical retirement in 1995. Woodrow Stamping Plant was paying less per hour when she was first retired. When Woodrow Stamping Plant brought Andrea back in 1999, wages had increased due to contract negotiations. Andrea's pay should have been adjusted to the current rate of pay. They weren't going to change her rate of pay because they were going to put her back in retirement. Therefore Andrea was underpaid from 1999 through 2002.

Andrea couldn't make the same rate of pay as the other employees in the same job classification because the company had to leave her retirement in effect, in order that they could continue to divert her retirement money electronically putting the money in special accounts each month. After all those years, Woodrow Stamping Plant couldn't officially bring her back because she was retired with the diagnosis of Degenerative Joint Disease. There is no cure for this disease, so why would they bring her out of retirement? They brought her back on one set of records, and eventually settled her second Worker's Compensation claim in 2004 with the extra set. It would have been very risky business if Andrea were injured in the plant. They had to take the chance in bringing her back so they could terminate her by means of the second set of records. They set out to get rid of Andrea for good and they succeeded by terminating her. Their concerns arose when Andrea started inquiring and asking questions with reference to her retirement. For this reason things didn't work out the way Woodrow Stamping Plant and Local 783 wanted. Andrea didn't cooperate the way they had planed. They were putting her on jobs her body could not withstand. They wanted her back out of the plant, but Andrea started fighting back by filing complaints with the NLRB, Labor Department, Equal Employment Opportunity Commission, and the unheard grievances with Local 783. Andrea was aware she was being treated differently when all of this was happening to her. That's one of the main reasons Andrea was hit by the truck—to frighten her enough so she would quit. It was clear that Woodrow Stamping Plant and Local 783 wanted her back out of the plant.

This is the same thing that happened to Linda Jackson when she was brought back to work upon request. Linda asked Woodrow Stamping Plant to work around her restrictions and they did not. Instead they sent her packing never to return again. This was so they could continue pilfering her retirement and monthly disability checks from Metro Craft Insurance Company. She too received nothing because she was offered $10,000 dollars and refused. Linda felt this was an unfair dollar amount since she had been off work for the period of 5 years at the time her first Worker's Compensation case was settled. Woodrow Stamping Plant worked in unison with Linda Jackson's attorney in filing a new claim in the Worker's Compensation court resulting in a denial of any Worker's Compensation benefits at all.

Woodrow Stamping Plant paid employees from their Worker's Compensation fund at the plant in which Linda worked. Linda Jackson's first Worker's Compensation settlement offer was settled without her agreeing to a settlement. They didn't need her to finalize the case since she didn't agree to the December

2002 settlement. Her medical condition did exist and the judge established that Woodrow Stamping Plant did cause and/or aggravate her medical condition. So why wouldn't Linda Jackson receive any compensation? Woodrow Stamping Plant filed a new claim for Linda, not recording any pre-existing injuries. They did this in order not to pay Linda Jackson any Worker's Compensation.

Woodrow Stamping Plant never paid Linda Jackson's money from her first Worker's Compensation claim. Woodrow Stamping Plant pays employees for occupational injuries through Worker's Compensation out of their plant fund. How can someone be on medical leave for 10 years and continue completing medical forms? Linda Jackson's doctor informed her she would never be able to return back to work, so what was the purpose of Linda Jackson completing medical forms twice a year? Is it only for the medical insurance? Woodrow Stamping pilfered her money and they continued to rob her each month directing her retirement into their special accounts.

In 2004 Andrea received a letter stating her Worker's Compensation was denied. Woodrow Stamping Plant did Linda Jackson the very same way, her first claim was decided in December 2002. According to Linda Jackson's decision, she was to be paid according to her settlement findings. She received nothing too.

How could Linda Jackson receive no money when the decision was granted in her favor? Her medical condition stayed the same and she has not returned to work since 2002 because the Medical Department didn't honor her restrictions. When she returned to work previously, her medical condition was further deteriorated due to her restrictions being disregarded. Her hands swelled twice their size. What were the odds of a judge changing their decision concerning a medical condition because a person didn't agree to the amount of money granted in the settlement? If Linda Jackson never received her settlement, what were the odds of the money being pilfered? Who was the person that was supposed to be paying her Worker's Compensation settlement? Woodrow Stamping Plant was supposed to pay Linda Jackson because Woodrow Stamping Plant caused and aggravated her medical condition. This was at least according to the Worker's Compensation findings regarding Linda Jackson first settlement.

The judge or referee made a decision on a claim and because Linda Jackson didn't agree the amount of money she should have received, she was denied anything at all. The money Linda Jackson was contesting was the issue, not her proven medical condition. Why would the judge or referee change the medical aspects of the case? Her condition will never change. This was proven when she returned back to work with swollen hands when Woodrow Stamping wouldn't work around her restriction. So why would the judge or referee in Linda Jackson's case resend the decision made in December 2002 regarding her medical decision? The money should have been paid 30 days after the first Worker's Compensation case was decided. Woodrow Stamping Plant should have paid Linda Jackson the Worker's Compensation benefits owed. As you read these circumstances, would you say Linda Jackson's situation was one of normal circumstances or do you think her money was pilfered?

Woodrow Stamping Plant hired Linda Jackson's attorney to make sure she received her Social Security settlement, and as a result she didn't receive a dime from any other entity. I will assure you this lawyer was paid. What did Linda Jackson get out of her Worker's Compensation settlement? Nothing! Because Woodrow Stamping Plant pilfered all of her money only leaving her with medical forms to complete even as of May 2007. Linda is only living on her Social Security benefits received every month.

After they pilfered all her money, they returned back to court and another decision was made. Linda Jackson received nothing from this new claim because when the new claim was filed in the Worker's Compensation court, it was filed as though there had never been a claim filed in the Worker's Compensation court prior on her behalf (Similar to Andrea's case.) This was done because Linda Jackson could have brought her claim back into court as a new claim, and they were making sure this didn't happen. All this was done without Linda's knowledge. The only knowledge she understood was that she was injured at Woodrow Stamping Plant and they pilfered all her benefits. They left her with a broken down body and they profited by her medical condition. This was big business for the company. With this second court decision, Woodrow Stamping Plant pilfered all her money not just in part—they took it all.

Metro Craft Insurance Company was paying Linda Jackson 'sick & accident' payments from 1997 until 2002. When she returned back to work, she only worked two days. Woodrow Stamping Plant dismissed all her medical restrictions in order to have her return on medical leave. Linda Jackson received a letter in September 2004, two years later, stating her Worker's Compensation was turned down. This last letter explained she was to receive no compensation. This left Linda as though her condition was of a personal nature and Woodrow Stamping Plant had nothing to do with her injury, which had been occupational.

Woodrow Stamping Plant never issued payment to Linda on the first decision made in December 2002 regarding her Worker's Compensation. She lost her seniority and couldn't draw her retirement because of what Woodrow Stamping Plant had done. Linda Jackson couldn't draw her retirement because they were already receiving her retirement benefits. She did not have 10 years of seniority. If

Linda Jackson's condition were aggravated or caused by Woodrow Stamping Plant, she would've been able to receive her retirement after 4 years with the company. Linda's medical condition was disabling and occupational. Linda didn't have enough seniority to take a medical retirement as a person with a personal injury. She needed 10 years for that, but under the occupational injury guidelines, she only needed 4. Linda and Andrea both had enough time to make a claim for retirement with their occupational injury. So Woodrow Stamping Plant retired them and pilfered their retirement instead of giving it to them. This is the reason Linda Jackson receives her medical insurance in part from her employer today. Why did it take two years for Linda Jackson to receive nothing when in 2002 the court stated she should have received Worker's Compensation? That's when Woodrow Stamping Plant stopped paying Linda Jackson 'sick & accident' benefits in 2002. This left her receiving only Social Security benefits.

They did Linda Jackson as they did Andrea Smith and tried to do me. I fired my attorney because he tried to make sure I didn't get my money. Woodrow Stamping Plant became angry with him because I fought for the money belonging to me. After my decision had been made in February 2002, I should have received my money approximately 30 days following. Woodrow Stamping Plant didn't pay my prior attorney because they became angry with him. He was supposed to make sure I didn't receive any of my out of pocket expenses once the first case was settled. They made him wait two years for his money from Woodrow Stamping Plant, and that was when I retired.

Andrea Smith was receiving 'sick & accident' payments from Metro Craft Insurance Company from 1995 until 1999 when she returned back to work. She was injured on the job and was later fired on the lie with the assistance of Local 783. If the company was sending Andrea the retirement's monthly supplement for her being retired, it should have been noted on her monthly check stub. Woodrow Stamping Plant continued to send Andrea 'sick & accident' benefits until she was fired. They fired Andrea because she was getting too close in finding out they had already retired her. When she filed a claim with Worker's Compensation, Woodrow Stamping Plant couldn't because she was already retired but they continued to say that she didn't have enough time to retire.

All these red flags should have reached from the grounds to the heavens above. Something was seriously wrong. Linda Jackson received 'sick & accident' payments for 7 years. I can't believe no one noticed this was a common practice at Woodrow Stamping Plant. Woodrow Stamping Plant paid into the Worker's Compensation fund for each employee working in the plant. They insured themselves leaving enough money into their fund, which subsidized every employee injured on the job.

Worker's Compensation was put in effect in the 50's to assure employees injured on the job would be compensated for being injured. This kept the company safe from large lawsuits. Worker's Compensation was set up to assist the injured employee by compensating the cost of medical treatment incurred on the job. Money was granted to employees through the courts and they weren't even receiving the money from Woodrow Stamping Plant's fund.

Woodrow Stamping Plant had been paying doctors, lawyers, judges, politicians, referees, and government agencies to see that injured employees didn't receive benefits granted by the judges or referees. Woodrow Stamping Plant was not paying their employees benefits from the Worker's Compensation fund. This meant the employer, Woodrow Stamping Plant, drafted the check for each settlement. They found a way to keep from paying employees and kept the money within the plant.

Worker's Compensation and Woodrow Stamping Plant granted my first decision in February 2002. I didn't receive the first portion of my money until 90 days from the settlement's decision—and only part of the money was allotted. The money from the expenses was not sent at the time because Woodrow Stamping Plant wanted to make sure I didn't receive that money. They disbursed the settlement amount agreed upon, although the check was made out to Attorney Silverman's law firm. My first Worker's Compensation attorney, Mr. Silverman, wasn't concerned when I started inquiring about the money I had not received. It was almost like going back in time when Attorney Bushe handled my discrimination case. The tactics were the same.

I contacted the Worker's Compensation Bureau in Lansing, Michigan myself. I later found out my lawyer made some kind of deal with Woodrow Stamping Plant. I questioned Mr. Silverman's logic because he had no characteristics of a person wanting to be paid. Mr. Silverman wouldn't get paid unless I got paid. Why wasn't he trying to get his money? Why wasn't he making a big enough deal to receive payment for the work he had done on my case? That sent another red flag to me that something was wrong. My payment was late and I didn't receive it all in the allotted time. In my grant, I was to receive my out of pocket expenses incurred while on medical leave, which was over $3,000 dollars. I didn't receive this allotted money until December 2002. I should have received payment no later than March 26, 2002 and Mr. Silverman was aware of that. I had to run my lawyer down in order to find out why it was taking so long for me to get my money.

There was much controversy between Mr. Silverman and myself. I hadn't figured how these lawyers were being paid for their services if they were making sure the employees didn't receive payment. Woodrow Stamping Plant kept the money instead of paying the injured employee. I noticed this when I was forced to fire my attorney and took on the case myself. Mr. Silverman didn't make sure I received my payment and he didn't seem to be interested in money at that point. Later when I received my out of pocket money owed to me by Woodrow Stamping Plant, here comes Mr. Silverman wanting to be paid for his services. If I had not received the money, he would not have been concerned in contacting me. Prior to this, he wasn't accepting or returning my phone calls. After I received payment, here he came to collect from me—the injured employee, after he sold me out to the highest bidder.

This also happened to my dear friend and co-worker, Andrea Smith. Linda Jackson didn't pick up her fight where her lawyer left off. Linda Jackson didn't fight Woodrow Stamping Plant as hard as Andrea and I did. For the most part she put her case in her attorney's hands and trusted he would handle it appropriately. He later betrayed her for the sake of Woodrow Stamping Plant.

In 2002, Andrea Smith stated (when she brought her case back into courts in an attempt to recover her Worker's Compensation benefits) all her medical bills were paid but she never received any compensation money. How could this be? Her medical bills and doctors' visits were paid, but she received no compensation. Andrea didn't know anything about what had happened but this seemed to be a pattern with Woodrow Stamping Plant.

This was almost like in 1995 when Local 783 settled my grievance in my favor. I ended up with nothing but the same seniority date I had when I first filed the grievance. I received no back money. Local 783 held onto the grievance for two years—only to do nothing. When I inquired about the various stages the grievance went through, there was never any paper trail. If there were an actual grievance, there would have been a paper trail of its various stages since the grievance procedure falls in line with the federal and state courts. This grievance started in 1993 and lasted until 1995, but Local 783 followed no guidelines. The grievance should have been completed in 120 days. I never knew you could settle half of a grievance in good faith when a grievance was never filed. Woodrow Stamping Plant pulled this same trick on Andrea.

My theory was these lawyers settled for a meager amount of money, making sure the injured employee received no compensation. My Worker's Compensation Attorney, Mr. Silverman, came out of the woodworks wanting to claim in part the money I had received. He wasn't concerned when I didn't get paid. I started to wonder about all this. After I fired my lawyer and started representing myself in my Worker's Compensation case, I received my out-of-pocket expense money that I should have received in March 2002. Woodrow Stamping Plant wasn't planning to release my out of pocket expense money and became angry with me because I continued fighting for my money when they had no plans on paying me. If I didn't fight for the money, I would not have received it.

I became a nuisance to them after I struck out without an attorney. I did this through correspondence and perseverance. Andrea's court days always seemed to be on the same day or just a few days apart from my court days. I really can't explain why this happened. Even when our cases were in the federal court, our dates were around the same date or just a few days apart.

On the day of my hearing, my attorney just happened not to be at court. I was told when I called his office he had forgotten about the court date. This was the day I fired my sorry lawyer. His boss, who took his place, became angry with me because I was complaining. He told me since I was speaking out, that was the reason I was *red flagged*. Mr. Silverman was aware of what he had done and he didn't want to face me knowing he was dealing in an underhanded effort.

My lawyer sent me a bill after I received my money and Woodrow Stamping Plant never paid him entirely or in part. Mr. Silverman chose to represent Woodrow Stamping and as a result he received nothing. This lawyer had the audacity to turn around and try to sue me. He had a lot of nerve! He sent a payment request to Worker's Compensation trying to obtain his money through the court system. After I received my Worker's Compensation in December 2002, I received a telephone call from Mr. Silverman asking if I'd received my out of pocket expense money. I said yes. He then asked me if the check I received from Worker's Compensation was made out in both of our names. I said no because it wasn't.

I have to admit I was a bit confused because Mr. Silverman had already been paid when I received my first half of the Worker's Compensation settlement. Once I thought about what was happening, I wondered why he was saying he wasn't paid. Mr. Silverman petitioned Worker's Compensation for payment. I guess he wasn't supposed to receive any of my out of pocket expenses because of the cost containment stipulation. Cost containment is when there are no taxes taken from the money received for Worker's Compensation benefits. Mr. Silverman wouldn't receive any of that money anyway.

In May 2002, Attorney Silverman received the sum of $2,542.35 (two-thousand five-hundred forty two dollars and thirty-five cents). Why was he asking for money after already being paid? When I received the first payment in May 2002,

Mr. Silverman took his money right off the top. Woodrow Stamping Plant was in no hurry to pay Mr. Silverman because he didn't complete his job by making sure I didn't receive my money from Worker's Compensation. I wondered what money was owed to Mr. Silverman unless Woodrow Stamping Plant paid him a percentage of the out of pocket expense money. Woodrow Stamping Plant finally paid Mr. Silverman in December 2004, a year and a half later.

I was able to later obtain another lawyer after the state police sealed off the Medical Department and took records out of Woodrow Stamping Plant in March 2003. There were about 13 or 14 employees that were walked out of the plant, along with files from the Medical Department. In September 2004, when the state police escorted Nurse Tootie out of the plant, they couldn't seem to find Tom Hemp, Local 783 Plant Chairman. He had lost the last election and disappeared. I'm not sure if the employees taken out of the plant in March 2003 ever returned. I heard only one or two people returned. From what I understood, Nurse Tootie was later charged with embezzlement, falsifying medical records, and falsifying government documents. Nurse Tootie wasn't arrested during the first raid in March 2003. They came back later for her and were looking for her partner in crime, Mr. Tom Hemp. Since they found out what Nurse Tootie was doing in the Medical Department, why didn't they re-open Andrea's Worker's Compensation case and review her complaints involving the fraud Nurse Tootie took part in at Woodrow Stamping Plant?

46

WOODROW STAMPING RETIRED CRISTA FOR THE THIRD TIME

In early 2000, I was put on a medical retirement. I returned back on December 8, 2000. I had asked the Department of Civil Rights to intervene and as a result, Woodrow Stamping had 15 days to return me back to work. While I was off work I received a newsletter from the Retirement Board at my home address. Woodrow Stamping Plant had to have retired me in 2000 in order for me to receive a retirement newsletter. Why would I receive a newsletter from the Retirement Board when I wasn't officially retired, when I was on medical leave? When I did retire in 2002, that was the second time I was retired, but I had no knowledge of my first retirement. Each time they would bring me back in the plant they would bring me back out of retirement. They were in hopes that I didn't have my 10 years because they would never have to pay me as they did Linda Jackson and Andrea Smith. The company used Andrea's and Linda's 4 years of service with the company as a personal injury instead of an occupational injury.

After I spoke to one of the attorneys for Famous Parts Company, I obtained an attorney with little or no difficulty soon after. It was in October 2003 that Woodrow Stamping Plant decided they wanted to sever all ties with me. I agreed to terminate my employment with a medical retirement but that shouldn't have had anything to do with my money that was to have been allocated to me through my Worker's Compensation Settlement. Woodrow Stamping Plant had their own reason that they wanted to retire me and it had everything to do with the pilfering even more money from me that I should have received from Metro Craft Insurance monthly. In my medical condition I would never work in the plant ever again, because they misused my body in order to make a profit. They wanted no more dealings with me ever. I had been through pure Hell dealing with Woodrow Stamping Plant pilfering money from me.

Larry Jackson (Worker's Compensation Representative for Famous Parts Company) and my final attorney, Mark Hess (who represented my claim against Famous Parts Company—Woodrow Stamping Plant), allowed me to retire without complications. Woodrow Stamping Plant and Local 783 allowed me to keep Mr. Hess. This time they weren't going to take any further chances with my suspicions since I was becoming too much trouble for them. Therefore they were going to retire me once and for all. They would never have to worry about me ever again. They decided that my condition was severe enough to grant me a medical disability retirement in 2002 but that didn't happen until December 9, 2004. Woodrow Stamping Plant's doctor had already agreed. All they needed were time to complete the paperwork. I found this information out after I had fired my first attorney. They decided they were going to retire me originally in June 2000 without my knowledge, but their plans were interrupted when I wrote a letter asking the company to work around my restriction.

I was put on a 'no work available' in June 2000, and some months later I was put on another 'no work available' when there *was* work in the plant I could do within my restrictions. They kept setting up court dates and each time, they would fall through. My attorney, the company's attorney, and Woodrow Stamping Plant's doctor in the Medical Department all said there were no jobs for me at Woodrow Stamping in 2004. Therefore they decided to retire me.

When my retirement neared, problems started arising from my Worker's Compensation case and there was a complete shake-up taking place at Woodrow Stamping Plant. The investigation resulted in the firing and / or demoting of the attorney for Famous Parts Company—Woodrow Stamping Plant. This was around the same time Nurse Tootie was arrested for embezzlement, falsifying government documents, and falsifying medical documents. This investigation continued from June 2002 to at least December 2004 when I was officially retired. Nurse Tootie was fired in September 2004 as a result of the investigation.

Attorney Mark Hess stated there was a problem regarding my retirement, although he never told me what it was. In June 2004, I became angry because if they were going to retire me, then they should have done so. Mr. Hess kept saying we had to wait. Mr. Hess and Larry Jackson, Lawyer for Famous Parts Company, had their hands tied. I was already retired and I explained to Mr. Hess what happened. He then made a statement that whatever was going on was illegal. Woodrow Stamping Plant had unofficially retired me. They needed to undo my retirement in order to retire me again. Once Woodrow Stamping Plant retired a person, they normally never went back to reverse the retirement status. Things had to be awfully hot because they took me out of retirement twice—once in 2000 and again in 2002 before they finally retired me in 2004.

In June 2004, I received a phone call from my lawyer saying there would be another hold-up and he couldn't settle my case as promised. Famous Parts Attorney, Larry Jackson, apologized for the inconvenience. Mr. Hess told me I would have to file for my retirement once again and I would not be able to receive my back pay for my waiting period for my retirement to start. How did he know this information if I had not been retired prior? What would have been the reason for being denied the money for the initial waiting period from the Retirement Board to make a decision whether to retire me? I was supposed to have already been paid for the waiting period leading up to my actual retirement. This was from the time I filed for my medical retirement until I received it. There was no back pay associated with my retirement.

I wasn't going to be paid that money at all because it had been paid once. I asked Mr. Hess why I would not be paid for the months while waiting for my retirement to go through. This didn't go according to the contract because I should have received back pay from June 2004 until December 2004 when my retirement first started. I completed the necessary paperwork and I should have been paid accordingly. He told me he didn't know exactly why, but something was going on at Woodrow Stamping Plant he couldn't discuss. I told him I knew I was already retired. I felt Famous Parts Company's Attorney, Larry Jackson, found out I was already retired too.

Woodrow Stamping Plant changed their records and stated I had returned to work in July 2004. This was in order for me to retire in December 2004, which would have been a six-month waiting period after coming out of retirement and returning back to retirement. I was unable to physically do the work once I returned because of my disability sustained at Woodrow Stamping Plant, according to Woodrow Stamping Plant's records. I was unable to effectively return because of my disabilities, so I was told to tell the Retirement Board to start my retirement from July 2004 and my retirement would then resume.

47

LINDA JACKSON'S &
ANDREA SMITH'S
WORKER'S COMPENSATION
DISASTERS

When Linda Jackson's Worker's Compensation case was granted, she had been off work from 1997 and returned in 2001. She only lasted two days without restrictions. Woodrow Stamping violated her restrictions in order to force her back on a 'no work available'. This way they wouldn't have to worry about her again. They wanted to continue receiving her retirement. After Linda's claim was granted, she felt since her case had been in the court for years, she should have received more than $10,000 dollars. This was all Woodrow Stamping Plant was offering and they weren't going to budge on the matter. Linda told the lawyer she wanted to challenge the amount of money because she thought it was unfair. Since, a new rule was put in place in the Worker's Compensation court that a case is to be complete in three sessions in front of the judge or referee. This rule was put in place to keep cases from being in the courts for years.

Linda Jackson remains on medical leave until present (2008). She received 'sick & accident' benefits until winter of 2003, but she was yet receiving her medical insurance when her 'sick & accident' benefit payments suddenly stopped. Why is she living on her Social Security benefits only? The amount she receives per month is $1,100 dollars. Why is she not receiving her retirement or Workers Compensation for her occupational injuries sustained at Woodrow Stamping Plant? Her condition is permanent and is never going to change. Why is Linda not receiving a monthly payment from Worker's Compensation? Her injuries were caused by and aggravated by her job. The only thing she has to show for her contribution to Famous Parts Company is empty pockets and a broken down body.

In Andrea's case, she was retired when Woodrow Stamping Plant put her on her first 'no work available' and was retired during her first filing in the court in 1995. That case was settled in July 2002. While they continued to pilfer her retirement from one file, Woodrow Stamping Plant took the second set of files and used them to submit a new claim to the court. I'm not quite sure exactly how they pulled it off with the social security number being the same, but they were bold enough to use any means necessary.

Woodrow Stamping Plant took Linda Jackson's seniority and money by stating she received time for time. This meant Linda Jackson was off on medical leave for a personal injury for the equivalent of her seniority she had with the plant. Linda Jackson was on a 'no work available' for 5 years before her Worker's Compensation case was settled, but Linda Jackson has never returned back to work on a continuous basis since 1997. As of September 2008, Linda Jackson continues to be on medical leave soon to be 11 years in total. Woodrow Stamping Plant's Medical Department sent Linda Jackson who had occupational injuries to Metro Craft Insurance Company when Famous Parts Company—Woodrow Stamping Plant was receiving her Worker's Compensation weekly benefit and she receives 'sick & accident' benefits.

When everything is said and done the employee such as Linda Jackson and I have to pay the money received from Metro Craft because it is said that Linda Jackson and I was paid Worker's Compensation while we were receiving Sick & Accident benefits at the same time. Therefore she has to pay Metro Craft back the money Woodrow Stamping Plant has pilfered through the Worker's Compensation Fund. Can you believe that Famous Parts Company was pilfering from themselves in the name of employees like Linda Jackson, Andrea Smith and me Crista Carry who is now paying money back for suffering from an Occupational injuries. The only reason Andrea didn't have to pay her money back is because they terminated her employment after they pilfered all of her money through her Worker's Compensation Settlement. When they did this there was to be no more questions asked because when Andrea was terminated all unasked questions ceased. Woodrow Stamping Plant would have employees with occupational injuries apply for benefits through Metro Craft Insurance Company. When Linda Jackson's "personal injury" was nearing her 7 years, Metro Craft informed her that she had received time for time, which meant Famous Parts Company no longer had obligation to employ her. Therefore her Metro Craft payments would stop.

Linda Jackson's Worker's Compensation was settled in 2002. Regardless of the fact she didn't receive any of her Worker's Compensation money, the decision was already made in December 2002. She is yet receiving her medical insurance from Woodrow Stamping Plant but no monetary compensation. That tells me she is also entitled to receive the money they've been pilfering from her for many years on a company's medical leave. Linda Jackson's settlement claim was final because Worker's Compensation had already had her trial. It was already established that her employer contributed to the onset of her medical problems. A claim can only go in front of a judge or referee three times, and during a five-year period those days were used up. The decision was final. Those involved in this scheme were guilty of embezzlement, money laundering, and other charges as well.

Linda was supposed to receive Worker's Compensation payments from Woodrow Stamping Plant's Worker's Compensation fund each month for her occupational injury. Her lawyer went back to court in a second claim, and that was denied. This is the same exact scheme they played on Andrea Smith to keep her from being paid the money owed from her Worker's Compensation settlement claim. If Linda received time for time, why do you think she is yet receiving medical insurance through Famous Parts Company—Woodrow Stamping Plant? Why is it Linda Jackson has to continue to complete her #6651 medical forms every six months? She's not receiving any money whatsoever under retirement or Worker's Compensation. What is the benefit of her completing her medical forms twice a year? Linda's doctor informed Woodrow Stamping Plant she would never be able to return back to work, so why does she continue to complete these forms? They won't allow her to take a buy out that many employees have an option to take a company buy out because she is already retired and they can't do that so Linda Jackson must continue to suffer at the hands of Woodrow Stamping Plant because of the money that they have pilfered from her.

Why did Metro Craft pay Linda Jackson 'sick & accident' benefits for so many years when after 6 months, according to contract, employees are supposed to apply for Social Security? If her injuries were occupational, she should have received a medical disability under the retirement plan. She had to apply for Social Security after six months whether the injury was occupational or not. If the employee was on an occupational injury, they should receive payments from Woodrow Stamping Plant's Worker's Compensation fund—not from Metro Craft Insurance Company.

Metro Craft was paying for employees who had occupational injuries and keeping the employees on extended medical leaves at the expense of Metro Craft. Metro Craft had to pay employees when there was an occupational injury and Woodrow Stamping Plant was saying the employee's medical condition was personal in order to keep from paying the employee's Worker's Compensation. Metro Craft was paying for the work-related injury instead of Woodrow Stamping Plant. All this additional money was going into special accounts.

It took Linda Jackson's case 5 years to be determined that her injury was occupational. It shouldn't take that long to determine if someone has an occupational injury or disease. Woodrow Stamping Plant was milking Metro Craft Insurance Company dry with the help of Local 783. Woodrow Stamping Plant got away with their scheme by stating all injuries were personal. They continued changing employees' diagnoses from occupational to personal. Nurse Tootie did this in Andrea Smith's case.

Linda Jackson now receives material from the Retirement Board from time to time, but the company says she doesn't have enough time to retire. She would qualify if they acknowledged her injury to be occupational. Again Linda was left wondering why. If Woodrow Stamping Plant credited Linda Jackson the Worker's Compensation they pilfered from her, then she would be eligible to retire. Until then, she can't. She will never be compensated for the years Woodrow Stamping Plant pilfered from her. She has called the Retirement Board and sent letters inquiring about her retirement—only to no avail. They pilfered her Worker's Compensation money and now they're taking her retirement. What will happen to Linda Jackson and Andrea Smith? God knows how many other employees Woodrow Stamping Plant retired without their knowledge.

Both women have complained, and as a result they are not receiving any compensation from the company that caused their injuries. Someone needed to look into these complaints and get the money diverted back in the hands of the employees where the money belonged. I don't think these two women should be living in poverty at the hands of others pilfering their money. The company found money being embezzled, especially when Nurse Tootie was arrested, and did nothing to correct the problem. If nothing was done, the company is just as guilty as the ones whose hands pilfered the money. I believed the CEO's of the company were aware of what was going on, but just did nothing.

Linda received a letter stating she was not going to get any money whatsoever in September 2004. She couldn't bring this claim back into court because this was the third time she appeared in front of the judge. The lawyer representing her filed another claim as they did in Andrea's case. Some two years later she received another decision regarding the last Worker's Compensation judgment. She wasn't aware her case was introduced in the court as a new claim (like in Andrea's case). This judgment was final 30 days after the decision was made. Linda's lawyer needed to be thrown in jail for partaking in this circus—never being allowed to do this again. Linda wondered why her decision changed. When this decision was made, it left her wondering what happened because the medical aspect of her Worker's Compensation was substantiated and supported by the court. Why was it she was going to receive no compensation? How did Woodrow Stamping Plant slither their way out of this one? There was much underhanded dealing with the Medical Department funneling the money back into the company.

Linda Jackson couldn't explain how Woodrow Stamping and her attorney pulled this off. What exactly did this plant do to keep from paying Linda Jackson's claim? The money should have been paid in January 2003, but she never received her money at all. Linda wondered why she received a letter some two years later stating she would not receive her Worker's Compensation money. Could it have been that another claim was filed with no acknowledgement of the old claim filed in the Worker's Compensation Court? Woodrow Stamping Plant never paid off on the first claim and she never returned back to work. She has been continuously on medical since 1997 until present when she returned back to work only for two days in 2001 and this was mention in the settlement which was made in the Worker's Compensation Court on December 20, 2002.

I assume they were diverting her retirement along with her weekly check from Metro Craft Insurance Company into the N account. Her 'sick & accident' payments stopped when she received her last decision from Worker's Compensation. She is receiving no retirement and no 'sick & accident' benefits from the company at this time. Since Famous Parts Company is in such disarray, what will happen to Linda Jackson? What are they going to do with her? Are they going to officially retire her? I will be patiently waiting to hear something. Linda is willing to take a *buy-out* since she has been on medical leave soon to be 11 years, but will the company give her that option? This will clearly be very interesting and I really want to know the outcome.

I do know one thing. This lawyer representing Linda should have been held accountable for his actions. Woodrow Stamping Plant didn't care how much poverty their employees found themselves in. They were pilfering their money at an alarming rate. There was plenty of fraud going around for everyone who wanted to indulge in the embezzlement of other people's money.

Linda Jackson's Worker's Compensation summation stated:

Hearing dates October 2 and December 12, 2001, with post-trial briefs submitted December 12, 2001.

Settlement Claim:

"… therefore, she is entitled to weekly wages loss benefits of $500.49 from May 2, 1997 through May 10, 1998 subjected to the stipulated coordination of long-term disability benefits based on her stipulated average weekly wage of $915.00, a tax-filling status of single, and no dependents to which all was stipulated. Moreover Plaintiff is entitled to weekly wage loss benefits of $487.24 from January 25, 2001 through May 7, 2001 subjected again to the stipulated coordination of the long-term disability benefits based on the stipulated average weekly wage of $864.60 single tax-filing status and no dependents.

Again, Linda Jackson never received any money after this decision. If she had, she would have been eligible to retire. This was something Famous Parts Company—Woodrow Stamping Plant didn't want to happen because they were already receiving her retirement benefits and Worker's Compensation prior to the court settlement. The document continued:

For medical benefits, plaintiff is entitled to same regarding the treatment she received from May 1, 1997 through May 11, 1998 and again from January 24, 2001 through May 7, 2001 all of which I find was reasonable and necessary to alleviate the effects of plaintiff work-related exacerbation of symptoms, subject to cost containment.

"… Defendant is entitled to credit for any and all wages and Worker's Compensation of Worker's Compensation benefits with payment of Sickness & Accident benefits to plaintiff, which plaintiff stipulated were coordinately per MCL 418.354 …"

This Opinion Order was signed on the 12 day of December 2002 in Detroit Michigan by the Magistrate in the city of Detroit. Plaintiff, therefore, is entitled to weekly wages loss benefits Linda Jackson vs. Famous Parts Company.

This meant Linda should have been reimbursed for any and all of her out of pocket medical expenses incurred while her Worker's Compensation was being decided upon. According to Linda, she never received any compensation from her Worker's Compensation claim, contrary to what her settlement agreement stated. Why would the courts go back a make another judgment unless there was another claim filed? I'm not sure how they worked this one out because some two years later, the claim should have been paid off. There was no other court dates set-up so why did Linda Jackson's decisions change? There were no disputes with her medical condition—only with the amount of money they were offering her. It was like a crumb thrown to a mouse. The amount was clearly unfair. At any rate, Linda Jackson's seniority was yet creeping up in years and she had not worked since 1997, except for two days when she tried to come back to work in 2001. How can a person continue to receive seniority when they haven't worked in over ten years?

Why Linda is living at poverty level and the ones who pilfered her money are having a comfortable night's sleep? Linda and Andrea wondered if their conditions worsened what would happen. How were they supposed to live? Linda yet has Blue Cross as a secondary insurance along with Medicare. This is a strong indication that Woodrow Stamping Plant is paying her medical insurance while she doesn't qualify for Worker's Compensation and retirement, this money was allocated to her but she's not receiving it because Famous Parts Company and Woodrow Stamping Plant is pilfering it. Her income is very limited. Woodrow Stamping Plant doesn't care if she lives in poverty or not as long as they are able to continue pilfering her money. Linda Jackson has paid enough to the 'White Supremacy Group' at Woodrow Stamping Plant. The world should know what Famous Parts Company Woodrow Stamping Plant with the help of Local 783 did to Linda, Andrea, I, and other employees. They should be held accountable in a court of law, but it looks as though the law is right by their side.

Keep a lookout for Part Two of this book to see what happens to Linda Jackson. Will she ever receive her Worker's Compensation? How long will Woodrow Stamping Plant keep Linda Jackson completing medical forms twice a year? Will Woodrow Stamping Plant offer her a buyout so she can sever ties with them once and for all, or will they continue pilfering her money until her death? Stay tuned to <u>Somewhere Hidden Between the Cracks—Part Two</u>. There may be justice for Linda Jackson afterall.

48

WHAT HAPPENED AFTER THE MISTAKE OF THE FIRST BOOK

I wanted to obtain a loan in the early part of September 2006, in an effort to get my book on the market as soon as possible. Tassam Abou, the man who took my loan application, stated he had just come back from Woodrow. I'm not sure exactly why, but I was skeptical why he would give me this information. As he made this statement, I really didn't know what I thought. At this point, Woodrow Stamping Plant was aware hundreds of copies of the unedited version of this book were mistakenly printed and dispersed. I figured the company knew I would most likely be seeking a loan to get the re-edited book on the market. I didn't tell Mr. Tassam Abou what I wanted the money for. My plan was to get a small business loan just until I got my proposal completed. That too, fell through and it seemed I couldn't get money from anywhere for my small business.

I applied for the loan on Tuesday, September 5, 2006. I was told I would have an answer regarding my loan on Thursday or Friday of that first week. The following week of the 11th through 16th, I had yet to hear from the loan offer. September 22nd was approaching and I knew it should only take about 24 hours to see if a loan was going to be granted once my credit report was accessed.

Woodrow Stamping Plant and Local 783 have constantly interfered with my private and personal business matters. I know they seem to get the blame for anything with regards to this book, but that's because they are a powerful entity and can pull strings in just about any direction. They were well aware of this book and its contents before the final edited copy was published. They knew it was only a matter time before my book would return to market for the second time. I'm sure Woodrow Stamping Plant, Local 783, and the Executive Branch of the Union didn't want to see this book released. When I tried to get this loan, I really didn't think it would be a problem using my house as collateral for my book. It was paid in full, yet I was denied. Every avenue in which I tried to get money, failed.

The day I applied for the loan, Mr. Tassam asked me what I wanted the loan for. I told him I was going to start a small business. He asked me where I worked and I told him I was retired from Woodrow Stamping Plant. He then informed me that he had just come from Woodrow, informing me he had some friends there. I then became skeptical of Mr. Tassam Abou. He was dragging his feet as though he didn't want to give me the loan, and as a result he *didn't* give me the loan. He told me I owed money on an old account, which was actually paid in full in 2002. This was his first reasoning for not giving me this loan. I faxed Mr. Abou the paperwork stating I'd paid the loan off in full. This man was determined to find fault and stated my credit score wasn't high enough and my lowest score was 625. My house was paid in full, there were no liens on the property, and taxes were current. Therefore I assumed my house was free and clear. I was wondered why Mr. Abou seemed as though he didn't want me to have the loan I was requesting.

I contacted the Department of Civil Rights to file a discrimination claim against this loan institution. After I filed a complaint with the Department of Civil Rights, I thought about what had transpired and decided to try another mortgage company or loan institution. I contacted Jason Warren at the Department of Civil Rights who was handling my claim. I told him I had decided I wasn't going to pursue the loan with this office any longer and was going elsewhere to apply for a loan. Mr. Warren then said I should continue with Countrydone Home Loans because the loan was going to be granted. A few days later, I received a call from Tassam Abou, the first loan officer. He only inquired about the loan after I filed a complaint with the Department of Civil Rights. He asked me how the loan was going and told me to notify him of the outcome of the loan. Please keep in mind that when I first applied for the loan and Mr. Abou took my application, it was obvious I was a Black woman.

It was the week of September 22nd when I received a call from a Mr. Shawn Burnout from Countrydone Home Loans. This was from another Countrydone office—not the office where I first tried obtaining the original home loan. Shawn was from the Southfield, Michigan office and my original loan application was at a Dearborn, Michigan office. Now Mr. Shawn Burnout was taking over the loan application. It really didn't matter from what office I obtained the loan. I just needed the money. When Shawn called me, he asked what I wanted the loan for. This time I told Mr. Burnout I wanted the money to publish my book. Within a week, Mr. Burnout had completed the inspection and the papers were complete.

I received a copy of the *Truth in Lending Disclosure Statement*, which itemized what I'd be paying monthly, the interest rate, and the amount of money I wanted to barrow. I signed and faxed the information back to Mr. Shawn Burnout that evening.

Since things were going so smoothly, it looked as though I was going to receive the loan. I then received a call from Mr. Jason Warren from the Department of Civil Rights. He stated since Countrydone was going to allow the loan to go through, I should withdraw my claim. I agreed. I met him in a parking lot on Greenfield Road in Dearborn, Michigan and signed the withdrawal form dismissing my discrimination claim. I wondered why he didn't want me to come into the office. I didn't figure it out until much later. If I had gone into his office, I would have signed the log sheet putting on record I visited the Department of Civil Rights. Even though the loan hadn't gone through yet, this loan officer had assurance the loan was moving forward. The closing was set up for September 30, 2006, although the papers I signed were dated for September 28, 2006. I later found out that this time when the loan went through, it was approved because my application stated I was a *White* woman in black & white. The first time I filed for a loan, I was denied because I was Black. I closed on September 30, 2006 with Mr. Shawn Burnout's agency.

After I brought the paperwork home and was reading the documents, I noticed they weren't in order. The paperwork discussed on the telephone wasn't the same as I had signed and returned to the company by fax. I explained that the current house I lived in had nothing to do with the loan and I wanted it nowhere in the paperwork. This was because the house was free and clear. As it turned out, the papers stated many other things I didn't agree upon. This included after I signed, I would have to occupy the home I was borrowing from within 30 days. The loan was set up as an adjustable mortgage rate and it would go up to 18% interest, whereas the original rate was supposed to be a flat rate of 11%.

I told Shawn Burnout what I wanted the money for, but he put in his paperwork that I took money out of the one house to pay off the house I am currently living in. I wanted my current house to have no ties with this loan, and I made that clear. Since I had a 3-day recession period, I quickly faxed Shawn, at Countrydone in Southfield, that same night. It was Friday, September 30, 2006. I faxed him again on the evening of October 1, 2006, and again on October 2, 2006 to acknowledge I no longer wanted the loan since the paperwork wasn't to my satisfaction. I then turned around and sent the same letter to Donna, at Primary Title Company, by certified mail stating I no longer wanted the loan and was resending it.

I received a call from Shawn at Countrydone, and Donna from Primary Title Company, stating I could not withdraw my loan because it was final. Shawn told me I could come and pickup the check on that same day, October 2, 2006, after he received my fax. I also sent the letter certified mail—return receipt, to Shawn and Donna on October 2, 2006 just to further acknowledge that they received my correspondence before the 3-day recession period was up. When Shawn received my certified letter on October 4, 2006, he held the letter as if he didn't receive the letter until October 25, 2006. Primary Title Company received their letter on October 4, 2006. I received a second call from Primary Title saying I could not resend the loan because my loan was commercial. I then told both Donna and Shawn, I was aware I had a 3-day recession to resend my offer and was doing so. I also told Shawn and Donna if the deal had been final, I would have received the check on the day I closed on my home. They sent the loan through anyway despite the fact I told them both I was resending the loan since the paperwork wasn't written up correctly. Countrydone paid my taxes two years in advance and paid my insurance before the 3-day recession period. They knew I no longer wanted the loan, but they were going to push this loan down my throat just the same.

Months later, I didn't know my house was being foreclosed on since I never returned any of the phone calls. As far I was concerned, we had nothing to talk about and I never received any money. The check was left at Primary Title Company. After I became tired of them calling me, I decided to write them a formal letter requesting them to stop the harassment. I didn't try calling until February 2007, when I received a letter attached to my property stating they were going to foreclose on my home. I had difficulty contacting them because I had no account number since I never received any paperwork. Their automated phone system prevented me from getting through to a live operator. I did finally get through by using the address numbers of my house. I was put on a long holding silence for about an hour on a few occasions—so I finally gave up. That was the real reason I wrote the letter to the Countrydone Customer's Service Center in January 2007.

I wrote Countrydone as to what happened because I found I had defaulted on the loan. I sent the letter in January 2007 and didn't receive a response until March 3, 2007 that they were looking into the matter. I later found out my house had gone into foreclosure by default on March 11, 2007. This was the first date they were going to foreclose on the property. They pulled the property off the foreclosure list until April 7, 2007 to investigate my claim. I called the number of the attorney involved in the foreclosure and explained to him the situation. He stated for me to call Countrydone. I told the attorney to give me a phone number so I could speak to a live operator. That was how I finally spoke to someone directly regarding the foreclosure.

When all this was happening, I went back to the Department of Civil Rights in an effort to file a retaliation claim against Countrydone for trying to force me in taking a loan. I told them I was aware of what my rights were and they weren't going to force me into an agreement written up differently. What I received from Shawn the first time around was supposed to be the same paperwork I received on the closing date of September 22, 2006. They didn't want to go back and fix the paperwork by taking my current home off. They didn't want to correct the loan as being a fixed rate loan. They did nothing to make amends and I rescinded for that reason.

I called the Department of Civil Rights to inform Mr. Warren of what transpired with Countrydone. He stated I got what I wanted and should be satisfied. I stressed this was done in retaliation since I forced them to give me the money, they didn't want me to have it in the first place. I went back down to the Department of Civil Rights and filed another complaint against Countrydone, but this time it was for retaliation. I gave them all the information regarding what I'd sent Countrydone, including the fax receipt that stated I'd completed all the necessary paperwork in a timely manner. This proved Countrydone yet processed the loan anyway. I contacted the Department of Civil Rights for the second time in February 2007. When they filed the second claim with regards to this loan, the Department of Civil Rights stated the incident would be reported to HUD, the government housing agency. However, I believe it wasn't recorded because of the following letter from Mr. Stan Glow, Vice-President and Senior Counsel at Countrydone, sent to Mr. Gram, Claim Representative with the Department of Civil Rights. I would like to share with you this letter in response to the complaint sent to the Department of Civil Rights on my behalf of Countrydone. It was dated April 27, 2007 and stated:

"Mr. Gram:

This letter is in response to your letter dated March 7, 2007, addressed to Countrydone Home Loans Inc., and forwarded on behalf of our borrower, Ms. Carrie.

We have conducted an investigation regarding Ms. Carrie's assertion that she filed a prior civil rights complaint against Countrydone. Countrydone is aware of such a complaint. It is therefore unclear how or why she believes Countrydone retaliated against her because of her complaint.

Mr. Brandon Lear, the Regional Vice-President, and Mr. Jim Falls, the Branch Manager, confirmed that Countrydone Loan Officer, Mr. Shawn Burnout explained the initial terms of the loan and also explained the final loan program and terms to Ms. Carrie. Additionally on Monday, October 2, 2006, upon receipt of Ms. Carrie's request to rescind, Mr. Burnout called Ms. Carrie to explain that her loan was not subject to rescission because it was secured by an investment property.

In her complaint Ms. Carrie also asserts that within the 3-day recession period, Countrydone illegally paid the property taxes and hazard insurance on her behalf in order to pressure her into continuing with what she states as an "unfair loan". Our records show that on September 29, 2006, Countrydone funded a non-impound loan in the original principle amount of $25,000 at closing.

We have enclosed a copy of the HUD-1 Settlement Statement signed by Ms. Carrie at her loan closing. In reviewing page one, you will find line 301 reflects the total gross amount owed in settlement charges from Ms. Carrie at the time of closing was $5,236.22. This amount is the total of lines 802 through line 1303, as itemized on page two of Ms. Carrie's settlement statement. Included in the itemization is a payment for the hazard insurance premium to Allstate in the amount of $1,481.00 as noted on line 903, as well as a payment to the City of Detroit Treasury for 2006 taxes in the amount of $944.00, as noted on line 1303.

Additionally, since Ms. Carrie had not made a single payment on her account, Countrydone reported derogatory information with the credit bureaus each month since November of 2006. Upon receipt of your correspondence, a block was placed on further credit reporting and we have placed the account in dispute with the credit bureaus. The foreclosure process has also been placed on hold.

With respect to the allegation that Ms. Carrie was treated unfairly due to her race, we at Countrydone take allegations of discrimination very seriously. Please note that Ms. Carrie's initial Loan Application (copy enclosed) was completed with the <u>incorrect race</u> entered for Ms. Carrie as being White. Mr. Burnout met Ms. Carrie for the first time at her loan closing which took place at the closing agent's office. Regardless of race, Countrydone would have treated Ms. Carrie's application in the same manner as any other similarly situated applicant. Ms.

Carrie's race would have played no part in how this loan transaction was handled. Ethical conduct and compliance with all applicable laws and regulations are the foundation for our position of industry leadership. At Countrydone one's ability to maintain its leadership position requires that each employee, officer and director exhibit a high level of personal integrity when interacting with Countrydone customers, business partners, shareholders, and each other. Our employees must allow honesty, common sense, and good judgment to govern their conduct and it is our position that we did so in this case. We therefore vehemently deny each of Ms. Carrie's accusations of discrimination.

If you become aware of any facts that may be contrary to our finding, I would appreciate you bringing them to my attention.

Finally, Contrydone without admitting any fault or wrongdoing has elected to unwind Ms. Carrie's loan. Our personnel with respect to the uncased settlement check will contact Ms. Carrie and her officer to pay Countrydone for the taxes paid on her behalf.

I hope we have satisfactorily addressed yours and Ms. Carrie's concerns. Please don't hesitate to contact me if you have any questions or require further information." The letter was signed sincerely, Mr. Tim Blow, Vice-President and Senior Counsel.

When I received this letter I was very angry because Mr. Blow stated there was no prior discrimination complaint filed. Since he didn't have a copy, I faxed him a copy of the complaint and stated in the note on the cover page that I didn't like to be called a liar. Why would I write a letter to a company claming discrimination if I didn't have any proof to substantiate what I said? This meant Mr. Jason Warren with the Department of Civil Rights never filed the first claim. That's why he had me meet him in the parking lot on Greenfield Road. I would assume Mr. Warren was paid by someone under the table not to file this complaint. What other reason would the corporate office of Countrydone not be aware that I hadn't filed a prior discrimination case? This was the reason the Department of Civil Rights was dragging their feet in filing my second complaint. I had knowledge of the law, but if I didn't I would have been "up a creek without a paddle".

Mr. Warren had me file a discrimination claim, but took some kind of compensation in order for the claim not be recorded and filed. That meant the Department of Civil Rights sent me misleading information if they stated they filed a claim and there was no record of if. What happened to the claim? Countrydone ultimately held my money, property, and my credit hostage, which made it impossible to obtain money for the period of 9 months, also making it impossible to put my book on the market.

My complaint was finally settled on May 25, 2007. I received a letter by express mail from Countrydone, which was addressed to the Department of Civil Rights in reference to my complaint. This letter was addressed to Ms. Coleson because the person handling my claim first, took a leave. My case was given to Ms. Coleson for representation. The letter read as follows:

"Ms. Coleson:

As I mentioned in my letter to you dated May 24, 2007, Countrydone Home Loans Inc., submitted a request to have a re-conveyance prepared in order to remove Countrydone's lien. Pursuant to said request, attached please find a copy of the Discharge of Mortgage for the above reference subject to real property. A copy of the same was sent to Ms. Carrie via FedEx Priority Overnight mail for delivery on Saturday, May 26, 2007.

Should you or Ms. Carrie have any additional questions or concerns, please do not hesitate to contact me directly." Countrydone Vice President and Senior Counsel, Jason Warren, signed the letter.

I actually received a telephone call from Ms. Coleson at the Department of Civil Rights, when this news was conveyed regarding Countrydone's final decision. She wasted no time in bringing the withdrawal form to my home for my signature. I really have a problem with how this was handled because the information was to be reported to HUD. Given the action by Ms. Coleson, I'm willing to bet this complaint never made it to HUD (government agency) as a complaint. Ms. Coleson's action was the same as Mr. Jason Warren's in filing the first claim. He went through the motions of filing, but in the end the complaint wasn't filed for discrimination in October 2, 2006. The last claim was for retaliation on October 2, 2007.

I called various lawyers regarding discrimination claims of this magnitude, but many lawyers wouldn't take these kinds of cases. There was a time when almost every lawyer in the telephone book took discrimination cases, but now very few attorneys do. I wonder why. It's because there's not a lot of money made on the cases any longer. Lawyers don't want to touch them even though discrimination is yet prevalent in our society.

What I have learned about the Department of Civil Rights Representatives they make deals with companies that discriminate, which is putting the lawyers out of business. The Department of Civil Rights agents make the deals themselves with various companies accused of discriminating in order to get the charges dropped. I'm assuming the higher amount paid for a withdrawal is unknown but the agent plays lets make a deal to get the charges dropped. It doesn't matter what the client thinks because the charges are withdrawn with or without their permission anyway. Those who discriminate don't want their actions made public, so they make deals. This simply puts the lawyers out of business. From what I've witnessed, the lawyers setting out to screw their clients have, screwed themselves in the long-run. I'm speaking of the dishonest lawyers employees have come across during their fate with Famous Parts Company—Woodrow Stamping Plant. This even applies to the National Labor Relations Board for forcing employees to withdraw their complaints whether they wanted to or not. Since all of this is happening, where can the harassed and the discriminated go when they have a legitimate complaint?

I have been discriminated against by my place of employment, by the housing industry, and by the court system. All that transpired in this book gave me a rude awaking. Since lawyers aren't taking these kinds of cases, it tells me there's no money involved because the companies aren't paying on these claims. The courts are set up to dismiss discrimination and harassment cases. 'Big business' remains sure to have all their areas covered.

When I called Countrydone, my first question was, "How can you foreclose on my house and property when you still have the check?" I never picked-up the check because I'd informed them I rescinded on the loan. It had been six months and that meant the check was no good. Therefore the money should've reverted right back to Countrydone. I was asking how they could foreclose on my property when they had their money and my house was going up for action on April 4, 2007. That meant they would have my house and their money *too*—leaving my good credit in jeopardy.

Do I think Famous Parts Company had something to do with these complications? Yes I do! As you saw in previous chapters, they believed in getting back at the person they felt caused them harm. If they're innocent, I sincerely apologize, but I really don't think I have to do that. They didn't want my book released. If they could delay its release, they would. They do as they please while putting road blocks in my way. My telephone has even been tapped. At one point I would pick up my telephone only to find my line was tied to my next-door neighbor's telephone line. I've always had problems with my telephone line in one form or another. I have problems with it more so now than ever. I'm not that important for anyone else to have tapped my telephone lines. My computer has been hacked into and things came up missing out of my book. (But rest assured, they will be replaced in Part 2 of this book.)

Mr. Tassam Abou, the first loan officer, should not have held up my loan. I didn't have bad credit. When I first went to see Mr. Tassam Abou, he told me I had some small amounts owed on my credit. He then named a creditor I supposedly owed. The one he was referring to was paid in full in 2002. I felt this man was knick-picking to stall my loan being granted. There was no reason for this agency to stall on giving me information regarding this loan pro or con.

49

OLD EMPLOYEES OUT—NEW EMPLOYEES IN THROUGH BUYOUT

I figured that my loan was stalled because the company in this book needed time to take care of their business. I figured the President and CEO of Famous Parts Company and Woodrow Stamping Plant were trying to delay my book so they could do what they had to do before my book hit the market. Famous Parts Company CEO, Robert Wart, handed the company to a new CEO to assume responsibility in hopes of bringing the company back in the black. This is supposed to be done by making steep cuts and laying-off many employees through *buyouts* and educational programs. If some employees elect not to take the buyouts, the company will make the decision for them. Lindale Marvin, the new President and CEO of Famous Parts Company, will be eliminating lots of jobs (white and blue-collared) while closing many plants in an effort to allow the company to make a profit.

They are going to allow all employees to take buyouts if they choose. I believe this was done in part in an effort to allow those employees involved in the schemes of pilfering from the company, the opportunity to walk out of the doors with no questions asked. The company wanted no witnesses left who had knowledge of the pilfering schemes that could be traced back to the Executive Branch of the Company. This way many employees have the option to leave. It will look much better for them to leave on their own terms instead of having the company eventually making the decision for them. These employees could lose everything just for knowing the company was pilfering from itself.

The employees at the Executive Branch of the Company were the ones targeted to leave. All those having involvement in the thief and money-laundering scheme had to go. They didn't want incriminating information leaking to the press, as if the press was going to cover the story anyway. White-collar employees, who were unhappy with leaving, were always considered disgruntled employees. Those white-collar workers having anything to do with the handling of correspondences regarding records and files or anything else having to do with the pilfering were encouraged to step down. The company didn't want any of those people left around to give knowledge of the Executive Branch of the Company condoning what transpired within the company.

I believe Robert Wart inherited this money-laundering scheme because it had been in existence for many years before him. However, I believe when he found out about the pilfering, he may not have known how to stop it. It had gotten out of hand by his time. I now know Robert Wart, former President and CEO of Famous Parts Company, allowed the pilfering from defenseless employees in order to put the money back in the failing business.

Woodrow Stamping Plant with the help of Local 783 was pilfering employees' retirement benefits, Worker's Compensation benefits, and any other money they could get their hands on. Famous Parts Company knowingly paid employees 'sick & accident' benefits and pilfered those weekly benefits from Worker's Compensation. When employees were put on a 'no work available', they just used the second set of records to do so. Metro Craft Insurance Company paid the benefits for an occupational injury, knowing Worker's Compensation should have been paying those benefits.

I handed out the first unedited edition of Part 1 to anyone who wanted a book. I didn't want the book thrown away. If there was someone willing to read the book with errors, they were welcome to do so. In each book I wrote inside the cover, "Unedited Version. This book can't be sold". I didn't want anyone else making a profit by selling the unedited version when the books were given out. I was giving the books away by the cases as a promotional ploy. I figured once the edited version hit the market, anyone who had an unedited version in their possession could do as they pleased with it.

In addition to the first version being distributed in various Famous Parts Company plants in Michigan, I gave Andrea Smith as many copies of the book she requested until they were all gone. Andrea sent unedited promotional versions of the books any and everywhere she could think of. She attached a cover page stating what pages and chapters to read pertaining to her unjust experiences. She sent the books to the local news stations 2 FOX, 4 WDIV, & 7 ABC. She gave copies to the Washington D.C. Branch of the National Labor Relations Board, Famous Parts Company CEO of the Executive Branch of the Company Robert Wart (who sent security down to pick up the book), the Local Branch of the Department of Civil Rights, and one was also sent to the Lansing Branch of the Department of Civil Rights. Andrea sent copies to the Governor, Dateline, and 20/20. There may have been more, but those are the places I know she sent books in an effort to get attention on her experience with Woodrow Stamping Plant and Local 783.

Andrea wanted to get some attention on how she was treated by her employer and the union that was supposed to be protecting her. She may receive some kind of justice afterall regarding the local National Labor Relations Board. She wanted to make notice of her retirement and Worker's Compensation she never received even though the case was settled just the same. She did receive a letter from the NAACP stating they would be sending a field representative to investigate her claims. However, this came to a dead end. The Department of Civil Rights stated they too, were going to investigate that was also a joke. This happened after Andrea had been trying to get both entities to look into her claims all along. Andrea just recently received a letter from the Michigan Worker's Compensation Board stating since she took her case to the Supreme Court, they were going to look further into the matter, but that never happened. Andrea's doctors were paid, but she received no payment after her case had been in the court for 7 years before it was settled in July 2002. Andrea wants the world to know what Woodrow Stamping Plant and Local 783 put her through. Until she sent a copy of the unedited version of Part 1, it seemed as though her story got no attention at all. I do hope Andrea Smith and Linda Jackson receive some kind of justice from what they have been through.

Executive Branch of the Union CEO, Don Hangem, stepped down two weeks after he was re-elected because of the same investigation. A local newscaster stated Don was leaving the Executive Branch of the Union to take a position with the Executive Board of the Company at Famous Motors Company, which had no affiliation with Famous Parts Company. When I heard this news, I was surprised. This investigation was years too late for many employees treated in the unjust manner as Andrea Smith and I experienced during our years of employment at Woodrow Stamping Plant with Local 783 as our representative.

I found out Don Hangem was indicted (under investigation) from a news article on the internet, which stated that out of the last eight Presidents and CEO's of the Executive Branch of the Union, 5 had been indicted. This was according to *UnionFacts.com*. What were the odds of the Executive Branch of the company and the Executive Branch of the Union stepping down only weeks apart amidst an investigation? Don Hangem resigned, slowly being fazed out of the media. Nosy Nort, former Director at the Regional 21A Office, took over as Union President and CEO of the Executive Branch of the Union. While Don Hangem was under investigation, he was not allowed to make any union decisions until the investigation was over. Since the publishing of the unedited version of Part 1, Robert Wart, President and CEO of the Executive Branch of the Company, also stepped down allowing someone else to take his place. He states that he feels comfortable with the predecessor taking over the company, but he will continue as Chairman of the daily operation of Famous Parts Company.

I know Woodrow Stamping Plant pilfered from Andrea Smith, Linda Jackson, and me with us not being able to do anything about it. They were so bold and blatant in what they were doing. My friend and co-worker, Mazzie Cane, could do nothing about them stealing her money or seniority either. Woodrow Stamping Plant and Local 783 pilfered Ronda Summers' money and seniority, and then sent her packing. They had the authority to do as they pleased and there was nothing we could do about it.

The bottom line is it's wrong for anyone to pilfer employees' retirement and Worker's Compensation especially when they're disabled and need the money themselves. I think if it were I, a minority with no clout, who was pilfering money, I would be tried and detained for the remainder of my life. It was alright to these large companies taking what didn't belong to them and never having to serve one day of time because money talked. It didn't matter what crime Woodrow Stamping Plant committed, their money bought them anything—Exemption, Redemption, Freedom, and Justice.

I am here to say I was strongly motivated to write this book. For many years I tried getting someone to listen. Each time I tried to get help, I was retaliated against in one form or another. I worked for this company for a total of 14 years before my retirement and I never saw justification for what they did to me and the others mentioned in this book. The people are real and the treatment received was real. That's what we all had in common. When you are poor and working hard to support your family, the last thing you need is the very company employing you to be stealing from you. We were all hard-working employees, and to be treated in this manner was inhumane. We were not animals, but humans with feelings. Any human in this type of hostile work environment would break and fall apart.

Was it democracy when the people who had money did as they pleased and weren't held accountable? I truly don't care at this point what happens to those who didn't care about me. Our memories of our work experiences are tainted because it was as though everyone ganged up on us while others stood by and watched. Everyone we reached out to for help failed to protect us. We clearly didn't count for anything. I learned no matter how good of a worker we were, we could always be replaced or removed because there was always someone waiting to take our places.

What about the discrimination, retaliation, harassment administered to us? Where was the justice system? Where were the lawyers who were supposed to protect us? Where were the judges and referees that were supposed to give use equal justice under the law? Where was the "justice for all"? I am sure if I were Caucasian, I wouldn't have to write this book just to get the attention of those who wouldn't listen to my cry for help. I know that sounds harsh, but it's the truth. When you are a minority, you have no rights even if you do have money and backings. I also blame the Blacks and other minorities who took part in the injustice when they knew the company was breaking the labor and contract laws.

I'm ashamed to say the judge handling Andrea's case allowed 'big business' to go against the law while throwing her case out in a Summary Judgment when she asked for a jury trial. This was a Black judge who sided with 'big business'. Andrea had much evidence proving her case, but with Woodrow Stamping Plant sitting on moneybags, it was as though she had no evidence at all.

The company used minorities to represent them in a court of law so their conduct wouldn't be viewed as discrimination. They used Black on Black discrimination. And you know what? It worked. The company had Black management, attorneys, and judges siding with 'big business' in an effort to discriminate against other Blacks. After all was said and done, discrimination was alive and well.

Organizations such as the National Association for the Advancement of Colored People (NAACP) need to close their doors. If they're not effective when "colored people" need them, what are they useful for? Is it to receive free money or handouts from outside organizations? The ones really needing help can't get it because of it jeopardizing the donations these entities receive from 'big businesses'. They want to maintain the loyalty and the flow of funding for certain causes.

Andrea and I reached out to so many organizations for help and were denied assistance. All we wanted was justice. Justice was a word with no definition because it didn't mean anything in the end. We Americans are supposed to be living in a democratic society. We are trying to teach freedom of speech to the world, but in essence we are living one big lie. All of our rights are slowly being taken away. It's gotten to the point where if we don't speak out, we will lose everything our fathers and forefathers have worked for.

Freedom of speech is a thing of the past, and if we're not careful our country will be under dictatorship. Can't you see what our Republican Administration is saying and doing? Don't you see how our country is being run at the approval rating of our President? Everyone is complaining, but he is yet making decisions unpopular to many. Our house of representatives seem to side with the President, and the senate is doing the same. This man is doing exactly what he wants and there is no one standing up to challenge his actions. In the end, we all have to pay the price of bad decisions made by our leaders. This is the story in our quest for justice. We have no voice and we have no justice.

50

NO RESPONSE FROM THE PRESIDENT OF THE UNITED STATES

This entire chapter (for the most part) is a letter sent to the President of the United States of America on Andrea Smith's behalf. The letter is a synopsis of her experiences with Woodrow Stamping Plant and Local 783.

Andrea was aware she wasn't going to get any help from the local sector or government agencies, so she started sending information to the Washington D.C. Branch of the National Labor Relations Board and the Department of Civil Rights. They finally re-opened her case and handed it back to the local branch of the Department of Civil Rights. It didn't matter how horrific the things were that Woodrow Stamping Plant and Local 783 did to Andrea. There were no charges brought against them when she was terminated unjustly. There were no investigations and when there were, the results were always the same.

Andrea couldn't get anyone in the state of Michigan to come to her defense and there had been a serious wrong administered to her by her employer. Andrea tried the governor, state senator, attorney general, the Executive Branch of the Company and the Union and of course various lawyers. Even the Local Union had never filed a grievance on Andrea's behalf. All of the above entities were contacted and this is where she remains today.

In January 2007, I figured if I could get politicians involved, including the President of the United States, it would be well worth my while just to get someone to listen and investigate. What was going on at the top level of Famous Parts Company and the Executive Branch of the Union, who were aware of everything happening to Andrea Smith? Everyone turned their backs with little or no remorse. I even contacted other senators with no Michigan affiliation and that was to no avail. With a problem of this magnitude, it's hard to comprehend that every door was slammed in Andrea's face—especially when her life depended on it.

I sent an overview of Andrea's experiences by e-mail to the President of the United States. I was only asking that someone look into the situation, but still no investigation took place. Everything has stayed the same. I didn't expect the President to get involved personally, but I did hope he would have a staff member address Andrea's issues. I stated I was contacting him for a friend in an effort to get some attention on the problem she was facing with regards to her employer and the union that was supposed to be protecting her.

I contacted the President of the United States by fax on December 21, 2006 and again on December 27, 2006, and I received no response pro or con. Andrea received no correspondence regarding her problem with Famous Parts Company, Local 783, or her illegal termination. At that point I guess Andrea's problems weren't important enough to reach the person at the highest level of the government. Here in Michigan, a woman called the President regarding a drug house in her neighborhood in which local agencies couldn't seem to close down. But according to the local news station, action was only taken after she called the White House to intercede. Why couldn't Andrea receive any intervention? Andrea's life depended on the President's help. Could the reason that we received no response have been because we were Black women seeking help? I also e-mailed the President of the United States on January 3, 2007 and again on January 23, 2007.

I knew my action may have been a little unusual in contacting the President, but I only contacted him because Andrea couldn't get anyone's help in the state of Michigan, leaving her reaching out for Washington D.C.'s help. My fax substantiated Andrea's problems surrounding her unjustified termination and explained there were many other employees experiencing the same fate as Andrea Smith and I. The fraudulent activity should have been investigated for these reasons. I received a response from the Speaker of the House saying I was out of her jurisdiction. I respected her for at least getting back with me. This was the only response I received.

My letter was dated January 3, 2007. The same letter was e-mailed on January 23, 2007. It read:

"Dear Mr. President,

I'm asking for help for a friend who was wrongfully terminated for something she didn't do while Local 783 (her union), allowed the termination to stand. I am writing this note because my friend, who was terminated unjustly from Famous Parts Company—Woodrow Stamping Plant, really doesn't know where to go for help. Andrea Smith found that Woodrow Plant, with the help of Local 783, was pilfering her retirement and Worker's Compensation claim money. Her attorney and Woodrow Stamping Plant settled her case, but neither her attorney nor the judge informed her of this most important fact regarding her Worker's Compensation claim. Her case was settled sometime in July 2002. All her medical bills were paid, but Andrea never received any compensation from the settlement.

Andrea Smith filed her case in the Worker's Compensation court in 1995. She filed another claim in 2002, unaware the first court's case was settled. A second decision on Andrea's Worker's Compensation decision was made June 24, 2004. She was hit by a hi-lo truck while working at Famous Parts Company—Woodrow Stamping Plant. She was hit with a broom by a White co-worker. This was the same co-worker whom cursed at her a week prior to the broom incident. The cursing incident was reported to Labor Relations and nothing was done. But one week later, he threw a broom hitting her in the chest leaving a large bruise. This incident ultimately led up to Andrea's major depression medical leave. Andrea's doctor pulled her out of the plant in 2002. Andrea called this kind of treatment "the slavery mentality of the 1950's".

Labor Relations did not investigate the incident with regards to her firing, but they all met in Woodrow Stamping Plant's Labor Relations Office. Those who in attendance were Andrea Smith who was hit in the chest with the broom; Silly Sally, Labor Relations Supervisor; Ronald Hatfield, the employee who assaulted Andrea Smith; and Andrea's immediate Supervisor, Joseph Fears. She was not allowed to say anything, but she did accept Ron's apology. She had no idea they were going to just let him walk out of Labor Relations with no disciplinary action taken against him whatsoever. She didn't think that Labor Relations was going to do nothing because his attack was done with intent.

He was told to assault Andrea by Woodrow Stamping Plant. They chose someone who didn't have so much as the knowledge to write his own name. Ron Hatfield had dedication for the place where he worked. Woodrow Stamping Plant had no intention on disciplining him because this was done in an effort for Andrea to quit her job. But things didn't go according to plan. They couldn't frighten her enough to quit, so they took the initiative to terminate her employment themselves, but not before she was hit with the hi-lo truck. It was the duty of Labor Relations to discipline Ronald, but they didn't. Instead they told Andrea Smith she was not allowed to talk to anyone about being assaulted with the broom, or the incident when she was hit with the hi-lo truck in the plant—even though she was taken to the local hospital in June 2002. She was treated and a bit shaken-up, but she was okay. The doctor in the hospital informed Andrea that being hit with the hi-lo truck aggravated her condition of Degenerative Joint Disease, but she was treated and released.

Andrea Smith was so distraught she went home for the remainder of the day without pay. The man who assaulted her worked and was paid a full day's pay. Famous Parts Company—Woodrow Stamping Plant professed they were a 'no tolerance' policy plant. What happened to their 'no tolerance' policy when Andrea was hit with the broom? That's self-explanatory because she was Black and he was White.

Soon after Andrea was hit with broom, she tried unsuccessfully to file a grievance against Famous Parts Company—Woodrow Stamping Plant. On the day she drafted her own grievance and handed it to Zeb Star, the Committeeman, she was later hit by the hi-lo truck going down the path where she worked. There were no other hi-lo trucks going down Andrea's aisle. They were forbidden in her area. But it was what happened after the fact that she found so disturbing. Woodrow Stamping Plant denied she was hit with the broom and when she was hit with the hi-lo, both incidents became alleged incidents only. Woodrow Stamping Plant destroyed everything having to do with Andrea Smith being hit with the hi-lo truck. They did the same with the incident when a broom was thrown and landed in her chest. It didn't matter. Andrea wasn't allowed to say a word in her own defense, even in the grievance process, which was the biggest joke of all.

Andrea is disabled under the guidelines of the Social Security Administration. She found out through the Social Security Administration that Famous Parts Company—Woodrow Stamping Plant, her employer, had her on a "retired" status. When she started inquiring about these allegations, she was brought back to work from medical leave. The harassment continued until she was terminated February 2003. During this time she contacted the Michigan Branch of the National Labor Relations Board and the Michigan Branch of the Equal Employment Opportunity Commission regarding Woodrow Stamping Plant. Each time she would receive a 'right to sue' letter that no lawyer in the state of Michigan would honor.

Andrea filed charges against Local 783 on numerous times through the Michigan National Labor Relations Board, the Michigan Department of Civil Rights, and the Michigan Equal Employment Opportunity Commission (EEOC) with six or more complaints, but they never followed through with any of the charges.

These are the cases she has filed with the EEOC:

- EEOC No. 153234   issued complaint January 13, 2006
- EEOC No. 147369   issued complaint August 9, 2005
- EEOC No. 309110   issued complaint July 28, 2003
- EEOC No. 23AA200356   issued complaint Mar. 3, 2002
- EEOC No. 288506   non-sufficient evidence Mar. 6, 2000
- EEOC No. 230950694   processed February 23, 1995
- EEOC No. 143180   issued complaint January 18, 1995

You would think this number of complaints would call for an investigation at the least—especially when one or more person is complaining about the same problem. This treatment continued because the company never had to be held accountable for their discriminatory actions. If there were no one there to stop them, why would they stop discriminating?

Where does a person go to obtain help when the Equal Employment Opportunity Commission won't even take all the complaints to court? Although I don't have the statistics of how many cases they take to trial, there is no reason for a person to have to file this amount of charges against one company. It was these claims, times two (at the least), because I filed many myself before I retired. This tells me that the government agencies in the State of Michigan condone these tactics used by the company and the union.

Famous Parts Company never learned from their discrimination practices because each time Andrea Smith would file a complaint, the same company would then retaliate against her. This should not be tolerated under the civil rights guidelines. When Andrea Smith would return to the Equal Employment Opportunity Commission and tell them she was retaliated against, again nothing would be done regarding the matter. In my opinion, there is no accountability at Woodrow Stamping Plant. They manage to pay their way out of everything.

Andrea having to file this many complaints tell me discrimination is alive, well, and growing in the state of Michigan. 'Big Business' owns this state and city government. This should not be. They say we have civil rights but when it comes down to it, we don't have any rights at all. The Department of Civil Rights and the Equal Employment Opportunity Commission could have taken Andrea Smith's case to trial, but instead they gave her a 'right to sue' letter in the providence where she lived. She couldn't so much as give the 90-day 'right to sue' letter away because it was a worthless piece of paper around the metro area.

I see that money rules the state of Michigan. If you have money, you do whatever you want with no accountability. Famous Parts Company maintained the authority to continue discriminating—even in a court of law. The media won't even cover Andrea Smith's story. They will not touch any story directly related to the powerful Famous Parts Company. Each local new channel has a 'Problem Solver' segment, but they are not interested in Andrea Smith's and Crista Carrie's problems. When is it that the news media isn't interested in a good news story? The local newspaper didn't even want the story. It was far too controversial. In my opinion, the only way a story is not covered is if it's censored.

At hand, I have where Andrea Smith filed charges with the National Labor Relations Board on:

* May 6, 2006   Charge No. 7-CB-15195
* January 2006   Charge No. 7-CB-15015
* May 9, 2002   Charge No. 7-CB-14801
* January 2002   Charge No. 7-CB-13116
* Nov. 16, 2001   Charge No. 7-CB-13065

There were more, but this is what I have access to. Each time she would file with Department of Civil Rights, the Equal Employment Opportunity Commission, or the National Labor Relations Board, she would be retaliated against for the charges she filed against Woodrow Stamping Plant and Local 783. This is the reason she was terminated and can't get any help from anyone as of today.

Each time she filed a complaint, she always had documentation to substantiate it. They would find "not enough evidence" to file a complaint against Local 783. Andrea Smith has also contacted the Governor of Michigan, the Michigan Attorney General, the Michigan Department of Labor, the Michigan State Senator, and the Michigan NAACP Branch. This was all to no avail. It seemed Andrea couldn't get one person to step up to the plate and help her in her efforts of representing herself against Famous Parts Company. In Michigan, this company is off limits from any wrongdoing.

Famous Parts Company is very charitable and when an organization is in need of money to help their cause, Famous Parts Company is very generous. The problem with this is those organizations receiving help from a large company such as Famous Parts Company, will protect their sponsor. Who is going to speak out against them? Famous Parts Company owns the state of Michigan and I wouldn't have believed a minority couldn't so much as get a case heard in the federal or state court when there were serious labor and contract laws violated.

I have been told on many occasions that the federal court would not find Famous Parts Company guilty of discrimination because of what they did for all the minorities that migrated to Michigan from 1918 until 1947 by giving them good paying jobs. I was told by the judge and lawyers that Famous Parts Company will not be convicted of discrimination. That was hearsay, but I'm beginning to believe there is some truth to this statement.

Just to make a point of what I'm speaking is true: In the November 2006 election, the civil rights proposal on Affirmative Action was defeated. If issues such as discrimination weren't so prevalent in Michigan, why was the affirmative action proposal put on the ballot in the first place? Some felt there was such a problem with affirmative action that it needed to be eliminated. The Caucasians spoke on how they actually felt behind voting booths, but it's not always apparent in front of your face. Behind the scenes, they stated minorities should have no rights. There are some serious discrimination issues facing minorities in various segments of the state.

By eliminating affirmative action programs, many minorities won't have a fair chance in colleges or in other areas. For example, my daughter Dorthia is an Occupational Therapist who very much wanted to become a Physical Therapist. She carried a 4.0 average all through Wayne State University when she was first denied entry in the program at Wayne State University. She applied at Michigan Eastern University and was denied for the second time. She always wanted to work in the field she so desired after becoming an Occupational Therapist, since receiving her two-year degree from Wayne County Community College. It wasn't because she wasn't smart enough. It was because she was a minority. There was a small quota or no quota at all of the number of minorities to be accepted, just as Famous Parts Company had a quota in hiring minorities in their skilled trade's field.

Affirmation Action programs were already in place when she attended Wayne State University and Eastern Michigan University At that point, she had no alternative but to go into the teaching field. My daughter Dorthia, is a teacher but not by her first choice. Can you imagine what minorities have to look forward to in the next ten years or so from now? For this reason, the Affirmation Action law should not have passed. Given the opportunity with these programs, it equals the playing field for those who are a minority to have a chance to participate in Affirmative Action programs. Nothing much has changed. Discrimination is just as prevalent now as it was before. It's just approached in a different manner.

Everyone has a right to their opinion and I respect that. I truly understand because there are always going to be those who don't like others because of the color of their skin. That will never change since it is a learned behavior. Those who think in this manner, think with a limited capacity. We know many minorities are behind bars in prison because of lack of education, opportunity, and above all else—lack of jobs. Felons find themselves back in the prison system because of these reasons.

We all play a part in society and we all have to respect and accept other people's ideas and opinions. But I see something wrong when I see mainly one race in any company, city, or state agency. When this happens, that's a sign that discrimination is a factor—especially when the surrounding area has many minorities. All communities: White, Black, Native-American, Hispanic, Arab ... we all need to work together for a common cause because we all have something to offer. There will always be people who want nothing in life. Those aren't the people who want to strive for their goals. Those who want nothing out of life shouldn't complain about those striving for a goal. It doesn't matter what color you are, anything worth having is worth working for. If it's not worth working for, then it is not worth having. Minorities with a drive shouldn't be hampered from accomplishing their goals just because they have a poor background or just because they are a minority.

How can a poor minority afford to go to collage with Caucasians catering to their own? The minorities don't have the same early educational backgrounds as Caucasians have. The school systems just keep passing the minority students whether they have learned anything or not. When some minority students complete school, they can't even read or complete a simple employment application. It's not the child's fault. The fault falls on the system. I'm not saying that they can't learn. When given the right atmosphere, minorities can be just as educated as Caucasian students. I'm saying if a minority makes it to college, they will never have the same opportunities as the Caucasian student. Discriminatory practices have never stopped. It's silently escalating whether we acknowledge it or not. We are taking a step back in history whether we acknowledge it or not.

The Caucasians spoke on how they honestly felt and they eliminated the very element that may have held our system together. Eliminating Affirmative Action will not stop those who are determined, though it may slow them down. I would rather have a person of any race dedicated to their job, rather than have someone of my own race with no dedication at all. If I were to only hire according to someone's skin color and not by their qualifications, I'd be shortchanging myself. I would be limiting my ability to grow and the opportunity to get to know what others were capable of.

We really won't see the ramification of eliminating Affirmative Action programs until years down the line. Just as long as large companies are as they are, we'll soon be back in the 1940's and 1950's as far as discrimination is concerned. The type of discrimination, harassment, and retaliation that Andrea and I experienced constantly goes unreported. It should not be tolerated by any company against Blacks or anyone else.

The letter continues:

Famous Parts Company—Woodrow Stamping Plant terminated Andrea Smith February 5, 2003 while she was on medical leave from the company. Woodrow Stamping Plant and Local 783 were in violation when they fired her while she was on medical leave for major depression. She tried to file a grievance regarding her firing and her grievance went ignored. She filed an Article 33 Grievance in a timely manner and they ignored that too. President and CEO of the Executive Branch of the Union, Don Hangem, stepped down in July 2006 shortly after he had been re-elected, because of this Article 33 and how it was handled. The NLRB wrote Andrea Smith a letter stating that she admitted that she didn't get her Article 33 in on time.

It didn't matter how much information Andrea sent Don Hangem stating she *did* file the Article 33 in time, they just ignored it and put words in her mouth. The letter Andrea received from the National Labor Relations Board stated she admitted she didn't get the Article 33 in on time. The NLRB made up a lie to save Don Hangem's job. That was wrong because her job wasn't spared. They made this decision for Andrea because they had the authority to do so. After she received this letter from the Washington Branch of the National Labor Relations Board, she filed an immediate response on October 2, 2006. Her response was in a form of an appeal, and that letter was ignored too. She hadn't heard anything else from the Washington Branch of the National Labor Relations Board until she filed an amendment to her claim in February 2007. At this time, the Washington Branch of the Department of Civil Rights accepted the added information from the contract between the union and Famous Parts Company.

The Washington D.C. Branch of the National Labor Relations Board had already received correspondence from the Washington Branch of the Department of Civil Rights. That is when the National Labor Relations Board stated they hadn't received any new information. Andrea had sent them the information in her appeal and they responded. Why would Andrea tell the National Labor Relations Board that she didn't get her Article 33 to the International Executive Board of the Union in a timely manner? What proof does the NLRB have stating Andrea admitted this to them? She had her proof, but the NLRB wasn't interested in what proof she had. The only thing they were interested in was saving Don Hangem's job. They were aware Andrea reached out to his office for help and was illegally denied.

She and I both have those copies and I am aware her information was indeed sent in a timely manner. I faxed this information to the White House in December 2006 and January 2007 in hopes that someone would investigate the fraud and money laundering at Woodrow Stamping Plant and Local 783. Andrea has no money, job, or health benefits, so what would be gained by telling a lie after all the events were over? Andrea is continuing her fight, which alone should say she's trying to get someone's attention in and effort for them to allow her to speak on her own behalf. She was never allowed to say anything in her defense. They all spoke for her and called her 'guilty'. This went for Woodrow Stamping Plant, Local 783, and the Executive Branch of the Company, the Executive Branch of the Union, the Department of Civil Rights, the Department of Labor, the Equal

Employment Opportunity Commission, the National Labor Relations Board, the Michigan Attorney General, the Michigan Governor, and our State Senator. I have always been skeptical of everyone yelling 'guilty' and not allowing the accused to speak out in their own defense. This was nothing more than a modern day lynching.

This is how Andrea Smith's complaints have always been handled. This went back to the early 1990's. She had written her own grievances to be filed on numerous occasions, but was never given the opportunity to have her grievance heard or participate in the grievance process. Through all of the appeals Andrea filed with the National Labor Relations Board, she was unable to find the charge of the appeals on the computer. There is no record of any claim or appeal in the NLRB Washington Branch regarding Andrea Smith or even Crista Carrie for that matter. Those appeals are supposed to be official public records.

At one point, I was bringing charges against Plant Chairman, Tom Hemp and Regional 21A Representative, Al Snake under Article 33. I asked Andrea Smith to appear at my hearing. She spoke on how she was treated by Woodrow Stamping Plant's Medical Department. She couldn't get Local 783 to file a grievance on her behalf. When the International Executive Board came back with their findings, they noted Andrea was at my hearing, but made no mention of her testimony.

Andrea wrote a letter dated March 17, 2003 addressing the Public Review Board on the matter. There was a letter written by Andrea to the office of Don Hangem, Executive Branch of the Union's CEO, requesting an investigation of Andrea's firing and how Local 783 handled it. The letter was dated February 16, 2004. The Article 33 was sent to Don Hangem on October 17, 2005, one month after the grievance was presumed to be settled. Andrea has her returned receipt and I have copies of those same letters. On March 17, 2003 one month after Andrea Smith was terminated, she wrote the Appeals Board of her concerns. She also wrote them March 21, 2003 in an effort to get her grievance addressed at the hearing. We both wanted to attend the Public Review Board hearings, but were denied. Andrea Smith wanted someone to address her termination and the lies surrounding her firing. Andrea also sent the newly elected Plant Chairman of Local 783, Larry Mean, a letter regarding her dissatisfaction of the outcome of her grievance settlement dated October 7, 2005. The grievance was settled in September 21, 2005.

When she sent this information to the Public Review Board, they had the authority to address Andrea's firing and other issues. They never addressed any of them. I felt Don Hangem, President and CEO of the Executive Branch of the Union, needed to step down if he allowed something like this to happen. Everyone has to work in order to survive and when they can't work, they can't survive. Woodrow Stamping Plant and Local 783 stripped all this away from Andrea Smith.

Andrea Smith went as far as going to Local 783's Union Hall and contacting the Vice-President, Mr. Moore, who was the newly elected Vice-President after Andrea was fired. Andrea tried to give a copy to Dorothy Rush, the recording secretary at Local 783, but she wouldn't accept it. She was the one the Article 33 should have been addressed to. According to the Constitution of the Union, the recording secretary handles the Article 33. Andrea went to the Regional 21A Branch of the Union and had the secretary of David Sanders, who's the representative for Famous Parts Company at the National Level, to sign for a copy of the Article 33. He told Andrea that he handed the Article 33 to Don Hangem himself. She believed him at the time because there was no reason for him to lie.

The question came about when Andrea refused to sign a wavier Local 783 made up just for her. This wavier was going to allow Andrea Smith to return back to work without any back pay. However, if she signed this waiver, she was to be on probation for the period of 12 months and would be forbidden to file a grievance against the union and the company for one year regardless of her guilt or innocence. She could be dismissed at any time. None of her medical leaves would go toward any contractual leave and her condition was originated at Woodrow Stamping Plant. She yet had to pay her union dues, but was forbidden to file a grievance. The newly elected Plant Chairman of Local 783, Larry Mean, stated he wanted nothing to do with Andrea Smith's grievance because it was illegal. He told Andrea as much.

The International Executive Board never forced Larry Mean to comply because they too, were aware the wavier was not standard. It didn't matter that Mean inherited this grievance and still should not have been able to deny representation to Andrea. They found no reason to bring charges against Local 783 for never filing Andrea's grievance or failing to represent her in her firing. Instead they took part in her termination, which was based on a lie. She was unable to substantiate what exactly was said that caused her termination. They didn't want anything Andrea Smith had to say on record because their lies couldn't stand up in a court of law. This is the reason Andrea's case was thrown out of court in a Summary Judgment. The judge wasn't going to allow her case anywhere near a jury. I wonder what favor these judges were granted or how much they got paid.

The deposition stated Andrea Smith threatened the doctor and/or nurse in the Medical Department. She was to have made threats on three occasions, the first being on October 14, 2002. The second threat was supposedly made on December 3, 2003, and the last was said to have been made on January 22, 2003. Andrea knew of none of these incidents until after she was terminated. She was terminated on February 5, 2003 on a lie—and not a very good one at that.

Andrea was on medical leave for major depression because of the treatment she received from Woodrow Stamping Plant and from everything I have explained I'm sure that you can understand why. If Local 783 was of any good or had represented her properly, she would not have been terminated while on medical leave because she was off company payroll. If she had returned and was back on payroll, Woodrow Stamping Plant would have terminated her anyway. They couldn't wait until she returned back to work for fear of their pilfering scheme being revealed. In order for a suspension to be justified, the person is to be physically at work. Andrea was not physically at work, but Woodrow Stamping Plant had her fired just the same. Local 783 allowed Andrea's illegal termination to stand.

Silly Sally, Labor Relations Supervisor who was on the investigation committee, was to investigate whether the termination that led up to Andrea's termination on February 2003 was justified. Everything was hearsay according to the deposition. Silly Sally stated in the deposition on February 28, 2005 that she knew nothing of the October 14, 2002 threat. Silly Sally's deposition stated she saw no records, notes, memorandums, or anything else regarding the October 14, 2002 threat. Silly Sally said she received a call from Andrea's doctor stating Andrea threatened both Dr. Slick and Nurse Tootie. We knew this was a lie because of the Privacy Act binding the doctor from doing such things. Andrea's doctor was forbidden to call the plant and slander her patient. If Andrea's state was so critical and she felt Andrea's mental condition was so severe, she would have called the police or an ambulance to take her to the nearest hospital for an evaluation. As far as Andrea's doctor calling Silly Sally and spreading this kind of gossip, it would have been very unprofessional to say the least. In this same document, Silly Sally stated Andrea was not hit with the hi-lo truck. Silly Sally then turns around and says in the same letter, Andrea was transported to the hospital and had x-rays administered by the hospital. All this was said in one letter from Woodrow Stamping Plant's Labor Relations Department and was signed by Silly Sally. None of these contradictory statements ever went under scrutiny.

According to another document Silly Sally wrote as to the reason for Andrea's termination, she stated when Andrea Smith was terminated under no circumstances was she hit with a broom by any of her co-workers. Silly Sally said this incident and the hit by the hi-lo were only allegations. Then she said in this same document that Ronald Hatfield made an apology for hitting Andrea with the broom. The incident may have been forgotten by Labor Relations and Ronald, but not by Andrea Smith.

On January 22, 2003 Andrea was called to the plant in the Medical Department for an evaluation. There it was said that she threatened the doctor and nurse. The supposed verbatim was never documented for the record. The specific threat that caused Andrea's termination was never expressed. There were three supposed events and not one document reveals what it was Andrea Smith said. Here we have someone terminated and not one person can say what was said that caused her termination. Everything seemed to be hearsay according to depositions. No one was able to say Andrea's exact words.

Andrea was truly afraid to return back to the plant because she felt they were trying to kill her. She called Don Hangem, President and CEO of the Executive Branch of the Union, and was told by his secretary they were going to send someone to meet her in the Medical Department upon her arrival. She also called the Regional 21-A Office and told them she was afraid to go back in the plant. She had already been cursed, hit with a broom, and hit with a hi-lo truck. She felt nothing would prohibit her from being killed in that plant since these people repeatedly got away with ruthless activity. Knowing all of this information on the day of Andrea's appointment, she walked in the Medical Department with her husband and there was no union representative anywhere in sight.

After all was said and done, Andrea was terminated for threatening the Medical Department staff. Andrea received another letter from Famous Parts Company on September 12, 2006 from the Labor Relations Manager of Vehicle Operations of North America. It stated Andrea was terminated once again. Was it that Andrea wasn't officially terminated in February 2003? Was the letter dated September 12, 2006 Andrea's official termination date? Was it because Andrea had not returned to work, therefore she was not officially terminated, but they continued pilfering her retirement and Worker's Compensation money from February 2003 until September 2006? She never did return to work since she didn't agree to the terms of the waiver.

Andrea filed a grievance in March 2003 soon after her firing, and the union wasn't answering any of her correspondences. Andrea tried to get Don Hangem to respond to her complaints. Local 783 didn't answer her grievance before she was fired, so I guess there was no cause for them to acknowledge her grievance at this late date either. If they did nothing before, what were the odds of them representing her after she was illegally terminated? It was fraud and they framed Andrea believing she would be desperate enough to do anything since she had no money for 2 years.

They felt they didn't need a grievance. Therefore they never filed one. They felt they would keep her out long enough to teach her a lesson, and after 2 years they decided they were going to tell her the grievance was settled and bring her back to work. They sent her a letter stating her grievance was settled in September 2005, but she received the letter in October 2005. Their plan was to protect themselves of what they had done by putting stipulations in the waiver. The last stipulation on the wavier stated they could terminate her at any time during that one-year period for no reason whatsoever, and she could not contest the termination.

Andrea became destitute and desperate due to her termination by Woodrow Stamping Plant and Local 783. They terminated her for threatening someone when she did not. She has been terminated for almost 4 years as of this day. She can't clearly say what she was terminated for, with the exception that after being asked by the Medical Department, "*What would you do if someone tried to harm you?*" she stated, "*I would protect myself*".

Woodrow Stamping Plant and Local 783 never met with her on the matter or ever inquired about any information as to what happened. There were no verbal or written warnings given on the three times this was supposed to have happened. She was just sent a letter by the Local 783 stating she was fired and not one person from Local 783 asked her any questions. Andrea felt threatened. She wasn't the one doing the threatening.

Andrea didn't want Don Hangem to get off the hook because she repeatedly contacted him regarding her issues ever since he took office as President CEO of the Executive Branch of the Union. This was long before Woodrow Stamping Plant terminated her. If she had signed the waiver, they would have terminated her anyway because they knew what they had done to her. They didn't really think Andrea would fight back, but she had no other choice. She wrote anyone who had a mailbox that she thought could help.

The company kept Andrea off work for so long they felt she would sign anything to get back to work. Woodrow Stamping Plant and Local 783 hadn't figured Andrea wouldn't sign the waiver. This was not according to their plan. They did everything they could for her to sign the waiver. Since Local 783 couldn't get Andrea to sign, they decided to go through the Local Branch of the National Labor Relations Board, who tried to get Andrea not to go through with the complaint and basically told her she had no other option.

Andrea said she had nothing to lose. So when she filed in May 2006, the NLRB told Local 783 they needed to come up with a grievance because Andrea had been requesting copies of what transpired while her grievance was in its various stages. At that point, they didn't really care how they got a grievance just as long as one was produced—and that's just what management at Woodrow Stamping Plant did.

Andrea received a copy of the grievance Woodrow Stamping Plant put together for her benefits. The papers were a classic case of fraud. Recording Secretary, Dorothy Rush, and the current committeeman forged all the papers. There was a special grievance created in the summer of 2006. Dorothy Rush forged much of the documentation that was supposed to be signed by the Plant Chairman, Tom Hemp, and by the National Representative for Famous Parts Company, David Sanders. The papers that were supposed to have gone to the Umpire stage had many pages with no names, but only typed initials. Anyone could have typed "LH". There was no full name of the Local Committeeman, Umpire, Plant Chairman, Regional Director, or Union Representative who would have taken part in the decision. Documents weren't dated and the recording secretary even signed the name of the new Plant Chairman of Local 783, Larry Mean, because he refused to have his name tied to this grievance. She signed his name and placed her initials next to his name.

It is against the law to forge someone else's name to documentation even when you initial the document. She should have signed the documents, stating she was the recording secretary in place of the original union representative. She was trying to fill-in for those people who no longer worked for the company and union. These papers should have dates going all the way back to 2003 when Andrea first filed her grievance, because those who were in office should have signed those documents during the time the grievance originated. There were no papers with the signature of Bargaining Committeeman, Pedro Stevens, from when Andrea first filed the grievance. His signature along with his statement should have appeared someplace because he wrote the grievance before he was voted out of office. Since the grievance was not written at the time, there would be no original signatures of those who were in office when Andrea first filed her grievance.

They had no original signatures because no one was in management to sign Woodrow Stamping Plant's documentations to keep this lie going. They just came up with a waiver for Andrea to sign to keep her from trying to sue Woodrow Stamping Plant and or Local 783 for unjustly terminating her. They had no idea that she wasn't going to sign. It's ironic how Woodrow Stamping Plant committed fraud and the National Labor Relations Board, which is made up of many lawyers who specialize in labor law, didn't know all these laws had been violated. I'm not a lawyer or a judge, but after reviewing all the facts provided, there is no reason charges should not have been brought against Local 783. But when dealing with Woodrow Stamping Plant, no matter how much evidence you had, there was never enough evidence to investigate.

Andrea's termination was the worst case of discrimination I ever saw since the 1950's. I had been discriminated against, harassed, and retaliated against when I was employed with the company. I thought my case was the worst. I even won a grievance against Woodrow Stamping Plant for discrimination, harassment, retaliation by their Medical Department. After the union went back and re-opened the grievance and granted it in my favor, I was to receive the settlement of $100,000 dollars, but they pilfered it—stating money was not negotiated. This was a lie. They just pilfered my money as they had done for many years. They said it was an error, but the error was never fixed. They continued to pilfer my money right in my face while there was nothing I could do to stop them. I eventually retired with a medical disability. My agreement under Worker's Compensation was that after the settlement was complete, I would cut all ties with the company.

I had already had a lawsuit pending in the federal court. Andrea had also filed a case in the same court. We both received a 'right to sue' letter and filed the charges in the court ourselves since we both were unable to obtain counsel. We both asked the judge handling our cases for counsel. Judge Patrick Turncoat and Andrea's judge, My Trader, presided over our cases to appoint us a lawyer. Andrea was granted a lawyer but never received one. Judge Turncoat told me on the other hand, if he saw a need to appoint me an attorney he would do so. He had no intention of giving me one because he was going to throw my case out of court. Andrea and I asked for a trial by jury, but instead we received bench trials.

Judge Turncoat threw my case out of court in a Summary Judgment and he lied in his finding. (1.) He didn't appoint me an attorney. (2.) I asked for a jury trial. This was made known when I filed my court papers and also in our first meeting with the judge in his chambers. (3.) I told him I was filing my lawsuit going back with the company for 13 years of discrimination, retaliation, harassment, and the theft of my idea. Yes, the company pilfered my implemented idea and they stole that money too. Andrea experienced all of the above except for idea theft.

There was nothing normal about our bench trial. We had no rights at all. We both took our complaints to the Michigan Tenure Commission about the judge's action on the bench. I too filed my complaint in the federal court and was denied. After that, I was unable to ever bring my case back to the federal court. As far as I am concerned, our cases were handled in the federal court like Woodrow Stamping Plant and Local 783 handled our discrimination issues and grievance concerns. Both of these federal judges had to be as blind as a bat, if they didn't see anything wrong with our cases. These judges can break the laws and sit back behind the podium while dispersing judgment to others. All their cases dealing with "The Big Three" need to be investigated. Andrea wrote a letter to the Michigan Judicial Tenure Commission regarding Referee Jackie Arnold's handling of her Worker's Compensation case. But it didn't matter what she did—money ruled and that was something Andrea and I didn't have. Referee Jackie Arnold was finally let go from her duties as a Referee.

Judge Turncoat was agitated with me because I would not accept the $7,500 as a settlement. What Woodrow Stamping Plant was offering me was actually an insult to my intelligence, so I declined. Judge Turncoat was biased and told me that I could not go back 13 years of discrimination. I was yet working with the company that had discriminated against me for 13 years at the time, so why couldn't I file for the whole 13 years. The question should have been what proof I had to document this abuse by my employer. I included all this information in my discovery, but he wasn't interested in the truth. He also lied when he stated the union didn't pay compensation claims when a grievance was won. According to the union contact, a grievance is supposed to follow the same laws and guidelines followed by federal and state courts. If the union is supposed to follow the same guidelines, Woodrow Stamping Plant undermined the judicial system with fraud by not processing grievances.

Allowing the Executive Branch of the Union to oversee the grievance procedures in our case was like asking the fox to tend to the hen house. Why wouldn't the union compensate me when a violation had occurred? What Judge Turncoat should have said was, "*I don't compensate minority employees for discrimination in my court for any reason concerning private companies or The Big Three. They are paying me to side with big business*". He didn't say it, but that's exactly what he meant. He told me I had to have a 'right to sue' letter specifically for racial discrimination. I received my discrimination under the Americans with Disabilities Act (ADA) and I didn't have a case for racial discrimination—so I was told. I told the judge that discrimination was discrimination. But it was his court and he was just as corrupt as Andrea's judge, My Trader. If he would have granted me counsel, I could have had my case presented accordingly, but I was just a visitor in his courtroom. He was as wrong as two left shoes. We didn't even have a fair bench trial between both of the federal judges put together. Something needed to be done about these kinds of judges.

This was the gravest case of injustice I'd ever come across. Famous Parts Company has everyone bought and paid for—no matter how much evidence one produced against them. Michigan Federal judge, Patrick Turncoat; and Judge My Trader, were not judging these cases on merit. It was bribery plain and simple. Judge Turncoat needs to step down from being a federal judge, and all of Judge My Trader's cases involving The Big Three need to be investigated. If one plant does something and gets away with it, then the other soon follows. I guarantee the other two large automobile manufacturers are doing the same thing Famous Parts Company is doing.

Andrea's case was thrown out of court in a Summary Judgment even though the court was aware of her termination and the circumstances surrounding it. Money always prevails over justice. Even after Andrea found Louse Lady (a lawyer out of Pontiac, Michigan), she robbed and looted an already defensive Andrea Smith, knowing she was not going to represent her. When Andrea first visited Attorney Lady, her fee was only $2,500 dollars. Andrea didn't have the money, but she was still going to try finding someone to represent her. After she couldn't find anyone to represent her, she went back to Attorney Louse Lady. This time Attorney Lady became greedy. Her fee went up to $5,000 dollars. For this reason Andrea borrowed another $5,000 dollars from the equity of her home. She eventually lost her home because she had no money and no job.

The first thing the Attorney Louse Lady did was notify the court she was going to represent Andrea's case. Ms. Lady told the court that she took Andrea's case on a *pro-bono* or on a *contingency* basis. This meant Ms. Lady would be paid only after money was recovered from the lawsuit and no down payment would be required. Andrea also stressed to her new attorney that she wanted a jury trial. The lawyer pilfered her money knowing she wasn't going to represent Andrea. Andrea informed her of what she wanted done and Ms. Lady did as she pleased. Attorney Louse Lady forgot Andrea employed her. That didn't matter because she was so confident she could get way with robbing clients like Andrea. Ms. Lady had no conscience and no fear in what she was doing to Andrea. She knew she wasn't going to represent Andrea, but Ms. Lady was in compliance with the opposing party. After the case was over, Andrea requested from Ms. Lady all files that pertained to her association with Famous Parts Company and Woodrow Stamping Plant. Andrea wanted to review the files Attorney Lady had in her possession. Andrea wanted to see something of what her $5,000 dollars paid for, yet Andrea was denied her own files. Andrea was losing all the way around. As of this day, Andrea has not received any files from Ms. Lady regarding Famous Parts Company. Andrea bought and paid for any and all correspondences in her possession. It seemed Andrea was the puppet and everyone else involved were pulling the strings.

Ms. Lady soon wanted Andrea to drop the charges against Local 783, but Andrea told Ms. Lady she wasn't going to do so because they were guilty of non representation. Ms. Lady continued to press the judge about dropping the charges against Local 783. These lawyers were so blatant they don't care how they treat their paying client that's going to loose their case anyway. This is because Famous Parts Company Woodrow Stamping violated many labor and contract laws between the both of them. The judge is not to give the opposing party so much as an attorney when they have been Black Balled. They continue to come forth smelling like a rose because of all the fraud that existed. These Lawyers knows Famous Parts Company was going to win, so the client that's paid the lawyer for representation doesn't give the client any respect.

The lawyer's knows Famous Parts Company is going to win, so they can extract as much money out of their client and do nothing in the client's defense. The lawyers are aware there is no one that's going to challenge Famous Parts Company Woodrow Stamping Plant, if they did it would expose Famous Parts Company and that's not going to happen. This was nothing but greed. When Ms. Lady asked the judge to drop the charges against Local 783 he should have sanctioned her in some form or another, or sent her straight to jail for not representing the client who paid for representation. This is clearly against the lawyer's code of ethics. There's no way the judge should have tolerated this kind of action in his court preceding—especially when the attorney switched sides, giving Andrea no respect and no defense at all.

Ms. Lady never removed the paragraph from court documents which stated Andrea wanted to drop the charges against Local 783 anyway. When Ms. Lady should have been representing Andrea, she was only concerned about Local 783. That alone was a conflict of interest. Andrea's case should have been her only concern. Attorney for Famous Parts Company—Woodrow Stamping Plant, Ms. Delia Hawker, told Attorney Louse Lady that the judge was going to throw her case out in a Summary Judgment. That was exactly what happened. Since the grievance was supposed to be in the process, that portion of the lawsuit was left open since the grievance wasn't final. Ms. Lady then relayed the message to Andrea. There were no questions or challenges to take this case to court by either side—just as simple as that! Attorney Lady did not represent Andrea, but took Andrea's money knowing she wasn't going to represent her. That didn't stop Ms. Lady from trying to extort more money from Andrea by telling her she needed more 'up front' money. Andrea asked Ms. Lady for a copy of the expenses she incurred, but obviously Attorney Lady could not provide that.

As a result, Andrea lost her home after 28 years through foreclosure, and her house was completely paid for. She had no money to move and nowhere to move. She left the majority of items in her house. She lost her husband (when he just packed up and left), her job, and her worldly possessions because she couldn't afford to pay someone to move her. Andrea became a squatter in the house that she once owned and was evicted from. She didn't have enough money to manage on a daily basis. Those who fabricated the occurring events stripped her of everything including her home. Andrea fought so hard with Famous Parts Company—Woodrow Stamping Plant because she was fighting for her livelihood. They destroyed her mentally and physically and left her with nothing. I'm in hopes that after all she has been through, she gets what she rightly deserves.

On December 21, 2006 the Department of Civil Rights again informed Andrea they wanted her to withdraw her complaint. Famous Parts Company—Woodrow Stamping Plant was free from investigation. Andrea refused to accept this information. With nothing to lose, she had to appeal the decision. After all Andrea went through, no one seemed to put themselves in her position. I guarantee they wouldn't ever trade places with Andrea. Famous Parts Company—Woodrow Stamping Plant couldn't care less that Andrea has nothing left. They wanted to make sure she didn't receive a dime.

Mr. President, this is why I'm asking your office to look into the fraudulent activity and money-laundering concerning Famous Parts Company—Woodrow Stamping Plant. Our rights have been stripped away by fraud. Maybe your office can direct us in the proper direction so we may achieve justice. We never received due process under the law. Our civil rights were violated and the only thing we received was a lack of respect. Why is it impossible to get your case heard in a court of law when citizens in the United States are supposed to have the right to bring their suits into a court of law? If you don't have an attorney, the law states a judge will appoint you one. We were denied that right too.

I believe Famous Parts Company is pilfering from itself and the employees by stealing employees' retirement by keeping them on long medical leaves and retiring them without their knowledge. The employees are receiving payments through Metro Craft Insurance Company. However, the company is making money off these employees because for an occupational injury, they are receiving over 100% of the employees' pay for an injury incurred in the plant. The company became so greedy that they started pilfering employees' Worker's Compensation benefits by having their Worker's Compensation lawyers betray their clients for a small fee. Woodrow Stamping Plant then makes the employee an offer to settle for a few thousands dollars. If the employee declines, the company uses their hard-lined tactics to give the employee nothing at all.

Andrea had no idea Referee Jackie Arnold wasn't going to consider her previous injury going back to 1992 with a sprained/strained upper and lower back sustained at Woodrow Stamping Plant. This information is even on Company documentations. It's truly unfair for the Michigan Worker's Compensation court not to consider prior occupational injuries. Jackie Arnold based Andrea's condition on two months of her working on the computer. Everything else regarding her other claims were erased. Why wouldn't Referee Jackie Arnold investigate when Andrea was complaining about being hit with the hi-lo truck? Why wasn't it considered in her findings? This referee used an act of deception when she purposely filed Andrea Smith's Worker's Compensation as a *new* claim. Andrea was now standing in front of the same judge she stood before the first time. Andrea was unaware her claim was settled and Jackie Arnold didn't even tell her at that point in June 2002. She waited until June 2004 when her final decision was made. Referee Arnold deceived Andrea when she went back in her courtroom for the second time along with the attorney for Famous Parts Company. Jackie Arnold knew Andrea's case was settled, but Andrea thought the cases were combined.

Woodrow Stamping Plant filed a new claim in the Worker's Compensation court as though Andrea Smith had never filed a claim against Famous Parts Company—Woodrow Stamping Plant before. If they had not pilfered her money through her retirement and Worker's Compensation, they wouldn't have been in this situation. It wasn't Andrea Smith's fault they were caught doing what they did. Jackie Arnold was wrong and should be handled accordingly. Andrea shouldn't have to suffer at the magnitude she has for something she had no control of. I guess someone had to take the blame. Andrea Smith's Worker's Compensation case had been filed in 1995 and the first decision was settled in July 2002—seven years later. She waited the total of 9 years while her case was in the Worker's Compensation court. As a result, she didn't receive a dime. Her condition hasn't changed and she yet can work. Woodrow Stamping Plant left her in a broken down condition physically and mentally.

The Worker's Compensation case would be denied, and the way the judge fixed it left it nearly impossible for Andrea to collect on the Worker's Compensation claim. The company would drop her from the employment roster since she was out on a medical leave for the extent of her seniority. They allowed her to keep her Medicare insurance, but that was it. This happened to Linda Jackson, but

Andrea Smith was terminated. Incase you were wondering, both of them are Black.

I have learned there were many employees who found out they were on medical leaves and retired at the same time. The company was putting this money in special accounts set up by their Controller. Woodrow Stamping Plant became so greedy by taking money belonging to employees. If there was a special project within certain programs to buy materials, the money was granted but went right back into the company. If employees were unaware they were to receive money, too bad—the money becomes the company's.

Andrea and I even contacted the Local FBI and informed them of the occurrences, but they ignored us too. We both contacted the Michigan Attorney General, Michigan's Governor, Michigan's State Senator, Directors of the Department of Civil Rights, the National Labor Relations Board, and the Equal Employer Opportunity Commission. We both contacted the company's CEO, Robert Wart, on numerous occasions. We also contacted Don Hangem, CEO and President of the Union. With all these acknowledgements, Andrea Smith remains terminated by Famous Parts Company—Woodrow Stamping Plant. It wasn't what they did, but how they did it. Not one person cared enough to investigate the complaining—not even the Department of Civil Rights, who contacted Andrea on December 23, 2006 and forced her to withdraw her complaint. A civil rights representative offered to meet Andrea Smith anywhere at her discretion to sign this withdrawal form dismissing her complaint for the second termination. This is because she was paid to get Andrea to withdraw. I have been there and done that—being forced to withdraw my complaints filed. If one disagrees to withdraw, they will withdraw the complaint anyway. Woodrow Stamping Plant was again spared from an investigation. It's almost as if these people can do no wrong and Andrea's claims have no validity.

Andrea Smith wasn't just terminated once. She has been officially terminated twice. Why did she receive two terminations? Was it because there was another set of records and she had to be terminated twice to officially close her file? Andrea Smith was terminated once on February 5, 2003 and again on September 12, 2006. She only received the last notice because the company became angry with her since she would not sign the waiver in an effort to save Don Hangem's job. They did manage to save his job. This was because the Washington D.C. Branch of the National Labor Relations Board lied and said Andrea admitted she didn't send her Article 33 in a timely manner. Everything that has happened with Andrea and Famous Parts Company—Woodrow Stamping Plant has been fraud. Andrea needs some kind of justice for all the adversity she's gone through.

When Andrea Smith appealed her complaint with the Worker's Compensation Appeal Board, it was concerning her hit with the hi-lo truck. Referee Jackie Arnold and Famous Parts Company were going to make sure Andre Smith would receive nothing at all. That would be her punishment for challenging their authority. Referee Jackie Arnold didn't tell Andrea her case was settled. She never required any additional information from Famous Parts Company's attorneys with regards to Andrea being hit with the hi-lo in the plant. Referee Jackie Arnold was aware of Andrea's termination, but everyone just took advantage and jointed in on the harassment, and the inhumane treatment administered by Woodrow Stamping Plant and Local 783. Andrea had a sprained/strained upper and lower back. She needed Carpal Tunnel surgery due to the work she had done. Woodrow Stamping Plant never honored her doctors' restrictions. They would even change the restriction to suit their satisfaction.

Jackie Arnold told Andrea that she hadn't filed a claim for Worker's Compensation. Therefore Andrea being hit with the hi-lo wasn't a factor in Arnold's decision. Famous Parts Company was prepared to fight Andrea with everything they had. They hired an outside law firm in Andrea's appeal process. Her first appeal was concerning the hit with the hi-lo truck in a Michigan Worker's Compensation court. Andrea's case didn't start in 2002 as Jackie Arnold implied in her final decision. Andrea appealed her case to the Michigan Appellate Court and the Michigan Supreme Court. Neither court would even hear her case. This proves corruption in the state of Michigan rules even to the highest courts. The courts in Michigan want to keep these cases private so corruption can continue without anyone's second-guessing. Cases are often bought and sold for favorable decisions.

Anything done in secret is not good. Why would the judges want to keep cases private if everything was legitimate? I see something wrong with not needing watchdog groups to keep corruption and cover-ups out of the legal system. When Famous Parts Company hired an outside law firm to take advantage of employees, laws didn't mean anything. Famous Parts Company normally had in-house attorneys to handle the Worker's Compensation cases. It is ironic that when court deadlines were set and Famous attorneys couldn't meet them appropriately, the court still accepted the late information. This happened on two occasions while Andrea's case was on appeal. Without proper notification to the court, such a case should be forfeited. It didn't matter what the rules were, they didn't have to follow them and they always come out smelling like a rose.

When Andrea received the decision in 2004 with no mention of the case filed in 1995, she was dumbfounded. It took Jackie Arnold two years to tell Andrea Smith that she: worked at Famous Parts Company, worked on a computer job, and received serious joint problems after two months. It's impossible for someone to acquire Degenerative Joint Disease and the serious mental problems Andrea experienced in two months. I'm sure Andrea would have been laughed out of court if this were the case. So why didn't anyone look at the underlying reasons this case was in court in the first place? Jackie Arnold said in her 2004 decision, "It is impossible to acquire these types of complaints in two months of work". If she knew this, why didn't anyone investigate Andrea's complaints? They all worked together to conceal the fraud by Famous Parts Company—Woodrow Stamping Plant. This included the deception of the courts.

The funny thing is that everyone took their portion of money and Andrea had none. She had no money, but she did have the truth on her side. Famous Parts Company's secret was well kept since they didn't have to return the money pilfered from Andrea for many years. This went on until 1995 when they retired her originally. How was Famous Parts Company going to explain Andrea being in the plant working, retired, and injured from an occupational injury at the same time?

I would not have thought discrimination existed to this magnitude from 1990 until Andrea's termination in February 2003 and until my retirement in 2004. I thought *my* experiences with Woodrow Stamping Plant were bad. At one point I thought Andrea's discrimination was equally as bad as mine, but looking back I think Andrea's discrimination and harassment far surpassed mine. I too was terminated unjustly, but I was able to recover through the hardship I endured. Andrea's treatment was the worst I've yet to see.

I'm asking you as the President of the United States, to have these allegations investigated in hopes that Andrea and other Famous employees will no longer fall somewhere between the cracks in the system of bureaucracy."

I sent this by e-mail to the President of the United States. The first copy in January 2007 was not edited. I also requested help from well-known figures in other states. The few governors from other states never responded back to Andrea or me in our quest for help. I guess Andrea just wasn't important enough. I was requesting help for my friend. Thus far, she is exactly where she was when she was first terminated—no money, no job, and no health insurance.

51

ANDREA'S LATEST COMPLAINT FILED WITH THE NATIONAL LABOR RELATIONS BOARD

The majority of chapter consists of Andrea's appeal for reconsideration filed with the Department of Civil Rights.

Andrea's last failed attempt to challenge Local 783 with the National Labor Relations Board was on September 2006. The Department of Civil Rights failed to file charges against Famous Parts Company in her complaint in a letter dated September 23, 2006. The Department of Civil Rights only re-opened this complaint because Andrea contacted the Washington D.C. Branch of the Department of Civil Rights, just to be forced to withdraw on December 23, 2006. The Department of Civil Rights would have ultimately dropped the case anyway. This is exactly what the local branch of the Department of Civil Rights did. Andrea filed another appeal with the National Labor Relations Board on October 4, 2006 because Local 783 just wouldn't represent her. She was not being represented through any of the grievance processes and the National Labor Relations Board and the Department of Civil Rights were aware of that fact too. Both organizations stood behind Famous Parts Company and Local 783 in an effort to protect Woodrow Stamping Plant and Local 783.

Andrea was aware she should not have been terminated while on medical leave. This was a corrupt cover-up by the National Labor Relations Board and the Department of Civil Rights. Andrea should have received union representation while she was employed and paying for it. It didn't matter what Woodrow Stamping Plant and Local 783 did. They always came out smelling like roses. Andrea went back into the contract book to find what the union was to have done during her quest for representation in an effort to obtain her job back. She wanted to prove Local 783 did not represent her through the grievance process. This is what Andrea wrote in her appeal to the Department of Civil Rights. The appeal was dated January 20, 2007.

"CLAIMANT AMENDMENT
FOR AN APPEAL AND REQUEST FOR RECONSIDERATION:

The Claimant Andrea Smith would like to amend her Appeal request for Reconsideration. She would like to include this amendment in all the Appeal Requests for Reconsideration because:

Claimant has found more proof that respondent Famous Parts Company violated the Union and Famous Parts Company's Collective Bargaining Agreement and her civil rights as an African-American female.

The Claimant Andrea Smith is requesting a waiver of the filing requirement under the rule that: If the discrimination occurred more than 180 days claimant can request that all prior complaints can be included in her claim, this would include all complaints filed with the federal, state, and local agency (all of which can be used in her current claim filed with agency*). The following complaints were filed with the U.S. Equal Employment Opportunity Commission, Detroit Department of Civil Rights, Michigan Department of Labor, and the National Labor Relations Board.*

I am African-American female hired at Famous Parts Company—Woodrow Stamping Plant on July 16, 1990 as a full-time employee.

I the claimant, Andrea Smith, am requesting this waiver so all changes can be examined and included in the current change that the discrimination and retaliation against me, an African-American woman, has continued by the respondent Famous Parts Company-Woodrow Stamping Plant.

In 1999, I returned to work because of Famous Parts Company's petition that they had a job fitting my disability. The job they promised never materialized. I found out this was not a permanent job, but it was just a job that ran occasionally. They continued to place me on jobs not fitting my disability or restrictions. Because of that, I suffered on these jobs. I ended up going back out on a medical leave due to Major Depression because of the constant harassment. I tried to return from medical leave in 2001. Both, my physical doctor and my psychiatrist approved this return. Nurse Tootie, RN at Famous Part Company—Woodrow Stamping Plant, continued to tell me there was no work available.

The union would not process my grievance so I went down to the National Labor Relations Board. After going to the National Labor Relations Board, my grievance was processed by Tom Hemp, Local 783's Caucasian Plant Chairman. Mr. Hemp made the statement, *"The only reason I'm doing this is because I'm being made to"*.

I returned to work on February 19, 2002 only to be harassed on a continual basis while they continued to give me jobs against my medical restrictions. I was not treated the same as my White co-workers, who were allowed to sit as they read the newspaper. Whenever I would sit, I was reminded I could not, even though I suffered with Degenerative Joint Disease. Part of my restriction was not to stand more than 2 hours and not to sit more than 2 hours.

I was assaulted in June 2002 with a broom by a White male co-worker. Ronald Hatfield was a known racist and couldn't so much as write his own name. Management had him hit me with the broom. He hit me in retaliation for telling the supervisor I could do his job due to my disability. Mr. Hatfield knew they would do nothing to him if he assaulted me, and they didn't. A week prior the broom incident, he cursed me out and Labor Relations at Woodrow Stamping Plant was aware of this incident. Again, they did nothing. How could they justify not doing anything to Ronald, who is White, when Famous Parts Company claimed of being a "zero tolerance plant"? Silly Sally, who is also White, used the excuse that Ronald apologized and I accepted, for not disciplining him. It was management's job to punish Ronald for this vicious act. When I went down to the Medical Department, my chest was sore and bruised. This was their way of showing me Whites were superior to Blacks—even if they have no education.

On June 26, 2002 while walking to the restroom, I was hit with a hi-lo truck driven by a White male co-worker. His delivery was to the left of me. As I was walking to the right, where no deliveries were made is where he struck me. This was intentional and premeditated. Silly Sally, Labor Relations Supervisor, later tried to say the accident never happened. I not only have medical papers to prove the hi-lo accident happened, but I have a statement from when the hi-lo driver came down to the Medical Department. Silly Sally also instructed me not to talk to anyone about the broom incident.

Joseph Fears, my immediate Supervisor who is White, has already instructed my female co-worker, who is not Black, that she was "*not to talk to Smith*". When he felt she was disobeying his orders, he instructed her again by saying, "*You are not to talk to Andrea*". All my White co-workers would talk to each other, yet I was ostracized as an African-American. All of this happened within a few weeks apart from the hi-lo assault, Ronald Hatfield cursing me first, and him later assaulting me with a broom.

I was discharged February 3, 2003 on malicious charges by U.S. mail. It took about two and a half years of waiting for Local 783 to settle my discharge grievance that should have taken only 120 days since a discharge is considered a priority case. When my grievance was settled, it was settled with a nonstandard waiver normally used for illegal drug users. This was not a standard grievance waiver. It was a continuation for any future discharge all over again. The one item that stood out was:

"Ms. Smith will be regarded for a period of 12 months with the understanding she will not have access to the grievance process to protest the reasonableness of any penalty including "*Discharge*" which she may receive during this probationary period for any infraction of Company rules."

They used this portion of the drug waiver and left out the part after "*Discharge*" which stated, "… *as a result of a positive test for illegal drugs or unauthorized prescription drugs during the 12-month period*". They made this grievance up just for me to have no access to the grievance process to protest the reasonableness of any penalty. This would leave an opening to discharge me at will. Again they could not have followed Famous Parts Company's Collective Bargaining Agreement. They had to make up a new rule for me—an African-American.

For one thing, I am not guilty of any charges that gave cause for them to discharge me. The wording of this waiver was for employees on drugs. The only drugs I used were prescription drugs. The purpose of this waiver was to enable them to terminate my employment upon a positive drug test result. The wording in the stipulation called for no access to the grievance procedure to protest the reasonableness of any penalty including discharge as the result of a positive test for illegal drugs or unauthorized prescription drugs during the 12-month period. This wavier should not have been applied to me.

It seemed like a set-up to discharge me on another unjustified act. Why would I have to sign a waiver when I was not guilty of any charges brought forth? I couldn't depend on my union for appropriate representation because they worked together with the company. Larry Mean, Woodrow's newly elected Plant Chairman, told me this was not a standard grievance. He even wrote a letter to that effect stating he had nothing to do with the waiver. It took from October 2005 to September 12, 2006 for me to get an official letter stating I was formally discharged for not signing the waiver. This would be considered my first of two official discharge letters after not signing the waiver.

Famous Parts Company is in violation of the union's Collective Bargaining Agreement. They violated the agreement to enable them to discriminate against me, Andrea Smith, as the Claimant. Famous Parts Company and Local 783 have violated the written agreement in the contract and they recognized the moral principle involved in the area of civil rights reaffirming them in the Collective Bargaining Agreement. Their commitment is not to discriminate because of race, religion, color, age, sex, sexual orientation, or against union activity, national origin, or against any employees with disabilities. This is what Famous Parts Company and the Executive Branch of the Union advocated. But this is not what they practice. Famous Parts Company has discriminated against me, retaliated against me, ignored my disability, and violated my civil rights.

In the case of my medical leave, I was only out on medical leave for 4 months when I was scheduled for an IME (Independent Medical Evaluation). Famous Parts Company was to refrain from scheduling an examination if any employee has not filed a claim for 'sick & accident' benefits for a period of 18 consecutive months immediately prior to the disability absence. The contract laws stated for them to:

"… make telephone contact with the employee or treating physician to determine the employee's current status if unknown and…. refrain from scheduling for a examination any employee who has not filed a claim for 'Sick and Accident' benefits for a period of 18 consecutive months immediately prior to the disability absence (not including time off the roll due to permanent separation) provided the disability absence does not extend beyond the anticipated duration of disability ..."

I went out on medical leave on August 5, 2002 for Major Depression. I waited approximately 6 weeks before I applied for 'sick & accident' benefits. I was scheduled for an IME just months later on December 3, 2002. This was in violation of my civil rights according to the agreement that applies to all employees. This is what I call discrimination. They made a difference in the ability to make or perceive distinctions regarding me, Andrea Smith.

Famous Parts Company scheduled me for an IME examination with their Dr. Cho of Taylor, Michigan. This was before the 18-month waiting period was over.

"... Every effort will be made to schedule an IME with an appropriate medical specialist. However in the event, an IME (Independent Medical Evaluation) is only possible with a General Practitioner. Such results, if in agreement with the findings of the treating physician, will be binding on the parties. If the finding of the General Practitioner, who conducted the IME, disagrees with those of the treating physician, an IME with an appropriate specialist must be scheduled to resolve the difference of opinion."

Dr. Cho's determination was the same diagnosis as my treating doctor's, Dr. Kindly. It stated I was "*Unable to work*". You will find this on page 3 of the enclosed letter addressed to Nurse Tootie concerning his diagnosis of me, Andrea Smith. The document is dated December 5, 2002.

After this determination, my Group Life and Disability Insurance benefits should have continued, but they were stopped. Famous Parts Company violated my civil rights according to the Collective Bargaining Agreement.

I couldn't understand the problem. There was no difference in opinion. Famous Parts Company's Dr. Cho and Dr. Kindly had the same diagnosis. The Executive Branch of the Union's and Famous Parts Company's agreement states:

"The result of any examination by an Independent examiner acting as an appropriate medical specialist will be final and binding on the company, the union, the employee, and the insurer."

So why was this not binding in my case? This rule of law applied to all employees. Famous Parts Company changed the rules when they wanted to and did not apply this to me, an African-American woman. Discrimination is to distinguish differences, the ability to make or perceive distinctions, perception, discernment, and showing of partiality or prejudice in treatment, action, or polities directed against the welfare of minority groups. This alone proves I was subjected to discrimination over and over again. They were prejudiced in treatment and I was singled out. They deliberately ignored the Collective Bargaining Agreement. This enabled those to retaliate against me by a premeditated discharge.

I had been on medical leave since August 5, 2002 and was still on medical leave under Dr. Kindly's care on February 3, 2003 when I was discharged. Famous Parts Company's Labor Relations Supervisor, Silly Sally, said on deposition "… not working does not justify a suspension because a person has to be physically at work" in order to be suspended. Coming to the medical facility does not constitute being at work. You cannot be at work and on medical leave at the same time unless there is more than one set of records on you.

I was not on active employment payroll because my medical leave had exceeded 90 days. Famous Parts Company could have sent a letter with a Notice to Expire Medical Leave if my medical papers were not up to date. My medical papers were up to date and my treating doctor had filled out all the necessary paperwork. Famous Parts Company's IME doctor, Dr. Cho, said I was unable to work. I should have continued on medical leave with my 'sick & accident' disability benefits. Again, my civil rights were violated when my disability benefits were discontinued.

I was called in for another medical examination by a non-psychiatrist after the IME (Independent Medical Examination) specialist had already stated I was unable to work. I should not have been at Famous Parts Company—Woodrow Stamping Plant on January 22, 2003. All of this was planned and they set me up to discharge me on deceptive unjust charges. Contrary to what the Executive Branch of the Union and Famous Parts Company said, the Union & Famous Parts Company Collective Bargaining Agreement stated:

"… Notify employee of the expiration of the 90-day leave period and request information as to their status by sending the attached from letter.

Send the letter at least ten working days (excluding Saturdays, Sundays, and holidays) prior to sending an Article VIII, 5(4) notice.

Consult with the plant physician concerning the employee's medical status prior to sending the letter to any employee.

Do not send Article VIII 5(4) notices in cases when a plant physician has personal knowledge or sufficient medical evidence to determine that the employee's absence will exceed ninety days.

The following procedures will be followed prior to sending Article VIII Section 5(4) notices to an employee removed from the active employment roll as Medical Leave of Absence expired because the employee's absence for medical reasons exceeded the maximum duration of 90 days ..."

Famous Parts Company Collective Bargaining Agreement stated I should not have been at Famous Part Company—Woodrow Stamping Plant on January 22, 2003. According to what the contract stated:

"At the present time, your medical leave cannot be extended based on the documentation you have provided us."

All my documentation was completed with the necessary information from my treating doctor, Dr. Kindly. Dr. Cho concurred with my doctor's diagnoses. The Collective Bargaining Agreement stated the IME would be binding. The Union & Famous Parts Company Collective Bargaining Agreement stated:

"... During these negotiations the Union raised a concern about the impartiality of the procedure by which difference of opinion between an employee's personal physician and the Company's Plant Physician, then the issue is resolved by referring the employee to an outside consultant for examination. This will confirm that the company is committed to assuring the present referral procedure continues to resolve differences in medical opinions in a fair and equitable manner ..."

My medical opinion *was* resolved. Both medical opinions were the same. I was unable to work. The question is why was I in the plant on January 22, 2003 for an examination when there was no basis for me to be there? The reason my medical leave was not accepted was because Nurse Tootie in the Medical Department didn't like the findings of Dr. Cho or Dr. Kindly. Woodrow Stamping Plant and Local 783 didn't get the results they hoped for. They needed a reason to terminate my employment. Since they didn't have one, they just made up one. Having me come into the plant gave them a reason to fabricate a lie in an effort to terminate me on unjust charges even though it was against the Collective Bargaining Agreement. Nurse Tootie and all others involved were up to no good. Nurse Tootie was not in agreement with the Union & Famous Parts Company Collective Bargaining Agreement.

This was all a fallacy because (1.) I was not yet out for a period of 18 consecutive months immediately prior to my disability absence for the Independent Medical Evaluation with an independent doctor. (2.) My treating doctor sent in the necessary paper work for my medical leave of absence, but this was ignored. (3.) Nurse Tootie, Head RN at Famous Parts Company—Woodrow Stamping Plant, received a letter addressed to her dated December 5, 2002 from Famous Parts Company IME doctor, Dr. Cho, stating I was unable to work. All this was binding according to the Union & Famous Parts Company Collective Bargaining Agreement.

I was blatantly discriminated against and had no union representation due to my race. My termination was allowed to stand because of the union working for the company and not for the union member.

While I was in Famous Parts Company's Medical Department for my physical examination by Dr. Slick, I was questioned by their doctor acting in the capacity of a psychiatrist. On January 22, 2003 while in the examining room I was asked a battery of question by Famous Parts Company doctor, Dr. Slick, such as, *"Do you have a gun?", "Do you know where you can get one?",* and *"If someone tried to harm you in any way, what would you do?"* To the last question I replied, *"I would try and protect myself".*

This was harassment and intimidation. The questioning was totally out of line. I had already seen an IME specialist and my treating doctor who both stated I was unable to work. All of the above questions were after the fact.

The Collective Bargaining Agreement stated, "… Every effort will be made to schedule an IME with an appropriate medical specialist". I had already seen Dr.

Cho and Dr. Kindly. Dr. Slick was not an appropriate medical specialist, nor was he a psychiatrist. The only time an IME is replaced with the General Practitioner is when they don't have an IME available. This did not pertain to me. I was examined by and Independent Medical Examiner who specialized in the field of psychiatry. I was not supposed to be seeing Dr. Slick at Famous Parts Company Woodrow Stamping Plant in an effort to change my medical status. The IME diagnosis was supposed to be final.

They had to show me who was superior, and as an African-American I had no rights. I have had Cancer causing toxic chemicals fall all over my body while working at Famous Parts Company. I was assaulted with a broom by a White male co-worker, and hit by a White hi-lo driver driving in an area where no deliveries were made. Now they wanted to question me to find a reason for discharging me after pilfering my Worker's Compensation settlement and reporting me as "retired".

These people had a lot of nerve. They needed me out of the plant before all their schemes and criminal activities where found out. This is why my termination was done intentionally. Nurse Tootie conspired with Local 783 to have me terminated. She herself, was later terminated and arrested for racketeering, falsifying medical records, falsifying government documents, and embezzlement. My medical records were falsified and I have the papers proving information was changed on my medical form. My Worker's compensation settlement was also pilfered in this embezzlement scheme. Famous Parts Company was sending information to the Internal Revenue Service stating I was retired when I wasn't. The FBI was also looking for Tom Hemp, Local 783's Chairman, for the same charges. A year later, their criminal activities were still being investigated, but my termination remained the same. I should have been reinstated, but instead they wanted to show me African-Americans had no rights. It didn't matter how much trouble they caused or what was found in their investigation. They proved they could investigate and arrest employees for criminal activities and still not restore my seniority or back pay.

The contract between the company and union stated:

"... *The company employee conducting the investigatory interview will advise the employee of the right to a Union Representative. Should the employee not desire Union Representative, the employee will sign a waiver to that effect* ..."

I was never advised of my rights to union representation and a waiver was never mentioned. In fact, I had asked for union representation. I had called the Regional 21-A International Office concerning my January 22, 2003 medical examination. I was scared to go into the plant. I was a nervous wreck because I felt they were trying to kill me. I was given an appointment to meet with a union representative, but no one showed up for the meeting. I never saw or signed a waiver.

I brought my husband to my appointment with Dr. Slick, but he wasn't even allowed in the examining room. They made sure they had no witnesses. Only the medical staff working under Nurse Tootie was present. They let me sit in the Medical Department waiting room with a co-worker for over an hour, but alleged it was a threat that caused them to terminate my employment. None of this made sense when I was the one being harassed.

Famous Parts Company's White Labor Relations Supervisor, Silly Sally, was one of the lead investigators of the alleged threats by me. Silly Sally testified in her deposition that an investigation of a hypothetical actual threat might last months and that they would analyze information from policy agency's disciplinary files, with discharge taking place only after a full investigation had been done. The first alleged threat was supposedly in October of 2002. Silly Sally was not even aware of this because it was never investigated. I never received a verbal or written warning as to these alleged facts—only my letter of discharge sent by U.S. mail. Silly Sally could not even recall the wording of any alleged threats. The company knew rules were being broken and lies were being told, but my termination still stood.

Woodrow Stamping Plant and Local 783 got away once again, with their conspiracy to cover-up, pilfer, and laundering the money of employees. It didn't matter what we did there was never any justice to be found to trigger an investigation. There should have been many red flags signaling that something was wrong at Woodrow Stamping Plant and Local 783. With the amount of complaints that Andrea and I have filed with these agencies especially the National Labor Relation Board, who oversees the union. All claims Andrea filed with the same company, for the same reasons, you would think that the agencies such as the National Labor Relation Board, Department of Civil Rights, Equal Employment Opportunity Commission, should have found reason to file charges against Famous Parts Company and Local 783 and make the charges stick but they did not. There was much government involvement on the State and Federal level in the State of Michigan.

For all the labor and contract violations that were going on at Famous Parts Company—this should have triggered and out of court settlement, but they didn't do that either. The Executive Branch of the Union needs to settle this claim and stop trying to cover for the union members for Andrea's termination and other unethical things they did in support of Famous Parts Company—Woodrow Stamping Plant. The majority of those who took part in the illegal events that was union members are no longer representing Local 783 in these matters, but I know it is business as usual and Woodrow Stamping Plant are pulling this same scheme on others because it a profitable business. Andrea Smith has the truth on our side and all Ford Motor Company—Woodrow Stamping Plant and Local 783 needs to do are settle this disagreement. The only thing they have is a stack of lies and contradictories to fall back on according to the depositions I've read. Therefore Andrea and I will not stop our fight until the truth comes out and we will win in the end.

I have tried obtaining interventions through various sources to no avail. I started contacting Local 783 to help me. When they failed to put me full-time and I was already full-time, I then filed a grievance on June 3, 1993. I assumed that the "#LB-710" stood for the Labor Relations Board, but the grievance number was #135381—LB710. I have filed charges and complaints on numerous occasions with the National Labor Relations Board. I lost count of how many times they refused to file charges and turned me back around to the door. I have listed dates and claim numbers to follow, but none of these charges were successfully filed against Local 783. Andrea's charges weren't ever filed either. The total number of complaints between Andrea and I is fifteen. Just the cases of myself and Andrea alone are far too many, let alone the complaints of many other employees. Something is severely wrong when a person files all these complaints and receive no results. There's a problem with poor representation with regards to Local 783 and the government agencies.

Andrea and I appealed our complaints when the National Labor Relations Board refused to file charges against Local 783. The Washington D.C. branch is where we appealed, but it didn't matter what the complaint was or where we filed it. Neither the local branch of the National Labor Relations Board nor the Washington D.C. branch found reason to file charges or to investigate Local 783's noncompliance. My seven complaints, which resulted in no charges being filed with the National Labor Relations Board, are listed below:

Dates	Claim No.
April 3, 1993	7-CB-0077
October 31, 1993	7-CB-10728
January 25, 1994	7-CB-9966
October 31, 1995	7-CB-10728
July 2, 1997	7-CA-45439-1
September 15, 2000	7-CB-12577-1
September 11, 2002	7-CB-13442-1/C-7-CA-45439-1

I later received a form from the E.E.O.C. for a 90-day 'right to sue' letter. The attorney on the case let all statutes of limitations run out. I contacted the Attorney Grievance Commission April 4, 1996 (File #0797196) and April 30, 2003 (File #23AA300100). I received another 90-day 'right to sue' letter in 2003, but I have been hampered by not being able to obtain an attorney. I never had my day in court. I contacted Attorney Beth Angel, of the International Union representing Local 783, and Attorney Wanda Scorn, who represented Woodrow Stamping Plant's Executive Branch of the Company & Union. Each time I filed a complaint with the National Labor Relations Board, I'd also contact the Department of Civil Rights and/or the Equal Employment Opportunity Commission. In my perspective, the names of these agencies need to be changed because their names don't apply to their titles. There was nothing "equal" about my experiences with my employer and my union. I have filed claims with the Department of Civil Rights. Some claims don't have claim numbers or dates, and other documents have dates and no claim numbers, but this is what I have been given.

Years ago the Department of Civil Rights would give you a list of attorneys whom would honor a 'right to sue' letter and take your case. I guess things have changed and it's almost as though racial discrimination doesn't exist any longer. Racial discrimination continues to exist. They're just using different methods to be more discrete about displaying hatred for minorities. The following is a list of the number of times I sought help through the Department of Civil Rights.

Dates	Claim No.
April 1993	230-93-1472
April 1996	0797176

July 1997	156345-EM 10/23A977160
September 2000	252194
September 2001	284334
April 2002	292313
September 2003	23AA300100

I have been trying to obtain my employment files since 1998. I was told I could see my records on computer only. I could not get copies of information pertaining to me. I've sent letters to the CEO Executive Branch of the Company, Mr. Robert Wart, and Woodrow Stamping Plant. Both letters were sent certified mail on three occasions requesting copies under the Bullard-Plawecki Employee Rights to Know Act (Public Act. N0. 397, of 1978) that guarantees both public and private employees the right to access their personal work file. I have requested my files in December 2000, February 2001, December 2001, and December 2002. I'm now trying to get a grievance filed on this problem. I have been told by Human Resources that they are unable to find my employment file at Woodrow Stamping Plant and Sarrow Stamping as well. My employment file seemed to have just disappeared, as far as they are concerned. It certainly seemed as though they weren't going to make any effort in finding it. I was also told my file couldn't be accessed because it was in a vault at the Executive Branch of the Company's Headquarters.

I was experienced a back injury in 1999 and was denied service in the Medical Department. They wouldn't provide me medical assistance after being injured on the job. I was forced to use the services of an emergency care facility. I have been diagnosed with Degenerative Joint Disease and Osteoarthritis of the spine. I've been fighting for Workman's Compensation because I was told by the Medical Department my problem is of a personal matter. I filed a case with the Department of Civil Rights under the Americans with Disabilities Act because my employer stated I was not able to return to work. As stated in my Workman's Compensation case, my lawyer and I have agreed under a voluntary payment form which will pay the out of pocket expenses I incurred while on medical leave from June 7, 2000 through December 7, 2000 and July 24, 2001 through October 10, 1991.

I think it is important to let the people in our democratic society know that in working for a large company such as Famous Parts Company, politics are often played, cover-ups are quite common, and unjust treatment yet exists against minorities. I know how easy it is to fall between the cracks with all the organizations setup to help minorities. It's only a hindrance when their heads turn away—making a simple problem much bigger. I even sent this information to the local TV channel seeking help but no one was interested.

I'm asking for your assistance in an investigation to see if you will agree there is unjust treatment. Please help me. I have documentation upon your request for viewing if interested in this story. I truly hope my story is interesting enough to find cause for investigation, because the lies, discrimination, cover-ups, and other unjust treatment were a constant problem. I will go more extensively into these allegations in Part 2 of this book. I don't want to put the cart too far before the horse, so to speak.

We have fallen through the cracks when this kind of inhumane treatment was allowed to continue for years. I guess the *Good Old Boys Club* carried a lot of weight—not only in the union and company, but also in our government agencies and court systems. This also includes doctors, lawyers, and government officials. They are all intertwined in a web of corruption. In the *Good Old Boys Club,* everyone has to do someone a favor because you get nothing for nothing in the business they're in.

COMMENT:

Changing the law seems to be the tactic White Americans use against African-Americans. This has happened all through history. They change the rules and make new ones for African-Americans—just as they did in my case. I have been discriminated against and retaliated against for filing charges. Until this day, nothing has been done about it. This takes us back to the 1950's when Blacks had no civil rights.

Various rules in the bargaining agreement were broken. Why am I still fighting for my rights when you have all the proof necessary? Why is outright discrimination being ignored? Why do we even have agencies allocated to help minorities when their civil rights are violated, if nothing is going to be done about it? It was said in the Michigan Citizen's Newspaper dated January 20, 2007 that:

"Attorneys for Famous Parts Company have stated as recently as 2006 in open court, that Famous is out to change the civil rights laws protecting us from the power of corporations."

I know from personal experience that Famous has used any means necessary to suppress the truth about the violation of its own 'zero-tolerance' rule. I want these issues investigated and something to be done about it. I want some kind of justice!" Andrea signed and dated this letter on January 20, 2007.

What's happened thus far has been done with regards to Andrea Smith's termination and a massive cover-up. She will be reinstated with full seniority and back pay. Someone needs to investigate Andrea Smith Worker's Compensation and how it was handled. All those involved should be held accountable. This is all I can express on Andrea Smith's saga for now, but it will be updated in Part 2 of this book.

In Part 1, there was no justice at all.

Will Andrea attain justice in Part 2?

See what this saga holds for Andrea Smith
while she remains
Somewhere Hidden Between the Cracks.

CONCLUSION

Famous Part's Company is restructuring the way they do business. They are trying to become more minority-friendly. They are now stressing commitment and most of all they want trustworthy and dedicated employees when they themselves can't be trusted. They are going to allow all employees to take *buyouts* if they choose. I believe this was done in part as an effort to allow those employees involved in the schemes of pilfering from the company, the opportunity to walk out of the doors with no question asked.

From what I have been hearing lately through the newspapers and the media, Famous Parts Company has decided to keep many of their employees instead of replacing them during their restructuring plan. The company wants no witnesses or employees left at the Executive Level who have knowledge of the pilfering schemes, just incase they have to testify against the company. In my opinion, since Mr. Marvin Lindale, the new Executive CEO of Famous Parts Company, took the position of the daily operation at Famous Parts Company, he decided to keep those old employees since they had the courts in their favor. So when things die down and the government gets out of their accounting books, they can continue pilfering from employees. After pilfering Worker's Compensation payments and employees' retirement funds for so long, why stop now? Everyone is on their side in terms of government officials, lawyers, courts, and judges. The road has already been paved for them. All they have to do is to sit tight and weather the storm.

Those who had involvement with the fraud and pilfering schemes with the company will be fired if they choose to stay with the company. By allowing the employees the option to accept a *buyout* program, this gave them a choice to leave without looking suspicious. These employees might've lost their job security just for knowing the company was pilfering from itself. All those having any involvement in the thievery and money-laundering had to go. They didn't want incriminating information leaking to the press if it ever came down to it.

White-collar employees who were unhappy when forced to leave were always considered to be disgruntle. The white-collar workers at Woodrow Stamping Plant having anything to do with the handling of correspondences regarding illegal activity with employees' records had to go. Those who had any knowledge of the pilfering that was going on The Executive Branch of the Union had to do the same. The Executive Branch of the Company knew exactly what was transpiring within the company, and the Executive Branch of the Company condoned this behavior. I believe that Robert Wart, President and CEO of Famous Parts Company, inherited this money-laundering scheme because it has been in existence for many years. I do believe when he found out about the pilfering, he may not have known how to stop it. Things had gotten too out of control by that time.

I now know Robert Wart was pilfering from defenseless people. This money was pilfered in order to put the money back in the failing business, and the union allowed the company to do so. I am aware Robert Wart came after the fact, but at this point he is aware of what has been transpiring within his company. Pilfering employees' retirement, Worker's Compensation, and any other money or benefits relating to occupational injuries is wrong.

Woodrow Stamping Plant pilfered employees' weekly benefits and when employees were put on a 'no work available', Woodrow Stamping Plant would collect Worker's Compensation payment for those employees. Metro Craft paid the benefits for employees with occupational injuries knowing that Worker's Compensation should have been paying those same benefits through the Worker's Compensation fund. Woodrow Stamping Plant and Local 783 kept two or more sets of records on employees. When employees were injured on the job, some of those employees receiving Worker's Compensation unknowingly had money directed to one set of the two separate files.

When there was a need for the Worker's Compensation files in the Medical Department, they would send for the files from the Brownstown Plant, which wasn't very far from Woodrow. The files would stay in Nurse Tootie's office until they were returned to their original destination for storage. These were the Worker's Compensation files that they were pilfering from. The other set of records were in the regular files kept at Woodrow Stamping Plant's Medical Department. The Medical Department had these same employees with occupational injuries listed as having a personal injury. All of the actual reports and true findings of Dr. Butt's (the Independent Medical Doctor), were all kept in the Worker's Compensation folder. This was along with other medical reports and opinions of the actual medical condition.

I'm not sure where the Union stored their records and/or files but the second set of files were in their possession. Those are the files they kept on the employees while they were on medical leave and still working in the plant. Employees were supposed to be receiving weekly Worker's Compensation payments for sustained occupational injuries. Local 783 kept the files used when employees were paid from Metro Craft Insurance Company, while those same employees were "working" in the plant while they were "retired" and receiving retirement payments that the company pilfered. This is why these employees were told they were '*double dipping*' and were forced to pay the money back to Metro Craft Insurance Company. After Woodrow Stamping Plant changed the medical information in the file folder, the union got something for their efforts in keeping the files. They kept an illegal set of records too. This was another scheme they sat down and dreamed up so the company would not having to pay employees what was owed to them. If an employee was to lose their check stub, Woodrow Stamping Plant wouldn't even pay their benefits for that week.

I know now Robert Wart, President and CEO of Famous Parts Company, was aware of what Woodrow Stamping Plant was doing. I sent him letters informing him of what Woodrow Stamping Plant was doing with the help of Local 783 and explained how they were running a criminal enterprise. I would say he took a special interest in the pilfering and fraud in 2006 at Woodrow Stamping Plant. When he heard there was a book about his company's behavior, he just came to work one day and fired many employees without any prior given notice. They received their notification by company e-mail and then were shown the door—according to a local newspaper.

This scheme was so widespread that when he did find out about the pilfering, he felt betrayed. No one had informed him of what his predecessors were doing. I think those who smiled in his face, were the ones deceiving him and cutting his throat behind his back. Robert Wart just terminated their employment. He would have to eliminate many more employees, but he was in fear he would cripple the company. Many people stepped down and they were later replaced after it was found out what was going on within his company. These events occurred soon after Andrea Smith delivered the free unedited 1st edition of this book that she handed out as a promotional ploy. When I sent the transcript of my book to my publisher through email, I accidentally sent the unedited version. As a result, many copies of the wrong version printed.

As a result of the unedited version's printing, Andrea recently received a letter from the Michigan Worker's Compensation court. They were going to look further into her complaints. As it turns out Andrea received this letter during the governor's re-election campaign in September 2006. Andrea thought the Worker Compensation Bureau was going to reopen and evaluate her Worker's Compensation claim, but that didn't happen either. Since my finished book never made it to the market, the Department of Civil Rights, the Local Branch of the NAACP, and the Board of Worker's Compensation stated they were going to review

Andrea's Workers Compensation case. The Local Branch of the Department of Civil Rights asked Andrea to withdraw her charge against Woodrow Stamping Plant in December 2006. But Andrea Smith heard nothing more after she received this letter in September 2006. The NAACP never got back with Andrea regarding the field representative they were sending out to investigate her allegations against Famous Parts Company. All that seemed promising soon came to a dead end. The Bureau of Worker's Compensation never responded back as to what they found in their investigation pro or con. The Department of Civil Rights, who suddenly picked up Andrea's claim to be investigated, closed her claim because Woodrow Stamping Plant paid someone at the Department of Civil Rights to force Andrea Smith to withdraw her claim in December 2006.

There was a hearing on December 1, 2006 with the Department of Civil Rights. Andrea Smith invited me to meet with her while meeting with the representative from Famous Parts Company—Woodrow Stamping Plant. This was a mediation hearing. I was surprised when Andrea and I spoke with the representative, who Woodrow Stamping Plant drilled on what to say and what not to say. The Civil Rights Representative started complaining that Andrea Smith didn't have a case because of the statue of limitations. This woman then asked me if I was the person who wrote the recently published book. I stated yes. She then said the book was very good. She went on to tell Andrea that the lawyer she conferred with at the Department of Civil Rights told her Andrea's case was too old.

Andrea and I were told by the representative at the Department of Civil Rights that they didn't know why the Department of Civil Rights re-opened Andrea's case. The representative at the Department of Civil Rights instructed Andrea to speak with a lawyer within the department. How could Andrea's case be too old when she was first terminated in February 2003 and received another termination in September 2006? She received another termination letter from Famous Parts Company—Northwestern Operation Division, stating she was terminated for the second time. It's not often that you can be terminated twice when you were only hired with the company once. This was new information regarding Andrea's complaint. This meant Andrea was not terminated in February 2003 afterall, unless she was terminated on another set of records.

Andrea was filing a new claim adding additional information regarding the second termination letter in September 2006. Andrea was specifically addressing information in her complaint that she received from Silly Sally, Labor Relations Representative at Woodrow Stamping Plant. She stated Andrea was neither hit with the truck nor a broom while working at Woodrow Stamping Plant. This was new information too. Silly Sally stated all these incidents were alleged. One paragraph in the letter Silly Sally wrote stated, "*Andrea accepted Ronald Hatfield's apology and the matter was closed, but not forgotten. She was hit with the broom and Andrea agreed to further elaborate on the matter*". It was a proven fact that Andrea had been hit with the broom and hi-lo truck. How could Silly Sally write this if these incidents never happened? In this same paragraph she stated, "*Andrea was taken to the hospital when she was hit with the hi-lo in the plant and the x-rays all came out okay*". All this information was given in one letter. Either Andrea Smith was hit with the hi-lo truck or not. There was no room for anything in between. Silly Sally's statement was full of Silly's lies.

Andrea and I discussed the well thought out plan full of lies and contradictories Woodrow Stamping Plant conjured up in an effort to terminate her. Andrea wasn't going to get any help from the National Labor Relations Board because they were siding with Local 783. Andrea and I also discussed the many flaws in the depositions and in her grievance. It was clear this grievance was made up for Andrea only. Even as all this information was being revealed, we discussed how Silly Sally and Andrea's Supervisor, Joseph Fears, were well aware of the broom incident, but did nothing in her defense.

This Department of Civil Rights Representative discussed all these facts and when we met with the Representative from Woodrow Stamping Plant, she set guidelines as to what we could and could not discuss. This was because she knew the courts had decided on Andrea's case in a lawsuit in 2003, but Andrea's grievance wasn't settled because there was never a grievance filed on Andrea's behalf. Woodrow Stamping Plant's Representative stated she couldn't discuss Andrea being hit with the broom or hi-lo truck because all this was to be settled in court. Andrea also discussed the stipulation the judge made because a determination on the grievance wasn't settled. Andrea stated she couldn't leave out the fact of being hit with a broom and by a hi-lo truck. Those were the same circumstances she was terminated under.

I told of my experience with the Medical Department and the harassment I received by Woodrow Stamping Plant. I touched on the subject when I had written Robert Wart, CEO of Famous Part Company—Executive Branch of the Company, about the Medical Department and how they were pilfering employees' retirement benefits and Worker's Compensation settlements granted by the courts. I spoke of when I told Robert Wart in a letter that Nurse Tootie was directing the various moneys to specific accounts. I told of her duties and of how Mr. Wart, President and CEO of the Executive Branch of the Company, soon terminated Nurse Tootie. I guess this information was something I shouldn't have had access to when I was speaking at this hearing.

Woodrow Stamping Plant's Representative said I was lying and that the letter I sent had nothing to do with Nurse Tootie being terminated. Her statement alone told me my letter was true. How could *she* have known what I discussed in my letter to Mr. Robert Wart? My letter to Robert Wart was *exactly* the reason Nurse Tootie was terminated. The woman from the Department of Civil Rights said to the Representative from Woodrow Stamping Plant, "Tell me something. Is Nurse Tootie working with the company any longer?" Her response was no. The Representative from the Department of Civil Rights also asked the Representative from Woodrow Stamping Plant if the company terminated Nurse Tootie. She responded by saying yes. This representative became very uneasy and nervously stated, *"I want you to put this statement in your records that I didn't say Nurse Tootie was terminated because of the letter"*. She seemed afraid that if she said too much, it would cost her job. This woman was serious and she wanted to make it very clear that she didn't say Nurse Tootie was terminated because of the letter I had written to Famous Parts Company CEO, Robert Wart. This lady turned as pale as a ghost when she made her statement. It was as though Andrea and I wasn't supposed to have known what happened regarding the termination of Nurse Tootie.

After the question and answer period was over, the Representative for the Department of Civil Rights stated she was going to have her colleague read the book, because many of the things discussed in the book actually happened. The big surprise came on December 18, 2006. Andrea received a telephone call asking her to withdraw the claim against Woodrow Stamping Plant and Andrea refused. The women handling her claim stated they were going to drop the charges just the same—and that's exactly what happened. Andrea's claim went from an all time high to an all time low, but there was one thing Andrea Smith wasn't going to do. She was not going to willingly withdraw her claim against Woodrow Stamping Plant for her pre-meditated terminations and the lies they told.

Andrea had already lost everything. What more did she have to lose? She surely wasn't going to lie and say this was all a mistake and it never happened. Realistically speaking, Andrea has no job, no money, and no insurance. Why in the world would she withdraw her legitimate complaint when she had already been through pure hell? Can you believe the nerve of all these people involved? The same thing happened to Andrea when she wouldn't sign an illegal waiver for threatening the medical staff—plus this was the waiver given to the employees who had drug problems within the plant. Andrea had no drug problem. She was terminated while on medical leave. What makes it so bad is that her treating doctor pulled her out of the plant for a stress leave. Woodrow Stamping Plant sent her to see an Independent Medical Examiner (IME) doctor and he concurred with Andrea's primary doctor's opinion. Yet she was terminated just the same. Andrea found they had pilfered her retirement and Worker's Compensation benefits when her case was settled. Woodrow Stamping Plant filed another claim in the court as though she had never filed a claim in the Worker's Compensation court ever. Andrea's termination was a well thought out plan by Local 783 and Woodrow Stamping Plant's Medical Department.

Nurse Tootie may get off, but the fact remains that she discriminated against others, lied on them, and had them fired. The company was aware of what she was doing because afterall, she was working for the company. If she does eventually get off, she will probably return to another plant and continue doing what she did to others since she was so good at her job. If it were I who was arrested for doing a job I was requested to do, I would sing against the company too. Nurse Tootie was Caucasian and she would be able to get an attorney to take her case. One was probably even provided by the company. Andrea and I were minorities, and that was our problem. Nurse Tootie was arrested for embezzlement, falsifying medical records, and falsifying government documents. I don't know what happened to Tom Hemp, Plant Vice-Chairman of Local 783. The last I heard the FBI was looking for him. I'm sure he's not that hard to find.

I learned much about the law after encountering a plight of lies and hypocrites while dealing with Famous Parts Company. I now understand laws don't have the same meaning for Caucasians as they do for minorities. The laws are about how much money 'big business' has to offer. Who really cares about the laws when justice can be paid for? I truly hope you have enjoyed reading this book. I am in hopes that you will purchase Part 2, which entails the challenges Andrea Smith and I experienced when we tried taking our cases to court and how we were treated once we got there. It will further explain how we were still caught SOMEWHERE HIDDEN BETWEEN THE CRACKS.

EPILOGUE

I have written this first book to let you know that we have come a long way since the 1960's and 1970's. Discrimination was once prevalent in our economics, entertainment, education, and so forth. But really, how far have we really come in terms of discrimination in the workplace? Workplace discrimination always has existed and always will—especially if the employers and government agencies condone it. It seems the very laws that were set up to protect Andrea and myself were the very same laws that failed us. Woodrow Stamping Plant and Local 783 breeched our contracts by allowing the company to do what it pleased. They turned their heads as though they would see no evil and therefore could speak no evil. All of the entities that Andrea and I contacted in an effort to obtain help from the system failed. We were simply reaching out for help and no one reached back, causing us to fall completely through the cracks in the web of bureaucracy.

What I found out through experience with employment at this large corporation is discriminating still exists at an alarming rate. We have many minority activists who are paid to say there is no need for affirmative action programs. Those programs were set up to eliminate discrimination, but have failed. There is no one watching over these companies to see that the laws are enforced. This alone is very disturbing because discrimination is alive, well, and growing in Michigan. In my opinion, this is a gateway to keep minorities with limited resources and not allow minorities to excel using their greatest potential. I can't see anyone being so naive to think we have advanced far enough to eliminate these kinds of programs. If we continue to turn our heads to what is happening with situations like Andrea's and mine, then the discrimination is clearly out of control.

Those who truly believe minorities have the same rights as Caucasians must live a very sheltered life. It is clear minorities have far more poverty because we do not have the same opportunities as Caucasians in our society. Some Caucasians have stated minorities don't want to work because they're lazy. That can be said about Caucasians too because they have all the opportunities. If perhaps they *don't* make anything with their lives it's not because of discrimination! If minorities were given some of the same opportunities as Caucasians, I feel minorities would commit fewer crimes and there would be fewer minorities in the prison system.

I see how our government and many Caucasians are turning their heads on discrimination in this country. This includes all minorities, not only Blacks. This is the reason discrimination has advanced to this extent. We seem to be backsliding into the old ways of discrimination only using different tactics. The government leads the way in not enforcing the various laws that are already put in place. I know this to be true because of the extent of harassment Andrea has experienced. This harassment is inhumane to any person—not just to minorities. Famous Parts Company and other big businesses that discriminated against minorities, such as Andrea and I, have an almost all-Caucasian management corporate sector. There actions explain how they feel about minorities and how they feel superior to all races. Above all, they can do as they please because they can pay for justice. They didn't care because they couldn't feel the pain and agony they were exercising on others. These companies lead the way in trying to eliminate the rights of minorities in court without using the word racism. Actions always speak louder than words.

I have realized our government and our elected officials are primarily Caucasian. They make the laws and own the majority of the land in the country. How can you think we have equal rights when minority employees are kept at a level only companies like Woodrow Stamping Plant can maintain? The laws are supposed to be enforced, but they are not. To what extent will these companies go through to keep the minorities down? Here we are talking about assaults on two minority women and you can't get one government agency to step up to the plate and help. Famous Parts Company Woodrow Stamping Plant and Local 783 have so much clout. They feel they don't have to be held accountable by any laws.

This is done in part by not following through with charges or grievances against the company. Government agencies allow complaints to go unnoticed by slapping companies on the wrist when they break the laws. This only gives them that much more power. Woodrow Stamping was breaking so many laws that I have lost count of how many.

- They were pilfering money from employees as long as I worked for them.

- I was terminated without my knowledge.

- I was called names such as "trouble maker" and "radical".

- The Medical Department took information out of my medical file.

- They retaliated against me when they got angry with me.

- My idea was pilfered and I never got the credit for coming up with it.

- They interfered with my doctor/patient medical treatment.

- I was put out of the plant and was told all of management agreed I could not return to Woodrow Stamping Plant.

- They made me work without restrictions, knowingly causing grave pain in order to make a profit off me.

- I was told none of management wanted me back. An employee at the Department of Civil Rights conveyed this message to me.

- I won a harassment grievance and never received a dime because they pilfered that money too.

The list goes on and on. This is just what happened to *me*. I'm not talking about Andrea Smith, Linda Jackson, Mazzie Cane, and others. The company used unfair labor practices on a daily basis. These agencies that were set up to help employees were a joke. "Money talks and bullshit walks." I have experienced more unfair experiences while working at Woodrow Stamping Plant than anyone could ever imagine, and since no one would listen I decided to put my experiences in writing. I complained for 14 years and it's a shame no one ever listened. There was nothing done to protect the employees. It was enslavement—plain and simple.

Holding responsible parties accountable would help eliminate discrimination. Our country hasn't advanced that far in terms of discrimination. Caucasians, who think discrimination doesn't exist, need to look at their neighborhood that is 95% Caucasian and ask why they themselves don't want minority to move next door to them. That tells us how far we have advanced in terms of discrimination. If you can't really see what is going on in our society, then there is a need to look within to see what part *you* play in the discrimination process. I think if we continue to allow the discrimination laws to erode, discrimination will become our silent killer. Segregation will once again become prevalent in our society. Everyone knows that all Caucasians don't discriminate, but I'm speaking of those who are in the dark—so to speak. You know who you are. Many leaders in our past (Black and White) have fought for discrimination laws. They have given their lives to attain what we have now accomplished. One must realize we have to continue fighting to preserve what we have before we relapse.

I feel this silent group that hides the fact they are superior, is the first group to say they don't discriminate or to say discrimination doesn't exist. I really don't know to what extent discrimination has eroded thus far, but it is grave enough to get the attention of the nation such as the Hurricane Katrina episode. Who is willing to stand up and vow to do something about what is happening? Clearly it's not our politicians who represent our best interest in government apparently. You would figure with all the laws in existence, the government agencies and the courts would be the watchdogs over all aspects of discrimination. You would think discrimination in these large companies would be at a minimum. But it was rampant in the company I worked for during all the years of my employment. If every agency that is put in place to denounce discrimination did their jobs, then discrimination wouldn't be as it is today. This tells me just how our laws convict others for the color of their skin. The laws don't mean as much in terms of democracy. If the discrimination laws were enforced, discrimination would be something of the past.

For those who discriminate, the word *"discrimination"* is just a word in the English dictionary. This is why they turned their heads to the discrimination Andrea, others, and I experienced. Those who complained to outside agencies regarding the harsh treatment they experienced by their employer, were just retaliated against. They continue to use their past practices in race priorities and don't have to worry about violating discrimination practices in the workplace. When I was a child, discrimination was prevalent. Therefore these laws were put in place in an effort to abolish discrimination in large private companies. If they did discriminate, the government agencies would do something about the law being broken. In our society now, we seem to be reverting back to discriminating ways of the past by allowing those who violate to continue violating. Those who violate discrimination laws regarding, color, race, sex, disability, religion, etc., should be held accountable. These laws of protection were written for Caucasians because from what I've seen and experienced, the laws don't apply to the discrimination of minorities.

Caucasians don't have to follow the same laws as minorities. Their consequences are always much lighter than the average minority. When a Caucasian feels they have been violated, they don't have to worry about obtaining a lawyer. Minorities have to get a lawyer to take their case, only to be told later that their case can't be taken when laws have been violated against them. I have learned lawyers consistently use a Lawyers Code of Ethics for determining if a person's name has been put in the computer after being *red flagged* or *blackballed*. Caucasians and big businesses have a different set of rules they follow. When the laws and rules are not followed, they don't have to be held accountable. I had a lawyer say to me, "*It doesn't matter how much proof you have to prove you are within your rights. They know how to get around the laws*". That was one of the truest statements this lawyer made. All my experiences related exactly. I had the necessary proof in reaching out for help and I fell by the wayside. No one listened to me and there were those who did listen but chose not to get involved.

This fact is very important because I became a victim and was in need of help. There were no laws to protect me because they weren't applied. There were no government agencies that would follow through with filing charging against companies for their accountability. The union was a total joke they needed to repay me every dime they took from me. I paid the union to expose me as a victim of Woodrow Stamping Plant and Local 783. But in unison they lacked to give me the necessary protection as the company relentlessly violated our contract.

Woodrow Stamping Plant was guilty of harassment, discrimination, retaliation, and wrongful termination. They were also guilty of pilfering my money for three years, underpaying me, and pilfering my idea (which they gave to a Caucasian employee). Andrea has experienced all of the above treatment with the exception of an idea being pilfered. I was never hit with a truck nor have I been assaulted with a broom. Woodrow Stamping Plant and Local 783 were clearly displaying criminal activities. They took my money and said it was an error, but the error was never corrected until I was wrongfully discharged to work at Sarrow Stamping Plant.

They took all my bonuses during that time, my profit sharing, vacation pay, personal days, and paid me part-time pay when I should have received full-time pay. All this money was taken during the three years I was full-time. Woodrow Stamping and Local 783 both said that I was part-time. I received a vacation check in 1992 and had to repay the money back to the company. However my Caucasian co-workers didn't have to pay their money back. The money didn't go back to the company because my check stub said it was paid to me. It took some months later for Woodrow to correct my check and confirm that I did pay the money back because I did.

They changed my eligibility status from December to the letter "S", whatever that meant. They didn't explain but stated the vacation amount as being paid to me. They couldn't take the amount off my pay because it was paid to me and pilfered. My check stub never reflected I paid the vacation money back to the company. This meant I received the money. I wasn't going to lie and say I received money when I did not and the money was directed to me in the first place. Not to mention all the money they previously pilfered from me. I also had to pay taxes on money I never received. The money was paid back from my paycheck through adjustments from my payroll check. During those three years the profit sharing was in the thousands of dollars. This money was pilfered with the help of the *Good Old Boys Club*.

The *Good Old Boys Club* was a group of all men who worked in management at Woodrow Stamping Plant and the union. I would hear supervision speak of the club during my first couple of years working at Woodrow Stamping Plant. They were a group of White men who stuck together for a common cause whatever the cause may have been.

This book is written for all the other employees who couldn't or wouldn't speak out in their own defense. After many years of being mistreated, lied to, harassed, and being caused bodily injury deliberately, I wrote this book to address some of these issues. The Medical Department knew I had Degenerative Joint Disease after they took the first set of x-rays. They allowed me to work without restrictions because their doctors said nothing was wrong with me. They hid medical information regarding my condition. If the Medical Department addressed my condition when it was first noticed, my disease wouldn't have escalated as much as it has. Now my condition is a permanent situation I will have to deal with for the remainder of my life. Woodrow Stamping Plant is where I worked from 1990 until 1993, and from 1997 until 2004. I was retired by Famous Parts Company with a medical disability retirement but not before many unforeseeable events occurred in the final years at Woodrow Stamping Plant.

I filed two harassment grievances against the Medical Department—2000, 2001, and I was in the process of filing the third in 2002 when the retaliation started. As a result I was put on medical leave in 2002. The first grievance I filed against Woodrow Stamping Plant in 2000 was finally settled in February 2002 in favor of Woodrow Stamping Plant. How the 2001 grievance was handled was with much dissatisfaction. When I returned in October 2001 the grievance had been settled and I had no knowledge of its settlement. Local 783 knew the grievance was settled but continued to lie saying the grievance was in its second stage.

In 2002 I was in the process of filing a third grievance. This time was against the Plant Chairman of Local 783, Tom Hemp, and his partner in crime, Al Snake Representative of the Executive Branch of the Union Regional 21A Office. (This was the middle branch of the Executive Branch of the Union.) I was bringing charges against both men under the Constitution of the Union under Article 33.

As a result of the 2001 grievance being filed, Local 783 reopened the 2000 grievance filed against Woodrow Stamping Plant and the Medical Department.

The grievance was granted in my favor. This was only done only after Local 783 botched the 2001 grievance. I was filing against the union because they eliminated my grievance filed in June 2001 against Woodrow Stamping and the Medical Department. The grievance could not have been settled without the knowledge of Plant Chairman Tom Hemp, and his partner in crime, Al Snake. The Bargaining Committeeman, Pedro Stevens, sent me on a wild goose chase by telling me the grievance was in the second stage when it wasn't. The grievance was settled on July 30, 2001 to be exact.

Local 783 could not have pulled this lie off without the authorization of Plant Chairman Tom Hemp, and Al Snake. The highest level of the Executive Branch of the Union tried to cover this mess Local 783 found them-selves in. These union leaders always stuck together and it didn't matter what they said or did—right or wrong. They stuck together as a result of the 2001 grievance that eventually was lost in the appeal I filed with the Executive Board. The Union failed to compensate me through the grievance procedure and the decision was appealed to the Public Review Board. Can you believe that Andrea and I were not allowed to participate in this Public Review Board hearing? Andrea was my witness and we were denied the right to participate. This grievance went to the Public Review Board and this was the first time my grievance had ever been to the Public review Board—contrary to what Local 783 said to me in my grievance filed in June 1993. The Executive Branch told that lie knowing the grievance had not been there. The Executive Board was aware the grievance had not been there, but they continued to side with Local 783 for all these years and wouldn't allow me to say a word in my own defense. Local 783 lied all those years while Woodrow Stamping Plant pilfered my full-time benefits package.

I never received a dime from the harassment grievance because it was said monetary payments were not discussed during the grievance. That was a lie! The grievance had been rewritten. Have you ever heard of a grievance that was derived from harassment and the person not being compensated? Where was the union? Clearly they were in the back pocket of Woodrow Stamping Plant.

Andrea and I thought maybe we could bring this thief scheme to the attention to the Executive Branch of both the company and the union. We had no idea they were the main perpetrators. It all started falling into place when the unedited copy of this book was sent to the publisher and was printed. When Andrea sent the unedited books out, she also sent a cover letter accompanying it directing the reader to what chapters concerned her condition and experience with the company.

The book just substantiated what I had been saying all along. When persons from the Executive Branch of the Union and the Executive Branch of the Company started stepping down, it showed exactly how involved these people were regarding Woodrow Stamping Plant and Local 783. When the CEO of the Executive Branch of the Company, Robert Wart, received a copy of the book, he just was interested in what the author said—fact or fiction. If he weren't involved, he would have contacted me in wanting to know more details. If it were I who someone made extreme accusations about, I would make attempts to contact them for clarification and further details of what was going on within the company.

Andrea and I didn't have a contract to follow because Woodrow Stamping and Local 783 weren't following what was in the contract. I read the contract with regards to the grievance procedures and followed it as if it were a roadmap. The contract explained the privileges of the full-time employees and the same for the part-time employees. The part-time employees were only to work on Mondays, Fridays, Saturdays, Sundays, and holidays if needed. This was their regular work schedule. Woodrow Stamping and Local 783 allowed us to work anywhere from 16 to 32 hours a week, which was considered full-time according to contract. We were working five days a week eight hours a day, which was clearly against the contract for the part-time employee. Part-time employees had to work six months before receiving insurance benefits. To receive holiday pay, part-timers had to work 90 actual days. Part-time employees were supposed to be allowed to work on weekends. As a full-time employee you started receiving benefits after you received 90 days. There was no waiting period for benefits if you were full-time.

This is how Woodrow Stamping Plant and Local 783 worked their thieving scheme. Woodrow Stamping Plant hired employees full-time. After they were hired, Woodrow Stamping told them they were part-time. Woodrow Stamping Plant would work employees two days for the company. Local 783 would have the employees on union paid days or on union business for the remainder of the three days on the part-time records they kept on employees. Local 783 had their own timekeeping records and had access to the payroll records as well. The benefits that came along with full-time employees (with the exception of insurance benefits) were transferred into the N account if they were monetary.

The N account was where Woodrow Stamping and Local 783 kept employee information separated. It consisted of days and times worked. Local 783 had access to the N account regarding part-time employees. Woodrow Stamping Plant and Local 783 would tell employees not to say anything to anyone about the full-time insurance benefits they were receiving because they would be taken away. The monies diverted were bonuses, profit sharing, vacation pay, and personal days. This is just part of the money that was diverted into the N account. The company would cover themselves by flagging employment records as "Auto Tender Line Worker (ATLW/Part-time.)" If there were any questions, it could easily be explained without rising suspicion by explaining that the employee was full-time and reverted back to part-time. This activity went on for years. The Controller set up the files so the money would be diverted to the N file. (By the way, the Controller is the same as an accountant.)

It was clearly a breach of contract in every aspect imaginable. For *one*: Local 783 was not allowing union members to file grievances. Number *two*: they were lying about various stages the grievance was in. There was no paperwork to show the grievance was in effect. *Three*, they lied about filing a grievance when a grievance was never filed. *Four*: they lied when they stated the grievance went to the Public Review Board. There was no paper trail contrary to the facts stating the grievance had been there. I have expressed how powerful Woodrow Stamping Pant and Local 783 were. They had people at the Executive Branch of the Company, Metro Craft Insurance Company (Famous Parts Company's insurance company), lawyers, referees, doctors, etc. I can't begin to express how far and wide this corruption extended. By them all working together, these entities were very powerful.

When Nurse Tootie was arrested in 2004, she was clearly arrested for doing a job the company was paying her to do. Nurse Tootie was very good at the job she did for Woodrow Stamping Plant. She was aware she was breaking the law. I can't see Nurse Tootie as being one of those employees that didn't think about her future. If in fact she were ever caught changing medical information on the medical forms and records, she would be fired. She was embezzling money, making sure the money was in its proper place, and forging government documents to the Social Security Administration. Nurse Tootie didn't strike me as being someone who would go down alone. She was smarter than that. Nurse Tootie was a very powerful person at Woodrow Stamping Plant. When they arrested her, they were also looking for the Plant Chairman, Tom Hemp. I'm sure they found him at his home or somewhere hiding under a rock, and arrested him for the part he played in Woodrow Stamping Plant's scheme of racketeering.

When Nurse Tootie was arrested in 2004, state policemen escorted her out of Woodrow Stamping Plant. She was then able to see how it felt, by having had others escorted out of the plant due to her lying on them. Nurse Tootie lied on Andrea by saying Andrea threatened to do bodily harm to her. The questions asked on January 22, 2003 were to get Andrea to say something incriminating to use for her firing. On the other hand, Nurse Tootie and Tom Hemp had their own plight of justice. They are now facing charges for doing what they were being paid to do.

The company is standing by doing nothing while these employees are taking the blame for what they were asked to do. The plight of injustice has fallen on them and them alone for a change. The company did to them what they had done to others. Do you think the Executive Branch of the Company would admit they told their employees to pilfer money from others? Do you seriously think they would admit to doing something of this magnitude? I truly don't think so. Famous Parts Company would not allow someone as small as Nurse Tootie to take them down. They'll just say they knew nothing about what she had done.

Andrea Smith has nothing else to lose at this point because when she lost her job, she lost everything. She even lost her house that she stayed in for at least 30 years. Andrea hoped the Michigan Supreme Court would hear her case after the lower court refused. What was the point in her going back to Woodrow Stamping Plant telling a lie to get her job back? If she went back to Woodrow Stamping Plant, they would fire her once again and there would be nothing she or any lawyer could do in her defense.

Andrea wonders why she was fired through the mail. If there were a problem, why couldn't the problems have been addressed while she was in the Medical Department? Why was Woodrow Stamping Plant not answering her questions? Why did they fire her unjustly? Although she didn't put anything past Woodrow Stamping Plant and Local 783, she never saw her firing coming on that day. No one gave Andrea the time of day. In fact, no one took the time and answered her questions or her grievance. Not even when she filed charges against Local 783 in how they were handling her grievance under the Constitution of the Union's Article 33.

They only left one option for her to come back. Andrea felt that saying she threatened the Medical Department staff was quite much. She also would not be able to file a grievance for a period of one year or be able to seek the union's help if there were problem. She yet has to pay union dues, but she will not be able to file a union grievance for one year. There were no other words exchanged—just a letter in the mail stating she was fired. Andrea was concerned about her safety at the plant. She had been hit by a truck and a co-worker hit her in the chest with a broom over a job assignment. Andrea found out by the Social Security Administration that Woodrow Stamping had her on a "retired" status. When Andrea started inquiring about the retirement, she came out of retirement and was called back to work.

When Andrea was fired, she was told if she came on company property she would be escorted off by plant security. Nurse Tootie kept notes of all the corruption she was involved in while employed at Woodrow Stamping Plant. When Nurse Tootie was arrested, she started singing like a bird—telling what had been going on at the plant. She talked about what they did to Andrea Smith along with the help of Labor Relations and Local 783. She also tried to blame Ruth More, another nurse, as being the one who was the guilty party in the embezzlement with the Medical Department. Chelsea More was involved too, but not to the extent that Nurse Tootie was.

After her arrest, a deposition was made and proved Woodrow Stamping was indeed aware Andrea had been harassed. Andrea retrieved the #5166 medical forms, which were altered by Woodrow Stamping Plant's Medical Department. Nurse Tootie explained carefully all the details of what happened to Andrea by changing her #5166 medical forms. When Nurse Tootie finished Andrea's edited medical form, the form stated: "*pain-restricted range of motion. SLR 20 degrees bilaterally from a fall at home*". Nurse Tootie stated Andrea couldn't lift anything over 25 pounds, which was 20 pounds more than her original restriction, stating only 5 pounds. Nurse Tootie changed medical information with reference to Andrea's restrictions to expire in one week before the restriction was supposed to be lifted. As for Andrea's disability being occupational, Nurse Tootie changed it from "yes" to "no". Nurse Tootie fraudulently changed Andrea's Medical information to fit the Medical Departments needs.

Andrea's original medical form was dated April 15, 2002. It said Andrea's diagnosis was "acute flare-up Lumbar Fibromtositis". Andrea's medical restrictions were:

> "Limited lifting and bending, limited prolonged standing or walking, lifting limited to 5 lbs., limited repetitive usage of both hands."

Her original document stated the duration of Andrea's condition was ongoing and permanent. The information had been typed and Andrea's doctor never typed her medical forms. He always completed her medical forms by hand.

Andrea was actually out on medical leave for CTC Fibromtositis, Reactive Depression, and a lumbar strain. The medical form #5166, which asked if the medical condition was occupational, had a box marked "yes" by Andrea's doctor. The original form stated Andrea's condition was occupational and listed Andrea's disability as being due to her occupation. The form asked if Andrea's condition was permanent and Dr. Cannon said, "Yes". This restriction was given prior to Andrea's leave for Major Depression.

The deposition made when Nurse Tootie was arrested, explained in detail of what happened to Andrea. This went back to 1992. They tampered with medical information in favor of Woodrow Stamping. The deposition I received revealed a calculated scheme. This is what they did to Andrea and those who were involved. The Medical Department was in hopes that what happened would never be revealed. They had hopes that this information would never come to surface. They harassed Andrea for no apparent reason, other than protecting their own asses. They gave less than a damn what happened to Andrea.

All this information was revealed under the nose of the CEO of Famous Parts Company until the arrests were made and depositions were taken. Andrea and I had been trying to expose the plant's corruption for years. This was the reason the Executive Branch of the Company fired employees in August and September 2005. Many were fired at a moment's notice. These people were supposed to be the *"family"* and they were not acting as though they were part of the family by undermining the company. The red flag came when they were 'fired' and not 'laid-off' due to cutbacks. There is a difference.

This was done in part to cover CEO Robert Wart's role in firing many employees at the executive level. At that point I thought Robert Wart had no involvement in this scheme, but some of what transpired revealed to be done on his watch—and he should have known. I later found he was just letting employees go so they wouldn't implement him in how and why they were pilfering money from employees. Taking money back that was granted to employees through the contract just isn't right. The game is called *"cover your own ass"* and reputation. This is why the CEO of Famous Parts Company just recently stepped down and handed leadership over to someone else. The Big Man always put the blame on the little man since they couldn't afford to defend themselves. The big executives got off with all that was done. As I have stated earlier, "money talks and bullshit walks" in every sense when you have money and clout.

Andrea lost each case she entered in court and it wasn't because she didn't have information to substantiate the truth. Andrea was trying to be compensated for her injuries that occurred at Woodrow Stamping Plant. The reason the court didn't recognize Andrea's condition was because Referee Jackie Arnold wrote her claim up as a new one. Although Andrea's medical bills were paid on her first claim, Andrea came out with the true facts of what happened. Woodrow Stamping Plant never paid Andrea anything from her first Worker's Compensation claim because she disagreed with the amount of money she was to receive. Andrea was asking for $300,000 dollars using the pay scale in the back of the Worker's Compensation manual. Woodrow Stamping only wanted to give her $10,000 dollars because Woodrow Stamping stated they paid her Worker's Compensation benefits on a weekly basis.

Since they couldn't pay Andrea the amount of money she was owed, they went on a campaign to get rid of her. Jackie Arnold never recognized the claim in 2002 because it was filed in the court as a new claim. The court never took into consideration that Andrea was hit by a hi-lo truck and was transported to the hospital. When Andrea brought it to the court's attention, she was completely dismissed. Andrea was trying to tell the court her complaint went further back than 2002, but the court wouldn't listen. This was the same referee that made a settlement of Andrea's first claim just two years prior. This was nothing more than a modern-day lynching.

Andrea wouldn't have had this much trouble pursuing her case if she were Caucasian. Since she was Black, it was less likely to get her case heard in a court of law. If Andrea were Caucasian instead of a minority, she could have easily gotten a lawyer because of the extent of Woodrow Stamping Plant's illegal activity. A Caucasian may have some problems, but they would be able to get *someone someplace* in the system to eventually handle their case. Andrea couldn't find an attorney—in state or out of state, to handle her case. I've heard the saying, "*Blacks always want to sue someone because they are too lazy to work*". If minorities were treated with dignity and respect, there wouldn't be a cause for a lawsuit in the first place.

Upon the condition of Andrea's return, she would receive no back pay for the illegal firing. The lie she was fired upon wasn't even investigated. She would not be allowed to file a grievance against the company. How can Local 783 say they represented Andrea when they were informed of all aspects of the grievance and she never returned back to work? Local 783 never allowed her to take part in the grievance procedure, even when she asked because there was no grievance filed. They did exactly what they wanted to do and there was no authority that could have intervened. She couldn't even challenge the decision made by the union according to the conditions given to her in a *so-called* grievance. Andrea's experiences will be explained in greater detail in Part 2 of this book.

They never tried to investigate the problem. There should not have been a reason for a grievance to take that long to settle—especially following the guidelines of state and federal courts. The Department of Civil Rights, National Labor Relations Board, and the Department of Labor, all stood by and did nothing while Andrea sought help. How could something like this happen to a person?

Laws had obviously been broken, lies had been told, and not one of the above agencies was there to protect Andrea. She had no other recourse but to fall completely through the cracks of bureaucracy.

With these complaints you would think Local 783 would have grounds for a grievance, but instead Andrea went completely ignored. With all that had happened, you would think the Executive Branch of the Union would have stepped in to investigate. We should receive every dime we paid to the union for representation we didn't receive.

After voicing how I wanted to take part in my grievance process, I was denied the opportunity. I was told I could not attend on any level of the grievance process. I was upset since I wasn't informed as to the findings in each stage of the grievance. Some grievances take years to settle due to the usage of all kinds of stall tactics. This allowed the statue of limitations to run out on the contracts and labor laws that had been violated. I wrote letters to the Executives of the Company in July 1995, September 2000, March 2002, May 2002, August 2004, and September 2004. I also contacted the union's CEO Executive on April 2002, May 2002, February 2004, and August 2004. Of course all this was to no avail.

Andrea is a very unique young lady and also a very smart one. I only mention her in detail in a few chapters in Part 1 of this book. I intend to go into greater detail in Part 2. I will prove the extent that the harassment, discrimination, and retaliation went to. There is nothing any organization did to alleviate the problems we experienced. We tried obtaining help in our quest for some kind of justice, which soon became a vendetta. Andrea is my friend and co-worker. The treatment she received by Woodrow Stamping Plant and Local 783 was despicable, insensitive, and inhumane.

Andrea was hit with a broom by one of her Caucasian male co-workers who had cursed at her a week earlier because he thought Andrea was going to take his job. Andrea was afraid. She came to work looking for her broom. (*Andrea's job was to sweep the floor on her feet all day. But her restriction stated she should alternate 2 hours on her feet and 2 hours off. With all of Andrea's restrictions she had on record, can you believe Woodrow Stamping Plant had her standing on her feet all day sweeping the floor and told Andrea she could talk to no one?*) Andrea's broom wasn't in its original location. Before she could completely turn around, Ronald Hatfield had thrown the broom, which landed in the center of Andrea's chest. Andrea was angry because just one week earlier, she'd reported to Labor Relations that Ronald cursed her angrily. This man did not so much as receive a reprimand for his actions even though the plant professed a 'no tolerance' policy.

She went to the Medical Department and reported the incident. Nothing was ever done to Ronald, and he was allowed to retire soon after. Then a week later, the hi-lo truck hit Andrea. This incident was never recorded either. Woodrow Stamping paid the medical bills for the incident, but no one seemed to care. They hid the incident, which made me think it was done purposely. The Medical Department got rid of all the information regarding Andrea being hit by the hi-lo. This was perhaps in the hopes the incident would have gone unnoticed and would soon be forgotten. Andrea went to the Labor Department, Department of Civil Rights, and National Labor Relations Board, but each time she was attacked by vengeance brought on by the company and union.

Andrea called me one afternoon in a panic, stating she was told to go back into the Medical Department to see the company doctor. She expressed how she called the Union Headquarters and the Regional Office. Andrea expressed her concerns and fears about entering into Woodrow Stamping Plant after she was hit by the hi-lo truck. I advised Andrea to go to the police and file a complaint of assault. Looking back on how things turned out, it would have been in Andrea's best interest if she had done so. Andrea feared going to the police because of how powerful these organizations were. She really felt the local police would be of no help, but at least there would have been a record of the incident that was less likely to have been ignored. Andrea believed Woodrow Stamping had the police in their back pocket too. She didn't want Local 783 to become angry with her again. She often faced retaliation issues because of her actions.

Andrea felt that she would at least be heard after she filed a grievance and explained the magnitude of what happened. This could not be ignored. Boy! She had no idea what she was getting herself into with Woodrow Stamping Plant and Local 783 joining together. Woodrow Stamping Plant mistreated Andrea and clearly she had no one to investigate what happened to her. As stated by one of Famous Parts Company's attorney's, it doesn't matter how much proof you have—it doesn't mean a thing. I have found his statement to be true. If you're Black fighting a big private company such as Famous Parts Company, how can you win? Lawyers are fearful of big businesses because they always seem to have reputations that lawyers don't want to touch. That is the reason big businesses have the union in their pockets. The unions have jumped ship by not represent- ing the working people, and now lawyers have jumped ship in fear of what big businesses can do to their law firms.

Andrea was wrong in thinking the union was going to assist her with the retal- iation she was experiencing from Woodrow Stamping Plant. Andrea thought everyone would know what happened to her. But things only got worse by filing the grievance against the company. The union wouldn't represent her in this matter at all. Why didn't Andrea receive any assistance from the union? I guess it was kind of like when the union and company were in a joint venture to terminate me in June 2002. I know they worked hard in an effort to terminate Andrea because they did the same to me on two occasions. Why was Woodrow Stamping so set on terminating Andrea and I? There had to be a valid reason don't you think? I will further elaborate on this in Part 2 of this book.

I had to return to work from medical leave in October 2001. Woodrow Stamping released my vacation pay while I was on medical leave. The company had to have me on active payroll in order for this to happen. In order for me to receive a vacation check, I had to be on active payroll and I should not have been. This wasn't the first time I brought this kind of problem to the Medical Department's attention. I informed the Medical Department I never returned back to work in June 2002. Woodrow Stamping Plant's records stated I was not on medical leave, but at work. If this were the case, there had to be two sets of records. While I was being paid by Metro Craft Insurance Company provided by Famous Parts Company, it was impossible for me to be working. I couldn't be working and on medical leave at the same time. This proves that something wasn't right surrounding these circumstances and no one took the initiative to investigate. This action happened on a continual basis until my retirement in December 2004.

In June 2001 I brought it to the company's attention I had not returned to work, but my medical papers stated I did. They were diverting my Worker's Compensation checks while I was on medical leave into one the N account where they kept the pilfered money from employees. I went into the Medical Department and had them remove the 'return to work' status, and they did. It happened again when I was on medical leave in September 2002. The company records stated I didn't start my medical leave until October 2002. They did this in part because I should not have been on a 'no work available' and receiving Worker's Compensation at the same time.

My injury was occupational, not personal. I should have continued to work with restrictions covered under Worker's Compensation guidelines, but instead Woodrow Stamping Plant kept the Worker's Compensation payments. I was left with the payments from Metro Craft Insurance Company. It appeared I had returned to work before I actually returned from medical leave. I had to meet with Labor Relations when I returned to work. They stated I returned to work in June 2002, when I actually did not. I then knew what they were doing. It was no accident at all.

I returned to work in October 1991 and went back on medical leave again in May 2002. I was called back on August 14, worked one week, and was sent back out on a 'no work available' medical leave. It didn't matter what Woodrow Stamping Plant said, I had my records to prove Metro Craft Insurance Company were paying my benefits. I had not returned back to work. Nurse Tootie told me I would have to complete a medical form while I was working 40 hours a week. I refused to do so, and the union later approached me. I was told that it was a "must" that I completed the form even though the medical form itself stated one must be "out of work" in order to complete the form. I would have been applying for medical benefits while employed. That was clearly against company rules. I'm not naive and I knew this was fraud. I was aware you couldn't be on medical leave and file a claim for medical benefits while working 40 hours a week.

There was another time I started seeing a new doctor because Woodrow Stamping Plant was interfering with my doctor/patient relationships. When I changed doctors, my new doctor completed my medical form and I picked it up. The Medical Department contacted my new doctor and informed him that he hadn't approved my medical leave. I contacted Metro Craft because I had been off work since May 2002 and had not received any payment and it was now July. When July came, I still hadn't received any money from Metro Craft Insurance Company. I called them to find out why. Metro Craft informed me my new doctor's office told them I was not authorized to be off work. Why do you think Metro Craft Insurance Company didn't inform me of what they were told by my physician earlier? I never received a 5-day or a 10-day letter of quit informing me to come into the Medical Department.

If my doctor's office told Metro Craft I was not authorized to be off work, then someone should have informed me. Wouldn't you think that would be a normal procedure? I told Metro Craft I was authorized to be off work and that I had the medical form from my doctor's office with his signature. I faxed the information to the insurance company and was later told I would be paid-in—full for the time I had been off work. When all this was happening, I contacted my new doctor's office and was told by the receptionist that even though she was aware I was authorized to be off, she was told to tell Metro Craft I was not. Why was this receptionist told to lie? In fact, why did the doctor lie when Metro Craft called his office for verification that he authorized me to be off work? You will later find out in Part 2 of this book. When I received my copy of the medical form on my second office visit, the new doctor's office had the original copy in their file. They had no idea I had a copy myself, at the time I spoke with

Metro Craft Insurance Company. The woman I spoke to at Metro Craft stated if I didn't have a copy of the medical form, I would have been terminated.

When I returned to work, I talked to the Plant Chairman, whom I was having investigated under Article 33 of the Constitution for working in the best interest of the company. When I asked Tom Hemp about what happened, he told me *"That's correct. If you didn't have a copy of the medical form you would have to be fired"*. From his expression that's exactly what he wanted. He was sorry I had gotten a copy of the medical form first. This is why I can understand why Andrea was so frightened. I was too. The Medical Department tried to fire me on more than one occasion.

Andrea was indeed frightened and she really didn't know where to turn for help. Andrea was assured by the assistant at the President's Office of the Executive Branch of the Union, that a committeeman would meet her in the Medical Department on the day of her doctor's visit. The Executive Branch of the Union's office asked Andrea not to go alone. When she arrived at Woodrow Stamping Plant, there was no union committeeman to meet her in the Medical Department as promised. Andrea took her husband along, but he was not allowed to go back to the examination room with her. Andrea asked Nurse Tootie if her husband could go back with her and she was told "No!"

The plan for the union was not to have a witness to what Woodrow Stamping Plant and Local 783 were about to do. The Medical Department lied on a defenseless person. They didn't want Andrea back in the plant from medical leave since they were already pilfering her money. Woodrow Stamping Plant was afraid they would soon be found out.

What are the odds of a person coming out of retirement after five years while receiving their retirement for an occupational injury, and not knowing they're retired while at the same time they're on a 'no work available'? Andrea would not have returned to work on her own accord, but Woodrow Stamping Plant stated they had a job for her to work within her restrictions. For Woodrow Stamping Plant to continue receiving Andrea's retirement when they brought her back to work, there had to have been two sets of records. Andrea was asking too many questions regarding her retirement because of what she was told by the Social Security Administration. They told her that Woodrow Stamping had "retired" her. Andrea was not receiving any benefits other than her Social Security each month. Where was Andrea's retirement going? I was aware the pilfered retirement accounts were diverted into the N account. The reason this thief ring got so strong and profitable was because no one oversaw the union and company. The union was supposed to protect. The local branch of the Department of Civil

Rights was not overseeing the complaints employees made regarding Famous Parts Company—Woodrow Stamping Plant.

There was no formal or informal meeting regarding Andrea's termination matter on her behalf. There was no meeting regarding this or any other problem with regards to the Medical Department or with Local 783 concerning her termination. Andrea wrote a grievance explaining what happened in her own words and gave the Bargaining Committeeman a copy. She then mailed other copies to the union official at the Executive Branch of the union. Andrea sent them certified mail. Again she went unnoticed without being given answers or acknowledgements of her correspondence. All I can say is that her grievance was put in existence in February 2003, and the grievance was yet to settle officially until September 2005. It was three years in February 2006. The complexities of Andrea's termination are yet to be completed and they are in no hurry.

What did the Department of Civil Rights, National Labor Relations Board, and the Department of Labor do to represent Andrea's defense? Nothing! They did nothing in my defense either. So there we were—two Black women who had very serious issues needing to be addressed. Yes we both received a 'right-to-sue' letter after the Department of Civil Rights and the Equal Employment Opportunity Commission (EEOC) found there was "no wrong doing" on the company's part. Truly they didn't look hard enough because Andrea and I had all the information they needed. They really didn't want to see what we had. They were too busy trying to support big businesses in their wrongdoings. They wanted no incriminating evidence proving to be true. That was a bunch of B.S.

Why didn't the Department of Civil Rights or the EEOC take these charges to court themselves or find a lawyer to represent us during these trying years of fighting the company? As a result, we both ended up representing ourselves in filing our claims of discrimination in court. No lawyer was willing to take our cases. Andrea did find a lawyer, but this lawyer was more interested in who was going to pay her the biggest kickback. Ms. Lady, Andrea's attorney, was totally for herself, not thinking about her client and all she was going through. It was all about money and had nothing to do with justice or fairness. The attorney didn't bother returning Andrea's calls. Andrea faxed the attorney information and made sure to receive a fax receipt. Therefore Ms. Lady couldn't say she didn't receive Andrea's information.

Andrea's lawyer was supposed to be representing her in her quest to sue for her firing. Andrea requested everything in her file regarding correspondences, legal papers, and briefs from her sorry attorney. Andrea never received her file in which she paid for. All papers Ms. Lady had, belonged to Andrea. When Andrea's claim was dismissed, the judges left the doors open so Andrea's lawyer could sue the union. That didn't happen either. Andrea's lawyer wanted to extort more money out of her and she was telling the judge the union didn't breech the contract. The judge made a statement that the union "*did* breech the contract". So if the judge knew that, why didn't he help Andrea? As of September 2006, Andrea's lawyer has yet to honor her request in sending her file with all correspondences regarding her case. I thought this woman was working for Andrea! Can you believe how unprofessional these lawyers were? Ms. Lady made it difficult for Andrea by representing the union.

Andrea suffers from Degenerative Joint Disease, which is the same condition I have. Andrea has had her Worker's Compensation case in the courts since 1995, and 'til this day she hasn't received any monetary compensation. The Medical Department fabricated her medical information and kept it in a separate file. They kept secret vital information about her health hidden. As a result she has not been compensated for any of her injuries.

Turncoat lawyers, who started out working for Andrea, ended up working for Woodrow Stamping Plant. Andrea's final decision was turned down for Worker's Compensation in 2004. Can you believe a truck has hit this woman at her place of employment and the Worker's Compensation referee didn't want to know more about it? *Anyone* should want to know what happened and why—especially the referee on the case. Can you believe the union didn't inquire more about what happened? This alone tells me there was something wrong with Andrea, her situation regarding Woodrow Stamping Plant, and their Worker's Compensation.

Andrea took her case all the way to the Michigan Supreme Court and they wouldn't hear her case. Andrea completed all of her appeals herself because she could not obtain a lawyer to represent her. The Appellate and Supreme Court didn't hear Andrea because she was *pro se*. This means Andrea represented herself in the court of law. In order for Andrea's case not to be denied or thrown out, she had to follow the same court rules and time lines as lawyers in the appeal process—but it didn't matter because it was denied just the same. It was Woodrow Stamping Plant and Local 783 who paid for information to stay dormant. They paid for justice and they received what they paid for when the higher court refused to hear her case. It wasn't that Andrea's cases weren't heard because she didn't know the laws to follow. She wasn't a lawyer, but that wasn't the problem. The court was bought and paid for. She knew exactly what she was doing while representing her facts. Woodrow Stamping Plant just had so much clout they could hide anything, and with enough money they made sure cases such as Andrea's never got heard.

There is much that Famous Parts Company doesn't want the public to know—especially on how they really feel about minorities. They kept this information secret for many years. They proclaimed they gave minorities (from the south) the opportunity to work and earn a good salary. Everyone who migrated from the south worked hard for a living and earned every penny of their salary. The work was hard then, and the work is hard now. The minorities did the actual labor many jobs Caucasians wouldn't do. When the plant gets finished working you to death, you are ill for the remainder of your life with a broken-down body or painful diseases.

The problems came after minorities were hired. The company showed their true colors in displaying no respect of minorities. One thing that comes to mind is how the skilled trades department was basically for the Caucasian worker. The company told Blacks and other minorities they didn't pass the skilled trade's test—no matter how smart they were. It was later proven the company used illegal hiring practices when it came to this department.

The God I serve is going to show he has dominion over all things, and when the higher power is involved, it will all turn out right in the end. These people forgot about the higher power having control of all things. I believe God is tired of how Famous Parts Company treated his children. The company thought they could not be touched. If you pay close attention, it seems Famous Parts Company can't get anything right for the company or for their local football team either. I believe they are being punished for treating the minorities—God's children, in such desperate manners with little or no conscience. Until Famous Parts Company changes their policy, they will continue to struggle.

Their plan was if Andrea was denied at the Appellate Court, for her to give up her fight—but that didn't happen. The referee who presided over Andrea's case, talked about her being hit by a hi-lo in the plant in her original order. Andrea's referee stated Andrea never filed a claim for that incident. This was a lie too. Woodrow Stamping Plant paid the medical bills, which derived from her being hit in the plant, but the ambulance bill has gone unpaid. No one claims to know what happened or why Labor Relations had no record of the incident. It's obvious she was hit in the plant. According to Andrea's Plant Treatment Incident Report from Woodrow Stamping Plant's Medical Department:

"EMP (employee) was sitting in chair in medical department quietly crying. A rack bumped her. She stumbled forward and she recalls another bump. She was not pinned. C collar placed on EMP. And EMP complained of left scapular pain with radiating pain down left arm. EMP will see Dr. Slain. (P. Favor RN. June 26, 2002 time 10:57). Andrea was sent by ambulance for x-rays & evaluation. (P. Favor RN. June 26, 2002 17:16.)"

Woodrow Stamping had many reasons they didn't want Andrea returning back to the plant. For one, Woodrow Stamping Plant had retired her without her knowledge although she never received any money from her retirement. Andrea's retirement benefits were diverted to the special account set up by Woodrow Stamping Plant and Local 783. There was a problem with Andrea's taxes. When she began confronting the problem, they called her back to work stating they had a job for her to do within her restriction. After Andrea returned, the Union Committeeman asked her why she came out of retirement. Andrea also found out she was being underpaid while under the same classification as her co-workers. At that point, we started putting many events together. I knew Local 783 and Woodrow Stamping Plant were laundering money by putting the pilfered money in separate accounts.

This time, when I had written a letter in August 2004 to the CEO of Executive Branch of the Company, there was an investigation taking place at Woodrow Stamping Plant. Soon after that, Head Nurse Tootie was escorted out of the Medical Department along with her files. Nurse Tootie was one of the head honchos and carried a lot of weight at Woodrow Stamping Plant. Not only in the Medical Department, but she carried a lot of weight when she would appear at Worker's Compensation hearings. Nurse Tootie was a very negative person. I didn't like her very well and I told her as much. I didn't like the lies she told me right to my face when she knew very well she was lying. I was well aware that money was being pilfered from employees through their retirement funds. They were pilfering money from the part-time employees, and also from the money employees should have received through Worker's Compensation.

Employees laid-off in the 70's who returned in the 90's should have received back pay with seniority. They held a full-time and part time status with the same company at the same time. The company kept the full-time benefit package including bonuses, vacation days, personal days, etc … and pilfered that money when they were called back to work. But Woodrow hired these same employees as new hires like they'd never worked for the company before. Employees who had just hired with the company were hired before them because former employees didn't have seniority as full-time employees. Woodrow Stamping Plant had been pilfering from these employees for over ten years and some longer because these employees never knew they were full-time. The reason Plant Chairman, John Hail, stated the part-time employees were going to get their seniority when they retired, was because their seniority continued as Woodrow Stamping Plant pilfered their money by having them full-time and part-time too.

Andrea and I weren't the average employees. We stood for truth and integrity. We felt our lives depended on us doing what we had to do in order to survive. I don't condone violence by any means, but I can truly understand how employees lose their character when they're backed up in a corner. They're just trying to get justice. This is *America*—so they tell me. When you work, you're supposed to get paid! That wasn't the case with Andrea and me—and we supposedly had a union to protect our interests.

I remember hearing something that happened to a couple of union officials and a management staff many decades ago. A man went into Famous Parts Company—Wright Steel Plant, shot and killed two union workers and one person from management. I truly understand why the media sat on the story so many years ago. I'm sure there were some unpleasant tasks the company had been putting this man through. What were the union and company doing to this man that caused him to literally lose his sanity? What were the odds that he just walked in his place of employment and started shooting up the place? The man completely lost it. From what I've experienced, there was a cause for this man to give up everything to get even if he had a grudge against Famous Parts Company for what they had done to him.

If he was treated in the same manner as Andrea, should the media not cover the reasoning and the outcome of the incident? Why should this kind of story not be followed through to its entirety? Do you think something like this was being covered up? Was he really justified? Should those who inflicted harassment, pain, and suffering pay a price too? Again, I don't condone violence, and there's no reason for him to have went to that extent. However, the story wasn't covered properly because the company wanted to keep it discrete. An incident like that was always smothered—especially if it was discriminatory on the part of the employer. This tells me there was something happening with employees that companies didn't want to be made public. The company paid for silence. The company used Black on Black discrimination—even down to a court of law. The company would tell a Black supervisor what they wanted done with the Black employees and how to carry it out. Management made sure the acts of discrimination were carried out the right way so the company wouldn't be held accountable.

The Executive Branch of the Company is responsible for the pilfering that went on at the local level of the plant. For the thief ring to have been at that magnitude there was no way management couldn't have known. There had to be many insiders working at the Executive Branch of the Company and the Union to help with their money-laundering scheme. The company had help from lawyers, judges, and other middlemen. The biggest hypercritical doctor was Dr. Butt, who worked for Woodrow Stamping Plant and was known for giving employees with occupational injuries incorrect diagnoses. Forcing employees back to work and denying their medical conditions put them through so much unnecessary pain and suffering. Dr. But would be aware of the actual medical condition, but would state the employee had nothing wrong when they actually needed restrictions.

I can't lie and say I wasn't afraid. The company knew I was aware of the discrimination and pilfering. That is the reason I was terminated. I sought help from the union, I wrote letters to the Executive Branch of the Union's CEO, and did the same for the Executive Branch of the Company. Local 783 didn't account for any of my complaints. Nothing was ever done about my problems. Therefore these entities must have been part of the problem if they weren't part of the solution. When I had no choice but to represent myself in a court of law, I was railroaded. The same went for Andrea. I was offered $7,500 dollars in a settlement offer against Famous Parts Company—Woodrow Stamping Plant. I turned the amount down because I felt it was an insult to my intelligence since they had pilfered from me for many years.

I decided to further my experience in law. I felt the judge was biased with directing me to take this money. It was as though he wanted me to accept measly pennies. My case was thrown out of court in a Summary Judgment. Judge Patrick Turncoat stated I didn't receive a letter from the Department of Civil Rights for discrimination. I was also denied access to a lawyer. I asked the judge to assist me in obtaining a lawyer and his reply was "No". He felt I didn't "need a lawyer". How can a person not need a lawyer when they can't get one to offer representation?

Regardless of what the judge said, he knew I wasn't sufficient in the area of law and should've assisted me in obtaining a lawyer. It really didn't matter if it was for discrimination under the ADA (Americans with Disabilities Act) or not, it was still discrimination. I really couldn't believe what the judge said. I told the judge discrimination was discrimination whether it was racial or pertaining to the ADA. Harassment is harassment just the same. All anyone has to do is to look at my track record with this company and see the company and union both violated my rights. If for nothing else, it was for breach of contract.

This case was a farce—a joke! Andrea had all the valid information on her original claim she filed prior to her lawyer taking her case. Andrea's attorney stated in her court records that she took Andrea's case *pro-bono* (meaning once Andrea got paid then the lawyer would get paid). This was a lie too. Andrea paid the lawyer $5,000 dollars before she would even look into her case. She told the court this information when she filed her papers with the courts.

When my case was thrown out of court in the Summary Judgment, I couldn't see any reason why the judge would throw my case out or wouldn't supply me with an attorney. I don't think the judge went through my exhibits of my discovery. There were letters sent to the CEO of the Executive Branch of the Company from 1995 until 2002. I sought help and I was trying to inform them of what was happening to me and why. The defense didn't cooperate by sending me the necessary paperwork I requested. I had no cooperation from the defense attorneys. I had to represent my case with a hostile defense. This was a trial bought and paid for by the Good Old Boys Club.

From my experience, the Good Old Boys Club was a group of doctors, lawyers, government agencies, and other people who worked together in the name of big businesses to keep cases from entering the courts. This group of people played golf together and were members of the same executive clubs. It was all tied together in an effort to keep big businesses from being sued. They seemed to be working around the laws by breaking the laws and not being held accountable. I often felt the people of big businesses were throwing stones then hiding their hands as though nothing happened.

I took an interest in Andrea's case just to show no matter what a corporation did, they weren't held accountable for their actions under the law. Big businesses break the laws and never give it a second thought. In my opinion, we as people are losing ground on our freedom. Our country was founded on the Constitution of the United States. Our country preaches democracy, but actions show we're losing our shares of freedom on a daily basis. We're leaning more toward a dictatorship each year. People are losing the freedom we've gained through the years and there is nothing we can do about it.

MY OPINION

I have written this book because I had no one to stand up for me in an effort to correct the wrong committed. There were organizations set-up to oversee that employees were not taken advantage of. These organizations were supposed to prevent employees from experiencing such unjust treatment while employed with Woodrow Stamping Plant or any other company. I believe Woodrow Stamping Plant and Local 783 thought they were pre-empting from any prosecutions and that nothing would ever be done about their illegal activities.

All in this book explains how Woodrow Stamping Plant was running a criminal enterprise. There's no reason any person should be mistreated in an effort to conceal a crime. The extent they went through would be classified as cruel and unusual punishment. I hope the company, union, and government entities do not continue to get away with the crimes they committed against the employees.

Employees reached out to anyone who would listen. But the various government agencies were bought and paid for in an effort to keep the company's scheme alive. We would not have fallen through the cracks at this magnitude unless favors were being granted. It doesn't take a rocket-scientist to see problems have gone unnoticed by both Woodrow Stamping Plant and Local 783. The union is the largest organized crime figure in this book. They used their power to persuade others to side with their unjust actions so other organizations would not bring forth charges for breech of contract. Local 783 didn't have to answer any questions regarding allegations.

Local 783 had done nothing in terms of representation. Therefore the employees had to go outside Woodrow Stamping Plant to file charges against the union and company. The union was so large and corrupt, it was impossible to get a fair chance in labor representation. The various organizations contacted were: The Department of Civil Rights, National Labor Relations Board, Department of Labor, the Attorney General's Office, the State Senator's Office, and the FBI. The FBI was another organization that didn't as much as reply by correspondence or by phone. It seemed they just weren't interested. I did receive a letter stating my problem was out of their jurisdiction and to go to another agency.

Andrea Smith sent a letter through e-mail everyone in the Michigan State Senate, but nothing was ever done about her complaint. I did get a response from the

Governor of Michigan. She was forbidden to get involved personally, but gave me a few options as to whom I could contact. Actually Andrea didn't get very much information from the Governor's Office that she could use. Andrea and I both wrote the Michigan Tenure Commission in reference to the judge overstepping their authorization. The judge failed to appoint Andrea and I a lawyer because there were no lawyers willing to take our cases. To my knowledge, every person has a right to have his or her case heard in a court of law according to the constitution.

Andrea's judge granted her an attorney, but in the end she never received one. My judge on the other hand, told me if he saw there was a need for an attorney, he would appoint one. The judge knew beforehand he was going to throw my case out in a Summary Judgment hearing. The people involved defeated our cases before our cases even got started. My grievance was complete before the grievance was ever discussed with the company or anyone else. Local 783 decided not to file the grievance, and the NLRB helped them to extort money from Andrea, Linda, Mazzie, and myself. They stood by and did nothing.

We have laws and we have the Constitution, yet a person can't get their case heard in a court of law. The United States is over in the Middle East fighting a war for democracy and we don't have democracy in our *own* nation. Many of our rights have been taken away in our country. We are losing the simple things—such as equal rights and freedom of speech. Here we are trying to give or teach other countries democracy when we don't have democracy at home. Here we have a president that everyone says they disapprove of. I blame the Congress and the Senate for not using their authority to take action against the President of the United States. We can complain all we want, but if our elected officials can't stand up for the people of the United States, they need be voted out off office. Everyone in Congress is complaining about what is going on, voicing their approvals and disapprovals, but the White House continues with business as usual. I believe the President of the United States is running the White House using the same tactics a union representative uses against its members.

I do wonder if the President of the United States is blackmailing the U.S. Senators and the House of Representatives in order to honor his wishes. I see the President, Woodrow Stamping Plant, the Executive Branch of the Company, the Executive Branch of the Union, and Local 783 all doing the exact same things. They hold all the cards and act as though they're indispensable. They don't have a worry in the world of ever being caught. The local newspapers and news stations won't carry the story about our experiences of the massive amount of pilfering within the company and union. There is no accountability as to what they do to the poor working people.

The union was very secretive in terms of filing a grievance. The contract stated you could participate in the grievance procedures, but that proved to be a lie. The union would not allow Andrea and I to take part in the grievance procedures. The President of the United States won't allow the media the freedom to access information. The media can't be the watchdog of what the President and his cabinet are doing in secrecy. I heard one newscaster say, "The White House and the Republicans are most secretive …" This is because the White House is doing more than they should be doing. The union uses the same tactics against the union members. The union members are always complaining about how the union is no good, but there doesn't seem to be anyone doing anything about it.

Robert Haste III was elected Plant Chairman in 2000 at Woodrow Stamping Plant. This was after John Hail stepped down as he was being indicted for racketeering. Plant Chairman, Robert Haste III, was a well-grounded person who won the April 2000 election because he wanted change. He wasn't honored as the Plant Chairman at Woodrow Stamping Plant or Local 783 after the election. Woodrow Stamping Plant and Local 783 both always worked in unison in doing anything unethical. The other ranking union members didn't include Robert Haste III in any of the union meetings. They always had their meetings without the Plant Chairman's knowledge or either they'd tell him of a planned meeting that wouldn't take place. They always had secret meetings. This is just how bold and calculating they were. Haste didn't stay Plant Chairman very long and later took an early retirement, which really didn't make much sense. He spent all that money and time in an effort to run for Plant Chairman and after his election, you didn't see him around the plant. I saw him some months later and he told me he was retiring to be at home with his family. I didn't think that was the truth, but I left it at that.

I had my own theory of what happened. Robert Haste III he had good intentions and he needed much more than that to be the Plant Chairman at Woodrow Stamping Plant. It was hard to fight a system that didn't want change. They were so corrupt that an honest man couldn't hold his position. I'm sorry to say that, but it's the truth.

Andrea and I experienced so much pain and suffering just so our money would be pilfered. Andrea had been hit by a hi-lo for God's sake and Woodrow Stamping Plant treated the incident as though it never happened. They were some very cold and calculating people. This type of treatment is inhumane to anyone, not just to us. These entities would actually get angry when we were fighting for what was right. *We* were the ones mistreated. The only thing I was doing was trying to recoup some of the money pilfered from me. When this happened, they would retaliate against me. What makes this crime so unforgivable is that they blocked Andrea's every effort for any kind of compensation. She could not receive a dime of the money that was supposed to be granted to her for her injury sustained on the job, nor her retirement.

This crime was so unique because they were pilfering from the very people that needed the money for their survival. My whole body was destroyed. I can't exercise because of the destruction to my body from the jobs I did. I'm also diagnosed as diabetic. Knowing I'm suffering from Degenerative Joint Disease and how it affected the body, why did these people put me back on the line? Why was I denied medical treatment while working in the plant when I was injured on the job? Why didn't Andrea receive any compensation after her Worker's Compensation claim had been in the courts for eight years? Why did the referees, lawyers, and doctors give Linda and Andrea such a rare deal? Was it because they were Black?

I have since retired from the company. I fired my first attorney and started representing myself until almost the end. The company cleared the way, so I became able to obtain an attorney when the company decided they were going to retire me. The extent I and other employees had to go to was pure injustice. I hope in the future, employees I'm speaking of receive justice.

Through all the years I worked for Famous Parts Company, the only thing I asked for was to be treated fairly with just a little dignity and respect. What I *did* receive was harassment, discrimination, and retaliation. They had the audacity to pilfer my idea and give it to someone else. I was made fun of by management because of all the devices I had to wear on a daily basis to perform my job. I had to wear a back brace, braces on both hands, wristbands, and a strap around my upper arm for the tennis elbow I suffered from. I was a laughing stock in the plant, but I did what I had to do to perform my job efficiently.

They didn't give it a second thought when they stole my idea to make improvements to the skilled trades department. There may have even been more pilfered ideas because I thought up many and turned them in. Someone always told me my idea had been thought of prior. I didn't follow the ideas through to see if they were pilfered because I trusted the process. If they pilfered one idea, why wouldn't they have pilfered others? As far as I'm concerned, if the idea becomes a loss for the company it's because they tried to get something for nothing. I don't expect the company to come back and ask questions after I had implemented the idea, and say it belonged to someone else. I was told it was impossible for anyone to steal an idea if the company implemented it. When I left the plant, someone received the credit I should have been given—and that was wrong. I truly believed them when they said my idea would be protected. I had proof my idea was pilfered, but again no one ever cared to investigate.

These people had no heart. They only cared about themselves and what they could pilfer. It was all about money. They transferred me and turned around and terminated me when I was supposed to be a rehire. When they hired me at Sarrow Stamping Plant, they hired me as though I had never worked for the company.

There were other employees who experienced many of the same problems that Mazzie Cane, Linda Jackson, and Andrea Smith experienced. As the book's main character, I speak of the many issues regarding my experiences in the plant. Prior to my experiences while working at Woodrow Stamping Plant and Sarrow Stamping Plant, I believed in the justice system. I was very defenseless and angry with everyone involved with blatantly pilfering my money for many years. I really didn't understand how something like that could have happened in the United States because of the various laws set up to protect employees.

I'd like my readers to know there is no justice in the justice system. The system works for the people who have clout and who can pay for justice. It is truly a sad scenario to know you have to write a book just to be heard. I endured many sad days because I had nowhere to turn when my job was in jeopardy and the retaliation treatment became unbearable. I was truly frightened when I returned back from medical leave. I knew they were trying to fire me and I had no way of stopping them. Woodrow Stamping Plant and Local 783 were working in unison. They had all areas covered from the courts, to the Medical Department, to the Department of Civil Rights, to the National Labor Relations Board. This book touches on how big businesses stick together and how unions can breech contracts without anything being done. That is the reason they are so powerful and can do anything they want to anyone.

They pilfered Linda Jackson's Worker's Compensation payments and her insurance benefits from Metro Craft Insurance Company. They pilfered Mazzie Cane's money, seniority, and her one-time lump sum payment. They paid her part-time pay per hour while she was full-time. They stole my money for three years saying it was a mistake, and they did the same thing to employees for even longer. Even after the mistake was acknowledged, they continued to pilfer my money. They pilfered my profit sharing (which was vast at the time), performance bonuses, vacation days, and personal days. They terminated me and harassed me when I did something that displeased them. My ability to stand up for myself caused me to have to work in a hostile environment.

I was retaliated against because of an article that I wrote for the union newspaper. They had always wanted me to write an article for the union paper, but when the article was a conflict of interest, they censored it. Local 783 never asked me to write another article for the union newspaper. I was called names like "trouble maker" and "radical". All the name calling was unnecessary.

They stole my idea at Sarrow Stamping Plant. I was denied entry to my *basic unit* or *home plant* because the Department of Civil Rights informed me Woodrow Stamping Plant didn't want me at their plant. It was obvious this was the case since they sent me back to Sarrow Stamping Plant in 1997. I didn't understand why the 'department' didn't protect my 'civil rights' by filing charges against Woodrow Stamping Plant and making them stick? I was aware Woodrow Stamping Plant didn't want me back because Sarrow Stamping Plant told me so when I entered their plant for rehire this was a conspiracy.

The Department of Civil Rights could have done something prior to this incident. They could have done something when I first arrived at their doorstep when they took back my vacation pay in June 1992. They could have brought charges against them and made them stick when I told them other employees had received performance bonuses in October 1992 and I had not. While I hadn't received my money, my Caucasian co-workers did. Again, the Department of Civil Rights found no reason to bring charges against Woodrow Stamping Plant or Local 783. During all this time, I was actually full-time on record. The company admitted this to be true, but did not stop taking my money. Verlinda Moose, Labor Relations Supervisor, told me I had to go back to Sarrow Stamping Plant because I wasn't welcomed at Woodrow Stamping. All this was done with Local 783's authorization.

I think Andrea lost more than anyone in this book. They pilfered her money, pride, dignity, and sanity too. She lost everything she had gained prior to her employment at Woodrow Stamping Plant. She has lost her physical health and her mental state is deteriorating—all this with no compensation. When her Worker's Compensation case was settled, her doctors were paid but she received nothing. Do you think this was fair treatment? The Social Security Administration told her the company she worked for had her listed as "retired". Woodrow Stamping kept all her money.

When Andrea was hit by the hi-lo truck, there was no record of what happened. When she was taken to the hospital, the Carrier's Report stated the plant paid her medical bills, but there was no other evidence of the incident occurring.

There was no record of when she was cursed by and hit with a broom by another co-worker. Andrea was fired (by mail) while she was on medical leave for Major Depression. Local 783 had been holding on to Andrea's grievance for over 2 years regarding her firing. Maybe this was because she gave them no reason to fire her.

In September 2005 she received a letter stating her grievance was settled and that she could come back to work with a letter from a licensed psychiatrist stating she wasn't a threat to herself or to others. They eventually accepted Andrea's treating doctor's letter, knowing Andrea was never a threat. The company may have thought there was a reason for some kind of reprisal for the treatment she was receiving from Local 783 and Woodrow Stamping Plant.

I do hope all these persons will take responsibility for their actions. This includes the judges when they didn't give the employees an attorney to represent their cases in court. All the corruption involved made it impossible for us to represent our own cases since we had no law degrees. There was no justice. Every law had been broken, and the judges in our cases lied if they said there were no laws violated. There had to have been pay-offs because the judges didn't allow Andrea or I a chance in the courts. We weren't given an opportunity to represent ourselves because Woodrow Stamping and Local 783 had enough influence to make sure our cases didn't reach a jury.

No one should read this book and say there were no laws broken or breech of contract. Local 783 owes those employees every penny extorted from them. I would like your feedback. I ask that you especially respond if you have been treated in this manner while working in a plant where there was supposed to be union representative protecting your best interest but instead, you found they were working for the company.

There is no excuse for poor representation. If you have paid for a service, you should receive it. I am aware of many who choose not to fight the system in fear of the consequences. I would like your feedback on some of the harassment, retaliation, and discrimination you've experienced. I would like to know just how many people paid for services from the union and never received results when their jobs were hanging in the valance. I'd like to know if you filed a grievance and the union did not file it on your behalf while stating they did. This is a breech of contract because every grievance has merit unless proven otherwise. This type of cruel treatment should never be extended to anyone.

If this kind of treatment has occurred, maybe everyone should go on a letter—writing campaign or e-mail our government officials regarding the treatment of the union member's and ask them to investigate. Since we can't count on the National Labor Relations Board or any other organizations for help, everyone should just bombard these politicians with letters of dissatisfaction. If your politician is bombarded by complaints, whether old or new, it should be enough to start an investigation on the union's unfair labor practices. One can't do it alone. We have to do it together and maybe someone will start getting proper union representation. We're paying for it, right? We have to start holding our lawmakers and union leaders accountable for their actions.

In my opinion, everyone who was involved may have thought they've gotten away with their illegal treatment. That may be true in a sense, but they *will* have to answer to the higher power regarding the unjust treatment. Those who administer unjust treatment need to be put in the same situation to see if they'd like it. They need to think about the tables being turned. If one doesn't want to be treated in an unjust manner, then it's wrong to mistreat others. I believe your conscience is your guide. I also believe in karma. The Bible says—"You reap what you sow". How you treat others will definitely come back to you. I believe you pay for the wrong you dispense to others *before* you die, not after.

I truly hope you enjoyed this book. I would like to hear from you—positive or negative. As for myself, my plans are to complete *Somewhere Hidden Between the Cracks Part 2*. My second book will further detail the discrimination, harassment, retaliation, and the circumstances surrounding the events resulting from working with Famous Parts Company—Woodrow Stamping Plant.

ABOUT THE AUTHOR

A retire autoworker from Michigan, who witnessed and experienced fraud, thief, and discrimination within the company and the union. The local news stations and newspapers wouldn't carry the story. We both were denied counsel. I was offer from Woodrow Stamping Plant offered me $7,500 dollars to settle. This Book expresses how big businesses have dominated the courts the judges are bought and paid for by big business. No government agency, local politician helped in seeking justice, Not even the president of the United States. Andrea Smith, was hit with a hi-lo in the plant and became afraid for her life. She was terminated while on medical leave. I wanted the President to intervene to investigate the money laundering and thief that was going on between the company and the union and Andrea's termination.

978-0-595-46029-8
0-595-46029-1

Printed in the United States
201665BV00003B/52-210/P

9 780595 460298